Juffie Kane

BEVERLY S. MARTIN

BANTAM BOOKS
TORONTO · NEW YORK · LONDON · SYDNEY · AUCKLAND

JUFFIE KANE
A Bantam Book/March 1989

Jacket photo fur courtesy of Goldin-Feldman, New York

All rights reserved.
Copyright © 1989 by Beverly S. Martin.
Book design by Maria Carella

Library of Congress Cataloging-in-Publication Data

Martin, Beverly S.
  Juffie Kane.

  I. Title.
PS3563.A723254J84   1989   813'.54   88-47825
ISBN 0-553-05345-0

Published simultaneously in the United States and Canada

Bantam Books are published by Bantam Books, a division of Bantam Doubleday Dell Publishing Group, Inc. Its trademark, consisting of the words "Bantam Books" and the portrayal of a rooster, is Registered in U.S. Patent and Trademark Office and in other countries. Marca Registrada. Bantam Books, 666 Fifth Avenue, New York, New York 10103.

PRINTED IN THE UNITED STATES OF AMERICA
DH   0 9 8 7 6 5 4 3 2 1

For my parents, who would have loved it

Prologue

Nobody who knew Juffie Kane was wholly surprised at the way she died, buried alive in an avalanche in the Swiss Alps on an October day in 1957. Juffie Kane's death was like her life—unexpected, unconventional, and dramatic.

Nothing in Juffie's thirty years had been run-of-the-mill, so it was somehow expected that she wouldn't have a funeral like an ordinary person's. Her battered frozen corpse was hastily interred in an obscure Swiss cemetery. A week later a memorial service took place in New York, mainly for the press. Organized by the agent who made a fortune out of Juffie while she lived, it was a media event, not an act of mourning. Half the world stood on the street and watched; most of the other half tuned in on television and radio. The event coincided with a weekly press conference at the White House; the president commented that the country had lost a national treasure.

There were a few who truly grieved for Juffie Kane; they found it hard to imagine life without her white-hot star lighting up their personal sky. Karen Rice, for instance. Karen would never forget the moment she heard that her oldest and dearest friend was dead. She was lying in Juffie's bed, with Paul Dumont, Juffie's husband.

At the age of twenty-nine Karen had just achieved her first orgasm. Which was cause for celebration, so Paul opened a bottle of vintage champagne and they sipped it while they sprawled— naked, languid, sated—on the enormous bed in the splendid penthouse overlooking the East River. The penthouse had been bought by Juffie's fame and fortune.

Paul had been in America for eleven years, but in many ways

he was still thoroughly tied to Europe. On his bedside table was one of the strongest links, a shortwave radio tuned permanently to London's BBC, the best station in the world for international news. He switched it on idly, in time to hear part of the closing summary of headlines.

". . . And former president De Gaulle of France has again insisted that Algeria must remain under French colonial rule. President Eisenhower has said that federal troops may be used to enforce racial integration in schools in the southern states. There has been a severe avalanche near Verbier in the Swiss Alps. Among those missing and feared dead is the celebrated American actress Juffie Kane. And that's the end of the news from London."

"Jesus!" Dumont sat up and frantically twisted the dial. Karen was too stunned to speak. She stared at Paul, willing him to say something that would tell her what he was thinking. "Jesus Christ," he repeated.

He kept on fiddling with the radio. "There's a Swiss station somewhere on this band . . . broadcasting from Geneva." Finally he located it. She heard a stream of unintelligible French. Paul listened intently. Karen heard Juffie's name again.

"Is it true?" she asked in a whisper.

He looked at her and she was astonished to note that his eyes were full of tears. If he could still weep for Juffie, maybe he didn't really hate his wife. "Yes, I think it may be true." He spoke in a dull monotone. "They say she was there in Verbier, and she's not been seen since the avalanche."

"Oh my God . . ." The real reaction began. Karen's throat tightened, she couldn't breathe, her hands started to shake. She was still holding the glass of champagne. Carefully she set it on the floor, on the wall-to-wall white carpet. Part of her was remembering that it was Baccarat crystal, that she mustn't break it. "Oh my God," she said again. "Paul, we have to contact somebody, maybe somebody official. There must be something you're supposed to do."

He shook his head. His hair was thick, dark, and curly, tousled now, a legacy of the passion of a few moments earlier. He looked disarmingly boyish, despite his thirty-three years. "I don't know. I just don't know what to do."

Guilt and grief did not numb Karen's professional eye. Paul's perfectly modeled profile seemed to blur, those suave good looks which had set so many female hearts pounding were coming apart. His chin and his mouth crumpled. His teeth began to chatter so loudly she could hear them. Paul Dumont, hero of the French Resistance, renowned impresario, was disintegrating while she watched.

Karen took a deep breath, gathering her reserves. Steady, she told herself, do what you have to do. This isn't the way you expected it to be, but things seldom are. At least that's what Juffie always said. So it was just like old times.

Chapter 1

On a summer day in 1927 there was a demonstration on Boston Common. One of many that had been staged there since the seventeenth century, this event was to protest the execution in the electric chair of Nicola Sacco and Bartolomeo Vanzetti.

Sacco and Vanzetti were immigrants, self-confessed anarchists, and draft dodgers. Seven years before, they had been arrested and charged with murdering two men in the course of a payroll robbery in Braintree. Many people thought the trial had been a travesty and the evidence a joke; they believed the accused were victims of raw prejudice. But the public outcry and legal maneuvering only delayed the inevitable. The governor had refused to grant clemency and unless President Coolidge intervened, the two men were to die at two P.M. About two hundred protestors were on Boston Common making a final plea for mercy. Among them were Myer and Rosie Kane.

Myer looked anxiously at his wife. "How are you doing?"

"Okay. I'm fine. Stop worrying about me." Rosie hoisted her placard higher. She had made it herself, with a broom handle and white cardboard and black crayon. It said DO NOT ALLOW OUR BELOVED AMERICA TO BE SHAMED.

She shifted the broom handle so her protuberant belly could take some of the weight. Rosie Kane was nine months pregnant, overdue by her reckoning, but glad of it because it meant she could be with Myer today on the Common. It was hard for her to imagine anything more important than being here, standing up and being counted, fighting for the American dream. "I'm okay," she told her husband again. She gave him her broadest grin. "This kid of ours has a great sense of timing. He'll wait until it's over."

Myer grinned back at her, then turned and added his voice to the chant rising off the Common and echoing toward the gold dome of the statehouse. "Justice for all! Freedom for all! Justice! Freedom! Justice!"

Rosie kept smiling until she was sure Myer was no longer paying attention. Then she went back to concentrating on the contractions and timing them. When they started getting closer, four or five minutes apart say, she'd tell him. But not until then. Nothing was going to make her cause Myer to give up his protest. She knew how important it was to him. She knew why.

A wave of pain started in the small of her back. She gritted her teeth and didn't make a sound. It didn't stop. This pain didn't ebb as the others had. It went on—one long, unending torment that finally she couldn't endure in silence.

"Myer . . ." Rosie gasped out her husband's name, but he didn't hear her. He'd moved away a few yards, to a group of men who were swaying in time to the rhythm of the two names they were half shouting, half singing. "Sacco, Vanzetti, Sacco, Vanzetti, Sacco, Vanzetti . . ."

Through the red haze of agony Rosie spotted a squadron of mounted men entering the Common from the direction of Beacon Street. Behind her a dozen or so women saw them too and began linking arms to form a human chain. It was a technique they'd perfected a decade earlier in the suffragette movement, and they were practiced and quick. "C'mon, honey, get in here with us. The blue boys won't charge a line of women."

Hands began plucking at Rosie's arms. She let her placard fall and it was trampled in the rush to close ranks. The police approached slowly, but with determination. "C'mon, dear," the same voice repeated. "We'll put you up front. When they see that you're—Holy heaven! What's the matter? Your time's come, is that it? You're in labor, aren't you? Hey! Somebody give me a hand, there's a lady here who's having a baby. . . ."

Thus the daughter of Myer and Rosie Kane was born on Boston Common on the same day that Sacco and Vanzetti were executed, at almost precisely the same moment the switch was pulled, sending two thousand volts of current through the bodies of the two Italian immigrants.

When Rosie first held her baby girl she didn't look at her. She looked at Myer, who had finally realized what was happening and fought his way to his wife's side. "What time is it?" she asked.

"About half past two."

"Did they do it?"

"Yes. That's what everyone says."

Rosie was silent for a moment, unaware of the dozens of strangers surrounding them, of the police ready to take them away in a hastily summoned ambulance. Finally she glanced down at the child she held. "A girl," she said softly. "But with a great sense of timing, like I said." She lifted her eyes to her husband. "Don't be sad, Myer. We tried to make them do what was right. Now we have a daughter, and she'll grow up and she'll try too."

Myer nodded solemnly in agreement.

· · · ·

The Kanes lived on Walnut Street in Newton in a three-story Victorian house of gray clapboard. It was a nice wide street, made to seem wider because the houses were set back behind deep lawns bisected by strips of concrete leading to pristinely painted front doors. With no fences, Walnut Street from the front was an open world where domains flowed into one another and privacy grew out of the owners' good manners and propriety.

Almost all these spacious front yards boasted big trees, mostly maples, one or two horse chestnuts. In summer they provided dappled shade the length of the block; in winter they caught the snow before it drifted and sometimes were hung with shimmering icicles. It was a perfect setting for the America of dreams.

There was no tree in front of the Kanes' house, but there was a discreet sign on the lawn. In letters carved into oak and gilded with gold, it said MYER KANE, ATTORNEY AT LAW. The first floor was given over to the office. What had been the front parlor held a secretary's desk and a large collection of law books. Behind it, in the original dining room, Myer had his private sanctum. The second floor housed a comfortable living room with nice mahogany furniture upholstered in blue tapestry and the gray carpet Rosie was so proud of, and the dining room, and a bright sunny kitchen. Upstairs on the third floor were four bedrooms.

The Kanes' baby daughter, the first installment on the big

family they hoped to have someday, was received with joy and delight. Not only did Myer and Rosie dote on the child they named Jennifer, but the little girl's two grandfathers, both widowers, competed for the privilege of spoiling her.

The Sunday Jennifer turned three months old Rosie's father, Dino Saliatelli, arrived bearing the biggest stuffed panda in captivity, and a small box containing diamond earrings. "The panda I saw in Jordan's window. I made them take it out. The earrings are only half a carat each, 'cause she's so little. But a good beginning."

"Thanks, Pa," Rosie said. "I'll put them away until she gets bigger."

"What bigger? They're for pierced ears, see? She can start wearing 'em now. Three months, that's how old you were when your ears were pierced. And my father, God rest his soul, gave you diamond earrings."

"She's too small to have her ears pierced, Pa."

"No." Dino shook his head. "Back in Palermo they did it when the little girl was three months. And after we came here the same thing. And for the Saliatellis, always diamonds for the firstborn daughter."

"This isn't Sicily, it's America. Babies don't wear earrings."

Rosie's father started to protest, but he was interrupted by the entrance of Benny Kane. He was carrying a panda identical to the one Dino had presented. The two men glared at each other. Benny was the first to break the hostile silence. "Those schmucks in Jordan's told me this was the last one. It was in the window."

"Mine came from Jordan's window too. I got the first one," Dino said. It was only a minor score. Not satisfying enough. "Yours is a copy," he added.

Rosie hastened to take the stuffed toy from her father-in-law's grip. "Thanks, Pop. It's great having two of these things. I'll put them either side of the door. See, they make a pair. Like a guard of honor."

The nursery had been duplicated from a picture in *Good Housekeeping*. It was a glory of yellow paint and white lace and stenciled flowers and clowns and animals. Myer and Rosie had worked on it together for nine months, almost from the moment she knew she was pregnant. Now the two pandas did indeed look like a guard of honor. Each one was almost as big as Rosie herself.

She found it hard to imagine what the tiny infant asleep in the lace-trimmed bassinet would do with them.

"Show Benny the earrings, Rosa." Dino was the only person who called his daughter Rosa and not Rosie.

She had put the box in the pocket of her apron; now she withdrew it reluctantly. "Diamond earrings, Pop. A family tradition. For when she gets bigger."

"For now," Dino insisted. "I'll bring your auntie Maria here in a couple of days. She'll pierce the baby's ears. She always does it."

"I'm not having her ears pierced," Rosie said. She wore an expression both men knew well. It was the way she'd looked when she stood beside Myer and said she was married to him, and there was nothing her Italian father or his Jewish father could do about it.

"Piercing babies' ears is a wop trick. It's cheap," Benny said. "Rosie is right."

"What the hell do you mean, wop trick? What kind of garbage are you talking? Diamonds you're calling cheap? These are perfect stones. You know how much they cost?"

"I don't care how much they cost. It's a greaseball custom. Where's Myer?" Benny looked around as if he thought his son might be hiding somewhere in the nursery.

"He had to go see a client. He'll be back soon."

"What kind of a *putz* idea is that? Go see a client. He thinks he's a doctor? Lawyers don't make house calls."

"It's an old lady, Pop. She was hit by a moving van and she can't walk. And the company says it was her fault and they're not going to pay her anything."

Benny sighed. "And I bet she's not going to pay Myer anything."

"If he gets a settlement for her he'll take his fee out of that."

"If. A thousand *ifs* we hear from these *shnorrer* clients of his. Thank God for me and Dino, otherwise nobody would pay him, and you and this gorgeous granddaughter of mine would be lucky to eat."

Rosie turned away and didn't answer. They'd all said everything there was to say before. And in a way, though she hated the fact, her father-in-law was right. The cases Myer really cared about, the ones he called *pro bono publico*, seldom paid. If it weren't for his other work, the jobs he undertook for Benny and Dino, he wouldn't be able to represent the poor and the downtrodden—and support his family. Rosie bit back a sharp reply. Dino started to say something more about bringing his sister Maria to pierce little Jennifer's ears. Then the baby cried. The three adults immediately converged on the bassinet.

"Whatsamatter with her?" Dino demanded.

"Nothing's the matter. She's hungry. You both go downstairs and have some wine. I'll feed her and bring her down afterwards."

Benny reached out one finger and little Jennifer immediately stopped crying and grabbed it. Her blue eyes turned to his. "She knows me, see?"

"Rosa," Dino demanded, "show her the earrings. I want she should see that her Sicilian grandfather knows how things should be done."

"You better be careful," Benny shouted. "You give a baby little earrings she'll put 'em in her mouth. Swallow 'em maybe. She could die from your goddamned diamond earrings."

The raised voices frightened the infant and she howled.

Rosie scooped her daughter into her arms. "Get out of here both of you! You're crazy. I can't stand any more of your bickering. Go downstairs. I'll bring Jennifer after I've fed her. Out! Out!" Her voice was rising and her eyes were blazing. The two men fled the approaching storm.

· · · ·

Little Jennifer Kane was fourteen months when she spoke her first words. By age two she had a sizable vocabulary and could talk in sentences, but she couldn't say Jennifer. She made it into something that sounded like Juffie. The name stuck; soon everyone called her Juffie. The child had worked her independent will for the first time.

In the soft, unformed, pudgy charms of babyhood Juffie's potential was already apparent. Her eyes turned from universal blue to smoky gray-violet with a wondrous dark ring around the iris. Her hair, a pale fuzz at birth, was fast becoming a thick honey-colored mane sweeping back from a pronounced widow's peak. And very early there was the hint, the mere shadow, of what a journalist would someday call ". . . those cheekbones that could cut paper." By the time she was six Juffie knew she was beautiful, because everyone told her so, repeatedly.

"My beautiful angel," Benny Kane called her.

"Beautiful little doll," Dino said when he bounced her on his knee.

"Daddy's precious little beauty," Myer murmured as he hugged her first thing in the morning and last thing at night.

"Mama loves her beautiful little darling," Rosie repeated a dozen times a day.

The four adults who dominated Juffie's existence were effusive in their praise and adoration. Maybe more than might have been the case if Rosie had managed to produce another child, which she did not. Too bad. Both she and Myer were only children and they'd hoped to spare Juffie that experience.

· · · ·

In 1893, when he was thirteen, Benny Kane knew the difference between crooks and regular people—crooks had money. They hung around in the back room of his uncle Jake's candy store on Myrtle Street in Boston's West End, and they wore silk shirts and had big gold pocket watches and flashed rolls of bills. "You think they worked for that gelt?" Benny's father demanded. "You think my brother Jake is so friendly with the cops because he goes to shul regular and is an upstanding citizen?"

Benny's arms and shoulders and thighs were solid muscle. For six years he'd been doing the milk round every morning at dawn, lugging crates of quart bottles up and down four- and five-story tenements, hefting them on and off the back of Mr. Polansky's horse-drawn wagon. But he was short, only five feet, and his precociously mature build made him appear oafish—until you studied his face. Benny had fine, almost aristocratic features, which had arranged themselves into a look of intelligence practically from birth. It wasn't a false impression; the boy was quite bright and had a naturally winning charm.

When he looked at his father and shook his head it was obvious he was being honest. "No, I don't think that. I sort of guessed about Uncle Jake. The cops are always in there because he pays vigorish, so they'll leave his place alone. That's the truth, isn't it?"

"Yeah, it is," his father admitted. "He's my own brother, but I ain't denying it. So tell me, Benny, what are you doing hanging around a place like that if you know what's going on? My only son, my only child, my *Kaddishel*, should be mixed up with lousy crooks?"

"I'm not mixed up with them, Papa. I only go to Uncle Jake's when Mr. Polansky sends me."

"To place bets. Hymie Polansky bets on the fights, right?"

Benny nodded. "Sometimes. Sometimes on other stuff, like numbers. Every week there's a winning number. Mr. Polansky always bets the same combination, three four six eight."

"Who decides what number is the winner?" the father demanded, his curiosity piqued despite his attitude toward gambling.

"Shlomo Kornblum. He pulls the numbers out of his hat Friday afternoons. Before sundown," Benny hastened to add.

"Shlomo! That *letz*! Polansky must be crazy. I guarantee, the only numbers that go in the hat are what Shlomo wants should win."

"I think so too," Benny agreed.

"So since Polansky is stupid as well as a *farshtinkener* gambler, he can do his own dirty work. I'll tell him myself."

Benny stared at the floor a moment, then fixed his father with the full impact of his sincere gray eyes. "Papa, lots of guys would like my job. I don't want to lose it."

The elder Kane was silent for a full minute, considering both morality and economics. He earned two dollars and fifty cents a week as a cutter in a small coat factory near North Station. Feigel, his wife, brought in a dollar or so more each week, stitching collars on the sewing machine in the kitchen. She got a penny apiece for the collars, but her eyes were going. These days she sometimes didn't manage a hundred a week. And Benny, the pride of their lives, the only truly wonderful thing that had happened to them in the twenty years since they came to Boston from Russia, was going to be a lawyer. They'd decided that the moment he was born. Benjamin Shmuel Kane would be educated, a big man in America. But putting him through college and supporting him while he apprenticed in a law office would cost a fortune, so Benny's job was important.

"Yes," the father agreed after some thought. "We don't want you should lose your job. Because you're going to college, Benny.

You're going to be somebody. A lawyer. And *mamzarim* like my brother and his friends who think the only way to get ahead in America is to cheat, they're going to see they're wrong. Benny, are you listening to me?"

"Yes, Papa, I'm listening."

"And you know I'm telling the truth. So you better do what Polansky wants, only so he doesn't get mad and fire you. But remember, those no-goodniks in the candy shop, they're all dreck. When you go in there, don't even look at them."

Benny tried to follow his father's command, but sometimes, clutching Mr. Polansky's dime, he had to stand in the back room of the candy shop for a long time before anybody noticed him. Finally Big Moishe the Lendler or Fat Yossel would look up. "You wanna place a bet, *boychik*?"

"Yes. For Mr. Polansky. Ten cents says John L. Sullivan will win tomorrow night."

Moishe the Lendler chortled with delight and stuck out his hand palm upward. "Put the money here, *boychik*."

Big Moishe was an exceptional man in many ways. Unlike most of the immigrants, he was not what they called a *tenor*, a tenant. Moishe owned property in Revere and Chelsea and Winthrop as well as in Boston. He was a *lendler*, a word added to the argot of Yiddish when the Jews discovered the existence of landlords, usually to their despair. A *lendler* could not, however, be kept entirely busy collecting rents, so Moishe dabbled in making book. "Tell Polansky I'm giving him six to one. Because I'm a kind man, and because I know for sure that Gentleman Jim Corbett is going to beat the kishkes out of Sullivan."

All the assembly laughed. Benny started to back out of the small smoky room. "Wait a minute, *boychik*."

Benny waited.

Big Moishe the Lendler eyed him up and down. "*Boychik*, those are some legs. Look, the muscles stick out from his knickers." There were approving nods. "So," Moishe continued, "how about you should give them a little exercise? Run down to Finkel's and get me a sandwich. Salami on rye with extra mustard, and tell Finkel not to forget the pickles." He took a gold watch from his pocket. "Tell you what, I got a nickel says you can't make it there and back in five minutes."

The delicatessen was two blocks away on Joy Street. Benny

ran through crowds of shawled women carrying trays of apples and darted among the pushcarts and the sidewalk displays of used clothing and secondhand household goods. Once he knocked over a barrel of fresh herring, but he stopped and righted it before too much spilled and the fishmonger's curses changed to thanks which Benny didn't pause to hear. Fortunately there was no one in Finkel's.

"Quick, a salami on rye with lots of mustard and don't forget the pickles."

The man behind the counter eyed him. "You're in a big hurry, *tateleh?* You're dying from starvation maybe?"

"Please, Mr. Finkel. I gotta make it back to the candy store before five minutes. It's a—" He hesitated, not wanting to say it was a bet. "A promise."

"Oh. Well, for a promise I can hurry too."

Benny completed the errand in four minutes twenty-seven seconds. Moishe the Lendler punched him on the arm in a friendly way when he handed over the nickel. Benny felt very grown-up and like a member of a secret society.

Doing little favors for the men in the back room of the candy store became a habit. Sometimes he wound up with twenty or thirty cents a week extra because of the needs of Moishe or Yossel or Shlomo. He couldn't give it to his parents because he dared not tell them the source of the money. Instead, he saved it in a glass jar kept in the corner behind his bed in the kitchen. Now that his mother's eyes were so bad she didn't clean as thoroughly as she used to. The money was safe, and it was Benny's secret. When he was sixteen and a sophomore at Boston English High School he had the incredible sum of thirty-six dollars and seventy cents hidden away. So he was almost a rich man when he met Zelda Bass.

Benny saw her for the first time outside Bass's Bakery on Cedar Street, where he went to buy bagels on Sunday morning. The bakery was some distance from his house, but his mother always said Bass made the best bagels in Boston, so he went there Sundays as soon as he had finished delivering the milk, and bought three still-warm bagels and carried them home for breakfast. He'd been doing it for years, but the tiny girl with very dark hair and eyes sitting on a folding chair in front of the store had never been there before. Benny stopped and looked at her. "Hello," she said.

"Hello. You new here?"

"Oh no, I live upstairs. I'm Zelda Bass. This is my father's bakery."

"I haven't seen you before. I come every week."

Her brown velvet eyes had been looking directly into his; now she lowered her lids. "I can't come down very often. But it's such a nice morning."

"Why can't you come down?" Benny had a direct way about him, a willingness to ask straight questions that his teachers encouraged. "They keep you locked up?"

She laughed, a little trilling laugh. It went right through him and trickled down his spine. It was a dainty laugh, just as the hands folded in her lap were dainty. "Of course I'm not locked up. But . . ." She lifted the skirt of her long blue and white striped dress. Just a little, so he could see the built-up shoes and heavy braces. "It's hard for Papa to carry me down two flights of stairs."

He felt sick, not with disgust but with pity. The sight of those black leather and metal cages buckled around both her legs was an obscenity, a sacrilege being committed right here on the street. "I'm sorry," he whispered.

Zelda shrugged. "So am I, but it can't be helped. I got polio a few years ago."

The following three Sundays she was waiting for him when he came to buy bagels and they chatted for a while and afterward, when Benny walked home, he was both ecstatically happy because he'd talked with Zelda and thoroughly depressed because she was crippled and her life was so terrible. On the fourth Sunday she wasn't outside the store.

"Mr. Bass, where's your daughter? Is she okay?" Benny demanded of the baker.

"My Zelda?"

"Yes, your daughter."

"I got four daughters. Zelda's the oldest. She's okay. It's just I hurt my back yesterday moving a sack of flour. I couldn't bring her down this morning."

"I can," Benny said immediately. "I can go up and get her if you'll let me."

The baker looked at the young man. Benny was five foot four now, and even more muscular than he'd been at thirteen. Still, he hesitated. "You gotta be real careful. It hurts her if she's not picked up just right."

"I'll be careful, Mr. Bass. I won't hurt her. I promise."

"You're Benny Kane, aren't you?" the baker asked. Benny nodded. Mr. Bass peered at him more intently. "Zelda told me about you. She says you're in high school. Then maybe you're going to college."

"Yes, in two years, when I graduate from English. I'm going to be a lawyer."

The baker smiled. "So okay, Benny the lawyer. I don't usually let anybody carry my Zelda but me, only it's boring for her not getting out. And she says you're a nice young man. So come upstairs and we'll bring her down."

Holding her in his arms was bliss. She was light as a feather; he could tell that what heaviness there was came only from the braces. And she smelled like fresh lemons. And when he set her down in the chair on the sidewalk in front of the bakery her cheek actually brushed his and it felt the way he imagined fine silk must feel, cool and exquisitely soft. Then she held his hands a few seconds longer than necessary while she said thank you.

Four months later Benny quit school. His parents didn't know; they thought he was attending classes as usual because he was gone all day. Instead, he was working full-time for Big Moishe, and earning four dollars a week. "You look tough, *boychik*. Sometimes the jobs I need done, they take a tough guy. Like when the *tenors* try to cheat and not pay the rent. You understand?"

Benny understood. He didn't particularly like the work, but he knew that if he was going to marry Zelda and take her to the best doctors so they could make her well, he needed money. Right away, not in seven or eight years when maybe he'd finally be a lawyer.

The only thing not absolutely clear in his mind was how to tell his parents of the decision and his new career. So he wasn't entirely sorry when the truant officer went to his house and told his mother that he hadn't been near English High School in over a month. "It's not illegal, Mrs. Kane," the truant officer said. "Benjamin is old enough to leave school if he wishes. It's just that he didn't tell us anything. And he's been such a good student. We thought it best that we check."

There was a big scene. His father's face was so red Benny

thought the old man might have a heart attack. And his mother cried so much her eyes were even more sore and swollen than usual. But the thought of Zelda was enough to strengthen him. Benny wouldn't relent.

"Get out!" the senior Kane shouted finally. "Get out of my house! All these years we've slaved so you'd be somebody. Now you're a crook and a chiseler. Get out!"

"No!" Feigel screamed. "No! He's my son. You can't throw him out of my house."

Benny dived under the bed and grabbed his jar of money. When he came up again his father was holding a furled umbrella over his head, ready to bring it down on his son's broad shoulders. Benny dodged artfully and managed to quickly kiss his mother's cheek. "I'm sorry, Mama. I'll come and see you—"

"You won't come into this house ever again! Never, you hear me? Cheat! Chiseler! Crook! We have no son, he's dead. We'll say Kaddish for our child who has died."

Mr. Bass paled when he heard this story. "Your own father is saying Kaddish for you, and you want to marry my daughter?"

"My father is mad because I'm not going to be a lawyer. But I love Zelda and she loves me. I'm going to take her to the best doctors. She's going to get well."

The baker was kneading a huge mound of dough. He was white from head to toe, even his beard and his mustache were covered with flour. He didn't stop working while he thought. He was a widower and had no one but his daughters. Because of the needs of Zelda the cripple, the three other girls couldn't look for husbands. Who would take care of the invalid and the house if they married and moved out? "Doctors cost money, Benny," he said finally. "A lot more than you can make delivering milk for Mr. Polansky. Even if you work full-time."

"I don't deliver milk anymore. I'm working for my uncle Jake." It was a fiction he'd determined on from the first; it was what he told everyone, including Zelda.

"Jake Kane who owns the candy store on Myrtle Street?"

"That's right. His business is good. I earn four dollars a week. And I have almost forty dollars saved. I can take care of Zelda, Mr. Bass. I won't hurt her, I promise you."

Which is just what the young man had said that first day when he carried her down the stairs. And that had been the truth. The baker punched the dough savagely and didn't meet Benny's eyes. He knew there was no way Jake Kane could pay his nephew four dollars a week. And he knew what went on in the room behind the displays of sour balls and licorice sticks and peppermints and chocolate-covered raisins. But Zelda was a cripple and it hadn't occurred to him that someone would marry her and solve almost all his most pressing problems. Maybe. "And afterwards? You want to live here with us?"

"Not afterwards, only until Zelda and I are married. Then we'll have our own place. In Chelsea." Big Moishe owned some nice buildings in Chelsea; Benny had studied them when he went to collect the rents. A couple were occupied by real deadbeats. He knew his boss would throw out one of the families in arrears and arrange a flat for him and Zelda.

"Chelsea? That's pretty far away. A trolley ride."

"Yes. But every Friday night we'll come here for supper. So you won't miss Zelda too much. I'll bring her in a taxicab."

"A taxicab. I see. And tell me, who will take care of this flat in Chelsea? Who'll cook your meals? Zelda can't do much."

"I know. I'll get somebody to help her. Just until the doctors fix her up so she can walk again."

Mr. Bass sighed. "Benny, you got everything figured out. So who am I to say no when so many plans have already been made? It's a mitzvah maybe, for Zelda and her sisters and probably for me. So okay, you can sleep here in the bakery until you're married. I'll talk to the rabbi."

Four years later the young couple still lived in Chelsea, but not in a rented flat. They occupied the entire ground floor of a three-story house which Benny Kane owned. A woman came every day to do all the cooking and cleaning. Another arrived each Wednesday to wash and iron, and a third came Friday mornings to shampoo Zelda's hair. Benny wanted to do that himself, but she wouldn't let him. "It's not right, darling," she insisted.

But she let him take off her braces each night before they went to bed and bathe her shrunken legs and massage a special cream into them. He'd gotten the cream from a woman in Revere who said it would cure her. It didn't, but Zelda found it soothing nonetheless. So he bought a very large supply. In fact Benny bought Zelda anything that he thought might please her. Gold earrings and a lace shawl and silk blouses and sterling silver Shabbat candlesticks were only a few of his gifts. His largess was never-ending and made possible because these days he earned a good deal more than four dollars a week.

Two years before, Big Moishe had died, and since he had no family except some distant cousins still in Poland, he'd left all his property to Benny Kane. The young man knew by then that Big Moishe had additional business interests, and there was a small war to take over those enterprises.

Benny Kane took on Fat Yossel and Shlomo Kornblum and a few other men, all of whom were much older and more experienced than he, and he won; because he was smarter and tougher than the others, and because the thought of Zelda and her needs made him determined to stop at nothing. He even arranged for Fat Yossel's grandson to be stopped on the way home from Hebrew school and given a note telling his grandfather how easy it would have been to do the child harm of the most intimate physical sort. After that it was easy.

In fact, winning most things had become easy for Benny, except the battle to make Zelda well. At least once a month he took her to a new doctor, but none of them succeeded in restoring movement to her withered legs or getting rid of the hateful braces.

In bed, however, Zelda didn't wear braces. And in the dark being a cripple ceased to matter. Benny and Zelda made passionate love almost every night. He was astounded at her appetites, at the way she could make him feel, at the things she thought of doing to him. He doubted that any of the whores in the Scollay Square houses of which he was part owner gave their paying customers as much pleasure as his wife gave him. "Zelda," he always whispered afterward, "you're incredible. You make me so happy."

"I love you, Benny. I love you so much," she'd reply. But one night nearing their fifth anniversary she varied her response. "I'm glad I make you happy, Benny, darling. I'm going to make you even happier. I'm pregnant."

"What! But the doctors said—"

"I know. I know everything they said. But it's true. I'm pregnant. Three months along. Our baby will be born in October."

Because of her ill health Zelda spent the final six months of her pregnancy in bed. She was very pale and the rest of her body seemed to shrink while her stomach ballooned. It was as if the child were sucking the life from her. Sometimes Benny found himself hating the unborn baby. Zelda, who was so perceptive she was almost prescient, knew just how he felt. "Don't blame the baby, Benny. He's doing just what I want him to do, growing big and strong like his father. He's going to be a beautiful baby and we're going to be so happy."

"So it's a boy," he said, smiling and stroking her cheek. "You got a direct line to heaven so you know?"

Zelda gripped his hand and pressed it closer to her flesh. She knew a great many things, but she was not ready to tell them to her beloved husband. "It's a boy. I feel it. And we'll name him Moishe, for your benefactor."

"Moishe officially maybe, in shul and for the bris. But we'll call him Myer, it's more American."

"Okay," Zelda agreed. "And he's going to be a lawyer, Benny. A wonderful lawyer. Promise me you'll make that happen."

"Hey, it's not just up to me," Benny protested, ignoring the sinking feeling in his belly caused by the implication of her words. "You're his mother. You'll have more influence over him than I will."

"A lawyer, darling. Promise."

"I promise," he whispered, pulling her close.

On the day of his birth in October 1901 Myer Kane weighed eight pounds four ounces and looked startlingly like his father. That would have pleased Zelda if she'd lived beyond the delivery.

· · · ·

Dino Saliatelli was born knowing what Benny Kane had to learn in the back room of the candy store. He was heir to eight generations of men who had responded to injustice with organized banditry; first in Sicily, then in the "little Italys" of various American cities. Dino's family was already powerful by the time he was born in Boston in 1885. Franco Saliatelli, Dino's father, imported olive oil from Palermo and sold it to groceries all over the North End and East Boston and Medford and Everett. He also protected his customers from a variety of unnamed dangers, for which he was paid handsomely each month.

Dino was the last child and the only son in a household of five daughters, and his birth was greeted with rejoicing and his progression to manhood watched over with infinite care by Franco. The child always had a tendency to be tall and thin, a thing the father found disturbing. *"Mange, bambino mio, mange,"* Franco said repeatedly. And to his wife, "Give him more meat, more pasta. What's the matter with you, Anna? My son is wasting away and you do nothing."

Dino ate and ate and ate, and all that happened was that he got taller and thinner. "It's his nature," the mother insisted, wringing her hands and calling on God to witness that she gave her son more than sufficient quantities of food. *"Mange, bambino mio, mange,"* Franco urged.

At fifteen Dino stood five feet ten and weighed a hundred and twenty-five pounds. One other thing was remarkable about this scion of the wealth and power of the Saliatelli family—his eyes. It was as if the countless great kegs of olive oil from Sicily which were decanted into gallon jugs and poured liberally into the pots and pans on Anna's stove had distilled their essence and transported it to Dino's eyes. They were liquid black, enormous, and almost from infancy they seemed to look through people, to see everything possible.

"Mama mia, look at those eyes," Franco said again and again. "They're the eyes of a capo, of someone to be obeyed." Sometimes his son's eyes frightened him, made him doubt who was in charge in his own home. "He needs to understand more than I can teach him," Franco mused aloud one night. "I am going to send him to Sicily for a while, to my father's house." Anna wailed and wept. It was madness to send her only son so far away, to the old country with its blood feuds and vendettas. Who knew what might happen?

"It's necessary," the father insisted. In the summer of 1901, when he was sixteen, Dino set sail for Palermo.

A number of things occurred during the four years the young man spent on that volcanic island. First, he came to understand in greater depth the code of family loyalty and structured honor that vivified the extensive clan to which he belonged, and the others which were its rivals. Second, he killed his first man.

It wasn't a murder. Murder as such, either for passion or personal gain, was *infamata* in their world, shameful and forbidden. What Dino performed was an execution. A man was caught in the act of stealing a chicken from his grandfather's henhouse.

The criminal was brought to the old man's terrace high above the aquamarine Mediterranean, and there, among the pink twining roses and pale blue irises which grew in profusion in the sweet cool of springtime, he was sentenced to die.

"You do it, Dino," the grandfather said. "You're a man now. It's time."

He wasn't a man, he was a seventeen-year-old boy who hadn't even had his first woman and he blanched and couldn't meet his grandfather's level stare.

"Here." The old man took a large pistol from his pocket. "Use this."

Dino took a step toward him. The accused man made a whimpering noise. He sounded just like a kitten Dino had found years ago in Boston. The kitten's foot had been mangled in a door and Dino had nursed it back to health. He couldn't look at the man who was to die any more than he could look at his grandfather. After that first step which indicated compliance, he didn't move. His feet seemed weighted to the stone terrace.

"Dino, *nipote mio,* do you understand why this man must die?"

"Because you have said so, *Nonno.* Because he stole your chicken."

"I was hungry!" the accused man interposed. "My wife is pregnant, we have no—"

"*Fa tacere! Silenzio!*" The grandfather turned toward his grandson once more. "He is accused out of his own mouth. That is just it, Dino. Did he need to be hungry? Did his pregnant wife need to suffer? Of course not. All he needed to do was to come here and show respect and ask me and I would have given him a chicken— no, many chickens. Instead, he comes like a thief in the night and takes. That offends my honor and for that he must die."

"*Sì, Nonno,* I understand."

He took the pistol and two others held the arms of the victim. They wanted to tie him but the old man would not permit it. "Cowards, he's my grandson, he won't shoot wild."

Perhaps because the grandfather had decreed it, Dino's first shot was amazingly accurate. It entered the man's forehead and knocked him backward over the wall of the terrace, so the bone and brains were splattered on the rocks, where the incoming tide would wash them away.

The third thing of importance occurred ten months before

Dino was scheduled to return to Boston. He fell in love. The object of his passion was a girl named Catarina, who was the daughter of Luigi Pasquale, one of his grandfather's lieutenants, a man wealthy in his own right. Catarina had violet eyes, hair the color of dark rich honey, and breasts that almost burst out of her blouse. Her hips were wide and her buttocks rounded, but her waist, which she always showed off with tight sashes, was so narrow Dino suspected he could span it with his hands.

Every Sunday afternoon the extended family of Dino's grandfather assembled on the big stone terrace above the sea and ate and drank and talked, and renewed their commitment to the man they called Don Fidelio. It was at these gatherings that Catarina and Dino eyed each other hungrily. It did not take long for the others to notice.

"Don Fidelio," the girl's father said. "Forgive me if I speak out of turn, but with all respect, your grandson needs a wife."

"You think so, Luigi?" The old man picked his teeth thoughtfully. "Well, perhaps you are right. He needs someplace to put his *pène*, that is for sure. Do you think it is as long and thin as the rest of him?"

Luigi laughed. "Long, yes. I'm sure of it. But big and thick. After all, he's your flesh and blood."

"Yes, I'm sure too. And what do you think? Should I tell my son to have a bride ready for Dino when he returns?" Don Fidelio was playing with the other man; he knew very well what Luigi thought.

"You could do that. And if you did I'm sure it would be wise, but . . ."

"Speak, Luigi. Say what is on your mind."

"With all respect, would it not be good for him to have a Sicilian wife?"

"Hmm . . . There is merit in that idea. But he must go home to America; there is no question about that. My son needs him. So any Sicilian father who gave up his daughter to my grandson might not see her again for many years. He could not hold his grandchildren in his arms."

"But, Don Fidelio, surely the honor of being more closely related to you would compensate for that loss."

Thus the arrangement was made.

At first Dino was wildly happy with his bride. Until then he'd only masturbated and dreamed, and waited until he would finally have a woman. All that was over at last, and what a woman he had!

Her body was as lush as it had seemed to him when he'd seen it clothed. Naked Catarina was more beautiful than he could have imagined. Her skin was as soft as the down of a peach and her breath as sweet as the orange blossoms in his grandfather's garden. Best of all, she was as eager to make love as he was. Their nights were marathons of pleasure, and even during the day, if they happened to be alone, she would rub up against him, and one somnolent afternoon of blazing heat she lifted her skirts and let him take her on the terrace while his grandfather napped a few feet away on the couch inside.

When the newlyweds embarked on the voyage to America in March of 1905 Catarina was six months pregnant and her belly was already enormous. Dino did not mind this alteration in his wife's figure; he delighted in the visible evidence of his manhood and in the fact that he was returning to his parents with such blossoming fortunes. "Listen, *cara*," he told her the first night on the ship. "I think I must leave you alone until after the baby is born. It could be dangerous for him."

"Not yet, Dino. My mother told me it's not dangerous until just before he is to be born. Look, we can do it like this." She turned over on her side to accommodate him. Dino couldn't resist thrusting himself inside her, but he didn't feel good about it. It simply did not seem right that he should do such things, particularly the things Catarina liked, with his child looking on, as it were. The next night he refused her offer. When they docked in New York he'd been celibate for almost three weeks.

Catarina looked around her in astonishment. "This is America? But there are no trees."

"This is New York. A big city. There are lots of trees in the country. Anyway, we don't get off here, we live in Boston. Wait till you see it, you'll love it."

After disgorging her New York–bound passengers, the Italian liner headed up the coast. The following morning she berthed at Long Wharf in Boston. Catarina was on the deck at sunrise, waiting for a glimpse of her new home. There were, she noted immediately, no trees in Boston either.

The girl's initial dislike of America was compounded by the

home of her in-laws. For all their wealth, the Saliatellis lived modestly. It was more prudent to do so in this country, where the families did not rule everything as openly as they did in Sicily. They had a large apartment on the middle floor of a three-story brick building on Margin Street in the heart of the North End. Men whom Franco Saliatelli trusted implicitly lived with their wives and families above and below. But that was scheduled to change.

"Dino," Franco told his son, "you're a man now with a wife and responsibilities. You should have your own home. Giorgio is moving out from downstairs. That apartment will be yours and Catarina's. The first floor, it's better when you have lots of little children."

The fact that she was to have her own home rather than share one with her mother-in-law did not compensate Catarina for the loss of a big stone Sicilian house and sea breezes. Neither did the familiarity of language and customs and even food. She felt a stranger in a strange place, and to make it worse, her husband was denying her sex. Catarina consoled herself with delicacies— pizza rustica crammed with sausage and *scamozze* cheese, ravioli stuffed with spinach, and roasted peppers swimming in the fruity first-pressed olive oil Franco imported only for the use of his immediate family. By the time her daughter was born she'd put on fifty pounds and she lost little of it following Rosa's birth.

"Make love with me, Dino," she begged every night after the baby had drunk greedily at her breast and was sleeping in the little basket beside the couple's bed. "It's been so long. I'm hungry for you."

But Dino looked at his sleeping infant and at his wife's spread thighs, which were now each the size of a watermelon, and he couldn't do it. His *pène* remained small and flaccid and would not respond. "I'm tired, *cara*, maybe tomorrow night." Most tomorrow nights were no different. Only occasionally did he manage a perfunctory, ritual intercourse. These performances bore no resemblance to the joy and abandon of the times they'd coupled in his grandfather's house, and they left Catarina even more frustrated and miserable than before.

"We should have a house of our own," she complained. "Someplace in the country with trees, by the sea. So our daughter can grow up proper. You want her never to know nothing but these narrow streets and brick buildings?"

"I can't move away," Dino explained time and again. "I'm my father's chief lieutenant, I gotta stay close by. Someday I'll be the padrone."

Despite the rarity of Dino's lovemaking, Catarina became pregnant again when Rosa was six months old. Anna, who found her daughter-in-law too pretty to like, was pleased that at least she was good for breeding. Franco was pleased because he wanted Dino to have a son. Dino was pleased because he loved children, and because now he'd have an excuse for avoiding sex with his wife. Catarina was not pleased. On top of all her other miseries she would again have morning sickness and swollen ankles and, after nine months, hours of agony, followed by another child to feed and care for.

In her fourth month Catarina miscarried. It was a terrible business of screaming and blood and a wild midnight chase after a midwife who in turn insisted on calling a doctor. Anna suspected her daughter-in-law of taking something to kill her unborn child, maybe even using a coat hanger or a knitting needle, but such thoughts were too terrible to voice.

Catarina survived the loss of her child and even seemed a little more cheerful and like the sunny, laughing girl she'd been in Sicily. Dino, however, managed only the infrequent penetrations of her body he'd achieved after Rosa was born. He did not know why the appetite for love had left him, only that it had. Maybe because he spent so much emotion on his daughter.

He adored Rosa. She was a wonderful baby. Beautiful and happy, with a fuzz of brown curly hair and gorgeous pansy-colored eyes like her mother's. But Rosa's eyes contained none of the accusations he read in those of his wife. The child spent hours upstairs in her grandparents' house and Dino loved best the time he spent with her there. Catarina was, by her own choice he would have said, alone a lot.

When Rosa was almost two Catarina conceived again, but once more miscarried after four months. This time Anna was sure Catarina had done something to herself. She tried to tell her husband her suspicions, but he grew furious with her and slapped her face. "*Infamata!* How can you say such things about the wife my own father chose for Dino? No more, woman, I don't want to hear such words in my house."

So they were not spoken. And when Anna was upstairs with

her granddaughter and Catarina was supposed to be alone but there were strangely suspicious noises from the first floor, she didn't dare tell Dino, much less Franco. Often Anna would see a man carry bags of groceries into her son's apartment and not leave for almost half an hour. The same thing happened with Tony, who delivered fresh fish twice a week. "All these deliveries," she told Catarina. "It's crazy. You should go and pick out for yourself. How do you know they're bringing you the best?"

"Why should I exhaust myself running up and down Hanover Street? Would they dare bring anything but the best for Dino Saliatelli's table?" the younger woman countered. And that was hard to rebut. To herself Anna acknowledged that Dino's wife was opening her legs for every man she could inveigle into her bed, but who to tell or how to stop this shame she did not know.

Anna could not imagine anything that would give her the courage to broach the subject to her husband again, but then she saw Josiah. He was a big black man whose family had been in Boston since they escaped slavery via the underground railway and he brought ice to the Saliatellis three times a week.

Anna had never classed him as a threat like the other delivery men. He was a *nero*, a nigger. Not a man like the rest. She wasn't even sure niggers had a thing between their legs like white men. But one sultry July afternoon when she'd taken Rosa down to the tiny patch of grass behind the house, she heard noises coming from behind the drawn blinds of Catarina's bedroom. She could not mistake those sounds. She'd heard them all her life. Anna crossed herself and pursed her lips, and hurried the little girl to the back of the yard so she wouldn't be tainted by her mother's sins.

Ten minutes later she was halfway up the backstairs, holding Rosa's pudgy little hand, when Josiah came out of Dino's home. "Hiya, Mrs. Saliatelli," he called out cheerfully.

Anna turned and stared over her shoulder at him. Josiah wore the heavy canvas apron he always wore, and he carried the great tongs with which he hefted the two-foot-square blocks of ice that fit into the zinc-lined compartment of the icebox. "It's you," she whispered.

"Sure it's me. Josiah, the iceman. You know. Hey, you all right, Mrs. Saliatelli?"

"Yeah, fine, fine." She fled upstairs and had to sit down and fan herself and take a tiny glass of wine before she could stop her heart from beating so wildly it almost burst out of her chest.

Now she knew she had no choice. "Franco, you gotta listen to me. I'm your wife, the mother of your children. You gotta listen and not get crazy."

"What are you talking about? Of course I'll listen. Why shouldn't I listen?"

"Because what I'm gonna tell you you don't want to hear. But if you don't, there's gonna be something terrible happen to this family. You hear me, Franco? Something so terrible you cannot dream of it."

Franco put down the tiny glass of Strega he'd been sipping. He always took a portion of the anise-flavored liqueur with him to bed; it helped him sleep. But the look on Anna's face told him he wouldn't sleep so well this night. "Tell me," he said.

"You won't scream and shut me up? Promise?"

"I promise."

She told him. Franco listened in silence and only the fact that he went very pale indicated he was registering the import of his wife's words. When she finished speaking, he turned out the light and rolled over onto his side and didn't say a word. That silence persisted for weeks. Between them Catarina's name wasn't mentioned.

For a while Anna thought he'd chosen to ignore her information, to do nothing. Then a scarlet fever epidemic came to Boston.

The disease was a recurrent scourge in turn-of-the-century America, coming usually at the end of a long hot summer and persisting, though no one knew quite why, until the onslaught of cold weather. There was nothing to be done but avoid the houses bearing the yellow mark of quarantine, the bonfires of clothing and sheets and personal effects which had touched a victim, and the frequent funeral corteges. And, of course, pray. Anna began a novena to the Madonna de Soccorso Perpètuo, taking little Rosa with her to church and lighting thirty-two candles every day, one for each member of her immediate family.

"Listen, Dino," Franco said to his son one late September afternoon. "Giorgio's sister runs a boardinghouse in Nantasket. Nice. Good food and right by the sea. I figure with all this sickness, maybe we should send the women down there for a few weeks. Safer."

"Yeah, Pa, you got a point. Better for little Rosa, and Mama and Catarina too, of course." Dino was going over the books. Business was off, particularly the receipts from the whorehouses in Scollay Square. No wonder. Who wanted to take the chance of getting scarlet fever just for a fast fuck? "Pa, I been thinking. How come we don't own the property in Scollay Square? The operations is all ours. Why do we pay rent?"

"Always been like that," Franco explained. "The Jewboys own the buildings, we own the whores. You wanna change things we gotta have a war. I'm too old for a war. I'll tell Giorgio to make arrangements with his sister. About Nantasket."

"Yeah, Pa, sure."

It was the most private of meetings, just Franco and Giorgio walking alone along Atlantic Avenue so there was no possibility they would be overheard by any but the sea gulls. "You got all that?" Franco asked finally.

"I got it, boss. Don't worry about nothin'. I'll do it all, just like you say."

"Thank you, Giorgio. And be very careful, I don't want there should be any trouble for your sister, or, God forbid, that it should get you." He sighed and Giorgio put a comforting hand on his shoulder.

"Nothing to worry about, boss. I'll make all the arrangements and leave my sister out of it. And I'll take care of myself."

"Good, I know I can trust you. But I can't tell you how it hurts me we should do this. After all these years, Luigi Pasquale's daughter . . ."

"Don't think about it anymore, boss. Just put it out of your head. Leave everything to me."

Nantasket was a beach town on the ocean side of a spit of land which began at North Cohasset and ended at Hull, and divided Boston Harbor from the Atlantic. Overland it was a long journey; by sea, less than two hours. The easiest way to get there was to take a ferry from Eastern Avenue wharf in the harbor.

This unusual means of transportation and the relative isolation made the resort seem exotic and wonderful. For Bostonians the name Nantasket conjured visions of cotton candy and taffy apples and ice cream, and the Ferris wheel and the roller coaster, and a hundred other summer delights. "Just look," Catarina said, holding at arm's length the murky picture Giorgio had given her. "Isn't it wonderful! We'll have a lovely time."

Anna snorted. She didn't know why Franco was doing this crazy thing, sending her and her daughter-in-law and her grand-daughter to Nantasket now at the end of September. Besides, in a place like that God only knew what the *puttana*, the whore, would get up to. Anna hated the idea. Rosa was just a little over three and didn't understand what was happening well enough to get excited. Catarina had a monopoly on joyful expectation.

The night before they were to leave, Franco announced that he'd just been informed of the arrival of representatives of the Donato family of Brooklyn. They were associates and an important meeting was to take place the next day. He needed Anna to stay and cook for the visiting men. "You go ahead, Catarina. Leave the baby here with us. Anna will bring her down day after tomorrow, but there ain't no reason you should miss a day of your vacation too."

Catarina agreed, because she hated every minute she spent in the North End, and she was accustomed to turning most of the care of her daughter over to Anna.

"Listen," Franco added. "I need Dino with me when the men from Brooklyn come. Giorgio will take you to the ferry."

Giorgio called for her at nine the next morning and drove Catarina to the wharf in his new Packard with the leather half roof and shiny brass trim. He was all dressed up for driving, with a long coat and a veiled hat and even gloves. He looked dashing, Catarina decided. Of course, he was a lot older than she, but that didn't really matter. Besides, she loved riding in the Packard. "Gee, Giorgio, this is such a nice automobile, why don't you ever take me out for a ride? Just the two of us, what do you say?"

"Sure, Catarina, when you get back. Hey, I almost forgot. Don Franco sent you a present."

"He did?" She was suspicious. Catarina was not sure her father-in-law really cared for her. And if he ever knew about— She rejected the thought as too terrible to consider. "What is it?"

Giorgio reached a gloved hand behind him and retrieved a parcel of wrapped clothing. "A new dress and a new shawl, because it'll be chilly on the boat. He wants you to look terrific when you get to Nantasket. So everybody'll know things are good with the Saliatelli family. In fact, he told me to say he wants you to change into this dress while you're on the ferry. So you arrive in it. He made a special point of that. You won't forget, will you, Catarina?"

"No, of course not. It's a pretty dress. I like red."

"Yeah, well, I'm sure it's gonna look terrific on you. And don't worry about finding my sister's when you get there. I've arranged for somebody to meet you."

Giorgio was as good as his word. A man approached as soon as Catarina descended the gangplank in her new red taffeta dress and bright blue wool shawl. "Signora Saliatelli? I'm Joe. I'm gonna bring you to the boardinghouse."

It was a three-story wooden structure painted white with green trim, one of many lining the streets behind the beach. It had a deep front porch with half a dozen rocking chairs and a sign in the window that said LODGING AND THREE GOOD MEALS, FIFTEEN CENTS A DAY.

The woman who greeted them was a redhead in her forties. She looked careworn and very tired. Catarina first shook her hand, then kissed both her cheeks. "You're Maria Forzi, right, Giorgio's sister?"

"Yeah, that's right, Giorgio's sister. Come on, I'll show you your room." What difference did it make? For twenty dollars she'd say she was anybody's sister. But it was crazy. On the next street there was a real Maria Forzi who took in lodgers. The woman decided not to think about it. The season was practically over, she didn't have any other boarders, and God knew she needed the money.

The man called Joe waited until Catarina was settled. Then he made his way to Boston and found Giorgio. "Everything's fine," he said.

"You have any trouble recognizing her?"

"No, she was wearing a red dress and a blue shawl, just like you said."

"Good. Thank you, Joe. I won't forget."

Neither would Giorgio forget that after he dropped Catarina off he'd had to burn everything he was wearing and even drive the brand-new Packard all the way to Neponset and roll it off a cliff into the sea. He'd balked at ditching the automobile, but Don Franco insisted on absolute caution, and he was probably right.

The following day Franco announced that the men from

Brooklyn were going to stay a week. He needed Anna at home, so she and little Rosa would have to postpone their trip to Nantasket.

"To me it makes no difference," his wife said. "But you're crazy, letting her stay down there by herself. Tell her to come home, Franco."

"No. Leave it to me, Anna. Catarina just needs a little change from all of us here. She'll be better when she gets back, you'll see."

Catarina Pasquale Saliatelli never returned to the house on Margin Street. Within five days of arriving in Nantasket she had the first symptoms of scarlet fever and the boardinghouse was quarantined. The landlady burned everything Catarina had brought with her, including the red dress and the blue shawl, but by then it was too late. Catarina died the following week, and the redheaded landlady followed her to the grave ten days later.

Chapter 2

*B*enny Kane and Dino Saliatelli knew each other only by reputation. Neither man was aware of the many similarities in their experience of fatherhood. It wasn't just that both were in the same line of work, nor that each, by remaining single, had made himself a rarity in an age when widowed men usually remarried swiftly. It was that the opening decades of the twentieth century were an era of enormous change in America.

With the advent of automobiles, a new entertainment called the "flickers," and soon afterward radio, life became more fluid; ideas and values were bartered across previously solid barriers, and customs sanctified by centuries began to alter. The melting pot was heating up. Inevitably Myer Kane and Rosa Saliatelli were children of their times, and neither father had a partner with whom to share perceptions of what this meant.

"Rosa, what the hell are you talking about?" Dino demanded of his daughter, who was fourteen on this May afternoon in 1919.

"Rosie, Pa. Everybody calls me Rosie. Why don't you?"

"Because we named you Rosa. Rosie sounds like some floozy."

"It sounds modern."

"Listen, you want to be Rosie outside this house, okay, I don't mind. But to me you're Rosa. Now, like I asked before, what are you talking about with this Congress business? What do you know about them bigshots in D.C.?"

"I know what I learn in school. Suffrage, Pa. The right to vote. Women are going to be able to vote. There's a Constitutional amendment being voted on by the States right now, and there's a good chance it'll be ratified. It should. Why can't we vote? We're people just like men are."

"Listen, if you're supposed to be so smart like all your teachers tell me, how come you say a dumb thing like that? Women are not just like men. At your age you need me to tell you there's a difference?"

"I don't mean that way," Rosie protested. She banged her fist on the kitchen table of the house on Margin Street. The dishes rattled. His daughter had a temper like all the Saliatellis, though she looked like Catarina. Her hair was a darker brown, but she had her mother's pansylike eyes and the lovely, even features. Rosa's figure, on the other hand, promised to be less voluptuous. She was tall and slim like Dino. Her father adored her, even when she made him angry, but he was grateful that Rosa probably wouldn't cause him the kind of worry old man Pasquale had with Catarina, God rest her soul.

The girl's hair was worn in two thick pigtails; they flapped over her shoulders as she made some further point about votes for women. Dino wasn't paying attention. "Rosa, where's your earrings?"

She didn't meet his eyes, but she didn't pretend not to understand. "In my room. In my drawer, Pa. They're safe."

"What's safe got to do with it? How come you're not wearing them? Your grandfather gave you those earrings when you were three months old. It's a family tradition."

"I know. And I love them. Only nowadays kids my age don't wear earrings." She kept turning the spoon in her bowl of thick minestrone soup, flipping chick-peas over bits of string bean.

"Eat," Dino said automatically, still thinking about the problem of the earrings. "Auntie Maria made it, it's good soup, eat." For the past year his sister Maria and her husband, Jocko, and their four children had lived in the middle-floor apartment. They moved in when Anna died, two years after Franco. Now Maria cooked for Dino and Rosa, and brought the food downstairs three times a day.

Rosie took a small mouthful of soup and pushed the bowl away. "I'm not hungry."

"Okay. Listen, what do you mean, girls nowadays don't wear earrings? Your cousin Natalie wears them. She's your age." Natalie was the youngest child of Maria and Jocko.

"Natalie's dumb," Rosie said.

"That's not how you talk about the family."

"I wouldn't say it to anyone else. But between you and me, Natalie's dumb. She's a guinea."

"Mama mia! What do you think you are, Rosa?"

"I'm Italian. Natalie's a guinea. It's different." She got up and began clearing the table. Her movements were quick and efficient. Anna had trained the girl well. Dino watched her in silence, too overwhelmed by everything this child was to argue about the difference between a guinea and an Italian, or whether or not she should wear her grandfather's earrings.

In a few minutes the dishes were washed and draining by the side of the sink. "I'm going next door for a little while, okay?"

"To Mrs. Rizzoli?"

"Yes. She's going to show me how to make gnocchi. You haven't had any since Nonni died."

"Ask Auntie Maria to show you how to make gnocchi. What can Mrs. Rizzoli know, she's not even Italian?"

"But since she married Paolo she's learned to make Italian things. She's a wonderful cook, everybody says so."

Jennifer Rizzoli was the wife of one of Dino's *soldati,* men who did the front-line work in the streets. So he should know how to control his wife, and it looked like he did. Jenny was a model of propriety and domestic arts, even if she was a Yankee whom Paolo had met somewhere and insisted on marrying.

God had punished this defection from the accepted way of doing things by making the woman barren, but Dino didn't hold that against her. As far as he could see, God distributed blessings and curses according to whim, and there was nothing to be done about it. Besides, Jenny did what she was told, and she really had worked hard to fit in with the ways of the North End. He didn't have any good reason to object to Rosa spending so much time with her. But it didn't make him comfortable.

"All the same, I think it's better you ask Auntie Maria to show you." In the old days that suggestion would have been interpreted as a command and instantly obeyed. Not now, not with Rosa.

"But Jenny is going to do gnocchi this afternoon whether I'm there or not. I may as well watch." She dropped a quick kiss on her father's forehead. "See you later, Pa."

Dino stared after her and shook his head. Maybe if he'd remarried it would have been different. Maybe he'd understand his daughter better. But he hadn't wanted to remarry. Because of his problem. For a while it loomed so large in his life he'd gone to a doctor about it. Not someone local here in the North End who, God forbid, could talk. He went all the way to Brookline and consulted a man named Harris with a dozen different diplomas hanging on his wall, who spoke like he had maybe eaten something that was stuck in his throat.

It hadn't been easy to tell Dr. Harris why he'd come. The man didn't seem to pick up any of his hints. Eventually Dino just said it plainly. "My problem is I can't get it up anymore. Most of the time I don't want to."

"Since your wife died?" Dr. Harris asked.

"Since before she died."

"I see. And have you been with a woman since her death?" He did not look at his patient, but kept writing something in the file he'd opened when Dino entered the office.

"Yeah," Dino admitted. "A few times. It wasn't any good." He didn't feel it necessary to explain that the women in question were Scollay Square whores who worked for him, so it didn't matter.

Dr. Harris examined him and took blood and made him pee in a bottle. A week later he went back and was told there was nothing physically wrong. "We don't understand a great deal about this yet, Mr. Saliatelli, but your problem may be something called hormones."

"Is it catching?"

The doctor didn't smile. "No, it's not a disease. It's something not quite in balance in your system."

"What does that mean?"

An explanation followed; Dino didn't understand it. "What you're saying," he summarized finally, "is I ain't got no sickness, but I got something wrong with me, and you can't fix it."

"Yes, I guess that's it," Dr. Harris said helplessly. "I'm sorry."

"Okay. It's not so terrible long as I know."

Dino was not an unhappy man when he left the office. He didn't really want another wife. He'd considered it only for Rosa's sake. Now he had an excuse, even if it was one only he knew. At least he needn't feel guilty.

The story put about was that he'd loved Catarina so passionately and her memory was so deeply enshrined in his heart that no woman could ever take her place. But Dino still wondered if it had been a big mistake where Rosa was concerned. Sometimes she really worried him. Like this business with the next-door neighbor.

The disturbing element in Mrs. Rizzoli's character was her intelligence, though Dino and the others didn't call it that, they only sensed something remarkable. Outwardly Jenny was docile and a model wife; inwardly she had the kind of mind that caused her to observe and question the ordering of a society she recognized as under siege. Had Dino known the nature of the conversations she had with his daughter, he would have done whatever was necessary to prevent Rosa from going next door.

"So you really think I could be a teacher?" Rosie asked, rolling the bits of potato-and-flour dough under her forefinger and trying to get the gnocchi to make artful little curls like Jenny's did. "You think I'm smart enough?"

"I know you're smart enough. Those gnocchi are terrible. They'll be like lead. Here, try it like this." She produced a fork and demonstrated a method for rolling the dough along the tines.

Rosie's technique improved slightly. A few morsels that at least looked like gnocchi began falling to the dishtowel spread on the kitchen table. "I'd have to go to normal school, wouldn't I?"

"You could, but I think college would be better." Jenny was a tall woman with big bones and drab hair and small, close-set eyes. At first sight she was homely and no one could figure out what Paolo Rizzoli had seen in her—until she smiled, or laughed like now. Then she was beautiful. "Thank God you don't need to get a degree in pasta making. You'd fail."

"I don't think Pa will let me."

"Make pasta?"

"You know that's not what I mean."

"Yes, I know." Jenny formed gnocchi silently for a few moments. Then, while she was lighting the stove to boil the huge cauldron of water in which the little dumplings would cook, she said, "Listen, about your father. He's not an absolute tyrant, not like some of them. He'll come around. The thing to do is get him used to the idea of college gradually."

"How?" Rosie gave up working with the sticky dough and wiped her hands of flour and bits of mashed potato. "He thinks all new ideas are terrible. Everything has to stay the same as it always was, like when he was a kid. I think he'd like to send off to Sicily for a husband for me when I'm sixteen."

Jenny grinned. "And would you marry him?"

"No. I'd run away or enter the convent or something."

"Yes, I believe you would." She paused in her cooking to put an arm around the girl's shoulders. "Rosie, I wish I'd had a daughter and I wish she'd been you."

"You're not old enough to be my mother."

"I know. But I still wish I was."

The girl hugged the woman. "It's okay, Jenny, we can be almost-sisters instead."

.   .   .   .

Growing up five miles away in Chelsea, Myer Kane, who was four years older than Rosie, also had an elder to whom he looked for advice and guidance. But Myer's mentor was his father. Unlike Dino's story about why he had never remarried, Benny's was true. He had loved his Zelda so utterly that he could not imagine filling her place with anyone else. But he didn't have Dino's large, close family into which to incorporate a motherless child. "It's just you and me, Myer," he frequently told the boy. "The two of us against all of them." It was a motto repeated often and believed firmly, at least by Benny.

Myer didn't know when he'd first understood what his father did for a living. It seemed he'd always known Pop was a *lendler,* owner of numerous tenements. Moreover, when Benny revolutionized bookmaking, he made no attempt to conceal his triumph from his son.

What Benny did was elegantly simple. The *Daily American* was a paper that came out in the late afternoon. Its biggest attraction was not the lurid stories of death, either murder or execution, in which most tabloids specialized; its appeal was to those who relished sports. It published on thin pink paper pages of game and event results—including those of the increasingly popular pastime of horse racing. "The numbers of the first four winning horses listed every day," Benny decreed. "That's the payoff number."

Good-bye to Shlomo Kornblum's hat, hello a numbers game anybody could play for as little as a nickel—and thousands did. In every neighborhood there were men, and sometimes women, who would take a bet, however tiny, and get it to Benny Kane. The numbers runner was born.

Myer saw all this as simply the way things were. It would be a while before he realized that some people viewed his father's activities with horror because many of them were illegal. What he understood first was that the way he and Pop lived cost a lot more money than a *kabtzen*, a working stiff, could make. "Poverty ain't no shame, Myer, but that's the only good thing you can say about it." That was one of Benny's favorite maxims.

"Is Mrs. O'Toole poor?" Myer asked when he was nine. Mrs. O'Toole was the lady who came in every day to clean the house and cook supper, which she left on the back of the stove for Benny to heat up later.

"For what I'm paying her she shouldn't be. Two and a half dollars a week, Myer. That's what my father used to make, and he was a skilled tailor."

"But she's always saying 'Poor me, poor me.' Like it was a song almost. She walks around the kitchen saying it."

"That's on account of she's Irish. The Irish like to cry and drink and fight. I'm not sure they have any other feelings."

"Do you give Mrs. O'Toole all your money, Pop?" little Myer asked. "Is that what you make, two dollars and fifty cents a week?"

Benny stroked his son's dark wavy hair and noted for the thousandth time that Myer had Zelda's big dark eyes. "No, *tateleh*. We couldn't live in this nice house and have a car and go to Revere Beach in the summer if I had to give all my money to Mrs. O'Toole. And you couldn't go to college and be a lawyer, like you're going to be when you grow up."

By the time Myer was ten he stopped asking questions. He learned not to press for details because he was discovering that a lot of people thought his father was a bad man. He'd overheard whispers when he was in the grocery store with Mrs. O'Toole, and some of the older kids at school said things. It was something he didn't want to talk about. But he did continue to wonder and worry about Mrs. O'Toole.

"Pop," Myer said one day when he was eleven. "I've been reading in the newspapers about Mr. Ford. They say the men who work for him don't get any time off to be with their families."

"Yeah, well they're all *goyim*. *Goyim* don't care about their families."

Myer shook his head. "No, Pop. That's not true. And Mrs. O'Toole cares about her family. Listen, I don't think she should work on Sundays. We can manage by ourselves. I'll learn to cook."

"I see. You're a union organizer now, is that it?"

"Pop, I'm serious."

Benny studied his son. "Okay, I'm serious too. Say I take your suggestion. Say she gets Sundays off. That means I'll pay her only two fifteen. She'll lose thirty-five cents a week. You think she'll want that?"

"No. That's not what I mean, Pop. Give her Sundays off but don't change her pay. Like a bonus, or a raise. She's been coming to us for a long time. She deserves it."

"Jesus," Benny said. "Jesus Christ. I don't believe it."

Myer was scared that maybe he'd made his father angry, something that had happened only a few times in his whole life but had been terrible when it did. Suddenly, though, Benny laughed. He threw back his head and opened his mouth and guffawed. "Myer, sometimes you remined me of myself when I was your age. Good-hearted and stupid. Only maybe not so stupid. You want it, okay you got it. Mrs. O'Toole gets Sundays off and the same pay."

The Sundays without help turned out to be a pleasure for father and son. Occasionally they went to a restaurant for a big lunch, more often they fooled around in the kitchen. They developed a specialty, potato *latkes*. Myer grated the potatoes and onion and mixed the egg and flour into the batter. Benny stood at the stove frying the pancakes. They both ate all they could stuff into their mouths as soon as they came out of the pan, so the waiting platter never got filled up and they never sat down to a proper meal, but eventually all the batter was used and they were replete and happy.

If it was a nice day they'd go for a walk when the orgy of *latkes* was ended. Everyone living in the streets around Benny Kane's building knew him; most were his tenants, though these days he never collected rents himself. A group standing on a corner and chatting would fall silent when Myer and Benny approached. The men would nod politely to Mr. Kane, but Myer sensed something other than respect in their attitude. He was fifteen before he dared put a name to it.

"Pop, they're all scared to death of you," he said one night. "That's what I really hate. Not that you break the law by making book, but that people are scared."

They were deep in a conversation about right and wrong and Myer was being as honest with his father as Benny had taught him to be. But hearing this from the boy's mouth, seeing the look on his son's face—that terrified Benny, and when he was frightened he got angry.

"Listen, you *pisher,* you think you know so goddamn much. What do you think I was supposed to do about your mother, who couldn't walk, may she rest in peace? Was she supposed to drag herself around the house trying to take care of me? Was she supposed to stay indoors all the time instead of having a nice automobile to go for a ride in? Was it better she suffered and I slaved in some goddamn sweatshop like my father?"

Miserable, Myer shook his head. "No, of course not. But there has to be some middle way, Pop. Something between starving to death and being a . . ." He couldn't say *crook.* He could not actually apply that word to his father. "Operating outside the law," he finished.

"There is," Benny agreed. "The way you're going to do it. Get an education and be somebody. I didn't do it. I was supposed to, but once I met your mother I couldn't wait that long. Don't give me a hard time, Myer. My Zelda's gone and it's for you, all of it. So go study and leave me alone."

Neither father nor son slept very well that night. The next day they pretended the conversation hadn't taken place.

In September of 1919 eighteen-year-old Myer Kane entered Boston University. B.U. was one of the fastest-growing schools in the nation. Its main building was on Beacon Hill, but its lecture halls and laboratories were spread all over the city. There was talk of a new unified campus on Commonwealth Avenue, but only talk.

Five months into Myer's freshman year, on January 29, 1920, the Eighteenth Amendment to the Constitution, which had been ratified one year before, went into effect. Like many others in his line of work, Benny had been preparing for the coming of Prohibition. It was going to make him richer than ever. He had a line to an illegal factory in Pittsfield that made grain alcohol, and by the middle of February he was bringing carloads of the stuff up to Boston and turning it into bathtub gin in some of the back rooms of his numerous apartments. A short time later he went to see the B.U. dean of students.

"You make sure my boy graduates and becomes a lawyer like his poor dead mother dreamed," Benny told the man, "and I'll see you get money for at least one new building on Commonwealth Avenue." It wasn't an idle promise. The amount of money already coming in from the sale of bathtub gin was staggering. "Maybe two buildings," he added. The dean nodded and quickly changed the subject.

Myer never learned of this conversation. In fact, Benny's bribe wasn't necessary. Myer Kane was a good student. At least he was when he paid attention to his studies and didn't go off on one of his many crusades.

Unions, women's rights, the unfair trial of Sacco and Vanzetti—Myer Kane joined the minority of students concerned about such things; most often he led them. He never stopped to analyze why he was swimming against the tide of the college experience of most young men during the twenties; he only knew he could do nothing else. Myer didn't slick his hair back in an attempt to look like Rudolph Valentino, he didn't carry a hip flask of homemade hooch, or join a "frat," or take part in marathon dances. When he thought about them, Myer despised those cynics and good-time-Charlies roaring with the twenties, but he didn't think about them often. It remained for Rosie Saliatelli to point out what he was doing and why, but first he had to meet her.

In 1923 Myer was graduated and went to work for a firm of lawyers on Federal Street in Boston. He would spend three years there as an apprentice, then take the bar examination. The apprenticeship involved long hours doing all the dog work in the office, but it paid nothing. He was still entirely dependent on Benny and he still lived at home in Chelsea. So he was there on the Sunday afternoon when his father said, "Myer, I want you should come with me to a meeting."

"What meeting? Where?"

"In the North End. I'm gonna see a guy named Dino Saliatelli."

Myer was reading the Sunday *Herald.* The funny papers. He kept his eyes on the doings of "Mutt and Jeff." "What do you want me for?" He had never been involved in his father's business dealings, and a meeting with some guy named Dino something in the North End had to be business. It couldn't possibly be social.

"I want you because I need a lawyer."

"Pop, I'm not a lawyer. Not yet."

"You're close enough," Benny insisted. "C'mon, get dressed. I gotta be there in an hour."

"I don't think—"

"Shut up." The words were spoken with great calm and no obvious emotion. "Shut up and don't say it, *tateleh*. Because I don't want to hear. I know what you're thinking, and I don't want to hear. Myer, you're twenty-two years old. Don't you think it's time you paid your dues?"

Myer was quiet for a moment, then he folded the paper neatly and laid it aside. "I'll get dressed."

Myer had a Ford his father had given him as a graduation present; Benny had an enormous, showy Lincoln. They took Benny's car, but Myer drove. Sitting alone in the back was Twitchy Cohen. Some people said Twitchy's nickname came about because of the tic that afflicted one side of his mouth, but it just as easily could have been inspired by the way his trigger finger worked. Myer was acutely conscious of Cohen behind him. Twitchy was a thug, a hoodlum, a crook. There was no other way to describe him, no euphemism that would mask the purpose of his presence or his relationship to Myer's father. Twitchy worked for Benny. He was along on this trip for protection.

"Here," Benny said when they came to Hanover Street. "Park near that restaurant on the corner, Freddie's."

The three men got out and stood for a moment surveying the street. It was four o'clock on Sunday afternoon and there was no one to be seen. The restaurant appeared to be closed. Myer started to lock the car. Benny waved a forestalling hand. "Leave it," he said airily. "Nobody's gonna touch my car."

Twitchy spoke for the first time. "This ain't our territory, boss."

"Say, is that so? And all the time I thought it was maybe Pinckney Street. Leave the car. C'mon."

Twitchy dashed ahead to open the door. It wasn't locked. A man wearing a tuxedo was standing inside. "Good afternoon, gentlemen. Mr. Saliatelli is waiting for you." As if they had a reservation for dinner.

He led them through the first room into a smaller one in the rear. Dino Saliatelli was sitting at a table with his back to the wall; a guy who looked like he could be Twitchy's brother was standing off to one side, near the corner, with his arms folded. Saliatelli spoke first.

"We had an agreement, one soldier apiece. How come you got two?"

"This ain't no soldier, it's my son, Myer. He's a lawyer. And we're in your territory, in your goddamn restaurant where God knows who's hiding in the kitchen. Don't give me one soldier, Dino. Can I sit down?"

"It ain't my restaurant, it's Freddie's. He's a friend, that's all. But all the same, you got a point." Dino gestured Benny and Myer to seats. "Freddie, bring some Strega." He turned to the younger man. "A lawyer, huh?"

"Not yet exactly—"

"He ain't passed the bar exam yet," Benny interrupted. "A formality, that's all. Let's get down to it. You got the place?"

"Yes. I bought it last week. The dock's gotta be fixed and reinforced. I got guys working on that now."

"Make sure the feds don't see them working. These days a dock's a dead giveaway."

Dino fixed his black eyes on Benny. Those eyes were still as remarkable as they'd been when he was a boy—compelling in their power, a shock because he was still tall and skinny and apart from the eyes didn't look at all strong or menacing. "Benny, you think you gotta tell me things like that, we ain't gonna be able to do business."

Benny hesitated a moment, then seemed to decide on the tone he would adopt for this negotiation. "You're right, Dino. I apologize. So let's get it on the table. I sell you the four houses in Scolley Square for a thousand dollars each."

"A thousand dollars on paper. I'm really gonna pay you four bucks. A dollar for each one."

"Of course, of course. Myer, we can do that? A deed that says one price when another is really paid?"

It was an asinine question. Benny Kane had bought and sold more houses than Myer had hairs on his head. His father just wanted to bring him into the conversation. "Yeah, Pop, sure you can do it if you want." Why his father should want to sell four extremely valuable Boston houses for a dollar each wasn't clear until Benny spoke again.

"Afterwards, when you got everything ready, my guys'll bring the stuff in on boats, you receive it, and take care of the distribution. We split the profits fifty-fifty."

"Yes."

The Strega arrived. It was a clear drink served in tiny glasses, each of which had two dark beans on the bottom. The beans created a slowly ascending haze of brown in the liqueur. Myer took a sip. The Strega was licorice-flavored, the beans coffee; they added a wonderful tang.

"You like it?" Dino asked.

"It's delicious."

"Yeah. I bring it in from Palermo, in the olive-oil kegs. You can't make nothing like this in a bathtub."

"Not Cuban rum neither," Benny said.

"Right," Dino agreed. "And on Cuban rum we're gonna make a fortune. I got thirty-two speakeasies lined up already."

"I want contracts with 'em. That'll be Myer's job."

Dino frowned. "They ain't gonna want to sign no contracts. This ain't Woolworth's we're dealing with."

"They'll sign," Benny said calmly. "Me and my boys, we'll see to it. Myer, you can make the contracts?"

"I can write them, sure, Pop." He wanted to ask how his father intended to enforce a contract made with an entity that wasn't supposed to exist to supply an illegal commodity, but he knew better than to do so.

Benny stood up. "Okay, that's it. Myer will bring the papers in a couple of days."

"Not here," Dino said. "I'm moving into the new place for a while. Just until we're sure everything's running smooth. He can bring me the contracts there, next Sunday."

"Good," Benny said. "A good idea." He extended his hand and Dino shook it.

Myer didn't say a word during the ride back to Chelsea, not until Twitchy Cohen had left them and they were back upstairs in their living room. "Pop," he asked quietly, "what the hell was that all about? What's with these cockamamy contracts that no court would enforce? Why did you take me along?"

Benny didn't answer immediately. When he did he spoke slowly and clearly. "I brought you 'cause I want you should understand how things are, Myer. 'Cause I want you should see that you don't have to be a struggling *putz* lawyer chasing ambulances and fire engines."

"Pop, I'm not even a lawyer yet. When I am, that'll be time enough to see what kind of a practice I should have."

"Yeah, maybe so. But there's lots you gotta understand, *tateleh*, 'cause your pop's not so young anymore and he ain't gonna change. Now let's not talk anymore about it. You just make the papers, okay?"

"Okay."

A week later Myer had finished the documents and he was instructed to take them to Dino Saliatelli's new home. "He's on Nahant. Way out in the woods with nobody around but sea gulls," Benny explained. "It's a perfect setup."

Dino had finally done it. After all these years he'd bought a place by the sea, like Catarina always wanted. But not for her reasons. Nahant was a neck of land jutting out from the town of Lynn on what was called Boston's North Shore. It was mostly summer houses and fisherman's shacks, and it was connected to the mainland by a narrow causeway over which a bus ran twice a day.

Dino's house was some thirty years old, built by an old New England banker as a summer home but hated by his wife and thus almost never used and finally sold. Dino had bought it furnished. The day he and Rosie moved in, the only thing they brought with them were their clothes.

"Pa, I can't stay up here. What am I going to do all day? Who can I talk to? I'll go crazy."

"You won't go crazy, I promise. Besides, you can take the bus into Boston whenever you want. And we won't be here long. Just a few months, just for the summer. Until my business is settled."

Rosie had a pretty good idea what the business was. She knew the dock was being reinforced and the cellar beneath the house deepened and made secure with specially built doors. She was indifferent to that just as she'd been indifferent all her life to her father's affairs. In the world she'd grown up in such things were what men did. Every man Rosie knew either worked for her father or was one of his rivals. Such were not the concerns that occupied her mind.

"Why can't I invite Jenny to come and spend a little while with us? She hasn't been feeling well. She can't get rid of that cough. She's had it since the winter."

"I don't want anybody here but you and me and your Auntie Maria, who's gonna cook. I got a lot of business to do."

Rosie knew that if she'd asked for any companion other than Jenny Rizzoli, the answer would probably have been yes. She flounced out of the house and went to sit under a tree. She spent a lot of time under that tree the first few days in Nahant. She was sitting there on Sunday when Myer Kane drove his Ford up the drive and parked it.

"Hi, I'm Myer Kane. I have an appointment with Mr. Saliatelli."

"He's inside," Rosie said, standing up. He was just fractionally taller than she, which wasn't wonderful, but she noted his nice wavy dark hair, his intelligent sort of refined face, and his smile that showed off remarkably white teeth. He looked at her tall slim grace, at her violet eyes, felt the strength in the grip of the hand she extended to him. They walked up the path to the house together.

· · · ·

All that summer they connived to meet, knowing without ever needing to discuss it that if either of their fathers learned of the blossoming romance, it would be ended. Rosie would be shipped off someplace far away, maybe even Sicily. Myer would be told that if he wanted to finish his apprenticeship and take the bar exam, he'd damn well do what his father wanted, and that would not include making whoopee with a girl guinea.

"That's what he'd call me, isn't it?" Rosie asked. "A guinea."

"Maybe," Myer admitted. "In my father's world the only real people are Jews. Everyone else is some kind of caricature existing only in his mind."

"How come they're working together, your father and mine? I've never known Pa to have a partner before."

"Neither of them has ever had a partner. But rum running is big business. You don't do it out of your pocket. The capital investment that's needed is enormous. And just last year my pop took two high-powered speedboats in payment of a debt. He wasn't sure how to use them until he managed the connection in

Havana. But it seems your father has most of the speakeasies tied up. So they had to get together."

They were in a little café on Beacon Hill which Myer knew from student days. It was not a place where they were likely to be seen by anyone connected with either Benny or Dino. Rosie played with the spoon in her dish of ice cream, studying Myer from under her long lashes. "Do you work for your father often?"

Myer shook his head. "This is the first time. I hate it."

"Why?"

"Rosie, listen, I know how things are with them, your pa and my pop, but I'm not like that. I'm not a racketeer. I don't want to be one."

Rosie didn't flinch at the word. She had an innate directness and honesty about her. It was one of the qualities that most attracted Myer. And she always said exactly what she was thinking, without any coy pretenses. "Then why did you agree to do this job?" she asked.

"Because my father made it seem very important to him. He said something about paying my dues. And . . ." He hesitated.

"And?" she prompted.

"I love him. I don't want him to think I'm sitting in judgment."

"I know," Rosie said. "I love Pa too. Even though he drives me crazy with his old-fashioned ideas. I want to go to college. So far I can't get him to agree."

Myer looked at the clock over the counter. "C'mon, we have to go if we're not going to be late."

He was taking her to a debate on minority rights to be held in the storefront office of the League to Free Sacco and Vanzetti. It wasn't Rosie's first brush with Myer's beloved causes; she'd already seen him march for the right to unionize and heard him speak on the abolition of capital punishment. Tonight he wasn't on the podium for once, but sat beside her in the back of the small, crowded room, and after fifteen minutes he was holding her hand.

"What did you think?" he asked when the debate ended and he was driving her home.

"I figured it out."

"What? The reason they convicted Sacco and Vanzetti? It was nothing but prejudice and spite; the state didn't prove its case."

"Not that. You. You use all these good works to salve your

conscience for spending ill-gotten gains. You're paying your dues, like your father said. But not the way he meant."

It was profoundly simple but he'd never thought of it before. Myer was silent as he maneuvered his Ford across Dock Square.

"You better let me out here," Rosie said. "I can walk to Jenny's." She was spending the night at the Rizzolis, a rare concession wrung from her father by endless pleading.

Myer slammed on the brakes and banged his fist on the steering wheel.

"What's the matter?" she asked.

"I hate all this sneaking around. And you're right, that is what I'm doing with my *pro bono publico* crusades. All the time I told myself it was altruism."

"I'm not sure what that means."

"Doing something with no thought of personal gain."

"Oh." She let herself out of the car, jumping off the running board with her customary grace. "Myer, get out, will you?"

He turned off the motor and the headlights and clambered down and walked around the car to join her. "Good," she said. "Now I can reach you." Rosie leaned forward and kissed his cheek. "That's to tell you that you are a very nice man. It doesn't matter what your motives are, what matters is what you accomplish."

He pulled her into his arms. It was the first time he'd kissed her and it went on a long time, and for the first few seconds Rosie thought about the fact that even though it was a moonless night and pitch dark in Dock Square, this was a very dangerous place for them to be embracing. Everyone within a radius of ten blocks owed allegiance of one sort or another to her father. Then she just thought about the way his mouth tasted and the way his tongue probing hers made her feel. Finally they broke apart.

"Rosie," he whispered. "I love you. I want to marry you."

She stared at him, or where she knew he would be if she could see him, and didn't say anything for a while.

"Rosie," he repeated. "I love you. Do you love me? Could you learn to love me?"

"I love you, Myer. I've loved you from the first moment I saw you."

"Then will you marry me?"

"Just say when," she murmured.

"Whenever we can. As soon as we can convince our fathers that they can't stop us."

"That day won't ever come," Rosie said. "We'll elope, Myer. Then we'll tell them we've done it. It's the only way."

.   .   .   .

The scene with Benny and Dino was the stuff of family legends. Myer set it up to take place on Nahant. He told both men they had a legal problem they had to solve immediately, and they could only do it together.

"I don't believe it," Benny kept repeating when the newly-weds stood hand in hand in front of them and made their announcement.

"I believe it," Dino said. "But I don't want to."

"Why?" Rosie demanded. "What's so terrible, Pa? You wanted me to get married and settle down and not go to college. Now I've done it. Why are you so upset?"

"I wanted you to marry one of your own, one of our kind. And have I been such a terrible father you would show me such disrespect? Sneak off and get married like some *puttana*, without a priest, without a proper wedding."

"We can't have a priest; Myer's not a Catholic."

"And you're not a Jew," Benny said. He was studying Rosie, trying to see what there was about this admittedly pretty but not beautiful young girl that would make Myer break his heart like this. "Your father is right," he said, "people should marry their own kind."

"Bullshit," Myer said. "You're talking bullshit, Pop. People should marry whom they love. Like you did when you married my mother."

That emotional appeal coupled with heretofore unknown impertinence set the fireworks going. Benny and Dino both gave up questions and calm reason. They ranted and they raved and they shook their fists, as much at each other as at their two disobedient children. It went on for nearly half an hour, and through it all Myer and Rosie stood and held hands and listened. Finally they could take no more.

"Shut up!" Myer bellowed. "Shut up, both of you! It's enough. We're not going to listen anymore. Rosie and I are leaving. If you come to your senses, you can let us know."

"You're not taking my daughter out of this house," Dino roared.

"He is," Rosie said. "We're married, Pa. We spent last night together. It's too late for you to do anything. Maybe I'm even pregnant."

The word dropped into a sudden silence. Benny was the first to break it. "You're gonna have a baby, that's what this is all about?"

"You stubborn old fool," Myer exploded. "If Rosie's pregnant, she's exactly twelve hours along. What do you think we are? We love each other. We're going to make a life together. We love both of you, too, so if you want to be part of our lives, fine. If not, that's your choice."

A month later Benny sought out his son in the furnished room in Everett where he and Rosie were living. It was a tiny drab hole in the back of a gloomy old house on Dean Street. "Some place you got here," Benny said.

"It's all we can afford just now," Myer said stiffly.

"How come you can afford even this?"

"I sold my car. And I've left the law office. I've got a job as a trainee salesman in Filene's. I start next Monday."

"Terrific. My son the salesman. Where's Rosie?"

"Gone to do some shopping." He gestured toward one corner. "We have a hot plate."

"Get packed."

"Pop, let's not start all over again," Myer said wearily.

"What start? I got a surprise I want to show you. A wedding present."

Rosie walked in just then. She looked at Benny and at Myer. "Hello, Mr. Kane."

"Mr. Kane you don't call your father-in-law. I'm Pop."

"I see. Okay, I like that better too. Hello, Pop."

"Put that stuff away." He gestured to the bags of groceries in Rosie's arms. "I'm taking you and Myer to see something. A surprise."

It was a house on Walnut Street in Newton. Big and sunny, with eleven rooms. A family house. "This isn't the fanciest part of Newton, but it's nice. A *goyisher* neighborhood—not Jewish, but not Italian either. Dino and me, we talked it over. Neutral territory, not his and not mine."

"You've spoken with my father?" Rosie asked.

"Of course. We're partners. We talk a few times a week. And now, God help us, we're *mishpocheh*."

"Related by marriage," Myer translated quickly.

"Yeah, and maybe even we're gonna be joint grandfathers. So we have to talk."

Rosie shook her head. "Not the grandfather part, not yet anyway."

"So you've only been married a month. What's the hurry? Besides, Myer ain't got his law practice going yet."

"Pop, I'm not going to be a lawyer. I told you. I gave up the apprenticeship. I'm a married man now. I have to earn a living."

"Yeah, selling *schmattes* in Filene's. Here, take this." He reached into his pocket and Myer expected him to withdraw money, which he intended to refuse. Instead, it was only a slip of paper.

"What is this?"

"All the stuff you need to know about the bar examination you're gonna take next month. Where, what time, all that stuff."

"I can't take the bar, I haven't completed the apprenticeship. It's a requirement."

"You can take it. I got it all arranged." Myer started to speak, but Benny held up his hand. "Shut up and listen, will you? Okay, I pulled some strings and used influence to get you on the list. But that doesn't make you a lawyer, *tateleh*. That you gotta do by yourself. You're smart enough to pass the test even though you didn't finish the apprentice business?"

Myer pursed his lips. "With a month to study, yes, maybe, I think so."

"Okay. So study. And if you can pass it, you'll be a lawyer and you did it yourself, not me. And if not, well, you can sell *shmattes* in Filene's. At least you don't have to live in a hole in the wall in Everett. The house is free and clear. A wedding present from Dino and me."

Two months later they erected the sign on the lawn. MYER KANE, ATTORNEY AT LAW. Both Dino and Benny were present for the occasion, and a way of life had been established.

Sometimes Myer thought it was crazy, that he must be the world's biggest hypocrite. His father and father-in-law were careful to keep him from actually doing anything illegal—he merely gave them counsel—but still he was working for racketeers and he knew it. Which made him financially secure and able to do the kind of work he cared about, to represent those who normally couldn't afford a lawyer and to take up the cudgel for whatever cause he was committed to at the moment.

"It's okay," Rosie said. "It's a compromise, Myer, but a good one. Not everyone would understand it, but the way you and I were raised, we do. And that's all that matters."

So that's how it was. And life was good, despite two sadnesses. Jenny Rizzoli died of tuberculosis, and for the first three years of their marriage Rosie didn't conceive, not until the winter of 1926 during a week's vacation they spent at cold, windswept, romantically foggy Nantasket Beach. Which is how their only daughter came to be born on Boston Common the day Sacco and Vanzetti were executed, and why she was named Jennifer.

Chapter 3

Religion wasn't an operative part of life at the Kanes on Walnut Street. Rosie wasn't much of a Catholic, and in theological terms, Myer wasn't much of a Jew. The couple thought of themselves and their daughter as Americans, living life a new way, a modern way. But that didn't apply to Benny and Dino.

The grandfathers were involved in a war to possess in some irrevocable way the little girl whom both adored. They loved their son and daughter, too, but the battle for their children they already deemed lost. Juffie was new and unclaimed territory. Each birthday, and on every occasion for which he could manufacture an excuse, Benny gave her a Magen David, a six-pointed star, on a chain. Some were sterling silver, some gold, some encrusted with tiny diamond chips, others with pearls. "A regular collection," Myer said wryly. "Maybe someday she can give them to a museum."

"Yeah," Rosie agreed. "They can display them next to her collection of crosses."

Naturally, it was Dino who'd given her those. He was as regular and lavish with his presents of jewelry depicting the crucified Christ as Benny was with stars. If anything, the crosses were more ornate. At first Rosie didn't let her wear any of the jewelry. But by the time she was five Juffie understood what each of her beloved grandfathers wanted. "Mama, can't I wear one of the stars today, since Pop's taking me to the circus?"

"You want to?" Rosie asked hesitantly. "You're sure?" She wondered if perhaps her daughter considered herself more Jewish than Italian.

"Yes," Juffie said. "I'm sure. Only 'cause Pop will like it. And

Pa won't see me. Next time Pa takes me someplace I can wear one of the crosses."

Rosie and Myer laughed till their sides ached when they reviewed the story later. "Incredible," Myer said. "Five years old and she's a diplomat."

"What gets me is that she's figured them both out. Myer, this little girl of ours is going to grow up to be some kind of dynamite."

Jewelry was not the only theater of engagement. There was also food. Rosie had learned well her lessons in Jenny Rizzoli's kitchen. She was quite a good cook. But naturally her style was Italian. "Suits me," Myer always said. "I love Italian food." It didn't suit Benny.

"Rosie, listen darling, how about I show you how to make some Jewish things? For Myer."

"Fine, I'd like that, Pop."

"And Juffie can watch too." He reached for the little girl, who was never far away, and pulled her onto his lap. "How about it, gorgeous? You want to taste some *Yiddisher* cooking?"

Juffie nodded enthusiastically. And she ate Benny's chopped liver and his famous potato *latkes* with delight. Not everything worked out as well. The gefilte fish was a disaster. Benny was philosophical about it. "It's difficult; even my mother couldn't make it good. Anyhow, Juffie doesn't like fish."

Dino was not without ammunition on the culinary front. Sometimes he took his granddaughter to the North End, to a bakery that had a few tables in the back and served coffee, and, after Prohibition was repealed in 1933, sweet liqueurs to accompany wonderful pastries stuffed with cream and morsels of chocolate and covered in drifts of white sugar. Other days he came to the house bearing the two-crusted filled pie known as pizza rustica, or spinach-stuffed raviolis made by his sister Maria, or five-gallon jugs of olive oil, or *scamozze* cheese, or big glass jars of succulent black olives. Juffie avowed as how she loved everything except the olives.

"When you get older, beautiful," Dino assured her, "then you'll like olives. It's what gives all little Sicilian girls like you their wonderful skin. So they grow up to be beautiful Sicilian ladies, only not half so beautiful as you're gonna be."

"Pa," Juffie questioned the day he made this speech, "why is it my eyes aren't like yours?"

"Because they're sort of like your mother's, and hers were like her mother's," Dino explained.

"But your eyes always look like you can see everything."

"You don't see good?" he asked in alarm, as if some flaw had been discovered in perfection.

"Yes, I do. I think so. But you seem to . . . I don't know, to look through things."

"I do," Dino assured her. "I do. And I see everything even when I'm not here. So you gotta be a perfect little girl and do everything your mama tells you."

Perfect Juffie was not. Normal. And almost as bright as she was lovely. She could read by herself before she entered first grade—Rosie, who really had wanted to be a teacher, practiced on her daughter—and she listened to every word said by the adults who surrounded her. Like many only children she developed a remarkable vocabulary. Once she astounded Myer by asking, "What's a tort?"

"Tort, where did you hear that, princess?"

"You said it yesterday. To Mama, I heard you."

"Yes, I guess I did. Tort is a legal term. It means somebody hasn't done what they're supposed to do, so you take them to court."

"So if I don't clean my room when Mama says, she can take me to court?"

Myer swallowed hard to suppress his laughter. "Not exactly. But you should clean your room, Juffie. Because Mama told you to. And because your toys are all over the place. I think the two pandas must be very unhappy living in such a mess."

Which was a genuine fault, not one imagined by her hovering grandfathers. Despite Rosie's continuing efforts to teach her neatness, Juffie was unbearably messy. Once one of Rosie's lectures took place in front of Pop, the standard one about keeping things where they belonged and not forgetting to put the covers back on jars and bottles and tubes of toothpaste.

"So what," Benny said, hugging the child. "Juffie, I ain't saying you shouldn't listen to your mama, of course you should. But when you grow up you're gonna marry a prince and live in a castle and have servants to pick up everything. A nice Jewish prince, right?"

Not if Pa had anything to say about it, Juffie thought. If it was up to Pa, she'd have to marry an Italian prince. But with Benny she only smiled and nodded her head yes and hugged him.

If Myer and Rosie, who, after all, had the full-time responsibility of raising the child, were not quite so constantly effusive in their praise of everything she did and every breath she drew, they were nonetheless the most devoted and loving of parents. Juffie was included in all their activities. They allowed her to participate in discussions and voice an opinion which was carefully listened to, and never was she left behind when there was a demonstration to attend. The only prerequisite was that it be peaceful, and most were.

When she was eight Juffie came across the word *fawning* in a book and looked up its meaning. After that she always thought of her parents and grandparents as "the fawning four," but she loved them as much as they loved her. The house on Walnut Street was a warm, secure haven; a place of laughter and humor despite the squabbles engendered by the ethnic clash, and Myer and Rosie's endless do-gooding. Rosie had become as committed as her husband to fighting for the rights of the oppressed—maybe because they didn't have to look far to find them during the painful Depression years of the 1930s.

In the first year of that fateful decade both Kanes flirted with the Young Communist League. But Rosie said she didn't trust the leader of the cell whose meetings they had attended. "He has a fishy look," she insisted. Myer wasn't sure about that, but unlike most of the members of the league, he actually read Marx, and he was uncomfortable with much of the doctrine.

"This withering-away-of-the-state business," he told Rosie. "I just don't see that ever happening. Not in the real world." So they stopped attending cell meetings. It left a void in their lives until Franklin Roosevelt announced in 1931 that he would run for president.

"Now, here's a guy making some sense finally," Myer said.

Rosie agreed wholeheartedly, and she and her husband founded an organization called "Newton for F.D.R.," and thus joined the ranks of Roosevelt's earliest and most ardent supporters. By the time he was elected, Juffie had come to believe that Roosevelt was another name for God.

The Kanes were also part of a group trying to silence the anti-

Semitic "radio priest," Father Charles E. Coughlin, and Myer joined a national organization of attorneys attempting to outlaw the Ku Klux Klan. But his first and most ardent concern remained the working classes and their right to form unions.

In 1936 Myer went to Michigan to support the strikers attempting to organize General Motors. He came home with a broken arm and a black eye, earned opposing Pinkerton men on the picket lines.

Juffie and Rosie treated him like the hero he was, and the child became her mother's ally in not allowing Pa or Pop to voice a single word of criticism about Myer's dangerous antics. Then, on two separate occasions, Walter Reuther and John L. Lewis each came to dinner on Walnut Street. Juffie knew they were great men trying to help the workers, and each time she told everybody in school about the visits. She also organized both her fourth and fifth grade classes to write letters to President Roosevelt in support of the New Deal and "being fair to *everybody* in America."

On the May day in 1938 when the *Herald* story erupted into Juffie's world of placards and marches and mailings on behalf of the righteous and the just and the good, she had no defenses against its revelations. In one afternoon, at the age of eleven, Juffie Kane had all her illusions shattered.

The Kanes didn't take the *Herald*; it was the newspaper of the Republican right, of Boston Brahmins. It opposed F.D.R. in 1932 and 1936. But Juffie passed a newsstand on her way home from school, and that particular afternoon she saw that the *Herald* had a picture of Pa and Pop. Her grandfathers occupied a quarter of the front page of the late edition, and they were both handcuffed and above them was a bold black headline that said, "A Blow Against Organized Crime."

She stood there for a moment, frozen in disbelief, then she searched through her pockets until she found a nickel, and she bought the paper and read it while she walked the rest of the distance to Walnut Street. "Benjamin Kane of Chelsea and Dino Saliatelli of Boston have been indicted by a special grand jury on charges of conspiring to defraud, engaging in illegal gaming, and operating houses of ill fame." Juffie didn't know what that last meant, but she had no time to puzzle about it. The next paragraph concerned her parents.

"This reporter has learned that an alliance of the two racketeers took place approximately fifteen years ago, at the same time
that Kane's son, Myer, married Saliatelli's daughter, Rosa. Myer
Kane is an attorney and it is alleged he has provided legal advice
for his father and father-in-law, but as yet no charges have been
brought. . . ."

Juffie broke into a run when she turned into Walnut Street. She
raced up the path and into the house and burst into her father's
office. Miss Gold, the secretary, wasn't there. Her desktop was
polished and empty, the way it was on Sundays and holidays,
when she wasn't working. The door to Myer's office was closed.
Juffie ran to it and turned the knob, but it was locked.

"Daddy!" She pounded on the door, but there was no reply.
"Daddy, are you in there?" Still no answer. She gave up and
dashed up the stairs. No one was in the living room, no committee
was meeting to stuff envelopes or make placards to carry in a
demonstration. "Mama! Mama, where are you?"

The house seemed to be empty. There had been very few days
in Juffie's life when she'd returned to an empty house. She ran to
the kitchen. Her mother had to be in the kitchen. But she wasn't.
Instead, there was a plate of Toll House cookies on the table, and a
note. "Precious, Daddy and I had to go out. We may be away until
dinnertime. Have some milk and cookies and be a good girl. We'll
be home before it gets dark."

Juffie wasn't in the least hungry. She sat down at the table and
pushed the plate of cookies away and spread out the newspaper
and read the story again. It was just as horrible the second time.
How could they tell all these lies about Pa and Pop and her father?
How could they get away with printing this stuff? They couldn't,
of course. *That's* where everybody was. Daddy had gone straight
down to that terrible newspaper to sue them. And Mama and
Miss Gold had gone with him to help. Juffie felt much better as
soon as she thought of that. She reached for a Toll House cookie.

Around five she realized that probably when her parents
returned there'd be lots of people with them. That's how it always
was when one of the causes was "heating up," as Daddy put it.
Normally Rosie would be in the kitchen preparing food for an
inevitably hungry crowd. But she was busy today, so Juffie would
have to take her place. At age eleven she wasn't much of a cook,

but in a house like hers, certain of the social skills had been absorbed through the pores.

She filled the big percolator with water and spooned coffee into the perforated metal basket. Lighting the stove was easy, it was new last year and had an automatic pilot. The bread box held a large loaf of rye, and Juffie sliced it and found mustard and salami and bologna and made open-faced sandwiches because she remembered Rosie saying if you were short you could stretch a loaf farther that way. She climbed up on the step stool to reach the top shelf of the pantry, where Rosie stored her homemade pickled green tomatoes. Doubtless both Pa and Pop would be with them when they came home, and her grandfathers loved pickles. But the *Herald* said that Dino and Benny were in jail.

She stopped in the middle of the kitchen floor, still holding the jar of bright green tomatoes, trying to imagine what jail was like. Would Pa and Pop be wearing striped suits with numbers on them like in the movies? And would they be allowed to share a cell so they could keep arguing the way they always did? No. No to both questions. Because they weren't in jail. Not now anyway. Her father would have gone down there and gotten them out. He always got people out of jail when they were put there for things they didn't do.

When she'd done everything she could think of, Juffie surveyed the table with its trays of sandwiches, and plates of pickled tomatoes, and a wicker basket full of the potato chips she'd discovered in the pantry. Rosie would have provided cole slaw and potato salad as well, and probably a bowl of white beans and tomatoes with olive oil and oregano. But Juffie didn't know how to make any of those things. Okay, it didn't matter. There was enough to get started with. Her mother would fill in the gaps as soon as she got home.

Juffie glanced at the clock on the wall over the almost new General Electric refrigerator. It was after six. But it was still light out. Nothing to worry about. She didn't mind being in the big empty house as long as it was light.

At a few minutes past seven, when the sun was just beginning to set, she heard the front door open. Juffie ran to the head of the stairs. Her mother was already halfway up them, and her father was right behind. That was all, only the two of them. "Where is everybody?" Juffie demanded. "Where's Pa and Pop?"

"They're not here, darling," Rosie said softly. "Why? Did you expect them?" She'd reached the landing by then and she put her arms around her daughter, but Juffie stiffened and pulled away.

"I read the paper," she blurted out. "I saw it on my way home from school." She turned to her father, who still hadn't spoken. "I figured you went to get Pa and Pop out of jail and to sue the newspaper for telling lies about us. You did, didn't you?"

Myer opened his mouth, but no words came out. He tried again. "Princess, I think we'd better have a talk. There are some things it's hard to understand when you're eleven years old—"

Juffie didn't let him finish. She turned and ran to the kitchen and began picking up all the platters of food and dumping them on the shiny linoleum floor. Myer ran after her and grabbed hold of her shoulders, holding her back and shaking her at the same time. "Hey! What's this? What are you doing? Juffie, for God's sake . . ."

Rosie came to the kitchen door and saw what had been done and what her daughter was doing now. "Let her go, Myer. She made food for a crowd and she's disappointed because they didn't appear." Her voice was quiet and controlled, a marked contrast to her daughter's choked sobs and Myer's shouts.

"What crowd? Why did she think there'd be a crowd?"

Rosie spoke to her husband as if he were a small child who required an explanation of the obvious. "Because all her life there's been a crowd. All her life we've been in the middle of crowds." She turned away from him and wrapped Juffie in her strong arms, holding so tight the girl couldn't pull away. "Darling, thank you for doing all this. It was wonderful. And you were perfectly sensible to think there would be a lot of people with us when we came home. But—"

Juffie interrupted her with a shout, tipping her head back so she could look directly into Rosie's violet eyes, so like her own but for the striking dark rings. "Where are Pa and Pop? Where are they?"

Rosie couldn't say they were in jail. She wanted to tell the truth, but she couldn't speak the words. "The police are holding them. Daddy's going to get them out. Just like you guessed. Of course Daddy's going to get them out."

The girl turned to her father, wrenching free of Rosie's embrace. "You can post bail. You always do that when somebody goes to jail for something they didn't do. I've heard you talk about it a million times."

Myer wished for a moment that his daughter were not so bright, that she hadn't been included from the first in so many of their activities. Now he could do nothing but tell her the truth. A part of the truth at least. She was too smart for anything else. "The judge has refused to set bail."

"Why? Why would the judge be so mean?" Juffie screamed the words, hurling them at him with the force of a blow.

"It's not uncommon in cases like this," Myer said. He spoke to her as if she were an adult, a client demanding an explanation of the law that was causing so much pain.

"Cases like what? That newspaper, the *Herald*, it told a lot of terrible lies. Just like you say it always does about President Roosevelt. Did you tell the judge that? Did you explain about the lies?"

"Juffie," Rosie tried again. "Juffie, please calm down and listen. . . ."

Juffie backed away from them, stepping unaware on the scattered slices of salami and bologna and bread on the floor, ignoring the mustard her shoes smeared over the linoleum. When she reached the wall she pressed against it, willing the plaster to give way and allow her to escape still farther from the expressions of despair and sorrow on her parents' faces.

The pain was terrible, a lump of it was stuck in her throat, another twisting in her stomach. Pop and Pa, Pop and Pa . . . She wasn't ever going to see them again. Nothing was going to be the way it used to be. The five of them had seemed a knot, never to be untied, Mama and Dad and Pop and Pa, and Juffie in the center of it surrounded by all of them, loved by all of them. Now the knot was coming apart and she was floating free. If such a thing could happen, there was no place safe, no place really secure in the whole world. There was nothing you could be absolutely sure wasn't going to change or go away.

Her voice became a hoarse whisper. Her eyes bored into her father's. "In the paper they said you were a lawyer for crooks and racketeers."

Myer felt a moment's relief. "That's plain libel and slander," he said firmly. "There's no evidence of any crime and nobody has charged me with anything. I haven't read the *Herald* article yet, but if that's what it says, I'll sue. Just as you guessed. You were dead right, Juffie. Maybe we'd better make you a lawyer when you grow up."

She wouldn't be diverted. "But what it said about Pa and Pop—that they were in charge of gambling and"—she couldn't remember the other words, houses of ill something—"and other illegal stuff. Was that true?"

Rosie and Myer looked at each other, communicating silently for a long moment. They both knew they had to remain true to some of their principles, to the compromise they'd lived with for so many years. They couldn't tell Juffie a flat-out lie; that was different from simply shielding her from the facts. "It's true in a way," Myer said at last. "But not the way—"

Juffie didn't listen to any further explanation. She ran from the room up the stairs to her bedroom and slammed the door.

Blackness surrounded her, but it was more than mere night. This was the dark of pure terror, of the sudden force-fed realization that the world was not as she wanted it to be, as she had until now believed it to be. Her rage and her anguish were beyond tears. There was only a terrible silence in her universe and in herself.

"Juffie, please, darling . . ." Rosie's voice, at the door.

"Go away. I don't want to talk to you, go away."

During that long night both her parents tried repeatedly to comfort her, and each time she made the same response. Eventually, they left her alone. "Some answers Juffie has to find for herself," Myer said finally. Rosie hated that, but she knew he was right.

She didn't return to school the next day or any of those that followed. Three weeks later the term ended without Juffie Kane being at the last-day party. No one was surprised. The newspapers were full of stories about her grandfathers and her father. It was even on the Yankee Network News at six o'clock. "Boston is fortunate to have a crusading district attorney who is determined to throw the mob and its foreign-inspired illegal activities out of our proud city" was the station's editorial comment.

The Kanes' daily life returned to a semblance of normality, but no one came to the house. The many friends of the causes and the committees had disappeared like snow in summer. Miss Gold came to work every day, sitting red-eyed and tight-lipped behind her desk, her devotion to Mr. Kane apparently undiminished by the present crisis. Vaguely Juffie remembered that a couple of times she'd seen Pop stop and talk with Miss Gold, and that he'd said she was an old friend of his. So whatever was happening, had happened, the secretary was somehow part of it. Which was why she wasn't surprised when it was Miss Gold who tapped on her door one afternoon.

Juffie was lying on the bed reading, or at least holding a book. "Juffie, please come downstairs with me. Your father is in his office and he'd very much like to talk with you."

"I don't want to talk with him."

The older woman stood her ground, looking at the girl upon whom so much love and affection and hope had been lavished. "You listen to me, young lady," she said finally. "All your life your parents and your grandfathers have doted on you. They've given you everything money could buy and adored you. Now there is trouble in this house and the only thing you can do is turn your back and ignore it, and act like something terrible has been done to you personally. Well, you're going to go downstairs and listen to your father if I have to drag you by the hair."

Miss Gold didn't understand; nobody understood. It wasn't herself she was worried about. It was Pa and Pop. "My grandfathers—"

"Don't talk to me about them," the secretary interrupted. "I can't bear it. I'm sick every time I think of poor Mr. Kane in that place, going through God knows what."

Juffie gasped. That was just it. What were Pa and Pop going through? What terrible things were happening to them in jail? How could her father allow this to happen? When she thought of that her anguish became anger. "Leave me alone. Just go away and leave me alone, will you?"

"No," Miss Gold insisted. "I most definitely will not." The woman stood barely five feet. Juffie was already three inches taller than she. But there was absolute determination in the secretary's eyes and in her stance. They faced each other silently for a few seconds. Finally Juffie got off the bed and walked to the door. "I'll come, but I won't believe a word my father says."

She was standing next to Miss Gold when she spoke and the words weren't out of her mouth before the woman brought up her hand and slapped Juffie full across the face. It was the very first time anybody had ever struck her. "You march yourself down-stairs. Now. And you show your father the respect he deserves. March!"

"Juffie," Myer began when she was seated across from his desk. "We've got to talk. I know you feel terrible, as if we've all betrayed you. Somehow I've got to make you understand."

Not me, she wanted to shout. It's not me you've betrayed, it's them, Pa and Pop. . . . She couldn't say it, couldn't find the words or the courage for such an accusation. The only response she could muster to this suddenly topsy-turvy world was hostility.

"Understand what?" she asked sullenly. Deep inside Juffie knew that the charges brought against her grandfathers were probably true. If they were not, the atmosphere in her house would be very different. Myer and Rosie would be building themselves up for a battle they meant to win, and dozens of people would be meeting in the living room every night planning what to do and how to do it. That's how it always was with the causes. It was nothing like that now, and so probably Pa and Pop were guilty and her father didn't for a moment believe he could prove otherwise.

"Understand the forces that drove the immigrants who came here in the last century," Myer said in answer to her question. "It was terrible for them, Juffie. There was wicked discrimination. They couldn't get work. Their families were starving. They tried to earn a living however they could. It was a jungle, and they had to eat or be eaten."

"Everybody in America is an immigrant of some kind. You always say that. But they're not all racketeers and they don't get put in jail."

"True," Myer said softly. "I can't fault your logic, Juffie. That's what has always bothered me too. That's why I've worked so hard to change things, so people wouldn't be driven by poverty to break the law."

She'd had a long time to think about it, and she had known that sooner or later she'd have this talk with her father. Her main question was waiting and ready. She stared straight at him. "Did you work with them, the way the newspapers said you did?"

"Sometimes," Myer admitted. "But not in an unlawful way. Everybody is entitled to legal advice, princess. The guilty and the innocent. There is no crime in a lawyer providing it."

"You helped them do the things they shouldn't do. Maybe if you hadn't, they'd have stopped, and they wouldn't be in jail now."

Myer shook his head. "It's not that simple, believe me. Your mother and I have talked about this a thousand times. We've done what we felt was right, Juffie. And we've tried to use what we have in your best interest first of all, because you're our first love and our first responsibility, and then for all the people out there who need a helping hand."

Juffie didn't say anything. After a few seconds of silence she stood up. "Can I go now?"

Sadly, Myer nodded agreement.

In the autumn they didn't send her back to the public school. She was enrolled at the Chestnut Hill Day School for Young Ladies. Juffie hated it. The other girls were different from her or anybody she'd ever known. They'd all been friends for years and they talked of people and places and events about which she knew nothing. They called F.D.R. and Mrs. Roosevelt rude names, and once Juffie found the words "a guinea and a Jew made you too," scrawled on her locker in red crayon. It didn't help in the least that she became more beautiful every day.

When she was thirteen it was all there. Her breasts had already matured sufficiently to require a bra, her waist was tiny, and her hips softly rounded. She was five feet five and still growing, but she never had the stretched-out awkwardness that some tall girls temporarily endured. Juffie was willowy from the first.

After age twelve most of Chestnut Hill's young ladies wore their hair up; not Juffie. She defiantly let her long dark honey waves hang free, simply brushed back from the prominent widow's peak. She didn't dare wear any makeup; Rosie would never permit it. But secretly she tweezed her eyebrows, desperately wanting them to look like Katharine Cornell's, and rubbed Vaseline into her eyelashes so they would look even longer than they were. She was always pinching her cheeks to intensify their rosiness. And she loved it when boys and even men looked at her on the street.

Pop and Pa had been sentenced to long prison terms, but Juffie and her parents never talked about it. A surface calm veneered life on Walnut Street. The Kanes ate meals together and were polite to one another. Rosie and Myer always asked Juffie about her schoolwork, and they often suggested she bring friends home, but they didn't press when her answers were brief and uninformative and no friends materialized. Their own friends had stopped coming too. There were no more fights for justice and freedom.

Myer had indeed sued the *Herald* for defamation of character and they'd settled out of court for a large sum. Moreover, he still had a practice advising the many men who once had come to the house with Benny and Dino, and now came alone. The Kanes' finances were the one element of their lives unchanged by the crusading district attorney who'd vowed to run the racketeers out of Boston.

In 1941, when she was fourteen, Juffie heard on the radio about the Japanese attack on Pearl Harbor, and right after that America entered the war that had been raging in Europe for three years. Her world changed yet again.

The frenzy and fervor and boom of the war years were exhilarating, particularly to Juffie Kane, who discovered that she thrived on excitement and vicarious danger. One Saturday when she was fifteen, saying nothing to anyone, she dressed up and went to Boston Common and applied at the U.S.O. kiosk to be a hostess, giving a false age and address. She told them she could help out only on weekends.

The United Service Organization had been created the year before, to coordinate the work of established charitable groups to provide recreational, religious, and entertainment facilities for American servicemen. Among their many activities they held open house in a club on lower Washington Street every Saturday and Sunday night.

Juffie told her parents she'd joined a theater group at school. This wasn't a surprise; Juffie had been stagestruck since she was nine, when Myer and Rosie took her to see Henry Fonda and June Walker in *The Farmer Takes a Wife* at the Shubert Theater on Boylston Street. "They'll be having rehearsals on weekends, in the evenings. Okay, Mama?"

"You won't be getting home too late, will you, Juffie?"

"No later than eleven," the girl promised.

"Eleven is too late," Rosie said firmly. "Ten-thirty at the latest. I'm sure the other mothers will feel the same way."

Okay, it wasn't so terrible. The sailors and soldiers and marines came in all day long, as soon as they had liberty. By the time Juffie got to the club at seven it was full and the dance floor was crowded. From the moment she walked in the door she had a line of young men waiting to swing her in a frantic jitterbug or lindy hop, or even better, hold her close for a fox-trot. She particularly liked one young sailor from Kansas whose ship docked frequently in Boston, and who rushed to the U.S.O. as soon as he could after arriving in port. He waited patiently for Juffie, ignoring every other young woman, and sitting by himself in a corner until she arrived.

His accent made Juffie laugh. It made him laugh that she could mimic him so accurately, as well as the regional dialects of all the other boys and men. "You oughta be an actress, sugar. You're terrific."

Juffie looked at him speculatively. "You know, I'm thinking about it. Might not be a bad idea."

"I'm full of good ideas. Let's you and me go out and walk around this here famous Boston Common and I'll show you some of my other good ideas."

She went out with him. They had to be discreet because it was against the rules, and she let him kiss her and even fondle her breasts a little, but that was it. The young sailor pressed against her, and sometimes tried to wedge his leg between her thighs, but Juffie wouldn't give in and he was too nice a kid to force her, even though sometimes he thought she was just a cocktease and he ought to drop her fast.

It wasn't difficult to neck on the Common or across the street in the Public Gardens in those days. All Boston was blacked out, and dark corners and crannies abounded. There were plenty of opportunities for Juffie and the lonely serviceman to go further— and God knew he was eager enough—but she held him off. She just wasn't ready. Put plainly, she was scared.

She could get pregnant. She knew that. And they said it hurt the first time. And anyway, she didn't want it to be quick and sneaky in the dark. She wanted candles and soft music and maybe even champagne. So the boy from Kansas never got beyond rubbing his callused fingertips over the tight erect nipples of Juffie Kane's generous breasts.

When Juffie was sixteen Rosie found out about her daughter's secret life as a hostess for the U.S.O. She told Myer and he was furious, and for the first time raised his voice in real anger.

"I haven't done anything bad," Juffie screamed back. "I wanted to help. They're just young guys and they're so lonely."

"It's not that," Myer answered, a little calmer now. "It's that you lied to your mother and me."

Juffie looked at him for a long moment, and in her eyes he read an accusation of other, earlier lies.

Rosie saw it too. "She's right about not doing anything bad," she said. "Juffie, I trust you. We both trust you. You mustn't think we don't. It's only because we love you so much, we can't stand the thought of anything awful happening to you."

"Nothing's going to happen to me," Juffie insisted. "I only dance with a lot of lonely guys."

Myer sighed. "Okay, okay. It's not so terrible. But why didn't you tell us in the beginning?"

"Because you'd have said I was too young."

That was true and they all knew it. "You're sixteen now," Rosie said. "So I guess you're not too young to go on doing your little bit for the war effort. But why not work with the Red Cross? You can roll bandages. I read in the paper where lots of girls are doing that."

"Lots of girls are U.S.O. hostesses too," Juffie said.

The parents looked at the exquisite young woman they'd produced and at each other, and they knew that the greatest contribution Juffie could make was to do exactly what she was doing. Rolling bandages in a back room wouldn't have been their style, and it obviously wasn't hers. "Take care of yourself," Myer said. "And see you're home both nights by ten-thirty."

．　　．　　．　　．

The girls of the Chestnut Hill Day School were not graduated in pseudo-academic caps and gowns. They wore long white dresses that came from Chandler's on Tremont Street. The style, chosen by a committee made up of representatives of the senior class, the headmistress, and a selected group of mothers, changed only slightly from year to year.

In 1945 they had no difficulty reaching agreement. Because of the war and all the restrictions and rationing, the model was simple: white piqué, with a skirt not full but flared, and a sweetheart neck and cap sleeves trimmed in just a bit of eyelet. Nothing could have suited Juffie better.

Each dress was individually made and fitted at the store; Juffie brought hers home one Wednesday in late April, carrying it in a dark blue Chandler's box tied with yellow ribbon. Rosie and Myer were waiting in the front hall outside his office, and she thought her parents wanted to see her in the first long dress she'd ever owned. "I've got it," Juffie said, breathless with excitement. "I'll go up and put it on right now."

"Juffie, wait a minute," her father said. "We've had some news. It's not very good."

Juffie felt her stomach knot then drop, the way it did sometimes in an elevator. She waited, but Myer couldn't seem to say more.

"It's Pop," Rosie intervened. "The authorities called us. He's had a heart attack and they don't expect him to last very long. We're on our way to . . . Bridgewater." Bridgewater was where the state prison was located, but not one of the Kanes had ever mentioned Pa or Pop and Bridgewater in the same sentence.

"Oh," Juffie said. She wanted to say so much more, to throw herself into her father's arms and tell him how sorry she was about everything, especially about the fact that his father was dying. But she couldn't; all she could manage was the single word, oh.

"Do you want to come with us?" Myer asked. "Pop would like it a lot. They'll let you see him. I asked."

Juffie had an immediate vision of Benny Kane old and ill, in a place with armed guards and bars on the window. She couldn't bear to see him like that. She wanted to remember him the way he was. She stared at her parents, then pushed past them and ran upstairs, still clutching the box tied with yellow ribbon.

After a while there was a tap on the door. "Juffie, it's okay. We understand; you don't have to come." Her father spoke the words with quiet sadness. "Mama and I are going now. We'll be back when we can." A moment later Juffie heard the front door open and close, and the sound of the prewar Oldsmobile starting up.

For a long time she sat on the bed staring at nothing, trying not to think of her once-beloved grandfather. Finally she got up and opened the box. Graduation was five weeks away, and she couldn't wait until then to admire herself in the white piqué dress. But when she put it on and stood in front of the full-length mirror, she could find no pleasure in the vision. All she could see was Pop making funny faces so she'd laugh, and frying potato *latkes*, and taking her to the circus, and holding out his two hands and asking her to guess which one had the quarter hidden in the palm. She felt rotten.

Juffie took off the dress and hung it away and slipped into a pink chenille bathrobe. The doorbell rang. She waited, but it kept ringing; apparently Miss Gold wasn't in the office. She was terrified that it would be a boy from Western Union bringing news that her grandfather had died. Or maybe they'd send a policeman to tell the family. They wouldn't know that her parents were already on their way to Bridgewater. Juffie wanted to ignore the bell, but whoever it was wouldn't go away.

She went downstairs, still in her bathrobe, and opened the door a crack and peeked out. It was a man. He didn't look like a policeman, or someone who worked for Western Union. He wore a dark suit and a dark shirt and a light-colored tie, and his hair was slicked back with a lot of brilliantine. She could see what she presumed was his car at the curb. It was a Cadillac and it looked new. Nobody she knew had been able to get a new car since the war started. "Yes?"

"I want to see Mr. Kane, the lawyer."

"I'm sorry, he's not here."

The man cocked his head, obviously trying to see more of her through the crack in the door. "Who are you?"

"I'm his daughter. If you leave your name I'll tell him you came by."

"What kind of a lawyer isn't in his office at four in the afternoon?"

"He usually is," Juffie said defensively. "But something came up, a family emergency. I guess he sent his secretary home too. Wait a minute and I'll get a pencil and write your name down."

The man smiled for the first time. He had very white teeth and that made Juffie realize that he had a dark tan. And it wasn't summer yet. "Do I have to wait out here on the porch like the Fuller Brush man?" he asked.

She couldn't very well refuse to admit a client of her father's. Juffie opened the door wider. "Come in. I'm sorry I'm not dressed, I was just—" She stopped speaking. There was no point in telling this stranger that she'd been trying on the dress for her high school graduation. "Wait here a minute and I'll get a pencil and pad."

She went into the office and opened the top drawer of Miss

Gold's desk. The paper and pencils were in their customary place. When she turned to go back to the hall she found the strange man right behind her. "Oh! You startled me. I thought you were—"

"Yeah. But I wanted to see your dad's office."

"He's not here, I told you."

"So you did. A family emergency you said." His eyes roved over her while he spoke.

"That's right. Now, if you'll just give me your name . . ."

"Angel. Angel Tomasso."

Juffie wrote it down and didn't comment on it being an unusual name.

"Tell him I just got in from Miami and I need some legal advice. I used to work for Dino in the old days before they locked him up and threw away the key. Hey, don't look like that. I'm sorry."

Coming as it did on top of everything she'd been feeling about Benny, the comment about Dino destroyed her. Juffie's face crumpled and her eyes filled with tears. She reached into the pocket of her bathrobe and fished out a handkerchief and blew her nose loudly.

"I'm an idiot," Angel Tomasso said. "I know Dino is your dad's father-in-law, so he's gotta be your grandfather. I just wasn't thinking. Sorry, kid."

"That's all right. It's not your fault."

"Yeah, it is. Have you got a name?"

"Juffie."

"Okay, Juffie. I know you must hear this a thousand times a day, but you're the best-looking thing I've ever seen. Any chance you'd let me make up for upsetting you by buying you dinner tonight?"

Juffie started to say no, then she reconsidered. Why not? Her parents were sure to be away for hours. She was all alone in the house and feeling miserable. It wasn't a weekend night, so she couldn't go to the U.S.O. There was no reason to sit here and feel sorry for herself. Besides, she was going to be eighteen in a few months and she'd never had dinner alone with a man. An older man at that. "Okay," she said. "I'd like that, if you don't mind waiting until I get dressed."

"I don't mind a bit," Angel said.

She stood in front of her closet for a long few moments, trying to decide what to wear. She didn't have anything that looked like the dinner dresses they wore in the movies or in magazines like *Vogue* or *Harper's Bazaar*. Black and low-cut. Nor did she have a little pouf of a hat with a tiny veil, or long white gloves. Damn! She didn't have anything that would make her look the way she wanted to look, like a grown woman, not a schoolgirl. Well, she'd have to wear something. She couldn't go out with Angel Tomasso in a chenille bathrobe.

Finally she chose the navy blue suit Rosie had bought her to wear on college interviews. But instead of the white blouse with the bow at the neck she'd worn on those occasions, she put on a pink angora cardigan and buttoned it up the back so it looked like a pullover, and added a strand of pearls and pearl earrings. And she applied her pale pink lipstick more heavily than usual, and rubbed some into her cheeks like rouge. Then she put on high-heeled navy blue leather pumps and white kid gloves and went downstairs.

Angel was waiting in the hall. "Kid, you take my breath away," he said softly. "C'mon. I can't wait till the guys at Freddie's get a look at you."

Freddie's turned out to be a restaurant in Boston's Italian North End. Angel seemed to know everybody, waiters and guests. "For a guy who just arrived from Florida, you have a lot of friends," Juffie said.

"I was born two blocks from here," Angel explained. "I went to Miami only a few years ago. It's been a live-wire town these last few years. Now the war is almost over, it's not so exciting anymore."

"Were you in the war?" she asked.

He guffawed. "Don't be nuts. Going into the service is a sucker's game. I'm too smart for that."

Juffie thought of all the boys she'd known at the U.S.O., but she didn't contradict him. He scared her a little. She'd thought her experiences as a U.S.O. hostess had prepared her for anything. She thought she was grown-up and sophisticated. But the way Angel studied her and touched her hand whenever he could, and the looks he exchanged with the other men in Freddie's made her nervous. He produced a pack of Camels and offered her one and she accepted. He lit it with a gold lighter. Juffie had smoked before, with the soldiers and sailors and marines, but she coughed on the first puff.

"Too strong?" Angel asked.

"Yes, I usually smoke Pall Malls."

He signaled a waiter and had a pack of Pall Malls brought to the table. She had no time to light up, however, because the stuffed clams they'd ordered as an appetizer came. Angel ate greedily and drank a lot of wine. But he didn't take his eyes off her while he did it.

"Stop staring at me," Juffie said finally.

"Why should I? There's sure as hell nothing better to look at. Jesus, you're incredible."

"Thank you," she murmured, "but it makes me nervous when you keep staring."

"Have some more wine." He refilled her glass. "That will relax you. What do you do, Juffie?"

She wasn't about to tell him she was still in school. "I don't have a job," she said. "I'm not sure what I want to do. Be an actress maybe."

"You've got the face and figure for it, that's for sure. There can't be anything better than you in Hollywood."

"Not Hollywood." Juffie shook her head in firm rejection of the idea. "I don't want to be in the movies. If I become an actress, I want to go on the stage. Like Helen Hayes or Lynn Fontanne."

"Never heard of either of 'em. But they can't be any better looking than you."

"It's not just looks," Juffie said. "You have to have talent. That's what I'm not sure of."

"Kid, believe me, you don't have to do a damn thing. Just stand there. In a bathing suit maybe. Any guy in the world will hock his grandmother to buy a ticket."

They left Freddie's at nine-thirty. "I have to get home," Juffie said. "My folks will be expecting me."

"Sure thing." He opened the door to the Cadillac and watched her slide across the seat.

Juffie sat as close to the passenger door as she could. Angel didn't say anything about that. But in a few minutes she realized he wasn't driving toward Newton. "Where are you going?" she asked when he entered the Sumner Tunnel.

"Just for a little ride. It's a nice night. Half an hour or so. No more, I promise."

She guessed he was headed for notorious Revere Beach, and

she was right. None of the stands along the boulevard were open yet, but there were plenty of cars parked facing the ocean. Angel kept going until he found a deserted stretch of road at the far end. Then he stopped. "Look at that," he said, indicating the moon on the water. "Isn't that pretty?"

It was, and Juffie said so. She knew very well what would happen next. Angel would kiss her, French-kiss her probably, and feel her breasts and try to talk her into going all the way. Well, it wouldn't be the first time a guy tried that. She could take care of herself. Anyway, he was a lot older and more exciting than the boys at the U.S.O. She was almost looking forward to it.

Nonetheless, the attack took her totally by surprise. Angel Tomasso made no pretense of gentleness, no attempt at seduction. He grabbed both her arms in a viselike grip and pushed her down on the seat. He didn't kiss her; instead, he hissed in her ear. "Don't fight me. I'll knock you out if you do. Maybe muss up that gorgeous face for good."

"Stop," Juffie said in a moaned whisper, terrified to raise her voice for fear he'd carry out his threat. "Stop. You've got me all wrong. I don't—"

"I got you all right, kid. A cocktease. I knew it from the first minute. But this time you're going to put out."

Those were the last words he spoke for some time. He was too busy pushing up her skirt and pulling down her pants. He used only one hand to do it; the other was occupied in holding her immobile. Juffie struggled to get free, to clamp her legs shut. Nothing seemed to deflect him. Finally she managed to get her head close to his shoulder and she opened her mouth and sank her teeth into his flesh, biting down as hard as she could through his suitcoat and shirt.

"Bitch!" He jerked away from her mouth and for a moment he stopped tearing at her clothes and used that hand to slap her hard across the face. Again, and yet again. "Now, listen good." There was no hysteria in his voice, no overt anger. Just cold determination. "I'm going to fuck you. Nothing you can do is going to stop that. I didn't have it in mind to beat you up, but if that's what you want, that's what you'll get. You understand?"

His voice was the most terrifying thing she'd ever heard. Juffie nodded.

"Say it. Say, 'Okay, Angel, I understand.'"

"Okay, I understand."

"Okay, Angel," he corrected her.

Juffie's mouth was so dry she didn't think she could speak. But her face was still burning from his slaps, and she knew he meant every word, that if she continued to resist, he'd methodically and thoroughly beat her up. Probably scar her for life. "Okay, Angel," she whispered.

He chuckled softly. "You learn fast, kid." He was more efficient now because he knew she was completely cowed, and he could use both hands to remove her clothes.

The rape was quick and methodical, almost mechanistic. It hurt like hell, but Juffie didn't make a sound. She lay there staring into the dark, trying to blank her mind and pretend it wasn't happening to her. It was over in less than a minute and Angel sat up and matter-of-factly buttoned his fly and adjusted his still-knotted tie. Then he leaned over and handed her a handkerchief. "Here, clean yourself up, kid. No need to advertise that you finally got what was coming to you."

She took the handkerchief meekly and did as he suggested. Her panties were ripped and she didn't put them back on, just shoved them into her handbag. Near as she could tell, the rest of her looked normal. When she was done she returned his handkerchief and he looked at it in the light of the moon.

"Blood. So you really were a virgin." He laughed softly. "I finally got even with that old son of a bitch, Dino Saliatelli. I stuck it to his granddaughter and got her cherry. He'd shit a brick."

He turned to Juffie, who was staring unseeing at the black expanse of ocean. "Tell you something, kid. The old man owed me money. I came to see your father today to collect. Now I figure we're even. I won't be back. You never have to see me again. But you're never going to forget your first fuck, are you?"

She knew he wanted an answer, and after some seconds she shook her head.

"Say it, 'I'll never forget.'"

"I'll never forget."

Satisfied, Angel Tomasso drove her home.

The house was dark. Myer and Rosie weren't back yet from their vigil at Benny's deathbed. Juffie was able to go in without being terrified that they'd see her and guess something horrible had happened.

She waited until she heard the Cadillac drive away. Then she slowly went upstairs and into the bathroom and ran a tub. While it filled she got undressed, dropping her clothes in a heap on the floor. She looked in the full-length mirror on the back of the door and she saw that her thighs had red welts on them. Her face was unmarked, however. The three hard slaps hadn't broken anything or done any visible damage.

Finally she got into the steaming water. The heat made her feel almost faint at first. She lay back and remained silent and unmoving for some moments. Then she opened her mouth and screamed.

She kept on screaming for a full five minutes, but she was alone in a solidly built empty house, separated from her neighbors by trees and hedges. No one heard her. If they had, and if they had known what had happened, they might have thought she was hysterical. She was not. What she felt was a monumental, overwhelming, permanent rage.

Chapter 4

On graduation day at the end of May, in her long white dress and carrying an armload of red roses, Juffie Kane stole the show. She had garnered no academic honors—all her teachers said she'd never really used her brains or worked up to her potential—but any girl who had would gladly have exchanged her prize and medal for Juffie's tall grace, her fabulous figure, her thick wavy hair of that extraordinary color that was neither brown nor blond, and her incredible eyes and perfect features.

Juffie knew everyone was looking at her, that Myer and Rosie were proud of her, but she took little pleasure in that fact. She'd missed her period that month.

She missed it in June too. When she didn't come around in July, she knew she was pregnant.

The summer had been planned as a time of relaxing and preparing for her September entrance to Simmons College. Her parents had always hoped for Radcliffe or Wellesley, but Juffie wasn't accepted to either because her grades were not good enough. They settled for Simmons. Juffie was unsure of a choice of major, but the admissions director told her not to worry about it. She didn't have to select a major for two years, and by then she'd probably have decided. In August of 1945 she had far more pressing concerns.

The war was rapidly coming to an end; victory in Europe had been proclaimed in May. Now the Pacific fleet was rumored to be steaming toward Japan to end it there too. The U.S.O. hospitality was much less important than it had been, and the club on Washington Street was almost deserted when Juffie arrived early on the first Saturday in August. But the girl she was looking for was there. "Rita, can I talk to you for a minute?"

"Sure, Juffie. You want to go outside?"

Rita Pine was in her early twenties. She was pretty in a dark blowzy sort of way that paled into insignificance next to Juffie's beauty, but she never seemed to resent the younger girl, as so many other women did. Rita was friendly and good-hearted and once, in a moment of unexplained intimacy, she'd confided to Juffie that she thought she might be pregnant but she wasn't too worried because she knew how to take care of it.

They left the club and strolled along Washington Street all the way to the Milk Street end, past the luscious displays of fall clothing in Filene's and Jordan's, and the sumptuous furs in I. J. Fox, on toward Raymond's, famous for its low prices and deliberately misspelled advertising. "What's the matter, honey?" Rita asked when Juffie's inability to say what she wanted to say became obvious. "You in trouble?"

"Yes," Juffie admitted.

Both women knew what kind of trouble they were talking about.

"Bad luck, kid," Rita said softly. "You want to marry the guy?"

Juffie shuddered. "God forbid."

Rita wore her dyed-black hair in a pageboy and a high pompadour; it bounced when she shook her head. "Like that, huh? Well, I know how you feel. Damned men are all alike, and marrying some jerk because he's knocked you up is a disaster. Don't do it, Juffie."

"I don't intend to," she said without further explanation. "But I've got to have . . . I've got to get rid of the baby." Saying it made her mouth go dry and her stomach churn. But there wasn't any choice.

"Okay." Rita was very cool. "I can tell you where to go. A woman named Leah Rice. She's okay. She does good work. The only thing is, you have to pay fifty bucks before she'll touch you. Cash money. But I suppose that's not a problem for you."

Rita lived in a Revere tenement with her folks. She didn't think a girl from Newton would have any difficulty getting fifty dollars. Juffie, however, didn't have any money of her own. She received an allowance of five dollars a week, which admittedly was generous, but she'd never saved any of it and she couldn't wait ten weeks. That would be much too late, she'd be showing by then. Despite that she said, "I can get the money. Will you give me the address and tell me what to do?"

"Sure." Rita stopped walking and took a used envelope and a pencil from her bag and wrote down a name and address. "Just go here any afternoon at five. It's sort of like a clinic. Knock on the door and say Rita sent you. I've sent Leah customers before, she knows they're okay. But be sure and tell her you've got the money."

"Where will she do it?"

"Right there in her apartment. Right away. Don't look so scared. You'll get through it. It's better than ruining the rest of your life, isn't it?"

The only remaining problem was the fifty dollars. But she'd anticipated the need for money, and even though it frightened her beyond words, she knew just what she had to do. Juffie didn't go back to the U.S.O. with Rita, she went to Freddie's Restaurant in the North End.

It was six-thirty and there were only a dozen diners at scattered tables in the room. "I need to find Angel Tomasso," she told the man in the black tuxedo who seemed to be in charge. "I was in here with him a few months ago. Maybe you remember me."

"Sure I remember you," the man said. A kid who looked like her he wasn't likely to forget. "They say you're Dino Saliatelli's granddaughter. True?"

"Yes. I am."

"So Benny Kane had to be your other grandfather." He chuckled. "That's some pedigree." Then he shook his head. "Benny I didn't know good, though them two met for the first time right here in this restaurant. But Dino did me a few favors back in the old days when I was starting this place. We was friends. How's he doing?"

Juffie didn't say that she hadn't seen him in seven years, not since he'd been sent to prison. "Okay. Just fine."

"Good. He's a tough old bird, your grandfather. Take it from me, he'll last until they let him out. What do you want with Angel?"

"It's personal."

The man hesitated. "Listen, doll, it ain't none of my business, but for old Dino's sake . . . don't mess with Tomasso, he's no good. He's got a real mean streak. And with your looks, you don't need a two-bit greaser like him."

"I just need to talk to him," Juffie said. "Only for a couple of minutes. Please."

The man shrugged. "He lives two blocks away, right off Dock Square. Maybe you'll catch him in; if not, his mother should know where to find him."

Juffie went directly to the address he gave her. It was a three-story brick building. The name Tomasso was written next to the bell for the first floor apartment and she rang it. An old woman dressed entirely in black came to the door. "I'd like to see Angel, please."

"He's sleeping. Come back later."

"It's important. Please," Juffie said again.

A voice from somewhere in the interior called out, "Ma, who is it?"

The woman grunted, then turned her head. "A girl. She wants to see you. I told her to come back later."

"Nah, it's okay." He appeared behind his mother, bare-chested with a crucifix on a gold chain hanging around his neck, wearing only trousers and no shoes. "Well, I'll be damned. What the hell are you doing here?"

Seeing him made her flesh crawl. She clenched her fists so her hands would stop trembling. "I need to talk to you." Juffie willed her voice to be normal. "It won't take long."

The woman still stood between them and he touched her shoulder. "Go in the kitchen, Ma. Make me something to eat. I gotta talk to this here young lady.

"Okay," he said when they were alone and he'd closed the door to the hall. "What do you want?"

"Fifty dollars," Juffie said.

He cocked his head and looked at her. After a few seconds he grinned. "Fifty bucks, huh? I don't need to ask what for. I knocked you up and you're gonna get rid of it."

She hated him so much it was almost impossible not to lunge at him, to scratch his eyes out and bite him until he bled to death. But all she did was nod.

"Get lost," he said with a quiet little laugh. "Go to hell. No way I'm going to pay to get you off the hook. Imagine, Dino

Saliatelli's granddaughter has a bastard in the oven, and I put it there. I like that, I really do."

"You won't like what his friends will do to you," Juffie said. She'd rehearsed all this for a week. Standing in front of the mirror in her bedroom and mouthing the words silently, planning them, planning the way she'd look and the tone of voice she'd use.

"My grandfather still has plenty of friends. They come to see my father. Benny Kane's friends come too. So far I haven't told anybody what you did. But if you don't give me the money, I will. And no matter how mad they are at me, they'll get revenge on you. You know they will."

For a moment there was a flash of fear in his eyes. Then he shook his head like a bull ridding himself of an annoying fly. "I don't believe you have the guts to do it. And if you do, you better remember something." He stared at her while he spoke, undoing his belt buckle at the same time and pulling the wide leather strap out of the hooks.

"Whatever they do to me, I'm gonna do worse to you. You won't be able to hide forever, and I'll get you. I'll fix you so no man will ever look at you again, not without gagging." He spoke the words with enjoyment. "In fact, I think I better give you a little of it right now. Just so you get my meaning."

He was playing with the belt while he spoke and he started to lift it. His mother appeared in the doorway that presumably led to the kitchen. Her eyes flicked from the strange girl to her son and his belt, reading the situation, if she hadn't already heard everything they'd said. "Angel, your food's ready. Get this *puttana* out of here. Tell her to go back where she belongs. I don't like girls like this in my house."

Angel looked first at his mother, then at Juffie. The arm holding the belt relaxed. "You heard her, get out of here. Quick, before I change my mind."

Juffie stood her ground for only a moment, then she left.

The man from Freddie's Restaurant was waiting in Dock Square. He saw her come out of the building the Tomassos lived in and he crossed the road and fell into step beside her. She was crying. "I figured maybe it wouldn't go so good, you and Tomasso. So I walked over to see how things worked out." He took a handkerchief from his pocket and handed it to her. "Here. And stop crying. Angel Tomasso isn't worth it."

"I'm just so mad," Juffie managed to say between sniffs.

"Yeah. He makes me mad too. Never could stand the little greaser. Listen, kid, like I said, your grandfather did me some favors in the old days. You need some help?"

Juffie stopped walking and turned to look at him. "I need fifty dollars," she said. "I can pay it back five dollars a week."

He was wearing his tuxedo and bow tie and it was a little after seven and still broad daylight in Dock Square. He looked silly but kind. He reached his hand into his pocket and produced a roll of bills and peeled off five tens. "Here. And I don't want nothin' back."

Juffie took the money and leaned over and kissed him. A couple passing by stopped and stared, but she didn't care. "I don't know how to thank you."

"Don't mention it. And maybe you shouldn't thank me. I don't have to be a genius to figure what you want this for. Otherwise you'd ask your mother and father. Okay, I ain't no priest. But just make sure you go to somebody good. You can die from what you're going to do if you're not careful."

.   .   .   .

On the fourteenth of August at approximately six P.M. eastern daylight saving time the people of the United States learned that faced with the devastation wrought by two atomic bombs, the Japanese had surrendered unconditionally. The war was over.

Juffie didn't hear the news bulletins that interrupted all the regular radio programs. She was sitting on a hardbacked chair in Leah Rice's long, narrow hall, waiting for her turn to be aborted. There was a woman ahead of her. Juffie didn't get a good look at her in the dim light, but decided she must be about the same age as Rosie. It hadn't occurred to Juffie that a woman so old would need to come here and see Leah Rice.

The woman disappeared into the rear of the apartment and the sound of her anguish was muffled. Not her own, however. Juffie heard her own screams of pain and terror while she lay on the cot in the back room off the kitchen. Then she blacked out for a while. When she came to, Leah Rice gave her a cup of strong tea with lots of sugar. "Here, drink this, you'll be okay. You gotta go now."

Juffie choked down the scalding tea and stood up. She couldn't feel much. Everything from the waist down seemed numb. Her legs moved without her being in control of them. The apartment was in the still largely Jewish West End, at the top of a ramshackle four-story wooden tenement, squeezed into the rear of a tiny cul-de-sac created from what had once been a spacious eighteenth-century back garden. The smells of food and urine permeated the hall and the steep stairs. Juffie descended them slowly, hanging on to the rickety railing.

Outside in the narrow alley a garbage can had been over-turned and she could hear a lot of noise. It sounded threatening. There were loud bangs. Like guns. She leaned against the brick wall, too weak and frightened to go out into the street. The smell of garbage was overpowering. A wave of nausea engulfed her and she barely had time to bend forward as she threw up.

Suddenly the numbness went away and a terrible burning pain began in her crotch and spread down her legs. She started to slip down the wall, but she resisted. If she fell, she'd land in her own vomit and the assortment of orange skins and coffee grounds and potato peelings that littered the ground.

A pair of strong arms were suddenly holding her up. "Hey, what's the matter?"

Her benefactor was a girl around her own age, short and skinny, with brown eyes and curly dirty-blond hair. "I'm sick," Juffie murmured.

"That I figured out. Too much to drink?" The girl was inspecting Juffie as she spoke and she answered her own question. "Oh no, that's not it. You're bleeding like a stuck pig."

Juffie looked down. Her skirt was stained dark red and there were trickles of blood oozing down her legs and puddling in the tops of her white bobby socks. Juffie moaned. "Oh my God."

"Oh Leah, more like," the girl said. She spoke matter-of-factly. "She just fixed you, didn't she?" Juffie nodded, too frightened and ill and miserable to deny it.

"Well, she usually does a pretty good job," the girl said. "I don't know why you have to be the exception." She pushed Juffie back a bit, out of the range of the worst of the mess on the ground, and eased her down so she was sitting with her back propped against the two-century-old brick wall. "Wait here, don't move. I'll get Leah."

She was back in a few moments, carrying a pile of things Juffie couldn't identify. The woman who'd performed the abortion was right behind her. "I don't butcher," the woman said smartly. "Nobody hemorrhages after I do them."

"She's hemorrhaging," the strange girl said. "Just look."

Leah looked. Juffie simply sat there and let her poke and prod. The noise from the street beyond the alley was becoming deafening. There was another series of loud bangs. "What's going on out there?" Juffie asked weakly.

"Fireworks," the other girl said. "Japan just surrendered. The war's over. Everybody's celebrating."

"Give me the towel," Leah said. "The dry one." The girl took something from the top of her pile and handed it over. The woman stuffed it between Juffie's legs. "You're bleeding a little, but most of it's already stopped. It's not a hemorrhage, whatever Miss Smarty-Pants here says. You'll be okay." She got up from where she'd been kneeling beside Juffie. "I gotta go back in. Your father's waiting for his supper. We're gonna go for a walk and see all the excitement."

"Go ahead," the girl said. "I'll stay and give her a hand. We can't have your reputation ruined, can we?"

The woman snorted. "Miss Smarty-Pants. I'll leave you something on the stove." She disappeared back into the tenement.

"My mother," the girl said. "I'm Karen Rice." She was swabbing at Juffie's legs while she spoke, washing the blood off with a wet towel. Luckily they were still alone in the alley. Everyone who could walk had left the apartment house as soon as the news came, swarming into the street to take part in the valediction to four years of war.

"I'm going to take your socks off," Karen said. "We better throw them away, they're ruined. It's okay, it's sure hot enough to go barelegged."

"My skirt," Juffie murmured. She wanted to say thank you, but all she could think of was her stained cotton skirt.

"That's probably ruined too," Karen agreed. "And you can't wear it out on the street. I brought you one of mine. If you can lift up a little, I'll get yours off."

Juffie did as she was bidden. In a few moments Karen Rice had deftly exchanged the stained garment for one that was clean. "Okay, you're decent. Can you stand up?"

"I think so." Juffie had to be helped, but she managed to stand. She was at least six inches taller than Karen Rice. And the skirt, a slightly faded green cotton dirndl with an elasticized waist, ended well above her knees.

"Damn! I didn't realize you were so tall. Here, let's pull it down and put your blouse outside so it doesn't show." When she'd finished her ministrations, Juffie looked like a scruffy kid but was presentable enough. "You'll do," Karen said, grinning. "Where do you live?"

"Newton."

Karen raised her eyebrows. "Lucky you. But that's so far to go the way you are. And God knows if the subway is running. They're going crazy out there. Well, c'mon, we'll just see what we can do."

They were at the edge of the alley, ready to step into the melee in the street, when Karen asked, "Hey, what's your name?"

"Juffie, Juffie Kane."

The shorter girl stuck out her hand. "How do you do, Juffie Kane. Nice to meet you."

.   .   .   .

It took them two hours to get to Newton by subway and trolley. "This is some place," Karen said, surveying the immaculate, well-cared-for Victorian house with its nice furnishings and spacious interiors.

"This isn't the fanciest part of Newton." Juffie felt as if she must apologize. "It's not where the really rich people live."

Karen grinned. "Rich is relative. Particularly if you live like Leah and Jake Rice among the oppressed working classes."

"Are you a Communist?"

"I'm not sure, but I don't think so. I've read a lot of stuff, but it doesn't really convince me." She walked around, unabashedly examining everything. "Looks like there's nobody home."

Juffie was reading a note that had been left on the telephone table. "No. My folks went out to join the celebrations."

"Good thing we didn't run into them in that mob on the Common." They'd had to skirt the Common to get to the subway station.

"I was born on Boston Common," Juffie said. She explained about the demonstration to reprieve Sacco and Vanzetti.

Karen listened wide-eyed, and when she spoke it was with new respect. "You mean your parents live in a place like this, your father's a rich lawyer"—she'd seen the sign on the lawn—"and they cared about Sacco and Vanzetti?"

"They care about the oppressed working classes," Juffie said. "Just like you. Look, I don't feel so great. I want to lie down. Do you want to come up to my room?"

"Sure. Have to see the patient is settled."

They climbed the stairs to Juffie's bedroom, and Karen helped her undress and get into bed. "The towel isn't stained much, Leah was right. You weren't really hemorrhaging."

She began looking around again. The wallpaper was pale blue with pink flowers. The spread she'd removed from the bed matched the pink exactly, and the curtains were the same color. There was a darker blue braided rug on the floor. In one corner was a vanity table with a mirror framed in gold and a skirt of blue satin. "This is a terrific room." Then, without any preamble, she asked, "Did you tell your boyfriend you were going to have an abortion?"

"I don't have a boyfriend."

Karen narrowed her eyes and studied Juffie. "That doesn't figure. Ma gets three kinds of clients. Married ladies who just can't afford another kid; nice girls with boyfriends who can't or won't marry them; and not-nice girls who say yes to everything in pants and are surprised when the inevitable happens. You aren't married. And I didn't figure you for the last type."

Juffie was feeling light-headed and still a little nauseated, she had cramps, she wanted to go to sleep, but she wasn't going to let Karen Rice's assumption go unchallenged. Moreover, everything that had happened had weakened her defenses. "I'm none of those things. I was raped."

"Jesus!" Karen sat down hard on the edge of the bed. "Are you kidding me?"

Juffie shook her head.

"Wow. And you got pregnant. What lousy luck. It almost makes me proud of Leah. Do your folks know?"

"Don't be ridiculous. Of course not."

"Jesus," Karen said again. "How did you find out about Leah?"

"I've been going to the U.S.O., as a hostess. A girl I know there told me about her."

Karen drew up her knees and hugged them, leaning back against the footboard of the bed. "In her own little way Leah's famous. So were her mother and her grandmother back in Lemburg. That's in Galicia, in Europe. That's where we come from. Leah is the last in a long line of experts on quick clean abortion. She says even her grandmother knew that between patients she should boil everything she used."

"Why the last? Aren't you going to follow in their footsteps?"

"Absolutely not. I'm going to study psychology." Karen glanced up. On the wall above the bed were two framed pictures. Karen recognized neither. "Who are they?" she asked, pointing.

"The one on the right's Katharine Cornell. The other's Lynn Fontanne."

"They're actresses, aren't they?"

"Yes. Listen, I can't talk anymore, I'm falling asleep."

"Yeah, sure. I wasn't thinking. Okay, Juffie, I'll go now. You're going to be fine."

"Karen," Juffie called to the girl's retreating back. "Will you come back and see me?"

"Sure. Tomorrow maybe."

The next day Juffie told her mother she had a headache and the beginning of a cold. "Stay in bed," Rosie said. "I'll bring you some lunch on a tray later."

"Thanks. And, Mama, a girl may come to see me. Her name is Karen Rice. I met her yesterday. If she comes, will you bring her up? Even if I'm sleeping."

Rosie said she would. The request delighted her. It had been years since Juffie had had a friend in the house. But when she returned with a lunch tray she was alone. "Nobody came," she told her daughter. "Maybe later."

By dinnertime Juffie had given up. Karen wasn't going to return. She'd only been pretending to be friendly. The thought made Juffie miserable. She felt so peculiar, so sick and so sad and so isolated. She really wanted to talk to someone who knew her secret. Worst of all, she'd never even thanked Karen for everything she did. Oh well, most girls didn't like her; either they resented her looks or they despised her background. Probably Karen Rice was no different.

There was a tentative knock on the door. Juffie thought it was her mother with supper. "Come in, I'm awake."

"Hi." Karen breezed in carrying a tray. "Your mother said I could bring this up. She said you had a cold." She winked conspiratorially.

"I've been practicing phony sneezes all day," Juffie said. "Want to hear?" She produced a convincing noise.

"You're good at that," Karen said, setting the tray on the table beside the bed. "You better be an actress like those women in the pictures. But first have your soup. It's good for you."

"I thought you weren't coming."

"Got a chance to work at the grocery store because the regular girl was sick. I'm trying to save some money for clothes for college."

"Are you going to college?"

"Yup. Simmons. In September."

"No kidding? I'm going to Simmons too."

"That's terrific! Can I have some of this toast?" Karen helped herself to a slice without waiting for an answer and again took the place at the foot of the bed she'd occupied the previous night. "That's not chicken soup, is it?"

"No. Minestrone."

Karen nodded as if that confirmed her suspicions. "I've been thinking of something. Myer Kane is a Jewish name, but you don't look Jewish. Are you?"

"Half," Juffie said. "My father is, but my mother's Italian." She hesitated. But they'd already shared so much drama and intimacy. And Karen really did seem different. "I'd better tell you about my grandfathers," she began.

. . . . .

Simmons was to provide the best time Juffie had known since she was eleven. Like all colleges, it was a world so self-contained and introverted that no one remembered about her grandfathers and her father, if they'd ever known. And she had Karen, her first real friend. They were both day students, but Karen didn't commute from the West End. During the week she lived at Juffie's house and had the bedroom next to hers.

Rosie and Myer welcomed her because they knew she was part of their daughter's newfound happiness. Leah and Jake accepted the arrangement because they were ambitious for Karen. For years most of the money Leah earned had been banked to pay for a college education for their smart daughter. The Rices lived on Jake's salary from his cousin's fish store, and saved everything else for Karen. And they understood that a lawyer's house in Newton was a better place for her to study than the noisy tenement with Leah's clients streaming in and out. That Mr. Kane was a Jewish lawyer helped make the arrangement palatable; Karen never mentioned her friend's Italian mother.

"Anyway," Leah said. "I did Juffie. Helped her out when she was in trouble. That makes her almost like family."

"Ma," Karen said, "if that's true, you must have the biggest family in America."

"Miss Smarty-Pants, like always. Just go get your education and live with the *gantze k'nockers* if you want."

The words meant literally big hits, a euphemism for people who thought themselves superior. Karen knew that Leah didn't really mean it. She understood that to her mother Newton represented a world she would never know but one she lusted after for her daughter. "Ma," she said gently, "it's just during the week. On weekends I'll come here. This is my home, you're my family. I'm not running away from anything."

"I know," Leah said softly. "I know, *mameleh*. Listen, you're a smart girl, it's all waiting for you out there. Go get it. For both of us."

So Karen moved to Walnut Street and Juffie was thrilled. One other thing made her life perfect, the drama society. Simmons didn't have a real theater department. What it had was Professor Leslie Wing, who taught a couple of token courses on the history of the theater, a sort of afterthought in the English department, and ran the drama society. They put on three plays a year in the college auditorium.

In November of that year Juffie saw the announcement on the bulletin board outside the student activities office: TRYOUTS WEDNESDAY AT THREE FOR G. B. SHAW'S *PYGMALION*. ROOM 742 IN THE MEMORIAL ANNEX.

"Go," Karen said when Juffie mentioned it later. "You're dying to, so just do it."

Juffie shook her head. "I haven't got the nerve. I won't get a part."

"Are you crazy? Juffie, look in the mirror, for God's sake. How can you not get a part?"

"Everybody thinks that's what it's about, how you look. It's not, it's a lot more than that. I don't think I have any talent."

"What about all those impersonations you always do? All those funny accents. You're terrific."

"It's more than that too," Juffie said glumly.

They were in the room on Walnut Street now known as Karen's. Before, it had been a catchall spare room, but when she knew Karen was coming Rosie repainted it pale green, and changed the curtains to yellow and white gingham trimmed in white eyelet, and added a matching bedspread and a bird's-eye maple dresser and desk. There was even a vanity table skirted in white eyelet with a little green velvet bench. When she first saw it Karen thought maybe she'd died and gone to heaven. To make everything complete, Juffie had given Karen one of her giant pandas.

"This is the Jewish one," she'd explained. "See, he's got a big nose. I kept the Italiano with the greasy look."

Both pandas were identical and both had buttons for noses.

Karen giggled. "What's his name?"

Juffie shrugged. "Hasn't got one. I just think of them as the kike and the wop." Long ago she'd called them Pa and Pop for their respective donors, but she couldn't call them that anymore. Not since Pop was dead and Pa was still in prison.

"Hymie and Luigi," Karen said. "I'll put Hymie right here beside the vanity table."

Now Karen was sprawled on the bed while Juffie sat cross-legged on the floor, using Hymie as a backrest. The huge black and white arms of the panda seemed to embrace her.

"Try out for a part," Karen repeated. "What have you got to lose?"

"My self-respect, my confidence."

"Bullshit. Those things you should lose if you don't even try. Juffie, how can anybody brought up the way you've been, with everything you ever wanted just handed to you, be so damned insecure?"

"I'm not. Not usually. It's just this. I want it so much. As long as it's a dream I can maybe have it. If I actually get up on a stage and I'm terrible, then the dream's gone for good."

Karen leaned down and picked up a book from the pile next to Juffie. *"The Plays of G. B. Shaw.* Is *Pygmalion* in here?"

"Page seven sixteen," Juffie said. Karen gave her a knowing look. "I just glanced at it, that's all," Juffie protested.

Karen opened the book. "Okay, I've got it. Now, which part's best for you?"

"I don't know." Juffie's tone was morose. "I'm not going to try out anyway."

Karen began to read. Five minutes later she looked up. "Eliza! It has to be. I mean look at the accent she's supposed to talk in."

"Sally Clements is bound to get Eliza. She's a senior, she's been in every play since she was a freshman."

"How do you know all this?"

Juffie shrugged. "I asked around a little, that's all."

Karen went back to reading. "Mrs. Pearce then," she said a few minutes later. "It's not such a big part, but she's English, right? So she has an accent too."

This time Juffie didn't shrug. "I sort of thought of that." She half whispered the words and kept her eyes on her notebook.

"Do it! Oh, Juffie, do it. You'll get it, I know you will."

Wednesday afternoon at three she was waiting in Room 742 with sixteen other girls. Juffie sat by herself in the rear. Nobody spoke to her, not because they were unfriendly, but because none of them actually knew her, and, besides, there was something in her manner that said she didn't want to talk. Five minutes later Professor Wing propelled his wheelchair through the door. "Good afternoon, ladies. Thanks for coming. Now, let's get right to it, shall we?"

He went along the ranks of would-be actresses, taking down any names he didn't know and asking each time, "Which role would you care to read for?" There were a number of requests to try out for Eliza, including Sally Clements's. Professor Wing simply wrote them down. Then he came to Juffie. "And you are . . . ?"

"Juffie Kane, Professor."

"Juffie? Can you spell that?"

She did, then added, "It's Jennifer really, but I'm always called Juffie."

He smiled. He was quite good-looking. Thick dark hair and a small beard that made him look very romantic. What a shame he was crippled. Juffie waited for his next question. "Which role, Miss Kane?"

"Mrs. Pearce, Professor Higgins's housekeeper." Damn! she didn't have to say that. He knew who Mrs. Pearce was. She'd done it because she was so nervous.

"Yes," Wing acknowledged. "I see you all have scripts. Let's begin. Miss Kane, will you turn to page eight, first scene, second act. Eliza has just come to Professor Higgins's home and Mrs. Pearce appears to tell him of her arrival."

Oh no! He was asking her to read first. It wasn't fair. She'd wanted to listen to the others for a while. If they were all much better than she could ever be, she'd simply have slipped out the back. Juffie's throat was too tight for her to get a word out, her tongue far too dry. She found the place, then just looked at him helplessly.

"I'll be Higgins," Wing said. "Don't be nervous, please. This is just a first reading, a tryout. Believe me, they're always terrible, even among professionals. Besides, I promise that everyone who's come this afternoon will have some part in the production. Backstage, if not on it. Now, Miss Kane, can we start?"

She took a deep breath.

"Mrs. Pearce has come to the door of Higgins's study," Wing said, "and he spots her. 'What's the matter?' " He spoke the simple words in flawless British English.

Juffie took a deep breath and said, "A young woman wants to see you, sir." She'd copied his accent, but she hadn't meant to do that. She'd already decided that the housekeeper wouldn't sound quite as high-class as Higgins and Pickering and the rest. Not like Eliza either, of course, but a bit more ordinary. A good idea, but she'd blown it.

If Professor Wing saw something wrong in her reading, he didn't indicate it. He gave her the next cue, "A young woman! What does she want?"

Juffie looked at him, then down at the copy of the play. But she didn't need the script. She'd memorized the role while she read it, automatically as it were, without making any real effort. She raised her eyes to the teacher's and tried to imagine herself onstage—her hair in a bun, wearing a stiff black dress with a white collar. This time the accent came out exactly as she'd meant it to be. An ordinary lady who wasn't educated but was trying hard to sound what she thought of as refined. "Well, sir, she says you'll be glad to see her when you know what she's come about. She's quite a common girl, sir. Very common indeed—"

"Thank you, Miss Kane. That will do."

Thirty minutes later he dismissed them all. "Thanks again for coming. I'm sure we're going to have a marvelous time and do a wonderful *Pygmalion*. Remember, I'm counting on all of you to produce boyfriends who'll read for the male parts. That's in this same room Saturday morning. And the cast will be posted on the student activities bulletin board on Monday."

Juffie didn't have any boyfriend to contribute, so she didn't attend the Saturday morning readings. Monday she got in very early. There was no one around except the janitor, and he ignored her. She went directly to the bulletin board, searching only for her name, skipping everything else for the moment. She found it finally: Parlor maid, Juffie Kane. The parlor maid had about four walk-on appearances and never said more than two words. Juffie felt tears well up and fished in her shoulder bag for a handkerchief.

"Don't cry," a voice said. Professor Wing was wheeling himself toward her. "And don't be disappointed. I'm so glad I found you here. Please, come to my office."

"No, that's all right. I'm fine. I have some studying to do. I'll go to the library."

"I wish you wouldn't, I wish you'd come to my office, it's just down the hall. I very much want to talk to you, Miss Kane."

She wondered whether she should offer to push his wheelchair, but he did such a good job of it himself that she didn't try. Then, in his office, he motioned her to sit down and pushed himself behind his desk. That made the situation much more normal. They were a professor and a student on opposite sides of a desk. That the professor was a cripple no longer mattered.

Juffie still wanted to cry, but she didn't. She clutched the handkerchief instead, twisting it between her fingers so tightly she almost cut off the circulation.

He wasted no time on small talk. "I understand your disappointment. You deserved the part. In fact, you should be Eliza."

Juffie stared at him, not sure she'd heard correctly.

"Nonetheless," he added. "I couldn't cast you in anything but a walk-on. You're a freshman, this is your first production. And this isn't a theater, much as I like to pretend it is. It's a girls' college. Miss Kane, this play was chosen because Sally Clements, who has worked very hard for the drama society for almost four years, will make a passable Eliza, and she's longing to do it. Sally's a nice girl. She deserves her moment of glory. Moreover"—he didn't look at Juffie directly—"her mother is president of the alumnae association, and the family have contributed a great deal of money to Simmons. If I put you onstage in any role big enough to be contrasted to Sally, I would ruin it for her, because you, my dear, would steal the show."

She was still staring at him, still not sure she understood.

"I'm sorry I let both of us get into this damned awful position, but how was I to know you were to drop from the heavens into my drama society, Juffie Kane? You didn't send an announcement of your impending arrival."

She'd stopped twisting the handkerchief; now she leaned forward. "Listen, please be honest with me. I don't mean to sound conceited, but I know about my looks. Is that why—"

He didn't let her finish. "Not because you're beautiful. And I don't think you're conceited. How could you help but know how you look? What you may not realize is that you have talent. I'm not sure yet how much, but you're a born mimic, and I suspect more. Is that enough for now? Will you stick with me through *Pygmalion* and be satisfied to know that you're going to get much better parts in the future?"

"Yes," Juffie said. "You bet your life, yes. Thank you, Professor Wing. I wish there were more I could say, but, thank you."

From that first day at the tryouts for *Pygmalion,* Leslie Wing did not respond to Juffie Kane the way most men did. He neither lusted after her nor was awestruck by her phenomenal good looks. Leslie had fallen totally in love with Juffie the moment he saw her. It was a selfless, devoted passion with no hope of a future. He knew very well that this extraordinary young woman was not going to spend the rest of her life with a paraplegic. But for the time being he was content to be near her, and to nurture what he recognized was a real if incipient talent.

In her way Juffie returned Professor Wing's devotion. Perhaps because it was he who introduced her to the bliss of being onstage.

No childhood dreams had prepared Juffie for how much she was going to adore acting, for the way it would fill her life and assuage needs in her that hadn't been met since the halcyon days of childhood with the fawning four. There was simply nothing like it. Nothing like feeling the waves of love sent toward her by the audience, nothing like loving them back.

Onstage she gave without stint, pouring everything inside her into what she was doing; because it so pleased the people watching her, because like her they wanted it never to end. The rapport between actress and audience was something alive and ecstatic. It was a drug that once sampled would addict her as long as she lived. Juffie knew it was so, and she blessed Leslie Wing because he'd shown her the way.

. . . .

One thing about growing up in the middle of a boil, Karen said, you got very observant of pus. Which was her pithy way of explaining why she always knew she was going to study psychology. "On the one hand there's the economics, obviously people in the slums don't have enough money. So if you give them more they should be better off. But I don't think that's the whole answer."

The professor who was listening to this commentary was named Bernard Hanrihan. He nodded. "I see. Why not?"

"Because what's going on inside them, what makes them different from the people who have more, isn't just money or education. It's something else."

"What?" Professor Hanrihan asked.

"I don't know. That's what I'm hoping you can teach me."

He smiled, but only slightly. He had thin lips and Karen had never seen him grin. His face was narrow and interesting, not handsome. It didn't lend itself to grins somehow. His voice was wonderful, however. Mellifluous and deep. Sometimes in his class she couldn't follow the words because she was so entranced by his voice. Now, alone with him in his office, it was easier. The voice, directed solely at her, commanded full attention. "I can't teach you a lot of pat answers, Miss Rice. There aren't any. I can merely train you to observe and formulate some workable theories."

"Okay, that's what I want then."

Hanrihan was head of the psychology department and this

interview was to determine if next September, when she began her junior year at Simmons, Karen Rice would be accepted as a psychology major. She'd taken one course with him. If she had her way, the next two years would be spent entirely under his aegis.

"We're a fairly new field, you realize," he said. "It's difficult to predict what career opportunities are going to be available to a young woman trained in psychology. Particularly if you don't go on and take an advanced degree." He took a pipe from his desk drawer and fondled it, though he didn't light it. "But I suppose you'll get married before any of that matters."

"No, I won't." Karen shook her head firmly and the short curls bounced. It was May, the spring had been unseasonably warm, already her hair was sunstreaked gold, and that did wonders for its dirty-blond coloring. She wasn't thinking of that just now, nor of the physical impression she might be making on Professor Hanrihan. She wanted only to convince him of her sincerity and commitment. "I'm going to go all the way with this. I haven't wanted anything else since I was a kid."

"Why?" He didn't really need to ask the question. He'd known before she walked into his office that Karen Rice was a suitable degree candidate for his department. But she intrigued him. Her passion and intellect for one thing, and the way her small pointed breasts lifted the front of her white cotton blouse for another.

Bernard Hanrihan did not think of himself as a sensual man. He was forty-nine years old, he'd been a widower for the past eight years, and after his wife's untimely death it never occurred to him to remarry. But today he found himself making excuses to keep Karen Rice sitting across the desk. "Why?" he repeated. "People often choose a career in psychology or psychiatry as a means of working out their own problems. Do you think you're doing that, Miss Rice?"

She hesitated a moment, not content with the glib no that was probably expected. "In a way, maybe," she said at last. "Because of my family and where I was brought up, as I said before. I always knew I was going to get out of the West End, but I've never thought of myself as simply rejecting all the people there. Does that make sense?"

"A great deal of sense," he said, smiling his thin smile once more. "We'll be delighted to accept you as a candidate for a degree in psychology, Miss Rice."

When she told Juffie about it Karen was ecstatic. "For a few minutes I thought he was going to turn me down. He kept asking me more and more questions, I was in that office for almost an hour."

"What's Hanrihan like to talk to?" Juffie asked. "I've seen him only from a distance. He strikes me as a dried-up old fig."

"No, he's not. There's something fascinating underneath. But I'm not sure what it is."

Juffie stretched out on her bed, raising first one long leg and then the other in a series of exercises she'd read about in *Vogue*. "Okay, if you say so. Anyway, I'm glad you're getting what you want."

"So am I. Juffie, what about you? How are you going to get from Simmons to a real stage on Broadway?"

Juffie flipped over onto her stomach. "I'm not sure. But Leslie will guide me when the time comes."

"Tell me something. Do you call him Leslie to his face?"

"Sometimes. When we're rehearsing alone together. When he's coaching me. He told me to."

Karen grunted. "He's head over heels about you— Oops, bad choice of words since he doesn't have heels."

"Karen!"

"Okay, sorry. Anyway, he is."

"I know," Juffie said. "I've known it for ages."

"Well, what are you going to do about it?"

"Do? Why should I do anything? Leslie doesn't think I'm going to do anything. He just wants to help me."

"Hah! I distrust such altruism."

"Karen, spare me your psychology. Save it for the poor folks in the slums." She smiled to take the sting out of the words. "Anyway, I'm too happy to get mad at you. I have a surprise. Leslie told me today we're going to do a kind of summer theater this year. Three productions."

"All starring Juffie Kane, I suppose."

"Starring Juffie Kane," Juffie repeated dreamily. The words exploded in her head, a golden bubble filled with the honey of pure joy. "Starring Juffie Kane," she said again. "Oh God, Karen, I'll do anything to make that come true. Absolutely anything."

Chapter 5

Leslie Wing was raised in England, the son of an American consular officer stationed in London. At the age of fourteen the boy's exceptional talents had been recognized, and he was apprenticed to the Royal Shakespeare Company. That was in 1926, and it was the start of what blossomed into a distinguished stage career.

In 1939, when Leslie Wing was twenty-seven, he had his fourth starring role in the West End, and a series of offers from Broadway. Then England declared war on Germany. Leslie tried to join the RAF but was rejected because of his age. He turned down the Broadway offers because he felt that if he left London he'd be deserting his adopted country in her time of trial. All that changed in 1941 when Pearl Harbor was bombed. He returned to America and enlisted.

Wing wanted to fight, but the army assigned him to Special Services and decreed that his function would be entertaining the troops. Six months later, walking across the base at Fort Detrick in Maryland, he was struck by lightning. He lost both his legs. It was among the more freak accidents of war, but it derailed Leslie Wing's life as thoroughly as any enemy bullet.

In 1943 he was released from the hospital to life in a wheelchair. He'd been through the period of suicidal depression; now he knew he was lucky—and was glad—to be alive. Wing looked around for something interesting to do. He had a full disability pension, but he didn't want a future of nothing but dreams of former glories. He was delighted to accept an appointment to the Simmons faculty.

.   .   .   .   .

Back in England they'd warned Antony Morton about the heat

and humidity of an American summer. He hadn't expected to mind so much. "Is it always this bad?" He pushed aside a still boyish-looking shock of blond hair and took another swallow of icy lager.

"In July, yes. One of the problems with a summer term . . ." Leslie Wing's voice trailed off. The silence grew awkward. He was finding it hard to look at the other man. Supposedly he had adjusted to being legless, but seeing someone from the old days hurt. Not enough warning, not enough time to prepare. Tony had called an hour before, and appeared twenty minutes later. "How long have you been here?" Leslie asked finally.

"In Boston, only since yesterday. In America, a week." Tony looked around. "This is very pleasant, you're in an excellent location."

"Yes," Leslie agreed. "Excellent."

Simmons College had no campus. It functioned in a nine-teenth-century former mansion on Fenway between Boston and Jamaica Plain, next door to the Isabella Stewart Gardner Museum. The museum's lovely gardens were made available to the college. So on this Saturday, July 5, 1947, at four in the afternoon, the two men were sitting under a sycamore tree in a shaded green glade edged with phlox.

Despite the beautiful setting, Antony Morton regretted the impulse that moved him first to spend the long weekend in Boston, and then to seek out Leslie Wing. He searched again for something to say. "I guess a week isn't long enough to develop a taste for beer out of the fridge." He glanced ruefully at the frosted bottle. "The chill takes away all the taste."

"Yes," Leslie agreed. "But in this climate you become accustomed to drinking everything very cold. Even tea."

Morton grimaced. "Don't remind me. I've been introduced to iced tea."

Leslie managed a smile. Crazy, this inane conversation. They'd known each other since they were fifteen-year-old apprentices with the Royal Shakespeare, worked together dozens of times; now they could find nothing to talk about. Leslie was painfully aware of the other man's eyes, as carefully averted as his own. "Tell me about your show," he said. He really didn't want to hear, but they had to talk about something besides drinks and the weather.

"It's called *A Small Miracle*. David Hope wrote it before the war. You remember David?"

Leslie nodded. "Of course. I did a play of his in thirty-seven, *The Trap*. At the Piccadilly. Had a nice run."

"So you did. I'd forgotten. Anyway, he wrote *Miracle* some years ago, then put it aside while he helped sort out the Germans. Takes place on a farm in Dorset. Just after the 'fourteen–'eighteen war as originally conceived. Naturally he's updated it now. Because our David found himself with a ready-made American backer. His wife has a new brother-in-law, Jack Fine, the producer. Fine thinks Broadway is enamored of all things English at the moment, victorious allies and all that. So here we are."

"And you're directing?"

"Yes. The cast is largely from London as well. David insisted that the show be entirely homegrown. Only the dollars are made in America. Of course we need to include a few locals to keep Equity happy. So we're not through casting, and rehearsals don't start until September. Still, there are the preliminary arrangements with the theater and the sets and such. And I was between commitments in London. It seemed sensible to come over early."

Leslie repositioned his wheelchair slightly, waved away the offer of help. "You don't have a role for a legless war casualty, by any chance?"

"Sorry, old man, but—"

"Don't be an ass, and don't look like that. I was making a joke. A poor thing, but mine own."

"Sorry," Tony said again.

"So am I."

Tony rose to go. Leslie was relieved. He couldn't handle all these reminiscences, all these reminders of a world that had once been his. "Let me know when you open," he said politely. "Maybe I can get down to see it."

"I'll do better than that," Tony said. "We're sure to do a tryout here in Boston. I'll send you tickets." He was wondering whether to lean down when he held out his hand. He'd never before considered the etiquette of bidding good-bye to a man who couldn't stand up.

"Do that," Leslie said. "I'll look forward to it. And remember me to David and—"

"Leslie, I was sure I'd find you here— Oh, I'm sorry, I didn't realize there was someone with you."

Juffie had approached from the rear, so that Leslie hadn't seen her coming. And if he had? What could he have done about it? And why would he want to do anything? Because he could see it all instantly. Even as he introduced them the whole scenario played in his head, as inevitable as sunrise and sunset.

"Juffie Kane, one of my students." Leslie's voice was normal, in no way indicating his impotent rage at yet another kick in the pants from fate. "Juffie, this is Antony Morton, a friend from the old days in London."

He watched them shake hands. He saw the look of astonished pleasure on Tony's face, Juffie's avid perusal of the slim, elegant Englishman with the unruly blond hair and the gray eyes that crinkled at the corners when he smiled. Tony had always been able to charm the ladies. Even his voice changed when he addressed a beautiful woman. The slight whine of discontent that had marked his comments about the climate and iced drinks disappeared. His words were cool balm in the hot still air, the trained Shakespearean declaiming from center stage. "Delighted to meet you, Miss Kane. One of your students, Leslie? Does that mean Juffie Kane is an actress?"

"Yes," Leslie admitted. His voice sounded gruff and petulant in his ears.

"I think the word is aspiring," Juffie added with a ripple of vibrant laughter.

Her hand was still in Tony's. When Leslie saw her finally disengage it, he noted how reluctantly the other man let go. He observed Juffie's smile, the special one she turned on for an audience. It was an audience of one. She was playing entirely to Tony, and Leslie might as well have been on the moon. "I take it you're in the theater, Mr. Morton."

"I'm afraid so, daft though I sometimes think that makes me. Started in the Royal Shakespeare years ago, with your professor here. Right now I'm directing a play on Broadway."

He'd spoken the magic words, but her timing was perfect. Juffie neither botched the cue nor showed anything of the excitement Leslie knew she felt. He had to marvel at her skill even while he hated it. Cut! he wanted to yell. But this drama was real, not one he could interrupt with a word.

"That's very interesting." Juffie's grin was properly self-effacing. The next line she delivered in thick Brooklynese, with such insouciant charm she might have rehearsed it for a week.

"Gee, Mister, maybe you got a part for me. I had the lead in my high school play."

Tony laughed. "You never know, Juffie Kane," he said. "You never know."

But Leslie knew. He knew while he spoke his line, the one that had been ordained for him by the great dramatist in the sky, the one he hated but had to say. "Juffie has a penchant for character roles. She's been doing Judy Holliday imitations since she saw *Born Yesterday*."

"A perfect imitation," Tony said. "Perfect delivery."

"I've been well taught," Juffie said.

Leslie had to try. "Tony was just leaving."

"For a little while," Tony interposed smoothly. "I'm spending the Fourth of July weekend here in Boston. Soaking up the atmosphere of where it all began. Leslie, you said your little theater group was performing tonight, didn't you?"

"Oh yes, we are," Juffie said. "Chekhov. *The Cherry Orchard*. You couldn't come and see us, could you?"

He tipped his head back and studied her. "Don't tell me, let me guess. You can't be Anya, the shallow child. You must be playing Lyubov Andreyevna, the woman of wealth and a past. Am I right?"

Juffie nodded.

Tony favored her with an even broader grin. "Wouldn't dream of missing it."

Curtain, Leslie thought. End of the first act. Oh God, why must this be such a painfully predictable script? But he was as good as Juffie. When he smiled at them his anguish didn't show.

Five weeks later, after Tony Morton had spent every moment in Boston that he could steal from New York, they played the next scene, just as Leslie had known they would when it began under the sycamore tree. "You're not ready," he told her.

"Tony thinks I'm ready."

"For what? The starring role as his mistress of the moment?"

Juffie stiffened. "That was a rotten remark."

"Yes," he admitted. "But is it true?"

"That's none of your business."

He spun the wheels of his chair furiously, turning away from her. "No, I suppose it isn't. Whom you bed is your affair, but I thought I was somewhat involved in your career."

She crossed to him immediately, fell on her knees beside the wheelchair, and took both his hands in hers. "Leslie, of course you are. I owe you everything, I know that. But this is such a wonderful opportunity. Everything you've been grooming me for is right here in the palm of my hand."

She turned up her palm in an expressive bit of business meant to emphasize her words. Unable to stop himself, he grabbed it and pressed it to his lips. The scent of her, the touch of her flesh, was exquisite—and a painful taunt. I was tall and good-looking and talented once too, he wanted to shout. The same smell of power hung around me. Given a fair chance I could have beaten Tony Morton. But not without legs. "It's a terrible role for you, Juffie."

He had no other ammunition; he could use only reason. And he was telling the truth. "I've read the script. Hannah Glemp is forty in the play, twenty years older than you. Which is okay for a college production, but not on Broadway. Besides, she's totally unsympathetic. Listen to me, you're a bit of an unusual package, my dear Juffie. You look like a leading lady but your great strength is character parts. We need to find the right vehicle. Give me a little time," he pleaded. "Tony Morton isn't my only friend from the old days. I'll get in touch—"

She interrupted the words by laying one finger across his lips. "Leslie, please. Don't keep talking, it will only make it worse. I have to do this. I just have to. I can't let this chance go by, please try to understand."

·   ·   ·   ·

"How did he take it?" Karen asked.

The two girls had seen less of each other this summer. Juffie was rehearsing or acting all the time, Karen had a job at the West End Settlement House and was living at home. They'd planned this lunch at Brigham's as a way to catch up on each other's news. But it was Juffie who had all the news. An offer of a part on Broadway, plans to leave Simmons immediately, an emotional confrontation with Leslie Wing. That last had taken place barely two hours earlier and Juffie could not shake the pain. "He didn't take it well at all. But I suppose that's natural."

Karen waited a moment before answering. The remark was so like Juffie. She accepted the adoration she inspired as her due. It was natural that people should love her, natural that she should have to disappoint them one way or another. It was all part of her destiny, part of the legacy she'd been handed with her looks and her talent. Karen decided she couldn't bear to dwell on the ritual discarding of Leslie Wing. "What about this Englishman, Tony whoever? Is he somebody special?"

"He's a director. Trained with the Royal Shakespeare Company, then did lots of things in the West End, that's London's theater district. This is his first Broadway show."

"Mmm. I wasn't asking for his professional résumé. Are you, how do the gossip columns put it, romantically involved?"

"I met him only last month." Juffie toyed with her strawberry frappe and didn't look at Karen.

"So what? Most men go crazy the second they set eyes on you. What's with this new one? Is he queer?"

"No, he's not queer." She still didn't look up.

"Juffie, this is me, Karen, remember? Now give. Are you having an affair with him? Is that why you're getting a part in his play?"

"Getting the part was altogether separate," Juffie said indignantly. "I read for it, and it was offered to me last week." She saw the expression on Karen's face and realized how much she'd given away. "Okay," she admitted. She was glad that she'd tricked herself into telling Karen. She leaned forward and lowered her voice. "Last night. The first time. For the real thing I mean."

"And?" Karen demanded breathlessly.

"And it was marvelous," Juffie announced in triumph. "Honestly, Karen. It's better than you can dream. Tony is so sweet, so gentle. He makes me feel . . . I don't know how to put it into words."

"For God's sake, try. You can't just leave me with hints, like they do in magazines."

"It feels . . . warm all over. Like there are lots of little explosions happening at the same time, each one generating a bit more heat."

"What about one big explosion?"

Juffie shook her head. "Not yet, Tony says it will come." She giggled. "I mean that *I* will."

"And while you wait he's whisking you off to Broadway and making you famous. Juffie Kane, I don't know what star you were born under, but you seem to have reinvented the word *lucky*."

"I hope my folks agree."

Karen's brown eyes opened wider. "You mean you haven't told them yet?"

Juffie shook her head. "Not yet. Tonight. I promised Tony. He wants to leave for New York tomorrow."

"And take you with him, carry you away from all this and off into the sunset where the hero and heroine live happily ever after. Jesus! What are you going to tell Myer and Rosie? Not about the part, that's self-explanatory, I mean about Tony."

"As little as possible," Juffie said.

But neither Myer nor Rosie needed the details spelled out. "Okay," Juffie's father agreed. "You want to be an actress and you've been offered a part on Broadway. So I guess it makes sense that you should take it rather than finishing college."

"It doesn't make sense," Rosie interjected. "Actresses live very unstable lives. They never know when they'll be working. If Juffie has a college degree, at least she'll have something to fall back on."

Something to fall back on. It had to be the slogan of every mother in America.

"What to fall back on?" Juffie demanded. "If I spend two more years at Simmons, majoring in English because I can't think of anything else, just what will that equip me to do? What is this wonderful reserve career you're describing?"

"You can teach," Rosie said.

"No, I can't. Not without returning to school and taking education courses. Besides, I hate the thought of teaching. It's so boring."

"You could work on a magazine maybe," Myer said.

"A job almost as hard to get as acting," Juffie insisted.

Rosie's shoulders sagged. Her daughter could be an invincible force, a hurricane sweeping away everything in her path. "It's not just leaving Simmons," she said tentatively, sending Myer one of those eye signals which twenty-three years of marriage had perfected.

"No," he agreed. "Not just that."

"What then?" Juffie knew what, but it was better if one of them said it first.

"This man Morton. The Englishman who was here the other night. You've been seeing a lot of him."

"He's the director of the show. If he hadn't seen me in *The Cherry Orchard*, I'd never have been asked to read for the part of Hannah Glemp."

Myer had been standing by the living room window. Now he sat down in his big, comfortable chair, the one no one else ever used. "Juffie, I think there's more to your relationship with Mr. Morton than the play."

She hesitated only a moment. "Yes, there is. I love Tony."

"How can you love him?" Rosie demanded. "You've only known him a month."

"Five weeks. And you and Dad were married when you'd known each other only a little longer than that."

"Are you going to marry Mr. Morton?" Myer asked.

This was the hard part. Juffie bit her lip and lifted the heavy hair off the back of her neck, a gesture that always meant she was concentrating on what she had to say. "Not yet," she admitted. "I'm not sure I want to get married." Besides, Tony hadn't asked her.

"Thank God," Rosie said.

"Maybe," Myer amended. "So if you're not going to marry him yet, what are you going to do? Move in with him? Is that the plan, Juffie?"

She went to him, kneeling beside his chair as she'd knelt beside Leslie's this morning. It was such a burden, being loved and loving in return. There was always so much to explain. "Dad, listen, life isn't the way it was when you and Mama were young. And the world of the theater, it's different from what people are used to in places like Newton."

Myer put his hand on his daughter's cheek. She was so gorgeous, so extraordinary. In a way, that had prepared him for this. People who looked like Juffie always thought the world had special rules for them, suspended laws. But it didn't. And learning that could be horribly painful. "You know what you're talking, darling? *Bubkes*. It's a Yiddish word for nonsense, but it means more than that. It means what you're saying. Nothing. Rubbish. Hooey."

"Bullshit," Rosie added.

Father and daughter turned to look at her. Neither had ever heard Rosie use such language. "She's talking bullshit," Rosie repeated. "The world has changed. The theater is different. That's genuine bullshit. Right is right and wrong is wrong, Juffie, and that doesn't change. If you live with this man and you're not married to him, not even sure you want to marry him, he'll think you're a tramp. Whatever he says, that's what he'll think underneath. And it's what everybody will think who knows about it."

Juffie started to deny it, but at the last second she chose another weapon. "I thought you two knew better than most that what the world thinks is right and wrong isn't always the way it is. Sometimes circumstances alter things."

There was silence for a moment. Myer spoke first. "That's a low blow, Juffie. Not called for."

"I don't mean it as a blow. Oh God, don't you understand, either of you? I could just have run away and done what I'm going to do and sent you a letter or something. I didn't because I love you both so much. Because I know you love me so much. And I don't want to sneak around behind your backs. Listen, when you got married, Pa and Pop were furious, you've told me so. At first they were going to disown you, but they accepted it finally. And we were all happy. At least until . . ." She couldn't go on. Her eyes were filled with tears and her throat choked with sobs.

Rosie was on the verge of crying too. But she wouldn't allow herself the luxury. "Okay, if you were saying you wanted to marry Mr. Morton and we were arguing against it because he's some English fellow whose world will never fit with ours or yours, then your argument would have merit. But that's not it, is it, Juffie? That's not what this discussion is about. What it's about is you wanting to tear up your whole life and quit college and go to New York with some man you've known a few weeks and live with him."

"And have a part in a play on Broadway," Juffie added. "You forgot that, and it's the most important thing."

Rosie and Myer looked at each other once more. "Juffie," Myer said softly, "did you hear yourself? The play is more important than the man you say you love?"

There was a moment, a brief second, when she knew he was right. Juffie wouldn't allow that fragment of insight to take root. She shook her head as if to clear it, then got up and started for the door. "I'm going to bed. Tony and I are leaving tomorrow and I have to pack."

None of the Kanes slept well. Rosie cried a lot, the tears she'd denied herself earlier. Myer held her and didn't say much until she'd quieted down and the bedside clock said it was after three. "You sleeping?" he whispered.

"No, of course I'm not sleeping."

"Darling, I think it's better if we . . . I don't know how to put it. Well, not give Juffie our blessing exactly. But let her know we're not throwing her out or disowning her."

"Like always. Maybe that's been a mistake. Whatever she wanted or did, we went along. Maybe if we'd been more strict and conventional she wouldn't be throwing away her whole life."

Myer sighed. "She isn't, you know. She's being very foolish, maybe. And I'm as sure as you are that she's going to get hurt. But in the end there probably won't be any permanent damage. And according to Professor Wing, she really is talented. And I think it's the way we raised her that gives her the confidence and strength to go after what she wants. Maybe she will become a big star on Broadway."

"I want her to be a star as a human being, a decent person."

"She is," Myer said. "In her own way. The Kanes and the Saliatellis, darling, they've always marched to their own drummer. Now sleep. We'll talk to Juffie again in the morning. It's going to work out. I promise you."

In the morning Juffie came into the kitchen early, but her parents were both already there and eating breakfast. Juffie had a tight look on her face and she merely murmured a terse, "Good morning," and poured herself orange juice and coffee.

"Stop looking like we're playing a tragedy right here on Walnut Street," Myer said mildly. "It's more like a comedy."

"I've missed the humor," Rosie commented.

"Me too," Juffie said.

"So okay. I'm the only one who sees the funny side. That's how it is with Jews. The whole world's falling down and they make a joke. Juffie, your mother and I have talked it—"

"You talked," Rosie interrupted. "I listened."

"And agreed."

"Yes, I agreed."

"Good," he said. "That's settled." He turned to his daughter. "We don't approve of what you're doing, leaving college and taking the first part you're offered, and especially this business with the Englishman. But we love you and we're your parents, and we don't want to be cut out of your life, or cut you out of ours."

Juffie stood silent for a moment, then she put the coffee cup down on Rosie's kitchen table, covered with a bright red cloth and centered with a big ceramic cookie jar in the shape of a clown, and started to cry.

They were so unbelievable, so marvelous. Of course she didn't deserve them, how could she? But the confidence and determination that had been her weapon the night before were in fact their gifts to her. Her armor. But it needn't protect her from Rosie and Myer. Once more they'd shown that they were on her side. Always. No matter what.

Juffie flung herself at her mother and sobbed against her chest the way she used to when she was a kid with a scraped knee.

Myer rose and put his arms around his two women, both crying now. He wanted to say something, but no words came. There was too much love for words. It was Juffie who finally broke free of the triple embrace. "If I don't stop, I'm going to look awful when I arrive in New York."

Rosie got up and busied herself at the counter by the stove. "How about if I make you a lunch to take on the train? They say the dining car's terribly expensive, and I don't think the food's very good. When Mr. Morton came for dinner, he said he loved Italian food."

Juffie managed a smile. "That will be great, Mama. Just skip the garlic."

They all laughed. "See," Myer said. "I told you there's always a funny side."

.   .   .   .

The Chelsea Hotel had history, character, and a certain shabby charm. Tony Morton's suite was big but sparsely furnished. In the sitting room there were two chairs with tattered covers, and a sofa that listed perilously because one leg was broken. The few tables were stained with the rings of long-ago drinks. "This place gives me the creeps," Jack Fine said.

"How can that be?" Tony asked. "A patron of the arts like yourself, Mr. Fine? Surely you're moved by the things this old hotel has seen. All kinds of famous literary Americans have lived and created at the Chelsea."

"Cut the crap," Fine said. "We're here to talk business. I think your play's a loser."

Morton took a sip of his tea and grimaced. Juffie had made it in the suite's service pantry—a large closet boasting some chipped crockery and a hot plate. She never managed to make proper tea. This tasted like colored water. He put down the cup and studied Fine. "Mind telling me where you got that impression?"

"With my eyes and ears, and they tell the truth. Look, I'm not trying to threaten you. I'm here to help. After all, for my wife's brother-in-law . . ." Fine had refused tea and asked for coffee. He drank it before he continued. Apparently there was nothing wrong with the coffee. "Thing is, like I told David, we have to change the slant."

"I see. And just what do you have in mind?"

Fine turned to Juffie. She was sitting some distance from them, in a chair by the window. She wore black linen slacks and a red silk blouse and high-heeled red shoes. A shaft of late September sun caught her like a spotlight and Tony wondered if she knew, maybe planned it. No matter, the effect was stunning. Both men looked at her.

"Miss Kane here," Fine said, "is an asset. And you're throwing her away."

It occurred to Tony that his entire conversation with Jack Fine was turning into questions. He asked another one. "How are we throwing her away?"

"This part she plays, Hannah Glemp. The woman's forty years old, a drunk, and a German. Tell me, does that young lady look like an old Nazi lush to you?"

"Hannah's not a Nazi," Juffie said. They were the first words she'd spoken. Until then she'd listened in silence to the two men.

"Juffie is a character actress," Tony said. "She's going to be magnificent as Hannah."

Fine shook his head impatiently. "I'm not saying she can't play the part. What I'm saying is it's dumb to put somebody who looks like her onstage in a shapeless dress and a gray wig. For Christ's sake, Morton, the war's over. Everybody wants a little sweetness and light. Audiences need to laugh. They want to look at pretty women, not Nazi hags."

"Mr. Fine, you read the script months ago. Before you agreed to produce the play. What's changed now?"

He hadn't seen Juffie Kane months ago, Jack Fine thought. But what he said was, "Look, let me introduce you to some facts of life, American style. In the twenties, when I began, you could produce a musical, a blockbuster, for less than a hundred grand. I'm talking gorgeous sets, a big band in the pit, everything. Now the same show would cost a quarter million, maybe more."

He stood and began pacing back and forth, punctuating his words with stabbing gestures aimed into the air. "In twenty-eight about two hundred new productions opened on Broadway. This year we may see sixty-five or seventy. It's a tough world out there. And my job is to produce shows that become hits. So the investors don't lose their shirts, and I can go back to them again and get money for another show. If I don't manage to do that, in a few years there isn't going to be any Broadway. I'm not just being a crass son of a bitch. I'm looking out for the future of our profession."

Fine stopped pacing and fixed Tony with a direct stare. "I've been talking to David. He has to make the show more upbeat." He paused. "And I want you to get rid of Sheila Wright and put Miss Kane here in her part. Otherwise I'm going to have to pull out."

The ultimatum was like the clash of cymbals in the suddenly silent room. Juffie didn't move. She almost didn't breathe. Tony stirred his cup of cold, insipid tea, watching the liquid swirl. "Sheila Wright is an actress of some stature in England," he said finally. "She's the leading lady, and she has a contract."

"Signed in London." Fine had obviously worked all this out. "My lawyer tells me it may not stand up in an American court. Anyway, I'm prepared to offer her substantial compensation for terminating."

"Juffie is all wrong for the part."

"She looks all right for it to me."

Tony hesitated a moment longer. "No," he said finally. "No. You're castrating my show, Mr. Fine. I won't agree."

An hour later they still had reached no compromise and Fine left. Juffie had been as silent while they discussed her as she'd been before her name came up. Now she exploded. "What the hell is going on here, Tony? Why were you so stubborn? It's not your doing or mine that Sheila is to be dropped. I didn't ask for the lead, but if it falls into my lap why shouldn't I take it?"

"Because you can't do it." Tony spoke the words coolly. "You aren't capable of playing that part, not yet."

"Damn you, I am!" Juffie flung herself at him, her fists pounded against his chest. "I am! I am!"

He grabbed both her wrists, ending the attack. "Shut up, you're becoming hysterical. This isn't a stage, Juffie. We're not acting. And you can't do this. If I allow it, I'll never work in London again. Everybody knows we're sleeping together. It will look as if I dumped Sheila so my girlfriend could have a starring role. That sort of dirty trick may be acceptable in New York, but in England it would blackball me for life."

"Ah," she growled through clenched teeth. "The truth at last. It's your own future you're protecting."

"And yours. For God's sake, listen to me. Will you do that? Can I let you go and will you listen?"

Juffie hesitated a moment, then nodded. He released her hands. He'd hurt her and she rubbed her wrists. Her breath was coming in short, burning gasps and her chest rose and fell with the effort.

Tony watched her breasts moving under the red silk blouse. "You're so beautiful," he said softly. "No wonder Fine is willing—" He shook his head ruefully. "Even I, Juffie darling, even I am tempted. But I'm not going to let you throw away your career and my own, not when we're on the verge of brilliant success."

"Mr. Fine says we're going to flop." But she was less sure of herself now, less certain that for some perverse reason Tony was trying to keep her from getting everything she'd ever wanted.

"Jack Fine is a money man, concerned with profit, as he was the first to admit. What you and I want, Juffie, is dramatic success, acclaim from the people who matter. I want every critic in New York to realize that you're not just a beautiful woman, but an immensely talented one. If I allow you to play a part for which you're neither naturally suited nor professionally ready, I'll set you back five years. Good directors, the ones that count both here and in England, won't imagine what talent you really have. You'll never even be asked to read for the parts you should get."

Juffie was still trembling, but now it wasn't rage. He was right, of course, and she was overcome with love for him. "Oh, Tony, why am I such a fool?" She moved close to him, wrapped her arms around his neck, tipped her head back to be kissed. "I love you," she murmured as he bent his head to kiss her.

Tony was an undemanding lover, gentle and sweet, as she'd

told Karen after the first time. He did everything she expected him to do in rather the way she'd always imagined it. He loosened the buttons on her blouse and unhooked her bra so he could caress her breasts and nuzzle them a bit, ran his hands over her skin, eventually undid her slacks and pushed them and her panties down. By the time they got to that stage she was lying on the tipsy couch and he was naked. A minute or two later he was inside her.

She quite enjoyed his thrusts. They made her feel a warm glow of pleasure. Her skin misted with the sweat of passion; her breath came hard. Then it was over and she sighed with satisfaction. "Okay?" he asked, kissing her forehead gently.

"Very okay."

He lifted himself off her and his glance strayed to the door. A pale yellow envelope had been shoved beneath it. Tony walked closer to examine it. "A telegram. The bellboy must have brought it up while we were . . . otherwise engaged. I didn't hear him knock, did you?"

"No. Who's it from?"

"Haven't a clue. Anyway, it's addressed to you."

Juffie had never before received a telegram. She jumped off the couch and ran to claim it from him. Her thoughts centered on her parents and she wasn't entirely wrong. The telegram was from Rosie. "PA RELEASED TODAY STOP DOING VERY WELL STOP LONGING TO SEE YOU STOP COME SOON AS YOU CAN STOP MAMA."

Tony had been reading over her shoulder. "Who is Pa, your father? Has he been in hospital?"

"No, my grandfather, my mother's father. And yes, he's been in the hospital." She felt no twinge of conscience. Rosie had worded the message in that ambiguous way for precisely that reason. "Tony, let's go up to Boston this weekend. You can stay at my parents' house; there's plenty of room."

"Daren't leave now, darling. Not while Fine has the wind up. You go ahead. We're not rehearsing Saturday or Sunday. Just see you're back here Monday morning."

.   .   .   .

Dino Saliatelli was sixty-two years old when he was paroled on the condition that he live with his daughter and son-in-law, and avoid his old haunts in the North End. He looked at least a dozen years older. He'd been nine years in prison and he was thinner than ever, flesh hanging like crepe on his bones. His skin was dirty gray and his mouth sunken to a thin line. His hair had turned snow white, but he still had all of it, and his black eyes hadn't changed. They still glittered and seemed to see everything. When she was little he'd told Juffie that he could watch her even when he wasn't with her. He said something like that now.

"I been keepin' an eye on you, gorgeous. Even though I ain't seen you since you were a little girl. Your mama's told me everything about how you're gonna be an actress on Broadway. Those New York jerks treating you all right?"

"Fine, Pa. They're treating me very well. My show opens next month. We think it's going to be a hit."

Dino nodded. "Good. Very good. I like you should be associated with winners. You need anything, let me know. I still got ways of helping my little beauty."

Juffie hugged him. Then she swallowed hard. "Pa, there's something I have to say. All these years, the reason I never came to see you . . . I wanted to remember you the way you'd been."

"I figured that. Said more or less the same thing to your mama. And she always brought me pictures. The one of you in the long white dress when you graduated, that's the one I liked best. Pure and beautiful. Like a bride sort of. You gonna get married, Juffie?"

"Not for a while. I want to concentrate on my career." Pure and beautiful, she thought. And she'd been pregnant when that was taken. Because she'd been raped by a guy who used to work for him. It occurred to her that she could tell Dino about that now. Looking at him, she knew without doubt that he'd have revenge on Angel Tomasso, even after all this time. But if she did, her parents might find out what had happened. And they'd want to know what she did about the baby, and nothing would make her cause trouble for Karen or her family. So she simply hugged her grandfather again and smiled at him.

"Look, darling," Myer told her before she left. "We were going to make up a party and come down for your opening night. Me and Mama and Karen, of course. And we were going to ask Professor Wing and maybe Mr. and Mrs. Rice. But now . . ." He made a helpless gesture.

"They won't allow Pa to leave the state, is that it?"

"That's it. I guess we could get someone to stay with him."

"No, don't. I prefer it, Dad. I sort of need to do this alone. A few months from now, when the show is settled and running, Pa will be more accustomed to things. That'll be the time to leave him for a couple of days and come see me."

·   ·   ·   ·

It was decided that *A Small Miracle* would not have an out-of-town run. Too expensive. The play was scheduled to open at the Morosco Theater on West Forty-fifth Street on November twentieth. A dozen times in the weeks before the opening it seemed it would never happen. Jack Fine backed away from his ultimatum, but he kept nagging David Hope and Tony Morton to change things. Right up to dress rehearsal on the nineteenth he was coming to the theater and shaking his head, and making suggestions that they largely ignored.

The Morosco was a small house, the kind referred to as intimate. It was well chosen for a production such as this, a quietly intense drama with a small cast. Every time Juffie walked on the stage, even now while the theater was empty of everything but ghosts, she felt a thrill so intense she was sure the others would notice. If they did they didn't say anything. They were all seasoned professionals to whom opening on Broadway didn't seem so wondrous a thing as it did to Juffie. They were even able to take in stride the producer's constant harassment.

"Mr. Morton," Fine would call out from the back of the theater, where he always sat. "Mr. Morton, sorry to intrude, but I think you should know that I can't hear your leading lady in the back. Perhaps we Americans don't have such good ears as you English. And can't she make her accent a little clearer?"

Tony would pause a moment, then turn around and project his voice to the darkened rear of the theater, addressing a critic he couldn't see. "The character is from Devon in the West Country, Mr. Fine. Miss Wright is interpreting the accent absolutely correctly. And I assure you that while she may save her voice a bit during rehearsal, you'll have no trouble hearing her at an actual performance." Then he'd return his attention to the stage, where Sheila Wright waited, apparently unconcerned by the carping.

Back at the Chelsea Tony fumed and raged about how difficult his job was being made by Jack Fine, but only Juffie ever saw these bouts of temper. "It doesn't matter, darling," she soothed him.

"We open in a few days, and once we're a hit Jack Fine will say how marvelous we are and how he knew from the first it would be that way."

Not quite. They opened on the twentieth in a terrible rainstorm that put the audience in a bad mood before they walked into the theater. Juffie had three scenes in the second act. Two in the third. The first act she wasn't on at all, so she stood in the wings and watched and listened.

For the first ten minutes she thought it was going quite well. The production had jelled in the past week. The subtle, moving story of simple people who have been on opposite sides in a war and now must follow their governments into peace seemed really to be working. The timing was excellent, nobody was stepping on anybody's lines, they were doing all the things Tony had worked for three months to get them to do. A few minutes later Juffie sensed that the audience wasn't doing its part. They weren't laughing at the quiet jokes, and she didn't feel any response from them in the poignant moments.

By the time she went onstage she was sure that nothing good was happening. There was no electricity. She felt no waves of love. Juffie played for everything she was worth, willing the people on the other side of the footlights to join her in making magic. Once she thought she felt a little something, but that was at the end of her first scene. By the time of her second entrance it was gone and the atmosphere was as dead as it had been earlier.

They went with a sense of doom to the customary party at Sardi's to await the reviews. Tony got very drunk; so did almost everybody else. Jack Fine didn't even bother to appear. Juffie sat silent at a table in the rear and mourned. Her first opening night was supposed to be a triumph; instead, it was a wake. Andrea Hope, the playwright's wife and the woman whose sister had married Jack Fine and thus made possible the entire venture, brought in the papers just before four A.M.

"David Hope's *A Small Miracle* opened last night at the Morosco," said Brooks Atkinson of the *Times*. "It isn't quite a miracle. It's a pleasant story deftly written but lacking the scope and impact that create stirring drama." He went on to precis the plot, and it did sound banal as he described it. "Having said that," the review continued, "it must be added that this is not bad theater. Mr. Hope is a seasoned professional and many things are right with his play. Moreover, it's competently directed, and the distinguished British actress, Sheila Wright, is delightful. Incidentally, the small part of Hannah Glemp is played by a newcomer named Juffie Kane. She's very good. In a role that better suited her she might be wonderful. Miss Kane bears watching."

Howard Barnes of the *Herald Tribune* said more or less the same things. "A quiet tale that never ignites although it pleases. . . . Good writing and direction. . . . Some fine acting. . . . Remember the name Juffie Kane. I suspect we'll hear of her again."

The *Journal American* wouldn't be out until evening, but as was customary, Robert Garland had a copy of his review delivered to the restaurant. He liked it less than Atkinson or Barnes. "Rather a yawn, as the British might say. Maybe that's why they sent it over here. . . . Sheila Wright's terrific, too bad she didn't make her Broadway debut with a stronger show. . . . A young lady named Juffie Kane—playing an old lady for whom she's miscast—shows a lot of promise."

"Well, they're not death notices," David Hope said. "I've read worse."

"They aren't exactly raves either," Sheila Wright said. "I think I'm going home to bed."

A lot of the others followed her, the party slowly breaking up in silence. Tony started to rise. Juffie, seated next to him, had been reading the reviews a second time. "Listen, these really aren't bad. What Brooks Atkinson says at the end: 'Perhaps this serious play is what New York audiences need in this season that seems so far to celebrate only vapid nothingness.' That's not bad, Tony. Why is everybody being so glum?"

"Because the only thing that was going to keep Jack Fine from pulling the rug out from under us was absolutely glowing notices. If the audience had loved it and the critics had said we were the best thing since *Antigone*, he'd have happily forgotten that he hates us and counted his profits. Now he's done his duty by his wife's family, gone as far as she can reasonably expect him to. He'll take what's left of his money and run. You can bet on it, my sweet Juffie, whose promise everyone recognizes, so you at least shouldn't be depressed. Let's go, I'm sober all of a sudden, and not enjoying it a bit."

Morton's analysis was accurate. On the twenty-third a letter was hand-delivered to the hotel. It was Fine's formal notice that financial backing was being withdrawn because response to the play did not allow "a prudent man to continue his exposure." He wished them well in the future.

Tony stretched out his arm and dropped the sheet of paper. It fell slowly to the floor, gleaming white against the threadbare rug in the tatty suite at the Chelsea. "That's it. Everybody take their toys and go home. Have you thought about what you're going to do, beautiful Juffie?"

She had. "Yes, I know just what I'm going to do. Tony, I can get us new backing."

He stared at her. "What are you talking about?"

"Backing for the show. Enough money to keep us going until word of mouth has a chance to build the audience. The way you said it would."

"Hoped it would," he corrected her. "And that is one hell of a lot of money, Juffie. I know your father is a successful lawyer and makes quite a bit, but we're discussing many thousands of dollars. Many, many thousands."

"Not my father." Juffie shook her head. "I can't explain. But will you keep quiet about Fine's letter just until tomorrow?"

"What is going to be different tomorrow?"

"What I said. We'll have money. I'm taking a train to Boston right after tonight's show. I'll be back before curtain tomorrow night. Will you wait that long?"

He stared at her a moment, then he nodded.

· · · ·

"You understand what you're asking me, gorgeous?" Dino looked hard at his granddaughter, the black eyes trying to see into her soul. "You know what it means if I get you financing the way you want?"

"I think I do. Pa, listen, let me be absolutely honest. When I first found out about you and Pop, what you both did, I was furious. I hated you for letting me down."

The old man was propped up in bed eating his breakfast and she was sitting beside him, leaning forward, looking at him as intently as he was looking at her. "I thought you'd disgraced us all." She took a deep breath. "I don't think that anymore."

Dino didn't seem shocked by her confession. He chewed a bite of toast, waiting until he swallowed it before he spoke. "So what changed your mind?"

"Wanting something as badly as you wanted not to be poor in the old days."

"Not just that. I wanted to do what my father and my grandfather wanted. The family. You know what I mean, Juffie?"

"I think so. That's why my father worked with you, too, at the same time he was running around shouting about saving the world. That's true, isn't it?"

"Yes. Because he was Benny Kane's son, just like Rosa is my daughter."

"And I'm your granddaughter. Yours and Benny's. I want something more than anything else in the world. To be an actress. I've almost made it. I'm right there at the edge, Pa, I have it almost here." She stretched our her hand in one of those wonderful gestures that had become so natural to her. "But a man named Jack Fine wants to take it all away."

Dino stretched out a scrawny arm and patted the black telephone beside the bed. "Your father got me this. Not an extension, a private line. You know how many strings he had to pull to get a second line in this house while the phone company got a list long enough to reach California?"

Juffie shook her head. Dino chuckled. "A lot of strings. Myer is Benny Kane's son all right. Anyway, I got a phone, so I can sort of keep in touch. I checked out this guy Fine when I first heard about you bein' in the play. He's pretty clean. I don't think I can make him do what we want."

"I didn't think you could. But there's a lot of money around that's looking for a legitimate home. I know there is, Pa. I read the papers, and I hear the things Dad says. I'm telling you where to put some of it."

He made a gesture at the coffeepot and she refilled his cup with the black, thick brew Rosie made only for him, and added two lumps of sugar and waited while he took a sip.

"Good," he said. "The only one ever made better coffee than your mother was my mother, God rest her soul. Listen, it's not like it was in the old days, Juffie. I ain't the top man anymore. I still got connections, I can get things done. But I ain't in charge, I'm retired. You gotta understand that. I won't be able to protect you. Not as much as I'd like."

"Protect me from what? Pa, all I want is to go on in my show. The backers will make a profit. What else is involved?"

He took her hands. "Gorgeous, when you buy from these guys once, you're a customer forever. I ain't gonna lie to you. No matter whether they make money, the way they see it they'll have done you a favor. You'll owe them."

"Owe what? How can I pay?"

"I don't know. And it won't be whatever you or I think it'll be anyway. It doesn't work that way. But someday somebody may figure he should collect, and you ain't gonna have no way to refuse." He paused, the black eyes studying her once more. "Think about that good, Juffie, then tell me if you still want I should do it."

She thought for a moment. It wasn't just the show, it was Tony too. She loved Tony and if the show closed he was going to return to London. But she couldn't go to London, she had to stay in New York and be the success she'd dreamed of being. She nodded her head. "Pa, this is the only thing I'll ever want. There's no price too high to pay for it."

"You're sure?" His voice was solemn.

"I'm sure," she said.

He patted her hand. "Okay, Juffie. You want it, you got it. Your old pa's word on it."

Chapter 6

*T*he Morosco's backstage facilities were as small as the front of the house, but no one called them charming or intimate. Juffie, never having known another theater, thought everything about the Morosco was wonderful, including her private dressing room the size of a postage stamp. She had it only because the cast of *A Small Miracle* totaled a mere five principals, and because she was Tony Morton's girlfriend. The hell with it, she loved her dressing room anyway.

She was there after the play's forty-seventh performance, on the first Tuesday of January 1948, sitting at the minute dressing table and creaming off the exceptionally heavy makeup required to make her appear forty years old. Behind her the door opened. Juffie didn't turn around, she looked into the mirror—and froze. There, framed by the light bulbs surrounding the mirror, was Angel Tomasso.

"Hi, kid."

After a few seconds she resumed rubbing cold cream into her greasepainted cheeks. "Get out." She spoke softly and still didn't turn around. "Get out of here, or I'll call some of the guys and have you thrown out."

"Nah, I don't think so." He moved another step into the room and closed the door behind him. "What gives? No crowds of people wanting your autograph, no lineup of stage-door Johnnys outside. It ain't like in the movies, is it?"

Juffie stood up. Only a couple of feet separated her from Angel in the tiny dressing room. She started to push past him and reached for the door. He grabbed her wrist. "Where do you think you're going?"

"Let me go," she said in a growled whisper composed of equal parts of hatred and terror. "Let me go or I'll scream the place down. And I'll have you arrested for attempted rape. Don't think I won't do it this time."

Tomasso threw back his head and laughed. "You really don't know how things are, do you, kid?" He still hadn't released her wrist.

"Stop calling me kid. It's Miss Kane to you. And what the hell are you talking about? What are you doing here?"

He let go of her. "You want I should answer your questions? Okay, Miss Kane"—the way he spoke her name made it an obscenity—"since you don't seem to know, I'll tell you. We work for the same boss. Vinnie Faldo. Mr. Faldo to you. Which sort of means you work for me."

"I never heard of Vinnie Faldo. I'll give you ten seconds to get out of here. Then I'm screaming for help. And any minute now the director will be arriving, because we're going out."

"Oh yeah, I know about you and the limey director. You're screwing up a storm in some fleabag hotel downtown. I suppose that's one way to get on Broadway."

Juffie opened her mouth, and this time a scream really did begin. Tomasso stifled it as the first sound escaped. One arm circled her neck in a choke hold, the other hand covered her mouth. "Shut up, you stupid bitch! I got business with you, and it don't include messing up that pretty face, much as I'd like to. Mr. Faldo doesn't enjoy his investments should be damaged."

His choke hold was still so tight, she could hardly breathe. Finally he moved his hand from her mouth and slightly relaxed the pressure on her neck. "Okay, now shut up and stay shut up. And put your ass in that chair and listen to me." He pushed Juffie to the stool in front of the dressing table. She remained there, too frightened and bewildered to move.

"That's better. Maybe you really don't know nothing, so I'll spell it out. Mr. Faldo put up the dough that's kept this lousy show open for . . . what is it now? A couple of months?"

Juffie nodded, beginning to understand though she didn't want to.

"Well, in eight weeks you ain't turned a dime profit. So it's over. No more checks from that Alliance Investment Company, which is wholly owned by Mr. Faldo and his associates. *Capisce?* You understand?"

Juffie nodded again. She wanted to throw up. She thought she was going to. Waves of nausea kept climbing from her stomach into her throat, but she just swallowed them and sat on the stool and nodded.

"Good. I told the boss you were a smart girl. And Mr. Faldo told me to tell you that he'd be in touch sometime when you can return the favor. Meantime, if you want backing for some other show that ain't such a loser, you let Dino know, and just maybe Mr. Faldo will consider it." Tomasso grinned. "Or you could get in touch with me, since I'm Mr. Faldo's right-hand man. I bet you'd rather do that, seeing as how we know each other so well. Here, I'll leave you my number."

He reached into his pocket and Juffie thought he was going to produce a card or a piece of paper. Instead, he palmed a tiny knife and snapped it open. She dived for the door again, but he grabbed her. Not in a choke hold from behind this time. He had both his powerful arms around her torso, pressed achingly against her breasts, and his hands held hers. He forced the right one open. Then he used his stiletto to carve four numbers into her flesh.

He didn't cut very deep and it wasn't terribly painful, and she was now too frightened to scream. The stinging sensation ended in less than a minute. Tomasso let her go. "In case my handwriting ain't too clear, that's two seven nine oh, in Boston. Make sure you don't lose it." He laughed again. "Take care of yourself, kid. See you around."

She was barely aware of the door opening and closing, of the fact that he'd gone. She kept staring at her palm, speckled with droplets of blood, oozing more. It took a few seconds before she realized that someone was knocking.

"Juffie, are you in there? We're all waiting for you."

She grabbed a wad of tissues from the box on the dressing table and made a fist around them, then she opened the door. Tony was lifting his hand to knock again. He dropped it and stared at her. "What's the matter? You look awful. Are you ill?"

"I was, a little. Something I ate maybe. I'm all right now."

"Okay. Can you hurry up? Everybody's waiting."

It was Sheila Wright's birthday and they were going to Lindy's to celebrate with enormous pastrami sandwiches and slabs of cheesecake. Lindy's was Sheila's choice. "I may never have another birthday in New York," she'd said. "And I want to remember this one as the essence of Times Square."

"Look, you and the others go ahead," Juffie said. "I'll be along later, when I feel better."

"You're sure?" Tony asked.

Juffie insisted she was. Then, alone again, she sat down in front of the mirror and stared at her half made-up face in the harsh light of the unshaded bulbs. "Oh my God," she whispered. "Oh my God."

Ten minutes later there was yet another knock on her dressing room door. "Miss Kane, you still in there? It's me, Bob. The janitor. I want to lock up, Miss Kane."

"Yes. Sorry. I'm just leaving. Two minutes more, Bob. Can you give me two minutes more?"

"Sure, Miss Kane, sure."

She heard the sound of his footsteps fading down the empty corridor and she grabbed another clump of tissues with her left hand and began swabbing at her face with vicious strokes.

Forty minutes later she was in the suite at the Chelsea. Tony was still at Lindy's celebrating Sheila's birthday, so she'd never have a better chance. Juffie took off her coat but kept on her gloves. They were black kid and the right one looked suspiciously damp, but the bloodstains weren't identifiable against the dark leather. She lifted the telephone with her left. "Hello, front desk? Can you get me a Boston number, please."

The phone rang only twice, then she heard her grandfather's gruff voice.

"Pa, it's me, Juffie. I'm sorry to call so late. Were you sleeping?"

"Nah. I don't sleep much these days. Anyway, like you know, the phone's right beside the bed. How are you, gorgeous?"

"Okay, I'm okay, Pa. Listen, who is Vinnie Faldo?"

There was silence on the other end of the line. "Why you wanna know?" he asked finally.

"A man came to see me tonight. Somebody I've met before, somebody I hate. He said he worked for this Vinnie Faldo, and that Faldo owns the Alliance Investment Company. He said they were going to pull our backing because the show still isn't making a profit."

"So?"

"So is it true?"

"Yeah," Dino said. "Most of it, I guess. Vinnie ain't alone, he's got partners. But he's the capo. And an old friend called me up a day or so ago. Said he knew I'd be interested, seeing as how you're in the play. The boys ain't happy with the investment."

"I see."

Again there was silence on the line. "Juffie," Dino said at last, "I can't do nothin' else to keep them interested. Like I told you, I ain't runnin' things anymore, just sort of looking on. But it ain't so terrible. You had a couple of months, right?"

"Yes, Pa. That's right. And I'm sorry I bothered you. How are you feeling?" she asked belatedly.

"Fine. Good. Your mama takes good care of me. And she and your dad are both okay too. I won't tell 'em you called, since this is just our business. But stay in touch, gorgeous. They worry about you."

"I will, Pa. I promise. Good night."

So that was that. She'd planned to ask him to do something to make sure Angel Tomasso was never sent to see her again. But the way he sounded, old and tired, she just couldn't. Pa was violating the terms of his parole by helping her, and she didn't want to get him in deeper. Besides, she suspected she knew what he'd say. "You let yourself in for this, Juffie. I warned you. It's too late to start crying now."

Which is rather what Tony said later, when he'd come back from the birthday party and she told him that she hadn't felt well enough to join them, and that she'd had word the investors in Boston were pulling out.

"Well, I'm not surprised. We've been playing to half-empty houses with disgusting regularity. It's a bit past time to weep. And I've been checking into some other possibilities."

For the first time in hours she started to feel a little better. "What possibilities, Tony? A new show? What is it? Will there be a part for me?"

"All in good time, dear heart." He finished buttoning his pajamas and crawled into bed beside her. "But I shouldn't worry too much about there being a part for you. The surest thing to have come out of this fiasco is that the star of Juffie Kane has begun its ascent." He rolled over. "Good night."

Juffie wanted to make love, to feel comforting arms around her. She reached out a tentative hand. The left one, which wasn't bandaged and hidden beneath the covers. "Tony?"

"In the classic phrase, not tonight, dear. I have a headache."

In minutes she heard him snoring.

Two weeks later she was again alone at the Chelsea. That was becoming a frequent occurrence because *A Small Miracle* had closed and Tony was out seeing people and arranging things, as he put it. What he was arranging she still didn't know. Juffie read the casting calls in *Variety* every day, but she didn't go to read for any of the plays. Tony had told her to sit tight. "I'm going to put you in something where you'll really shine, Juffie. And I shall bask in the glory of having discovered you."

She was lying on the couch, dreaming that old wonderful dream in which she took curtain call after curtain call to a tumultuous roar and a standing ovation, when the telephone rang. "Miss Kane, I'm so glad I found you in. This is Cecily Abrams, I'm Jack Fine's secretary. Mr. Fine would like to speak to you."

"Hi, Juffie," the producer said a moment later. "Sorry the show closed. But it could have been worse. It ran eight weeks."

"No thanks to you," she said.

"I know that. You still mad at me?"

"No, I'm not mad. You were probably right. We should have changed things before we opened."

"The hell with all that," Fine said. "It's over. Listen, is Tony there?"

"No. But I expect him later. Shall I have him call you?"

"That's not necessary. It's you I want to talk to. Can you meet me for a cup of coffee? Say in twenty minutes?"

Half an hour later they were in Schrafft's on the corner of Fifth Avenue and Fourteenth Street. "I picked this place because nobody from our business ever goes below Twenty-first Street," Jack Fine explained. "And this is a private conversation." He reached over and took her hand. It was the right one, which had only yesterday emerged from the bandages. "Very private," he repeated.

Juffie started to pull her hand away. Jack held on to it. "You haven't met my wife, have you, Juffie? Her name's Vanessa. She's

English and I adore her. We've both been 'round a couple of times before. Third time lucky we think. So this isn't a pass. Even if you are the most gorgeous thing I've ever seen. I'm forty-nine, old enough to be your father, and like I said, I love my wife. I also love the theater."

She didn't speak because there was nothing to say until she knew what he wanted, but she left her hand in his.

"Listen," he continued. "I've got to ask you a personal question. How committed are you to Tony Morton?"

Now she did pull her hand away. "Very committed. Tony and I are more than friends. You know that, Mr. Fine."

"Jack. And yes, I know it. That's why I wanted to see you alone. Look, I'll lay down all my cards. Word is that Morton's trying to make a deal for a new show with a major part for you, a starring role, and him as the director."

Juffie nodded. "Yes, I know that."

"Okay. But maybe you don't know the property he has in mind."

It was a question and he was waiting for an answer. Juffie shook her head.

"I thought you wouldn't," Fine said. "I know how guys like Morton operate, everything close to the chest. And I know the play. It's another war story. This one has a French heroine who stands up to the Nazis, and gets herself hung in the third act. The girl's not a bad part, she has some terrific scenes."

"Mr. Fine, why are you telling me all this? Why are we here?"

"Because I think you're a wonder, Juffie Kane. And because the play Morton's touting is another loser. It's a terrible story. Sour, heavy, depressing. This is not the time for depressing plays. Not after what everybody's been through in the last few years. It's time for comedy. Like *Born Yesterday*. Did you see *Born Yesterday*, Juffie?"

"Yes. I loved it. Judy Holliday is marvelous."

"So she is. Someday, sweetheart, you are going to be even better." Juffie started to say something, but he held up a silencing hand. "Let me have my say, then you can talk. You are going to be the greatest if—and it's a big if—you're showcased in the right vehicles. You're as smart as you are beautiful, so you know it doesn't do a young actress any good to be in a series of flops."

This time she wouldn't be quiet. "Yes, I know that, so does

Tony. He's an experienced director, Mr. Fine. You're talking as if he can't tell a good play from a bad one."

"Experienced in England, not here. And if he's such a good picker, how come *Miracle* was a disaster?"

"It wasn't a disaster. It ran almost three months."

"Only because some new money from, God help us, Boston, took a flyer. I'll never figure out how a bunch of guineas from Boston thought they knew more about my business than I did. They must have money to burn. But that's beside the point. Juffie, I have a new show in the works. It's called *Delilah*. Nothing biblical. Delilah's a Tennessee girl who comes to New York and makes it big running a cathouse." He paused. "You know what a cathouse is?"

Juffie nodded.

"Good. Okay, what happens is Delilah's whole hillbilly family comes to live with her, but of course they don't know what this place she runs is. They think it's a girls' school. Meanwhile Delilah gets the idea that one of her customers is the president of the United States. It's very funny, Juffie. How come you're not laughing?"

"It's a farce, isn't it?"

"Yes. An old-fashioned farce. With a laugh a minute and wonderful writing. The dialogue is fabulous. And Delilah's the whole show. She's on almost every second. That's a damned hard thing to do, so the director doesn't want to hear about some unknown that I think would be great. Somebody who's not only as beautiful as Delilah is supposed to be, but who can handle the accent and the humor. He wants Kitty Carlisle, or maybe Nanette Fabray. But since without me he hasn't got a show, he's agreed to hear my choice read. Tomorrow. What do you say, Juffie?"

"You haven't spoken to Tony about this, have you?"

Fine pushed away his empty coffee cup and shook his head. "No, I thought I made that clear. There's nothing in this for Tony Morton. John Duquesne is directing. And Morton wants to hold on to you. I don't mean personally, that's between the two of you and none of my business. He wants you professionally, Juffie. He knows as well as I do how big you could be. But not if he keeps *shtupping* you into losers."

She didn't comment because she couldn't find the words. Maybe Jack Fine was right. Maybe she should throw her arms around his neck and thank him for the opportunity of a lifetime.

But her self-confidence was at an all-time low. She'd just made an awful mess because she wanted so desperately to keep *Miracle* alive. It hadn't worked, it had only delayed the inevitable, and to achieve that small thing she'd put herself in debt to somebody named Vinnie Faldo whom she didn't even know, and Angel Tomasso whom she knew only too well. Now Jack Fine was making a proposition that would give him a claim on her too.

Juffie ran the fingers of her left hand over the palm of her right. There was only the faintest welt, but she imagined she could feel the numbers Angel had carved.

Fine stood up. "Okay, you're quiet this long, I have to figure you're not enthusiastic. And without enthusiasm this isn't going to work. Juffie, if you change your mind, you know where to find me. It'll be too late for *Delilah;* Duquesne's bound to get his star pretty soon. It's a terrific show. But you give me a ring and I'll see what I can do. Right now I think I was wrong and you're not smart, you're dumb. But I'm never going to change my mind about how much talent you've got."

It was a gray, cold winter dusk, but she walked back to Twenty-third Street and the Chelsea. Tony hadn't returned. By eight she was still alone and starving. There was no food in the service pantry, nothing but some tea bags, a can of coffee, and a bottle of scotch. It was starting to snow, so she pulled on boots and her coat and tied a wool scarf around her hair. Then she rode the creaking elevator downstairs and went out into the dark empty streets to a restaurant on Sixth Avenue. It was more a coffee shop than a restaurant, but she and Tony had often eaten a combination late lunch and early dinner there before going to the theater.

"Hi, Miss Kane. You alone?"

"Yes, Sam, it looks that way. Mr. Morton's been held up on business."

Juffie took a seat at the counter and ordered meat loaf and mashed potatoes. The food wasn't bad, but it didn't taste like Rosie's. Which made her think about home. She wanted to think about it. She did not want to dwell on her conversation with Jack Fine, or the incredible fact that she'd just turned down an opportunity to read for a starring role. If she did, she might begin to wonder if maybe Fine was right and Tony was wrong—and she was a prize jerk. Juffie pictured her family instead.

There would be supper on the table by now. Lasagna maybe,

or ravioli. Pa loved ravioli. Of course it might have been steak or roast beef or even meat loaf. Rosie didn't cook exclusively Italian. "Your mother makes good in any language," Karen had said when she first moved in. Karen.

There was a pay phone at the rear of the restaurant. Juffie fished in her bag. "Sam, can you change a couple of dollars for quarters?"

"Sure. Hey, something wrong with the meat loaf?" Half the food remained on her plate.

"No, nothing. I guess I'm not as hungry as I thought. I want to make a call, then I'll have some coffee." She took the handful of quarters and stepped into the booth.

Rosie and Myer had invited Karen to continue living in Newton during the week, but she'd refused. "It won't be the same without you," she'd told Juffie. "I'll sleep at home and do my studying at the library." That's where Leah said she was now.

"Studying, Juffie. At the library. It's so noisy here. How are you, darling?"

"Fine, Mrs. Rice. You?"

"Fine, except for my arthritis."

They chatted a moment more about such things. The way in which Leah met Juffie had not affected her feelings about the girl. She was Karen's friend and Leah was fond of her. She simply assumed that Juffie had made a mistake and learned from it. "Men always want to do it and women always get pregnant," she said. "That's the way it is." Which was what she said now.

"That's the way it is, Juffie. Here Karen's all the time saying how much she misses you, and you call and she's not home. I can't even tell you what time to call back. Sometimes she stays real late at the library."

"It's okay, Mrs. Rice. I'll call again in a couple of days. Give her my love."

Juffie went back to her seat, wondering about how late the library stayed open, and found Sam had put a slice of apple pie next to her coffee. "On the house. You have to keep your strength up, Miss Kane. After all, I bet you're going to be starting another show pretty soon."

"Maybe, Sam. Maybe." Juffie tasted the pie and thought about Karen. It would have helped a lot to talk to her. Karen was always so sensible.

. . . .

Professor Bernard Hanrihan, head of the Department of Psychology at Simmons College, had never before taken one of his students to his home on Brighton Avenue in Brighton. Maybe he was dreaming that Karen Rice lay beside him in the double bed he'd formerly shared with his wife. "Karen, you're really here, aren't you? I'm not making all this up in my fevered imagination."

"No, you're not making it up." She lay on her back, her nakedness covered only with a thin sheet. In the darkness of the room she thought her voice sounded disembodied. "If you are, we're sharing a joint hallucination. Do such things exist, do you think?"

"No, not really. Of course there's mass hysteria. That comes close."

"Is that a clinical explanation for something like the Nazis, mass hysteria?"

"Karen," he said gently. "I don't think this should turn into a class. How do you feel?"

She hesitated. "A little strange," she admitted at last. "Like all girls, I've always wondered what the first time would be like."

"That's what I'm trying to find out. How was it? Did I—" He hesitated, and when he spoke he sounded disarmingly shy. "Did I satisfy you? I don't really have a lot of experience. No, don't laugh. It's true. I know it sounds ridiculous since I'm fifty-one years old, but I was married quite young, and there's never been anyone other than my wife."

"I wasn't laughing at you. At us. A couple of innocents. And, Bernard, I feel very satisfied."

He sighed and rolled over and took her in his arms. "I'm so glad. I care for you deeply, my dear Karen. This would never have happened otherwise."

"There haven't been any other students, then? Not in all the years since your wife died?"

He'd told her about it, how nine years ago Bess Hanrihan had drowned in a boating accident on a New Hampshire lake. The story had come out two months earlier, after they met in a public library and somehow left together, and strolled through Copley Square and had a cup of coffee and talked for two hours.

That had led inexorably to this, and all the while Karen was allowing it to happen—no, helping it happen—a secret corner of her mind told her she was probably one in a long line of willing students.

Now he was insisting that wasn't so. "No one else," he said. "Certainly no other students. Just my wife, as I said." He stroked her back while he spoke, petting her as if she were a kitten.

Karen felt waves of pleasure engulf her, not just because of his touch, but because she knew he was telling the truth and she was special, not merely the latest in a series. It felt better than the sex, though she'd never tell him that. She sighed and snuggled closer to him. Bernard's body didn't seem old. It was slender and he didn't have a paunch and his hair wasn't gray. The thirty-one years between them didn't matter. That was just a silly convention they would ignore. She sighed again.

"I hope you understand how risky this is," he murmured.

"You mean because if anybody found out you'd lose your job and I'd be expelled? Yes, I understand that."

"And you're willing to chance it?"

"Yes."

He did not ask why. She was glad, because she could not have answered. What it was that drew her to Bernard she couldn't quite identify. She admired him enormously, that was part of it. He was tremendously intelligent, he'd even published a number of books on psychology. But it was more than that. In her head she heard Juffie's voice. What kind of more? And the only answer she could give was, I think I love him.

He was still holding and petting her. "What are you thinking?"

"Nothing I can put into words. Bernard, did you love your wife?"

"Yes. It sounds corny, but I married the girl next door. We sort of grew up together."

"And there were no children?"

"No. There never seemed to be time. She had a career of her own, you see. We were both in college when we married and we went on and took our masters' and Ph.D.'s together. She had an income from a family trust, so it was possible."

"What was her field?"

"I thought you knew. Psychology. In fact, she wrote three of the textbooks we use in class. She pioneered in intelligence testing."

A Ph.D. who pioneered in psychology and came from a rich

family to boot. Terrific. She had one hell of a chance of competing with that. Karen made a small sound in her throat and he took it as a groan. "Is something wrong, am I hurting you? Are you cold?"

"A little cold maybe. Let's pull up the quilt."

He did, then said, "Listen, it's nearly ten. I hate to say it, but I'd better set the alarm in case we fall asleep. You must leave here soon, my dear. I'm sorry," he repeated.

"Don't apologize. It's all right, Bernard. Really."

"There's a twenty-four-hour taxi stand around the corner. I'll take you down there and send you home in a cab."

"We can have another hour though," she said. "I'll go at eleven."

"Very well, at eleven."

. . . .

In New York it was nearly eleven when Tony returned to the Chelsea. "You're late," Juffie said. "I was worried."

"Sorry."

He said it perfunctorily and she wasn't sure he was sorry at all. But he soon distracted her. Tony removed a script from his inside coat pocket and handed it to her. "Have a look at this, will you? If you're not too tired."

"No, I'm not tired at all." Juffie carried the blue-bound folder to the single reading lamp in the room. *The Passionate Defender* was hand-lettered on the cover. "It's a drama?"

"Yes. Takes place in France during the war." He got the bottle of scotch from the service pantry and poured himself a large drink. "Care for some?"

Juffie shook her head and concentrated on the script. She only skimmed it, because Tony was sitting and watching her, obviously waiting for her to finish. The heroine's name was Yvette, and as Jack Fine had said, she had some wonderful scenes. But the other things he'd said were also true; it was a desperately serious story. "Very heavy going," Juffie said when she reached the final page.

"Yvette's a great part."

"Yes. Lots of meat, that's for sure." She began to warm to the idea of playing a classic-style heroine who dies in the final act. Katharine Cornell had been a smash in *Antigone* at the Cort last season. But Juffie couldn't forget everything Jack Fine had said. "You don't think it's too heavy for the Broadway audience of the moment? I'm just remembering what they said about *Miracle*, of course."

"It may be," Tony agreed. "It's hard to get a lot of laughs out of the Nazis."

"But you want to do this anyway?"

Tony took a long drink of scotch. "I think it should be done, and I think you'd be a wonderful Yvette. But not on Broadway. At least it shouldn't open there."

Juffie closed the script and put it down before she spoke. "I'm not sure I understand what we're talking about, Tony. Maybe you'd better explain."

"The New Stages Theater on Bleecker Street. In Greenwich Village. They want to produce it."

"Off-Broadway," Juffie said. "That's what you have in mind?"

"Yes, to start, as I said. Plenty of plays have moved from off-Broadway to a major theater. It's much cheaper initially, of course. By the time the show's a hit at the New Stages, there'll be enough interest to generate the funds for a full-scale midtown production."

Juffie lifted her hair from the back of her neck and considered her next words carefully. "Listen, I'm not shooting you down, and I suppose it's okay for me since I'm a newcomer, but do you really think a director of your stature should do an off-Broadway production just now? Wouldn't it sort of be acknowledging that *Miracle* was a flop?"

"Yes," he agreed. "It would. A very ill-considered move." He rose from his chair and crossed to where she was sitting and took both her hands in his. "Cut's healed, I see," he said. "You took the bandage off."

She'd told him she cut herself opening a can of tuna. "Yes, it's healed. Tony, I still don't understand. Please explain again. In words of one syllable maybe. So I get it absolutely straight."

He pulled her up to stand with him and took a deep breath. "Okay. Words of one syllable. I can't find anyone who wants to stage a major production of *Passionate Defender* with you as Yvette. Not with anyone else as Yvette either. This city is full of the most crass businessmen in the universe. Art and great theater are not high on their list of values. But the New Stages has a regular company, and quasi-permanent financing. The people down there are interested. The director saw you as Hannah, and he thinks you'd make a superb Yvette."

"The director. So you don't plan to direct the show?"

"No. For all the reasons you just outlined."

"What are you going to do?" Juffie asked the question in the most normal of voices, but she moved away from him and went to stand by the window. It looked north to the lights of midtown and Broadway.

"Sheila Wright's been asked to do a revival of *Medea* in London. She wants me to direct."

"You'd go back to London?"

"I can't very well direct *Medea* long distance, Juffie."

She waited to see if he was going to ask her if she'd rather go to London with him than play Yvette off-Broadway. After nearly half a minute she knew he didn't intend to.

"Right," Juffie said, crossing to the table where the script of *Passionate Defender* still lay. "That's settled then. When do you leave?"

He didn't look at her. "Tomorrow actually. Sheila lucked into a couple of tickets on the weekly Pan American flight. First they said they were booked for a month, then there were two last-minute cancellations. *Medea* goes into production mid-February, and there's a lot of preliminary work to be done."

Juffie managed a weak smile. "Well, you always move fast, don't you, Tony? But surely you didn't decide just today to return to London."

He shook his head. "End of last week, when I'd had my third turndown on a major production of that." He nodded toward the script she was holding.

"Oh yes, this." Juffie handed it to him. "You can take this, Tony. I won't need it."

"I don't understand. Don't you want to do the show? It's a wonderful part. I spent two days getting everything arranged for you. And, Juffie, I've paid the rent here until the end of February."

She should have been furious; instead, she giggled. "Did you? Well, thanks, I'll stay on until I find an apartment. Poor Tony, you should see how forlorn you look. Sorry, but I won't be playing Yvette off-Broadway. I was waiting for a chance to tell you without it being too painful. Jack Fine's offered me the lead in his next production. But since there wasn't anything for you . . ." She shrugged expressively.

He stared at her, open-mouthed. It was worth everything just to see that look on his face. "Tony," she added before he could say anything. "Would you mind getting the hell out of here? Right this minute? Before I call the front desk and tell them you tried to rape me or kill me or something? I'm sure Sheila Wright will be glad to give you a bed for the night."

He was gone minutes later. And she had to face the consequences of her lie, and make it the truth. Juffie began paging through the telephone book, frantically looking for the F's. "Please God," she whispered fervently, "let Jack Fine live in Manhattan." She didn't have any other phone books. She found a J. Fine at 960 Park Avenue. The telephone rang half a dozen times before a man answered. He'd obviously been sleeping.

"This is Juffie Kane. Am I talking with Mr. Fine the producer?"

"Yeah, Juffie, this is me. What the hell time is it anyway?"

"After midnight, Mr. Fine. I'm sorry. But you said that Kitty Carlisle or Nanette Fabray would probably sign any minute. And that I had to read tomorrow. I want to do it. Please, I want to read for the part of Delilah."

There was silence for a few seconds, then Fine chuckled. "I already told Duquesne you weren't interested, but I'll wake him up too. Be at my office at ten."

She didn't sleep all night. Not because of Tony Morton, the bastard. Because she didn't have the script of *Delilah*. She'd have to read cold. If she'd been smart enough to say yes the minute Jack Fine asked her, she could have spent the night studying the part. Now all she could do was try to remember what a Tennessee hillbilly was supposed to sound like, and practice the accent.

When she finished worrying about that, she started on what to wear. How would John Duquesne expect her to look? Like Delilah? Like a Boston college girl? Like a sophisticated New York actress? What had Fine told him about her? At nine she was still standing in front of the closet in a bra and panties trying to decide. There was a knock on the door. Juffie threw on a robe and went to answer it.

"Front desk sent me up," the young bellhop said. "Mr. Morton asked for his things to be packed."

"Okay, but it has to wait another fifteen minutes. I'm getting dressed to go out. When I leave, you can come in and pack Mr. Morton's things."

"The guy from the express company's waiting downstairs. He's supposed to bring the suitcases out to LaGuardia."

"Screw him—and Tony Morton." Juffie slammed the door and shot the bolt. Then she felt sorry for the kid, who was only trying to do his job. "Fifteen minutes," she called, and ran back to the closet.

It was nearly nine-thirty by the time she was on the street hailing a cab. She was wearing a black wool dress, relieved only by a strand of pearls, under a three-quarter-length red coat. She'd decided on sophisticated New Yorker. Her hair was completely hidden by a black felt hat with a turned-back brim and a long red feather. Thank God it wasn't snowing, so she didn't need boots over her black pumps.

"Miss Kane," Cecily Abrams said when she arrived at Fine's office on East Forty-third Street. "How nice to meet you at last. I've heard a great deal about you." She held out her hand and Juffie shook it. "I'll take you right in," the secretary said. "Mr. Fine is expecting you."

He was alone and he got up from behind the desk and showed her to a chair. "Sit right there. Take off your coat so you don't boil in here. This is the script."

Juffie took it with nervous eagerness she couldn't conceal.

Fine smiled at her. "Relax. You've got forty-five minutes, maybe an hour. John's due between eleven and quarter of."

"I won't have to read cold then," she said with a sigh of relief. "Thank you."

Jack Fine patted her cheek and left her alone. The next thing she knew he was back. It seemed as if five or ten minutes had passed, but it must have been longer, because he had another man with him, whom he introduced as John Duquesne. Juffie stood up to shake the director's hand. He was about Fine's age, maybe a few years older, and he was short and stout and thoroughly unimpressive. But Juffie knew his reputation. "It's a pleasure to meet you, Mr. Duquesne. I've been reading about your work for years."

"Hmm," Duquesne said. To her that was all he said. He looked Juffie up and down, then turned to Jack Fine. "Beautiful, I agree. Exquisite. A great body. But she's much too cool and sophisticated for Delilah. We need a bouncy, vibrant type, like Kitty Carlisle. Not a high-class Boston lady."

"Just hear her read, John. That's all I'm asking."

"Of course. That's what I came for." He turned back to Juffie, as if by paying attention he made her reappear. Clearly, when he discussed her as if she were a slab of meat she was supposed to be absent. "Whenever you're ready, Miss Kane."

Juffie looked from the director to the producer and back again, seeing on both their faces that she'd made the wrong first impression, and this was going to be a waste of time. "Look, I'd like to do it from Delilah's second-act entrance. Is that okay?"

Duquesne shrugged. "Whatever you like."

"I'll just step out then, and come in the way she does." Juffie didn't wait for comment, she ducked out the door of the inner office and closed it behind her.

Cecily Abrams was seated at her typewriter and she looked up. "Is there something you need?"

"No." Juffie didn't have time to explain. She was too busy yanking off her hat and pulling the pins out of her hair so it would hang free. Then she took off her dress.

"Miss Kane!"

"It's okay, Miss Abrams. Don't shout, please. I don't want them to get nervous and come out here." She was unhooking her garter belt while she spoke, and stripping off her stockings and shoes. Finally, hair hanging down her back, barefoot, wearing only a black slip which she'd hitched up into the legs of her panties so it looked like a very short dress, she threw open the door to Jack Fine's office.

"Is there anybody in this heah place wants a little nooky?"

It was the most risqué line in the show. They weren't sure they'd be able to leave it in, and it wasn't Delilah's entrance line but one she delivered later toward the end of the second act. Juffie had improvised to serve her own needs. The two men stared at her, thoroughly unnerved because she was half naked and she hadn't said what they expected her to say. Then they both roared with laughter.

Juffie waited. Leslie Wing always said she was born with perfect timing. When she'd milked the laugh for all it was worth, she went on. "Just look at this crowd! I'm feared to say you gentlemin are gonna wear out my hospitality, and they don' sell no more o' that at Macy's neither. Maybe I oughta try Gimbel's."

She crossed to John Duquesne and pressed his head to her

half-naked breasts. "Mr. President, ah think the reason you come to Delilah's so often is jus' 'cause you need a ma—"

"Cut!" Duquesne yelled. The word was half muffled because he was being smothered by Juffie's cleavage, but she heard him.

"Right," she said, pulling back and stepping instantly out of Delilah's character. "That's a first reading, Mr. Duquesne, and I had only a few minutes with the script before you arrived. But is it anything like what you had in mind?"

He looked at her, and nodded slowly. "Something like it," he admitted. "Now, Miss Kane, would you care to put your clothes back on before we discuss the contract?"

Twenty minutes later she was being stubborn because she had decided that she'd done all the damn fool things she was going to do for a while. No more crazy decisions made for crazy reasons. Besides, she was a lawyer's daughter. "I'm sure this contract is fine, and everything's standard, just as you say. But I'll feel happier if I can take it home and read it over and come back and sign tomorrow."

"It's not an unreasonable request." That was Duquesne placating Jack Fine. The roles of the two men had reversed; now it was the director who was prepared to do whatever was necessary to get Juffie Kane into the show.

"No," Fine agreed. He turned to Juffie. "But asking for more money, that would be unreasonable, Juffie. You're a complete unknown, we're taking a big chance."

"It isn't that," she said. Which was true. Four hundred dollars a week probably wasn't half of what they'd have to pay a big-name star, but it seemed more than fair to her. She'd been making ninety-five in *Miracle*. "It's all the fine print," Juffie explained. "I just want to read it carefully and understand everything. I'm enormously grateful to you both for giving me this opportunity, and I don't want hard feelings later because I misinterpreted some words."

"Reasonable," Duquesne said again.

"Twenty-four hours, Juffie," Jack Fine said. "Ten o'clock tomorrow morning you come in here and you sign. Otherwise we haven't got a deal."

She didn't wait to get back to the hotel. Juffie went across the street to Grand Central and located a bank of telephones in the marble-lined grand concourse, and called her father at his office number.

"Dad, I'm looking at a ten-page contract, all of it written in lettering so tiny I can barely make it out, and I've got to sign it by tomorrow morning or lose the best chance I'll ever have. There's a train leaving for Boston in half an hour. Should I take it?"

"No," Myer said instantly. "We'd love to see you, but it would be a wasted journey, darling. You need an expert on theatrical contracts, and I've never seen one. Stay where you are and call me back in thirty minutes."

When she did, he had a name. "Matthew Varley, 501 Fifth Avenue. Go straight there, he's expecting you."

Varley's office wasn't far away. It was on the corner of Forty-second Street, right across from the Public Library, and looked down on the lions guarding the entrance to all wisdom. "I'm sort of a two-headed beast myself," he explained. "I'm supposed to be an attorney, but more often than not I function as a theatrical agent. I think I got into it because I've been stagestruck since age ten, but I don't have any talent."

"Except for legal things, I hope," Juffie said. She pushed the contract across his desk. "I'm supposed to sign this tomorrow morning. I desperately want to; it's a wonderful part and I'm satisfied with the pay, but I don't understand all the other clauses. I don't want any nasty surprises down the line."

"Very wise," the lawyer said. "It looks standard, but I'll take a minute to check it out, if you don't mind." He bent his head over the pages and seemed to forget she was there.

Juffie took the opportunity to study him. Matthew Varley was young, no more than thirty, she guessed. She hadn't expected that. He had straight sandy hair and pleasant features and a sprinkling of freckles, and his eyes were dark brown. He was wearing a tweed suit that looked rather more casual than she'd expect a Manhattan lawyer to wear.

Old money, she decided. The kind that doesn't care what other people think. Harvard or Yale or Princeton. He even smoked a pipe. She elaborated on the image while she waited. Mother— Philadelphia main line probably. Father—a broker or maybe a doctor. Some school like Groton or Choate before college. And all the while he was growing up, summers at the lake. It didn't matter which one, some lake where wealthy WASPs congregated. At that point in her reverie he looked up.

"It's boilerplate, and thus minimally acceptable. Except for clause nine."

"Which one is that?"

"The one saying that if the show remains open, you can't leave it for twenty-four months." He leaned forward and showed her the clause. "The point is, if a show is a hit, the names of the principal actors become thoroughly associated with it. The backers don't want to lose a star until they've wrung a property nearly dry. The star, on the other hand, wants a chance to take another offer while his or her name is most valuable because of being in a hit. So it's an inevitable conflict of interest."

"And twenty-four months isn't usual?"

"A year is usual. I've seen eighteen months, never twenty-four."

Juffie nodded her head. "Okay, that's what we tell Mr. Fine. I'll agree to a year. If he really balks, we compromise on eighteen months."

Matthew Varley grinned. "That's supposed to be my line. The agent gets to spell out the terms."

Juffie didn't smile. "Look, I want to explain something. It's not because of my looks."

"What's not?"

"The reason I've got the part. I'm a very good actress, Mr. Varley. Please believe that."

"There's nothing wrong with being beautiful either. Some of our best actresses labor under that handicap. Though offhand I can't think of any in your league."

She shook her head impatiently. "It's important to me that you understand."

He leaned his chair back on two legs and clasped his hands behind his head. "Why?"

"Because you saw me today as a favor to my father or some friend of my father's."

"Not true," he explained. "Mr. Kane called the New York Bar Association and asked about someone experienced in theatrical contracts. They gave him my name, and he called me. I did agree to see you immediately as a courtesy to a fellow attorney, but that's all there is to it."

"Okay," Juffie said. "But it's not all I want. I want you to be my agent. But only if you understand about me."

He dropped the chair forward and leaned on the desk and

studied her. "I'm beginning to. I think I'd be delighted to represent you. In fact, I'm sure of it. I get ten percent off the top. Can you live with that?" She nodded. "Fine, then let's try each other for a year. After that we'll see."

Juffie extended her hand. "Deal, Mr. Varley," she said.

"Deal, Miss Kane," he agreed.

Juffie sighed and relaxed in her chair. "I feel wonderful. I've got a fabulous part and an agent all on the same day. If I were a drinking woman, I'd go out and get drunk."

The lawyer didn't smile but he buzzed his secretary on the intercom. "Miss Wilkins, could you come in here with a thirty-nine, please."

"What's a thirty-nine?" Juffie asked.

He was looking at the contract again, making notes, and he acted as if he hadn't heard her. Two minutes later the secretary appeared, carrying a tray with a bottle of champagne and two glasses.

"Bollinger thirty-nine," Matthew Varley said as he popped the cork. "An excellent year. I keep it on ice only for very special occasions. Ordinary signings get nonvintage stuff."

· · · ·

Jack Fine suspected from the first week of rehearsals that he was incubating a huge success. *Delilah* was written by Sadie and Phil Leonard, a husband-and-wife team who already had five hit comedies to their credit, and he had gifted them and their play with Juffie Kane. "It's a marriage made in heaven," he told his wife. "I know it in my kishkes."

"Then why are you worrying?" Nessa Fine demanded. "Why are you sleeping so poorly?"

"Because I keep thinking that if we're going to take this all the way, if we're going to make history like I think we can, I have to do something more. I have to start building the word of mouth."

The legitimate theater did not live on hype the way Hollywood did. Broadway did not indulge in outrageous press stunts and "spontaneous" demonstrations of "fans" hired by the studio. Jack Fine had as much disdain for the movies as everyone else of his profession and his era, but he couldn't ignore the evidence. Never mind that Mayer and Warner and those schmucks didn't know *gornicht* about acting, directing, or writing; they'd proved that sometimes clever public relations could make a success into a smash.

"Juffie, we have to get you talked about," he said six weeks before the show was to open. "I've got a story I'm trying to get into the papers."

"About what?"

"About how you're a college girl from Boston, a lawyer's daughter, almost a virgin as far as acting is concerned, and here you are with the lead in what's going to be only the best show to open in this or any other season."

"Oh, that."

They both chuckled. "Juffie, you've been hanging around this town too long already. You're starting with the one-liners."

She wasn't listening. "Does your story mention my father's name?"

"Of course. I looked it up in your file at Equity." He pulled a notebook from his pocket. "Myer Kane. And your mother is Rose. Did I get it right?"

"Near enough." She waited for him to say something about her grandfathers. He didn't. So he couldn't know. Which was a good thing. Dino Saliatelli and Benny Kane were no part of the image he wanted for his "almost virgin" actress. But what if it all came out? She blanched. She wanted success, wanted it desperately, and swallowed hard at the taste of fear.

"Anyway," Fine said. "A couple of stories isn't enough. You should be seen around town."

"Mr. Fine, you know what a slave driver John Duquesne is. I haven't got time to be seen around town." Inside, she was tingling with apprehension, praying that Fine would drop this plan.

"How often do I have to tell you to call me Jack? And you're going to make time. You seeing anybody, I mean since Morton went back to London?"

"No." She felt guilty and couldn't look at him.

"Okay, how about Varley? He's single, and he looks like a nice all-American young man. You have to know him like I do to know he's a goddamn shark. Yeah, I'll talk to Matt."

Let him refuse, Juffie prayed. Let Matt think this is a terrible idea. Later, when I'm a star, it won't matter. But right now I do not need to have my past life in the newspapers. . . . She kept remembering that time so long ago when the *Herald*'s front page featured Pa and Pop. Please, God, let Matt say the whole idea is terrible and he has no time to squire Juffie Kane around the New York hot spots.

He didn't. Matt agreed that what Jack was suggesting was in the best interests of his client. The only way she could stop this train Jack had set in motion was to tell him the truth, and she simply hadn't the courage for that.

Matt and Juffie began appearing at Peacock Alley, the fabled bar in the Waldorf, and the "21" club, and Toots Shor's, and the Stork Club. Fine saw to it that judicious tipping assured the couple seats in the most prominent areas of these legendary establishments. They were on display; the appearances were brief, and so carefully orchestrated that the pair didn't have much personal conversation. Juffie didn't feel she knew Matt Varley any better after these command performances. But they achieved their end.

Juffie Kane—with her tall, gorgeous figure displayed in a low-cut cocktail dress from Bergdorf Goodman or Saks Fifth Avenue, with her thick honey-colored mane of hair waving to her shoulders, with her dark-ringed violet eyes and pronounced cheekbones and full plummy mouth—attracted attention. The added spice was the story Jack was assiduously spreading that she was a huge talent who had come from nowhere to be discovered by him, and now she was rehearsing the lead in a new show that was going to be a winner.

They began to get results quite soon. In March full-length features ran on the theater pages of both the *Times* and the *Herald Tribune*. In April Walter Winchell's column mentioned her four times, and Leonard Lyons, who wrote the nationally syndicated "Lyons Den," gave her three paragraphs on one occasion and four on another.

They also had another piece of good fortune. Before they went into production they'd commissioned a Tin Pan Alley regular to compose incidental music for the show. He came up with what Jack Fine called "the genuine article," a catchy tune that was half ragtime, half burlesque striptease music. It was so good they wrote in an extra bit of business for Juffie in the second act. She did an exaggerated bump and grind to the number. It was straight from Minsky's—on one of Minsky's better nights.

Jack brought a man from Columbia records to a rehearsal one

afternoon. He watched Juffie roll her hips and swing her breasts to the foot-tapping tune and he loved it. Three weeks later Mitch Miller and his orchestra recorded the music, and it was released as a 78 rpm single, with Juffie in her scant hillbilly regalia on the cover. What they called "Delilah's Song" went to the top of the hit parade.

.   .   .   .

On the first of May, 1948, three months short of Juffie's twenty-first birthday, *Delilah* began its run at the Cort on Forty-eighth Street east of Broadway. The theater hadn't seen a bigger, more instantaneous hit since it opened its doors in 1912 with *Peg o' My Heart*. Within a week the marquee didn't just announce the name of the show, it said JUFFIE KANE in lighted letters two feet tall.

By the end of the month everybody in New York was talking about her; by the end of the summer everybody in the country. Juffie kept the word of mouth going. She started dating her leading man, Harry Harcourt. They were seen in all the places she'd gone to with Matt, and the gossip columnists kept writing about her. Cholly Knickerbocker said that Juffie Kane and Harry Harcourt were thinking of marriage. The day after that item appeared, Harry took Juffie to a little-known place on Ninth Street in the Village for supper after the show.

"Listen, beautiful, we've got to have things square between us. Because you are the nicest lady I know."

"And you're worried that I planted that story in Knicker-bocker's column to get you to consider the idea."

He smiled sheepishly. "It crossed my mind. I think you're wonderful, Juffie. And us going around together is fun, and good for the show. But marriage isn't in the cards."

"I know that, Harry." She took his hand. "I understand more than you think I do. And I did not, repeat not, slip that silly rumor to that equally silly columnist."

"Thanks," he said softly. "Like I said, you are one very nice lady, as well as the best actress in captivity. Now finish your food and let's go uptown where the folks who matter can see us."

Delilah went from strength to strength. The SRO sign was out for every performance, and they were booked solid for five months. "We're not just a smash," Jack Fine said. "We're a goddamn revelation. Juffie, you know that award they started a couple of years ago? The one in memory of Antoinette Perry?"

"The Tony? Of course I know it. In 'forty-seven they picked Ingrid Bergman and Helen Hayes as the best actresses on Broadway. This year it was Judith Anderson, Katharine Cornell, and Jessica Tandy."

Fine smiled. Juffie Kane had an absolute dedication to the theater. He'd seldom seen devotion so intense in one so young. Trust Juffie to know all about the Tony awards. "I hear they've decided not to give any more multiple awards," he said. "Just one for a dramatic actress, one for a musical. Well, I say you're going to get the Tony for best dramatic actress this year."

She stared at him, unable to speak for a moment. When she did, her voice came out in a hoarse whisper, because just the idea of such a miracle had constricted her throat with excitement. "I couldn't. How could I, Jack? My God, look at the competition." Gertrude Berg was starring in *Me and Molly* at the Belasco, Irene Rich was in *As the Girls Go* at the Winter Garden. The immortal Tallulah Bankhead was packing them in at the Plymouth in Noel Coward's *Private Lives*.

"You're going to get it," Jack repeated.

On the 24th of April, 1949, in a ceremony held in the ballroom of the Waldorf-Astoria, Juffie Kane received her first Tony for best dramatic actress of the previous season. *Delilah* was a comedy, but for purposes of the award a play was either a straight or a musical production. *Delilah* was straight. And there was some sweet poetry in the fact that the actress John Duquesne originally wanted to play Delilah, Nanette Fabray, won the Tony for best actress in a musical for her role in *Love Life*.

Rosie and Myer were at the Waldorf for Juffie's triumph; so were Karen and her mother. Mr. Rice didn't come, he said he was happy for Juffie, but he wouldn't be comfortable with all those fancy people in New York. Dino wasn't well enough to make the journey even if the terms of his parole had allowed him to leave Massachusetts.

As soon as she knew of the nomination, Juffie invited Leslie Wing, but he begged off on the grounds that the Simmons Drama Society was opening its spring production the same night. "But I'm not a bit surprised, my dearest Juffie," he wrote. "And very proud." His letter made her cry. Even after she won there was no word from Tony Morton in London, which didn't make her cry at all.

.   .   .   .

In 1957, when *Time* ran a two-page story on the memorial service that followed the avalanche in Switzerland, they remembered *Delilah*: "So it was for the lady who suspended most of the rules. Juffie Kane paid no dues in summer stock, she pounded no pavements, she waited anxiously in no darkened theaters for her turn in the dreaded ritual of casting calls, she did not chew her nails beside a silent telephone, or scheme to meet a particular director or producer. Juffie Kane began her professional career miscast in a small part in a flop; a short while later she exploded on Broadway as zany, wonderful, hilarious Delilah, and instantly became the full-blown, magnificent, unsinkable, inimitable, incomparable star which she was to be for nine glorious years. Thanks for the pleasure, Juffie. We shall miss you, and we know we may not see your like again."

Chapter 7

"Karen, I don't believe it." Juffie spread her arms in one of those gestures she'd made famous. "You and that dried-up old fig, Hanrihan? I just don't believe it."

It was two days after the Tony awards, and they were in Juffie's apartment in Tudor City. She'd lived there for sixteen months, since *Delilah* went into production. It was a step up, and uptown, from the Chelsea. Tudor City was a vast complex of buildings on Forty-second Street between First and Second avenues, a world unto itself, partially raised above the street, and threaded with artificially created lanes and alleys. The only thing Tudor about the stacked cubes with their hives of apartments was the red brick construction.

From her window Juffie could see the exciting tower of the city's latest aluminum and glass landmark, the United Nations building, but that was the one luxurious touch. There were quite nice apartments in Tudor City, but hers was basic New York studio—one room with a Murphy bed that folded into the wall, and a tiny kitchenette. For this Manhattan cell she paid sixty-seven dollars a month. She could have afforded more, but not much. After Matt took his ten percent and after taxes, her take-home pay was two fifty a week. Not a great deal considering what she was spending on taxis and clothes.

When Karen made her announcement, Juffie was displaying her worldly wealth, her wardrobe. Dresses and suits and blouses and lingerie and shoes and jewelry were spread all over the room. Almost buried in a colorful jumble of clothing, they were a pair of potentates exulting in the riches of the kingdom.

Karen wriggled out of the ice-blue satin cocktail skirt she'd been trying on. "He's not a dried-up old fig. Bernard is a wonderful, sensitive, brilliant man. I thought you of all people would understand."

"How old is this sensitive, brilliant person?" Juffie demanded.

"Just turned fifty-two." Karen went to the tiny refrigerator and poured herself a glass of V8 juice. "You want some of this?"

"Yes. Karen, you are almost a year younger than me. You've been twenty-one for only a few weeks!"

"Imagine, and all this time I didn't know that. Here." She handed the drink to Juffie.

"That's what, thirty-one years difference? He's thirty-one years older than you. I wouldn't care if it was just a fling, but you're telling me you love this guy. Karen, how can you do this? Did you go crazy the minute my back was turned?"

Karen drank her V8 in one long swallow and looked for a place to put the empty glass. She had to push half a dozen lace bras in assorted pastels off the coffee table. "I never expected this from you, Juffie. I thought you'd be happy for me."

Juffie's tone softened. "Sweetie, I want to be happy for you. I want your life to be wonderful. It's just—"

"Just that you're making all the conventional noises. Bernard and I don't think conventions should rule our lives."

"Are you getting married?"

"No, that's another convention," Karen said defiantly. "I'm starting at B.U. in the fall, to get my master's. Bernard's working on a new book. We don't have time to get married."

"Where are you going to live? With him?"

Karen made a face. "No, we'd prefer that, but it isn't possible. A professor and a student, even a former student, is verboten. Too many people think like you do. I'm getting a little apartment in Brighton. A couple of blocks from Bernard's house."

Juffie shook her head. "Do your folks know?"

"Don't be an idiot. Of course not. Not a single soul knows. Except you. One of the main reasons I stayed in New York for a few days was to have a chance to tell you." She leaned forward and put her hands on Juffie's shoulders. "You're my best friend. So you've got to understand, Juffie. Please. I have to have someone to share it with."

Juffie wrapped her arms around Karen's slight frame. "Of course I understand. If you're happy, then it must be okay."

"I am. Really happy. My life's just about perfect."

"Something must be." Juffie pulled back and eyed her. "You're looking great."

Karen's dark blond hair was cut shorter than ever, in close curls that hugged her scalp. It was a style made instantly popular by Mary Martin when she opened the month before in *South Pacific*. A lot of the women wearing it probably shouldn't have, but the cut suited Karen. It accentuated her pixie look and made her brown eyes seem even bigger. And she glowed. "I wish you didn't have to go home tomorrow," Juffie said. "We could go shopping. You could get some new clothes to complement the new you."

"Can't afford it," Karen said. "I'm still an impoverished student."

"That doesn't matter," Juffie said airily. "I have charges everywhere. Bergdorf, Altman, Saks, Bonwit, Bendel—everywhere."

"And they don't send bills at the end of the month? Funny stores they have here in New York."

"Oh, they do, of course. I pay them all a little bit each time, enough to keep them happy."

"And you're a star, so they don't balk. Juffie, you really are a star, exactly the way you dreamed of being. And that's marvelous. But"—she waved her hand at the pedestrian little apartment—"why aren't you making millions of dollars?"

Juffie explained about the contract for four hundred dollars a week. "I'm locked in until October. Of course, now things will be a bit different." She reached out and touched the gold medallion on the end table beside the sofa. It had the masks of comedy and tragedy on one side and a profile of Antoinette Perry on the other. "Now that I've got the Tony, Matt will put the screws on them. They'll probably kick in a few hundred extra."

"Your Matt's adorable, by the way. When you stood up to receive the award, he clapped so hard I thought his hands would fall off."

Her Matt. Juffie felt a tingle of pleasure, then pushed it away and began stuffing selected items of clothing into a big brown bag. "Take some of this junk home with you; you'll only need to have it shortened." She added the blue satin skirt to the things in the bag. "He's not my Matt. He's my agent. Believe me, he's made it perfectly obvious that that's all he is. He was clapping himself to death because after I leave *Delilah* I'm going to do another show right away. And make a lot more money. Ten percent of more is more. Matthew Varley has a dollar sign where his heart should be."

Which might be true, but he wasn't pushing her into the first thing that came along no matter how much money was offered. "We've got to find the right property," he kept saying. "Something where you're really showcased. We've got to build on what you've accomplished."

Juffie agreed, but it was easier said than done.

The scripts poured in from producers and directors and writers' agents and would-be writers without agents. Everybody had a play that was a surefire smash if it could just star Juffie Kane. Matt weeded out the obvious turkeys and sent the others to Juffie. She spent most of the hours she wasn't onstage reading. So far nothing tempted her.

"They're all *Delilah* warmed over," she complained. "I don't want to make a career of being a hillbilly."

"You want me to stop passing on anything that's full of country corn?"

"Yes," Juffie agreed. The result was a week when she had no scripts at all to read.

She went shopping instead. It was July, hot as hell, and she was running around the stores trying on wool suits and fur coats. She was determined to buy a fur, even though she wouldn't be able to afford one until she went into her next show. That didn't matter; what mattered was that her first fur coat be perfect. Like her next part. So far she hadn't found either.

She came home one afternoon with an hour to shower and change before she was due at the theater. The telephone was ringing when she opened the door. She dived for it and grabbed the receiver. "Hello."

"Hiya, kid. You know who this is?"

"No." She knew, but she didn't want to. She wanted to hang up. But she hesitated.

"I'll nudge your memory a little. What hand you holdin' the phone with, kid?"

Angel Tomasso. Oh God. "What do you want?"

"Me and Mr. Faldo and some of the boys is in town. We wanna

see your show. But them jerks say they ain't got no tickets for tonight."

It could be worse, so she allowed herself to feel a little relief. "How many seats?"

"Eight. And Mr. Faldo would like a box. Real close to the stage."

"Listen, I may not be able—"

"A box," Angel interrupted. "Best seats in the joint. We'll pick up the tickets when we get there. You can leave 'em in my name. You remember my name, don't you, Juffie?"

"Yes."

"Okay, you ain't said it, so I thought maybe you forgot and I should come over there and remind you. Forty-second and First. Number Five Tudor City Place, Apartment Twenty-four B."

She swallowed a gasp, he had her telephone number, it shouldn't surprise her that he knew where she lived. People like Angel Tomasso made a career of knowing things. "The tickets will be there."

"Okay. There's somethin' else. After the show Mr. Faldo and his guests is gonna be at Sardi's. I mean he wants to do it right, a real Broadway night on the town. He wants you should join him."

"I can't," Juffie said. "I don't go out after a performance. I need to rest."

"Sardi's right after the show," Angel said as if he hadn't heard her. "Mr. Faldo's table."

He broke the connection. Juffie hung on to the receiver until it made beeping noises of objection. She was sweating. And she didn't know how to get Angel his tickets. It was crazy, but these pockets of ignorance were always tripping her up. Her apprenticeship to stardom had been so brief, there were thousands of things she didn't know about the world that had suddenly become hers.

Juffie thought for a moment, then dialed the Fines' Park Avenue apartment. A maid said no, Mr. Fine wasn't in. Would Miss Kane care to speak with Mrs. Fine? Juffie said she would.

She'd met Nessa a number of times in the past year, and she liked her. She never felt obliged to pretend to knowledge she didn't have with the Englishwoman. "Look," she said. "I need eight tickets for tonight's show and we're supposed to be sold out. How do I get them?"

"That shouldn't be difficult," Nessa said. "Larry can always pull some seats out of a hat."

Larry Machefsky was the show's general manager. Juffie had thought of him, too, but that didn't entirely answer her needs.

When John Cort came from California at the turn of the century to build his East Coast theater, he wanted it to be the most splendid in New York. The Cort was a Louis XVI fantasy. It had a marble facade, Corinthian columns, and a lobby decorated with murals of Marie Antoinette. And the owner had built himself a box bedecked with gold leaf and velvet, so close to the stage it hung over the apron. Juffie knew that if she provided the men from Boston with any less she'd be in trouble.

"That's not the whole problem," she told Nessa. "I don't just need eight seats, I need the John Cort box." They still called it that though the man himself was long dead and the owners of the theater were a consortium of businessmen. "Do you think that's possible?"

Nessa laughed softly. "Juffie, you're a star. As far as the Cort is concerned, you're *the* star. Of course it's bloody well possible. Would you like me to call Larry and arrange things?"

"Could you? I still haven't showered and I'm due at the theater in forty minutes."

"Consider it done. Does he leave the tickets at the box office in your name?"

"No. Angel Tomasso." She had to spell it.

"Right," Nessa said. "I've got it now. Listen, Juffie, Jack and I are having a few people for dinner this evening. Why don't you join us after the show? We eat late, you'll be in time for dessert."

"Thanks, but I can't tonight. Ask me again, please, Nessa."

Later, when they were dressing for the evening, Nessa Fine spoke to her husband about Juffie. "I worry about her, Jack. She's twenty-two years old, the hottest ticket in town, and she's like a little girl in some ways. She doesn't even have a boyfriend. I invited her here tonight, but she refused. Could she still be pining for Tony Morton?"

"Maybe," Jack said with a shrug. "But I wouldn't have thought so. Besides, she dates Harry Harcourt a lot."

"Harry Harcourt is queer." Nessa fastened a diamond earring. "What bloody good is that?"

"What kind of garbage are you talking? You want to cast a muscular he-man all the ladies will swoon for, you get Harry Harcourt." He hesitated and looked at her. Nessa was smart, she didn't open her mouth just to hear herself talk. "You sure he's queer?"

"Of course I'm sure. Juffie knows too. She told me so months ago. I think she goes around with him only to keep everyone else at bay." She turned from the mirror to face him. "Know what I really think? It's Matt Varley she has the hots for. And he's only interested professionally. But why? That's the thing I don't know."

"It's too much for me." Jack started on the jet studs of his dress shirt. "I can't figure Varley and I sure as hell never picked Harry for a pansy. If he is, I wouldn't have figured Juffie would run around with him. Who knows what you broads are going to do?" He went on fiddling with his studs and his wife dropped the subject, but neither of them forgot it.

. . . .

All during the opening scene Juffie was conscious of the people in the John Cort box. Four men and an equal number of women. Her eyes kept darting to them. Once she almost missed a cue—and that brought her up short. She didn't look at the box or its occupants again. She turned the full force of her personality on the rest of the house, and within seconds the magic was under way. Juffie and her audience established their customary rapport, and nothing else mattered.

But after the show she had to decide what to do about Angel Tomasso and his party. Juffie considered not going to Sardi's. She could go home and go to bed. She knew if she did she wouldn't be alone for long. Angel Tomasso would arrive with his knife and his belt and . . . She'd brought evening clothes with her and she changed into them.

"Good evening, Miss Kane. A pleasure to see you." The headwaiter at Sardi's spotted her as soon as she came through the door. He glanced at the bookings recorded in the ledger on his stand. "Let's see, how many are there in your party?" It was an act, he knew there was no reservation in the name of Juffie Kane. Some shithead must have fucked up. He'd spill blood over this. Now he had to figure out how to give her the table he was holding for Danny Kaye.

"I don't have a reservation," Juffie said. "I'm meeting Mr. Faldo's party."

The man had not become maître d' at Sardi's by being shockable. He didn't bat an eye. "Of course, right this way please, Miss Kane." He'd sized up the Faldo party the minute they arrived, out-of-town hoods with the cheap broads they'd rented for the evening. They were in the dimmest corner in the back. And the schmucks weren't even smart enough to stand up when he brought Juffie Kane to join them. But he couldn't leave her at a table like this.

"You should have mentioned that Miss Kane was joining you," he reprimanded them softly. "Perhaps you ladies and gentlemen would prefer something over there in the center of the room."

A small fat man looked toward the table the headwaiter indicated; it was exposed to everyone entering and leaving. He couldn't have his back to the wall the way he could here. He shook his head. Angel spoke for him. "Nah, we're fine where we are. Just bring another bottle of scotch."

"Champagne," the small man said. "For Juffie here it's gotta be champagne."

"You heard Mr. Faldo. Bring some champagne," Angel said. "No garbage neither. Your best stuff."

"Right away, sir." The headwaiter snapped his fingers and another chair was produced.

"Put it here next to me," the small man said. "You move over, honey," he said to the peroxide blonde sitting on his left. Juffie took the blonde's place. The maître d' disappeared. The little fat man held out his hand. "Vinnie Faldo, Juffie. A pleasure to meet you. We liked your show. Loved it, in fact. You were terrific."

"Thank you," she murmured. Juffie wore a short white chiffon dress with a full skirt and a strapless top. It had a matching stole and she wound it tighter around her shoulders, conscious that each of the four men at the table was trying to peer down the front of her dress.

"She don't look nothin' like Dino Saliatelli, does she, boss?" Angel asked, chuckling.

"Not like Benny Kane neither," Vinnie Faldo agreed. "Where the hell's that champagne?"

Angel leaned back and signaled a passing waiter. "Mr. Faldo's waiting for his champagne."

"Right away, sir."

It arrived. The bottle was displayed for Faldo's approval, but he waved it away. "Pour," Angel said. "If it ain't all right we'll let you know."

Juffie watched her glass being filled and felt a hand on her right knee. She pushed it off. Seconds later it was back. She grabbed the glass of wine, drank it straight down, and someone poured her another.

The evening seemed to have no end. Vinnie Faldo's hand had worked its way under her skirt and into her panties. Angel kept looking at her and smirking, as if he knew what was happening. The men drank scotch, lots of it, and told dirty jokes. The women sipped the champagne and didn't say anything. Neither did Juffie.

"So this guy says, 'Well, a cock's a convertible, ain't it?'"

The man telling the joke signaled its end by exploding in laughter; the others joined in. The fingers inside Juffie's panties were trying to excite her. She couldn't bear much more. Abruptly she pushed her chair back, smoothed her skirt, and stood up. "Excuse me."

"Yeah, sure, Juffie," Vinnie Faldo said. "You go have a nice pee." He lifted his fingers to his nose and sniffed deeply. "But come back quick."

Everybody laughed. Juffie felt her cheeks burn and she was suddenly lightheaded, as if she might faint. She fled to the ladies' room. Just before she opened the door she felt a touch on her shoulder and she nearly jumped out of her skin. She turned around, expecting that Angel or one of the others had come after her, but it wasn't any of the four men from Boston.

"Juffie, I saw you head this way and I followed you. How are you?"

"Fine. I'm fine, thanks, Mr. Winchell."

"Congratulations on the Tony. You deserved it."

All New York knew that Walter Winchell finished every night of the week at Sherm Billingsley's Stork Club, at table fifty, which was always reserved for him, but he sometimes hit a few other night spots first. Tonight he happened to have dropped into Sardi's. He was also known for never taking off his beat-up fedora, except in church for a wedding or a funeral. Sardi's wasn't a church. He took off his hat, however, and leaned his arm against the wall so Juffie couldn't get past him.

"I'm going to speak out of turn," he said. "You don't like it, I'm sorry. What the hell are you doing with those creeps? They're a bunch of cheap wop crooks. I can smell 'em a mile off. I don't want to put this in my column, Juffie. But how can I avoid it?"

She knew this was her one chance. If she muffed it, in a short time she'd be forced into bed with Vinnie Faldo. "I don't know, Mr. Winchell. Someone I know from Boston called, asked me to get them tickets to the show and say hello . . . I had no idea what sort of people they were. Now I simply don't know how to get away." She'd never played an ingenue, but she was good.

"You say good night," Winchell said. "Short and sweet. And you go home."

Juffie shook her head. "I can't. They really are sort of scary. I'm nervous about just getting up and going."

Winchell thought for a moment. "Okay, leave it to me. You go to the ladies' room, then back to the table. After that sit tight and wait for your cue."

She managed to smile when she rejoined the Faldo party. But she leaned as far away from the little man as she dared, and she crossed her legs. Seconds later she felt a vicious pinch on her thigh. It hurt so much it brought tears to her eyes, but Juffie didn't uncross her legs. Faldo leaned over and started to whisper something. She didn't hear it. Mr. Winchell and another man were approaching the table.

"Juffie Kane, I thought it was you. How're you doing?"

"How nice to see you, Mr. Winchell." She turned to Vinnie Faldo and the others. "I'm sure you gentlemen know Walter Winchell, the famous columnist."

Vinnie looked as if he'd swallowed his Adam's apple, the others not much better. "Pleased to meet you," Winchell said. "I'll have to get all your names for my column before you go. Meantime, this is my buddy Jim Baxter, from the Bureau. He's been dying to meet you, Juffie. Even G-men go to the theater sometimes."

Winchell's friendship with J. Edgar Hoover was well known; his column often lauded the exploits of the FBI. Juffie jumped up and stepped forward to shake the strange man's hand. "Listen,"

Winchell said. "Jim's wife is with us. She wants to meet you too. How about coming to our table for a few minutes, Juffie?"

She swept up her bag and stole and went with him without a word to Vinnie Faldo and his friends.

Winchell's table was right up front, so he wouldn't miss anyone coming or going. The tables in the rear had a much less clear view. "Okay," he said, "they can't see you from where they are. C'mon." He rushed her out the door. There was a cab waiting. "I'll stay behind. Any of those lugs try and follow you, me and my friend'll slow 'em down."

"Mr. Winchell, is that man really with the FBI?"

He grinned. "What difference does it make, Juffie?"

"None," she admitted. "Thank you. I'll never forget this."

"I don't intend for you to forget it. Any news about the fabulous Juffie Kane, I expect Mr. and Mrs. America to read about it first in my column."

"Promise," she said. And she kissed him before she got into the taxi.

"Where to, miss?"

She didn't hesitate. "The Pierre." It was on Fifth Avenue, one of the most luxurious hotels in the city. And it had a full staff on duty day and night. It was a good deal safer than her studio apartment in Tudor City.

Early the next morning she called Matt. "I'm at the Pierre and I'm in the middle of an emergency. Can you come right now?"

He was there in fifteen minutes. "What's up, Juffie? What the hell are you doing here dressed like that?"

She was still wearing the white chiffon cocktail dress because she didn't have anything else. "I got into a mess last night." She told him pretty much the same story she'd told the columnist, that she hadn't realized what kind of people she was with until she was too frightened to leave.

"Jesus," Matt said. "And Walter Winchell knows about this?"

"Yes, he helped me, as I told you. I'm sure he won't print it. He said he didn't want to. That's why he approached me in the first place."

"Okay," Matt said. "But don't you ever do anything that dumb again. For Christ's sake, Juffie, you're no Hollywood starlet, you're a legitimate actress. The college girl from Boston. Your public expects you to be a lady, not hang around with racketeers."

"Stop yelling at me! Don't you think I know that? Why else did

I jump at the chance to get away? Why am I here?" She was furious and horribly disappointed. She wanted comfort and praise for her resourcefulness; instead, Matt was mad at her.

"Calm down," he said, lighting his pipe and pouring the coffee she'd ordered. "Let's both calm down." He sipped in silence, puzzling over what to do next.

"I need my clothes," Juffie said sullenly. "The first thing I need is something to wear."

"Yes, and you'd better not go back to your apartment. Not if you're sure they know where you live."

"I'm sure."

"Okay, give me your key. I'll send my secretary to pack your things. I'll bring them over this afternoon. Meantime, you stay out."

He returned a little after three. The front desk called and said Mr. Varley was on his way up, but she didn't open the door until she heard his voice.

"It's me, Juffie. Matt. It's okay."

She let him in. He was white-faced and obviously shaken. "What's the matter? Oh God, Matt, what's happened? Are you all right?"

"I'm fine. Juffie— Look, we'd better sit down." He led her to the sofa beneath the window overlooking Central Park. It was a beautiful day. She'd drawn the drapes, and the afternoon sun streamed through the sheer curtains.

"I sent Miss Wilkins over to your place," he said. "But somebody had been there first." He took her hand. "It was a terrible mess, Juffie. And there weren't any clothes to pack. Whoever got in had cut every single thing to shreds. They even hacked up the shoes."

She started to cry.

"Don't," he said, putting his arm around her and drawing her close. "They're only clothes, Juffie. Not worth crying about. You can buy more."

"Idiot," she said, her voice muffled against the smooth linen of his summer suit. "I'm not crying for what my father would call a few *shmattes*. I'm just scared. Oh, Matt. I'm scared to death."

She thought she felt his arms tighten around her, his cheek bend to touch her hair. Juffie almost told him the true story then. She wanted to. If somebody else knew that a long time ago Angel Tomasso had raped her, and then she'd been stupid enough to talk

Pa into making a deal that put her head right back in the lion's mouth—well, maybe she wouldn't feel so alone.

But she'd imagined his response. She must have because Matt pushed her away and handed her a handkerchief. "Here. Blow your nose. And stop crying or your eyes will be all red. You've got a show to do in a couple of hours. Meanwhile, I've worked a few things out.

"First, you don't go back to Tudor City ever again. I've been in touch and told them we're breaking the lease. It will cost, but not a hell of a lot. Second, I've talked to the desk downstairs. You've got a monthly rate on this room and I told them you'll be here eight, maybe twelve weeks. Meanwhile I'll start looking for an apartment for you. Something in a building with maximum security." He cocked his head and studied her. "You okay now?"

Juffie nodded. He might not offer the kind of comfort she craved, but at least Matt was taking charge. She desperately needed that.

"Okay, here's the rest of it. I've hired a bodyguard for you. A guy from Pinkerton's. And no more taxis—a limousine with a driver. From now on you don't go anywhere alone. At least not until we're sure these bastards have gone home and forgotten about you. And I called Winchell and told him he'll know what your next play is as soon as we do."

"Matt, you're wonderful. What would I do without you?"

"God knows. But you don't seem to have added all this up. It's going to cost a fortune, Juffie. So we've got to stop horsing around and sign you into a new show. We can't be as fussy as we've been. You have to go after the biggest bucks."

A dollar sign where his heart should be, just as she'd told Karen. "I see," Juffie said. "Okay, we'll take another look at the scripts we put aside as maybes. But there's one thing you forgot. I can't go to the theater tonight dressed like this." She fingered the skirt of the white chiffon dress.

"I didn't forget that either," Matt assured her. "Miss Wilkins has gone shopping, she should be here any minute."

. . . .

Three months later Juffie was living in the penthouse of a new building on the corner of Second Avenue and Sixty-eighth Street. The building was beautiful—fifteen stories of white brick separated from the street by a space filled with gardens and fountains.

Inside it had every modern convenience and the latest in security systems. There was twenty-four-hour service, a closed-circuit television system, and the penthouse was reached by its own elevator. East River Tower was billed as the apartment house of the future, and it was incongruous as hell among its down-at-the-heels neighbors.

For years Lexington Avenue had marked the eastern edge of the world of expensive midtown housing. But the old elevated railway along Third Avenue, the infamous El, was slated to be torn down, and everything east of Lexington was poised to take off. A few gutsy builders were getting their oars in early. Equally gutsy buyers could get good deals. Juffie didn't rent the nine-room penthouse, she bought it for a hundred thousand dollars.

"On Park or Fifth it would be three times as much," Matt said. "And someday Second and Sixty-eighth is going to be terrific. It's worth putting up with a less than wonderful neighborhood for a while."

Juffie didn't need to be convinced. She had what her grand-fathers would have called a nose for class: the building and location just smelled right. She'd unhesitatingly borrowed twenty thousand from her father for the down payment on the pent-house, and Matt got her a mortgage for the rest. She wasn't nervous about owing so much, or about the salary of a bodyguard, or the monthly tab she ran with the limousine company. She'd even bought the fur coat of her dreams, a luscious full-length blond mink. It was all possible because she was going to be making eleven hundred a week when her new show opened.

It was called *The Visitor,* a comedy about a girl called Penelope, somehow transported from Roman times into twentieth-century Manhattan. Juffie thought the idea better than the play itself; the writing didn't sustain the pace for three acts. But they were working on that, and it was a good showcase role, and at least she wasn't playing another hillbilly. And eight hundred a week during rehearsals, eleven hundred for the first three months the show ran, and sixteen hundred after that wasn't bad. In fact, it was terrific.

"And they let you out at the end of a year," Matt said. "If you want to go."

"I'll want to go," Juffie said. "Start looking for my next show right now. I want something marvelous lined up for after *Visitor.*"

"Okay, Juffie. Whatever you say."

As long as it pays big money, she thought. That's what's important to you, Mr. Matthew Varley. Well, it was important to her too. Meanwhile she'd give Penelope everything she had. Maybe she could make it into a hit simply by trying.

．　．　．　．

On the seventh of January, 1950, *The Visitor* opened at the National on West Forty-first Street. It was a turkey but not a flop. The critics said the only good thing about the show was Juffie Kane, but audiences liked it. They played to full houses most nights. And Matt was sending her scripts to read. Nothing wonderful yet, but she had hopes. Matt, however, was impatient; he had other ideas.

"Look, television's getting bigger and bigger. I think you should do a couple of appearances."

"No, I act on the stage, I told you that."

She'd resisted every attempt to get her to star in the movie version of *Delilah*. Matt still hadn't gotten over it. "I hear Fox has signed Joan Blondell to play Delilah," he told her.

"Yes, well, they were bound to get somebody."

"Juffie, why are you so damned stubborn?"

They were in his office, she'd been looking down on the lions, now she turned to him. "Matt, remember the first day I came in here, I told you I was a very good actress. Was I lying?"

"No, you weren't lying. You're wonderful, that's why I can't understand your being scared of the camera."

"I'm not scared of it. I simply know I can't love it, and it can't love me back. That's what I do onstage, Matt. I love the audience. Whatever else I'm doing, that's what's happening underneath. And they know it. That's why it works."

He grinned at her. Long, lanky Matt with his pipe and his tweeds and his Ivy League manner could seem hard-hearted sometimes, but he had one of the nicest grins of any man she knew. It always made her want to grin back. "You could just imagine the audience was there," he said. "Or how about this, I'll be there. Every day, whenever you're performing. You can play to me. Could you love me, Juffie?"

That startled her, there was a fleeting moment when she

thought he was asking for real, that the question was unrelated to contracts and performances. Then she reminded herself of who he was and who she was, and what was the nature of their relationship. "I like things to be what they seem, Matt. I don't like make-believe."

He stared at her for a moment. "Strange words for an actress," he said finally. "But I'll remember them."

A week later he tried again. "Juffie, the TV people are offering big money. They want you to appear with Ed Sullivan. He's hosting a program called *Toast of the Town*." She started to protest; he held up a hand to stop her. "At least listen to the numbers. Three and a half thousand for one show. And you don't have to go to the coast. Sullivan's going to broadcast from right here in New York."

"No," she said.

He slammed down his pen. "Have it your way, Juffie. Just as you always do."

It seemed as if she would, then Myer called her. At midnight of the first Sunday in March. "Juffie, it's Dad, darling. Can you come right away?"

"Is it Pa?"

"No, not Pa. It's your mother."

.   .   .   .

Rosie Saliatelli Kane's heart gave out at four P.M. Monday afternoon. "It was such a big heart," Myer said, still holding his wife's lifeless hand. "But you used it up, Rosie darling . . ."

"Dad, we have to go now." Juffie put her arm around her father's shoulders. "The nurses and doctors have things to do. Come on, Dad. Let's go home."

The Pinkerton man was waiting in the corridor. His name was Mike Ryan and he'd stuck to Juffie like glue from the moment she boarded the plane that morning at LaGuardia. Juffie had never wanted to fly. The idea terrified her. Probably nothing but the overwhelming need to be with her mother right then, that minute, could have made her board the plane. She wasn't sorry to have Mike's company. And now he was useful for running interference. The Boston papers had sniffed out Juffie Kane's presence at her dying mother's bedside. They were outside the Massachusetts General Hospital in force.

"A bodyguard," Myer said incredulously as they were led out

a back entrance to a cab. "My little girl needs a bodyguard right here in the West End. Pop would never have believed it."

There was no wake and no church service. Rosie had strayed too far from her religion for either. They said their last good-byes on Tuesday at a funeral home that prided itself on being nonsectarian. The ceremony was private. Juffie had even told Matt and Jack and Nessa Fine that she was grateful for the thought, but they needn't come to Boston. It had been an instinctive reaction, but why? The grief was too intense, she realized, the shock of loss too sudden to share with anyone who hadn't also known and loved Rosie.

The only people present were Myer and Juffie and Pa and Karen and some dozen Saliatelli relatives, plus a few women who'd been Rosie's close friends, including Leah Rice. There were flowers, though, a veritable garden of flowers. The sterile chapel of the funeral home was stuffed with them, so was the house.

The smell of the flowers was overwhelming when they returned to Walnut Street. It was just the three of them. They'd asked for it to be so. "Tomorrow or whenever," Myer told the friends and relatives. "We'd love to see you. But this afternoon, I think it's better . . . It was all so fast, no warning. We need . . ." He'd shrugged helplessly, but they understood him and his wishes were respected. Now they stood in the front hall, fending off an olfactory attack from roses and lilies and gladioli. "Juffie, I'll be in my office for a while. If you don't mind, I'd like to be alone a little."

"Sure, Dad, I understand." She was holding her grandfather's hand. Dino was very quiet. It almost seemed as if he'd gone away somewhere, to a far country, where his daughter wasn't dead.

"Take Pa upstairs," Myer said.

"Yes. We'll be there whenever you want us."

They went to Dino's room. Juffie wanted to help him get into bed, but he wasn't having it. "I ain't so old I need a young girl to undress me. You wait outside. I'll call you."

She stood in the hall, looking at the world her mother had made and fighting off her choking tears. She had to be strong, for Dad's sake and her grandfather's. The way Rosie herself would have been strong. Downstairs she could just see the top of the Pinkerton man's head. He'd taken up a position by the front door. Her mother would have accepted his presence with her usual aplomb. By now she'd have made him sandwiches. Juffie went to the kitchen.

"Corned beef on rye okay?" she asked when she handed him the tray.

"Fine, Miss Kane. Thanks. I think the news hounds here in Boston are a little nicer than the ones in New York. They seem to be leaving you folks alone today at least." There wasn't a soul outside on Walnut Street who didn't belong there.

"Thank God," Juffie said. "Listen, the kitchen's at the top of the stairs. There's more beer in the refrigerator. Help yourself."

He said he would and she went back to Dino's door and knocked. "Come in," he said gruffly. When she did, she realized that the gruffness was because he'd been crying, which choked her up all over again.

She sat on the bed beside him and rested her head on his chest. "Oh, Pa, what a lousy piece of luck. What are we going to do without her?"

"We'll manage, gorgeous," he said, stroking her hair. "We'll manage." They stayed like that awhile, taking comfort from each other's physical presence. Then Dino laughed softly. Juffie looked up at him. His cheeks were still wet with tears, but he was laughing. "I hear you really stuck it to Vinnie Faldo," he said.

She laughed through her tears too. "Sort of. How much do you know?"

"Just that he ran outta New York like he had a firecracker up his ass. And you were the reason."

"Not exactly." She told him the story, an edited version that did not include Faldo's hand in her pants.

"Walter Winchell and the FBI!" Dino said when she finished. "I love it, Juffie. Best story I've heard in years. And that's it?" He narrowed his eyes and studied her. "That goddamn Faldo didn't do nothin' to get even?"

She shook her head. "Nothing, Pa."

"You're lying. I can tell. Ever since you was a kid I told you I can see right through you. What did he do, the *stronzo*? He tries to hurt you, I'll kill him."

"He didn't hurt me, Pa. Somebody went to my apartment and cut up all my clothes, that's all. Nothing important, a few *shmattes*, like Dad would say."

Dino put his hand on her cheek, rough skin against smooth. "Gorgeous, you know it was the clothes only 'cause you weren't there. 'Cause you used your head and went to that hotel. And after, that's when you got the bonzo downstairs? Not because you're such a big star the fans'll maybe pull you apart? Because of Faldo?"

"That's it," Juffie admitted.

"I like it. A smart idea. He's a good bonzo?"

"I think so. A Pinkerton man."

"Yeah. I was watching his moves this morning. I think he's a good soldier."

Downstairs, in his office with the door locked, Myer Kane was saying Kaddish for his Rosie. He'd donned a yarmulke that was in the drawer from God knows when, and he was rocking back and forth in that prayer rhythm which was part of the primeval Jewish memory, and saying the ancient words. *"Yis gadal vey yis gadash . . ."*

He cried a lot after he finished, but he felt better. This morning had been so . . . sterile. Inhuman. Okay, a rabbi would be appalled at Kaddish for a shiksa, but Rosie wasn't a goy, she was his wife. Now he could go upstairs and be with his father-in-law and his daughter. A family should be together at a time like this.

He'd just joined Dino and Juffie, when there was a knock on the door. "Miss Kane, there's a package I think you'd better see."

Mike Ryan led Juffie to the kitchen. Dino and Myer followed. What waited was a long cardboard box, the kind that roses usually came in. But it didn't smell like roses. A terrible stench pervaded the room. "It was addressed to you," Mike told Juffie. "I always open everything addressed to you." In the background Dino nodded approval. The bodyguard lifted the cover from the box and stepped away. Juffie leaned forward, then clamped her hand over her mouth and ran from the room.

Dino and Myer peered into the box. It contained a full-length picture of Juffie as Delilah, a colored print doubtless cut from some magazine. The picture of Juffie lay on a slithering, bleeding mass of something unspeakably horrid, it was thick with maggots. They crawled through the blood and slime over Juffie's face and body.

"Liver," Ryan said, lifting a bit of it in his fingers. "Ground up raw liver."

"*Stronzo!*" Dino shouted. He turned and headed back to his bedroom.

Myer followed him, not speaking until the bedroom door was

closed behind them. "What's this about, Pa?" he asked through clenched teeth. "Who'd send Juffie a thing like that?"

"I ain't sure, but I'm gonna work the phone until I find out."

"I knew it wasn't Faldo," he said later. "It had too much imagination for a guinea like him. Too classy. A chicken with its neck broken, maybe. Not raw liver and maggots and a picture."

"Then who?" Myer demanded. In the past hour he'd gotten some of the story out of Juffie. She told him about Alliance Investments backing *A Small Miracle* for a couple of months, how that had obligated her to Vinnie Faldo, and how he'd tried to collect by making a pass at her. She left out the cut-up clothes, and she certainly hadn't begun at the beginning, with Angel raping her in his car. Not even Pa knew that part. But right now it was Pa who knew more than any of them.

"Faldo sold your paper," he told his granddaughter after a dozen telephone conversations.

"I don't understand," Juffie said.

It was Myer who explained. "It's what a private lender often does. Say you buy something on credit, thirty-six months to pay. The lender, the guy who sells cars for instance, can't really afford to carry you. He takes the contract to a finance company, maybe even a bank, and sells it for something less than face value. You owe him three thousand dollars principal and interest, he sells for twenty-five hundred. The buyer is going to make five hundred on the deal, as long as he's prepared to wait. It's perfectly legal in the case I've described."

"But I don't owe Vinnie Faldo any money," Juffie protested.

Dino shook his head. "Juffie, Juffie. I told you from the first day. You owe. Okay, it ain't money, but you owe. You got a debt, and Faldo sold the right to collect it."

Myer wanted to scream at his father-in-law, to tell him he was insane ever to have allowed Juffie to get into such a situation. He didn't. It was too late and they were all hurting too much as it was. "Who did he sell to?" he asked.

"Guy named Finky Aronson. From New York. Brownsville. Seems he's a good pal of Bugsy Siegel."

Myer went cold at the name. Bugsy Siegel headed an organization called Murder Incorporated. Juffie didn't know that. Nonetheless, it was she who said, "And this Finky whoever wants to kill me?"

"No," Dino said. "He don't. You're no good to him dead, Juffie. He can't collect nothing from a corpse. Even a beautiful corpse."

"Then why did he send me . . . that thing?"

"A warning, that's all. He wants you to know what he could do."

· · · ·

When he negotiated her contract for *The Visitor*, Matt had thought of everything. There was a provision that allowed Juffie four days off in the event of a death in her immediate family. Rosie died on a Monday, today was Thursday; Penelope could be played by her understudy for one more night. That gave her time to meet Karen and Bernard Hanrihan for dinner.

Karen picked the place, The Marliave, in a narrow alley off Bromfield Street. It was in Boston's shopping section, not the North End, but the restaurant was Italian. Perhaps not what Juffie would have chosen at the moment, but she didn't say anything to Karen about that, just agreed to meet her.

After the box of rotting liver arrived, Mike Ryan had sent for reinforcements from the Pinkerton office in Boston. There were four bodyguards now, and one of them remained in Newton on Thursday afternoon while Mike and two others examined The Marliave. "It's okay," he told Juffie when he returned. "We can cover it and still leave one guy here with your father and grandfather." Juffie had insisted on that, though no one but she thought it necessary.

She was the last to arrive at the restaurant. Ryan drove her to town in a rented car and went in before her. Then he returned and escorted her to the table where her friends were waiting. He and the two men with him took up their stations.

Karen and Bernard watched these preparations without comment, assuming it was part of the life of a star. If nothing else, it would make the service attentive. Hanrihan rose when Juffie came to the table. She kissed Karen, then turned to Hanrihan and shook his hand. Nothing in Bernard Hanrihan's appearance explained Karen's fascination to Juffie. He still looked like a dried-up old fig. "Good evening, Professor."

"Please, it's Bernard." He murmured condolences, which

Juffie brushed away. The tears were still so close to the surface. A word of sympathy could start them flowing again. "I remember seeing you at Simmons," Bernard said, "but you were never a student of mine, were you?"

"No. I'm afraid psychology isn't one of my talents."

"You seem to have a great many others," he said. "Anybody who reads a newspaper knows as much, even if they've never been in a theater."

"Juffie, why don't you go on television?" Karen asked. "It would give so many more people a chance to see you."

"Not you too."

"Not me too what?"

"Everybody's at me to do TV lately. My agent mainly, but Pa and my dad also think it's a good idea. They've been driving me nuts with it."

Pa had an eleven-inch television at the foot of his bed, the last in the long line of comforts Rosie had provided. They'd watched it endlessly in the many hours Juffie spent consoling her grandfather during the past few days. *What's My Line* with Arlene Francis and Bennett Cerf, *Your Show of Shows* with Sid Caesar, whom she thought wonderful, and Milton Berle, whom she didn't. When the variety and the quiz shows were absent, there were heart-tugging stories such as *Mama,* a warm tale of an immigrant family. Pa even watched kids' shows, like *Howdy Doody* and *Kukla, Fran, & Ollie.*

"I can't imagine myself on television," Juffie said.

But it was no longer quite as true. For one thing, she recognized that unlike movies, television was an intimate medium. Watching someone from the privacy of your home was almost like being with them in the theater. And she was intrigued with the fact that most of the performers were drawn from the world of the stage, not Hollywood. There was a connection, she was sure of it, but she hadn't yet figured it out. When she did, maybe she'd change her mind about doing TV. Until then she'd stick to her refusal.

"Now, we mustn't talk about me. Everything I do is splashed all over and you know about it. Tell me about the two of you."

They did, at least Bernard did. Most of the evening was devoted to a discussion of his work, what it had been, was now, and would be. Karen sat silent and looked at him adoringly. Juffie was glad the party broke up before ten, even if the reason was that Bernard had an early class the next day.

"Isn't he wonderful?" Karen said when she telephoned first thing Friday morning.

"Oh yes, wonderful," Juffie agreed. Someday maybe she could talk sense to Karen; right now she recognized that her friend was deaf and blind with adulation. But she couldn't hang up without some small word of warning. "Karen, look, sweetie, if there's ever a problem, come and tell me, will you? Don't be too proud or stubborn to say if you think you've made a mistake."

"Of course I won't be. But there isn't going to be a problem, Juffie. Bernard and I are going to live happily ever after."

Juffie wanted to take the train back to New York. The *Yankee Clipper* left South Station at noon and reached Grand Central at five. She'd be in time for tonight's show. "No good, Miss Kane," Mike Ryan said. "On a train there are too many stops, too many people getting on and off. It's very difficult to keep the situation in complete control. We could drive if you like. But I'd suggest we fly."

"I hate flying, you know that."

"It's the safest thing, Miss Kane."

Which was paradoxically true, so they took a two o'clock flight from Logan Airport, which would have them in New York at quarter past three. And Juffie Kane met Paul Dumont.

. . . .

He was the best-looking man in the waiting lounge, so she couldn't help but notice him. Besides, speculating about a stranger took her mind off Rosie, and the two desolate men she was leaving behind. He wasn't sitting in one of the plush red seats of the terminal, he stood by the window watching the airplanes arrive and depart. He had curly black hair, cut just a trifle longer than expected, and a marvelous profile. He was tall, probably six feet, and very slim, but his shoulders were as broad as a football player's and the suitcoat he wore over them was a perfectly tailored dark blue pinstripe. He was almost too elegant, but for the tan trench coat slung over his shoulder and the way he kept his hands in his pockets as he leaned against the plate-glass window in an attitude that was so offhand it was outrageously sexy.

Juffie wore a belted black cloth coat and a black hat with a wide brim and a veil. She hadn't brought her blond mink from New York; it didn't seem appropriate when she was racing to her mother's sickbed, and today she'd chosen the hat in hopes it would keep anyone from recognizing her. It seemed to be working. She was totally unmolested and she was pretending to read a magazine she held in her lap. But she kept darting glances at the handsome stranger.

At one-forty the flight was called. "That's us, Miss Kane," Ryan said.

It was just the two of them again. One Pinkerton man had been left on Walnut Street. "Only for a few days," Juffie told Myer. "So I won't worry." The others had been dismissed.

"A crowd of bodyguards attracts too much attention," Ryan had said. "It's okay in a crisis, but that seems to have passed." Now he gestured to her black leather hatbox with the initials *J.K.* embossed in gold and her matching makeup case. "I'll have to ask you to carry those. And walk just ahead of me, please."

Juffie did as she was told. They approached the gate. The man in the pin-striped suit joined the line from the side and managed to insert himself between Juffie and Mike Ryan. Instantly Ryan shouldered him out of the way. "Hey!" the man said. "Sorry if I took your place, but you don't need to be rough."

"Excuse me," Ryan murmured, but he didn't move from just behind Juffie. They were practically at the gate now; in a moment they'd be out in the wind. Ryan took Juffie's arm.

"I did not realize you were together," the stranger said. "Where I am from a gentleman carries the luggage of the lady he's with. Mademoiselle, may I assist you?" He reached for Juffie's two small suitcases.

"Get lost, bud," Ryan growled under his breath.

"You get lost," the man growled back.

So far none of the other passengers had paid attention. As the men's voices rose, the people just behind the threesome craned their necks to see what was happening, and a few in front turned around. Juffie had been silent and biddable, doing exactly what Mike Ryan told her to do. Now she turned and looked directly at the stranger.

All along she'd thought there was something foreign-looking about him. His first words had indicated that perhaps she was wrong. He didn't have an obvious accent. But to her trained ear there was something, and the use of the word *mademoiselle* gave him away. The man was French. He couldn't be a racketeer connected with Vinnie Faldo or Finky Aronson.

"It's all right, Mike. I'm sure this gentleman is just trying to be helpful." She smiled her best, most brilliant smile at him, and surrendered the hatbox and the makeup case. "Thank you, you're very kind."

"And you," he said in tones of almost exaggerated surprise, "are Juffie Kane. I had no idea!"

They were going through the gate now, out onto the tarmac, where the icy March wind was sweeping in off the ocean. Juffie clutched her coat closer and hung on to her hat. They climbed the steps of the DC4 in tandem, Juffie in the lead, Ryan just behind her, and the stranger behind him. Getting inside the aircraft was a relief. "All the way to the back," Ryan murmured in her ear. "I reserved the last two seats."

They made their way to the rear. Juffie was aware of people looking at her. Someone had overheard the Frenchman's exclamation and the word had already spread. So there wasn't any need to remain incognito. She stood in the aisle beside her seat and took her hat off, then her coat. Her dress was two piece, more of a suit really, in cream-colored faille with a double-breasted jacket and wide lapels. "Stunning," the French-accented voice said softly as he stowed her bags in the overhead compartment. "You are even more beautiful than on the stage."

Ryan wanted her inside in the window seat. Juffie insisted on taking the one on the aisle. The Frenchman had the seat immediately opposite. Whether by luck or design was impossible to say. The stewardess passed up and down asking the passengers to fasten their seat belts. Juffie started to get nervous again, just as she'd been on the earlier trip. What if she became airsick? She might throw up all over everything, in full view of a hundred people who now knew who she was—and the best-looking man she'd ever seen. She'd finally gotten a look at his eyes. They were a fabulous aquamarine blue; they lit his whole face.

Why was she thinking these things? How could she be thinking them now, with her mother so recently . . . That's why, because she could not bear to examine the dimensions of her loss, and a handsome foreigner was a welcome diversion. If Rosie were with her they would have exchanged knowing glances, little secret smiles between mother and daughter, because he was, whatever else, a man incredible to look at.

He waited until she was buckled in, then leaned across the aisle and extended his hand. "Please, permit me to introduce myself. I'm Paul Dumont."

She shook his hand. "Juffie Kane."

"I know. Oh yes, I know."

Later, a long time later, he would tell her that he'd spotted and recognized her the moment she entered the terminal. And he'd bribed the clerk at the ticket counter to tell him what seat she was in and give him the one next to it. "But I decided to make my move a little earlier, when we were on our way to the plane. I guessed that the man with you was a bodyguard and had to keep his hands free, so he wouldn't be able to carry your bags."

By the time she knew that, Juffie knew a great deal else about Paul Dumont.

Chapter 8

"*J*ack, take a look at this." Nessa passed a newspaper to her husband.

It was the Boston *Record American*. Hearst had bought the old sports paper, the *Daily American,* and combined it with his evening tabloid. The hybrid wasn't printed on pink sheets the way the *Daily American* had been in Benny Kane's day, but it still carried more results than news. What filled the first few pages of the new *Record American* was gossip and scandal, the juicier the better.

"Where'd you get this rag?" Jack demanded.

"A friend sent it to me." She pointed to the picture that occupied the top half of page two. It had been shot from some distance and wasn't particularly clear, but it was easy enough to recognize Juffie Kane in the rear of a big car. The caption explained that she was going to her mother's funeral. The headline said, "Racketeers' Famous Granddaughter Mourns." "Read it, Jack," Nessa said.

He looked at her for a long moment, then dropped his gaze to the page. "Juffie Kane, darling of Broadway who scored a triumph in Jack Fine's production of *Delilah,* came home to Boston a few days ago. Juffie's mother, Rosa Saliatelli Kane, had had a heart attack. On Tuesday Rosa was buried. Juffie Kane, her father, Myer, and Rosa's father, Dino Saliatelli, were the chief mourners. Saliatelli was paroled two years ago after serving nine years for, among other things, running houses of prostitution. Benny Kane, the man credited with inventing the numbers racket, and Myer's father, died in prison before being eligible for parole. Kane and Saliatelli were tried and convicted together when—"

Jack raised his head and looked at his wife. "You read this?"
"Yes."

"Shit," he said softly.

"Read the whole thing, Jack. You have to know."

He went back to the paper and learned about the trial and about Myer Kane, who was implicated but never charged, and who to this day had legal, but questionable connections to what the *Record American* called the Syndicate. "Shit," he said again when he finished.

Nessa sat on the arm of his chair and put her arms around him. "I'm sorry, love. And I've always liked Juffie. But you had to be warned."

Fine kissed her, then looked at his watch. It was noon, Juffie was likely to be home. But he didn't want to go there, not the way he was feeling right now. He went to his office, which Nessa called his study, and dialed her number. "Juffie, Jack Fine here. Listen, remember that Schrafft's on Fourteenth and Fifth? Can you meet me there in an hour or so?"

• • • •

Juffie got to the restaurant first and took a table in the back. Mike Ryan stationed himself near the front door. Very few people knew she had a constant bodyguard because Ryan was so expert at being unobtrusive. Jack Fine was apparently not among the few. He didn't look around for the Pinkerton man when he arrived. He just joined her, sat down, and handed Juffie the paper. She read it, then put it aside and didn't look at him. "I'd like another cup of coffee."

Jack motioned to the waitress. They didn't speak until the fresh coffee came. Then he asked, "You hadn't seen this?"

"No, I hadn't seen it."

"Ran a week or so after your mother died. Friend of Nessa's sent it to her."

"And she took it straight to you. How nice."

"You bet your goddamn ass she took it to me. Juffie, Nessa and I aren't your enemies. We're your friends. We like you. I guess we even love you. Only I'm waiting for something, but I'm not hearing it."

"What, Jack? What are you waiting for?"

"For you to tell me it's a crock of shit. A lot of goddamn lies."

Juffie sipped her coffee, then put down the cup. "It's not lies. The facts are all pretty much as reported."

"Jesus!" He started to shout, then remembered that even down here on Fourteenth Street they were still in public. "Juffie, how could you do it?"

"Do what? Get myself born into a family of 'racketeers,' as they're so quaintly labeled?"

"No, of course I don't mean that. But when I began the big publicity campaign, when *Delilah* was still a dream and everything was riding on making the smart moves and doing it right, why didn't you tell me then? Before I plastered this town with stories about the college girl, the lawyer's daughter, why didn't you warn me?"

"It isn't an easy thing to talk about, Jack."

He leaned forward, pinning her with anguished eyes. "Juffie, they would have made hamburger out of us if they'd found out. You, me, Duquesne, the Leonards, Matt Varley, everybody connected with that show could have been dumped in the shit. And I would have put them there. You let me pull my pants down and stand there with my *tochis* hanging out."

Juffie was battered by so many emotions she didn't know which to give in to. Rage won. "What about me? What about my *tochis*? What would you have done if I'd told you? Dropped me from the show? What about my father and my grandfather? Can you imagine what it must have been like for them when this miserable filth was dragged up again a week after we buried my mother? But they haven't come to me, they didn't send me the story. You did that, Jack. You and Nessa."

He hadn't heard anything after she mentioned dropping her from the show. "You think I'd do that? Drop a wonderful actress from a role that was made for her because her family had skeletons in the closet? You're crazy, Juffie, you must be. What I'd have done is found a cover story. Protected you and me and all of us." He took out his wallet and put a couple of dollar bills on the table. "I don't think we have any more to say to each other." He started to leave.

Juffie reached out a hand to him. "Jack, wait . . ."

"Yes?"

"I don't know." She turned and stared at the empty coffee cups.

"I know, Juffie. I know that you're never going to be a whole person until you learn who your friends are. Someday you have to trust somebody. I hope you pick the right one."

"She never even said she was sorry," he told Nessa later. "If she had, I'd have forgotten the whole thing, figured she was just a scared kid who didn't know any better. But not one word of apology."

"Let it go, love," Nessa said. "You're not doing a show with her now. *Delilah* is wonderful history."

"Damn right I'm not doing a show with her. Not now and not ever. Juffie Kane may be God's gift to Broadway, but she'll never be in another production of mine. I'd be scared to death."

. . . .

Juffie walked for seemingly endless blocks, deep into the Village, hands in the pockets of her windbreaker, hair hidden under a plaid wool scarf, dark glasses hiding her eyes so no one could see she was crying. She wasn't likely to be recognized, and she wouldn't have cared if she were. She was too miserable to care. Too hurt, too angry. She spotted a telephone booth on the corner of Hudson and Christopher streets and fished out some coins.

She didn't have enough money for a long-distance call; she had to make it collect. "Dad, it's me. I'm not home and I didn't have enough change. How are you?"

"Okay, darling. Pa and me, we're both okay. It's not something you get used to, but we're managing."

"I just saw that rotten story."

"The one in the *Record American*?"

"Yes."

"I hoped you wouldn't know about it. Crazy of me, I suppose."

"Someone I thought was a friend went to the trouble of being sure I knew about it."

"Yes, that kind of thing happens. They killed it after one edition, Juffie. I threatened a suit and that was the end of it. None of the New York papers picked it up, did they?"

"No, not yet."

"Then they won't. It's yesterday's news, darling. Than which there's nothing deader, as they say."

"Okay. I didn't call about that anyway. I was just worried about you and Pa."

"We're fine, like I told you. Juffie . . . have you had any more packages?"

"Nothing. Listen, I'm in a phone booth and somebody's waiting. I'll call again in a few days."

By the time she hung up the man waiting for the telephone had moved on. She hesitated a moment, then knew who she most wanted to talk to. She had one more nickel and she used it to call Matt's office. "I'm sorry, Miss Kane," Miss Wilkins said. "He's not here just now. I'll have him get in touch the moment he comes in."

"No, I'm not home. It's okay. I'll catch him later."

She spotted Ryan waiting a few yards back in a doorway, but she ignored him. She'd become accustomed to ignoring him; it was the only way she could endure the constant surveillance and remain sane. Juffie walked on, thinking about Matt.

There were other people she could talk to, Karen for instance. Or Paul Dumont. She'd seen Paul a dozen times in the three weeks she'd known him. But somehow neither of those alternatives appealed. She made her way as far as West Street and the highway skirting the Hudson River. By then it was four o'clock. She was working that evening. It was time to find a cab and go home. But this was a bad place for taxis.

Juffie started to retrace her steps. She'd been on this end of Christopher Street only once, with Harry Harcourt. He'd taken her to a homosexual bar a couple of years before, when they'd both had so much champagne it seemed like a "fun" idea. She recognized the place as the one on the corner of Washington Street. She'd missed it when she walked by before.

She was looking at the black-painted door when it opened. Matt Varley stepped into the street. Juffie started to hail him, then stopped. He was with another man. The man had very bleached blond hair and arched eyebrows. He and Matt were having some kind of terrific argument. They didn't notice her. Juffie stared at them until they flagged a taxi and got in and drove away. Matt. Oh Jesus. No wonder he never . . .

Mike Ryan came up and took her arm. "It's getting late, Miss Kane. Hadn't I better get you a taxi?" He must have recognized Matt too. He'd seen the agent often enough at her place. She nodded miserably and waited until he found a cab, then let him hand her into the back as if she were the rag doll she felt like. A very battered rag doll.

. . . .

She had a date with Paul that night after the performance. *The Visitor* was not a long show; it finished at ten-forty. By eleven Juffie had changed and was on her way to yet another theater. This one was called La Venue and it had a screen, not a stage.

La Venue was just off Sutton Place on Fifty-fifth Street. It hugged the edge of an enclave of enormous private wealth. Nobody living in the East Fifties was poor, but Sutton Place had snob value and economic worth all its own. It also had a reputation for being more cultured than most of Manhattan. The Steinway family of piano fame owned a home in Sutton Place, and their presence seemed to have attracted musical and literary types, which is why Paul Dumont had chosen to turn an old Fifty-fifth Street brownstone into what he called a cinema, and what New Yorkers knew as an art theater. La Venue showed only foreign films, with English subtitles when required.

"True snobbery would be to skip the subtitles," Paul had told Juffie that first day on the plane. "But that would also be true economic suicide."

When she saw his theater, Juffie wondered how Paul Dumont could avoid economic suicide. The auditorium of La Venue was very small. The center section was ten seats wide, there were two narrow side aisles of three seats each, and the whole thing was a mere fifteen rows deep from front to back. That made a capacity of two hundred and forty. Paul charged a dollar fifty a ticket, as much as Radio City Music Hall, but he seldom played to a full house.

"I'm holding my own," he'd said. "But I know this place will never make me a millionaire. So my eggs are in many baskets." She'd chuckled. "Why are you laughing at me?" Paul demanded.

"I'm not laughing at you, not the way you mean. It's your English, it's wonderful but you do funny twisting things sometimes. The expression is, 'Don't put all your eggs in one basket.'"

"That's what I said, my eggs are in many baskets."

"Forget it. Tell me about the other baskets."

"Well, I'm a distributor, for one thing. I bring these films from France and Italy and England and show them at La Venue, but I also have the exclusive right to distribute them to other cinemas across the country."

They had this conversation in a restaurant called The Original Joe's on Third Avenue. It had sawdust on the floor, scarred oak booths, and a menu of foods either fried or boiled. Along with shoeshine joints and cheap hairdressers and places selling second-hand girlie magazines, and with restaurants like Clarke's and Manny Wolf's, The Original Joe's was part of the dark netherworld that existed under the perpetual shadow of the Third Avenue El.

Since Juffie and Paul both worked evenings, their dates were of necessity late-night affairs. Either they went to a fancy after-theater spot, where Juffie would instantly be part of a crowd of Broadway people, or they patronized the places on Third Avenue. More often, as tonight, they chose the latter.

Juffie finished her deep-fried codfish cakes and sipped the last of her wine. The Original Joe's didn't serve wine, at least nothing a Frenchman would call by the name. Paul brought a bottle with him in a brown paper bag and poured it into their water glasses when the waiter wasn't looking, which meant it always had to be white wine. So they always ordered fish. "I'm going to grow gills and fins pretty soon," Juffie said.

"Fish is good for you. But it should be delicious." Paul frowned at his plate. "A lightly poached fillet of sole with sauce Véronique and garnished with truffles and asparagus tips . . ." He prodded the remains of soggy fried haddock. "The chef didn't quite bring it off this time, did he?"

Juffie laughed. Paul made her laugh a lot, and he was wonderful to look at, two of the reasons she kept seeing him. "Paul, your English isn't just good, it's fabulous, and so colloquial. How did you learn?"

"I started in school at age seven. And the war was an advanced course."

"What did you do in the war?" It was an innocent question, one Americans often asked each other. Juffie was amazed to see how dark his face became.

"Nothing I want to remember. I speak fluent German too." He emptied the bottle of Sancerre into their glasses and drank his quickly.

Juffie recognized the need to change the subject. "Tell me how you got started in the movie business."

"I never did really. I just happened to know a lot of people in Europe who made films before the war and were eager to start again as soon as it was over. So I got the idea of bringing their work to America."

On other occasions she learned more. Paul didn't want to import just motion pictures, he wanted to bring live entertainment. "There's a great deal of talent in Europe, and since the war Americans have become more sophisticated, more aware that there's life on the other side of the ocean. There's a market, I know there is. If I can just put the right deal together."

On the night that followed her meeting with Jack and the revelation about Matt, Juffie didn't want to talk about Paul's plans for the future. She got to La Venue at eleven-fifteen. According to the discreet posters by the door, Paul was showing an English picture called *The Lavender Hill Mob* with somebody named Alec Guinness. A substantial crowd was exiting from the lobby.

She hurried past them and made her way up a narrow flight of stairs to the projection room. Paul was waiting for her there. "Juffie, this is really a terrific film. Three nights after it opens look at the crowd. You've got to see it— What's the matter? You look terrible."

Nothing of what she felt had shown onstage. Penelope was as funny and winsome as always. Only after the final curtain had her mood of black despair returned. "I'm just tired. I only came by to say I think I'd better go home and go to bed."

"No," Paul said instantly. "You're *over*tired. I can tell by looking at you. You won't sleep." He was slipping off the navy silk raincoat she wore over navy slacks and a pale lavender cashmere sweater. The coat was damp. "It's still raining out?"

"Yes, it's never going to stop. Every day so far this April. I'm keeping a record."

"Then we won't go out. We'll stay right here."

"Paul, no. I'm sorry, I really am very tired—"

"Stop talking. I'm not going to listen anyway. Where's your shadow?"

She knew he meant Mike Ryan. "Downstairs in the lobby."

"Don't move, I'll be right back."

Juffie collapsed into a chair behind the projection equipment, too exhausted to protest. Paul returned in a couple of minutes. "I've sent what's-his-name for Chinese food. He wouldn't go until

I swore to lock all the doors and not let you out of my sight until he gets back." He took both her hands in his. "You must have the most determined fans in the country, all threatening to do you bodily harm. Funny way for fans to behave."

She looked at him, her violet eyes studying his blue ones. "Paul, don't pry."

One hand stroked her cheek. "I'm not prying."

"Yes, you are. You want to know why I have a bodyguard. Not tonight, Paul. I'm not up to it."

"Very well. Tonight you are going to be entertained. I'm going to give you a private screening of *The Lavender Hill Mob*. You'll love it. And we'll sit here and eat and laugh, and an hour and a half from now you'll feel like a new woman."

It wasn't a bad prescription. Juffie decided to go along with it. Mike Ryan returned with a brown paper bag that felt warm and smelled deliciously garlicky. Everyone else around Juffie Kane ignored her bodyguard; they either didn't know she had one or pretended not to know. Paul Dumont was different, he tried to co-opt him. "We're going to see a new film from England. Care to watch?" Paul asked.

Ryan shook his head and turned to Juffie. "Miss Kane, I'm getting a bad cold. I wonder if I could leave you with Mr. Dumont here and call the office and have them send someone to take over for a day or two."

That was the routine they followed on Ryan's days off; Juffie was used to it. "Sure, Mike. And really, whoever it is doesn't have to show up until the morning. Mr. Dumont will see me home, won't you, Paul?"

"Of course."

Ryan left and Paul produced some plates and forks and napkins from one file drawer, a bottle of red wine from another. "I sometimes have lunch here," he explained.

The napkins were damask, the forks silver. "In style, I see. What, no crystal?"

"It's too breakable for a file drawer. These are safer." He put two heavy glasses on the desk, unaware that she was teasing him, and led her to a leather couch with a stack of pillows on one end. "You can see the screen perfectly from here. Now, put your feet up, I'm going to take off your shoes. There. Better?"

"Heaven," Juffie said.

He piled two plates with pork strips and fried rice and subgum chow mein and chicken chop suey and handed one to her. "Your wine's right here on the table. And I'll sit here." He drew a chair to the side of the couch. "Now we're ready." Paul flicked a couple of switches. The theater and the projection room were plunged into darkness, and images began flickering on the screen.

Alec Guinness was wonderful and in a silly sort of way it really was a very funny picture. All about a bunch of bank robbers posing as musically minded bankers and living on Lavender Hill in London, in a house owned by an eminently respectable old lady. The mob, led by Guinness, decide to get their latest heist of gold out of England by making it into models of the Eiffel Tower— which operation takes place under the long nose of the old lady.

After twenty minutes of this amusing nonsense Juffie was really laughing. In another ten minutes she didn't know what was happening on the screen and she didn't care.

Paul was kissing her, not urgently, not as if he were in any sort of hurry. His lips were moving over her forehead and her eyes and her cheeks and her nose. They paused on her mouth and stayed there for some time, but he did not thrust his tongue inside. It wasn't one kiss so much as a series of gentle, tender kisses. Eventually he moved to her neck. He spent a long time there too.

When he pulled the cashmere sweater over her head she didn't try to stop him. She was almost somnolent; nothing was required of her but that she drift with this slow, attentive lovemaking. He removed her bra and cupped her full breasts in his hands and buried his face in them.

Now at last she felt his tongue. It was tracing circles around her nipples. Over and over and over. He went on until the tips of her breasts were so sensitized she couldn't bear it. Juffie put her hands on the back of his head, trying to guide him to what she wanted, but Paul did not take her nipples into his mouth. Instead, he disengaged her hands and stretched them up over her head so they hung limply off the end of the couch. Then he began playing his fingertips over the incredibly sensitive skin between her breasts and her underarms. It was bliss. Juffie started to tremble.

It seemed ages before he got to her midriff, but when the feathery stroking began there, it went on even longer. Just the tips of his fingers moved over her skin, awakening nerves she didn't know she had. He did not say a word. The music of *The Lavender*

Hill Mob played on in the background. A few times Juffie sighed, once she moaned. "Shh," Paul whispered. "No sounds. Not now. I will tell you when. Now you hold all your pleasure inside."

He removed her slacks and her panties and her garter belt and stockings. There was no hurried fumbling. Everything was done with care and deftness. He began to pay attention to her belly, kissing it softly, repeatedly, as he had her face and neck. She moved one leg up over the top of the couch, exposing herself to him. Paul ran his fingers across the insides of her thighs. Up and down and around, a sequence of movements as ordered as a minuet.

She could barely breathe; what she wanted was choking her. "Please . . ."

"Shh," he said again. "Not yet."

The tips of his fingers were still on her thighs, high in the fold of skin between them and her torso, but his thumbs moved to the honey-colored hair between and spread the lips. He lowered his head but didn't touch her. Instead, he breathed softly on the crevices and valleys he'd exposed, blowing over them a breeze that did not cool but intensified the heat.

Juffie arched up to him, thrusting her pelvis toward his face. Finally he drew his tongue from her clitoris to her anus and back. Slowly. Once again. He lifted his head. "Now, Juffie. Now I want to hear your pleasure." He bent toward her once more, tonguing hard, squeezing her flesh closed with his hands so it seemed as if all of her were in his mouth. Juffie screamed. She kept screaming for a full two minutes.

When she finally stopped, he lifted her off the couch and onto the floor. There was a rug of sorts, but it wasn't particularly thick. Every inch of her body was so sensitive, the unyielding wood seemed to press into her flesh. And the pain of that was somehow part of the pleasure. Paul lowered himself on top of her and something that felt enormous and rock-hard slowly inserted itself between her legs. She gripped his narrow hips with her knees, clung to his broad shoulders with hands that had never felt so strong.

"Now, *chérie*," he whispered. "Now we will begin."

It was a half hour before he allowed them both a screaming, frenzied climax. The movie was long since over. The screen glowed a ghostly white and the hum of the projection equipment was the only other sound in the little art theater. "See," he said. "I told you you'd be a new woman after the film."

. . . .

He was a drug; she was addicted to him. They stopped going out when they were finished working; instead, they met at Juffie's and made love until dawn. Nothing she'd experienced with Tony Morton had prepared her for Paul Dumont; he was an artist, a creative genius whose medium was sex.

He didn't need anything other than his hands and his mouth and the rest of his wonderfully disciplined body, but on occasion he could make inspired use of props. Butter, for instance. It had never occurred to Juffie that you could do things with butter besides eat it. Paul slathered half a pound of it over her body and licked it off. He spent an hour doing that. Then there was the time he covered the dining room table with pillows and lay her on her belly and used a piece of smooth rounded wood to massage every exposed inch of skin. His flesh didn't touch hers once during the hours he spent doing it. He didn't let her turn over either. He just kept working the wooden tool over the back side of her, from her scalp to the soles of her feet. In the end she was begging him to stop. "Take me, oh, God, Paul, I can't wait any longer. Take me."

"Not yet." The wood was slick with her sweat. He was kneading her buttocks with it, drawing it up and down the crack, sometimes reaching tantalizing close to the orifice that was shuddering with contractions induced by longing. She began to sob.

"*Maintenant, chérie,*" he murmured. "You can have a little bit now." He inserted the wood into her vagina, pushing it so high she thought she could feel it in her belly, and held it there. Finally he actually touched her, one hand pressed down on her buttocks, all his weight behind it. That was all, no thrusting, no friction. Just the dual pressure of the wood inside her and his hand bearing down on her ass. She came with such force her fists beat on the sides of the table and chipped the pearl ring she was wearing.

Then he flipped her over and put her legs on his shoulders and stood there and screwed her like that. And he could still wait for her to build another orgasm before he had his own. It was incredible.

"Jesus, Paul, where did you learn such stuff? Is that wooden gizmo French? Does everybody in France do these things?"

He laughed and pointed to the instrument he'd used to bring her such exquisite pleasure. "That isn't French, it's Japanese. The French have the reputation, but the Japanese are the real masters."

"Then you must have some Japanese blood."

"I wish I did. It would make my present negotiations a little easier."

"What negotiations?" It was morning, they were eating breakfast in Juffie's kitchen. The sphere of wood was in the middle of the table, like a centerpiece.

"A film, a fantastic film from Tokyo called *Rashomon*. I want to bring it to New York. They have no objections to that, just to making me the exclusive U.S. distributor."

Juffie frowned. "Look, I don't want to tell you your business, but the war's been over for only five years. I'm not sure American audiences are ready for a movie from Tokyo." She gestured to the thing in the middle of the table. "Now, if you could import that . . . I think people might be willing to forget their prejudices."

Paul laughed again. "We'll see. I'd better get out of here. The bird dog will be arriving any minute."

He meant Mike Ryan. Their frenzied sex life had necessitated certain changes in Juffie's arrangements. She'd reduced the hours she had a bodyguard to days only. Ryan saw her home after the show, then left. If he knew why she'd established the new routine, he didn't say.

Paul grabbed his jacket and kissed her good-bye. "See you tonight. I may be an hour or so late. I'm meeting a Japanese lady who might be able to do the subtitles for *Rashomon*. I need to check out her English."

"She's Japanese and you're French and you're going to check out her English?" Juffie laughed.

Paul bristled, as he did sometimes when she teased him. "My English is as good as yours. Believe me, if it weren't, I wouldn't be alive right now."

. . . .

"Good night, Miss Kane. I'll leave you here tonight, okay? I have a date and I'm running late." The Pinkerton man had brought her as far as the door to the private elevator leading to the penthouse.

"Yes, sure, Mike. Thanks." Juffie pressed the button and waited for the elevator.

A man came through the great glass doors of the apartment building. He pushed past the doorman and headed straight for Juffie. "Miss Kane, may I speak to you, please?" Panic welled up; she looked desperately for Mike, but he was gone. He'd left the building at the same moment the stranger entered it.

"Please," the man said. "Don't be alarmed. There's no need to recall your bodyguard." He was about fifty, maybe more, short and slim, with a thin pure-white mustache and white hair. He carried a black bowler, and a camel's-hair coat was neatly folded over his arm. "I would suggest we go up to your penthouse, but perhaps you'd feel safer if we talked here."

The lobby of East River Tower was marble and mirrors and crystal. But it was not dimly lit, that was a security risk. It was bright, and there was a small reception desk with a clerk behind it as well as a doorman and a security guard. Juffie knew that all three men were unobtrusively watching her, waiting for any signal that she required assistance. Finally she shook her head. "Very well, we can talk. But here in the lobby."

She led him to a corner delineated by a washed-silk Chinese rug and black bamboo chairs upholstered in shades of soft rose and pale lime green. "Who are you and what do you want?"

"My name is Morris Aronson. I have the misfortune to labor under the nickname Finky."

Juffie stared. "I don't believe it," she said finally.

"Nonetheless, it's true. And I apologize for the melodramatic gesture of the picture and the rotting offal. One of my employees overstepped himself; he has a macabre sense of humor. It won't happen again."

She narrowed her eyes and studied him. "Mr. Aronson, as you are well aware, I have known guys like you virtually all my life. You don't look like them, you don't sound like them, you don't even smell like them. So what are you doing here? What in God's name do you want from me?"

"As to how I look and sound and . . . smell"—he spread his hands—"I am as you see me. As I have made myself. Perhaps as I have invented myself, Miss Kane, just as you invent a new self every evening on the stage. For the rest, a man earns a living however he can."

"Yes. Well, some do so in more acceptable ways than others. I repeat, what do you want from me?"

"At the moment, nothing. I merely came to tell you that this ridiculous charade with the gentleman from Pinkerton's needn't go on unless you wish it to. You are in no danger from me, Miss Kane. I can understand your believing otherwise after the incident in Boston. But it isn't true."

"How kind of you to let me know," she said. "How very kind to come here and apologize for your thoroughly rotten, despicable, illegal behavior. Look, you bastard, I don't care how you've polished up your image. I know only too well what's beneath it."

He flicked an imaginary piece of lint from the lapel of his gray serge suit. And he did not rise to her bait. "I quite understand your reaction. Considering that formerly you were under obligation to Vinnie Faldo. The man's a pig."

"But you're not."

"No, I'm not. I'm a businessman. Admittedly, some of my associates are not the sort of people one would choose to be with on a social occasion, but that's an unfortunate fact of life. The other fact, the one I came here this evening to discuss, is equally true. You are in no danger from Faldo or anyone around him. Not even that sadist known as Angel Tomasso. I paid a high price for your IOU, Miss Kane. But I own it now. And in my world, as I think you realize, such transactions are honored. No one can touch you."

"Except you."

"I have no intention of doing you bodily harm."

"What do you want, then? You still haven't told me that."

"At the moment, nothing. Merely to make your acquaintance and release you from a silly arrangement which anyway wouldn't have worked if I'd chosen otherwise. It was, for instance, ridiculously easy to arrange that Mr. Ryan would leave you at the elevator this evening. A matter of a paltry few dollars. Ah," he added, seeing her expression, "you don't believe me. Mr. Ryan usually accompanies you upstairs, doesn't he, Miss Kane?"

He did. So it was the truth. Mike had sold her out. She nodded agreement.

"Good. I admire people who recognize the facts and acknowledge them. Now, you may do as you wish about this bodyguard business. If just seems silly that you should have an unnecessary expense because of me."

He stood up, obviously preparing to leave. "Someday there will be something I need, Miss Kane. A way for you to discharge your obligation. When that day comes, I will let you know. Until then I doubt that we'll meet again." He actually bowed slightly before he left her.

Juffie sat in the elegant black bamboo chair and stared after him. Paul came in just then. He saw Juffie and passed Finky Aronson, and realized the two had been speaking. "Hi." And after a moment's pause he asked, "Were you talking to that man?"

Juffie stood up. "I guess I was. But he's nobody real. I think he's somebody who stepped out of a play. A comedy by Oscar Wilde maybe. Let's go upstairs."

She was crazy that night. Crazy because she realized she was free. It had hit her on the way up in the elevator.

Whatever else, there would be no more visits from Angel Tomasso. And Finky Aronson with his mustache and his bowler was never going to humiliate her in public, or stick his hand up her skirt, or expect her to go to bed with him. Moves like that clearly weren't his style. And Mike Ryan was a rat who'd sold her out, so she could fire him without a qualm. No more bodyguards. Aronson said she didn't need one, and she believed him. All right, she had a debt, but it was to a white-haired gentleman who spoke like a college professor, not a hoodlum. Someday he'd call it in and she'd pay. How bad could it be? Meanwhile, she was free.

She turned on Paul the moment they stepped into the apartment, flinging her arms around him and kissing him and biting him and tearing at his clothes. "Vixen," he murmured, "gorgeous little fox," tearing at hers in response.

"A fox, yes. One that bites." She sank her teeth into his shoulder. "Here. And here. And here." Her mouth worked the length of his body, biting and sucking and leaving angry red marks. "Maybe here." She nipped at his balls.

"Hey!" Paul jumped back, then lunged for her. "I'll teach you to attack me, Juffie Kane." He picked her up and carried her to the couch. Already both naked bodies were sheened with sweat and slick with the juices of love. He sat down and flung her over his knees and spanked her naked buttocks with his open palm. Four hard slaps, each one making the room echo with the sound of flesh on flesh.

Juffie screamed, then wriggled away from him, but not too far. She pulled him onto the floor and on top of her. "No waiting. None of your games tonight." She reached for him, trying to force him into her body. "Fuck me, goddamn you. Fuck me."

He did, driving himself with no restraint for once, letting his passion run headlong into hers, forsaking his customary disci- plined control. Seconds later they both came and he collapsed on top of her. "Silly child," he murmured in her ear. "Look at all the hours of pleasure you deprived us of with your impatience."

"No, I didn't. But tonight it will be my turn to do things to you."

She did—incredible things that she never would have thought she could even imagine. A trick with her douche bag and warm soapy water, another involving just her long hair and only the tip end of his penis. By two A.M. he'd climaxed three times and they both fell into exhausted sleep. He woke up two hours later and wakened her by putting his fingers inside her and rubbing his thumb hard and fast over her clitoris. He didn't stop after she came, even though she begged him to. He went on doing it until she came again a few minutes later, though she'd sworn she couldn't.

"Okay," he whispered. "Now you can sleep. That's just the way I am, *chérie*. I always have to have the last word in an argument."

In the morning she telephoned Matt as soon as Paul left. "Hi, it's me. Listen, I want you to call Pinkerton's and tell them I don't need a bodyguard anymore. And you can tell them that Mike Ryan isn't trustworthy. He took a bribe to let somebody get to me."

"Juffie, are you all right? What's going on? Why don't you need a bodyguard? And how do you know Mike did something like that?"

"I know. And I don't need a bodyguard because there are no more racketeers after me. Not so you'd notice."

"Are you sure?"

"Positive. And Matt, there's something else. I've been think- ing about television."

"At last! Juffie, you'd be great. I get offers for you every day. You could even have your own show if you wanted."

"Absolutely not. I do not want my own show. I don't want to

be a television regular, Matt. I just want to dabble a little. Get me a guest spot. Something short but very sweet. Let's have lunch and talk about it."

. . . .

They ate at the Oyster Bar in Grand Central. Matt adored oysters and he was a regular there. Juffie loved every kind of shellfish, including oysters. The two of them had often been in the restaurant together. They took seats at the far end of the counter, where they had a good deal of privacy. The service was attentive but unobtrusive, and they could speak freely.

"I still think the Sullivan show, *Toast of the Town*, is the best bet. You can pretty much write your ticket, but if I understand what you're after, Sullivan's best."

"Hmm. What do you think I'm after?"

"Simple. The opportunity to show everyone that Juffie Kane can do anything. And be better at it than anybody else."

He understood her far too well. But she understood him now too. Finding out about Matt had hurt like hell, except that it explained why he never seemed to see her as anything but a remarkably successful client. And discovering that Paul Dumont was a sexual athlete without equal had followed so quickly on the revelation that she didn't have time to brood about it.

"I guess that's more or less it," she agreed. "But it's only anything in front of an audience. That's the difference between TV and the movies, Matt. It's why I'll do the former but not the latter. TV shows go out live and they have an audience. That's why they use theater people, not Hollywood types."

"You must have figured that out ages ago. Why did it take you this long to do something about it?"

"It's because I'm free," Juffie told him, stretching her arms over her head in a gesture of marvelous abandon. "I want to spread my wings because I'm free, free, free."

"I hope so, Juffie," Matt said. "I sure as hell hope so. If not, we're taking an enormous risk. I let Pinkerton's go right after you called. And I told them what you said about Ryan."

"Good. The man he sold me out to wanted only to talk. He didn't mean me any harm. To be fair, Mike probably knew that. But it was still a rotten thing to do."

"Not just rotten, totally immoral and unethical. Mike Ryan's through as far as Pinkerton's is concerned. He'll probably lose his detective's license."

"Never knew he had one." Juffie ate the last spoonful of her oyster stew.

"Of course, all Pinkerton's senior staff are private eyes in their own right."

"A possibly useful bit of information," she said. "I'll file it. Tell me what I'll do on the Sullivan show."

"Depends. It's a variety hour, a little bit of everything. You could do a sketch maybe. Something written for you. Or you could do a scene from *Delilah*. They'd love that."

"Nope. No *Delilah*. Listen, I've got an idea. You know George Bernard Shaw's play, *Pygmalion*."

"Yes."

"I had a walkon in that when I was a freshman in college. The parlor maid. I'd love to do a bit of Eliza Doolittle. And Harry Harcourt would be a wonderful Henry Higgins. Call Harry's agent and see if he's interested, Matt. Then see if Sullivan's people will buy it. A couple of scenes from *Pygmalion*, me and Harry."

They bought it to the tune of four thousand dollars for a twenty-minute appearance by Juffie Kane. Harry Harcourt got twenty-five hundred for being her co-star. The network hyped the show for three weeks before it played. And they got more mail after it than any single act on *Toast of the Town* had ever garnered. "Matt," Juffie asked, "do you think anybody would care to stage a revival of *Pygmalion*?"

"It was done in forty-five with Gertrude Lawrence. A short run as I recall."

"Well, this is 1950, not 1945. Try Jack Fine. I'd adore to do it. Eliza's a better part than anything I've been offered in months and months."

Three days later he told her that he'd approached Jack and been turned down. "He didn't say anything specific, but I get the impression that at the moment you're not on his list of wonderful people. What's that all about? It isn't something to do with your new boyfriend, is it?"

"No." She shook her head sadly. "It's nothing to do with Paul Dumont." There wasn't any point in being coy; of course Matt knew about Paul. She understood now why it didn't matter to him. But there was no need to tell him what Jack Fine was mad about. Especially not since the threat from Faldo and his friends was past. "Just a disagreement we had a while ago. I thought he'd forgotten about it."

"Apparently not. And no one else I've approached is excited by the *Pygmalion* idea. Even if the package comes with Juffie Kane. Shaw's too highbrow for the current market. At least that's how Broadway sees it."

Juffie shrugged. "Okay, it was only an idea. We'll simply have to keep looking for my next role."

Six years later, when Rex Harrison and Julie Andrews were knocking them dead at the Mark Hellinger in *My Fair Lady,* Juffie cursed herself as every kind of a fool for having given up so easily. She had two more Tonys by then, and another year before the avalanche in Verbier, Switzerland. But she never managed to play the role she'd secretly coveted so long ago when she read for Leslie Wing in Room 742 in the Memorial Annex at Simmons College.

Chapter 9

*T*he weather was wonderful in Cedar City, Utah, on this July day of 1951. Bernard Hanrihan, never before having traveled west of the Mississippi, had expected unbearable heat, but today a breeze from the surrounding mountains tempered the blistering sun. He sat happily on the campus of the College of Southern Utah, on a folding chair set on soft green grass, in the shade of a towering tree of some variety with which he was not familiar, and listened to his colleagues discuss Rorschach testing.

"Of course, it's all in how the psychologist interprets the results," one man said. A woman contributed her insight—what the patient saw in the inkblots depended on the order in which they were presented.

Bernard cleared his throat. Eight pairs of eyes turned to him, respectful of the eminent professor from the east who had delivered the keynote paper of this conference. "It's not entirely interpretation or order," Hanrihan said. "Everything ultimately depends on the experience of the psychologist. His wisdom. That's a word sometimes ignored in our profession, wisdom."

The others nodded and there was a moment of respectful silence before the discussion continued.

Bernard stopped paying attention; he let the voices drift around him and looked at the low buildings of the small college set in this quintessential western American setting. A nice little town, Cedar City. So different from Boston, it might be on another planet. He wondered if possibly Karen might agree to— No, she wouldn't. Karen was wedded to the big city, with its slums and its sidewalks teeming with the ethnic types that so fascinated her. If she'd just give herself a chance, she might learn to value a place like this.

Karen wasn't creating the opportunity for that to happen. She had attended only the main session of the conference, when he delivered his paper, and a minimum number of seminars. Now, when she should be here talking to her peers, getting to know them and let them know her, she was stuck away in the building to the left. Bernard knew exactly what she was doing. Karen was watching television.

Half an hour later he sought her out in the faculty common room, given over to the conferees this week. The shades were drawn and the room was dim. The only light came from the flickering gray images on the ten-inch screen. Karen was sitting on a leather couch a few feet from the set. She was hunched over, elbows on her knees, chin in her hands, absolutely rapt with attention.

"Karen . . ."

"Shh, not now, Bernard. That's Halley, the crime committee's chief counsel, questioning Frank Erickson."

Bernard listened for a moment.

"What is your business?" Halley asked the witness.

Erickson looked like a baldheaded cherub. He had a fat, round face and he smiled a lot. "My business? I have no business, I'm in jail."

Halley tried again. "What was your business before you were convicted? Were you a bookmaker?"

Erickson's smile disappeared. He seemed pained, saddened that the lawyer knew no better than to ask such a question. "I refuse to answer on the grounds that it might tend to incriminate me."

Bernard sighed. That was all any of them ever said. But Karen, like so many in America, was riveted by the televised hearings of Senator Estes Kefauver's Organized Crime Investigating Committee. Perhaps because he took their minds off the war in Korea, the senator from Tennessee had become a folk hero overnight. Even movie theaters interrupted their films to show the hearings.

There were a few more interchanges between Halley and Erickson, then the day's session ended. Karen stood up and switched off the set. "Now, dear, what were you saying?"

"Nothing important, Karen. I simply wanted to tell you that it was lovely out. A nice breeze. I thought perhaps you'd join me and some of the others."

"Sure, a great idea. Let's go now."

She was wearing a navy cotton dress with white piping and a little white bolero. She looked adorable. He could forgive her anything when she looked like this—so fresh and young and bouncy, the way she was when he first saw her as a Simmons freshman six years before. Bernard led her out into the sunshine.

The group had dispersed while he was gone. The chairs under the tree were all empty. Here and there conferees strolled or sunbathed in groups of two or three. This was a free afternoon, preceding the final dinner and general meeting of the Association for the Advancement of Psychology, but like Karen and Bernard, many of the visitors had eschewed a trip to the nearby Mormon memorial or the small town of Cedar City itself, and chosen a relaxed few hours on the campus.

Karen watched her lover out of the corner of her eye. They didn't touch, much less hold hands. She was here as a psychologist in her own right, she had her master's now, but everyone knew that she and Bernard weren't married. Discretion remained an absolute requirement. Still . . . "Bernard, let's go to my room." She whispered the words though there was no one within hearing distance.

"Now? Do you think we should risk it?"

"It's the only time to risk it. That awful woman from Texas I'm sharing with is tramping off in those mountains somewhere. She won't be back until five. Come on, Bernard, say yes."

He hesitated a moment. "Yes."

Karen grinned. "I'll go up first. You come in about five minutes. The second floor in that building over there. Fourth door on the left. I'll leave it open a bit, so you won't make a mistake."

She turned to him and shook his hand, saying a formal good-bye for the benefit of any observers. "I'll be naked by the time you get there, Bernard," she said from behind the restrained little smile suitable for a neophyte to offer one of the great men of the profession. "I hope you have something nice and hard for me."

The sex was better than usual, enhanced by the fillip of danger lent by the circumstances and the surroundings. Bernard was more energetic than he'd been the past few months. Cedar City obviously agreed with him. He lasted three or four minutes before he collapsed on top of her in a heap of shivering satisfaction.

Karen hugged him and kissed his shoulder. It wasn't his fault that she never quite got to where she thought she was going when the lovemaking was at its peak. She'd read everything she could lay her hands on about female orgasm, and Bernard must have read it all, too, though they never discussed it. He was thoughtful about foreplay, he always spent at least fifteen minutes exciting her before intercourse. And she became excited. It was just that the actual act never seemed to last long enough, their bodies never seeming to connect in exactly the right place. It was like having an itch she never quite managed to scratch. Which was her problem, not his. Didn't Freud say that a mature woman transferred her sexual feeling from the clitoris to the vagina? she asked herself. It wasn't Bernard's fault that she hadn't managed to mature yet.

"Good?" he murmured against her cheek.

"Wonderful," Karen said. She always said that. She'd been faking a climax for four years now; she was an adept. She told herself that it didn't matter, because in every other way they had a totally honest relationship. She wriggled out from under him and propped herself up on her elbow.

"Bernard, I have a terrific idea."

"What's that?" He was twining his fingers in her short curls. He loved the feel of Karen's hair. It was so springy, so full of life. Just as she was.

"Let's go to Las Vegas for a few days on our way home."

"What?"

"You heard me. Let's spend a weekend in Las Vegas."

He sat up, drawing the sheet to his chest. "What in God's name would you and I do in Las Vegas?"

"Rent a room together for one thing. Mr. and Mrs. John Smith from Kalamazoo. Nobody there will ever have seen either of us. We can relax and be ourselves, even in public."

"I see. Well, that has a certain appeal. But it doesn't have to be Las Vegas, my dear. The two-thousand-plus miles between here and Boston encompass a number of locations where nobody knows us."

"I said that was one thing. The other is that these days Las Vegas is the headquarters for the Syndicate. The Kefauver Committee has made that very clear. The mobsters own the town."

"Am I supposed to see that as a recommendation for a weekend's holiday from care?"

She flipped over on her back, staring at the cream-colored ceiling. "Don't be dense, Bernard. You know, I've got this great idea for my doctoral dissertation—organized crime and the ethnic experience. That's too general, but I'm narrowing in. I'll get a specific peg to hang it on pretty soon. I know it will help if I can actually see Las Vegas."

Bernard frowned. "You still don't like it," Karen said. "You don't think it's a good idea for a dissertation."

"It's just that it's so sordid. It's so different from my image of you, my dear. If you'd do that research we were discussing about intelligence testing among children from non-English-speaking homes, you'd be staying close to the question of the immigrants, which interests you, but in a way that the academic community as a whole will find more sympathetic."

Bernard had been telling her for months that if she wanted a teaching job in a decent college, she had to give up her fixation on crime. But then, he didn't know about Leah, the last of the abortion queens. He knew a lot about Karen's background, but not that.

"Okay," Karen said. "I'll think about it some more. But I still want to go to Las Vegas." She rolled over and put her head in his lap. "Say yes, Bernard. It's only for a weekend. You can stand being among the riffraff for two days."

They went to Las Vegas.

The population of this improbable city, erected with malice aforethought in the middle of the desert, was barely fifty thousand. Given the size of the town, the prevailing architecture was grandiose in the extreme, but it wasn't intended for the residents. It was designed to attract tourists; it was the embodiment of the fantasies of men whose notions of glamour came from Hollywood and Coney Island. Las Vegas was a grid of wide roads planned for flashy automobiles. At their heart ran a street called the Strip. In 1951 there were just four huge, garish hotels on the Strip. The most prominent among them were the Flamingo and the Desert Inn.

Karen and Bernard stayed at the Flamingo. For seven dollars and fifty cents a night they had a large room with wall-to-wall red carpeting and an enormous bed draped in red satin. The room also boasted a gold telephone, white and gold vaguely French

Provincial furniture, and the biggest television Karen had ever seen. Too bad the Kefauver hearings weren't on over the weekend. This television had a sixteen-inch screen, and on the rare occasions when a program was transmitted in color, it could show pictures of people who seemed to have orange skin and green hair.

The room was cheap because Las Vegas hotels did not expect to turn a profit on renting beds. They preferred that their guests never go to bed. The profit was far greater when the tourists spent their time on the main floor, in what any other hotel would call the lobby.

In Las Vegas that space had been enlarged and became the casino, a shrine of gambling open twenty-four hours a day where, mirabile dictu, all the action was absolutely legal. As long as the cards weren't marked, the dice weren't loaded, the roulette wheels not out of balance, and the government of Nevada could take its cut, gaming was permitted in the state that had invented the six-week divorce. For guys like Bugsy Siegel and Meyer Lansky and Moe Dalitz, the men who had conceived and labored into being the dream of Las Vegas, it was paradise.

"Jeezusss . . ." Karen stood on the carpeted steps leading to the Flamingo's sunken casino and marveled. At ten in the morning the huge area was completely devoid of any natural light. Neither sun nor cloud nor moon nor stars could affect the ambience here. The casino was lit only by electricity, and the intensity never changed. Perpetual night or perpetual day, whichever notion turned you on, you could nurse the illusion in this windowless space.

There was a crowd. It thickened and thinned as the hours wore on, but there was always a crowd. A player was on a roll at the craps table on her left, and while Karen watched he threw the dice against the padded parapet of the table and made his point. The man cheered, those who'd bet on him cheered, a small group of losers walked away. A croupier wearing a black vest and a green eyeshade used his rake to scoop in some chips and pay out others. "Jeezusss," she repeated.

"I don't think you're praying, are you, Karen?" Bernard asked. "I rather think this isn't the place for it."

"Oh yes, Bernard. Yes. I expect a lot of praying goes on right here."

He looked at her, noting that her cheeks were flushed and her eyes were shining. "Karen, this is a side of your character I shall never understand."

"It's research, Bernard. Field work. How can I do a doctoral dissertation on crime if I don't study Las Vegas?"

He smiled indulgently. "All right, we're here. We won't start that argument again. Are you actually going to play any of these games?"

She hesitated. "I might, for a little while. Just to see what it feels like." She already knew what it felt like. Simply standing there was the most exciting thing she'd ever done in her life.

Bernard patted her cheek and gave her a twenty-dollar bill. "A Christmas present in advance. I believe you can change it down there."

"Yes, I believe I can." She grinned at him. "Thanks, and Merry Christmas to you too. Are you going to watch me?"

"Absolutely not. We've been in here ten minutes and I already have a headache. I brought a book. I'm going to find a bit of shade out by the pool and sit and read. Meet you right here at noon and we'll go have some lunch."

She didn't take the time to answer, she merely nodded and headed down into the pit.

When Bernard returned, Karen wasn't waiting on the steps. He had to look for her and it was a chore. The casino was much more crowded than it had been earlier. He finally found her. One small, tight buttock rested on a stool in front of what he knew was called a one-armed bandit, a slot machine. He watched her for a moment. She was putting in dimes and pulling the heavy lever with a kind of strange grace; a rhythm existed between Karen and the machine. It seemed to be wooing her. But that was ridiculous. Machines did not have rhythm, and if they did, they couldn't match it to a human's.

He approached and placed a hand on her shoulder. "Hi."

"Hi." She didn't stop playing. Insert the dime, pull the lever, watch the three rolling bands of symbols, have your next dime in the slot before they came to a halt. Three cherries appeared in the lighted strip that bisected the machine. A jangle of coins fell into the metal tray at the machine's base.

Bernard glanced down. The tray was full of dimes. "You're winning," he said with some surprise.

She finally turned her face up to his. "I'm winning a lot." Karen lifted a cloth bag from her lap. "They gave me this to use. It's full."

"Good Lord! How are we ever going to count them all?"

"We don't have to. They do it for you at that booth over there." She nodded toward a kiosk in the middle of the floor. Lines of people stood waiting to buy chips or cash them in or change coins for bills. She opened the drawstring of the cloth bag and added handfuls of dimes from the tray. "Tell you what, you go get this counted and changed. I'll play another couple of minutes. Just till you get the money."

"Karen, I don't want to stand in line with those people. And you've been playing for over two hours. You must be going blind, staring at those spinning circles. I should think you'd be bored silly."

It was the first time he'd sounded impatient. And he'd come to Las Vegas only because she wanted to. She stood up. "Okay, I'll do it. Then we'll have lunch. But it isn't boring, Bernard. It isn't a bit boring."

They left Las Vegas a little after midnight on Sunday. In the forty-eight hours they'd been there, they had attended an extravaganza in the Flamingo's Showroom—high-kicking half-nude chorus girls and Teresa Brewer singing her hit, *Music, Music, Music*—and eaten two steak dinners in the hotel's Beef Baron restaurant. They had also spent some time in the big bed making love, but not a lot. For the vast majority of the forty-eight hours Karen played the slots and Bernard sat by the pool and read. He was tanned dark brown. She was pale, but her cheeks still had two high spots of color. She'd wound up winning three hundred dollars and seventy cents. "You really enjoyed yourself, didn't you?" Bernard asked.

"I really did. What about you?"

He shrugged. "Oh well, the flamingos on the lawn were nice. Remarkable-looking birds really."

Karen pursed her lips the way she did when she was concentrating. "Bernard, what do you think could be the fascination racketeers have with flamingos? The racetrack in Miami, Hialeah, it's famous for its flamingos too."

"I don't really know, my dear. Perhaps they're simply the most exotic thing such people can imagine. Are you going to include flamingos in your doctoral dissertation?"

"Maybe, Bernard. Maybe."

.　.　.　.

On the Saturday night that Karen was tasting the joys of Las Vegas, Juffie was playing Penelope, the misplaced Roman maiden, for the last time. *The Visitor* closed in July 1951, after a run of eighteen months.

Juffie remained with it six months longer than she had to because she hadn't found another show she wanted to do. She still hadn't, but recently she'd discovered a way to maintain her income. It was easier than being onstage for seven performances a week, though a good deal less exciting.

In March Clifton Fadiman had invited her to join him for a guest appearance on his popular TV show, *This Is Show Business*. Juffie knew and liked Cliff, so she did it—and she was wonderful. After that she was in demand for other TV spots, and she found she quite liked doing them. Especially the talk shows, where the interaction between performers and audience was so intense.

Juffie started entertaining the night owls on the first of the late-night shows, called, appropriately enough, *Broadway Open House*. After that she appeared with Steve Allen and Dave Garroway and Jack Paar. She did three or four shows a month and she worried about being overexposed on what the intelligentsia already called "the idiot box," but it seemed as if America couldn't get enough of Juffie Kane.

The magic she could create speaking lines a writer had put in her mouth was just as effective when she was ad-libbing and being herself. The fan mail poured into the networks every time she was on, and she earned as much for one television appearance as she did in a week in a play. An added bonus of this routine was that she had a lot more free time.

A good part of that time she spent with Paul Dumont. He had opened two more art theaters, La Venue II on Eighty-first Street and Lexington Avenue, and La Venue III on Ninth Street in the Village. His distribution net had widened too. All over America interest in foreign films was increasing. But Paul wasn't satisfied. "Live entertainment," he kept saying. "An opera company from

Vienna, or a ballet, say. From France, maybe even Russia. The Bolshoi Ballet from Russia! Wouldn't that pack them in, Juffie?"

"Of course it would. But would the Bolshoi come? I don't think the Russian government would let its dancers just hop in a plane and fly off to New York."

"No, probably not. All right, a ballet from Paris, then."

The idea was constantly on his mind, but the capital required for such a venture was staggering. More than Paul could amass even with three art theaters doing a reasonably good business. A lot of the time he and Juffie spent together was devoted to discussion of Paul's schemes to get backers for his ideas. The plans didn't come to much. And each time another door was closed he would be morose and difficult.

Juffie didn't mind too much, because if he really started getting on her nerves, she either turned the encounter into one of their sexual marathons or sent him home. They might be sleeping together, but one thing Paul Dumont did not do was live with Juffie Kane. He kept no clothes at her place and he usually left sometime during the night and returned to his single room in a residential hotel downtown. It had a bed, a chest of drawers, an electric hot plate, and a minuscule bathroom, which didn't prevent him from criticizing the penthouse.

"*Mon Dieu,* Juffie. Look at this place. A celebration of the bourgeoisie."

"What's wrong with it?" When Juffie first bought the apartment at the top of East River Tower, Rosie had come from Boston and spent a week with her daughter choosing furniture. She felt a mixture of joy and pain remembering that. They'd gone to Altman's and Macy's and Lord & Taylor and selected a mahogany table and chairs for the dining room, a living room suite upholstered in nubby green bouclé, and a variety of comfortable, practical pieces for the other rooms. Most of the floors were carpeted in pale gold shag, and the drapes were beige shantung throughout. They'd had such a good time together, and Rosie had been dead so soon afterward. "What's wrong with it?" Juffie repeated. "My mother picked out most of this stuff."

"I'm sure your mother was a lovely lady, but—"

"The best," Juffie interrupted.

"But her taste was strictly middle-class nothing. Hire a decorator, Juffie. You can afford to live in beauty, why don't you?"

"I don't want a decorator. In case you haven't figured it out, darling, what I spent on that would not be available for other things."

"Your clothes, for instance. Those seven closets filled with clothes."

"That's right." Juffie narrowed her eyes and cocked her head and studied him. "Paul, do you have something to say about my clothes, about the way I live my life?"

He always knew when he'd gone too far. "Only that I adore you. And you would be the perfect Mrs. Paul Dumont."

He'd started asking her to marry him—frequently. "I love you," he insisted. "You're the first person I've really cared about in years. I want us to be together always."

Juffie didn't want a husband. Marriage meant absolute commitment, exposing yourself completely to another person, perhaps having children. Marriage was giving hostages to fortune. The idea terrified her. "It's got nothing to do with my feelings for you," she told him. "I just don't want to get married."

"Why? No, don't answer, I know. You had an unhappy childhood, your parents didn't get along." Paul was attracted to hidden motives and early influences. He'd read Freud.

"Exactly the opposite. My parents adored each other, they adored me. Rosie and Myer did everything together. They were as close as two people can be."

"Then why—"

He'd picked the wrong childhood influences, but she didn't say so. "I simply can't see myself married." Juffie wanted the subject closed, but Paul wouldn't give up. He said she really didn't know him, not deep down underneath, and he began telling her stories of his experiences during the war.

"I grew up in the Loire Valley, near Sancerre. When I was seventeen years old I was working in my family's vineyards. I expected to take them over someday. Then the Nazis came. The panzer tanks arrived and everything changed."

"It must have been awful. What did you do?"

He hesitated, not quite looking at her. "I joined . . . the Maquis. You've heard of it?"

"The French Resistance. Of course I've heard of it. Paul, were you frightened? I know you must have been brave, but were you scared at the same time?"

"Scared shitless," he admitted. "All the time. I was picked to work in Nazi headquarters for the area. They'd taken over the chateau at Fontainebleau. I was a courier. I rode my bicycle all over the district for them, delivering papers, things like that. They had cars, of course, but fuel was precious."

"And all the time you were secretly working for the Resistance?"

"For the Maquis. Yes, that's right. Juffie, can you imagine what it was like, never knowing which of your friends would be found out and tortured and then killed? Never knowing if someone would talk and give the rest of us away? I didn't let myself care about anyone. Just concentrated on saving my own neck."

"And your country."

"Yes, and my country." They were drinking a bottle of Sancerre at the time—now she knew why he so loved that particular wine—and he'd poured himself another glass and downed it quickly.

"What happened to your family's vineyards?" she asked.

"Torn up. The Nazis even salted the earth so nothing would grow later. They wanted to make an example because of an incident in my village."

"And your parents?"

"Dead. All my family is dead. Marry me, Juffie."

She laid her hand on his arm. "I can't. I care for you deeply, Paul, but I can't see myself married."

He asked at least once a week. "Let's not start that again," Juffie would say. She'd go back to the script she was reading—she never stopped looking for a new play—or perhaps reach out and stroke the back of his neck in a way which had become a signal that it was time to make love yet again.

Thus passed the second half of 1951. Then, two weeks before Christmas, Juffie was asked to appear on the immensely popular *Dinah Shore Show.* "In a sketch?" she asked Matt.

"Sort of." He handed her a sheaf of papers. "Take a look at this."

Juffie sat down opposite his desk. She crossed her long legs in their ultrasheer stockings. The skirt of her russet silk dress rode up above her knees. For a moment she thought Matt's eyes had flickered toward the accidental display. No, Juffie, she reminded herself. You are not Matt's type. Boys are Matt's type.

She adjusted her dress and began leafing through the typed sheets. After a moment she looked up. "Matt, what the hell are you giving me here? This is a part for a singer. It calls for a duet with Dinah Shore."

"Not exactly a sung duet. It's a parody, Juffie. A couple of housewives talking over the back fence."

"Not talking. Singing." She waved the script. "It says so right here."

He ignored that for a moment. "They come onstage dressed like ladies of the 1890s. And they progress by decades up to now, 1951. All the costume changes take place in full view of the audience. It's clever as hell, Juffie. Look at the lyrics."

"That's just it, they're lyrics. Dinah Shore is a singer. I am not a singer. Is that fact too difficult to absorb?"

"Have you noted the setting of that back fence, Juffie? The Deep South. Georgia, someplace like that."

"Shore's southern."

"I know. And who is the best actress in the world for dialect parts and character roles and that combination funny-sad-we're-all-in-this-together humor that made *Delilah* a legend?"

"I don't sing. Not even in the shower."

"Look, Miss Shore loves you. She thinks you're terrific. She's a very nice lady, Juffie. First class. And she got this idea herself. She'd dying for you to do it with her."

"That's nice to hear. I think she's very talented and I appreciate the compliment. But what do I do for a voice? Maybe she could get Patti Page."

"She doesn't want Patti Page. Another southern singer is exactly what she doesn't want. In her position, you wouldn't either. Miss Shore's idea is that you'd sort of talk the songs. A kind of slightly musical patter. Will you meet her and discuss it?"

Juffie hesitated. Matt didn't usually push. If she had an instinctive no response to a part, he respected her judgment and backed off. But she also respected his. And she knew he was no more well served by having her, God forbid, bomb onstage than she was. "Okay, don't say we'll do it, but set up a meeting."

It took place in a scruffy rehearsal room in what had been the Longacre Theater on Forty-eighth Street between Broadway and Eighth Avenue but was now leased to NBC television. A good many legitimate theaters had gone the same route, and Juffie, like so many others, mourned every time another one caved in to escalating costs and shrinking audiences. Being reminded of that didn't put her in a good mood to meet Dinah Shore. And for the first time in years, she was nervous as hell.

The two women were entirely alone in the small room. Dinah Shore was waiting when Juffie arrived. A remarkable concession. Or maybe she just never played the prima donna. "Miss Kane," the blond darling of movies and television said, oozing the famous southern charm, "what a pleasure."

"Miss Shore." Juffie shook her hand. "The pleasure is mine."

"Can we sit here and sort of talk about this?" Dinah indicated a couple of beat-up straight-back chairs.

"I'm not sure what we have to talk about," Juffie said, sitting down. "I think your sketch is a terrific idea. With the right partner you'll be great. But I doubt that I'm the right partner."

Dinah smiled. "Can we try a little bit, just so you can sort of see what I had in mind?" She flipped a couple of sheets of the script on the rickety table between them. "This part here, say when it's the 1920s and the ladies are flappers. I sing the line, 'What do we do when the bathtub gin runs out?'" She sang it. A nice voice, sweet and true and clear.

Juffie looked at the line that followed Dinah's, the one meant for her. She looked from the page to the other woman. "This is precisely the problem. I can't sing."

"Talk it," Dinah Shore said. "The way you'd deliver it if it weren't a song."

That was easy. "What're we gonna do, honeychile, when the rum runners run no more rum?" She made it broad and silly and funny as hell. Dinah smiled.

"That's it. That's why you and I simply have to do this together. Now, Juffie, say as a for-instance you lifted that line a tiny bit more. Got it up from your diaphragm to right here." She indicated a spot on her chest with her hand. "Then sort of let it slide out from your throat in a way that isn't singing but isn't quite talking either. Do you see what I mean?"

Juffie had always been a director's dream, a natural. "Like this?" She tried it. One false start, but she went back to the beginning and tried again. When she got to the words "rum runners" they came out like a cross between the two Ethels, Merman and Barrymore—pitched low and belted forth.

Dinah Shore clapped her hands together. "Perfect! It's perfect, Juffie." She sang her next line, "We're gonna be sad without Southern Comfort . . ."

"But we don't intend to like it or lump it," Juffie chimed in, using the crazy half-basso-profundo tone.

"Okay," Dinah said quickly, "together now. 'We're gonna get by. My, my, we're gonna get by.'"

It was the reprise that occurred throughout the sketch, and the combination of the Shore sweet high tone and Juffie's half growl, half roar was nothing short of fabulous.

"Why was she so determined?" Juffie asked Matt later. "I think she was right, but what made her so set on getting me to do it?"

"Easy. She's smart as hell."

Apparently so. Seconds after they went off the air, the telephones began ringing at NBC. The ratings went through the roof. And a whole new world opened for Juffie Kane.

Nothing was more Broadway than the Broadway musical comedy, the big show with the big orchestra and the drop-dead costumes and the fabulous sets. Nothing could still attract the crowds like that proven combination which, when it worked, worked like nothing else ever staged.

On November 10, 1952, *Whaddaya Say* starring Juffie Kane opened at the Imperial Theater on West Forty-fifth Street. In 1923 the Imperial had been the fiftieth playhouse to be built in New York by those brothers from Syracuse named Shubert. Twenty-nine years later the Shuberts were in the audience when Juffie and her co-star, Timothy Frank, stopped the show toward the end of the first act.

Whaddaya Say was set in thirties Hollywood, where Myrtle, a girl from Brooklyn, and her fabulously rich boyfriend, Danny, have come to make Myrtle's dream of stardom come true. But despite the fact that Myrtle is gorgeous, she hasn't a hope. When she opens her mouth, thick Brooklynese comes out. It was the kind of part Juffie had dreamed about since she first saw Judy Holliday in *Born Yesterday*. One of the things that made it so wonderful was that Myrtle really loved Danny. She was dumb and naive and greedy, but genuine.

"'You're my star, babe,'" Tim sang in his rich tenor in the last scene of the first act. "'I really just love you,'" Juffie counterpointed in her throaty, nonmusical imitation of song.

The pair were alone onstage, in a canoe floating on a real lake—a bit of technical virtuosity that set the audience to gasping. Now they were listening to this warm, bravura duet celebrating all life's most fundamental emotions, and when the last note died away, they came to their feet applauding. In the classic phrase, the number brought down the house. When calm was finally restored, Juffie stood up and overturned the canoe and both stars fell into the water. Curtain.

Among those who gave the company a twenty-minute ovation that opening night was a man sitting on the aisle in the seventh row center. Finky Aronson, in black tie and diamond studs, enjoyed every second of Juffie's latest triumph. Who could fail to delight in an investment that increased in value while you watched?

"Bouncy, witty, tender—in a word, a joy. And Juffie Kane, Juffie Kane, Juffie Kane—which says it all." That was Howard Barnes in the *Herald Tribune*. "America's favorite funny lady, Juffie Kane, honking the patter songs specially written for her in a voice somewhere between a train whistle and a foghorn, manages to make us love every minute of the noise," exulted the *New York Post*. According to Atkinson in the *Times* the show was "Enchanting, simply wonderful. No audience has left the theater so thoroughly delighted since *South Pacific* opened. Juffie Kane tries to sing and her voice is terrible. But we adore it. Miss Kane just keeps getting better and better and better. Long may she reign."

She was twenty-five years old, playing in her fourth Broadway show, and the critics had elevated her to the role of legendary theatrical grande dame; someone who had always been there, and would never let them down.

· · · ·

Everyone said she was a sure bet for another Tony. By March of '53 Juffie, too, thought she'd get the award. She cast aside superstition, and bought a new dress for the awards ceremony. It was a black satin sheath, an utterly simple wrapping of lush fabric for her glorious body, with two thin shoulder straps relieving the bareness. The dress came with its own wrap, a three-quarter-length black satin cape that ended in a triple flounce of twelve-inch ruffles. The cape was lined with pale lavender silk that exactly matched Juffie's eyes.

When she brought the dress home the last week in March, Paul was at the penthouse. "Want to see it?" She motioned to the box.

Juffie seldom showed off her purchases. She knew Paul disapproved of the fortune she spent on clothes. So the question was unusual. "What is it?" he asked.

"A new dress for the Tony awards. Of course it was expensive, but considering the occasion . . . It's spectacular, Paul. Just look." She opened the box and extracted the black satin outfit.

He was slouched on the couch and he didn't get up. "Pretty spectacular," he agreed. "Should look great on you."

"That doesn't sound very enthusiastic. What's wrong, Paul?"

"The negotiations to get that Spanish dance troupe over here fell through. And I heard today that Sol Hurok is talking to the Russians about maybe bringing the Bolshoi Ballet to New York."

She dropped the dress and sat down beside him. "I'm sorry, darling. Really. But you've been trying so hard, you're bound to get a break. Please don't give up."

He looked at her for some seconds before he answered. "Juffie," he said finally. "Has it ever occurred to you that when somebody who has it all the way you do, says something like that, somebody like me wants to puke?" He got up and left the apartment before she could think of a reply.

The awards ceremony was always on a Sunday, the one day Broadway theaters were closed. Juffie came backstage after her final curtain call on an April Saturday night to find the whole cast of *Whaddaya Say* standing in the wings and waiting for her. Not surprising perhaps. Juffie had never developed a prima donna's habits. Even the people who envied her liked her.

Tim Frank stepped forward. "We all just want to wish you luck, Juffie. For tomorrow night. And whatever the American Theater Wing in their wisdom decide, we want you to know that as far as we're concerned, you're our star, babe."

Kisses and hugs all around. Juffie was still teary-eyed when she left the theater sometime after eleven. The taxi that always waited for her was by the curb, and she started for it. A man stepped out of the shadows. "Miss Kane, I'd like to speak with you."

She peered into the darkness and recognized Finky Aronson.

Her heart gave a funny little lurch, not so much fright as foreboding. "You startled me."

"Excuse me, that wasn't my intention. I believe that taxi is waiting for you." She nodded. "Then suppose we just ride uptown together."

They didn't speak in the cab. Juffie had the length of a fifteen-minute journey in which to imagine the worst. They got to Fifty-ninth Street and the driver headed east. He'd gone six blocks up Third Avenue when Aronson leaned forward and tapped him on the shoulder. "Stop here. Miss Kane and I will walk the rest of the way."

There was no fare to be paid, the cab company billed Juffie at the end of the month. Aronson climbed out first and turned and extended his hand to help her. Juffie didn't take it. He pretended not to notice. They began walking the few blocks to her building. "It's time for you to do me a small favor," Aronson said.

"What favor?"

"I want you to appear in Las Vegas. At the Crystal Room in the Desert Inn."

"Mr. Aronson, you don't seem to understand my profession. I'm an actress, which is a different kind of entertainer. I've never in my life played a nightclub. I wouldn't have the faintest idea what to do."

"You're very talented, Miss Kane. The toast of Broadway at the moment. I imagine you'll think of something."

"No, I won't. I can't do it. I'm sorry."

"Miss Kane, I thought we understood each other. You have an obligation to me. I've kept my part of the bargain, have I not? You've felt no need for a bodyguard for almost two years now."

She was thinking fast, trying to analyze the situation, determine the risks. "Why the Desert Inn in Las Vegas? Do you own it?"

"I have a small interest. And my friend, Mr. Moe Dalitz, is the entertainment director. He's in need of something special. A headliner, I believe it's called."

They were at Sixty-eighth Street and Second Avenue. Juffie had no intention of inviting him up to the penthouse. Aronson apparently didn't expect she would. He took her arm and steered her across the street to a small coffee shop that was still open. Juffie said she didn't want anything. He ordered tea with lemon.

"This Mr. Dalitz," she asked, "doesn't he have a whole list of nightclub-type entertainers that he uses regularly?"

"Of course. Every major name in the country has played the Desert Inn. But Mr. Dalitz wants something very special at the moment. Something extraordinary. You've heard of Frank Sinatra?"

"Of course." Who hadn't heard of Frank Sinatra? "But Sinatra's a singer. He's the sort of person who plays in nightclubs." She kept thinking that if she could simply make him understand the difference between what she did and what a nightclub performer did, everything would be fine. Finky Aronson would just go away and leave her alone.

"Mr. Sinatra is appearing at a new hotel in Las Vegas, the Sands. In what they call the Copa Room. He's . . . I believe the expression in your business is, packing them in."

"That's not my business, Mr. Aronson. Not hotels in Las Vegas."

"It's merely for one night, Miss Kane, only Sunday evening. Because at this critical moment the person Mr. Dalitz had booked into the Desert Inn has had a ruptured appendix. He's arranging for someone else next week. I understand perfectly that you must be back on Broadway in *Whaddaya Say* by Monday."

She leaned forward. "Wait a minute, are you asking me to perform in Las Vegas *this* Sunday night? Tomorrow?"

"Yes, exactly."

"That settles it, then. I can't, Mr. Aronson. The Tony awards are being presented tomorrow evening. I'm possibly going to get one."

"I know. You'll simply have to designate someone else to accept on your behalf. Mr. Varley perhaps, or Mr. Dumont."

Icy chills crept up her spine at this proof of how much he knew about her life. But there wasn't time to worry about that now. "I can't do that. I know it sometimes happens at the Academy Awards in Hollywood. But never at the Tonys, not unless someone is practically dead."

"You'll have to be the first, then, Miss Kane." He extracted an envelope from his pocket. "I've arranged a private airplane for you. You're to be at LaGuardia Airport at two A.M. The same arrangements will be made for your return to New York after the show. All the details are written down in here."

Juffie didn't touch the envelope. She shook her head. "No. I can't do it. Not the night of the Tonys. I know you can do something terrible to me, Mr. Aronson. But what good will that be for either of us? I'm not saying I don't have an obligation to you. Simply that this is not the way I can repay it."

"Miss Kane, you are an intelligent young woman. Kindly open that envelope."

He was such an unthreatening-looking little man with his pencil-thin mustache and his white hair. He had watery blue eyes and they were watching her intently. Juffie reached for the envelope. It wasn't sealed. She opened the flap and extracted the contents. It consisted of a typewritten sheet of paper containing the flight information he'd already explained, and an old picture.

The picture was a still that seemed to have been taken for a newspaper or a magazine. Juffie had never seen it before, but she recognized her father instantly. Myer's head had been circled by a black grease pencil, though surely she didn't need that. He was a great deal younger in the photograph, still, it was unquestionably he. He was in the front row of a group of people on some sort of march or demonstration. He was carrying one end of a large banner that proclaimed THE YOUNG COMMUNIST LEAGUE IS THE FUTURE OF AMERICA.

"That was taken in 1930, Miss Kane. A long time ago, admittedly, but presumably you've heard of the House Un-American Activities Committee. And Senator Joseph McCarthy from Wisconsin."

Juffie didn't look up, just kept staring at the picture. She nodded. There was a fever loosed in the land, a virulent infection spread by ravening wolves. And with this photograph, delivered anonymously to some office in Washington, Finky Aronson could throw her father into their jaws.

"Did you know that Alger Hiss is still in prison?" Aronson asked in a conversational tone. "He's serving four years. For perjury, I believe. And there are any number of people in your own profession—" He spread his hands eloquently.

Juffie wasn't thinking about what the red-baiters could do to her. That was more a problem in Hollywood than Broadway. But it was impossible to imagine Myer being hauled before some congressional committee. It would open the whole thing yet again. Her father was fifty-two years old, but since her mother died he seemed so much older, and he had high blood pressure. The last time she saw him he was taking a small mountain of pills every day. This could kill him. Not to mention what it would do to her grandfather.

Aronson looked at his watch. "It's after midnight. You'd better go up and get packed, Miss Kane. I'll wait for you here and accompany you to the airport. These days the city isn't safe for a woman alone at night."

Paul wasn't there, thank God. He was still mad at her because of that argument last week when she bought the dress. Juffie threw some clothes into a suitcase. At the last minute she realized she needed something to perform in and she added the black satin gown with the matching cape. She felt like bawling her head off and banging her fists against the wall, but she did neither. She found her address book and looked up Varley.

Matt didn't live in Manhattan; his home telephone was a New Jersey number. She'd never been to his house, and she did not call him there very often. She was always afraid that some man would answer. It wasn't that she had anything against homosexuals, there were plenty of them in the business. Juffie knew and liked a great many, and Harry Harcourt remained one of her closest friends. But this was different, this was Matt.

She dialed. The telephone kept ringing, but there was no answer. Goddamn men, never around when you needed them. She flipped through the pages of the address book until she came to the H's and Harry's number.

He answered on the third ring. The sounds of a party echoed in the background. "Who is this? Juffie, is it you? You sound peculiar."

"I feel peculiar. Listen, Harry, I need a favor. A big one. Are you sober enough to understand and remember in the morning?"

"I'm rapidly getting that way. What's up, doll?"

"I have to go away, to Las Vegas. I won't be at the awards ceremony tomorrow night. Harry, if I get it, will you accept for me and make some kind of excuse?"

"Juffie, are you crazy? You can't go to Las Vegas of all places. Not the night you're supposed to be getting the Tony. They'll have your head on a platter."

"I have to go. I can't explain, Harry. I just have to do it. Will you be my stand-in?"

There was a long pause. "Okay," he said finally. "I'll do it, Juffie. Only because it's you and I love you. But don't say I didn't warn you. And what do I tell them? What excuse do I make?"

She didn't dare say she was sick. Not if she was going to do a show at the Desert Inn. The truth would be known in a matter of hours. "I don't know." She couldn't think of anything. "No excuse," she said finally. "Say I'm sorry not to be with them and I thank everybody very much. You'll have to brazen it out, Harry. That's if I get it, of course."

"You're going to get it. In every sense of the word. Take care, Juffie. I hope Las Vegas is worth it."

. . . .

The flight west took ten hours. The airplane Finky Aronson had chartered for her had a small cabin with a real bed; Juffie lay on it and stared at the padded blue leatherette ceiling. She felt so rotten she didn't have time to think about her fear of flying. Besides, a nice crash right now might not have been unwelcome. Not if it was quick and final.

There was no crash. They landed uneventfully at the small airstrip in the desert on the outskirts of Las Vegas. It was nine A.M. local time, and the sun was still fairly low on the horizon, but already the heat rolled up off the tarmac in waves. Juffie descended the steps of the aircraft carrying a raincoat over her arm and cursing herself for forgetting dark glasses. By the time she walked into the squat terminal building her printed silk dress was clinging to her perspiration-soaked body. All that stuff about dry heat being different was a myth.

"Miss Kane, welcome to Las Vegas. Right this way please." A man in a light tan sport coat and an open-necked shirt led her to an enormous bright yellow Cadillac limousine. Vulgar maybe, but air-conditioned. And Las Vegas might be the new Jerusalem to some, but it was not the City on a Hill.

The place was absolutely flat, almost naked of vegetation, and ugly in its glittering newness. The Desert Inn was seven stories of white concrete fronted by the biggest marquee she'd ever seen. TONIGHT ONLY, it said in enormous letters, JUFFIE KANE, DIRECT FROM BROADWAY.

Pictures of her were plastered all over the lobby. They showed her as Delilah and as Penelope and as Myrtle, and just as herself, in a shot taken by Richard Avedon the year before for a *Vogue* feature. The magazine called her not only one of the most beautiful women in America, but one of the best dressed. How the publicity department of the Desert Inn had accumulated all this stuff in a few hours was a mystery she didn't care to solve.

Her suite was big enough for a sultan's harem and overlooked the spacious gardens behind the hotel. Here, at least, the desert was relieved by green. There was greenery inside as well, flowers on every available surface in the bedroom and sitting room, and a basket of fruit so big she couldn't lift it. A bar in one corner was stocked well enough for a bar mitzvah.

Juffie wanted a shower, but she was too exhausted and emotionally wrung out to move. She sank down on a couch upholstered in tufted white velvet and just lay her head back and tried not to think about anything. There was a light tap on the door.

"I'm Moe Dalitz," the man said when she admitted him. He held out his hand and she shook it. There wasn't any point in not doing so. "Thanks for coming on such short notice," he said. As if she'd had a choice. She wondered how much he knew. "You're even more gorgeous than your shots," he said. "We're proud to have you here at the Desert Inn. You seen the Crystal Room yet, Miss Kane?"

She shook her head.

"You'll love it. Terrific. Best stage and best lighting in town. And we seat six hundred. We've got Jack Hanes and his band to back you up. They're going over your music right now."

"I don't have any music, Mr. Dalitz. I'm not a singer. I hope you understand that."

"Sure I understand. Everybody knows Juffie Kane is an actress. I meant the music from your shows, your Broadway hits. And you do sing a couple of numbers in your latest, don't you?"

"If you can call it that."

He smiled. "Don't worry about a thing. You get some rest now and later on, whenever you like, you can go and run through your act with Jack and the boys. Just phone downstairs and give 'em five minutes. Everything will be set up. The first show ain't until ten, so you got plenty of time."

Her act. What the hell was her act supposed to be? She decided against asking Moe Dalitz that question. He started to leave, then turned back to her. "I was born in the West End, you know. I knew your grandfather. He was older than me and my crowd, but once in a while Benny would play stickball with us. I lived with my cousins, the Swerlings, in those days, on Joy Street. We were so damn poor we all three slept in one bed, me and my cousins Moe and George. A nice guy, Benny Kane. Smart. I always liked him."

.   .   .   .

"And now, ladies and gentlemen, the award for best actress in a musical." Katharine Cornell spoke into the microphones that carried the ceremony to the nation over WOR radio and the Mutual network and turned her famous wide smile on the audience in the ballroom of the Plaza. Her scarlet nails slit the envelope. "The best muscial actress of the season is . . ." She dropped her focus to the card, looked up once more, milked the drama for yet another second, then breathed forth the magic words, "Juffie Kane for Myrtle in *Whaddaya Say!*"

Cornell was one of the great troupers of all time, and she genuinely admired others of the same breed. It was she who led the enthusiastic applause.

A spotlight rigged for the occasion panned the room, then rested on the table where Matthew Varley and Paul Dumont and Karen Rice and Bernard Hanrihan sat. Myer Kane hadn't been able to make it this time. His doctor wouldn't let him travel. And Dino still wasn't permitted to leave Massachusetts. There was only one empty seat at the table, the one meant for Juffie.

Matt had been phoning everybody he knew for the past hour, but nobody could tell him where she was. Paul said he went to pick her up at six. They'd had a quarrel a week or so before, but he still expected to escort her to the awards. "But she wasn't there. No note or anything else," he explained. "I thought she came without me, so I came anyway." Karen didn't know anything either. She and Bernard had taken the train to New York that afternoon; they'd expected to meet Juffie at the Plaza.

Just before the actual ceremony began, while they were still having dinner, Matt had buttonholed Harry Harcourt. "You don't by any chance know where Juffie is? She hasn't arrived and I'm worried sick."

"She's okay. At least I think she is."

"You've talked to her?" Matt demanded.

Harry explained about the telephone call the night before. "So if she gets it, I'm going to accept on her behalf. That okay with you, Matt?"

"No. None of it's okay with me," Varley had snarled through clenched teeth. "Las Vegas. Is she out of her mind? What the hell is she doing in Las Vegas? Why didn't she call me?"

"I don't know. She just said she had to go and I should brazen it out."

"Yeah," the agent said as he turned away. "You do that, brazen it out. And I hope Juffie has some small goddamn idea of how grateful she should be for her friends. She won't have many after this stunt."

Katharine Cornell was still standing alone at the small podium next to the head table. Everybody was waiting. The fact that Juffie wasn't at the ceremony had been noted earlier, but they'd expected her to appear before the award was announced. Now the spotlight stayed on Juffie's empty seat, proving she hadn't slipped in while the lights were dimmed.

Cornell was one of the theater's empresses; she'd been thrilling audiences for nearly a quarter century, and there was nothing she didn't know about performing, but even she couldn't find an instant ad-lib suitable for this occasion. Finally Harry Harcourt rose and made his way forward. The actress turned to him with obvious relief.

"Juffie couldn't be here tonight," Harry said. "She asked me to thank you all very much. She's thrilled with the honor and she'll never forget it. Just as we'll never forget Juffie Kane." He lifted the medallion by its base and waved it at the crowd and headed back to his seat. The applause was decidedly restrained.

In Las Vegas the reception was equally cool. They'd fronted her in with a juggler and a kid called Frankie Avalon, a singer nobody had ever heard of. Avalon was pretty good, but everybody was waiting for Juffie Kane. When the emcee introduced her, the news about the Tony had just come over the wire.

"Ladies and gentlemen, tonight Juffie Kane was awarded the highest honor Broadway can give. For the second time she's won the Tony. And she has chosen to spend this evening of celebration here with us at the Crystal Room of the incomparable Desert Inn in Las Vegas." He turned and stretched out his arm. "I give you the first lady of the stage, Miss Juffie Kane."

The Hanes band struck up the overture from *Whaddaya Say.* Juffie came on wearing the black satin sheath and the swirling cape and immediately went into Myrtle's first act finale, "I Just Love You."

But there was no Tim Frank for her to bounce off, no smooth tenor to cover the high notes. It wasn't any good. Just as doing the housewives' number from the Dinah Shore show wasn't any good without Dinah. And the gag lines from *Delilah* didn't work. Nothing of the makeshift act she'd cobbled together that afternoon worked; because her heart was in New York and there were tears in the back of her throat. And for once she couldn't love the audience, and they, sensing that, didn't love her back.

Chapter 10

$\mathcal{M}$onday morning Matt found a telegram in his office saying she'd be back that night by six. He was waiting at the penthouse when she got in.

He was sitting on her green bouclé couch. Juffie dropped her suitcase and tried to smile. "Hi, I didn't expect you to be here."

"Paul loaned me his key."

She blushed. And that had to be the most stupid and inappropriate bit of business ever seen, onstage or off. Juffie headed for the kitchen.

"We have to talk," Matt called after her. "Where the hell are you going?"

"I'm getting some wine." She returned with a chilled bottle and two glasses. "There's nothing to talk about. Do you want a glass of this?"

"No I don't want any wine. I want a goddamn explanation. Juffie, are you listening to me?"

"Yes, Matt. I'm listening."

"Then say something!"

"Stop shouting at me. What can I say? I had to go to Las Vegas. As you know by now, I did a show at the Desert Inn. I was terrible."

"Everybody in town knows you did a show at the Desert Inn. They knew it some time ago. They did not know it at seven o'clock last night, when one of the greatest ladies of the stage was standing in the ballroom of the Plaza with egg on her face. When everybody who is anybody in the theater was waiting to tell you how terrific you were, and how much they loved you. When your friends from Boston, and Paul, and I were sitting at a table with an empty chair and not knowing what the hell happened. Not to

· 225 ·

mention Harry Harcourt, who played the nasty little scene you wrote for him, and had his evening ruined for his pains."

She didn't move during his speech. She simply stood and waited until he ran out of breath. "Are you finished?"

Matt ran his fingers through his hair. "Ah, Juffie, Juffie, Juffie . . . Yes, I guess I'm finished. Now it's up to you. You've got to tell me what happened. What do we say to everybody? How do we clean up this mess?"

"There isn't anything to say; we just have to brazen it out."

"That's what Harcourt said you told him to do, just brazen it out."

"That's right."

"Jesus!" He grabbed the bottle of wine and poured himself a glass and drank it in one gulp. That calmed him a little. "Okay, Juffie, if that's the way it has to be, then that's how we'll play it. But what about me? Aren't you going to tell me why you did it? Don't I get some special consideration?"

She turned from him, afraid she'd start to cry if she didn't. "I can't, Matt. I'm sorry. I just can't."

He reached out a hand as if he were going to touch her, then dropped it. "Las Vegas is full of crooks, guys from the rackets. Is that what's behind this, Juffie? Is it something to do with those creeps who cut up all your clothes?"

"Not exactly."

"What the hell does that mean, not exactly?"

"Matt, that's all I can say." She refilled her glass and her hand was trembling. "One thing though, I did try to call you as I was leaving just a little after midnight. The Jersey number."

"I was there, Juffie. I was home. I didn't get a telephone call."

"You weren't there. I let it ring and ring."

He stared at her for some seconds, then set down his glass. "I guess there's nothing more to say, is there?"

Juffie shook her head.

"Then I'm getting out of here. Suddenly I don't like the smell in this apartment. And may I remind you that you've a show to do in"—he looked at his watch—"just under an hour. One other thing, the people from that show—you know, Tim Frank, your co-star, and Mike Winters, your director, people like that—they were at the next table. They came to cheer, Juffie, and they stayed to be mortified. Maybe between now and eight o'clock you can figure out something to say to them."

She watched him walk to the door. Then, as he opened it, "Matt, are you still my agent?" in a small, weak voice.

He hesitated. "Yeah," he said finally. "Yeah, I guess I am."

. . . .

Three months later, in July, Manhattan sweltered in a heat wave. The thermometer topped a hundred for six days running. On Thursday, the hottest afternoon of them all, Dino arrived at his granddaughter's door.

"Pa, what are you doing here? No, don't try and explain yet. First come in and cool off." Juffie led the old man to a chair in the living room.

He told her he'd come by bus, decided to do it on the spur of the moment and walked into the Greyhound terminal in Boston's Park Square and bought a ticket. "It's okay. I called the house and told your dad before I left, so he wouldn't worry. He said I should give you a big kiss for him."

Dino wore a white linen suit and brown and white shoes and a panama hat. She took his jacket and his hat and made him take off his tie, and she insisted on unlacing his shoes and taking them off too. The air-conditioning was reviving him while she watched. "What do you want to drink, Pa? Wine, beer, a Coke?"

"A glass of milk, darling." He was as tall and skinny as ever and he pressed his hand to his flat belly. "I got a little ulcer. That's what the doctor called it, a little ulcer. It hurts just like a big one."

She brought him the milk and waited until he drank it, then sat down across from him. "Pa, didn't you take a big chance? Your parole . . ."

"Is finished. The parole is over. I'm a free man. Which don't mean I'm gonna do anything very different. But if I want to come and see my beautiful granddaughter in New York, nobody can stop me."

"That's why you came? Just to see me? How come you didn't let me know?"

"Spur of the moment, like I told you. Besides, I figured you'd try and talk me out of it. And we need to have a discussion, Juffie. You and me have to *degli affari*. You know what that means?"

"Talk shop."

"Right, we gotta talk shop, Juffie. You need a *consigliere*, and I'm the best you got."

She stood up and fiddled with the controls of the air-conditioner. "What shop do you want to talk about, Pa? My shop or yours?"

He shrugged. "It's the same thing. The *stronzi* are always out to get us, but the family stays together. Juffie, I been reading what they're saying about you."

A lot of people had been reading what they were saying about her. Every columnist and critic blasted her after the Tony awards. "How greedy can you get?" Winchell demanded. "They pay big bucks in Las Vegas, but the respect and admiration of your peers isn't something money can buy. And," he added, "the irony is that according to my sources, Juffie Kane laid an egg at the Desert Inn."

"When is a one-night stand in Las Vegas more important than the highest honor Broadway can bestow?" asked the man writing as Cholly Knickerbocker. He answered his own question. "When you're Juffie Kane, and success has been so fast and so easy you think all the rules of decent behavior don't apply to you."

There was a lot more, even an editorial in the *Post*. It was summer, there wasn't much happening. New York papers like the *Journal American* and the *World-Telegram* kept the story alive; so did the syndicated columnists whose words were printed across the nation.

"It will pass, Pa," she said. "It hurts, but I keep reminding myself everybody will forget about it sooner or later."

"Sure they will. But that ain't the real question. The real question is what I came down here to ask. Why'd you do it, Juffie?"

"Finky Aronson called in my IOU."

Dino nodded. "It figures. He's got money tied up in Vegas. All the boys got investments there. I thought it must be something like that."

"Okay, now you know and we can stop talking about it." She tried to make her voice gay. "Tell me what you've been doing at home. Tell me how Dad is."

"He's okay. The blood pressure stays down as long as he takes them goddamn pills. If your mama was alive he wouldn't need no pills." He took a large white handkerchief from his pocket and blew his nose loudly. "But we still ain't settled nothing, Juffie. I told you I figured it was Finky made you do the Vegas thing. What I wanna know is if it's finished. He shoulda told you the debt was paid off. It wasn't such a big debt that he should get more than you make your name lousy by going to Vegas and saving his ass when you shoulda been in New York."

"I suppose it's finished." She reached for his empty glass. "Would you like some more milk?"

"No, I don't want any more milk. I want you to tell me the truth." The black eyes studied her. "What do you mean, you suppose it's finished? Either it is or it ain't, and Finky's gotta tell you. That's the way it is. That's the rules."

"Finky Aronson doesn't play by the rules."

"Yeah, Juffie, he does. *La cosa nostra*'s got rules. And nobody gets as high as Finky if he don't stick to 'em. Believe me, I know. So what did he say?"

She couldn't deny his eyes; she never could. "I still owe him. I'll owe him until I die."

Dino expelled a long sigh through clenched teeth. It came out a whistle. "I was afraid of that. I been having dreams about you. You and my Rosa when she was little. What's Aronson got on you, Juffie? Besides what he bought from Faldo."

She was barefoot and wore white shorts and a pink shirt with the sleeves rolled up and the tails tied around her waist, no makeup, and her dark honey hair pulled into a ponytail. When she sat down hard and sprawled her long legs out in front of her she looked like a little girl again.

"Tell me, gorgeous," Dino pleaded softly. "I'm your pa, and I love you. Tell me."

"It's Dad. Aronson has a picture of him marching with something called the Young Communist League. He's threatened to send it to the House Un-American Activities Committee, or to Senator McCarthy."

"The Young Communist . . . You know how long ago that was? You were still a baby. I don't think they ever really joined, him and Rosa. They fooled around with everything back then. Everything they thought was a good cause. But your dad's a loyal American, just like me. He organized for Roosevelt, supported him all four times."

"That doesn't cut much ice now. Eisenhower's a Republican. Anyway, those committees in Washington are madmen. They're out for blood. Any blood."

"Even an ordinary mouthpiece, if maybe his father was Benny Kane and his daughter is a big star on Broadway . . . Yeah, I see it, Juffie. I don't like it, but I see it." He closed his eyes and thought for a moment, then added, "Listen, you said you got some *vino*?"

"Yes, but what about your ulcer?"

"My *little* ulcer. The hell with it. I wanna think. I think better with a glass of *vino*."

She got a bottle of Sancerre from the refrigerator and opened it and brought it to the living room.

"It's not Italian *vino*," Dino said.

"No, French. It's delicious, try it."

As he took his first sip a key turned in the lock. Paul let himself in. "Juffie . . . I'm sorry, I didn't realize you had company."

She was annoyed with him for using the key. The agreement was that he always rang the bell first, in case she was home. If she was home, she'd told him, she'd open her own door. "No, obviously you didn't. This is my grandfather, Mr. Saliatelli. Pa, this is Paul Dumont. He's from France, but he lives in New York now."

Dino stood up, the two men shook hands. "France," Dino said. "That must be why Juffie has this *vino*." He didn't comment about the man's possession of a key. The world had changed and Juffie wasn't a kid anymore.

"It's Sancerre," Paul said. "The wine of my region. My father made it, and his father before him."

Dino nodded; he understood such things. "It's good *vino*. A little weak maybe, but good."

"Not weak, just smooth," Paul said. "Have a couple of glasses, Mr. Saliatelli. Then you'll feel the kick."

"That's just what he mustn't do," Juffie said. "He has an ulcer. One glass, Pa. Sip it and make it last. I'm putting the bottle away."

Dino sat down. "Just like your mama. Always giving orders." He resumed his sipping and thinking.

Paul followed Juffie to the kitchen and took the wine bottle from her hands. "Look, I'm sorry I barged in. But don't be mad at me. Not today."

"Why shouldn't I be mad at you today?"

"Because I've just had marvelous news. I came straight here to tell you. The Spanish dance troupe, the flamenco performers from Seville. I've got it all set up. I'm bringing them to New York. A week's engagement at Carnegie Hall. Pretty classy, no?"

"Pretty classy, yes. But why a concert hall and not a theater?"

"Because theaters book a production for what they hope will be a long run. A hall is accustomed to booking for a week or two. Something like this is more like a concert than a play."

"Carnegie Hall," she repeated in tones of awe. "God, Paul, where did you get the money? Just the guarantee to the management must be a fortune."

He was putting away the wine and his head was in the refrigerator, his back to her. "It is. I found an angel."

"Who? Where?"

"Someone from the old days. A man I knew during the war. He wants to reward me for my heroism."

There was something odd about the way he said it. But she didn't pick up on his tone. She was too happy for him, and she knew how he hated to remember the war. "It's wonderful, Paul. I'm thrilled for you, really."

He hugged her and kissed her hard. "That's a promise for later. I have to get back to the theater, but I wanted to tell you in person, not on the phone." He glanced toward the living room. "Is your grandfather staying long?"

"I don't know. Two or three days, I imagine. You'll have to sleep alone for a few nights, lover."

"Don't be so sure," he said, tweaking her nose. "Because you're sleeping alone doesn't mean I am."

Juffie opened the top buttons of her shirt and pulled his hands inside the cotton. She wasn't wearing a bra; she didn't need to. Juffie's breasts weren't just large, they were extraordinarily high and firm. "Where are you going to find anything better than this?" she asked in a husky whisper.

Paul groaned softly. "Nowhere. There isn't anything better. Not in the whole damn world. Marry me, Juffie."

"Not today. I have to take care of my grandfather."

Dino remained in New York for three days. That first evening Juffie took him to Mama Leone's, the most flamboyant Italian restaurant in the city, then seated him in a box at the Imperial.

He'd never before seen her onstage and she played her heart out that night. For Dino. The things the theater community were saying about Juffie had not affected the audiences of *Whaddaya Say*. They loved her. Juffie took six curtain calls, and on the last one she looked up to the box and blew a two-handed kiss to her grandfather.

When she'd changed, she offered to take him to Sardi's for a drink. "It's the traditional place for after a show, Pa. Would you like to go?"

"Not tonight, Juffie, if you don't mind. I'm not as young as I was. All this big-night-on-the-town stuff ain't for me anymore."

She was relieved. She hadn't been in Sardi's since the disaster with the Tonys, and she wasn't eager to go now. They left the darkened theater and rode uptown in the taxi that, as usual, was waiting for Juffie.

In the back of the cab Dino took her hand and held it. "You were wonderful, gorgeous. Wonderful. But one thing I can't figure out. You get all wet at the end of the first act. Then a few minutes later you come back and your hair's dry."

"It's a wig, Pa. I wear a real tight bathing cap over my own hair for that scene, and a wig over that."

Dino nodded. "Yeah, it figures. Every business, you got tricks. Ways of doing things the civilians don't know nothin' about."

Friday the heat broke and they walked together in Central Park, and visited the zoo, and ate peanuts and fed the monkeys. Dino wanted to see Macy's. It was the only New York department store he knew about, because he always watched the Thanksgiving Day parade. And he told her he'd seen *Miracle on 34th Street* three times, twice when it was shown in the prison, once on television.

Dino bought six shirts: three for him, three for Myer. Juffie bought gold key rings for her father and grandfather, and had a little gold charm attached to each. "See," she pointed out. "It's a replica of the Statue of Liberty. A souvenir."

"Juffie," Dino said solemnly, "liberty ain't no souvenir. It's the most important thing in the whole goddamn world."

She arranged for him to take the *Yankee Clipper* back to Boston on Saturday afternoon. The train left before she was due at the theater to get ready for the matinee, but they had time for an early lunch. Dino said he wanted to go to Lindy's. "Benny was all the time talking about it. He came here a coupla times in the twenties."

They ordered corned beef sandwiches on rye. Dino said he wasn't going to worry about his ulcer the one time in his life he got to Lindy's. "Save some room, Pa. You have to taste the cheesecake afterwards. That's what they're famous for, the cheesecake."

"Hope you and your guest enjoy it, Miss Kane," the waiter said when he brought two enormous slabs of cake topped with cherries.

Dino looked at her. "You eat here a lot?"

"Pa, if I ate like this all the time, I'd weigh so much I'd collapse the stage. But today's a celebration. Today I'm in Lindy's with my grandfather, and I don't give a damn about calories."

Dino ate a few mouthfuls, then pushed the cake away. "It's delicious, but too rich. Listen, gorgeous, I've been thinking about our problem."

"Don't," she said. "Don't worry about it, Pa. It's my problem, not yours."

"That's crap. We're family, you're my flesh and blood. Besides, I'm your *consigliere*, and a *consigliere* is worth nothin' unless he gives good advice."

"Okay, what's your advice?"

"We gotta get something on Aronson. So's we can trade."

"What? How?"

"I'm not sure yet. But I'm going to work on it. When I got it figured out I'll let you know."

When they left the restaurant there was a man with a camera waiting for them on Broadway. He aimed it quickly. "Smile for the birdie, Miss Kane."

She was startled but not astounded. The friendly waiter had probably tipped off the photographer; it happened all the time.

Dino started forward, as if he were still young, as if he meant to snatch the camera away from the reporter. Juffie placed a restraining hand on his arm. "Don't, Pa. It's okay. I'm used to it."

"Not me," he grumbled in a low voice. "I ain't used to it. In the old days he'd have died for trying that."

"It's not the old days, Pa," she said gently. "Come on, we'll take a cab to Grand Central and I'll put you on the train."

She insisted on sending him home in a first-class seat in the parlor car, and she bought the ticket and led him downstairs to the departure level. They had a few minutes to spare, so they walked along the platforms. There were no trains to be seen, they were behind closed bronze doors set in marble. Grand Central wasn't merely a railway station, it was a shrine of sorts, a magical gateway to the city that believed itself the top of the heap.

Dino was fascinated by everything, especially Track 34, where a red and gray carpet was rolled out along the platform. The words "Twentieth-Century Limited" were woven into the carpet. It was the name of the express that left the station every night at six for the sixteen-hour journey to Chicago.

"More and more people are flying everywhere," Juffie said. "But for my money, this is still the only way to travel."

"Things change," Dino said. "You gotta change with 'em."

Juffie laughed. "That should be my line, you should be insisting that everything stay the same."

"I see things like they are, gorgeous. Not the way I want 'em to be."

It was time. They went to the open doors behind which waited the gleaming cars of the *Yankee Clipper.* She kissed him good-bye and hugged him hard. Then, just before he boarded, Dino turned to her. "I almost forgot. I saw your friend Karen a week or so ago. Ran into her on Tremont Street near the Common. She looked a little funny."

"How funny? Is something wrong?" She talked to Karen on the telephone once or twice a month, but she hadn't seen her in ages.

"I don't know, probably not. But she looked a lot older. Her hair's different, maybe that's it."

"Maybe. And she could be tired. She had a big disappointment a little while ago. Her doctoral dissertation wasn't accepted. She didn't get the degree."

Television had widened Dino's world sufficiently, so he had at least some idea what she was talking about. "Too bad, Karen's a nice girl. They probably were looking for a little grease."

"I don't think so, Pa. I don't think you get a Ph.D. with vigorish."

The conductor called, "All aboard," and she kissed her grandfather good-bye again and made a mental note to see Karen as soon as she could.

. . . .

The week after Dino's visit *Confidential* ran a story about Juffie Kane's background. It was largely a rehash of the things that had been printed in the Boston *Record American* five years before when she was playing Delilah, but they updated it with a picture taken a few days earlier outside Lindy's on Broadway. "Juffie Kane with her grandfather, ex-Syndicate boss, Dino Saliatelli," said the caption.

Confidential was a bimonthly rag, a scandal sheet that was constantly being sued for one or another kind of libel, which made their sanctimonious closing paragraph particularly hard to take. "No one can be blamed for the family they're born to, not even Juffie Kane. Juffie's mistake seems to be in not disassociating herself from her family's sins. And this while she provides what's sometimes called family entertainment . . ."

Things were very strained between Juffie and Matt, but he remained her agent and their professional lives were thoroughly intertwined. He called her a few hours after *Confidential* hit the stands.

"You've seen it?"

"Of course. With my face on the cover it was hard for me to ignore. Besides, they carry it in my neighborhood candy store. I went down for some Cracker Jacks and got a surprise before I opened the box."

"Do you want to sue?"

"What's the point?"

"I don't know. I'm asking what you want to do."

"It isn't libel if it's the truth, is it?"

"Not exactly. Though we could claim invasion of privacy and grievous mental anguish."

"What would it accomplish?"

"Not a great deal," he admitted. "A dozen people have sued them on those grounds. Mostly they've lost."

"And it would keep the whole thing alive, make more headlines."

"Yes."

"Let's forget it," Juffie said.

"As you wish." He hesitated. "Juffie . . . can't you tell me something? If you'd just explain the whole story, maybe I could help."

"There's nothing for me to explain. You can read all about it in *Confidential*." She didn't exactly slam down the telephone, but neither did she say good-bye.

She was sorry as soon as the connection was broken. Matt didn't deserve such treatment. But she was so angry and so hurt, and so frightened for her father and her grandfather and herself. And Matt's was one of the few opinions she really cared about. She'd rather he think she'd had a terrible lapse in judgment than know she'd been dumb enough to let somebody from the *cosa nostra* take control of her life. Moreover, she was terrified every time she thought of the possibility of Finky Aronson sending that picture of Myer to McCarthy, or of somebody else getting hold of it and printing it.

All the ifs were too terrible to contemplate. She wanted to keep her mouth shut, and curl up in a corner, and be quiet until it all went away.

Meanwhile there was Paul, and he seemed oblivious to the gossip swirling around Juffie. She found that comforting. He held her and loved her and told her how much he adored her—and he never spoke about racketeers or the Syndicate. The only time he mentioned the disastrous night of the Tony awards it was to ask about Karen. "What does your girlfriend from Boston see in that old guy she runs around with?"

"God knows. I've been trying to figure it out for years. And she's so cute and smart and funny, she could have any man she wanted."

"Smart maybe," he agreed. "But she didn't strike me as cute or funny. I was surprised when I saw she was older than you."

"She's not. Karen's almost a year younger than I am."

"Doesn't look it," Paul said. Then he changed the subject. He was full of his plans for the Spanish dancers; he was sure they would take New York by storm.

·   ·   ·   ·

Juffie's contract allowed her to leave *Whaddaya Say* in November 1953. In August she started asking Matt to keep an eye out for something new.

"There's not a lot coming in," he said. "Maybe you should stay put until the right property comes along."

"I don't want to stay put. This thing I do that is supposed to be singing and isn't is killing my throat. I'm using sprays and taking pills, but nothing seems to help."

"Gargle," he said curtly. "But stick with Myrtle. You can't afford to be between shows."

Good old Matt, still a dollar sign where his heart should be. She flounced out of the office, and to console herself she went to the fur salon at Bendel's and bought a six-thousand-dollar fitted lynx coat with a wide sable hem and a sable collar.

Toward the end of the month she learned that Moss Hart was casting a new comedy called *Anniversary Waltz*. She heard about it from one of the kids in the chorus of *Whaddaya Say*. The girl, Lucy Warren, adored Juffie and always told her about the casting calls she'd been on and her hopes for the future. Juffie always listened. "I know we're going to run forever, Miss Kane," Lucy said. "But I don't really want to be a dancer. I figure if I can get a speaking part, well . . ."

"You're right, Lucy, keep trying. What's the Hart show like?"

"Terrific, very funny," Lucy said. "The leading lady's show all the way."

Juffie called Matt first thing the next morning. "How come I haven't seen a script for Moss Hart's new play?"

"I think he's going to use his wife."

Hart was married to Kitty Carlisle. "Was the show written for her specifically?" Juffie asked.

"I don't know. I don't think so."

"What you're saying is that whoever else has seen it, we weren't sent the script in advance."

"No. We weren't."

"I see."

"Juffie, look, it will blow over. You're working, the paying customers love you. Just ride with it, huh? As soon as something good comes in, I'll let you know."

The problem was that she couldn't live without a new challenge, a new role to create. She owned Myrtle, she'd done everything she could do with the would-be actress from Brooklyn, explored every nuance of the character. It was getting boring. Besides, her throat really did hurt a lot.

In September Ramón Viera, the flamenco dancer from Seville, arrived in New York with his company. All told, there were forty of them, and case after case of costumes and props and instruments. And Paul didn't speak Spanish. The logistics were a nightmare despite the painstaking preparatory work he'd done. For a full week after the Spaniards arrived, Paul spent every waking hour running around Manhattan with an interpreter in tow.

The few times she saw him, Juffie reassured him with all the old theatrical platitudes, promised him it would be all right on opening night, but he looked so frazzled and harried, she couldn't help but worry.

"The lighting's all wrong," Paul complained. "I've got to bring in another lighting expert, nobody on the staff of the hall can fix it. And the stage is too small. Viera's having to adjust his routines. He just loves that, as you can imagine."

"He should love it," Juffie insisted. "Playing Carnegie Hall in New York City is worth a little extra effort."

"Try telling him that," Paul said.

Juffie didn't make it to a rehearsal of the flamenco dancers, so she never had the opportunity to lecture Ramón Viera on his good fortune. And she certainly never told Paul she thought it might have been a mistake booking them into Carnegie Hall rather than into a theater despite the difficulties about the length of the run.

It might not have looked to the principals as if they'd ever manage to open, but the publicity appeared on schedule. "Paul Dumont Presents Ramón Viera and His Spanish Dance Company," the full page ads in the newspapers proclaimed. "One Week's Exclusive Engagement at Carnegie Hall." The advance sale was good. On Thursday Paul told her they were sold out for Saturday's opening night.

"I'm so sorry I won't be there. I'll get away the minute after the final curtain."

"No you won't; your fans won't permit it. Take all your curtain calls, darling. Just come be with me at the party afterwards."

The party was at the Russian Tea Room on Fifty-seventh Street, next door to the hall. By the time Juffie arrived, the decibel level announced that the show had been a success. The restaurant's enormous paintings on pine-green walls, its cranberry glass hurricane lamps on pink tablecloths, and its glittering brass samovars all reflected the glow of people immensely pleased with themselves.

Juffie slid in beside Paul and kissed him. "I don't have to ask, but I will. Was it wonderful?"

He put his arm around her and pressed her close. "*Magnifique,* marvelous! They brought down the house. Seven curtain calls and two encores. The audience didn't want to let them go." He turned to the interpreter on his right. "Please tell Señor Viera I want him to meet my fiancée, the famous actress, Juffie Kane."

He always did that, introduced her as his fiancée. She'd stopped remonstrating with him about it. She leaned across the table and shook the dancer's hand. "*Felicidades,* Señor Viera. *Bienvenido a Nueva York.*"

"Hey," Paul said. "I didn't know you spoke Spanish."

"I don't. Two years of it at the Chestnut Hill School for Young Ladies, but that's about my whole vocabulary."

Viera had come to the same erroneous conclusion; he was leaning across Paul and chattering in Spanish to Juffie. She simply smiled and nodded. The interpreter sized up the situation. "He says you are the most beautiful woman he's ever seen," he explained. "He says some time he must dance for you—privately."

She kept smiling and reached for the tiny glass of vodka someone had set in front of her. It was icy cold, bottles of vodka in ice buckets ringed the tables, and it went down easily, soothing her parched throat. She poured herself another. "Easy," Paul said. "That stuff's dynamite. You'd better eat something." He spooned caviar and blinis onto a plate and put a fork in her hand.

This affair had to be costing the earth. "I suppose it's crazy," Paul had said earlier. "A Frenchman brings a Spaniard to America and they celebrate in a Russian restaurant. But there aren't any really classy Spanish places. I've checked. And The Russian Tea Room is classy."

It certainly was. And exceptionally popular with performing artists. The room was crowded with them. Juffie smiled and nodded to at least a dozen familiar faces. They nodded in return, so she was probably imagining that their smiles seemed cooler than in the past.

Not Finky Aronson's though. His smile was broad when he approached the table. "Good evening, Miss Kane. I want to congratulate Mr. Dumont here. A triumph. I was in the audience and I loved it. So did everyone else."

Paul murmured his thanks. Aronson moved off through the crowd.

"How do you happen to know him?" Juffie asked. She'd been

lifting a forkful of caviar to her lips when Aronson arrived. She was still holding it, but she didn't feel like eating.

"He's a film buff. Comes to the Fifty-fifth Street theater all the time." He turned away from her to speak to another well-wisher who'd approached from the other side.

Juffie stared after Aronson's retreating back. The caviar tasted of ashes.

· · · ·

The Viera company was held over an extra week at Carnegie Hall, by popular demand, as the notices said. Before the opening, Paul had been trying with little success to book a nationwide tour for them. Now he was buried under requests for appearances in St. Louis and Cincinnati and Chicago and Los Angeles, and all points between. Best of all, Ed Sullivan's people called. They wanted the flamenco dancers to do a spot on *Toast of the Town*.

"I'm on my way," Paul said exultantly to Juffie. "Nothing can stop me now. Screw that guy Hurok and the Bolshoi. They're not here yet, are they? But I am. Oh yes, I am."

They were in bed together for the first time in ten days. The sex was fantastic. It was always good, but a ten-day drought caused by Paul's hectic schedule made it superb. At first he didn't linger, he took her and allowed them both a swift, almost superficial orgasm. After that he exerted all the skill and control that gave them such exquisite pleasure. He was stroking her while he talked, running his fingertips over the inside of her thighs.

"Yes, you're here." She groaned. "Oh . . . oh . . . there, touch me there."

"Beg me," he whispered. "Beg me."

"Please. Please, Paul. Please."

"Please what? What do you want me to do?"

"Put your fingers inside me. Let me come."

"No, not inside. Like this." He used one finger and brushed lightly over her clitoris. It drove her crazy. She arched toward him, put her hand over his and tried to increase the pressure. "No," he whispered. "I say when. You just lie there and let me do what I want to do." He continued the feathery stroking, so light it was almost no touch at all.

"I can't stand it." She moaned. "I can't wait anymore."

"Don't move. Don't let any part of you move or I'll punish

you. I'll spank you hard. Lie absolutely still and let it build. Even when you come, don't move."

It was different from any climax she'd ever reached before; utterly internalized, an implosion of feeling that lasted almost a full minute. "My God," she said breathlessly afterward. "I'll never get over what a maestro you are."

"Because you are a perfect instrument." He bent his head and kissed her breasts. "Marry me, Juffie. I'm on my way to the success I've dreamed of. I need you to make it complete."

For once she didn't say no. "Maybe. I'm not sure, Paul. Give me more time."

. . . .

At the end of the month she went to a new throat doctor. The old one wasn't helping her a bit. Dr. Merton was recommended by an opera singer she'd met because they both used the same hairdresser. One day at the salon Juffie confided her problem, a throat that was always irritated, and the diva sent her to an office on Madison Avenue.

The doctor examined her thoroughly, then invited her to the consultation room. He sat at a huge mahogany desk, bare except for a spray of fresh orchids. There was a large oil painting on the wall behind the desk. The painting looked like an old master; it probably was. His fee for an initial visit was three hundred dollars.

"Strain, Miss Kane." He pronounced the word as if it were an exotic disease. Slowly and with feeling. "Strain. Not just your throat, though that's the most acute symptom. Your entire body is showing the result of stress. When was the last time you took a vacation?"

"I don't remember. I did a lot of television before my present show. I had more free time then, but I wouldn't call it a vacation."

"No, neither would I. Well, what you do is up to you, but I will tell you my prognosis. If you don't take a rest, stop singing in this peculiar voice you've affected"—he'd obviously seen her on-stage—"you will lose both it and your normal speaking voice. I don't wish to be an alarmist, but you could do permanent damage."

"How long a rest?" Juffie asked.

"I can't say exactly. I'll give you something to deal with the immediate discomfort, but you must give your larynx at least two or three months to recover. I cannot overemphasize how dire the results will be if you do not. Two or three months, then we'll see."

Paul was in St. Louis with the Spaniards. But it wasn't he who first occurred to her anyway. As always in a crisis she went to Matt. She telephoned him the moment she left the doctor's office. "I need to talk to you, right away."

He heard the sob in her voice. "Juffie, where are you?"

"Madison and Eighty-ninth. In a phone booth."

"Listen, you're near the Croydon Hotel. Eighty-sixth Street. I'll meet you there, in the Peach Tree Lounge, as soon as I can get uptown."

He was with her in twenty minutes. It was three in the afternoon, there were few people in the tiny bar. Juffie was at a small table in the corner of the room. "Hi." He leaned over and brushed her cheek with a kiss of greeting. He hadn't done that in months. "What's up, doc?" he asked in a funny Bugs Bunny voice.

"That's what's up," she said. "Funny voices. I've just left Dr. Merton, a throat man who specializes in opera singers. He says if I don't shut up for two months, maybe three, I'm going to lose my voice altogether. Possibly forever. I may be dumb, Matt, but I can't face being dumb, if you see what I mean." She took a handkerchief from her alligator bag.

He waited until she'd dabbed at her eyes, then reached for her hand. "There's no debate about what you have to do, Juffie. If that's the best medical advice, you have to follow it. Exit Myrtle, stage left."

"Leave the show? You said I shouldn't."

"I said that before Dr. Merton. Now we're in the post-Merton era. Your contract's got another two months to run, but they'll have to let you out early for illness. And I happen to know they've been covering their bases, talking to Gwen Verdon. They want her to play Myrtle if you leave. If she says no, they'll probably take a road company to the West Coast. Nothing seems to be decided, but I don't think there's going to be a problem."

"I'm the problem. What will I do with myself? I've been working steadily since 1948, that's almost six years. I won't know what to do."

He grinned. "You'll think of something. I know you, Juffie; you'll think of something."

"I'll read scripts. That is if there are scripts to read. Matt, has anyone asked for me?"

He looked away. "Not exactly, but I'm working on a couple of things."

"Don't lie to me. One slip, one false move, and I'm a pariah. What's that poem, 'It was roses, roses all the way.'"

" 'With myrtle mixed in my path like mad.' Then something, something, something, I can't remember. Then, 'A year ago this very day.' It's Browning, 'The Patriot.'"

Trust Matt with his tweeds and his pipe and his neatly brushed sandy hair and his horn-rimmed reading glasses; trust him to know the reference. "How does it end?"

He furrowed his brow. "Can't remember the very end, but I know what you're thinking of. 'I go in the rain, and, more than needs, a rope cuts both my wrists behind. And I think, by the feel, my forehead bleeds, for they fling, whoever has a mind, stones at me for my year's misdeeds.' That's it, isn't it?"

"That's it. And only one misdeed."

"But it was a pretty big one, Juffie. The *Confidential* story wouldn't have been half as damaging if people weren't still smarting from the Tony fiasco."

It was the first time in months that they'd mentioned it directly. "I know," she said. "Matt, I didn't mean to drop you in at the deep end. I really did try to call you the night before. I wasn't lying."

"No, I know you weren't. I was home, but apparently my line was out of order. I found out later, but I thought it was better to let the subject lie. Anyway, it doesn't matter. If I'd told you not to go, would you have listened?"

She shook her head. "Matt, believe me, I had no choice."

He leaned forward, holding both her hands now. "Juffie, are you mixed up with the mob, the Syndicate, whatever they call them? I don't mean through your family, I mean you yourself."

She knew that was the word around town, not just that she'd rebuffed her own profession when they wanted to honor her, or that she had notorious relatives. The gossip said that Juffie Kane was somehow tied into the rackets. That she worked for hoods.

"No, I'm not. Not the way you mean. Let it rest, Matt. It's done and over."

"Okay. We won't talk about it again. And about the show, I'll call Mike as soon as I go back to the office." Protocol demanded that the director be told before the official word to the management. Juffie knew that as well as Matt. She nodded. "Let's say I tell him you have to leave by the end of next week," he added. "Can you go on that long?"

"Yes, of course. And I'll make it my business to see Mike tonight after the show, tell him how sorry I am."

"Good. That's settled, then."

"Yes. Matt, you will keep looking for something for me, won't you. The doctor said I need only two or three months off."

"Of course." He hesitated. "Look, I wasn't going to say anything yet because it's premature. But you need some cheering up, and a little bird told me that Sadie and Phil Leonard are just finishing a new play."

The Leonards were the husband and wife team who wrote *Delilah*. "That's wonderful!" Juffie clapped her hands in delight. "We got along marvelously. I'm sure they—"

"Don't get excited yet. Let me see what they've got, if anything."

Three days later he called her. "Juffie, I'm sorry, it's no go with the Leonards."

"Why not? Isn't the lead right for me?"

"I don't know. They didn't let me see the script. They're talking to Deborah Kerr. And Jack Fine's the producer. You know how he feels."

She did, all too well.

The following Saturday she gave her final performance as Myrtle. It was a tearful occasion. Verdon had turned them down and the management had decided to close the show on Broadway and take it on the road with a lesser star. Juffie felt as if her life were closing. She spent all Sunday alone in the apartment brooding. Monday morning she made up her mind to take the initiative.

. . . .

Juffie had been there before; she knew what she'd see when the door opened. Nessa Fine spent a great deal of her husband's money. But she did it very well. The foyer of the apartment on Park Avenue and Eighty-second Street was lined with walnut paneling. The floors were parquet and the carpet was an exquisite Oriental in jewellike colors. Ultra chic combined with perfect taste, the sort of thing Paul had in mind when he kept nagging her to get a decorator for the penthouse.

Nessa herself answered the summons of the discreet door chimes. If there were servants, they weren't in evidence. "Juffie, you're a surprise. Did you want to see Jack? He's not in at the moment."

"No, not Jack. Nessa, I'd like to speak with you. I would have phoned first, but I wasn't sure you'd see me."

"Of course I would. Come in here, we'll be more comfortable." She led Juffie into the library. Another Oriental rug, and more walnut paneling, and shelf after shelf of books bound in the same mulberry leather. There was also a sofa upholstered in pale blue linen. Nessa sat down on it and patted the place beside her. "Sit down and tell me what's on your mind."

"The Leonards' new show," Juffie said, coming straight to the point. "Matt says I wasn't even sent a script. And I've been playing to constant full houses in *Whaddaya Say*, Nessa. Not to mention that I packed them in as Delilah."

"You're the greatest, Juffie, a superb actress. Nobody is denying it."

"Then why is Jack freezing me out? Even if the gossip were true, Nessa, which it isn't, what would that have to do with my ability to fill a theater?"

"Jack's not freezing you out, as you put it. He's . . ." Nessa hesitated. "I guess the word is frightened."

"Frightened! Of me? That's absurd. I work damned hard in any show I'm in. Jack of all people should know that. Matt says—"

"He's frightened because he feels he can't trust you," Nessa interrupted. "He was more hurt than angry over that business with *Delilah*. Terribly hurt. The thing he can't get over is that when he confronted you, you never even said you were sorry."

"I did!"

"Jack says you didn't. The way he remembers it, you didn't."

She thought for a moment, trying to reconstruct the long-ago scene in Schrafft's on Fourteenth Street. "Maybe I didn't, I can't remember exactly. I just know how hurt I was. I thought he was accusing me, not even trying to understand my feelings. And when Matt called him about my *Pygmalion* idea, he didn't want to discuss it. He wouldn't even talk to Matt or to me."

Nessa shook her head sadly. "Not talking. That's how most misunderstandings happen. Look, wait here a moment, I'll get us some tea."

She left the room and Juffie had time to study the books and pictures. There was one wall devoted to still shots from all the Fine productions. The turkeys were up there as well as the hits. She was represented twice, once as the ill-fated Hannah Glemp, once as Delilah.

"Jack says he wants an accurate record even if that means it's sometimes a painful one." Nessa had returned with a tea tray. She put it down and came and stood beside Juffie and looked at the pictures. "It's hard to think there'll never be another picture of you in our gallery," she said softly. "I don't believe it's true. Jack's afraid to work with you because he thinks you'll let him down somehow, that he can't trust you. But I think he's wrong, and I know a talent like yours doesn't come along every day in the week."

"Thank you for the kind words," Juffie said. "But I have the feeling you're avoiding a direct discussion about the Leonards' new play. I don't even know what it's called."

"*A Time for Lilies,* and they're signing Deborah Kerr this morning. That's where Jack is right now." She poured the tea and handed Juffie a cup.

Fussing with the tea gave Juffie a chance to regain her composure. That she'd come here and laid bare her soul when it was already too late hurt like hell. She didn't want to humiliate herself further by crying.

"How's your throat?" Nessa asked. "We heard you had to leave *Whaddaya Say* two months early on doctor's orders."

"Yes, but it's already getting better. It was that crazy singing, if you can call it that."

"I call it wonderful," Nessa said, smiling. "Do you know I saw it three times?"

"Did you?"

"Yes, three consecutive Saturday matinees. I just couldn't get enough."

Juffie set down the teacup. "Thanks. For everything. I can't think of a terrific exit line, so I'd better just leave."

Later Nessa discussed the visit with her husband. "What's she worried about?" Jack asked. "She can always work for the mob. Anyway, her boyfriend's raking it in just now. That Spanish dance troupe is making him a fortune."

"You know, it's funny," Nessa said thoughtfully. "She mentioned Matt Varley's name every other sentence, but she didn't talk about Paul Dumont once."

"Matt's her agent. It's natural she should talk about him."

"No, I think it's more than that. I told you ages ago, Jack. I think she fancies him."

"Fancies him, another one of your English expressions." He patted her rear end. "I love it when you talk dirty. Anyway, if there was anything between those two, they couldn't have kept it secret for six years. You're imagining things. My wife, the *shatkin*."

"What's that?"

"A matchmaker. How the hell do you English Jews manage to know so little?"

She ignored that question for one of her own. "Are you going to call Juffie?"

"Why should I? We signed Deborah Kerr this morning."

"Not about the show. To make up. She's down now, Jack. This is when she needs her friends."

"I used to be a friend of hers. Not anymore. What's for dinner?"

A week later she raised the subject again. "Jack, I've been doing some checking."

Nessa had been a newspaperwoman in London before the war, and during it she'd worked for some kind of intelligence operation he preferred not to know too much about. "What kind of checking?"

"Just checking. On Matthew Varley. After we talked, it occurred to me that he's a bit mysterious."

"Why should you care about Matt Varley? And if you'd ever sat in a negotiation with him, you wouldn't say mysterious. A shyster's more like it. He squeezes out the last penny. And there's a clause for everything that could maybe bother his client if the world just happened to come to an end during the show." He took a long swallow of the whiskey sour she'd made him when he came in. "What did you find out?"

"I thought you didn't care."

"You're sitting there with a look on your face like the cat that got into the cream. Of course I care. C'mon, what?"

"Jack, he's married."

"Married! I don't believe it. In all these years I've never seen him with a wife. Not with any woman, come to think of it. Where the hell does he keep her? In a locker in Grand Central Station?"

"No. In Englewood Cliffs, New Jersey."

Chapter 11

"Karen, what is all this garbage?"
Juffie had restrained herself during lunch at the Union Oyster House on Canal Street in Boston, but by the time they got to coffee her frustration exploded. "What's going on?"

"I don't know what you're talking about. And don't shout, Juffie. People are staring."

"People stare at me. I'm an actress, an infamous one at the moment. Staring goes with the territory. The hell with people. I want to know about you. What is this crazy talk you've been giving me for over an hour?"

"There's nothing crazy about intelligence testing for children from non-English–speaking backgrounds. That's what I've been trying to explain. It requires a different approach, but psychologists have been ignoring the fact."

Juffie shook her head impatiently. "I don't mean that. As much as I can understand what you're saying makes sense. And I think it's great that you're trying again, not giving up on the Ph.D. It's just—"

"I wouldn't dream of giving up on the degree," Karen interrupted. "It would be such a disappointment for Bernard."

"There you go again! That's what I'm talking about. Sweetie, you haven't spoken one sentence that doesn't include his name."

It was true. She'd put off this trip home until the third week in September in large part because she didn't want to field a lot of questions about what really happened the night of the Tony awards. She expected Karen to probe incessantly, to insist on "the straight story." But now that she'd come, galvanized because Pa was ill, Karen said almost nothing that wasn't related to Bernard Hanrihan.

So it was Juffie who brought up Las Vegas, to fill the silence that ensued after she accused Karen of being fixated on her lover. "I'm sorry about the way I let you down the night of the Tonys. I had to go to Las Vegas, no choice. Karen, it's the most incredible town—"

"Don't!"

"Don't what?"

"Talk about Las Vegas," Karen said through clenched teeth. "I hate it. And I'm not mad at you about the Tonys."

Juffie narrowed her eyes and studied her friend. "What can you possibly know about Las Vegas?"

"I went there once, with Bernard. After we came home I had these terrible dreams . . ." She actually shuddered; Juffie saw the tremors. "I don't want to talk about it," she repeated.

"Okay, we won't talk about it. What I can't accept is that we have to talk exclusively about Bernard. It's weird. It's almost as if you've exchanged your personality for his. Where's the Karen I knew and loved?"

"Nobody else loved her." Karen stirred a spoonful of sugar into her coffee. "The doctoral examining board didn't think she was worth much at all."

Juffie was watching the bit of business with the coffee. "Karen, you don't take sugar. You've never put sugar in a cup of coffee in all the years I've known you."

"What? Oh, that. Bernard does. His wife, Bess, did too. So he usually puts it in mine, absentmindedly. And I got into the habit."

"Hmm. And did you get into the habit of forgetting to have your hair cut? Is that why you're wearing it in that godawful bun thing?"

Karen touched her hair. "I don't think it's godawful. It's professional looking."

"Maybe. If your profession is grave digger." She leaned across the table and grabbed Karen's hand. "Sweetie, something is happening to you. I don't like it. It scares me. Look, I'm between shows. Come to New York for a few weeks. You've met Paul only once, at the awards. And the circumstances were strained, to say the least. But he's a lot of fun. We'll have a marvelous time. We'll go shopping, and to the movies, and to lots of shows."

"I can't, Juffie." Karen smiled to take the sting out of the refusal. "It's very sweet of you to ask me, but I have my work to do. Do you know that Bess got her doctorate and taught at Radcliffe, and wrote textbooks on intelligence testing to boot? Isn't that amazing? She did all those things so well, and she hung on to Bernard too."

Juffie fished a pill out of her bag and reached for a glass of water. In the time it took to swallow Dr. Merton's medicine, she thought she'd figured it out. "Is that what you're worried about? Do you think you're losing Bernard, the almighty paragon?"

"No, of course not. We love each other. But . . ."

"Yes? Come on, Karen, give. As you used to say, this is me, Juffie. But what?"

Karen smiled at the words, but it was a weak imitation of the old pixie grin and it quickly faded into a frown. "He was crushed when my thesis was rejected. For me, of course, because he knew how disappointed I was. But he was a little annoyed too. He'd warned me not to choose that subject. Crime and the immigrant experience. He thought it was too sordid. The examiners said it was too sociological, not sufficiently specific to the discipline of psychology. That's a direct quote, but the real reason was the one Bernard gave. He was right."

"The fact that you bombed doesn't make him right. Maybe you just didn't do it as well as you should have. Maybe you should try a different angle rather than a different subject."

Karen shook her head. "No, Bernard was correct. He's very wise. Bernard has a lot of wisdom."

"Oh, Jesus, I give up."

But she couldn't. Not when she was looking at Karen in an extraordinary outfit that made her look like a forty-year-old with advanced jaundice. A dark brown tailored suit and a beige rayon blouse primly buttoned up to its Peter Pan collar did nothing for Karen's coloring. And oxfords yet. Lace-up oxfords. Juffie almost didn't recognize her when they met. But the real Karen was there underneath; she had to be.

Juffie tried again. "Why didn't you talk to me when you were writing the thesis? My family should be a prime example. Of course your own can provide plenty of material as well."

Karen pursed her lips. "I didn't want to bother you. And I don't see much of my parents these days."

"What does that mean? What's much?"

"I said not much. Infrequently. On rare occasions. All proper English expressions, I believe."

"Proper English expressions and proper horseshit. Karen, are you ashamed of Leah? Have you forgotten what got you into Simmons in the first place, so you could start on this brilliant career in psychology? Not to mention meet Bernard the sage."

"Of course not."

"Then why are you telling me you don't see your folks?"

"Bernard isn't comfortable with people like my parents. And they aren't comfortable with him. They don't understand our decision not to go through the formality of a wedding ceremony."

Juffie opened her wallet and took out two five-dollar bills. "No, I'll bet they don't get along, Bernard and Leah and Jake. I don't find that hard to understand at all." She stood up and dropped the pair of fives on the table. "I can't talk to you when you're like this, Karen. Besides, I have to go see Pa. He's in the hospital, as I think I mentioned."

"I'll come with you."

"No, don't bother. Your boyfriend, the fount of wisdom, would doubtless disapprove of your visiting Dino Saliatelli. Just one thing—someday the curtain will come down on the Bess and Bernie and Karen show. Let me know when that happens, will you? I had a friend I loved a lot. I'd like to see her again."

. . . .

Dino wasn't in the Beth Israel Hospital on Brookline Avenue because of his ulcer. He had a blood clot. "They think they can maybe dissolve it," Myer had told his daughter when he telephoned, "but it's a dangerous situation and there aren't any guarantees. You'd better come and see him while you still can, Juffie." So of course she had.

"They tell you a lot of stuff to make you worry, gorgeous?" Dino had demanded the first day she arrived at the hospital. "You listening to all the crap these doctors hand out?"

"Not a chance. I know you better than they do. I just figured it was time for a few days at home. I'm between shows, giving my voice a rest. It was the perfect opportunity."

"About your voice, that's good. I thought you sounded a little hoarse when I came to New York in July." He lay back on the pillows and smiled. "That was a good time, wasn't it? I'll never forget you standing up in that canoe and tipping it over. And the way everybody clapped. And those restaurants . . . A good time."

"The best, Pa. Now you have to get well quick, so we can do it again."

"Sure, sure we'll do it again."

But he looked gray and very tired and she didn't stay long. "What does the doctor say?" she demanded of her father later.

"He says everything that can be done is being done. The Beth Israel's a wonderful hospital. But you should have seen Pa's face when he found out where we were sending him. 'Myer,' he said to me, 'you think it's okay they have a wop in there? They won't figure it's a time to settle old scores?'"

His imitation of his father-in-law was perfect. Juffie laughed. "I wonder which old scores he was thinking about. I don't imagine Pa's very familiar with the history of relations between Jews and the Catholic Church."

"Not on your life. He's worried in case he and Pop left some bases uncovered when they were running rum. Made some hard feelings maybe." He put his arm around his daughter. "What about the hard feelings, Juffie? Do you blame all of us for the problems we've caused? It's been pretty rough on you, this family. Lately more than ever."

She hugged him hard. "Don't say it, don't even think it. I know what a snot-nosed brat I was years ago when I first found out how things were. But I wouldn't trade my family for any other in the whole damn country. All the love and support I've always had—what could be more important than that?"

He'd started to cry. Tears had run down Myer's cheeks and he had to blow his nose. Which made Juffie cry too. And she realized that what she'd said hadn't been just words. It was the truth. Okay, she didn't approve of them, but she loved them. Anybody who didn't like that she couldn't be bothered with. Even if anybody included the entire theatrical establishment.

She remembered the conversation with Myer when Karen said what she did about her parents, which is why the remarks at lunch made her so angry. She forgot her anger when she arrived at the hospital. Dino was in a private room. The shades were down and there was a tube leading from a bottle of something into the vein of his thin left arm. The intravenous setup hadn't been there when she came yesterday. "What's this?"

"Some new medicine they're trying. They gotta drip it in. That's what this guy Toomey tells me. Imagine, here I am, a wop in a Jew hospital, and I got an Irishman for a doctor."

Juffie grinned. "Only in America."

"Yeah. You still seeing that Frenchie?"

"Yes."

"Juffie, you want to marry him, darling?"

"I'm not sure, Pa. He keeps asking, but I'm not sure."

Her grandfather patted her hand. "Take your time. You gotta be sure about somethin' like that. But he comes from people who must be okay. They make wine for a living, they gotta be good people. Listen, since your dad ain't here, I better tell you I been checking every which way to see what we can get on you-know-who. So far I come up zero."

She did indeed know who. And she shared his reluctance to mention the name aloud. "He's very odd. Not like anyone I've ever met, I mean anyone in your . . . in his line of work."

"Yeah, that's what I been hearin'," Dino agreed. "Lives by himself in a big mansion in Brooklyn. No wife, no kids. Most of the boys hang around together. Not him, unless it's strictly necessary for business. He's a loner. They say he reads more books than a college professor. And he goes to the opera and the theater and places like that."

"How did he ever get involved in . . . what he's involved in?"

Dino shrugged. "Grew up in Brownsville, used to pal around with Bugsy Siegel. Siegel was rubbed out a coupla years back. Our friend was maybe involved. Been up eight times for grand larceny and fraud and aggravated assault, and five times for the big one."

She knew the big one was a murder charge, but not what Dino meant by "up." "You mean he's served time for all those things?"

"Nah. He's been lucky. They keep hauling him in, but they never make nothin' stick. I only wish that bastard made all the trouble for me and Benny had took a crack at him. Now there was a prosecutor what knew how to make a charge stick. 'Course, it was easier years ago. Judges and juries, they weren't so particular about what was good evidence and what was bad."

He sounded proud of the improved sensibilities of the law. Juffie squeezed his hand. "Stop worrying about all that. Concentrate on getting well. I brought you some grapes. The nurse said you could have them."

She picked the lush purple fruits from the stem and popped them into his mouth one by one. There was a television at the foot of the bed. Myer always insisted on the best of everything for the family. "Do you want to watch something?" she asked.

"Nah, not yet. The game later. Second in a four-game series with New York. Those goddamn Yankees are in first place, even though Cleveland's got all the hitters. The Indians got Al Rosen, but the goddamn Yankees are gonna snatch the pennant."

All her life they'd been the goddamn Yankees. She used to think the expletive was part of the official name of the club. In the old days Dino was a Red Sox fan while Benny was crazy about the Braves. As with the crosses and the stars, it was a contest for her allegiance. They used to compete to take her to games, and she always claimed to prefer the team favored by whichever grandfather she was with. With Pop gone she only needed to be a Red Sox fan. "How's Williams doing this year?" She fed Dino another grape.

"Not so hot. He got injured early in the season. Worst luck in the world, that's what the Red Sox got. The worst. No more grapes, Juffie. I'm full. You remember the forty-six season? When Joe Cronin was the manager and Williams was hittin' like a son of a bitch? Everything they threw at him he hit it outta the park, and the Sox won the pennant. I was inside. All I could think of, if I was out now, I could take Juffie to the World Series."

Dino died of a pulmonary embolism at two A.M. the following morning. Before they buried him, Juffie put a Red Sox pennant into his coffin.

Karen came to the house on Walnut Street the day after the funeral. She looked as terrible as she had when they had lunch, but the warmth with which she hugged Juffie and Myer was the old Karen returned. "I didn't know in time to get to the funeral. My mother told me this morning because I happened to telephone her. I'm so sorry."

"It doesn't matter, Karen honey," Myer said. "You're here now. Thanks for coming."

"Yes," Juffie said. "Thanks."

"What do you mean, thanks? Where else was I going to be today if not here with both of you?"

With bloody Bernard, Juffie thought. Trying to make yourself over into his beloved wife, Bess. Which is why I didn't call you right after Pa died. But she didn't say it, and she was more comforted by Karen's presence than by anything else. Karen and the fact that the Red Sox took the last game of the series with the goddamn Yankees ten to six. Williams hit three home runs. "Those were for Pa," Juffie said, and Myer and Karen nodded agreement.

. . . .

New Year's Eve, 1953. Juffie and Paul were at "21." People were jammed in like sardines and the restaurant provided streamers and whistles and funny hats. On the television behind the bar were Guy Lombardo and his orchestra intercut with scenes of the ball descending in Times Square while a frenzied crowd called out the passing of the last thirty seconds. ". . . Nine, eight, seven, six, five, four, three, two, one!" the announcer yelled with enough excitement to portend the Second Coming. "Happy New Year, everybody!"

Paul kissed her. "Happy New Year, my beautiful, adorable, wonderful Juffie." He spoke the words into her ear, so she could hear them despite the noise. "Marry me. Marry me in 1954."

She pulled back and looked at him, and she had to shout to be heard over the din. "Paul, do you mean it? Really?"

"I have been meaning it for three years," he yelled back.

"You're sure?"

His blue eyes looked into hers with the dawn of a hope he almost didn't dare entertain. "I'm very sure. Will you marry me, Juffie?"

"Yes. Yes, I'll marry you Paul."

"Mon Dieu, c'est incroyable, je ne le crois pas. . . ."

"Speak English. You know I don't understand French."

"I said I don't believe it," he yelled. "I don't believe it, but if you back out I'll kill you." He picked her up and tried to swing her around, but the place was too crowded for the maneuver. "I love you," he whispered in her ear. Then he shouted it. "Listen everybody, I love Juffie Kane! And she's going to marry me. She just said so!"

It was quite a night.

She woke up alone on New Year's Day, Paul wasn't beside her. Rosie had bought twin beds for Juffie's room when she furnished the apartment. Juffie and Paul had long since pushed them together. She stretched out her arm. His pillow was still creased and the sheets were warm, but he wasn't there.

Juffie opened her eyes and looked at the clock: a little past one in the afternoon. Not surprising; they hadn't come home until three, and it was hours after that before they actually went to sleep. She smiled at the memory, then opened her eyes wide and really looked at Paul's side of the bed.

Mrs. Paul Dumont. The words were written on the blanket in large white letters. Juffie leaned over and touched one, then put her finger to her tongue. Salt. He'd used a box of salt with a pour spout to write the message. She laughed, then lay back and stopped laughing.

Okay, she was going to marry him; she'd promised, she couldn't back out. But why did she vote aye after so many nays? She ticked off the reasons in her head. He loves me, he wants to take care of me forever, he makes me laugh; unlike a lot of rotten producers and directors, he doesn't think I'm secretly working for a bunch of gangsters; he's the best-looking thing in captivity and sex with him is fabulous. So, Mrs. Paul Dumont. Why not?

You've forgotten one of the reasons, a little voice inside her said. You didn't include the fact that Matt Varley is married.

She'd found out three weeks before. She was Christmas shopping in Saks and she ran into Nessa Fine. "Juffie, how nice. You look marvelous. How's the throat?"

"Getting better, Nessa. Not as fast as I'd like, but it's improving." She asked how Nessa was, she even asked how Jack was.

"We're both wonderful."

Juffie knew that *A Time for Lilies* had opened the week before to rave reviews. The critics loved Deborah Kerr. "Congratulations on the new show." She managed a genuine smile.

"Thank you. Juffie, are you pressed for time? If not, let's have lunch."

"I've plenty of time," Juffie said. Which was true. She still wasn't working; time wasn't one of her problems.

They went to Longchamps and sat at a table behind a polished brass rail and they both ordered grilled cheese and tomato sandwiches. "What's new, Juffie?" Nessa asked when the sandwiches came.

"You mean what scripts am I reading? Nothing wonderful." The only scripts she'd seen lately were such obvious turkeys that their backers were willing to chance the stench attached to her name because maybe her talent could perform a miracle on their pedestrian properties. "Matt says we might as well hold out for something terrific, since the doctor wants me to have a few more weeks rest."

"Yes, of course. Good advice. How is Matt these days?"

"Fine, the same. You know Matt, he's an even-tempered sort most of the time."

"Mmm . . ." Nessa took a sip of the tea she'd ordered with her sandwich. "Terrible. Why doesn't anyone in this land of plenty know how to brew a decent cup of tea? Juffie, I'm about to open my mouth very wide and put my foot in it. I want you to know I'm doing it fully compos mentis, and I'm not being bitchy, I'm genuinely concerned. You do know Matt's married, don't you?"

She wasn't shocked, not at first. She shook her head. "He's not, Nessa. Where did you get that idea?"

"From the Department of Public Records of the State of New Jersey."

Juffie put down her sandwich and stared at Nessa. "It's a mistake, it must be."

"No mistake. He's been married for thirteen years, since 1941; they live in Englewood Cliffs. I checked, Juffie. A long time ago I earned my bread and butter ferreting out facts. This particular one is correct."

"But he's . . ." She stopped in mid-sentence, before she said he was a homosexual. Because the whole thing didn't add up. And it wasn't any of Nessa's business. "May I ask why you were checking, as you put it, on Matt?"

"Because you're twenty-six."

Juffie nodded.

"Okay, but I'm fifty, almost twice your age. And I've been married three times, and the first two times were disasters, but this time it's perfect. And I like you very much, Juffie Kane. And I don't have any children, but I guess I'm basically a Jewish mother at heart."

She couldn't just let it drop; she told herself she should, but she couldn't. A week later she called the taxi company she always did business with and arranged a cab to take her to New Jersey on an afternoon when she knew Matt had a series of meetings in Manhattan.

She dressed in black slacks and a long black raincoat with two sweaters underneath, so she looked twenty pounds heavier, and she tied her hair into a black kerchief, and put on dark glasses. She might look like the Witch of Endor, but not like Juffie Kane.

She knew Matt's address and she'd bought a street map of Englewood Cliffs. She had the driver leave her a few blocks from his house and wait. Then she walked the rest of the way. It was the most ordinary of suburban roads. Newish type single-story ranch houses were set back behind lawns that had gone brown with the heavy frosts. There were bikes in evidence, and she saw a couple of kids playing at the end of the block. It was nearly four in the afternoon and the dusk of winter crept upon the scene. Christmas lights winked on here and there.

Matt's house was shingled a kind of driftwood gray and had maroon trim. It also had one of the ubiquitous picture windows. Here, as in most of the homes, the curtains weren't drawn and there was a Christmas tree behind the glass. At Matt's the tree had apparently just been put up. As yet it was bare of lights.

Juffie stood across the street and peered at the house. She dared not stay long. In a neighborhood like this a woman who looked as odd as she did today would find herself answering a cop's questions if she loitered. But she didn't need more than a minute or two. A woman appeared in the window. Small and blond, Juffie couldn't tell anything else about her. She began hanging ornaments on the tree. A second woman joined her. Much older and heavier. Her mother perhaps. They went on putting up the Christmas decorations.

Juffie watched for two or three minutes, then turned and walked back to where the cab waited.

She told herself that she was so upset because it was a blow to her perception of the closeness she shared with Matt. She wasn't crying because he was married, dammit. She was crying because he'd never told her about it. If he was gay and didn't mention it, that she understood. Being a homosexual was something a lot of men thought they had to keep secret. But a wife?

If he'd told her years before, if occasionally the woman came with him to a show, or joined them for dinner, or even if she just appeared at the office once in a while . . . Like if she'd come into the city to shop and Matt was taking her to lunch . . . She'd have accepted the whole thing as inevitable and natural if any of those things had ever happened. But they hadn't, not once in six years. And that's why she was crying, because it was such a shock. And it made it seem as if Matt didn't feel close to her at all. He thought of her as almost a stranger, a business associate, nothing more.

Later she tried to make sense out of the scene she'd witnessed years ago on Christopher Street. Maybe the guy he'd been arguing with was a client? No, it hadn't crossed her mind then and it didn't fit now. There was something totally personal in the way Matt had looked at him. Something that made it absolutely clear theirs was an emotional involvement. She'd recognized it instantly because it was a way that Matthew Varley almost never looked at her.

So maybe he had both a wife and a male lover. Maybe that's why the wife never appeared in public. Maybe things were rotten between them because the little blond woman knew she was sharing him with a man, perhaps a lot of men.

Juffie tried to imagine Matt cruising the gay bars, going out for a night of what Harry Harcourt had told her was called rough trade. "Some homosexuals feel so guilty about themselves they want to be beaten up, treated like dirt," Harry had said. "They go looking for such treatment, usually with a one-night stand, somebody who doesn't even know their real name. It's pretty sad really."

Juffie couldn't imagine Matt doing something like that, even wanting to do it. But she couldn't imagine him in a suburban ranch house in Englewood Cliffs, New Jersey, either. And he didn't care enough about her to explain anything about his personal life. Not one goddamn word in six years. So the hell with him. And so on New Year's Eve she agreed to become Mrs. Paul Dumont.

Paul returned to the apartment at three in the afternoon on New Year's Day. "Awake at last," he said, kissing her. "Hung over?"

"A little. Champagne always does that to me."

"Have some tomato juice."

"I already did, with a raw egg in it. It tastes foul, but it works. Where did you go?"

"I had to do an errand."

"Today? It's a holiday, everything's closed."

"Not if you have influence." A smile lit his remarkably handsome face, a tender smile that made him look like a beautiful little boy, the kind whose pictures are painted on sentimental Christmas cards. "I had to get you a present."

"Christmas was last week. You already gave me more presents than I can count." He'd spent money with wild abandon, because this year, unlike last, he had it to spend.

Ramón Viera and his dancers were still causing a sensation wherever they appeared. And Paul had them under exclusive contract. Now he was scheduling both an English ballet and a Viennese chamber orchestra for cross-country tours in the fall, and negotiating to get the legendary French singer, Edith Piaf, into Carnegie Hall for two weeks in June.

"Not a Christmas present," he said. "An engagement present. Close your eyes and put out your hand. No, the left one."

She changed hands and waited. He slipped something on her finger. Juffie opened her eyes. It was the biggest diamond she'd ever seen. A square-cut stone in an austere platinum setting that showed off its glittering perfection. "Paul! My God, I don't know what to say. It's beautiful, incredible. But I don't understand. Where did you get it today?"

"I called my friend Harry Winston, the jeweler. I've known him for years. He likes foreign films. I told him the most beautiful woman in the world had agreed to marry me, and I needed to put a ring on her finger right away. Before she changed her mind. This came from Harry's private collection. Six carats. He says it once belonged to some Russian princess."

"It's . . ." Juffie searched for a word. "It's exquisite." She held out her hand and the ring flashed its blue-white fire. "Thank you. It seems the understatement of all time, but thank you."

"You're welcome, but that's not what I want to hear."

She looked at him, trying to read a message in his eyes. She'd never told Paul she loved him. Juffie was terribly aware of that, she didn't know if he was. "What do you want to hear?"

"That you haven't changed your mind. That in the cold light of today you still mean it. You'll marry me."

"The cold light of day, not today," she corrected him gently. "And no, I haven't changed my mind. I'll marry you, Paul. And I'll do everything I can to be a good wife."

He chuckled and pulled her close. "That's a corny line; it's not worthy of you. Besides, all I want is for you to go on being wonderful, beautiful Juffie."

. . . .

Two days later Matt telephoned first thing in the morning. "Juffie, I've had an interesting offer."

So have I, she thought of saying, but she didn't. She'd tell him later. "Yes, what?"

"I'd rather not explain on the phone. Can you come down to the office?"

She was there a little after eleven. She sat in the chair across from his desk and slipped her lynx and sable coat from her shoulders, but she kept on her black kid gloves. She'd have to show him the diamond and say she was getting married; but not now, later. "Tell me, I'm dying to know."

"It's not a show," he said quickly.

Her heart sank. "Then how can it be interesting?"

"It is. Because it's steady, and it will keep your name in the public eye. Not to mention your face."

"A movie. That old obsession of yours. Juffie goes to Hollywood."

"No. Television, a regular program."

"My own series. I don't want that any more than I want to make a movie. I'm not Dinah Shore, Matt. I don't want to be America's favorite hostess."

"Stop playing guessing games and listen to me. I'm not talking about you doing a series. Though the right sitcom wouldn't be a bad idea if it came along. It hasn't. What's up for grabs is a spot on *What's My Line*. It's a panel show."

"A quiz program. I've seen it once or twice."

"It's not a serious quiz, there's nobody in a sealed box showing off what he knows about the love life of the tsetse fly. The format's simple—somebody they call the challenger comes in with an offbeat job, putting the sticks in Popsicles say, and the panelists try to guess what he does for a living by asking questions he can answer yes or no. The questions are really an excuse for clever banter."

"About putting sticks in Popsicles. Just what I've always wanted."

Matt ran his fingers through his hair. "Juffie, I know what you want. A terrific show. But you've seen every script you've been offered for the past six months. I passed every damned one on to you in case you saw something I missed. We both agreed that none of them was terrific."

"Is six months forever, Matt? Do I quietly retire to the land of the flickering little screen and forget about Broadway and theaters and the career I thought I had?"

"Of course not. We're simply buying time. Until the country stops having its fit of ultra-morality. It will, you know, it always does. Remember Prohibition?"

"How much time?" she asked.

"The *What's My Line* offer is pegged to a year's contract."

"A year. Fifty-two weeks of talking about Popsicle sticks."

"Forty actually. In television a year is forty weeks. They show something else during the summer."

Juffie sat back. Without thinking she peeled off her gloves. The big diamond winked in the pale winter sun that streamed through the window. Matt looked at it. "I see you got something special from Santa Claus."

"What?" She followed his glance with her eyes. "Oh, you noticed."

"Hard not to. That's some rock. Paul?"

"Yes, of course."

"Of course. Does that mean you're going to marry him?"

She thought she heard something like regret in his voice. But that had to be fantasy. "That's what my mother told me an engagement ring meant." Smart cracks to cover up what she was feeling; business as usual for Juffie Kane.

"Congratulations," Matt said. "When?"

"I'm not sure. We haven't decided."

"It's just that if you want time off for a honeymoon, I'd better get that into the television contract."

Ah yes. "If I agree to do the show," Juffie said.

He leaned forward. "Juffie, you pay me for advice as well as for reading the fine print. Take it. The show's got a certain amount of class. And staying power. It's already been on five, maybe six years. And there's no indication the public's getting tired of it. Class and staying power, you need those things right now."

Juffie shook her head and sighed. "Why, Matt? Why is everybody being so rough on me? I know what I did and what they think I'm doing—which I'm not—but why does it matter so goddamn much? Frank Sinatra and Dean Martin and the rest of those guys who are rumored to have mobster friends—I don't notice them having any trouble finding work."

"First of all, they're men; you're a woman. Which makes a huge difference in the public mind. Second, they're based in Hollywood, and when they leave tinsel town it's to play club dates. You're an actress in the legitimate theater, which you well know looks down its nose at anything that isn't played on Broadway. Hell, you do it yourself. I could call you in here and offer you the moon with peanut butter on it, and if it isn't a Broadway show you don't care what it is."

"True," she admitted. "Matt, are they ever going to get over hating me?"

"Nobody hates you. They're scared of you. Look, the guys with the big properties, the ones everybody feels in their bones are going to be hits, they have their pick of the best actors and actresses around. You've been number one on that list until recently, but now there are question marks after your name. If somebody's sinking hundreds of thousands into what should be a sure smash, he can't take a chance on a question mark. So he drops down to the next name on the list. Still a big star, still a talented lady who can do the part. So it's not Juffie Kane, so what? Better safe than sorry."

"And the ones who don't have surefire potential hits are the ones willing to take a chance on me."

"Right. In the normal course of things they wouldn't even

have a crack at you. The way things are now, they take a shot and send us the script."

"What if we picked out the best of them, the one that was least awful, and I did it? Maybe I could make it work, Matt. Like with *The Visitor*."

"Nobody was gunning for you when you did *The Visitor*."

"But they are now."

"Yes," he agreed. "It's all tied up with the Kefauver hearings and that bastard McCarthy. The country's having a fit of moral mania, as I said. And somehow your name has become associated with that which isn't moral, upstanding, and 'the American way.' It will pass, Juffie. Don't do a turkey because you can't wait. Do this TV show, and let everybody see you and hear you and remember how much they've always loved you. And the minute a wonderful show comes through that door, I'll get you out of the television contract even if we have to plead temporary insanity."

. . . .

They decided on a small quiet wedding in Boston. Paul said something about a church, Juffie looked at him in amazement. "I'm not a Catholic, I can't get married in a church. Anyway, you've never been inside a church since I've known you."

"I'm French. Every Frenchman is a Catholic. So what if I don't go to mass? Getting married is different. Besides, you're half Italian."

"Yes, but that doesn't make me half Catholic. There's no such thing. No church, Paul. I never knew that clause was in the contract."

He shrugged. "It isn't. I just thought it would be nice."

"Not a bit nice. Dad's arranging for a judge, an old friend of his. And he's reserved a private room in Joseph's Restaurant in Back Bay. It's a lovely place, Paul. It will be perfect, you'll see."

Juffie was to start on *What's My Line* the first week in March, the wedding was scheduled for the last Sunday in February. Paul had a few unbreakable appointments and couldn't leave New York until Saturday evening. Juffie took the train to Boston on Friday.

Seeing Myer alone in the big house on Walnut Street was painful, but he insisted he had no desire to move. "I've lived here since 1925, why should I go somewhere else?"

"It's so big, Dad," she pleaded. "And there are so many memories."

"Good memories," Myer said. "I have no desire to put them behind me."

The memories had become more important than ever. Pa's death had broken a major link with his beloved Rosie, Juffie realized. She was the only tie left. She and the pictures. Her father dragged out boxes of snapshots Saturday morning while they lingered over coffee and toast in the bright kitchen. "I've been going through these. There's a lot I don't think you've ever seen."

She looked at photographs of her mother and father before she was born. They seemed so young, so vulnerable. Rosie in 1924, for instance, in a short shapeless dress that ended in a flounce above her knees, with long ropes of beads and a cloche hat. "She was so pretty," Juffie said.

"Of course. You had to get your looks from somewhere. See, this was taken in 1930, when you were three years old." Juffie and her mother on Boston Common, with the stores of Tremont Street in the background. "Remember how we used to go to the Common all the time on your birthday and tell you the story of how you were born there?"

"I remember." She flipped through a few more shots from the same period. "Dad, when you and Mama were into joining all the causes, did you ever become Communists?"

He laughed. "Not quite. We nibbled at the edges, but we never joined the Party. Your mother said the guy in charge of the cell we went to had a fishy look. That settled it."

"Then you weren't a member of something called the Young Communist League?"

He looked at her. "Yes, as a matter of fact we were for a very brief time. But that didn't constitute actually joining the Party. It was more like an initiation ceremony, an application to join." He stopped short and looked intently at her. "Juffie, it suddenly occurs to me that you aren't asking idle questions. All this goddamn red-baiting in Washington, those rotten blacklists. Are you on some entertainment blacklist because your mother and I were Young Communists for maybe twenty minutes a quarter of a century ago?"

"No, of course not."

"Don't lie to me, Juffie. The truth."

"I'm telling you the truth. I don't think there is a 'blacklist' for New York theater people. Hollywood, not Broadway. Anyway, if there is, I'm not on it. I wouldn't have been offered this television job if I were."

"Why are you taking a year's contract on television anyway? I thought you were looking for a new show?"

"I am. But nothing good's come along. Nothing right for me. Matt says the TV program is good exposure. If I find something marvelous, we'll wriggle out of the television contract."

Myer chuckled. "I like Matt Varley. A good lawyer never says you can't do something, Juffie. He tells you what the risks are, then he explains how you can do it if you really want to."

"I'll remember that. I'll write it down in the little black book I'm keeping. Advice from my father."

He kissed her cheek. "So much for breakfast with the Kane family. I have to read some papers for a client. What are you going to do?"

"Check on the flowers."

"Everything's arranged. I told you."

"I know. But I have to find out what Karen's wearing and make sure her bouquet matches."

She'd asked Karen to be her maid of honor as soon as they set the date. "I'd love to, Juffie, but what should I wear?"

"Anything, as long as it's not a brown suit. I'm not getting married in white with a veil and a train. It would be a little silly at this stage. Get a pretty dress, sweetie, the sort of thing you'd wear to a party."

"Blue," Karen told her when she called that Saturday morning. "A blue dress."

"Fine. I just wanted to know because of the flowers."

Myer, as usual, insisted on the best of everything for Juffie's wedding. Which in Boston in 1954 meant flowers from Penn the Florist on Arlington Street. Juffie went to the shop.

"Miss Kane, it is you! I said it had to be when Mr. Kane made the arrangements. I told everybody, it has to be Juffie Kane the actress. I'll never forget that duet you did on TV with Dinah Shore, the one where you were both housewives. You were wonderful."

The clerk kept fussing; Juffie kept smiling and saying thank you. Finally they talked about flowers. "Mr. Kane said you were wearing pale lavender and you wanted something small, so we've chosen a single spray of orchids and some sprigs of white stephanotis. Is that all right?"

"It sounds lovely. My maid of honor will be in blue. We didn't know until this morning. Is it too late to make sure she has something that will look good with blue?"

"No, of course not." The woman led her to a refrigerator case full of blossoms. "The sweetheart roses are lovely just now. Either pale pink or pale yellow would be nice with a blue dress."

"No, I don't see Karen with sweetheart roses. What about those daisies? Or the pansies, they're wonderful."

"How about a mixed spring bouquet—daisies and pansies and a few violets? We could do them as a nosegay, an old-fashioned tussy-mussy with lace and blue ribbons."

"Perfect," Juffie said.

It wasn't perfect. The tender, gay bunch of flowers showed up the awfulness of Karen's dress. It was heavy blue crepe with a side drape and ungainly sleeves that were neither short nor long. If she'd gone out searching for something to make her seem twenty years older, she'd found it. Juffie took one look and buttoned her lips shut. It was her wedding day, she was not going to ruin it by having an argument with Karen. So her best friend was flushing her life down the drain. Today was not the day to worry about it.

Moreover, it was unlikely that anyone would pay attention to Karen when Juffie was around. "You look so beautiful," Paul said. He spoke the words in an almost prayerful tone. "Like a goddess."

She wore silk peau de soie in a color somewhere between palest gray and lavender. It was the color of smoke, and what it did for her eyes was fabulous. The bodice was tightly fitted. The sleeves were long and the neck was a deep square. The fabric was gathered around her body to flare out in the back from a point between her shoulders. The dress was knee-length, but it hinted bride to just the degree she'd wanted. Juffie's hair was swept up in a sleek coil at the top of her head, and in place of a hat she wore a whisper of very fine lavender veiling held with a diamond clip. That and Paul's ring were her only jewelry, and her silk high-heeled pumps were dyed to match her dress.

"You're a vision," Myer said with tears in his eyes yet again. "I only wish Rosie could see you, and Pop and Pa. . . ."

"So do I," Juffie agreed with a lump in her throat. "I think it's time, Dad."

They'd decided that the ceremony as well as the wedding luncheon would be in Joseph's. The judge was waiting in the flower-bedecked private room beside a window that looked out on the Public Gardens. It had snowed the night before; all the world seemed frosted sparkling white, decorated for the marriage of Juffie Kane and Paul Dumont. Myer tucked his daughter's arm through his own and they walked the few steps to where Paul waited.

Paul hadn't know whom to ask to be his best man. When he first brought it up it struck Juffie that he had masses of acquaintances but no friends. Not surprising perhaps, considering that he'd been in America only eight years. All his real friends must be back in France. "Do you think I could ask Matt?" he'd said.

"Not Matt," she'd objected quickly. "Too much mixing of business with personal life," she added. It wasn't a bad excuse and Paul accepted it without question.

"What about your father then? I saw it in a film once, a man ushers his daughter down the aisle, then steps beside the groom and acts as his witness, his best man as you call it here."

"Why not?" Juffie agreed.

That's the way it was. Myer delivered Juffie to Paul, then stood beside him. Karen was on Juffie's right. Bernard Hanrihan, Jake and Leah Rice, and half a dozen Saliatelli relatives were the guests. The judge said things about the laws of the Commonwealth of Massachusetts—Juffie hadn't realized that the words of a civil ceremony were so different from the religious phrases everybody associated with a wedding—and finished up by pronouncing them husband and wife. Paul kissed her.

She was happy, she realized as his lips touched hers. She really was. He was a great guy, a good man, and the marriage was going to work. She was really happy.

Just then a man poked his head into the private room and motioned to Myer. He went and conferred with him a moment, then returned. "Reporters," he told Juffie. "I'm sorry, I thought we'd kept this a secret, but they're six deep outside the restaurant. I told the manager to say that we were having a very small wedding with a few close friends and family, and if they tried to get in, I'd call the cops. But I had to promise that you'd pose for a few shots when you left. Okay?"

"Yes, fine."

"I'm sorry, darling." Myer turned to his brand new son-in-law. "Forgive me, Paul. I hope this won't ruin a very special day."

"Not at all," Paul said. "Juffie and I are in the entertainment business. Being seen and written about is part of our lives. We're accustomed to it."

It certainly was true for her, but Juffie hadn't before associated that reality with Paul. She'd never seen anything in the press about him, nothing personal, only his name in connection with the Spanish dancers. He seemed prepared to change all that. When they left Joseph's, Paul chatted amiably with the reporters and the photographers. He even alluded to his experiences with the French Resistance.

Chapter 12

*T*he following week Juffie began appearing on *What's My Line*. Doing the show didn't make for a strenuous schedule. On Thursday afternoon they had a quick run-through that couldn't really be called a rehearsal, then on Sunday night at ten-thirty they went on the air. The questions were fairly standardized: Do people come to you? Men and women? Are they happier when they leave? Is a product involved? Can I hold it in my hand? Is it bigger than a bread box? Smaller than an elephant?

"Simple-minded," Juffie said. But the viewers liked it, and they loved her. They loved the way she looked, the stunning clothes she wore, her clever one-liners. CBS got lots of fan mail about Juffie Kane. "Did it ever occur to you, we could spend the rest of our lives doing this?" Bennett Cerf, the publisher who'd been with the show since it began, asked her one evening backstage. "We could even arrange for our corpses to be propped up on camera. They could get a ventriloquist to ask the questions."

It was a joke, but she didn't laugh. The thought made Juffie gag. She'd enjoyed the TV guest spots she did before *Whaddaya Say;* she did not enjoy being a regular on *What's My Line*. By the end of the month she was calling Matt every day to ask if he had any word, even a hint, of a new show for her. He did not. Juffie grew more and more discontented and it was a mark of her consummate professionalism that her mood did not affect her performance. The audience saw only smiles and laughter.

In late April a man named Joseph N. Welch, a Boston lawyer named Special Counsel for the army, began to take Joe McCarthy apart on television. Welch was a Boston Brahmin whose world in normal times would never touch that of ordinary folk, even a fellow lawyer like Myer Kane; now destiny had made him the conscience of America. The nation saw the pieces of the Wisconsin senator disassembled and left flapping in the wind, and they were at last revolted by everything he'd been and done. America was waking from a long nightmare, and according to Matt, that boded well for Juffie. But it didn't cheer her up.

She hid her mood from the television cameras, but she couldn't hide it from her husband of two months. "We're newlyweds. You're supposed to be happy," Paul said. "Why are you miserable?"

"It's nothing to do with you, darling. Really. It's this damned thing I used to call my career. I can't stand it being stalled at twenty miles an hour."

"Matt's looking for a show for you. He'll find something."

He didn't look at her when he said it, and it occurred to Juffie that they had never talked about the reason for her problems on Broadway. She had loved him for not questioning her about hoods and the Syndicate when everyone else was screaming about her "connections with the rackets." Suddenly it seemed strange. "You do know why everybody's mad at me, don't you? You're not having one of your foreigner's lapses of understanding?"

"I know. The Tony awards." He still didn't look at her.

"Sort of, but not just that. The story in *Confidential*, and—"

"Listen, are you going to be home tomorrow afternoon?"

"Yes, I guess so. But what does that have to do with anything?"

"I'm changing the subject. Because I have a surprise for you. Tomorrow at three. I want to make sure you're going to be here."

"Okay, I'll be here."

The surprise was an impeccably dressed small man with a faint southern accent and a gentle smile. "Juffie, I'd like you to meet Billy Baldwin," Paul said. "Mr. Baldwin, my wife."

"Miss Kane, it's a great pleasure. I've thrilled to your performances many times."

"Not Miss Kane, not in our home. Mrs. Dumont." Paul was smiling, but Juffie didn't think he was pleased. "And we are not going to talk about the theater."

The man looked pained to think his simple gallantry had offended. She made an effort to smooth things over. "Please, just call me Juffie." She turned to Paul. "Darling, I know Mr. Baldwin is the surprise, but what am I to be surprised about?"

"See," Paul told their guest, "I warned you. She could live in a cage in the Bronx Zoo and not notice. Juffie, you must be the only woman in New York who doesn't know that Billy Baldwin is the most wonderful interior decorator in the world. He's going to do this place over top to bottom."

"Oh." Juffie tried for a more articulate response. She gestured to the beige shantung drapes and the gold shag rug and the green bouclé furniture. "My mother picked all this out. Paul says it's horrible."

"A bit outdated, perhaps. I'm sure it was lovely when she first did it. What's that French expression, Mr. Dumont . . . ?"

"There are a number of them," Paul said. "*De trop, déclassé*. I just call it bourgeois."

"Ah, yes. I was thinking of *passé de mode*. And for you, lovely lady, a house must be a setting worthy of the jewel."

They toured the nine rooms of the penthouse. "Do you really need six bedrooms?" Baldwin asked when they'd seen everything.

"No, I guess not," Juffie said. "But we had to put something in all this space. Beds and chests of drawers just seemed sensible."

"Mmm . . . I was thinking of a study for Mr. Dumont, and for you a classic boudoir. It doesn't mean bedroom, by the way, that's an American misuse of the term. A lady's boudoir should be her special place, a room where she can keep her treasures, and relax, and be alone if she wishes, or entertain an intimate friend. So a boudoir and a study, and perhaps a library. And we could join a few rooms together to enlarge the master bedroom into a suite with a dressing room and a nice little sitting area."

"Exactly!" Paul was overjoyed. "That's the sort of thing I've been trying to get Juffie to see for years. That's the kind of home you deserve, *chérie*. And that's what you shall have. When can you start, Mr. Baldwin?"

"Well, if you'll both agree to call me Billy from this moment forward, I'd say we've already started."

Which is how they were to acquire a living room done in soft cream and dusty rose chintz with accents of black, and an Aubusson rug, and a Louis XV dining room with a crystal chandelier, and a walnut-paneled library furnished in English oak, and more English oak coupled with red leather in a study for Paul, and a little room for Juffie that was to be all violet-sprigged curtains and velvet slipper chairs and chaises longues, and an enormous yellow and white master suite with the biggest bed imaginable, and wall-to-wall white carpeting. The total effect would be breathtaking, Juffie realized, but she worried about the cost.

"Paul, how are we paying for all this?" she asked in May when the apartment was full of workmen, and cans of paint and fabric swatches, and Billy Baldwin and his associates.

He waved a dismissive hand. "Money is no problem, *chérie*. The advance sale for Piaf is so good, they're already talking about an extra week at Carnegie Hall. I'm trying to get her to agree to a three-week engagement."

But in June, when it was almost done and the bills began pouring in, money became a very big problem. Paul came home one evening looking gray and exhausted. Juffie had never seen him like this. "Paul, what's the matter? What is it?"

"Piaf. The bitch has cancelled."

"No! How could she? What about your contract?"

"It doesn't mean a thing. She's in the hospital. They're not sure she's going to live. Drugs, alcohol, God knows what else."

"Oh, Paul."

He went to the newly installed bar, which had a sink and a tiny refrigerator cleverly concealed behind a mahogany fretwork screen, and poured himself a very large whiskey. "Why are you hanging on to that newspaper?"

"I wanted to show you this." She passed him the *Herald Tribune* opened to the theater page. It bore a large headline, "From Hero to Impresario."

"Oh, that. I've seen it."

"Have you? Where did they get all this stuff?"

"I gave them an interview."

She was surprised. "I thought you hated to remember the war. This is full of stories about your exploits with the Maquis. It even talks about the chateau at Fontainebleau."

"Yes, the reporters love that sort of thing. And it's good publicity."

"I know, but—"

"Juffie, my whole world has just collapsed. I don't want to talk about some goddamn newspaper story."

She crossed to him and pushed the dark curly hair off his forehead. "Not the whole world, darling. Just one booking. The hell with Piaf, you'll get someone else. And there's still the Viennese orchestra and the English ballet."

"Not without Piaf there isn't. Without her there's not a damn thing."

A cold chill was starting at the base of her spine and moving upward. "Why? What do you mean?"

"I mortgaged the three theaters and all my distribution rights to pay the Carnegie guarantee for Piaf. She was supposed to earn enough to pay that off and provide seed money for the other two events."

"And now the guarantee is forfeit?"

"That's right."

"Oh my God." Juffie found a bottle of white wine in the little refrigerator behind the bar and poured some into a glass. She sipped it without taking her eyes off Paul. He was standing by the window looking out toward the East River. His perfect profile was as remarkable as when she'd first noted it in Logan Airport in Boston. But just now the slightly aggressive chin was quivering.

"Okay," she said. "Okay, Paul. It's not the end of the world. We can sell some things. My furs, the diamond. And I can borrow a little money from my father."

"Thanks, but it would be a drop in the bucket. The ballet, the orchestra, and all this on top of it . . ." He waved his arm at the newly decorated apartment. "It's hundreds of thousands, Juffie. Hundreds and hundreds of thousands."

And she was earning nine hundred a week asking "Is it bigger than a bread box?" She glanced at the newspaper he'd dismissed so casually. "Darling, what about the angel? The one who backed you when you brought over Viera. The man from the old glory days in France?"

Paul stared into his glass. It was empty; he'd drunk the whiskey in three fast gulps. "Yes. I've been thinking of that. I hate to do it, but I don't see any choice."

A couple of days later he told her he'd be away until late in the evening and she shouldn't wait dinner. They didn't have live-in help, just a cleaning woman who worked days. When they ate at home Juffie cooked. That night she broiled a steak, made a salad, and ate a solitary meal before going to bed with a new Agatha Christie mystery.

She intended to wait up for Paul, but around midnight she fell asleep. It seemed only a few minutes later that she felt his hand on her shoulder. She sighed and turned over, trying to press herself against him. But he wasn't in the bed, he was standing beside it. "Juffie, wake up, darling. I'm sorry. I hate to disturb you, but can you put something on and come to the library?"

"The library . . . Paul, what time is it?"

"A little after two. Please, there's someone with me. I want you to speak with him."

She struggled out of bed, still groggy with the deep first sleep from which he'd wakened her. By the time her eyes were fully opened he'd left the room. The master suite provided each of them with a bathroom. Juffie's was done in royal purple tile and had marble fixtures with gold taps fashioned to look like dolphins. She splashed water on her face, didn't bother with makeup, brushed her long hair back, and slipped on an emerald-green hostess coat that zipped up the front. Then she went to the library.

Paul was sitting at the round English-oak table in the middle of the room, in an oversized Queen Anne chair upholstered in hand-woven burlap imported from Malaya which had cost thirty-five dollars a yard. She'd been dumbfounded by that. Thirty-five dollars a yard for burlap. Billy Baldwin said it was magnificent and worth every penny. He'd said the same thing about an old oak tantalus they'd found in an antique store on Third Avenue in the shadow of the El. It cost two hundred dollars, but it was "magnificent and worth every penny."

The tantalus was kept on the table in the library; it housed two heavy crystal decanters. Paul kept one filled with dark aged cognac, the other with pale single-malt whiskey. He was drinking the cognac. So was the man with him.

For long seconds Juffie just stood and stared at them. Sitting with her handsome husband in her perfectly appointed library was Finky Aronson.

. . . .

"It has to be you," Paul said. "Believe me, I'd give anything if that weren't so. If there was any way I could do it in your place, I'd feel a lot better about this. But Mr. Aronson says it has to be a woman."

"A famous lady is the very best insurance," Finky Aronson added. "The customs people go out of their way to be quick and courteous. They don't expect any trouble, so they don't make any."

"No," Juffie said. "I won't do it. You can both just forget this idea. I'm not going to Mexico and I'm not bringing back any packages."

"You have to," Paul said. It wasn't a command, he was pleading. "Juffie, don't you understand? If you don't do it, I lose everything. We lose everything."

"The only thing we lose is this . . . this piece of filth you've dragged into our home."

Aronson ignored the insult. "He is quite correct, Miss Kane. Or do you prefer Mrs. Dumont these days? Well, it doesn't matter. Your husband has made a most accurate assessment of the situation. As things stand now, he owes somewhere in the vicinity of half a million dollars. That is a very large sum of money. I was prepared to advance him a hundred thousand to bring Señor Viera and his dancers from Spain, and that proved a most advantageous transaction for both Mr. Dumont and myself. The loan was paid back in full. But half a million is not an amount I can simply lend. My colleagues would never permit it."

He took another sip of his cognac, replacing the heavy crystal glass on a coaster with fastidious care. "A lovely table. Does it mark easily?" Neither of them answered.

"As I was saying," he continued. "Half a million dollars is beyond my ability merely to lend, so you will have to earn it. Three consecutive monthly trips to Mexico, to a clinic where the doctor will treat your frayed nerves. And each time you return you bring a package worth a million dollars to myself and my associates. Your share is ten percent. As to the remaining two hundred thousand, I'm prepared to advance that on the same terms as my previous arrangement with Mr. Dumont."

"No," Juffie said. "It's drugs. It's filthy."

Aronson rose. His coat and his bowler hat were lying over the arm of another of the burlap-covered chairs. He reclaimed them.

"I'll show myself out and leave you two to discuss it. You know where to reach me, Mr. Dumont."

Neither of them said a word until they heard the sound of the front door closing, and in a few seconds the soft whirring noise of the descending elevator. Then it was Juffie who broke the silence. She screamed. She kept on screaming.

Paul jumped up and grabbed her shoulders, shaking her. "Stop it! Stop it, Juffie! You're hysterical." She didn't stop until he slapped her face. Then she collapsed in sobs and he pulled her close, crushing her to his chest.

"I'm sorry," he murmured into her hair. "*Mon Dieu*, I'm so sorry."

She pulled away from him, wiping her eyes with the backs of her hands, sniffling until he handed her a handkerchief. He poured her a large portion of the cognac. "Here, drink this. It will help."

"Nothing will help." But she drank it. "How did it happen?" she demanded after the spirit had begun to warm her icy insides. "How did you ever get mixed up with him? You said it was somebody from France, somebody who knew you from the old days. Finky Aronson is from Brownsville. He lives in Brooklyn. I don't think he's ever been to France."

"I had to tell you something. Someone from France was the only story I could think of."

"Why did you have to lie?"

"Because there was no way I could tell you that I'd taken a loan from the Syndicate to get me started. But if I didn't, nothing would have happened. I'd tried all the conventional routes, the legal ways. They all dried up and blew away. You know it, you heard my stories week after week. No, no, and more no. That's all I ever heard from banks and legitimate backers."

"Was it so important, Paul? Was bringing flamenco dancing to New York so damned important?"

"If I didn't get out of the rut I was in, you were never going to marry me. That was important enough for anything." He refilled his glass and held the decanter out to her, but she shook her head and just kept looking at him as if the answers to her questions might be written on his face.

"Juffie," he said after a moment. "Doesn't it seem a little funny to you, asking me that? Was the dance troupe important? Who was it who went to the mob to get backing for a show that closed anyway after three months? At least Ramón Viera turned out a smash hit."

"You know about that? About the business with *A Small Miracle*? How?"

"Aronson told me."

"I don't understand. When he went to La Venue to watch foreign movies he talked about how he had his hooks into Juffie Kane?"

"No, not like that. Don't be ridiculous. I saw him that first night he came to talk to you. Don't you remember, when he cornered you downstairs in the lobby and you two talked? I came in just as he was leaving. I recognized him from the theater. I wasn't lying about that; he really is a foreign film fan. So I knew who he was. But when I asked you, you didn't admit it."

He was looking at her, and his bright blue eyes were moist. "I didn't care if you had business with the Syndicate. I didn't even want to think about it. But you were so crazy that night, so wild. Like a bird who'd just been set free. And the next day you fired Ryan, the bodyguard. So I knew you'd made some kind of a deal with Aronson. When I finally faced the fact that I wasn't going to get the money to import European talent any other way, I decided what was good for you was good for me. I approached him. He told me about the two of you while we were negotiating the terms of my loan."

She was hanging on to the back of one of the chairs to keep herself upright. Finally she managed to move around it and sit down. "Paul, what you said about my not marrying you if you didn't become a success. That wasn't true. It isn't true. I didn't marry you because your name's on posters saying 'Paul Dumont Presents.' How can you think that?"

He shrugged. "It doesn't matter. We're two of a kind, Juffie. We like to play with the high rollers. We like to win."

"No." She shook her head. "I'm not like that. I just love being onstage, in front of an audience. It's what I was born to do. It's like air to me. I can't live without it. I don't care about all the other stuff. The clothes and the jewels and the furniture, it's all nice to have. But it's not the thing that really matters."

"It matters. You're only saying that because you've never been without it. Juffie, don't you realize that in your whole life you've never wanted anything you didn't get? Your parents, your grandfathers, the public—everybody has fawned all over you from the minute you were born. It hasn't been like that for me."

"They're not fawning over me now. At least the public isn't."

"Not true. The fans still adore you. It's just a few producers and directors who aren't happy with you at the moment. They'll get over it. Matt keeps telling you they will, and it's true. But not if you start smelling like a loser, Juffie. Not if we wind up on the streets with nothing to call our own and half a million in debt."

Later she told herself that had nothing to do with her decision. It wasn't because Paul raised the specter of her never getting another decent role. It was because she was married to him for better or for worse, regardless of the fact that those weren't the words the judge pronounced in Joseph's Restaurant in the Back Bay. She was his wife, the way Rosie had been Myer's wife. She could not stand by and see Paul destroyed.

So in the end she agreed to go to Mexico and bring back packages for Finky Aronson. They weren't very big packages. The first one fit in a clay flowerpot decorated with handpainted designs typical of the country. A souvenir of her trip south of the border.

• • • •

The clinic of Dr. Juan Santiago de Rodriguez was about two hundred miles east of Mexico City, on the Gulf coast, in the tiny village of Tichipol in Veracruz. The complex that made up the clinic was many times larger than Tichipol itself. It was a forest of private cabañas artfully placed among lush tropical gardens.

Juffie's cabaña was number thirty-four. It was exactly like the rest, a low, whitewashed adobe structure with a red tile roof and painted blue trim. Inside there was a sitting room and a bedroom and a bath. The floors were covered in terra-cotta tiles and decorated with vivid handwoven rugs; the furnishings were dark, heavy wood with wrought-iron trim. Meals were brought three times daily by a smiling girl with long black braids and laughing black eyes, and served on gay blue and white earthenware plates. Juffie had a private terrace and a small private pool.

"You are to swim twice a day, Señora," Dr. Santiago told her. "At least half an hour each time. The water is special. I add certain minerals and salts. Very soothing for the nerves."

He came to see her each morning of her three-day stay, and he examined her as if she were indeed a patient. She saw no one else. The universe was peopled by herself and Santiago and the little maid. On the last day, just before Juffie was to leave, the girl with the braids and the laughing eyes brought her a present. "A souvenir, Señora, something to remember us by."

The first time in July it was the flowerpot. She wondered what it would be this second time in August.

She arrived very early on a Tuesday morning. The heat was cruel. She knew the sea lapped the shore beyond the bougainvillea and the hibiscus and the palm trees and the high walls, but if there was a breeze, it did not penetrate this man-made tropical jungle. At eight the maid brought her sliced mangos and herb tea, and toast made from chewy cornbread pebbled with specks of the grain. Soon after nine the doctor came to her cabaña. He was a great bull of a man with a florid face and a thick neck and shoulders like railroad ties.

"Ah, Señora Dumont, welcome back. How are the nerves?" His English was perfect; he'd told her he had a British mother and had attended a boarding school in England for a few years.

"My nerves are holding up, Dr. Santiago." Juffie eyed him, wondering the same things she'd wondered last month. Why? For money. But this incredible complex, this haven for ultra-rich pampered ladies with imaginary ills, it must make him a fortune. How much was enough? "How are your nerves?" she asked him. The tiredness that followed the long journey and the heat combined to make her reckless. "Are your nerves steady, Dr. Santiago?"

"I have learned to control my nerves," he said softly. "As you will learn to control yours. The water in the pool, the herbal teas, they will strengthen you."

Juffie stared at him. He wasn't giving anything away. "Yeah, sure they will." She diverted her attention to an arrangement of hibiscus blossoms and waited for him to go.

Santiago started for the door, then turned back. "Señora Dumont, I do serious work here. What I might call seminal work. The research is enormously expensive."

"I'll bet."

He shrugged and left the cabaña. Juffie ran after him. "Wait a minute. Listen, if I want to get out of here, where can I go?"

"Where do you want to go? It's only for three days; we do our best to make you comfortable."

"It's not that. It's being confined to this elaborate shack, these few square yards. We're on the coast, how far is the ocean, is there a beach?"

He shook his head. "No, it's not prudent. And against the rules. After ten, if you like, you can walk in the gardens. The other patients will all be in their cabañas." He hesitated. "But you must go to bed early, Señora, it is part of my prescription for your nerves."

The heavy growth around the little terrace provided complete privacy. After he left she stripped off her clothes and plunged naked into the pool. The water was tepid and it was too small for proper swimming, she could only paddle a bit or float. When she came out she didn't dry herself, just tied on a cotton sarong and went inside and started the fan, and sat and tried to read the books and magazines she'd brought with her.

After lunch she slept for an hour. Then back to the pool. Then it was time for dinner. The boredom was stultifying, much worse than it had been the first time. Because of the heat, she decided. When ten o'clock came she bolted out the door like a prisoner who has just heard the locks click open.

During the day the gardens were gay with exotic birds, everything from hoopoes to peacocks. She'd caught sight of their plumage and heard the fluttering of their wings. Now they slept, and it was like walking in an enchanted forest—silent except for murmuring insects, heavy with scent, and lit only by a full orange moon. It was still very hot. She wore shorts and a shirt tied around her midriff and rope-soled sandals, but the absence of the blazing sun made it seem cooler. Juffie strolled along the winding paths, knowing she should take note of where she was going so she could find her way back but too glad to be beyond the confines of the cabaña to care.

After a while she glanced at her watch: ten-fifteen. She'd been walking for fifteen minutes and she hadn't come to the end of the property. She was still surrounded by the carefully created domain of Dr. Santiago. The sweet smell that permeated the air was heavier now. She traced it to a patch of white flowers with narrow green leaves and she knelt and picked one and buried her nose in its heart. She didn't know its name, but it was obviously one of those plants that scattered its perfume at night to attract some nocturnal creature necessary for pollination.

"Juffie? It is you, isn't it?"

She remained where she was, kneeling by the flowers, and didn't turn around. "Matt?"

"Yes."

"How did you find me? Why?"

"I didn't find you. I wasn't looking for you. I left my cabaña to walk in the garden."

She stood up and turned to him. He wore cut-off jeans and a T-shirt. She'd never seen him in clothes like that. "You're a patient here?"

"No, not me."

"What are you doing here then?"

"Shh. It's after curfew, we're not supposed to be here. There are guards." He approached her and took the flower she held and tucked it behind her ear and put his hands on her shoulders with a touch both gentle and insistent. "It's a tuberose. Native to Mexico. Juffie, are you ill? Something you haven't told me about?"

He asked the question so gently, she knew he expected her to say she had some terrible disease. "No, nothing like that. I'm fine. I just . . . needed a rest."

He studied her face, trying to see if she was lying. "You're sure."

"Of course I'm sure. My nerves, that's all. I've been depressed, as you know. Somebody told me this was a good place for nerves. Mineral waters and herbal teas, stuff like that."

"Yes. I heard Santiago also did that kind of thing."

"Okay, that's why I'm here. What about you?"

For answer he led her farther down the path she'd been following. "I've been here ten days; I found a chink in the armor."

"Ten days? That's when you closed the office and started your vacation, ten days ago."

"Right," he said, but he offered no further explanation.

They'd reached the wall. Like everything else, it was built of adobe and was whitewashed, but behind a tangle of vines there was a small break filled by a wrought-iron gate. "Is it locked?" Juffie asked.

"It was. I jimmied it a few days ago." He lifted the gate slightly on its hinges and swung it open. "Through here, come on."

They came out onto a dirt track; a few spindly low shrubs marked it off from a sweep of bare grassland. "The jungle is confined to inside," Matt said. "This path goes to the beach. Be careful, it doesn't seem to be used much, and there are lots of rocks and potholes." He took her hand and guided her forward.

They didn't speak until they came to the sea and the sand. Suddenly it was blissfully cool. The only sound was that of gentle waves slapping the shore. They walked to the edge of the dunes and sat down. "I guess it's time I explained," he said.

"Yes, I think so."

"I'm here with my wife. I'm married, have been since forty-one."

"I know."

"You do? How did you find out? Practically nobody knows."

"How I found out isn't important. Why is it such a big secret, Matt? How come it's taken over six years for you to tell me?"

"If I'm going to answer that, I have to begin at the beginning. Do you know where I grew up, Juffie?"

"Only what I've guessed. Philadelphia, Chesapeake Bay, someplace like that. And you spent summers at some lake, and went to Groton or Choate, then to Yale or maybe Princeton. Not Harvard. I'm from Boston, I recognize the Harvard type. You're Ivy League, but not exactly Harvard."

He laughed softly. "Is that the characterization you've written for me?"

"Yes. I worked it all out that first day in your office."

"You lose. The panel is defeated and the challenger wins. It's a part, Juffie. I act it rather well, I think, but it's a role. I was born on West Forty-ninth Street, over near the docks in what is generally known as Hell's Kitchen. I never knew my father, and my mother didn't know much besides a bottle. I have one brother, he's a homosexual. The kind who isn't at peace about it and never was."

And that explained Christopher Street. "Do you see much of your brother?"

"Not much. When I do, we fight. I don't care that he's homosexual, just that he lives the way he does. It's such a . . . a marginal life. I don't know another word for it."

"I understand. And your mother?"

"She's dead. Which is a blessing for her and for me and my brother. So much for the villains. Enter the hero, stage right. A teacher at the old Haaren High School on Columbus Circle. A Mr.

Durant. He showed me that I might be as tough and filthy-mouthed and amoral as every kid on my block, but I was different. I had a brain. 'It's your one piece of luck, you little shit,' he told me. 'You going to use it or piss it away?' That's the way he talked, which made him different from every other teacher, and which is why I listened to him. Act Two, Rutgers on a scholarship, followed by Columbia Law, ditto."

Juffie was transfixed. She didn't move, almost didn't breathe, while he spoke. When he paused, she didn't say a word, simply waited for him to continue.

Matt picked up a handful of sand and trickled it through his fingers. The moon was high now and no longer orange; it had to be past midnight. He opened his palm and dropped the rest of the sand back to the beach, then reached out and drew his fingers the length of her bare thigh. She felt as if he'd stroked her skin with fire. He must have felt something of the same thing. He pulled back as though he'd been burned.

"Tell me the rest," she said. "When did you meet your wife?"

"In thirty-eight, my first year at law school. Patsy was a student too. And neither of us had any money; she came from a background that was just a variation on mine. I admired her guts before anything else. It took a lot more for a woman to escape the slums, particularly going the route she chose. Most girls who dreamed of better things managed to marry up. Patsy decided to study her way out.

"We both worked at a restaurant near Columbia. I washed dishes and she waited tables. When the place closed, we'd make a meal on the leftovers. The boss was nice about it. We'd sit at the worktable in the kitchen and eat and talk. After a few months we were in love, but she didn't want to get married until she got her degree. Anyway, we couldn't afford to get married."

He didn't touch her again, just crossed his arms behind his head and lay back and stared at the stars. "Juffie, am I boring you with all this? I've never told the whole story from start to finish. Not even to Santiago when I gave the medical history."

She wanted to ask what medical history? Whose? But she didn't want him to jump ahead, she wanted it all, every detail. "You're not boring me, Matt. Go on," she added softly, hoping to encourage him. "When did you pass the bar?"

"In late 1940, and I got a job with a firm of admiralty lawyers on Wall Street. Foley & Martin. A lot of their work was concerned with the commercial barges on the East River. They were always either blowing up or sinking or ramming each other and having claims. It was lucrative for the partners but boring as hell for me. After a year I was going out of my skull. Patsy was a senior at Columbia and we were saving all our money to get married. I was living in a furnished room near where I worked. It was the dullest existence imaginable. J. A. Martin took pity on me, had me to his house for dinner a few times. A remarkably kind man as well as a fine lawyer.

"He was also a great opera fan and he knew lots of singers. One day he handed me a contract a friend of his was about to sign with the Met. 'Take a look at this, Matt. See what you think.' I did and made a few suggestions. The lady asked me to see the Met's management and talk them into accepting my version. I did and they did. Happy endings all around."

He rolled over and propped himself on his elbow, looking at her in the moonlight. Their eyes met for a moment. She wasn't ready for that. Juffie shut hers. "Go on. You said you got married in 1941."

"Yes. In June, the day after Patsy was graduated. J.A.'s wedding present was the down payment on a brand-new ranch house in Englewood Cliffs, New Jersey. And he began talking to me about specializing in contract law, suggested I concentrate on theater people. I'd never even been to the theater."

"That first day I came to your office you told me you'd been stage-struck since you were a kid."

"I lied. My introduction was a flop that ran for a few weeks in forty-one, called *Papa Is All*. At the Guild on Fifty-second Street. The show was terrible, but Celeste Holm was great. I was hooked. That first summer Patsy and I were married we used to get in line for SRO tickets to something every Saturday night. She'd taken a job as a teacher in the New Jersey public school system, but she wasn't due to start until Steptember. We didn't actually have a honeymoon, couldn't afford it, but that whole long summer was like one. We were young and just married and we loved each other, and we ate cheap spaghetti dinners in places that watered the Chianti, and went to the theater and stood up for three acts. And the future looked wonderful."

"Then?"

"Then we were in a train accident going home to Jersey after a show. I had a broken arm, Patsy wasn't so lucky. She had severe head injuries. She's never spoken a word from that day to this. She looks perfectly normal, but she can't speak and she doesn't know anything. Not who she is, or who I am, or if it's winter or summer, or if she's in New Jersey or on the moon. The doctors say it's a tumor on the brain caused by the trauma of the accident. But they can't operate because of where it's located.

"They told me to put her in an institution, I wouldn't do it. A whole life of shit and she crawls out of it and then, just when she's breaking free, God or fate or what have you has the last laugh. So I keep her at home and keep someone with her around the clock. A little while after it happened J.A. helped me set up on my own. Then the war came, and the draft. I was exempt because of Patsy, so I was more or less the only game in town and I started doing well right away. But Patsy takes every cent I earn. We still live in the same little house in Englewood Cliffs."

She was crying, but she ignored her tears and rolled over, grabbing his arm. "Why are you here, Matt? Why have you brought Patsy here?"

"Santiago has a big research operation and he does unusual things. He's not like those guys at home who won't breathe unless the A.M.A. tells them to and are afraid to try anything until it's been tested for fifty goddamn years. I know a guy who swears this clinic cured his wife of cancer. Santiago's giving Patsy injections of some new medicine that may dissolve the tumor."

She jumped to her feet and ran to the water's edge, choking on her sobs and the words she couldn't say. Santiago's a crook, he's tied into the Syndicate, he's running drugs, and the reason I know is because I'm his courier. But that wasn't the only reason she couldn't tell him, not just because of what she'd have to admit about herself. And not because of Paul and the fact that Finky Aronson owned them both. She couldn't say anything because she could not bear to destroy Matt's hope.

"You okay?" He'd come after her. He was standing beside her now, lightly touching her arm. The contact was as electric as it had been when he stroked her thigh. The barriers between them were breaking and the current was bursting free and building.

She nodded. "I'm okay."

"I didn't mean to upset you. It's just . . . Juffie, do you know how many times I wanted to tell you all this?"

"Why didn't you?"

"Partly for the same reason I never tell anyone else. I don't want anybody's pity. Patsy wouldn't want it. Besides, I realized I had no right."

He touched her again, this time with only two fingers, tilting her chin, tipping her face to the moonlight. "Because I love you, Juffie Kane. I've loved you from the moment you walked into my office in your little black hat with the red feather and told me you weren't going to play Delilah because you were gorgeous but because you were a damned good actress. I looked into those violet eyes with the unbelievable dark rings and I thought, I love you, I will love you until the day I die. And I'm never going to tell you so, because I will also be married until the day I die, or the day Patsy dies, which comes to the same thing."

"And do you know how I feel?"

"Yes. You love me. I've known that for a long time too, Juffie. You're a wonderful actress, but not that wonderful. Not with me, at any rate, not in your unguarded moments." His fingers touched her cheek. "I don't know why you should love me when you can have any man in America, but I know you do."

She put her fingers lightly over his. "When I told Paul I'd marry him, it was a few weeks after I found out you were married."

Matt took his hand away and broke the tenuous physical contact. "I see. I knew he'd been asking you for years, he told me so himself. I wondered why you finally gave in." He turned his head away so he wasn't looking at her. "Juffie, it's okay, isn't it? It's working? I figured it would, because he obviously loves you so damned much."

"Yes, I think it's working. But at the moment that's rather beside the point." She moved in front of him and lifted her face. "Kiss me, Matt."

He did, a slow, gentle kiss, and they held it a long time.

"That's it," he said when they broke. "That's the end of it, Juffie. I can't leave Patsy, not ever. I could never live with myself if I did. I've never wanted an affair with you, something we have to snatch at in out-of-the-way places, and hide from everyone who knows us. I still don't want it. I'm ten years older than you, I've seen a hell of a lot of that kind of thing. I won't let you settle for it."

They stood silent for some seconds, not touching, separated only by inches, and by a chasm impossible to cross.

"I want to swim," she said, suddenly breathless with the heat and the still night air. She tore off her clothes and left them in a heap on the beach, and struck off into the sea. A few moments later he was beside her and they swam together, matching their strokes. Finally she was exhausted and she turned on her back and let the ocean support her body.

"You're so beautiful," Matt whispered. "Oh Christ, Juffie, you're so goddamned beautiful."

He kissed her again. Not gently this time, but with the pent-up hunger that had gnawed at them both for so long. She clung to him and wrapped her legs around his torso and opened her mouth wider to taste yet more of him. Then a light played over the water, missing them by only a few feet.

Matt pulled back. "What the hell's that?"

"I don't know."

They studied the black horizon. "It's a boat," Matt whispered. "Over there to the left. Do you see it?"

"Yes, a shape in the water anyway. Who are they? Fishermen, do you think?"

"No, that's not what I think. Fishermen don't come up so quietly, and run without lights, and check the beach with a searchlight."

"Oh," she said softly. "I understand."

"Drugs or guns or money. It could be anything down here. Stay absolutely still, keep treading water, and try not to splash. If they turn the light back on, we go under and hope it passes before we run out of breath."

"Santiago?" She made it a very tentative question, and was grateful for the cover of darkness and the water that put some small distance between them.

"No reason to think so. A deserted stretch of beach, the only thing nearby a clinic full of self-absorbed sick people. The location could appeal to anybody."

She didn't have to answer because something was happening on the speedboat. They lowered a dinghy and two men rowed to shore. The men dragged the small craft onto the beach and left it hidden among the dunes and headed inland on foot. Whatever they were carrying was either too small or too well hidden to be seen. Is it bigger than a bread box, Juffie wondered. No, it's no bigger than a flowerpot. What she said was, "What about our clothes? They're on the beach."

"At the other end. And they're not looking for anything. We'd better stop talking. Voices carry over the water."

A few minutes went by. Finally they saw the speedboat start to leave. It still showed no lights, just a shape on the horizon, and it ran almost silently, with only a low hum identifiable because they were listening for it. "They've muffled the motor somehow," Matt said.

"Where are they going?"

"God knows. They've probably got a rendezvous time arranged with the guys from the dinghy, and they'd rather wait it out farther offshore." The boat passed beyond sight. They were alone again. "Come on," he said. "We've got to get out of here while we have the chance."

They swam to shore and found their clothes and hurried up the track to the gate in the adobe wall. It was as they had left it. There was no indication that the men from the dinghy had entered before them.

Matt stayed with her while they walked the paths in Dr. Santiago's forest, looking for her cabaña. Once they almost ran into a guard, but fortunately the man didn't see them. By the time Juffie spotted the number thirty-four on her door it was nearly morning. Dawn was rising pink in the eastern sky. "Come in," she whispered.

"No. It's no good, Juffie. It'll just hurt all the more afterward. Besides, it's almost time for Patsy's injection. She gets it before breakfast. It's pretty painful. I want to be with her." He leaned forward and kissed her forehead.

"I'll be here until Thursday evening. We could go to the beach tomorrow night." She was shameless; she wanted him and she didn't care about anything else.

"No," he said again. "No. I'll see you in New York next week. Business as usual, it's the only way."

She put her hand on his arm to stop him leaving. "Matt, I hope the injections help Patsy. I mean that, I really do."

"I know. Good night, sweet princess."

"Sweet prince," she corrected him, managing to grin. "Don't start feeding me screwed-up cues, Matt. Not after all this time."

"Never happen, Juffie. Never happen."

·   ·   ·   ·

Years later—after Valachi spilled his guts, and Mario Puzo created his godfather, and the whole country was familiar with the name Mafia and the words *la cosa nostra*, which was some time after the avalanche in Switzerland—one of the few men who knew talked about it one night in a bar in Las Vegas.

"Get this," he said. "Before the commission okayed we should take the drug business away from the sambos, a few of the guys got impatient. So Finky Aronson sends this actress broad down to Mexico, and she carries a couple of pounds of powder back with her. A couple of pounds. In a flowerpot first, then in some candlesticks, and the last time behind one of them fancy Mexican silver mirrors. You know how many nickel bags they made outta that much pure junk? A lot of nickel bags. Can you figure doing that now? I mean, the customs guys and the T-men was so innocent in them days. No sniffer dogs, no X rays, no nothin'. Just this dame and some goddamn spic souvenirs, worth at least a cool million when they was cracked open."

Chapter 13

*M*att acted as though nothing had happened, nothing had changed. A couple of times Juffie made some tentative gesture, spoke some provocative word, but he always cut her off. As in December, when they were having lunch at Joe Madden's on West Fifty-sixth, and she grabbed his arm and said his name in a way that made it much more than merely his name.

"No," Matt said. "No."

She pulled back, feeling not so much rejected as despairing. She didn't think of Paul, didn't feel disloyal. Juffie had drawn a line down the center of her mind. Her husband and their life together was on one side of it, Matt, whom she loved, on the other.

"Eat your steak," Matt said gently. "You need to keep up your strength."

She produced a weak grin. "For what?"

"To stay healthy, so you can succeed in this brilliant idea of mine."

His idea was that Juffie should do one of the television dramas which provided some of the very best entertainment available at the moment. The irony was that they had become so because of Hollywood's fear of competition from the new medium.

"Movies Are Better Than Ever" was the slogan of a campaign to lure people out of their living rooms, and the Hollywood studios refused to provide their rival with old films. The resultant hours of empty air time created a vacuum, which became a vortex, which spewed forth dramatic shows such as *Studio One, Hallmark Hall of Fame, Playhouse 90,* and the *U.S. Steel Hour.* The insatiable needs of these programs could not be satisfied by the existing repertoire; theoretically one show could go through all of Shakespeare in a single season, so in turn a new generation of writers was called forth. Many of them were fine talents.

"Chayefsky's very good," Matt said. *"Marty, The Bachelor Party*—those were great shows, Juffie."

"Yes, but I think he's more a man's writer." She pushed away the remains of her filet mignon. "Anyway, Matt, they do very little comedy, and I haven't done a dramatic role since I played Hannah Glemp. And I've told you what happened to her." Certainly not that she'd sold her soul to keep a turkey alive and hung on to a lover who didn't give a damn about her—only that the show had been a flop. She didn't elaborate now, but only said, "The idea scares me a little."

"Don't be scared." He rested his chin on his hand and gazed at her. "You're not just another pretty face, you know. You're the inimitable Juffie Kane. You can do anything."

"Maybe. Matt, if we find the right thing, and if you can make a deal, and if I do it, will it get me back on Broadway?"

"It could. I think it will."

"And you haven't heard anything more about that show with the crazy name?"

"Will Success Spoil Rock Hunter? Yes, I heard something more. They've signed Jayne Mansfield for the lead. And Tony Guthrie tells me he wants Ruth Gordon for the revival of the Wilder thing that used to be called *The Merchant of Yonkers."*

"What are they calling it now?"

"Not settled yet, but looks like *The Matchmaker."*

"Starring Ruth Gordon."

"Yes, if they get her. Do you want some dessert?"

Juffie shook her head. "Just coffee. What bothers me is that mostly those TV shows use newcomers. After you mentioned it I checked the listings for the past couple of months. Anne Bancroft, Eva Marie Saint, Joanne Woodward . . . Nobody's ever heard of these women. It's the same with the men—Rod Steiger, Paul Newman. There's not a famous name among them. Am I kidding myself, Matt, or am I still a famous name?"

He looked into his coffee cup for a few seconds, then raised his eyes to hers. "At the moment, yes. But just barely, Juffie. This business is beset by a collective short memory. Very short."

"I see," she said quietly. "Well, that's telling it like it is, isn't it?

And you're right, of course. So it's the only thing left for me. A television drama."

"Maybe not the only thing, but if we can find the right property, it will move you off the dime." He signaled the waiter and asked for coffee. The remains of their steaks were cleared away. No one asked if they'd liked them. Madden had a slogan printed on his menu: "If you enjoy your meal we are glad, and if you don't, well, go somewhere else."

Juffie was thinking about that. "Take it or leave it, like the steaks. Okay, if we can get it, I'll take it."

"Good. I'll start sniffing around and talk to a few people. It could be terrific, Juffie. A lot of the writers really are wonderful. Rod Serling, Gore Vidal, a fellow named Reggie Rose. They're doing some fine stuff."

"Okay." Then, before they left the restaurant, she asked, "Matt, is Patsy any better?"

He shrugged. "I don't know. Sometimes I think she is, just a little. At other times I think I'm kidding myself. But it's been only three months. Santiago told me it could take as much as six. Anyway, we're going to try another course of the injections over Christmas."

There wasn't any point in saying more, and she didn't, but what she thought must have shown on her face. "There's nothing to lose," he said. "I have to try. What about you, Juffie? Are you going back for more soothing of your nerves?"

For a moment she thought he was asking if she wanted to meet him at the clinic. But he wasn't, the question was no more than it seemed. "No. I won't be going back."

That at least was true. "I am not a greedy man, Miss Kane." That's what Finky Aronson had said. "We have been very successful, there's no need to take unnecessary risks." So she didn't have to go to Mexico again, or bring home any more souvenirs. Thank God for that, and for the fact that Paul had survived his crisis and was once more on top of the world.

The music critics loved the Viennese chamber orchestra, and the English ballet was the success of the holiday season. To frost the cake, audiences were fascinated by an Italian film called *La Strada*. It ran for four months at La Venue II in the Village, and every screening was a sellout. The same was true across the country. Paul had taken a fancy suite of offices on Madison Avenue and Forty-seventh Street, and formed a corporation called Paul Dumont Enterprises, and he had a staff of six now. "It's all thanks to you," he told her repeatedly. "If you hadn't been so brave, I'd never have made it."

Juffie didn't think she was brave. She got sick to her stomach every time she thought of what she'd done. But each time she'd remind herself why she did it, and that she'd had no choice, and that if she'd not gone to Mexico she might never have known that Matt Varley loved her.

She hugged that fact to herself, a bittersweet secret to ward off the demons of a sleepless night. The other cure was Paul's mouth and his hands and the tireless, inventive, enthusiastic sex that remained as much a part of their lives as ever. Sometimes she had to fake it. Unwittingly she'd think of Matt or of Dr. Santiago or of Finky Aronson, and excitement would disappear, its heat chilled by the ice of memory. But the last thing she wanted was to discuss any of those subjects with Paul. And she was a terrific actress.

But maybe not so terrific as all that, not in her unguarded moments, as Matt had pointed out.

"Juffie," Paul said one night. "Where are you? In the last few minutes you've gone away."

"No, I haven't. I'm right here, Paul."

"You're here, but you're not here."

"You're imagining things. Look, I'll prove I'm here. Like this. And like this." She slid her tongue down his chest and his belly until she got to his crotch, and took him in her mouth, and made him forget his questions.

It was just before Christmas, on another of those nights when he'd sensed some distancing in her and she'd responded by becoming the aggressor, that he raised the issue of children for the first time. They were at last sated and exhausted and Juffie was dropping off to sleep, but Paul whispered her name. "Juffie. Don't go to sleep yet. I have an idea."

"No more ideas, my love. Not tonight."

"It's not that kind of idea. Juffie, let's have a baby." She didn't answer immediately. "Juffie, did you hear me?"

"I heard you."

"What do you think?"

She rolled over and tried to see him in the dark. She could

distinguish only his shape beneath the wildly expensive hand-stitched yellow quilt Billy Baldwin had told her was magnificent and worth every penny. "Paul, I'm not ready. Someday maybe, but not now."

"We can't wait too long, not if we're going to do it. You're twenty-seven, I'm thirty. We don't have all the time in the world, *chérie.*"

"Funny, I didn't realize I was turning into an old hag."

"Don't be ridiculous. You know I didn't mean that. But people should have children while they're young, while they can enjoy them."

"I agree about the enjoying part. And I wouldn't enjoy a baby right now. I have to feel that my career's back on track first. I have to prove that I can still do more than ask absurd questions of people with crazy jobs. There aren't too many parts for pregnant ladies."

"No, I suppose there aren't. Very well, we'll wait a while. But not too long." He chuckled and patted her belly. "To tell the truth, *madame*, I want to knock you up."

She laughed too. "Okay, but not without permission. Promise me that. No tricks." The only time they'd taken a chance was that first night in the projection room of his theater. Subsequently they'd been supercautious. They used two kinds of birth control, his and hers as Paul called them. "No punching pinholes in my diaphragm or forgetting your rubbers when it rains. Promise me, Paul."

"I promise. When we do it, we'll both have decided to go ahead. I mean it, Juffie. You can trust me, I won't jump the pistol."

"Jump the gun. And I do trust you. If I didn't, this would be no marriage at all."

· · · ·

Trust was something Karen Rice thought about a great deal during that Christmas season of 1954. She trusted Bernard. She had to. He'd been so right about so many things. She had her doctorate now, and her career was flourishing, and while they maintained separate apartments in Brighton, they had a tiny cabin in the wilds of Maine where they went together many weekends and lived like an old married couple. Old was the operative word.

In recent months she'd suggested repeatedly that they should give in to convention and get married. "No," Bernard said. "I'm too old, Karen. I'm fifty-seven. I can't change my ways now. Besides, you'll meet a younger man someday. You'll want your freedom."

"I won't! Darling, how can you say such a thing? You know how much I love you. You must know."

"I do. I also know that I'm moving toward the end of my life, and you're at the beginning of yours."

She hated to hear him say things like that. Invariably she changed the subject. But even when they didn't talk about it, Karen thought about it. Her thoughts never included any speculation that he might be right. Not in this instance. What she thought about was how to convince Bernard that she meant to stay with him always. She wasn't a flighty child, she was a mature, settled woman. Her campaign to prove that had begun three years earlier, in 1951, after the trip to Las Vegas. When the earth had opened, and Karen had looked into the chasm yawning at her feet.

The euphoria produced by that single weekend at the Flamingo Hotel lasted five days. Then she became depressed. It took her weeks to figure out what she was unhappy about, what she craved. Then one August day when she was in a café near the B.U. campus and she glanced at the jukebox, with its rows of buttons and flashing lights and garish painted designs, she knew. She was possessed with longing for the jukebox to turn into a slot machine.

She wanted to sit with an endless supply of dimes and keep feeding them into the machine and pulling the lever. She wanted that long-drawn-out buzz, that peculiar intimacy, that sustained thrill of watching the symbols spin and waiting to see if she was a winner or a loser. She wanted it so much she could taste it, and being without it gave her such a sense of acute deprivation, she became nervous and irritable and depressed.

Karen had no desire to find a bookie and bet on the horses or the numbers, or even to go to a racetrack. What she hungered for was to be in a womblike casino in Las Vegas, staring at the whirling cherries and lemons and oranges that spelled instant success or instant failure, and always gave you an immediate second chance.

The literature on compulsive gambling was not extensive, but Karen read everything that existed. She had no difficulty recognizing herself in the archetypes depicted in the learned tomes. Jesus! Oh, Jesus! How did this happen to me? What crazy gene got into my makeup? What did Leah and Jake do or not do? She racked her brain, but she could think of no explanation. Nonetheless, she recognized the truth, and she was determined never to give in to the obsession lying in wait beneath the surface of her conscious mind.

"What's wrong, Karen?" Bernard had asked frequently during that painful period. "What's the matter? Is it me? Something I've done? Are you unhappy about us?"

"No, of course not. It has nothing to do with you. I'm just nervous about my thesis."

He accepted that excuse because it was logical. Karen clung to it and went on fighting her secret battle. A few times she thought of confiding in Bernard. He was a psychologist, after all. Besides, he loved her. But she couldn't say anything. It was like confessing to leprosy. He'd be understanding and he'd pity her and try to help, but underneath he would be revolted. As she herself was revolted.

She attempted to use that revulsion to her advantage. She used aversion therapy, told herself how much she hated gambling, how degenerate it was, how self-destructive. She formed a detailed mental image of herself: slack-mouthed and dirty, probably toothless, living in a hovel somewhere in Las Vegas, where she begged in the streets for money by day and gambled it away by night. It was an exaggerated picture perhaps, but it worked.

Gradually she came to associate her craving with that thoroughly repellent image, and when she pushed away the mirage of Karen as a mindless slut, she was pushing away the gambling as well. For a while she thought she'd beaten it and she was triumphant; then in early May 1952 her dissertation, *Crime and the Immigrant Experience*, was rejected. The disappointment plunged her right back into dreams of running away to Las Vegas and playing the slots until her arm fell off.

What saved her then were the snapshots. She was sitting in Bernard's house, at his desk, waiting for him to come home, and she saw the corner of an envelope just visible under the blotter. It was the kind of envelope used to return developed pictures, and because it was that and not something more personal, she gave in to temptation and looked inside.

The envelope contained old black-and-white snaps, late thirties she judged, maybe early forties. They were of Bernard and a woman who had to be his dead wife. In the pictures she was very much alive. Karen had always imagined Bess as a sophisticated Jennifer Jones type. But the female standing beside Bernard on the sidewalk in front of this very house had her hair in a bun—there was no way it could be called a chignon—and her clothes weren't of the chic-little-black-dress-with-pearls variety.

"R. H. Stearns," Karen said aloud in the empty room. "She had to buy that stuff at R. H. Stearns." It was where rich Yankee ladies shopped, proper Bostonian types who cared more about quality than style. There was one snap of Bernard and Bess under a tree, God knows where, and it showed her full-length. She was wearing lace-up shoes with Cuban heels.

So that was what attracted Bernard, a no-nonsense professional woman who looked as sensible and intelligent as she doubtless was, and didn't fuck up when she went after her Ph.D. Not a smart-mouthed schoolgirl who always chose the highest possible heels and bright colors and cinch belts that showed off her tiny waist. Certainly not one with a latent addiction to playing the slot machines in Las Vegas. After that she made a conscious effort to change outside as well as in.

"Bernard, do you like this suit?" It was dark brown and it came from Stearns and it looked almost exactly like the one Bess had been wearing in one of the pictures. She'd had to perform contortions with her budget to justify invading her meager savings to buy it. She'd been working only part-time since she left Simmons to allow time for studying for her master's and then her Ph.D. Wool suits cost a lot more than the little cotton dresses she usually chose for spring. The brown suit meant she could look forward to an entire summer of scrimping. "Well, do you like it? I think it's quite smart."

"Er . . . yes, of course it is, Karen. It makes you look a lot older."

"More professional too," she agreed. "I'm going to take very good care of it, so next May, when I face the board again with my new thesis, I'll look the part of Dr. Karen Rice. Don't give up on me, Bernard, I'm going to make you proud of me yet."

He'd kissed her and petted her and told her he was already proud of her, but the spring day in 1953, when Karen was actually awarded her Ph.D., was the first day she'd felt absolutely sure of him.

Soon afterward she got a part-time teaching appointment in the continuing education department at Northeastern, and was made assistant head of the guidance division of the West End Settlement House, where she'd worked since her sophomore year at Simmons, and she was named as a testing consultant in the neurology department of the Peter Bent Brigham Hospital. Karen was very pleased with herself for managing to arrange her life to include three jobs. She thought it gave her a lot of kudos to pursue simultaneously three different elements of her discipline.

Bernard agreed, and congratulated her on each achievement. Meanwhile he was deep in the writing of a new book, so the fact that they seldom made love could be attributed to their busy lives.

The day she got her doctorate was also the day Karen stopped thinking about slot machines all the time. Moreover, she stopped waking up in a cold sweat because she'd been dreaming about Las Vegas. She told herself what a happy, fulfilled woman she was. Some months later, aware of a vague and inappropriate discontent, she decided that the thing needed to make life perfect was that she become Mrs. Bernard Hanrihan de jure as well as de facto.

It was early 1954 when she faced that yearning of her secret heart. She'd had enough of being Bernard's clandestine mistress. She wanted the whole world to see the final accolade, the ultimate confirmation that little Karen Rice had made it out of Leah and Jake's tenement flat and wasn't ever going back.

That realization happened to coincide with Bernard's buying the cabin in Maine. So she began her overt quest for a wedding ring amid the Arcadian pleasures of the rural haven he acquired thirty miles northwest of Biddeford. That's also where he started saying he was too old, and implying their relationship wasn't permanent and she'd find someone more her own age one day.

"I'll never leave you, Bernard," she assured him repeatedly as they walked beneath the pines. "Never. I love you and I always will."

In 1954 they went to Maine for the Christmas holidays: a whole week alone together in the woods. The snow was four feet deep outside and the telephone was out of order, but they were snug and cozy. The cabin had no electricity to worry about, they used candles and cooked with bottled gas, and the heat was supplied by a wood stove. There was enough cut wood stacked out back to last three winters, even in Maine. "It's perfect here," Karen said, stretching her legs toward the fire. "Just perfect."

"Yes, I think so too. Karen, wouldn't you be more comfortable in slacks?"

She was wearing a woolen skirt and a twin sweater set, and thick lisle stockings with her sensible oxfords. "I never wear slacks, Bernard. They're not very professional looking."

"You used to wear them."

"When I was much younger. Before I grew up."

"I thought the point of this hideaway was that we could be together with no concerns about the outside world, the way it was when I first knew you. Really knew you, I mean."

"You really know me now. I owe everything to you, Bernard darling, you showed me the woman I truly was, the woman I wanted to be."

"That's a big responsibility," he said softly.

"Not too big for you, my darling." She kissed him lightly on the forehead on her way to the kitchen. "It's almost midnight. I've made some spiced cider. We can drink a toast to 1955."

· · · ·

"Happy New Year!" everybody yelled. Gold and silver streamers danced in the currents of air created by the moving crowd. Balloons and confetti descended from the ceiling. The band struck up "Auld Lang Syne." Juffie and Paul were at El Morocco this year, not "21." There was no television and they were spared the sight of the ball dropping in Times Square. El Morocco, with its swank zebra-striped decor and its ladies in ermine and pearls, suited Paul's mood. He toasted Juffie with a glass of Pol Roger 1947. Each of the four bottles their party had consumed so far would appear on his bill at something close to fifty dollars, but Paul seemed unconcerned. "Happy New Year, _chérie_."

"Happy New Year." She flicked a piece of red confetti from the lapel of his black dinner jacket and leaned forward to be kissed.

The shouts of the merrymakers around them subsided somewhat, and they could hear the band, and they could talk. "I'm a little sorry to say good-bye to 1954," Paul said. "It was a very good year."

"Mixed," Juffie amended. "I give it mixed reviews." She could be frank because the two couples with them, associates of Paul's, were on the tiny dance floor, and for a few minutes they were alone.

"It's the year we got married," Paul said.

"Yes, but also the year of Piaf."

"And your trips south. Which were my fault." He looked glum. "Juffie, will you ever forgive me for that?"

It must be the champagne. He'd never before taken the exclusive blame for that episode. "There's nothing to forgive," she said. "It wasn't anybody's fault. It just happened. We got ourselves into a bind."

"And you got us out." He kissed her again. "I adore you, *chérie*. Do you know that you're the most beautiful woman in the room? Emeralds suit you." He'd given her emerald earrings for Christmas. Tonight she wore them with a strapless black gown and a chinchilla wrap. The fur was another of Paul's Christmas gifts.

Juffie touched the earrings. "These would suit any woman as long as rigor mortis hadn't set in. They're so gorgeous I'm almost afraid to wear them."

"Don't be. They're insured. I want you to wear them every day. At breakfast."

"Right, as soon as we buy the solid gold plates."

"Is that what you want?" He sounded serious. "You shall have them. I'll order them tomorrow."

She laughed. "No, Paul, I was joking. I do not want solid gold plates, and I think you're a little drunk."

"No, I'm perfectly sober. And I want you to have whatever your heart desires, whatever you can think of. What do you want, Juffie? Tell me."

"Only for us to be happy together," she said gently.

"Aren't you going to ask what I want?"

"Yes, I am. What do you want for 1955, darling?"

"A son," he said. "I want a son. Or a daughter if that's what comes. I want a child, *chérie*. Our child."

"Paul, we talked about it, we agreed. Not until . . ."

"Until your career is back on course," he supplied. "Yes, I

know. What does Matt say? Has he found a television show for you?"

"Not yet. He's talking to people, but you know how it is over the holidays. Nobody's in, and if they are, they don't return telephone calls."

One of the other couples rejoined them then, and the Dumonts did not again discuss emeralds or children, or the secret wishes of either. Not that Juffie was prepared to disclose her true secret wish. Most of the time she didn't even allow herself to think about it.

On the fourth of January, when New York was settling back into a regular working schedule, she called Matt. He had nothing good to report. "Paddy Chayefsky said normally he'd jump at a chance to write a show for you, he's a longtime fan. But Hollywood's taking all his creative energy at the moment, he's doing a film version of *Marty*. I haven't been able to reach Serling or Vidal."

"What about something already written? Something that's casting now."

"It's possible," Matt agreed. "And I've got feelers out, but what I'd really like is a specially tailored package we take to the networks. Maybe even get them to bid against each other."

"It's not about money, Matt."

"Of course it is. That's how they vote, sweetheart, with dollars. I want to engineer a landslide victory for you. So be patient, please."

"Okay." She took a deep breath. "How was Mexico?"

He didn't answer right away. "Lonely," he said finally. "I went for a walk on the beach."

"Matt—"

"Forget I said that," he interrupted quickly. "I spoke out of turn, Juffie."

"No, you didn't. But you think you did, so we'll let it lie. How's Patsy? Any response?"

"No, none. And she was awfully sick this time. I think maybe she's allergic to something in the new medicine. Her . . ." He swallowed hard; she could actually hear him swallow on the other end of the line. "Her hair is falling out. They tell me it will grow back, but Christ, it's awful. The only consolation, if you can call it that, is that she isn't aware it's happening."

"It *is* a consolation," Juffie said. "Hang on to that, Matt. She doesn't worry about medicine or her hair or anything else. You keep her comfortable and looked after and that's wonderful. It's all she needs."

It was not, however, all Juffie needed. When she hung up she put on her coat and went out for a long walk. Walking, she'd discovered, sometimes helped. It was one of those January days that make winter in New York tolerable—crisp, invigorating cold, and bright sun in an azure sky. She went west to Lexington Avenue, then uptown as far as Ninetieth Street. There was a Whelan's drugstore on the corner, with a soda fountain. She realized she was hungry, so she went in and ordered coffee and an English muffin.

While she was eating, a boy came through the door. She guessed he was about sixteen. He hesitated, looking all around the drugstore before he took the stool next to hers. He had a notebook with him and he ordered a Coke, then busied himself writing. But every few seconds he'd sneak a glance at her when he thought she wasn't looking. Finally he worked up his courage. "I don't mean to be rude, but you are Juffie Kane, aren't you?"

She smiled at him. "Yes."

"I knew you had to be. There can't be two ladies who look like you."

"If I have a double," Juffie said. "I haven't met her. What are you writing? Homework?"

"No, I know I look like a school kid, but I'm twenty-three." He blushed. "I'm too embarrassed to tell you what I'm writing."

"Oh, that sort of thing," she said, laughing. "Well then, I don't want to know."

"No, you've got it all wrong. I mean, I've given you the wrong impression." He shoved the notebook toward her. "Look, I know this is more nerve than brains, but here I walk into an ordinary drugstore, Whelan's for God's sake, and I find Juffie Kane sitting at the counter, and she actually asks me what I'm writing. I can't let an opportunity like that pass by, can I?"

"I don't know. You still haven't told me what it is."

"It's a play." He blurted out the words. "I'm a playwright."

"Oh, I see. Ever had anything published? Or performed?"

"Only in college. I don't work at it full-time."

She motioned for the man behind the counter to refill her coffee cup. "What do you do full-time?"

"Work for my father, he's a stockbroker. I didn't go into the office today because I think I'm getting a cold. At least my mother said I was. We live across the street. I'd like to move out and get my own place, but living with my folks means I have a lot more time to write." He realized he'd been displaying his nervousness by chattering, and he stopped. Juffie didn't say anything, only took another sip of her coffee. He waited until she set down the cup, then asked, "Miss Kane, will you read this? Please. I know it's an outrageous request, but . . ."

Juffie's heart sank. He was a nice-looking kid with freckles and a crew cut, and he did look at least six years younger than his claimed age of twenty-three, and she hated the position they'd been put in by this casual encounter. If she refused to read his play she was a bitch; if he didn't ask he'd curse himself as a coward ever afterward; if she read it and it was terrible she couldn't say so, because she could be wrong, and even if she were not, it was too unkind to be conceived. She didn't take the proffered notebook. "What's your name?"

"Henry Whiteman."

"Look, Henry Whiteman, do you really want me to read your play? It's probably a first draft and I'll be judging something you haven't finished, which may be entirely different when you do. Besides, actresses aren't necessarily good at telling about plays in general. I can say for sure only that something is right or wrong for me."

"It's not a first draft. It's a story I've been working on for a couple of years. Of course, I'm sure I could improve it. I mean, if there was something you didn't like you could tell me, and I could change it." He hesitated. "Maybe. If I agreed."

She chuckled. "You're a writer all right. Okay, if you're sure. Let's see what you've got." She slid her cup to one side and he pushed the looseleaf notebook closer. Juffie bent her head and started to read. His handwriting was very neat and legible, that was one good thing. She didn't say anything for a few moments. And she turned the page. Finally she looked up. "Mr. White-man—"

"Henry, please," he interrupted. "Please call me Henry."

"Okay, Henry. Do you have a typewritten copy of this script?"

He shook his head glumly. "No. I don't type and I don't like to ask the secretaries in the office." His face brightened. "Maybe I could get it done by some agency. I could send it to you in a few days."

"No, that's all right. Your handwriting's pretty clear. I asked because I'd like to borrow this and take it home and read it more carefully. But you won't want to let your only copy out of your hands."

"Sure I will! Take it, please take it. You can send it back when you're done. Or I'll come and pick it up. Or send a messenger."

"You're sure you trust me with your only copy?"

"Of course I do. You're Juffie Kane."

They exchanged addresses and shook hands and he went across the street and disappeared into an old brownstone. Juffie tried to get a cab, but it was lunchtime and there wasn't one to be had. She glanced up Lexington for a bus, but there wasn't one of those either. She started walking, then broke into a run, clutching the looseleaf notebook under her arm.

Ninety minutes later she called Matt's office, but he wasn't in. Miss Wilkins promised to have him return her call the minute he arrived. She paced the apartment for an hour. Finally the telephone rang.

"It's me, Juffie, Matt. What's up?"

"Me. I am up. Up over the moon."

"Why? What's happened?"

"Matt, I have just read the most marvelous script. It's written for television, about a woman named Tilda Patchik who escapes the Nazis and comes to America and becomes a doctor and makes a success of her life. Then she gets called before a Senate committee investigating so-called Communists and sees everything disintegrating around her yet again. It's a superb story and she's got the most marvelous lines—"

"Hey, hold on a minute. Whose script is it? Where did you get it?"

Juffie took a deep breath. "I hope you're sitting down, Matt. Because you're not going to believe this."

.   .   .   .

Just Like Home starring Juffie Kane was broadcast on Wednesday, April thirtieth, at nine P.M. on the *Kraft Television Theatre*. The show was over at ten. It took a mere sixty minutes to raise Juffie Kane from the dead.

There were no reruns, no delayed broadcasts, no sales of the show abroad, not even any permanent record. Videotape would not arrive until 1957, two years later. Juffie played Tilda Patchik only that once, and her performance, heralded though it was, was never seen again. But in that single hour she was watched by more people than had seen productions of *Hamlet* in the three hundred and fifty years since it was written.

"It's not just that you were so incredibly, unbelievably marvelous," Matt said right after the show when the thunder already rumbled and they knew the storm would soon break. "It's partly because you and the story rubbed so many raw nerves. The whole damned country feels guilty. And I figure that's a damned good thing."

"They don't feel guilty about me. I was never accused of being a Communist. I don't even think the general public knows what's been happening to me."

"Probably not, but a wave as big as this is going to be makes lots of little waves. And they'll nudge the people who do know what you've been through, the people who matter as far as we're concerned. Take my word for it, sweetheart, we're going to have to hire a truck to lug the scripts from my office to your place."

They had this conversation at midnight on the evening of the broadcast, on the roof of the Astor Hotel at Forty-fourth and Broadway, and they spoke over the sound of "Delilah's Song" as played by Harry James and His Music Makers. "Juffie, here you are." Paul came up and grabbed her hand. "Excuse us a minute, Matt. There's someone I want Juffie to meet."

It was Paul's night as well as hers. He'd guessed how it would be while they were still in rehearsal, and laid all this on—twenty tables reserved at the Astor Roof with Harry James, even though normally he played the Astor only Sunday nights. "You're going to have a triumph, *chérie*, and we are going to celebrate it in style."

"What if I bomb?" Juffie asked in protest. "I haven't done heavy drama in seven years. What if I'm terrible?"

"Then we'll say it's a birthday party. We'll move your birthday from August to April this year."

"That's crazy."

"It doesn't matter because you won't bomb. The way NBC's

building this is sheer genius. They've been plugging it every day, the ratings will top anything they've seen."

It was too early to know about the ratings, but the telephones began ringing the minute they went off the air. By the time Juffie had removed her makeup and changed into the gown she'd bought for the occasion, yards of floating purple silk, the first load of telegrams had been delivered to the studio in a postal sack.

Now Paul was tugging her away from Matt, and she started to follow him, then turned back and said over her shoulder, "Matt, forget the truck. I'll come to your office and read the scripts."

They made their way across the crowded room. Everybody waved to Juffie and she waved back. She spotted Harry Harcourt and his party and blew them a kiss. A couple of times she tried to stop and talk to someone, but Paul kept pulling her forward.

The man he was so eager for her to meet turned out to be English. His name was Simon Barnes, sixty-some, Juffie judged. Heavyset with pronounced pouches under his eyes and thinning hair. Somebody, as Matt might say, who'd been the course. "My wife," Paul said as he introduced her. "Juffie, this is the man who got me started importing British films. He's the biggest distributor in London."

"A pleasure, Miss Kane, a real pleasure."

For once Paul didn't insist that she was Mrs. Dumont. Juffie flashed the Englishman her brightest smile. "Thank you for being clever enough to realize what Paul could do for your movies over here."

"I can't reform her," Paul said. "She insists on calling them movies, not films. But she loved *The Lavender Hill Mob*. Didn't you, Juffie?" He grinned, and from behind, where nobody in the crowded room could see, he rubbed her ass through the layers of purple silk.

"Oh, yes," Juffie agreed. "I adored *The Lavender Hill Mob*. It was a unique experience." She kept an absolutely straight face. Paul was drawing his finger along the crack between her buttocks.

"Guinness was brilliant, wasn't he?" Barnes said. "A real artist, as you are, my dear. Have you ever met him?"

"Sadly, no, not in New York. And I've never been to London."

The Englishman cocked his head and gestured with the large cigar he was smoking. "Now, that's something we'll have to remedy. You and Paul must come and be my guests."

"That sounds wonderful." She tried to move out of reach of her husband's hand, but not because she didn't like what he was doing. Juffie had visions of that first night in the projection room of La Venue, Paul doing incredible things to her while the movie played on unobserved. For a moment she thought she might have an orgasm where she stood. In full view of some hundred guests. It was Tim Frank who saved her.

He pushed his way through the crowd and came to where she and Paul and Simon Barnes were standing. "Juffie, I happened to be downstairs in the restaurant and I heard you were up here. I wanted to add my congratulations to the rest."

She hadn't seen him since *Whaddaya Say* closed a year and a half earlier. When he'd opened eight months ago in yet another hit, she'd sent him a note. He had not replied. Not one telephone call, not one word. Not since they parted onstage for the last time. Ah, the hell with it. "Thanks, Tim. And I'm delighted you came. Have a drink."

"Yes, you must." Paul stopped a waiter carrying a tray and snared a glass of champagne for the new arrival. "Did you see the show?" he asked as he handed it to him. "Did you see Juffie tonight?"

"I saw. Fantastic. But then, she always is."

Except sometimes, Juffie thought. Except when you're afraid a little notoriety might rub off. "Where's Henry?" she asked her husband. "He'd love to meet Tim."

The young playwright was still starstruck. His success had come with such speed it hadn't had time to change him. He was as gawky and adolescent and ingenuous as he'd been the day Juffie met him in Whelan's. She never got over marveling that such powerful emotion and thrilling dialogue came from the mind behind the crew cut and the baby face and the freckles. "Have you seen Henry?" she asked again.

"About twenty minutes ago," Paul said. "His mother was insisting he had to go home because he was coming down with the flu."

"Oh, no! Not tonight."

"Tonight," Paul insisted.

A man Juffie didn't know approached them. "Miss Kane, Mr. James asked me to say that if you and Mr. Frank here might like to do a number, he has the music all ready."

Harry James had obviously seen Tim Frank arrive. Juffie looked at her former co-star. "To coin a phrase, Tim, whaddaya say?"

"How's your throat?" he asked.

"Good enough for a few bars."

They sang a lot more than that. The crowd wouldn't let them go. Finally Paul whispered something to Harry James and he nodded, then leaned over and took the mike.

"These two wonderful talents are getting tired, folks. And Juffie's already given us more than our money's worth tonight. So how about we get one more number out of them and let them go? Whaddaya say?" Applause and laughter. James lifted his trumpet and turned to his band and gave them the beat. They broke into the famous first act finale.

"You're my star, babe," Tim sang.

"I just love you," Juffie counterpointed in that throaty tremolo that had brought her so much adulation and so much grief. When they got to the end, she addressed the line to the people beyond the footlights, as she had so many times. "I just love you." She stretched out her arms and included them all in the declaration. And unaccountably, miraculously, her eyes found Matt's among the many gazing up at her. "I just love you . . ."

They left the bandstand to a tumultuous ovation. James finally ended it by leading his band into Irving Berlin's "There's No Business Like Show Business."

"Miss Kane, excuse me, Miss Kane." A man from the hotel staff was tapping her on the shoulder. "Telephone for you. They say it's urgent."

Dad, Juffie thought as she followed him to a private office near the checkroom. Don't let it be something bad about Dad. She'd spoken to her father that afternoon. And he'd told her that of course he'd be watching, and he was only sorry he couldn't be with them tonight. The doctor still wouldn't let him travel, because now his blood pressure was complicated by his heart. "A little murmur, it's nothing. He's an alarmist, but for what I'm paying I'd better listen to him."

Please God, don't let anything have happened to Dad. Nothing had. It wasn't Myer.

"Juffie, is it you?"

"Yes, it's me. Karen? What's the matter? You sound awful. What's happened, sweetie?"

"It's Bernard." Juffie had to strain to hear, because Karen was whispering. It sounded as if she could barely open her mouth and say the words. "He's left me, Juffie. He got married."

"Married! To who?"

"An idiot. One of his students. A fat little eighteen-year-old blond poopsie without a brain in her head."

"Oh shit. I don't believe it, Karen. When did you say it happened? How long have you known?"

"It happened today. That's when he got married and that's when I found out. Bernard wrote me a letter."

Chapter 14

*H*ow do you know she's a fat blond poopsie?" Juffie asked.

"Because I met her. Once. For about five minutes." Karen sat on a chaise longue covered in sprigged-violet chintz, in what Billy Baldwin insisted on calling Juffie's boudoir. She was shivering despite the cashmere lap rug Juffie had spread over her knees. Her voice sounded metallic and scratchy, an old record played on a poor machine, but she kept talking, spewing out words as if mere sound had the power to comfort.

"It was about three months ago. Bernard and I were together in public in Boston, which was rare. We'd gone to an art gallery in Back Bay, because he wanted to see an exhibition of Russian icons. The blonde came in and he introduced us. Her name's Gloria Finkelstein. At least that was her name. Now she's Mrs. Bernard Hanrihan."

Behind the flow of words Juffie heard another noise. Finally she realized what it was: Karen's teeth were chattering. "Look, you'd better have some brandy; you're shaking." She poured some from the crystal decanter she kept on a small mahogany piecrust table. Karen took the snifter, but she didn't say thank you and she didn't drink. The record had apparently come to an end. She was staring into space.

"This Gloria What's-her-name," Juffie said, desperate to pull Karen back from the edge of whatever hole she was prepared to jump down to escape reality. "She can't be all that dumb if she goes to art galleries."

It worked. Karen turned on the record again. "Oh yes, she is. Totally dumb. She simpers and bats her eyes. Really, she bats her eyes. We talked long enough for me to know she was nothing but a poopsie with big boobs and long eyelashes. It just never occurred to me—" She broke off, unable to utter the horrible truth which hadn't occurred to her. "I'm sure she showed up at the gallery just because Bernard mentioned he was going."

"Maybe he said he was going with you. Maybe she wanted to get a look at the competition."

Karen hugged herself and bent over. Juffie remembered her doing that years ago when she had menstrual cramps.

"God! You know, you're probably right. Oh, Juffie, they must have talked about it. That's what hurts most. Bernard had to have been seeing her for months. While he was still with me. So they must have talked about a lot of things. I can almost hear him, 'Poor Karen, how can I hurt her? She loves me, you know.'" She took a long swallow of the brandy and coughed, then lifted her eyes to Juffie's. Karen's were the eyes of a whipped puppy. "But in the end it was easy for him, wasn't it? He just sent me a letter."

"And that's what hurts most? That he was cheating on you?" Juffie prized the brandy snifter from Karen's stiff fingers and tugged her to her feet. "Sweetie, take a look at yourself. Just take a look."

One wall of the room was mirrored. Karen and Juffie were reflected in the glass, side by side. The actress with her heavy bronze mane loose around her shoulders, and her fabulous figure wrapped in a white silk Japanese kimono; the psychologist with mouse-brown hair pulled back in a bun, and a wrinkled peach-colored blouse half out of a gray wool skirt. Juffie was barefoot, each toe tipped in shocking pink polish. Karen wore navy blue oxfords and flesh-colored stockings in what was referred to as "service weight."

"I never was much next to you, Juffie," Karen said quietly. "Nothing's new about that."

"Karen, you were adorable! You were always such a little pixie, with your short curls and your grin, and those big brown eyes. And even when the rest of us wore loafers and bobby sox, you always wore high heels. They did terrific things for your legs."

"And that's what I should be mad about? Not the fact that the man I love has married an eighteen-year-old nincompoop, but that I'm getting older?"

"You're deliberately missing the point."

Juffie had decided to be tough, not sympathetic. She'd made up her mind to that as soon as she hung up the telephone at the Astor Roof the night before. After she made Karen swear she would go directly to South Station and get on the first train to New York. Apparently the first was the early morning milk train, because Karen had arrived at Grand Central a little after eleven and telephoned, then took a taxi to East River Tower. Juffie had still been sleeping when Karen's call came. She'd had time only to shower and make some coffee and toast, and carry it on a tray to her private hideaway so they could talk. And also enough time to rehearse exactly what she was going to say.

"Karen, when you first got involved with that goddamned Bernard you were a delightful young woman with double her share of brains and a fabulous sense of humor. You were ready to gobble up the world. And he squeezed all that out of you. He made you into some cardboard imitation of his dead wife. Then he decided he didn't like the result, and dumped you for a blonde with big tits. That's what you should be mad about. All the time you wasted on that creep Hanrihan."

Tears rolled down Karen's cheeks, and in a few seconds she was sobbing. "I'm sorry. I didn't mean to do this."

Juffie grabbed her, holding her friend in a tight hug. "You go right ahead and do it. You're entitled. And that's what you're here for, a shoulder to cry on."

An hour later Karen had stopped crying and she'd showered and changed. She had arrived with no luggage whatever, nothing but the clothes she was wearing. So now she had on one of Juffie's robes. It was bright green quilted cotton, and though it was much too long, the color brightened her skin. The fact that she'd washed her hair and it was drying in soft curls around her face helped too.

"You're beginning to look more like your old self," Juffie said. "When you sleep away those black circles under your eyes, you'll be a new woman."

Karen lay back beneath the lace canopy of the bed in the Dumonts' blue and white guest room. "Like in the stories," she said. "The fairy godmother waves her magic wand and everything is perfect. It won't happen like that, Juffie. But thanks for trying."

"Of course it won't happen like that. I know what you've been through has made scars on the inside. I'm only saying that the outside matters too. It reflects how we feel about ourselves. And if the reflection is a good one, we can't help feeling better about what's inside."

"Maybe you should have been the psychologist," Karen said wearily.

"Not me, I deal in common sense, and an occasional helping of nostalgia. Look over there in the corner. I brought you some company to share your room."

Karen looked. Propped next to a charming old-fashioned washstand was one of the giant stuffed pandas. "I have only one here," Juffie explained. "The other one's in Newton. So I call this one Hymie-Lou. A southern cousin." She waited, Karen made no response. "Of Hymie and Luigi," she added. "The names you gave them."

"Yes, I get it. Sorry, Juffie, even your jokes are lost on me today. What was in that pill you gave me? I'm getting woozy."

"Something to help you sleep. I'll be here when you wake up, honey. Whatever time it is. I haven't anything scheduled for this afternoon or this evening. Now, get some rest." She turned to go, but Karen called her back.

"Juffie, one thing wasn't right about your analysis. It wasn't Bernard who made me over into Bess. I did that myself. Because I thought that's what he wanted. I guess I got it wrong."

Karen slept nearly twenty hours. It was probably the first sleeping pill she'd ever taken, Juffie realized, and she was exhausted to begin with. So naturally it hit her hard. Karen said the same thing when she appeared at Juffie's bedroom door at nine Friday morning. "Whatever you gave me really knocked me out. Am I intruding?"

"No, of course not. Paul's gone to his office and I'm lying here doing domestic things like ordering the groceries and the meat and some flowers. Paul insists on having fresh flowers in all the vases. Everything's delivered, thank God, otherwise I'd spend my life shopping for boring domestic necessities. Come sit down and have some coffee. I brought an extra cup in case you surfaced." She filled it from a silver pot on a tray beside the bed. "Are you hungry? I can make some fresh toast. How about an egg?"

Karen shook her head. "No, nothing yet, thanks." She was inspecting the master suite. "This place has had some transformation. I've been peeking into the other rooms. Did all this happen after you got married?"

"Yes. Paul hired a famous decorator. He's sensitive to his environment. Not the decorator, Paul. Everything has to be just so. I didn't mind it as it was, but I have to admit all this is pretty nice. Do you like it?"

"Of course. Who wouldn't like it? What's that?" She pointed to an enormous black box with a dozen dials and a tall antenna beside Paul's side of the bed.

"It looks like something out of Buck Rogers, doesn't it? It's a shortwave radio. I gave it to Paul for Christmas. He fiddles with it constantly. Mostly late at night because that's when the reception is best. He can pick up French stations sometimes. And he can almost always get the BBC from London. They broadcast news from all over the world, every hour on the hour."

"I see." Karen didn't seem very interested in news from all over the world. Her glance lit on the white telephone with the extra long cord that Juffie had pulled from the night table to the middle of the bed. "Do you mind if I make a couple of calls?"

"Of course not." Then, eyeing her suspiciously, she asked, "Who are you calling? Not Bernie and Gloria, the newlyweds?"

"Don't be an ass. I'm not going to start heavy breathing on the phone and lurking in dark corners to spy on them. I've been stupid and blind as hell, but I'm not psychotic."

"Okay, whoever you want, then." She passed over the telephone and started to get up.

"Don't go unless you want to," Karen said while she dialed. "This isn't personal. I have to make some excuse to my various employers. I left without saying a word to anyone."

"Tell them you're sick," Juffie said. "Tell them you'll be out of work at least a week."

Karen made her excuses to the university and the settlement house and the hospital, and finally she agreed to remain in New York. Even though at first she said a lot of things about not wanting to be in the way. "You're not in the way," Juffie insisted. "How could you be in this enormous place? Besides, I don't have a thing to do. I finished my contract with *What's My Line* two months ago. And I'm between shows, as we politely say in this crazy business. I don't suppose you saw *Just Like Home*, did you?"

"The thing you did on television Wednesday night? No, I'm

sorry. I meant to watch, but that was the day I got the letter, and I wasn't thinking too clearly. When I decided I had to talk to you I phoned here, but there wasn't any answer. So I called your dad and he told me where to find you."

"I wondered about that. But I'm so glad you did it. Being here is exactly what you need, sweetie. I know it seems as if it will never stop hurting, but it will. Meanwhile we'll keep your mind occupied. First thing on the agenda, let's go buy you a few things to wear. Nothing of mine will fit you, and you can't go around in that peach blouse and the gray skirt."

"It's a suit," Karen said. "There's a jacket. I can just get some different blouses."

"Absolutely not," Juffie said firmly. "I won't allow it."

She was as good as her word. They were in Saks by noon. Either Karen knew nothing about New York stores, or she was too preoccupied with her pain to argue. In any case, she didn't insist on somewhere cheaper like Macy's or Gimbel's. Juffie took her straight to the dress department and quickly selected a couple of silks in size eight. "These are both nice. And you can wear them almost all year round. Silk is super under furs in the winter."

"Juffie, I don't own any furs."

Juffie giggled. "Remember Delilah? She had a great line, 'Honey, the only way ah'll ever get mink is the same way the minks do.'" She waited, but Karen didn't even smile. "Okay, so you don't feel like laughing today. They're still good dresses for you."

One was a soft blue shirtwaist style, with a tight waist and a full skirt; the other was a yellow two-piece. The yellow dress had a fitted bodice with little shoulder straps and a pleated skirt, and a matching short jacket meant to be worn as a cover-up by day. Juffie dragged Karen into a dressing room and made her try the things on. Karen just stood there and let the dresses hang from her thin frame; she didn't even look in the mirror.

"Great," Juffie said nonetheless. "They're both great. You look terrific." She charged the dresses to her account and led the way to sportswear.

"These linen slacks," she said immediately. "In black because they'll go with everything. And that red cotton dirndl skirt." She turned to Karen, who was still acting like a woman befogged. "Do you remember your green dirndl skirt? The one I had to pull down over my hips so it wouldn't look so short?"

Karen smiled. She actually smiled. It was the first time in hours. "I remember. It was on V-J Day. When I thought you were hemorrhaging and Leah said you weren't." She took Juffie's hand. "That wasn't such a great day for you, but it just may have been the luckiest in my life."

"A good day for me too, as it turned out," Juffie said. "Come on, let's choose some tops to go with these things."

She did the choosing, Karen nodding agreement to whatever was suggested. Juffie flicked through the racks with the rapid hand of experience. "This white blouse with the bow, and this red and white print. And we'll take this black sweater too. It will go with both the slacks and the skirt." She looked for a saleswoman, spotted one, and with Karen trailing behind her, carried the armload of clothes across the floor.

The woman gave Juffie a quick double take, then took the things and asked if she wanted to try them on. "It's not necessary," Juffie said. "They're for my friend, and she's a perfect eight." She took her charge card from her bag. It identified her as Mrs. Paul Dumont. The woman looked at it, then at Juffie again.

"Excuse me, but you *are* Juffie Kane, aren't you? I know it doesn't say so here, but—"

"Yes, I am." Juffie turned on the smile she saved for fans. It was her warmest, most vibrant smile, because she genuinely adored their attention.

"I thought so! I saw you on television the other night. As that poor woman . . . what was her name?"

"Tilda Patchik."

"Yes, Tilda Patchik. What she went through! It was criminal, that's all, criminal. I told my husband—" She broke off. "I'm sorry. I shouldn't be rattling on and wasting your time. But I was so moved, Miss Kane. So moved. You were wonderful."

"Thank you." A few minutes later Juffie took the box of clothing from the woman's hands and reclaimed her charge card. "I'm very glad you enjoyed the show." She found a piece of paper on the counter, and a pen. "Now, what's your name?" The woman told her and Juffie wrote it down and added the words, "Warmest thanks for your help, Juffie Kane."

"It's like that everywhere you go, isn't it?" Karen asked. "The whole world falling over themselves just to get near you."

"Sometimes. Sometimes people prefer to think I don't exist."

"I don't believe that."

"It's true. There have been times when I've been decidedly unpopular. This way. You need some kind of coat. May can be chilly in New York."

"I have a coat." Karen fingered the tweed sleeve of the coat she was wearing. It was the sort of thing sometimes referred to as classic. Single-breasted with narrow lapels and falling straight from the shoulders to well below her knees.

"Your grandmother wouldn't have been seen dead in that coat."

"What do you know about my grandmother? What do grandmothers have to do with anything?"

"Me you can't fool," Juffie whispered. "I know you're coming from Molka, the abortion queen of Lemburg. So whom are you kidding, darlink? And you shouldn't look like a celebrity, maybe?"

The exaggerated Yiddish accent achieved another small smile; it got them as far as the coat department. Juffie chose a reversible black and white faille rain and shine coat, with a tight waist and a full skirt and a Mandarin collar, and puffed long sleeves with tight wrists. She held it up in front of Karen and studied the effect, then nodded. "Right. It's perfect."

"I am going to be broke for six months when all these bills come in," Karen said.

"Forget about the bills. Shoes next."

"High heels," Juffie told the salesman. "The highest you've got. Size five." She turned to Karen, still silent and bemused. "Your feet haven't spread, have they? God knows what wearing those ugly things did to you."

"No. I still take a five." She looked ruefully at the navy oxfords. "I haven't worn high heels in three years. I'll teeter."

"You won't. It's like riding a bike—once you know how you don't forget."

The shoe salesman also recognized Juffie, and talked about how wonderful she'd been as Tilda Patchik and asked for her autograph. "I've been pretty egotistical, haven't I?" Karen asked as they left the store laden with packages. "I never even asked you how the show went the other night."

"So ask."

"I don't have to. For the past couple of hours I've been hearing people tell you how wonderful you were."

"Not just wonderful," Juffie said. "I was stupendous. I knocked 'em dead. C'mon, let's go across the street to Rockefeller Center. We'll have a drink above the world in the Rainbow Room, to celebrate the rebirth of Karen Rice as we all knew and loved her."

That night, after a lot of pleading and insisting by Juffie, Karen changed into her yellow dress and turned the coat to its black side, and wore the spike-heeled black shoes Juffie had made her buy. Then Paul took them to Le Pavillon for dinner. The owner, Henri Soulé, was from Paris, and a friend of Paul's. "This is the only place in Manhattan that serves real French food," Paul said. "I'll order for everyone. May I, Karen?"

She nodded. She seemed shy with Paul, but she didn't know him very well, and this was not a time when she'd feel comfortable making new friends. Juffie was content that Karen, who had refused food all day, managed a few mouthfuls of the coquilles St. Jacques Paul selected as their first course.

Afterward she drank a bit of consommé garnished with tiny profiteroles, and took a bite or two of salmon in puff pastry. She refused strawberry mousse, but she drank three glasses of chilled Sancerre. Best of all, she started really wearing her new clothes, moving in them a little, doing the subtle things with her body that women do when they know they look good. Juffie's eye was trained for such small gestures. She didn't miss one of them, and she was triumphant, though she didn't let it show.

"What are you ladies doing tomorrow?" Paul asked over the tiny cups of strong black coffee that finished the glorious meal.

"We're going to the hairdresser's," Juffie said firmly. "The sheep to the slaughter. Karen's going to be shorn."

.   .   .   .   .

On Tuesday Matt telephoned. "I know your girlfriend's visiting and you're busy, so do you want me to send that truck?"

"What truck?"

"The one that will bring you all the scripts piling up in my office."

"Matt! Really? They're really coming in?"

"Of course they're coming in. I said they would, didn't I?"

"Yes, you marvelous genius, you did. Matt, is there anything really good? Anything absolutely made for me?"

"I haven't had time to read them all yet. But there are one or two that show a lot of promise, Juffie."

"Tell me. I can't wait, Matt, tell me."

"Jule Styne's got something in the works I think may be great. They're calling it *Bells Are Ringing*. A switchboard operator has a telephone romance with a client."

"Jule Styne? Then it must be a musical."

"Yes," Matt agreed. "As planned now. But Styne thinks maybe it could be adapted for your honk."

"No," Juffie said. "Tell him thanks, but no thanks. I can't go through that throat strain again. What else?"

"There's a comedy based on the life of the millionaire, Anthony J. Drexel Biddle. It doesn't have a title yet, but they're talking to Walter Pidgeon about the male lead, and looking around for a lady co-star." He hesitated a moment, "Then there's my favorite."

"Matt, you've been leading me on! All this stuff is a buildup for something you think is terrific. What is it?"

"Do you read the funny papers?"

"Never, not since I was a kid."

"Too bad. Then maybe you've never heard of Li'l Abner."

"Of course I've heard of Li'l Abner. I live in America, don't I? Are you telling me that Al Capp is going to let them make a show out of his strip?"

"That's exactly what I'm telling you. And who do you think would be a perfect Daisy Mae?" He waited. "Juffie, are you still there? Say something."

"You're not going to like what I'm going to say. *Another* hillbilly."

"I know but—"

"Okay," she interrupted. "Let's not talk about it now. I'll stop by tomorrow afternoon. Paul's arranged an advance screening of some new picture from Sweden. He can take Karen. I'll beg off and come see you."

"We don't have to argue about Li'l Abner," he told her the next day when she arrived at his office. "Turns out it's going to be a musical. So if you don't want to do your bullfrog imitation again, it's out."

"I can't, Matt. My throat won't stand up to it." Juffie didn't sit, she prowled the office with its shelves of legal books and stacks of bound presentation manuscripts on every available surface. "I've been thinking."

Matt tilted his chair back and nursed his pipe and watched her. His reading glasses were perched on the edge of his nose, and his eyes followed her restless movements over the top of the horn-rimmed frames. "What have you been thinking?"

"The plays we've been sent, every one of them is a comedy or a musical. Hasn't anybody suggested a drama?"

"Your name is synonymous with spoof and comedy. Say Juffie Kane and break into a big heartwarming grin."

"*Just Like Home* wasn't a comedy. There was nothing funny about Tilda Patchik."

"Sometimes there was. Sometimes you got real humor into her character. That's one of the things that made it so wonderful."

"If it was so goddamn wonderful, why hasn't anybody sent me a dramatic script to consider?"

He let his chair drop back to all four legs, put the pipe in a heavy crystal ashtray, removed his glasses, and rubbed his eyes. "Juffie, you always ask me a variation of the same question, and I always give you the same answer. You know as well as I do that mounting a major Broadway show costs more money than most people see in a lifetime. Nobody putting up that kind of dough wants any unnecessary risks. You played Tilda Patchik for one hour on one night. You've been funny ladies for thousands of hours on hundreds of nights."

Juffie leaned against the window frame and looked out at the stone lions on either side of the entrance to the library. It had turned unseasonably warm for May. She wore a little navy linen dress that skimmed her body, and navy pumps with an open toe and red piping and a tiny red leather rosette. Her hair was up and the sun coming in the window backlit her long neck and the elegant slope of her shoulders. "You're looking exceptionally beautiful today," Matt said softly.

Not so much the words as the tone pierced Juffie's heart. She looked at him a moment. He looked at her. Their gazes locked. Then Matt turned away and opened the bottom drawer of his desk. "I've been debating about showing you this. It depended on whether any of the other things excited you."

He removed four notebooks from the drawer and set them on

the desk. They were looseleaf notebooks with blue cloth covers. Juffie stepped closer and opened one at random. She looked at it a moment, then at Matt once more. "Henry Whiteman?"

"Yes. He says he wrote it in the last three months. With you in mind. But this time he wanted to 'be professional' as he put it, so he sent it to me and not directly to you."

"He still can't type, I see." The thing looked so patently amateurish among scripts in their official black and brown and gray bindings held by large silver clips. Juffie turned back a few sheets until she came to the title page. "*When Morning Comes*," she read aloud. "Have you read it?"

"Yes. The night before last."

"Well?"

"It's brilliant," Matt said simply. "The most moving thing I've read since . . . well, since *Just Like Home*, though it's entirely different. It's a costume piece, set in eighteenth-century America. It covers the thirty years before the Revolution. Marjorie, the heroine, is a young woman when it opens and she's still young at the end of Act Three. In between, in sort of interposed scenes, we see her as a much older woman, living the consequences of the decisions the country has made."

"Wow." Juffie whistled softly. "It sounds like quite a challenge. Just the staging . . ."

"Exactly. And there's an enormous cast. And I figure it will run close to four hours, played as it stands now."

Juffie let the top notebook fall closed and stared out the window once more. Then she turned and reached for the cape she'd flung over a chair when she came in. It matched her dress, navy linen with a red silk lining. She slipped it over her shoulders and began gathering up the four notebooks. "What are you going to do?" Matt asked.

"Take it home and read it."

"Juffie, you're probably wasting your time. It's a pipe-dream kind of project. It's something that can probably only ever live in the theater inside Henry Whiteman's head."

"Tilda Patchik was born inside his head too. And she was a lady who did very well by me. The least I can do is read it, Matt. I owe him that."

She couldn't do so immediately, much as she wanted to. Juffie had promised to meet Paul and Karen at La Venue I off Sutton

Place. The advance screening was over when she arrived, and the theater was empty except for Karen and Paul. They were sitting in the tiny outer lobby, drinking cups of the espresso coffee Paul served, compliments of the house, to patrons waiting for show-time. Paul rose to meet her when she came in, kissing her and taking the stack of notebooks from her arms. "Hi, what's this?"

"A new play by Henry Whiteman. I'm going to read it later." She slipped off the cape. "How did the screening go?"

"Very well, I think. *The Seventh Seal* is a difficult kind of film, and God knows Bergman isn't a director who makes it easy for the audience, but I think the critics were impressed. Karen certainly was."

Juffie crossed to her. Karen was staring into space, not an unusual thing for her these days. Juffie leaned down and kissed her cheek. "Hi. How are you? Did you like Paul's new movie?"

Karen seemed to pull herself back from a far place. "No, I didn't like it. But it mesmerized me. There's this scene where a man plays chess with death . . ." She trailed off. "I can't describe it."

"Sounds depressing," Juffie said. "All Paul's most successful movies are depressing. Where shall we eat?"

"I thought Karen might be amused by some local color in the form of a Third Avenue joint," Paul said. "But it's a mess over there. They're tearing down the El. So how about that Italian place?"

The Italian place was called Luigi's and it was at Seventy-second and First, just a few blocks from their apartment. It suited Juffie only because the service was quick. Nothing Luigi's produced tasted like the food that had come from Rosie's kitchen, or that of any of their Saliatelli relatives. But tonight she ate overcooked spaghetti and bland meatballs, and didn't complain.

She chatted with Paul about how to get the American public to appreciate Ingmar Bergman's work, and thought about how quiet Karen was, but how nice she looked with her hair short again and wearing her red and white blouse and red skirt—and all the while, inside her head, there was a little buzz of excitement waiting to become a big buzz. *When Morning Comes*, it repeated, *When Morning Comes*.

By morning the buzz had become a roar. She sat up all night

reading the play; in the bedroom at first, in the sitting alcove Baldwin had created from a small adjacent room. She moved because Paul seemed restless. He was twisting and turning beneath the yellow quilt, so Juffie decided the lamplight was disturbing him and she turned it off and gathered up the notebooks and padded across the hall to her violet-strewn hideaway. It was more comfortable there. She could move around, try bits of business, even say a few lines aloud. She was still doing it when the door opened and Paul appeared.

"Good morning," he said.

Juffie was startled. "Is it morning?"

"It is. Seven A.M. Have you been in here all night?"

"Yes, I guess I have. Paul, listen to this." She ruffled the pages of the notebook she held. "Here it is. It's 1769 and Marjorie, the heroine, is arguing with her husband about loyalty. To the British king. He's for independence, Marjorie can't see how they can turn their backs on the mother country."

She took a deep breath, then spoke the lines. "'Will you spit out the milk of the breasts that suckled you? Will you deny the womb that bore you? For what? A town you call Boston? A few more towns? All clinging to the coast just beyond the reach of an encroaching wilderness. Is this your independence? The freedom to cut yourself off from the culture and wisdom and beauty of home, and rot here in this tiny pinprick of civilization, besieged by the ocean on one side and savages on the other?'" She stopped reading and looked up. "Well, what do you think, isn't that incredibly powerful stuff?"

"Powerful," he agreed. "But not likely to be popular with the great American public. Are you going to play this Marjorie?"

"It will be popular," Juffie insisted. "Marjorie was born in England and comes to America as a young woman. So her feelings are understandable. And she struggles inside herself with the whole thing that every American immigrant has to fight. It's the same to this day. The pain of letting go of the old so you can succeed with the new. It's fabulous, Paul. And if I can find any way to do it, I sure as hell am going to play Marjorie."

He shrugged. "Okay, but do you think you could wait until after breakfast? And don't forget that Karen goes home today. I have to go to the office, but I'll meet you at Grand Central to say good-bye."

"Paul, that's awfully sweet of you. I really do appreciate how nice you've been to Karen. Eggs or oatmeal?"

"Neither. A croissant and some proper café au lait would be perfect. But since they're not available, toast."

Paul was an example of exactly what Marjorie suffered, Juffie thought. He couldn't entirely give up the old life either. Aloud she said, "One order of toast coming up."

She waited until Paul had gone before calling Matt. "I have to play Marjorie," she said. "I absolutely have to."

"Yes, I expected you to think that."

"Well, don't you? Tell the truth, Matt. Isn't this the best thing you've read in years?"

"I already said it was. I told you that yesterday."

"Then why do you sound so unenthusiastic?"

"Juffie, we have just broken you out of prison. You're free at last, to continue the analogy. More to the point, you're hot again after nearly two years. The time to do a new show is now."

"I want to do Marjorie now."

"How the hell can you? There is no show, Juffie. There's nothing but four notebooks with Whiteman's scrawls. No backing, no producer, no director, no theater, no nothing. It could take months to get this project off the ground. Years. Maybe in the meantime you can take it down to Union Square and stand on a soapbox and declaim the lines."

"Matt, don't get mad at me. Not now. It's the role of a lifetime. A dream. I have to try. We have to try. I'll never be able to do it without you. Will you help me?"

He sighed. "Yes, of course I'll help you. I knew you'd want it and against my better judgment I've been racking my brain trying to figure out where to start."

"Money," she said. "We have to start with backers. You look for angels. Meanwhile, I'll call Henry and set up a meeting. There are some things he'll have to change. At the moment it's more complex than it needs to be. It won't be easy to persuade him to rewrite, but I'll do it."

But first she took Karen to Grand Central and the *Yankee Clipper.* She insisted on sending her home in a parlor car, as she'd done with Pa. That seemed a very long time ago. "Take care of yourself, sweetie. And don't forget to have another haircut in a few weeks. You know how fast your hair always grows. It looks wonderful short, keep it that way, won't you?"

"Sure," Karen said. "I will. Juffie, thanks for everything. Mostly for being there."

"I'm always here, always."

Karen started to say something, but Paul joined them and she clammed up. He kissed them both and took Karen's hand. "Glad I didn't miss you. I had a long-distance call as I was leaving the office. Ran all the way down here."

They exchanged more kisses and more good-byes. The porter shouted his final boarding call, the doors were closed, and the first hissing train sounds began as the *Yankee Clipper* edged forward. Juffie stood and watched it go. "I wish I felt better about her. I did a lot with the outside, but I don't think I touched the inside Karen."

"She has to find her own way back out of the forest," Paul said. "Like we all do. Juffie, I want to talk to you. Come and have a drink."

They went to the cocktail lounge at the Biltmore. "I made my first film deal here," Paul said. "I met a guy 'under the clock at the Biltmore' and we came in here and had a drink and made a deal."

Juffie reached over and patted his hand. "You've come a long way, Mr. Dumont. I'm proud of you, you should be proud of yourself."

"I am. Sometimes. Listen, the call that came before I left, it was Si Barnes from London. He's on to something hot. A chance to maybe bring the D'Oyly Carte Opera Company over here. They've been before, but not since the war."

"I thought Barnes was a movie distributor."

"He is. But he—what's the English word?—dabbles. He has a finger in a lot of cakes."

Juffie smiled. "A lot of pies. And that's what my father calls a *tumler*. It's a Yiddish word meaning somebody who makes things happen."

"I suppose all Jews are like that."

For some reason she was offended. "Not all Jews. Any more than all Irishmen, or all Frenchmen, or all anything else. Sometimes I think you're a bit anti-Semitic."

"Don't be ridiculous. I'm married to you, aren't I?"

"Sorry, I'm tired. Skipping a night's sleep is catching up with me."

He let it drop. "Juffie, Si wants me to come to London. To discuss the D'Oyly Carte idea. I want to go."

"Yes, if it's important to your business, you'll have to go. When?"

"Right away. In a couple of days."

"Wow! Well, okay. If that's how it has to be, I understand. What can I do to help?"

"A lot." He leaned forward and took both her hands in his. "I want you to come with me. I need you, *chérie*."

"Paul, I can't! Matt and I are going to move heaven and earth to get Henry's new show produced. And that's what it's going to take. He's a virtual unknown, and Marjorie's the kind of part nobody thinks of in connection with me. We've got to build the entire project from the ground up."

"Juffie, I haven't left America since I arrived in forty-six. I don't know how I'm going to feel about being back on the other side of the water. And the English are such snobs. Not Si, he's different. But the rest of them . . . snobs. The people connected with the D'Oyly Carte will be, you can bet on it. A beautiful, famous wife will open a lot of doors. Please, *chérie*," he said again. "I need you."

"I'm not famous in England. I don't think anybody's ever heard of me there."

"Not true. Si had heard of you. He was dying to meet you at the party the other night. And you're beautiful anywhere."

"You make me feel like a commodity, a possession to be displayed."

"You know I don't mean it that way." He turned her hand over and drew his finger lightly across her palm. It was an intensely sensual gesture. "Besides, how can we manage being apart for weeks? I'd miss you too much." He kept up the stroking. "And you'd miss me."

Juffie stared at the tip of his finger as it traced circles on her skin. He was making her feel things, he could always do that, but it was happening in a separate place, a place apart from her thoughts and convictions. "That's not what this is about, Paul," she said softly. "I love going to bed with you and I'd miss it, but that's not why I'll go."

He was exultant. "You'll go, then?"

"If I can set the wheels in motion with Henry's show so

something is happening while I'm away, yes, I'll go." She took his hand with her free one and deliberately moved it away, breaking the erotic contact. "But not because you can always turn me on. Because I'm married to you, you're my husband. And in the only other marriage I know anything about, my parents', that's how it always was. You stick together whatever happens. That's what makes it work."

She called Henry Whiteman as soon as she got home and made an appointment to see him the next morning. And she called Matt and arranged that they'd meet in the afternoon to start making a list of possible backers, and maybe producers and directors, and figure out the best approach to them.

The meeting with Henry took place in Juffie's cream and black living room and it was stormy. He was ecstatic about her reaction to his play, but he resisted the simplifications she wanted him to incorporate.

"All this back and forth in time business, it's not necessary, Henry. It doesn't add a thing. We have to see the progression of Marjorie's life, the way it changes her thinking, but we don't need to know everything at the same time."

"That's the way I conceived it," he insisted. "That's the play I've written. If I lose that, I don't have anything."

"Yes, you do. You have a brilliant drama. And one that can be staged for something less than a million dollars, and doesn't require technical expertise that hasn't yet been invented."

"It's not that difficult. I've done some work on it. Look." He dragged yet another notebook from his briefcase and flipped through the pages, and made her look at set designs involving winches and ropes and pulleys and sliding screens.

"Maybe," Juffie admitted. "Maybe it could work like that. But it will terrify any producer who looks at it. Henry, put this idea away. Save it. Don't breathe a word to anybody about it. Someday, when you've a string of hits to your name and you can write your ticket anywhere on Broadway, then do it. Write a show with this time-change element, this to-ing and fro-ing, and you'll probably be hailed as the most inventive playwright of the century. But not now. Not with *When Morning Comes*. Because the show doesn't need it, and because what we're trying to do is difficult enough without adding unnecessary complications."

"They're necessary," he said again.

Juffie went through all her arguments once more. And he

reiterated his. Then they began at the beginning and did it a third time. "Listen," she shouted finally. "Just listen, goddamn you!" She grabbed the handwritten script and found the page she'd quoted from to Paul the day before. "You've got this speech in the first act, a flash forward in one of your time leaps. But listen to it and imagine it coming near the middle, as the fulcrum on which all her feelings turn. The place where she comes to the fork in the road, and she's convinced she has to go one way, though in the end she'll go another."

Juffie was exhausted. She was pale, and the black slacks and sweater she wore accentuated her pallor. But inside there was fire, an erupting energy that overcame her tiredness. Her hair was loose. She tossed it back and stood in the middle of her Aubusson rug and took a deep breath and began Marjorie's speech. She held the notebook but didn't look at it because she'd already memorized the lines. They'd burned themselves into her brain by their sheer power.

" 'Is this your independence? The freedom to cut yourself off from the culture and wisdom and beauty of home, and rot here in this tiny pinprick of civilization, besieged by the ocean on one side and savages on the other?' "

She stopped and looked at the young man whose life and talent had become entwined with hers in such a serendipitous fashion. "Well?"

He was crying and he couldn't answer for a few moments. When he had control of himself he said, "I'll do anything, Juffie. Anything to hear you say those lines onstage. I wrote it for you, but you're an even more perfect Marjorie than I imagined you'd be."

That was on Friday. Sunday evening she left with Paul for London, knowing that because young Henry Whiteman was more than a little in love with her, he was home furiously revising his masterwork, and that Matt had appointments the following week to see three possible angels, and the first director on their short list.

·   ·   ·   ·

Si Barnes was an effusive host. He met Juffie and Paul at the door of what he'd called his "cottage in Sussex" and shook their hands and kissed both Juffie's cheeks, and took their coats and overnight bags—all at the same time. "Come into the drawing room and have a drink. Everybody's been waiting for you to arrive."

The cottage was a Georgian splendor built of flint-gray Sussex stone, and the drawing room was enormous and filled with overstuffed furniture and flowers and rugs and framed hunting prints. "This place gives me the strength to cope with London during the week," Si said as he led them into the room. "Best of all is sharing it with my friends. Look everybody, Juffie and Paul have come."

Everybody turned out to be David Hope, the playwright who wrote *A Small Miracle,* and his wife, Andrea, neither of whom Juffie had seen in eight years. There was also a Frenchman named François Fibon, and there were Nessa and Jack Fine.

She wasn't surprised to find the Fines in England. She and Paul had been in London for five days. For Juffie every minute had been charged with the thrill of the different and the new. She adored the accents all around her, the big red buses, the squared-off black cabs. And the sense of history. So it was a special delight to learn that a revival of *Delilah* was planned for the West End. Still, she was nonplussed when it came time to greet Jack. She and Nessa had kissed, should she kiss Jack Fine, who hadn't spoken to her since that day in Schrafft's when he had confronted her with the story from the *Record American?*

He looked a lot older and very tired as he struggled up out of a deep armchair. "Hello, Juffie. How are you?"

"I'm fine, thank you, Jack. You?"

"Older. Less hair and more aches and pains, but I'm here and I'm breathing." He offered his hand and Juffie shook it. Apparently they were not going to kiss. "I've been in London for a month, so I didn't see it," he said. "But I heard you were fantastic in that television thing."

"It was a marvelous show," Juffie said. "I had only to say the lines."

"I expect you did a little more than that."

The conversation was interrupted by Si, bringing a sherry for Juffie and a whiskey refill for Jack. "Ah, I'd heard you two were old friends," he said. "Having you both here this weekend was my little surprise. Chatter on, children, don't let me interrupt."

But they had nothing more to chatter about. Juffie drifted over to David Hope and asked what he'd been doing in recent years.

Jack began a conversation with his sister-in-law, David's wife. Paul, Juffie noted, was in a far corner speaking animated French with his compatriot, who had been introduced as a businessman from Nice. In twenty minutes a butler came to the door and announced lunch.

Barnes was a bachelor, but he didn't live like one. They'd dined at his apartment in London, and Juffie had been impressed with the graciousness of the setting and the way things were done. It was a way of life she'd seen before only in movies and plays. With Si Barnes it was real, and his country style wasn't much different from the one he adopted in the city.

There was still food rationing in England, and Juffie heard Nessa and her sister discussing the servant problem, but Si Barnes did not seem affected. The table was beautifully appointed, and successive courses were elegantly served by the butler. Soup was followed by a fowl said to be something called guinea hen, then there was a bright red concoction identified as a summer pudding. It was all good, but Juffie found it heavy. Which was also her opinion of the conversation around the table. And it was more than a little strained.

Paul and the man called François had stopped speaking French; they seemed to have nothing to say to each other in English. Jack kept avoiding Juffie's eyes and thus the need to make any direct comment to her. David and Andrea Hope had some kind of domestic squabble simmering beneath the surface. Only Si and Nessa were animated and apparently relaxed. At last the end of the meal was signaled by the appearance of a great wheel of Stilton cheese and a decanter of port. "The ladies don't have to leave unless they want to," Si said. "We're not bound by tradition here at Coom House."

"Oh, do let's leave," Andrea Hope said, standing up. "It's very warm. I'm going for a walk in the garden."

Nessa reached over and took Juffie's arm. "Yes, that's a lovely idea. Come walk in the garden with me, pet, and tell me all about Billy Baldwin. I heard he did your flat over and it's a wonder." Her husband shot her a dark look, but Nessa persisted in tugging Juffie gently from the room.

Paul's eyes sought Juffie's. For a moment she thought he was sending her a silent plea, but she couldn't be sure, so she followed Nessa through the French doors.

"Mmm . . ." Nessa breathed deeply. "This is what I miss, almost the only thing. The smell of an English garden on a June day. If, by chance, the sun happens to be shining. In my memory it always is. But not too often in reality. You've had good weather for your week in London. How long are you staying?"

"Another few days," Juffie said. "Maybe a week more. Paul's negotiating with the D'Oyly Carte."

"Yes, so I hear. Very clever, your Paul. He's done well, hasn't he? Do you think he and that François whomever are old friends? They were rattling on in French for ages."

"I don't know, perhaps." Juffie stopped halfway down a narrow path between two ranks of rosebushes and cupped a lush yellow flower. She bent her head, then frowned. "No perfume. I didn't think there were roses without any smell in England."

"Sometimes. Juffie, you know we're doing *Delilah* here, don't you?"

"Yes. I've seen the advance publicity. Good luck with it."

"We need it. It was all my idea. Jack's been very tired since *A Time for Lilies* closed. And a little bored. Nothing really interested him. So I thought a change of scene, something that was a little bit of a challenge but not too much. After all, whatever wrinkles there were in *Delilah* had been ironed out years ago. . . ."

"But? It sounds as if there's a but."

Nessa's smile was rueful. "There's a big but. It's turned out a rose that looks good but doesn't smell so wonderful. Beryl Randolph, the actress who was to play Delilah, broke her contract two days ago. She's got religion of some sort. She's going to Africa with a missionary group that believes the end of the world is imminent and the natives have to be warned."

"My God! I've heard a lot of reasons for breaking a contract, but that's a new one. Who are they going to get in her place?"

"That's the problem."

Juffie stopped walking. "Oh, no. I have suddenly realized what this conversation is about. No, Nessa, I can't. And Jack wouldn't want me to."

"He'd hate you to," Nessa agreed. "But you'd be saving his life. Juffie, hear me out. It's not a long-term commitment. There is someone who can replace Beryl Randolph. Someone wonderful whom Jack and the director wanted in the first place. But she's tied up for a month more in another show and the timing didn't work, so they went with Beryl. The timing still doesn't work. The new actress wants to do it, but she won't be free until the middle of July. All our commitments are made. We have to open in ten days, on June fifteenth. That means four weeks with no Delilah in sight. They're running around London right now trying to find a stop-gap. And I suppose they will. But she won't be Juffie Kane."

"You engineered all this, didn't you? This cozy country weekend was all your idea."

"Of course. When I read that you and Paul were in England, it was an opportunity from heaven. I called Si immediately. I knew he was doing business with Paul. Si and I are old friends; we go back twenty years. He was a perfect lamb and delighted to set it up for me."

"And did you talk to Jack about it?"

"If you mean your playing Delilah for a month, I pleaded with Jack about it. His mouth keeps saying no, but his heart keeps begging me to pursue it. I know him, Juffie, I can read him like a book. He's dying to make it up with you. He loves you, and he thinks you're the finest actress he's ever known. And to top it off, he's worried sick about this show. His pride's involved. An American producer trying to revive a Broadway show in the West End . . . well, a lot of people are waiting for him to fail. They'll cheer when he does."

"I can't," Juffie said. But her voice carried less conviction than previously.

"Think about it," Nessa said. "Just think about it. Talk to Paul, sleep on it. We're all going to be here for another twenty-four hours. You don't have to decide this very instant."

The first chance she had to talk to Paul was when they were getting ready for bed. There hadn't been time when they'd been changing before dinner. "Well," she said after she repeated the conversation with Nessa, "what do you think I should do?"

"How the hell do I know what you should do? You've never asked me questions about your work, Juffie. Why start now?"

"For heaven's sake, Paul. You don't have to bite my head off. What's wrong with you? You were surly and preoccupied all evening."

"It's these damned English. Can you believe there's no heat in this place? *Mon Dieu*, it's 1955, not the Middle Ages."

Their bedroom had an electric heater. Si called it an electric fire, but its two glowing bars didn't do much about the chill in the large old room with its drafty mullioned windows. "The log fire downstairs was lovely," Juffie said placatingly. "And all week you've been raving about the charm of London."

"This isn't London. It's some goddamned place at the end of the world." He was removing the ebony studs from his dress shirt and he dropped one and had to crawl around on the floor searching for it. "*Merde!* They haven't got any decent light bulbs either."

Juffie didn't say anything, but she spotted the stud at the foot of a huge Victorian chest of drawers and reclaimed it and handed it to him. His thanks were mumbled.

They finished undressing and crawled into the double bed beneath a tapestry canopy. "Hey, this is great!" Juffie said enthusiastically. "There are hot water bottles in here." Her toes brushed the welcome warmth. "Someone must have put them under the covers ages ago. The bed's nice and warm." He didn't reply. "Paul, is there one on your side?"

"Yes."

She waited a moment. "Listen, I've been wanting to ask. Did you know that François What's-his-name before? In France, I mean. You and he seemed to find a lot to talk about."

"No, I didn't know him in France. It's a big country. I never saw him until today."

"Oh, I just wondered." She moved a little closer to him and stroked his back.

"I'm tired, Juffie. I'm going to sleep."

"Okay." She pulled back to her own side of the bed, but she didn't fall asleep for a long time.

Chapter 15

W hat did Nessa tell you?" Jack demanded.

"That you're stuck for a Delilah for four weeks."

He shrugged. "They'll find somebody in London. There are plenty of actresses looking for work. There always are."

"Of course," Juffie agreed.

They were at the far end of Si Barnes's country garden, under the sheltering roof of a curlicued wrought-iron gazebo. The gazebo's white paint was the brightest thing to be seen. The good weather had fled and Sunday was gray and sodden with mist; even the colors of the flowers seemed faded. Nonetheless, Juffie had invited Jack into the garden after breakfast. "I want to talk to you," she'd said without preamble. "Come outside."

He'd followed her silently, and they'd walked to the gazebo silently. The first words spoken had been his question about Nessa. Now she repeated her agreement with his assessment of the casting problem. "Of course they'll find a Delilah, but as Nessa put it yesterday, she won't be Juffie Kane."

"Jesus, I'll never get over the egos in this goddamn business. Yours is bigger than most, and that's saying something."

"Yes, I know. Without it I'd have been dead long ago. You know what's happened to me, Jack. You don't have to pretend you don't."

"I'm not pretending. Of course I know. But maybe there's something you don't know. I never said a word to fuel the fire. Not a goddamn word, Juffie. The only person who knows what happened between us is Nessa. I never made your name lousy."

"I never thought you did. Anyway, you didn't have to, I did a great job all by myself."

He shrugged. "You said it, I didn't."

"Yes, and I'm saying something else. This time you really are standing with your *tochis* hanging out. Like you said that day in Schrafft's. Only it's not my fault."

"Who said it was your fault?"

"Nobody. I'm simply stating the facts. You are bare-assed in the shooting gallery, Jack. And the best chance you have of getting out alive is me. Am I correct so far?"

He lit a cigarette, cupping his hands around the flame and drawing deep before he answered her. "Yeah, I guess you are. I'm not going to be jerk enough to tell you they'll turn over a rock in Hyde Park and come up with a Delilah as good as you were."

"Better than good, great. I made that role, everybody over ten years of age associates my name and my face with it, even here in England. I've had London cabbies quote me lines from the show. God knows how they know them, but they do."

"Okay, Juffie. You can stop being your own best press agent. You're the greatest. I know it and you know it. Where do we go from here?"

"I go on to the stage of the Garrick Theater on Charing Cross Road for four weeks. And save your bacon. I'll give you a London smash, Jack."

"Thanks, but I'm waiting for what I believe is called the other shoe to drop. You aren't doing this for free, Juffie. And I have a feeling you're not doing it for money."

"No, you're right about that. I'm going to charge you a fortune—Matt will screw it out of you—but that's not what I want in return. It's simply what I deserve for my professional skills. What I want is a favor for a favor."

"I can't say yes or no until I hear it."

"It's extremely simple. I want you to read a script."

"What script?"

"A thing called *When Morning Comes* by Henry Whiteman. I know you've never heard of him, but he's the guy who wrote the television drama I did last month. His new play is absolutely brilliant. The best thing I've seen in years. The best thing anybody's seen."

"All right, if it's so wonderful, why am I doing you a favor by reading it?"

"Because I want to play the lead, Marjorie. And nobody would imagine me in the part. And it will run over three hours, even after the cuts the author is making right now. And the cast is enormous. And it's a period piece that will cost a fortune to stage." She took a deep breath. "And we have no backers, at least as of three days ago when I called New York we didn't, and no director and no theater. As Matt puts it, no nothing. Just a dream of a play and a part made for me in heaven."

He took another drag on the cigarette, then flicked it over the railing of the gazebo into the wet grass. "That's what I said about you and Delilah; that the part was made for you in heaven."

"This one was created by a more senior choir of angels."

"The college girl. Smart literary references, you and Nessa." He didn't say anything more for a few moments, then, "Okay, I'll read it. That's all you want?"

"As long as it's a fair reading, not one where you've already made up your mind that it can't work and you're only going through the motions of keeping your word."

"I won't do that."

"I didn't think you would." She leaned over and kissed his cheek. "Jack, I don't want to be your enemy. I never did. I'm sorry I was so stupid, but I was a scared kid having her first big chance and terrified of blowing it."

"Juffie, why the hell didn't you say that years ago? That's all I wanted to hear, and if I had, everything would have been different."

"I just told you why. I was a scared kid years ago."

.　.　.　.

Juffie and Paul shared a train compartment with the Hopes on the return trip to London. There was no opportunity to tell him of her decision until they were back in their room at the Dorchester. "I told Jack I'd do Delilah for a month. In return he's going to read Henry's play. I hope he'll agree to produce it."

"*Bien,* sure. Okay, Juffie. Whatever you want."

He still seemed preoccupied. And he usually didn't pepper his sentences with quite as many French words as he'd used that day, as if half the time he couldn't remember the English he normally spoke so well. "Paul, I don't need a lot of rehearsal time for Delilah, and we don't open for ten days. I'll be with you most of next week while you're here."

"I'm going back to New York tomorrow."

"What! Why? You said you hadn't finished your business. You said you wanted another few days to tie things up with the D'Oyly Carte."

"Don't keep telling me what I said. *Je ne suis pas fou.* I remember. Si and I have agreed to be partners on this one. He can finish the negotiations. *Ils sont presque finis.* They're practically done anyway. I'm more useful making arrangements in New York."

He left for the airport Monday morning at ten, and he didn't ask Juffie to come see him off. Moreover, she didn't feel like offering. She wanted to stay in the hotel and count the hours until it would be nine A.M. in New York and she could call Matt.

She booked the international call with the hotel switchboard for two P.M. London time, and ordered her lunch sent up to the room. The telephone rang a little after one. She grabbed the receiver anxiously, though it couldn't possibly be her call to America. "Juffie, it's Jack. I've arranged for a rehearsal Wednesday afternoon. And if it's okay, I'd like to bring the director by your hotel later today. Just for a drink, just so you can meet each other. I know it's premature until I speak with Matt about terms, but we don't have a lot of time to get this rolling."

"No, I know we don't. It's okay, Jack. We won't have any problem. And I have a call in to Matt right now."

The Fines were staying with a cousin of Nessa's in Belgrave Square. Juffie promised that Matt would call Jack there after she spoke to him. Then there was nothing to do except wait some more. But however slowly the seconds passed, they did pass. At a few minutes past two she was connected to the office on Fifth and Forty-second and talking with Matt. "So I said I'd do it, and he's agreed to read Henry's play," Juffie finished up. "What do you think?"

"I think maybe you're a genius. Or incredibly lucky. Of course that presumes that Jack will love the show as much as we do, and be willing to pull out all the stops to get it produced."

"He will. He's got to. Have you spoken with Henry? How is the rewrite going?"

"I haven't talked to him; writers hate to be disturbed when they're working. But there's a fat package on my desk I haven't opened yet. I think it was left outside the door over the weekend. And the handwriting looks like Whiteman's. Hang on, I'll check."

She heard him tearing open the package while they chatted about the weather. Then, "Yup, this is it. The boy genius delivers fast."

"How does it look?"

"Juffie, how the hell can I answer that? I just opened it. I don't have any idea what he's done."

"Yes, I know. Sorry. But listen, can you have it typed right away? Sort of finished yesterday?"

He chuckled. "Day after tomorrow. I'll get three typists working simultaneously and have a typescript Wednesday. And I'll have read the new version by then. So we should talk on Wednesday. Meanwhile, what's Fine offering you for this four-week stint?"

"We didn't talk about it. Except that I told him he was going to pay through the nose. He's waiting for your call." She gave him the number. "And Matt, thanks for everything. Talk to you Wednesday." She didn't remember until after she hung up that Wednesday was also the day of her first rehearsal with the London company of *Delilah*. Because of the time difference, she'd have to call Matt from backstage at the Garrick.

They offered to send a car for her, but she refused. Wednesday, a little before two, Juffie took a cab to the theater. She found the stage entrance in St. Martin's Place and let herself in.

The show was scheduled to open in a week. The theater was thick with carpenters and painters and electricians, and all the other people necessary to create a set, as well as costume people, and, of course, the cast. They were all scurrying around, intent on their own tasks and worries, nobody noticed her.

Juffie found the stage manager's office more or less where she expected it to be, where it was in most of the theaters she'd been in. The door was open. The office was the size of a large closet, but it was empty, and there was a telephone visible among the clutter on the desk.

She closed the door while she dialed, but it was still noisy as hell, and to make things worse the line was bad. ". . . Terrific . . ." That was the one word of Matt's conversation she was sure of.

"The rewrite, you mean? It's terrific?"

"Fabulous . . . show it to that guy . . . money . . ."

"Matt, I can hardly hear you. I'd better call again later. But listen, we have to figure out the fastest way to get the typescript to Jack. While he's still feeling grateful."

"Yes . . . 'em dead, Juffie."

"I think you've told me to knock 'em dead. I intend to. Talk to you later."

She heard the director yelling, "Places everybody. Places, please. First scene, first act." Juffie hesitated by the door of the little office. She took a deep breath. Because this was her first legitimate show in almost two years, her first time on what she thought of as a real stage in twenty-two months.

"Where's Miss Kane?" The voice of the director again. "Has anybody seen Miss Kane? Didn't we send a car for her?"

"No," someone answered. "We offered but she refused."

Juffie pushed open the door. "I'm right here," she called. "Coming."

Juffie walked into the wings, paused, felt the eyes of the entire company turn to her. She wore jeans and a sweatshirt, her usual rehearsal gear. Her hair was pulled back in a ponytail and her face bare of makeup. She did not look like a legendary beauty, a star whose name was spoken in hushed tones of awe.

She knew they probably expected Paris clothes and temperament; that was the image most Londoners had of famous American actresses. Well, they'd learn fast enough. She took the six magic steps that carried her to center stage, the place Delilah occupied at the rise of the first curtain, the place she commanded throughout most of the show. No one had to tell her where she was supposed to be; every movement of this role was part of her being, graven into her flesh and blood. "Sorry to be late," she said. "I had to call New York. Are we ready to begin?"

A hush had fallen with her entrance. Even the stagehands were eager to get a look at Juffie Kane. "Yes," the director said quietly. "We're ready if you are, Miss Kane."

"I'm ready."

And she was. She could sense the theater around her, smell it. Her blood started to sing, her stance changed subtly, so did her expression. In seconds she was Delilah, hillbilly mistress of New

York's finest whorehouse, and convinced that the president of the United States was one of her best customers.

They ran through only two acts, but the rehearsal lasted two and a half hours. When it was over and Juffie spoke her second act curtain line for the final time that day, they applauded. The whole cast and the whole crew, the entire company rose to their feet and clapped for her. Not just because she was a brilliant Delilah. Because they recognized in Juffie Kane that blood tie to the theater that was in themselves. That's why she was there on three days notice, and prepared to re-create for four weeks the role that was part of the myth of her past.

It was ten P.M. in London, five New York time, when she called Matt again from her hotel room. "How did the rehearsal go?" he asked first thing.

"Very well. They're a good company. No nonsense, completely professional." She wouldn't tell him about the applause; that was something between her and her fellow theater people. Even Matt was excluded. "The sets are great," she said. "Better than the originals, I think. Matt, you did tell me that Henry's rewrite was terrific, didn't you?"

"I think I said fabulous. It is. And a hell of a lot easier to read now that it's been typed. I've sent it to a few possible angels. And I'm checking into air freight as a means of getting a couple of copies to you fast. They'll make too big a package for ordinary air mail."

She hesitated, then plunged. "Listen, I've been thinking . . ."

"What have you been thinking?"

"That the safest and fastest way to get the script here is for you to bring it. You must be due a little vacation, Matt. Why not come to London for a few days?"

He hesitated. "I don't know, I hadn't thought of it."

"Of course you hadn't, I just suggested it. Can you leave Patsy? That's the one thing I don't know."

"Yes, that's no problem. Patsy's stable at the moment, and the woman with her is wonderful, she's been with us for years. But, Juffie, listen . . ."

"Yes?"

"Nothing," he said after a few seconds. "What the hell, I'll do it."

He arrived on Saturday evening. Juffie met him at the airport.

She waited for him to look around and ask about Paul. She hadn't told him that her husband was no longer with her in London, that he'd returned to New York. She didn't mention it because she was sure it would have made him decide against the trip.

But he said nothing about Paul. They were in the back of a big London taxi, heading into town. It was Matt's first time in England, but there was really nothing to see on this part of the journey. He didn't look out the windows. He looked only at her. "You look marvelous. I've never seen you looking better."

"I guess London agrees with me. I know rehearsing for a show agrees with me. Even if it's warmed-over *Delilah*."

"You're not going to give them a warmed-over performance, are you?"

"You know me better than that. Besides, I promised Jack a smash. It's part of our deal. I only hope the English critics and the audiences cooperate."

She'd reserved him a room at the Dorchester. "Okay?" she asked when they arrived at Park Lane and stood in front of the gracious old dowager of a hotel. "That's Hyde Park across the road."

"Very okay," he said. And in the lobby, sotto voce, he added, "Not bad for a kid from West Forty-ninth Street."

He registered and was told his room was on the fourth floor overlooking the park. "I'm on the fifth," Juffie said. "And I forgot to mention it, but I'm on my own. Paul had to go back to New York last Monday."

"I know," he said as he lifted his briefcase and waited for the bellman to load his luggage onto a cart. "I ran into him Tuesday, as it happens. We were both having lunch at Joe Madden's." He didn't look at her.

"Oh, I see." She didn't look at him either. "Are the scripts in there?" Pointing to his briefcase.

"Yes. One for you and one for Jack Fine."

Juffie read her copy that night, in bed after an early dinner with Matt in the hotel restaurant. They had talked only about her contract for the short run in *Delilah*, and a couple of new parts she'd been offered in New York but didn't want to take, and about the fact that Matt was close to getting a commitment of twenty-five thousand out of one of the men he'd approached about backing *When Morning Comes*. And he'd told her again that Henry had done a wonderful job straightening out the time line of the play.

Now, reading it alone in the big double bed of her rose and gray room on the fifth floor of the Dorchester, Juffie agreed. It was marvelous. Henry was a genius. She finally fell asleep with the script beside her in the other half of the bed, and she slept all night with her fingers curled around it.

Delilah opened at the Garrick on Wednesday, the fifteenth of June. Jack had managed to get a big advertising campaign organized in the previous week. "For one month only, Juffie Kane in the role she created on Broadway. . . ." And her name was the only one on the theater marquee. Opening night was sold out, but all during the first act Juffie had a sinking feeling in the pit of her stomach.

The house wasn't responding as it should. She'd been warned about English audiences. They were said to be cooler than those in New York, harder to please because they were spoiled by a surfeit of great theater at affordable ticket prices. But she'd also been told that they loved a spoof and broad humor and genuine farce.

In the short break before the second act she cornered the English director. "Listen, do you think they're having trouble understanding me? Is the hillbilly still too broad?"

They'd worried about that, and worked on it during the few rehearsals for which there had been time. "Maybe just a bit," he said. Juffie thought she saw a shadow of fear in his eyes.

"Right. Don't sweat it. Just leave it to me."

At the start of the second act she smoothed out the vowel sounds still further, and let some of the words stand on their own rather than sliding into the next. She could feel the house warming up, feel the response building. By the time she delivered the show's most famous line, "Is there anybody here want's a little nooky?" they were roaring with laughter.

. . . . .

Two on the aisle, seventh row center—those were the seats Jack Fine took for the opening night of any production. He was fiendishly superstitious about them; if somehow, somewhere, they should not be available, he doubtless wouldn't go near the theater. No such tragedy had struck tonight at the Garrick. He and Nessa sat in their ordained places, and when the final curtain came down and there was that moment's magic hush, followed by an explosion of applause, she leaned over and kissed his cheek. "Congratulations, bigshot, you've done it again."

The curtain calls began, and a torrent of affection poured from the audience toward the stage. Bit players first, then principals, and finally Juffie. They brought her on to two bars of the burlesque queen's theme from *"Delilah's Song"* and she gave them one more bump and grind, then blew a kiss. The response was thunderous. Jack stood up. "C'mon, we've already seen this part, I want to get to the restaurant before the others."

The West End had its own traditions, not necessarily like those of Broadway. After the opening night of a new show, for instance, they didn't go to one special place and wait for the reviews. Those restaurants and pubs known to cater to theater people closed long before the morning papers became available, and waiting for them would have seemed interminable. These days London shows started at seven or seven-thirty, and got out well before ten. The war had made this a city of people who wanted to be home early, and the habit hung on, because almost everything, including electricity and fuel, was still in short supply.

All this had been explained to Jack, but he'd still decided to do it his way. "I'm giving a party for everybody tomorrow night," he'd told them after the dress rehearsal. "The Grill Room at the Café Royal on Regent Street. Everybody, front and back of the house."

He picked the Café Royal because it was big, and because Nessa told him that in Victorian times Oscar Wilde was a regular customer. The restaurant had changed a lot since Queen Victoria, but the Grill Room still looked as if Wilde might drop in any minute. It was gaslit and hung with red velvet drapes. A fire burned in a corner grate, and there was soft music coming from somewhere unseen.

The night of his party Jack wondered if all that was enough. When he and Nessa arrived, the atmosphere was quiet and decidedly subdued. The room was empty except for a handful of late diners in evening dress who had reached the point of coffee and liqueurs. "What are we going to do to liven up this joint? Sardi's it's not."

"Relax," Nessa said. "They'll do their own livening up, you'll see." She began checking the arrangements of cutlery and flowers on their ten reserved tables. Half an hour later the cast and crew arrived, boisterous and loud and very un-English in Jack's opinion. All of them were still reeling from the rush of adrenaline induced by five curtain calls. The sound of popping champagne corks began punctuating their laughter. Jack surveyed the scene and grinned. "See," he said to his wife, "I told you everybody loves a party. Even the stuffy English."

Juffie was the last to arrive. She floated in on Matt's arm, wearing diamonds, her hair up, and a full-length black satin cape over the purple silk gown she'd bought the month before for the party at the Astor Roof. She was finally giving them the one thing she hadn't thus far produced, a glimpse of her glamorous high-fashion image. But it wasn't just the clothes that made her look so wonderful, it was the exultant glow created by the pure joy of being onstage again.

Matt slipped away and left her to yet another of her moments of triumph. There was a lot of kissing and hugging, a lot of exchanging of compliments and a few complaints, as if the company needed to convince itself that what had happened had really happened. You were marvelous, darling. . . . Fabulous, Juffie, simply fabulous. . . . Who the hell forgot that glass of water in Act One? . . . I don't know, does it matter? . . . Where's Phil, I want to tell him he finally got it right. . . . Incredible, Miss Kane, I'll never forget it. . . .

This last was the shy, heartfelt comment of a nineteen-year-old boy with a bit part and big dreams. And a big future, Juffie thought. He had something special.

"You'll have a triumph of your own someday," she told him softly so no one else in the noisy throng was likely to hear. "I hope I'm there to see it."

The boy couldn't reply, he just looked at her with ecstasy writ large on his adolescent face. Juffie smiled and started to move on. She felt a touch on her shoulder and heard a once-familiar voice. "Juffie, I just wanted to add my congratulations. I hear you were sensational tonight."

She turned and looked into the blue eyes of Tony Morton. They still crinkled at the corners, and his smile was just as captivating. He was grayer and had many more lines, but he was still the kind of man women sighed over. "Hello, Tony. Thank you."

She started to push past him, but he slipped his hand beneath her cape and held her back. His fingers on her bare arm were somehow proprietary, almost intimate. "I knew you were in town, but I couldn't find the courage to ring you." He was actually gazing deeply into her eyes, speaking with sincere urgency. "I prayed we'd meet like this, by chance. We had to, it was fated. I've never forgotten you, Juffie, never got you out of my system. How could I?"

"I don't know, Tony. Did you try Ex-Lax? I'm told it always works." She reached up and patted his cheek. "We must have lunch sometime, darling."

Juffie turned back to the young boy whose exciting future she'd predicted and ostentatiously took his arm. "See that tall lanky guy over there, the one with the pipe? Do you think you can get me through this crowd and over to him?"

He set about it as if he were running interference for Notre Dame.

At five in the morning Jack telephoned her room at the Dorchester. "I know I'm waking you up, but it's worth it. I just got the morning papers. They're crazy about us, every goddamn critic is crazy about us. I'm not going to tell you what they say about you, because you'll want twice the king's ransom I'm already paying you. Okay, go back to sleep. Love you, Juffie."

"Love you, Jack."

She'd kept her end of the bargain. She'd given Jack Fine his London smash.

· · · ·

"Stay a few more days," she begged Matt.

"You don't need me anymore. The show's opened and they're sold out for your whole month, you're a hit. Jack has the script and he says he'll read it over the weekend. Besides, I have a business to run."

"I do need you. You can help me persuade Jack to produce *When Morning Comes* after he's read it and loves it. He will, you know. Nobody with any feeling for the stage can help but love it."

"He's a hard-headed businessman, Juffie. Don't get your hopes too high. Even if he loves it, he's going to see the enormous difficulties it presents. Despite Henry's revisions, it's still a costume drama with a huge cast and a zillion sets and—"

"That's just my point," she interrupted. "You can help convince him that they're not insurmountable difficulties. They're not, Matt, I won't let them be."

"Okay," he said finally, convinced by the sheer force of her determination. "I'll stay until Monday. Maybe we can sit down with Jack on Sunday. I'll try to set it up."

Sunday. The one day they didn't perform. The London stage was like New York in that regard, but in the West End they did more matinees than on Broadway. Juffie was very tired by the end of the week. "I've been out of harness too long," she told Matt. "I'm really feeling this."

"Have to get you back in training, like an athlete." He'd waited for her after the last show Saturday evening. Now he slipped her raincoat over her shoulders and took her arm and led her out the stage door. "Hungry? I spotted a nice little restaurant around the corner. They serve late suppers."

She shook her head. "No, I'm not hungry. Are you?"

"No. So I'll find a cab and we can head back to the hotel."

"Not right away," Juffie said. "Let's walk a bit first. It's a nice night."

It was ten-thirty and the sky was just darkening. That had been a shock, the very long hours of daylight of an English June. "I can't get used to sunset after ten P.M.," Juffie said. "It's nice. Makes it feel like fantasy land."

"Not fantasy land, just latitude fifty degrees north. But I agree, it's nice. Let's walk this way, toward the river."

They headed east across the broad avenue known as the Strand and through some small side streets that emptied onto the Embankment, a wide boulevard fronting the Thames. "You know your way around," Juffie said. "I'd never have found my way over here on foot."

"I've been wandering around playing tourist while you were doing your bit for the British theater. Yesterday I actually saw the changing of the guard at Buckingham Palace. Very impressive." He pointed up river. "According to my guide book, that's Waterloo Bridge. And that"—he indicated a tall obelisk set by itself on a granite pediment—"is Cleopatra's Needle. It was made in 1500 B.C. and given to England by Egypt in 1887."

Juffie looked at it for a moment, then walked to the wall separating them from the river. "A lot of history has floated down the Thames, hasn't it?"

"One way or another. Warm enough?"

She wore slacks and a blouse and her raincoat, and she hadn't applied fresh makeup when she creamed off the face she wore as

Delilah. Juffie Kane at her least glamorous. "Yes, plenty warm." She looked up at the stars and a rising moon. "I think the weather's changing again. Maybe summer is returning."

They were almost alone. A few taxis sped along the road and an occasional pedestrian passed in one or another direction, but everyone else was hurrying to some destination. They were the only people out so late simply for a stroll. On the side of the Embankment not edged by the Thames was an area filled with greenery. It bore a sign: EMBANKMENT GARDENS.

There were a number of statues in the small park and they wandered from one to another. "At least these survived the pounding," Matt said. "It's amazing how much rubble is left. Particularly when you realize they've already cleaned up most of the bomb sites."

"That's one thing I find terrible in London, the rationing and all the remaining evidence of war. But this is an enchanted wood in fantasy land," she added softly. "Listen, I hear music."

They listened, there was music. A dance band. "It's Glenn Miller, 'Tuxedo Junction,'" Juffie said. "Wasn't he killed here during the war?"

"Lost over the channel. But I don't think that's his ghost. I think it's a radio being played someplace with the windows open."

"You're a killjoy." But she smiled when she said it. "Matt, dance with me." She moved into his arms.

He held her a moment, but he didn't move. "I can't dance," he confessed. "It's something I didn't manage to learn on my scramble out of the slums."

"It's easy. I'll show you." She maneuvered them into position. "Okay, like this." She led him through a simple two-step. "The Glenn Miller sound is easy to follow," she said. "The beat's so clear. Good, you're doing fine. You catch on fast."

Suddenly the music stopped, although the song hadn't ended. "Somebody must have closed the window," Matt said. He stood with his arm around her waist, looking down at her in the moonlight. Juffie leaned her face against the rough tweed of his jacket. "I think it's time we got out of here," he whispered. But he didn't let her go.

"No, listen. More music. They didn't close the window, just changed taste."

It was a waltz this time. "Strauss," Juffie said. "This is easy too. C'mon, you've seen it in a million movies. Just pretend you're Fred Astaire and I'm Ginger Rogers."

He spun her round the small park and her raincoat belled out behind them as if it were a ball gown. They turned faster and faster, following a rhythm of their own, unrelated to the violins in the background. "I'm getting dizzy," Juffie said, laughing. And while her lips were parted he bent and kissed them.

Minutes later they were in the back of a taxi, though neither had said it was time to return to the hotel. The window separating passengers from driver was closed, they had privacy, but he didn't kiss her again. Neither did they speak, they simply held hands until they got to Park Lane. At the desk they both claimed their keys, but Matt didn't get out of the elevator on the fourth floor. He went with her to the fifth, took her key from her trembling fingers, and unlocked the door.

A maid had turned down the bed and laid Juffie's pale blue nightgown and peignoir across the foot. Matt left her standing at the door and crossed to the window and opened the curtains the maid had drawn. Moonlight poured in. He came back to her and put his hands either side of her face and tipped it upward, and bent down and put his lips on hers. After many seconds he lifted his head. "Juffie, yes?"

"Yes," she whispered. "Oh God, Matt, yes, yes, yes."

· · · ·

In the early English dawn, as disarming as the tardy sunset, she rolled over and propped herself on one elbow and watched him sleep. Straight sandy hair tousled a bit, the too-thin face cutting a narrow swathe from the oversized white pillows of the Dorchester, he was not a handsome man—but she thought him wondrous. Ah, Rosie, she thought, don't be mad at me. I know I haven't played by your rules, but it was just this once.

She'd understood that all the time. While he kissed her and held her and while she took off her clothes and gave herself, a complete gift, to his touch and his possession, she'd understood. When he was at last inside her, filling that hollow in the center of her being which had been carved over years by the knowing and the not knowing of him, she'd understood. Through the hours of caressing and tasting punctuated by the soft laughter of discovery, she'd understood. Here was a time out of time, a fleeting voyage to a far shore where neither of them could establish residence or apply for citizenship.

Matt opened his eyes and looked into hers. "Good morning."

"Good morning." She leaned down and kissed his lips. "I love you."

"I love you." He put his hand behind her head and pressed her close for another kiss, then moved away. "I'd better go. They'll be bringing your breakfast soon."

"Not for ages, it's only six. Anyway, it doesn't matter. We're a long way from New York, nobody knows us and nobody gives a damn."

"You're Juffie Kane, everybody knows you. And I give a damn."

He got up and went into the bathroom and she heard the water running. When he came out he wore the flannel trousers he'd stripped off so hurriedly the night before, and his shirt and tie. "You forgot something," Juffie said.

He glanced down at himself. "What?"

"You're barefoot."

He grinned and sat down and pulled on his socks and shoes. "Better?" he asked when he'd tied the final lace.

"Depends on your point of view. I prefer you raw to cooked."

Matt moved to the bed and sat down beside her, laying one hand along her cheek. "I never meant for there to be a last night, but I'm very grateful that there was."

"Didn't you? Didn't you mean for it to happen sooner or later? I think you did, Matt. I think you knew as well as I did that it was inevitable. That's why you came, even though you knew Paul wasn't here."

He did not answer immediately. Eventually he nodded. "Yes, perhaps I did. You're painfully honest, I guess that's a virtue."

"Not always," Juffie said. "And I'm not always the winner in the tell-the-truth stakes. But I don't want lies and half-truths between us. More important, I won't have everything spoiled by guilt. We both know how it has to be, that last night was special, a one-act play with a limited run and no encores. Today can be special too. It's our day, Matt. Our personal private day to use however we want, the only one we're probably ever going to have. Do you really want to run off and spoil it?"

He looked at her for a long time. "You're right," he said finally. "Our day. Until six o'clock, when we have to go and see Jack."

Juffie glanced at the little travel clock by the bed. It was six-fifteen. "We have almost twelve hours. So will you please take off that damned shirt and tie and get back in bed?"

He was not a world-class lover, not like Paul. He had neither the inventiveness nor the control, coupled with utter hedonistic abandon, of the man to whom she was married. But he was the man she loved. She gloried in his directness, his total lack of artifice, the almost primitive dimensions of his hunger for her. And hers for him.

By noon they were replete with love, and starving for food. They shared the scant comfort of Juffie's spare, untouched breakfast tray; drinking one cup of cold black coffee each and munching a single slice of dry toast. "No butter?" Matt demanded. "No marmalade? Where are we, Siberia?"

"I eat very little when I'm working. I have to stay lean and hungry, like Cassius. But not today. I'm ravenous. Let's go eat the biggest, most traditional English Sunday lunch we can find."

They went to Simpson's in the Strand. It was full of American tourists, but they ignored them and gorged on roast beef and Yorkshire pudding, served with two different sorts of potatoes and four different overcooked vegetables. Then they walked clear across town to Regents Park and finished up feeding peanuts to the elephants at the zoo. "During the war they closed this place and moved all the animals to the country," Matt said.

"Were the Nazis likely to bomb a zoo?"

"They weren't that accurate. Besides, they'd bomb anything. The whole point was to demoralize the citizens. It wasn't really about military advantage."

Juffie shuddered. She didn't want to think about Nazis. She saw a sign for the bird house and drew Matt toward it and they spent some time admiring the incredible colors of parrots and peacocks. Neither of them mentioned the birds in Dr. Santiago's Mexican garden. When they'd looked their fill Matt checked his watch. "Quarter to six. We'd better get a cab to Jack's."

Belgrave Square was back in the direction from which they'd come, not far from Buckingham Palace. The taxi ride took about ten minutes, and while Juffie waited on the sidewalk for Matt to pay the fare, she thought about closing scenes and curtain lines. "I haven't got one," she said when the driver had pulled away and Matt was facing her.

"One what?"

"A terrific exit line. You just played the final bit of business, my love. That's the end of the trip. We've come back to the near shore."

He looked at her a moment. "Hello," he said finally. "That's my exit line. Hello to all the times we'll be together in the future, the way it was before. But now, hidden away inside each of us, there'll be the memory of last night and today. And sometimes, just sometimes, I think we'll look at each other and we'll laugh and be very happy, and we'll be the only ones who know why."

Juffie stood silent for long seconds, too choked with tears to speak. Then she nodded and turned from him, and led the way up the short flight of steps to the elegant Georgian front door of the house in Belgrave Square.

．　．　．　．

"Yeah," Jack Fine said. "I read it. You were right, it's a great play. An enormous story, a titanic story. Moving as hell. Nessa read it too."

"What did she say?" Juffie asked.

Jack smiled a small smile. "That if I don't get it on Broadway she's going to file for divorce."

They were sitting in front of a coal fire in a square room with an Adam ceiling of elaborately worked plaster and pale cream wainscotting below damask-covered walls. It was a glorious room filled with glorious furniture. Everything about it spoke of comfort and money, and the leisure to enjoy both. "This is what Marjorie hungers for, isn't it?" Juffie said. "The world this room and this house represent."

"Yes, just this," Matt agreed. "We have here a living model of a set for *When Morning Comes*."

"Just one set," Jack said. "One among many. Whatever this play may be, a drawing room comedy it's not." He tapped the script lying beside his chair. "I made only a quick count, but I figure there are eight, maybe nine different sets."

"Some of them are just variations on a theme," Juffie said quickly. "The same room years later. The differences won't be all that great."

"True," Jack agreed. He sipped his whiskey and soda and asked Matt if he wanted a refill, Juffie if she'd like more sherry.

"No more sherry. Jack, I can't stand this. Are you in or out?"

He tapped the script again. "There's thirty-two people in the cast. Did you realize that? Thirty-two people."

"Twenty-four of them are virtual walk-ons," Matt said. "There are just eight principals."

"Yeah, eight."

"Jack . . ."

He turned to Juffie. "Hold your horses. I know, I know how you feel. If I were you, I'd be the same. You're right about Marjorie. She's a dream role, and personally I think you could do wonders with her. You may never get another chance at anything half so good."

"So what's it to be?" Juffie demanded.

"It'll cost minimum half a million to get this thing up and running. Matt, you've been looking for backers, what have you got?"

"Twenty-five thousand. Maybe. The guy's not absolutely sure."

Jack snorted. "Twenty-five thousand maybe dollars. So we're only short a fast four hundred thousand, give or take a few bucks. Jesus."

Juffie picked up on the pronoun. "We? *We* are only short four hundred thousand?"

"Of course we. You don't think I'm gonna let you take this to some jerk producer who doesn't know his ass from a hole in the ground, do you? You brought it to me, it's my show now. Of course we."

They made only one irrevocable decision in that first of what were to be a great many meetings. It was Fine who verbalized it. "The thing that's certain, we have to put it in the Lyceum. It's the best stage in New York for a show like this, and there's enough room backstage to take care of all the scene changes. And the house is intimate but big enough so maybe if we can sell out every single performance for two years we won't lose our shirts. I'll get on to them right away. From here."

"Jack, what do you think we can shoot for as an opening date?" Juffie asked.

"We have to do more than shoot. If we're setting up a theater, we have to decide when we're going to open and make it. Six months," he said after a moment's pause. "January 1956. That's late enough for us to have a chance to put it all together—and early enough so Juffie has time to get her third Tony."

They all laughed, then Jack turned to her. "Only, you have to promise me one thing. On Tony night, Juffie, you show up. I don't care if they offer you a million bucks to play one show in Vegas. You show up on Tony night."

"I'll be there," she promised. "You can bet your life on it."

"That's just what I'm doing," Jack said. "We're all betting our lives on it."

.   .   .   .

During the month Juffie was in England Paul called her every few days. He sounded fine. Whatever mood had overtaken him in London was apparently dispelled. She called her father once a week, and Karen a couple of times. Myer was cheerful and insistent that his health was good, and delighted to hear how well things were going with her. Karen she was less sure of. "How are you doing?" Juffie demanded. "I mean, how are you really doing?"

"Okay, I'm hanging in. Stop worrying about me."

"Have you seen Hanrihan?"

"Don't be ridiculous, why would I see Bernard? He's married."

"I just wondered. Your apartment is near his house, isn't it?"

"Not too far."

"Karen, get out of there. Find someplace else to live. A new apartment is just what you need right now."

"I don't have time to look for a new apartment. Maybe during the summer when I'm not teaching. How are things going in London?"

"Fine. Terrific. Listen, did you get your hair cut again?"

"Not yet. I probably will next week."

"It must be getting straggly, sweetie. Make an appointment." She paused. "I sound like Leah and Rosie rolled into one, don't I?"

"A little."

"It's just that I'm concerned about you."

"I know, Juffie. And thanks for caring. Now, stop worrying about me. I'm doing fine."

They were the right words, but there was something in her

voice when she said them, some quality of distancing that Juffie found terribly disturbing. Each time she hung up after talking to Karen she felt a cold chill of fear in her belly. She knew in her gut that Karen was still walking perilously close to the edge.

Juffie's life was too busy and too full to allow her much time to brood about it. She had to put Karen and her troubles aside until she was back home and might be able to do something about them, and she did. Just as she put Matt and the magic time with him out of her mind. Do your job, Juffie. Drink deep of the delight of performing again. Be grateful that Jack's enthusiasm for *When Morning Comes* is building daily. The future is going to be wonderful and the present is pretty damned good. What more do you want?

On the fourteenth of July her run as Delilah came to an end. The English actress they'd been waiting for took over the role and Juffie flew home to New York. The second airport the city had been building since 1942 was fully operative now. Idlewild was where international flights landed. Paul met her there on a Tuesday evening.

"Let me look at you." He put his hands on her shoulders and studied her, then pulled her close in a hug. "You look fantastic. *Mon Dieu, chèrie,* I've missed you so damned much."

"I missed you too," she said. She did not allow herself to think of the words as an automatic response.

"Wait till you see the neighborhood," he told her in the taxi on the long ride into Manhattan. "It's changing so fast you don't know what you're going to find when you wake up in the morning."

"Changing how?"

"For the better. Since the El came down every developer in New York wants a piece of Second and Third avenues. We're becoming fashionable."

Juffie looked out the window of the cab at still-rural Queens. "They didn't exactly put this airport in a fashionable location, did they? We'll be forty-five minutes winding our way home through the potato fields."

"Just wait," Paul said. "All this will be developed too. Idlewild makes it inevitable. I wish I had enough cash for some land speculation."

"Don't be greedy, you're doing all right as it is." Then she thought about what he'd said. "Paul, are you having cash problems again?"

"No, nothing like that. I'm stretched to the limit, but not over it. That's inevitable in my line of work." He saw the fear in her eyes and he knew what frightened her. "It's okay. I haven't taken any unusual loans. I do business only with banks these days."

It had been in her mind to ask if he wanted to buy a piece of *When Morning Comes,* become one of the angels for her next show. With Jack Fine as the producer she wouldn't hesitate to recommend the investment to anyone. Well, maybe she would ask him. Later, when she'd sounded him out a little more thoroughly. Now was not the time for that. She smiled and put her hand in his.

That same hand was trembling the next day when she dialed Matt's number. As it happened, he answered himself; his secretary must have been out. "Varley here."

So brusque and businesslike. And still his voice sent shivers down her spine. She could picture his mouth forming the words, those thin, mobile lips that had satisfied primeval hungers far beyond the physical. "Kane here," she said, matching his tone. "How are you, my love?"

A second or two passed before he said, "Fine, Juffie. Welcome home. How was the trip?"

Still businesslike, that moment's pause had been to allow him to get control, to remember as she must remember that nothing had changed. They were agent and client, warm friends; they could be nothing more. Juffie swallowed the lump in her throat and responded to his cue. "The trip was fine, if you like airplanes, which I don't. I saw Jack just before I left. He'll be back in a few more weeks, as soon as the new Delilah seems settled in for a long run. Meanwhile he says the Lyceum looks all set."

"That's what I hear," Matt agreed. "Juffie, do you know that they wanted a seventy-grand guarantee and Jack paid it out of his own pocket?"

"My God! No, I didn't know that. He never said a word."

"I've never heard of him doing anything like that before. It's a mark of how much faith he has in this show."

When she hung up she went into the bathroom and had one good cry. Just ten minutes worth of howling anguish because here in New York the poignancy of all they'd missed, all that might have been, was a million times more painful than it had seemed in a foreign city, where everything had been slightly strange and thus unreal. Then she blew her nose and washed her face and summoned the inner strength she had to have, knew she had. It was over before it had begun, and that's how it would remain. Okay, get on with your life. Think about Jack's incredible gesture. Seventy thousand dollars out of his own pocket.

Juffie thought about it all morning. She realized the one thing that hadn't occurred to her until now. For the first time in her career she was involved in mounting a project from the beginning, and it hadn't crossed her mind to put her own money into it. Because she didn't have any money. Good times and bad, she always spent every cent she earned. There was Paul, of course. And she was going to talk to him about investing, but that was different.

She paced her bedroom, trying to figure out how she could come up with a wad of capital to back her own commitment. After ten minutes she'd narrowed the possibilities to two. She owned this apartment and her jewelry. The apartment still carried a sixty-some thousand dollar mortgage, though she could probably refinance it. The neighborhood was burgeoning, just as Paul had said. But dealing with the bank was bound to take time. Her jewelry would be quicker.

An hour later she was on her way to Phil Wineberg's in the Fuller Building on Madison Avenue. Wineberg was a jeweler, but not exactly in the retail business. He bought and sold for a select list of clients. Many people, like Paul and her, came to Wineberg when they needed an appraisal for insurance purposes. They brought a velvet-wrapped roll of treasures to spill before the man reputed to be one of the most knowledgeable gem experts in the city, just as she had done that day.

They were alone in the office-cum-shop on the third floor of the building and Juffie was entirely frank. "I'm getting a new show into production, Mr. Wineberg, and that takes a tremendous amount of cash. I'd like to put some money of my own into it, and the only way I can think of doing that is to sell my jewelry. Or pawn it maybe. I'd prefer that, of course, if I could get enough. Because I'd rather not lose the things permanently."

"How long before you could pay back a loan, Mrs. Dumont?" He always called her that. It wasn't surprising; she usually went there with Paul.

"Nine months to a year," Juffie said. "We're planning to open in January. Then it will take a few months for the backers to see some profit."

"If you stay open a few months." The jeweler smiled. "I don't mean any offense, but Broadway shows aren't famous for being the safest investment in town."

"Not usually," Juffie agreed. She matched his smile with one of her own. "But I'm playing the lead in this one, Mr. Wineberg. I've never been in a flop yet." Which wasn't exactly true, but true enough for the moment.

"Hmm . . . Let's see what you want to offer as collateral."

She took the velvet roll from her handbag. "I've been seeing purse snatchers around every corner since I left the house."

He shrugged. "Not to worry, that would solve your problem maybe. Everything's insured."

Now, why hadn't she thought of that? It would have made for a much less nervous cab ride to Fifty-ninth and Madison.

The jeweler spread a black velvet mat on his counter. She unrolled her carefully wrapped treasures. "My husband gave me these pearls as a wedding gift. You assessed them at five thousand, and the diamond studs are worth two thousand, the diamond ring eight, and, of course, the emerald earrings. I believe you valued those at eleven and a half thousand."

The man looked at the things on the counter, then at her, then at the jewelry once more. He fingered the pearls and the emeralds, picked them up and set them aside. "Using the diamonds as collateral I could myself make a loan of five thousand at nine percent interest for one year. Which is very generous. You never get full value if you sell stones. The insurance is replacement value. You sell, particularly in a hurry, and you'll get three, maybe four thousand."

"Well," Juffie said slowly. "Five thousand would be a start. What about the pearls and the emerald earrings? The emeralds are the most valuable things I own."

He fingered both pieces again, then sighed. "Mrs. Dumont, these are worthless."

"Worthless! I don't understand."

"They're copies. I'm sorry, I figured Mr. Dumont would have told you. He brought them to me about a month ago and sold the originals and had the copies made. He netted nine thousand out of the arrangement."

. . . .

"How did you find out?" Paul's voice was dull, matter-of-fact.

"I took them to Wineberg because I wanted to make a loan so I could invest some of my own money in the show. He told me. That's the thing that kills me, Paul. Why didn't you tell me? Okay, you're stretched. As you said, in your business that's normal. And the pearls and the emerald earrings were here. I had the diamonds with me in London. I understand all that. I just don't understand why you didn't tell me."

"I couldn't." He walked to the bar and poured a scotch.

"Why the hell not? Did you think I'd say no? You're my husband. If you need money and I can help, then I help. Those are the rules, that's the way the game is played."

He looked at her over the rim of the glass. "Is this a game, Juffie? Is that what marriage is, a game with rules?"

"You know how I mean it. Paul, listen, my parents—"

"Ah, yes, the sainted Rosie and the noble Myer. The happiest marriage in the world. Stop, Juffie. I'm sick of listening to stories about your parents' terrific marriage. It doesn't apply. For one thing, they had a child. For another I don't imagine dear old Rosie slept around. But then, she wasn't a famous actress and she didn't have an agent, so maybe she never had the chance."

She stared at him, unable to answer. There were a lot of possible words. She could find the dialogue for this scene in a dozen plays. Nothing seemed appropriate, however. Not just at the moment.

"Listen," he said finally. "Don't look like that. I didn't mean to hit you with it. A couple of people I know saw you and Matt having lunch in London. They told me about it, and just the way they put it . . . You looked like lovers. That's what they meant. And I happened to see Matt last week, and a couple of times the week before that. He never said he'd been in London, and you never mentioned that he was there. So I just figured it out."

"Matt's my agent."

"I know. I already said that."

"Paul, I—"

"Don't," he interrupted. "Don't talk about it, don't deny or confirm it. I don't want to hear. Juffie, I'm sorry about the jewelry. I just needed a few thousand quick and that was all I could think of. I'll buy you more as soon as the D'Oyly Carte tour happens."

"I don't give a damn about the jewelry," she whispered. Her throat had gone hoarse. No reason, they weren't shouting. It just had. It was like when she was playing Myrtle. Her throat felt lined with sandpaper.

He came to where she sat and perched on the arm of her chair and put his hands either side of her face. "Juffie, listen to me. I adore you. I can forgive anything as long as I still have you. The only thing I want that I don't have is a child. Our child. When, Juffie? You said when your career was back on track. Well, it is, so when?"

Now, she wanted to say. Right this minute. Take me in the bedroom and fuck the hell out of me and don't use anything and we'll make a baby. Because I owe you. I broke the rules. But she couldn't say it. "Jack Fine put up seventy thousand of his own money to guarantee the Lyceum Theater for January. He did it because he believes in me and in this play. I can't let him down, Paul. I can't be pregnant in January."

"When?" he asked again.

"When the show is up and running. When it's such a tremendous hit they can replace me with no loss of revenue. It will be, Paul. That's not a pipe dream. This is a truly great play, and if we can just get it onstage, we're going to win big."

He looked into her eyes for long seconds. "When the show's a hit. Is that a promise, Juffie? A solemn promise?"

"Yes. Yes, it is. I promise. Give me six months in *When Morning Comes*, then we'll start a baby." She wouldn't show for three or four months, so she could stay with the play for almost a year. It was long enough. "I promise, Paul," she repeated.

"*Bien,* I accept the promise. Now"—he leaned over and kissed her. "Don't you think we should rehearse this promise a little? Just a . . . what do you call it? . . . a run-through."

While she followed him into the bedroom Juffie was thinking that he'd never really explained why he needed the cash. And that it was very odd he hadn't told her what he was going to do before he did it.

. . . .

Juffie remortgaged the apartment for an additional twenty-five thousand. It was easy, just as she'd imagined it would be. Her credit rating was good, she'd never fallen behind with the mortgage payments, and Sixty-eighth and Second was looking like an excellent investment these days. She told Paul what she was doing and that the money was going into her new show. He said it was okay with him and she should do whatever she wanted. The penthouse, after all, was hers. She'd bought it and it was still in her name.

That business out of the way, she found herself with a weekend free. She decided to go up to Boston and spend a couple of days with her father and see Karen. Paul agreed to that too. He couldn't get away from the city, but he let her go without a fuss. He was very happy these days, very content since she'd solemnly promised to have his child the following year. They never mentioned Matt again; she could almost convince herself her husband had forgotten about her infidelity. So she took the train to Boston Friday afternoon.

Myer looked better than she'd seen him in months. "This new medicine," he told her. "It's doing wonders for me. I get out and walk now. Half an hour a day. Doctor's orders, but I love it. And I've taken up bridge. I'm playing with a bridge club two evenings a week. While you're here I'll teach you the game. It's fascinating, Juffie. You'll love it. We can play two-handed. Honeymoon bridge they call it."

God, she admired his courage. Myer Kane was not a quitter. He did not sit around and moan about his empty house and his lonely life and the pains of old age. Feeling thoroughly buoyed up by that, she telephoned Karen. There was no answer. She called again Saturday morning. Still no answer.

Maybe it was Myer's example. Don't sit around and *kvetch*, do something. However bad you think it may be, face it. Juffie went to Brighton and rang Karen's bell repeatedly. When there was no reply she found the building superintendent and tipped him ten dollars to let her into the apartment.

The terror lurking in the back of her mind did not materialize. There was no body hanging from a light fixture or lying in the bathtub with slit wrists. Of course there wasn't. She was being crazy. Karen wasn't suicidal. But she also wasn't home. And there was a stench coming from the kitchen that would have reached the hall in a day or two and brought the super in here even if Juffie hadn't insisted he unlock the place. She opened the refrigerator door. That's where it was coming from; the smell was over-powering.

"Spoiled hamburger," the man said, peering over Juffie's shoulder into the refrigerator. "It stinks somethin' fierce. Gotta do somethin', the other tenants will complain."

"Yes. Look, I'll take care of the refrigerator. But how long is it since you've seen Miss Rice?" She glanced around her while she spoke. One coffee cup and one saucer were in the dish drainer beside the sink. As if Karen had her breakfast this morning and washed up hurriedly before she went out. But not in such a hurry she would leave a pound of ground chuck rotting in her refrigerator. Not if she'd been here this morning.

"Dunno," he said with a shrug. "A few days, maybe a week. I ain't the nosy sort. Don't keep tabs on nobody long as they pays their rent and don't make no trouble."

The man left her to get on with cleaning out the refrigerator, but first she called Leah. She had to be careful, she didn't want to alarm Karen's mother.

"Juffie, how nice to hear from you, darling. Where are you? Home with your dad?"

"Yes, I am. Just for a couple of days. But I seem to have missed Karen. I didn't let her know I was coming, so probably she made plans for the weekend. I wondered if maybe you knew what they were. I mean, if there's someplace I could get in touch with her."

"No, Juffie," Leah said quietly. "I don't know anything about Karen's plans. I never do. She doesn't come around much anymore. Not since she got involved with that man."

"She's through with him, Leah. Do you know that?"

"Yeah, I know. But it ain't made any difference. Karen hasn't called me in three weeks. Maybe a month. It's been like that for years."

She brooded about it all Saturday afternoon and Sunday. And she stayed in Boston until Monday morning so she could telephone Karen's three offices and find her, and maybe see her. But Karen wasn't at the hospital or the university or the settlement house. It was when she made that last telephone call that Juffie managed to worm out of some secretary that nobody had seen Karen Rice for two weeks.

"She just didn't show up one morning. We've telephoned her home and sent registered letters, and even a telegram. But there's been no reply. The settlement house board is probably going to take action pretty soon. It's most irregular. Most irresponsible of Dr. Rice."

Chapter 16

The idea came to Karen in mid-June, after Juffie called from London and suggested she get a new apartment. Karen decided that was silly, her three-room apartment on Commonwealth Avenue in Brighton suited her perfectly. The only reason Juffie wanted her to move was that it was two blocks from Bernard's house on Brighton Avenue.

What Juffie didn't realize was that Karen didn't need to go to Brighton Avenue unless she wanted to. The trolley ran right past her door, taking her to the Park Street subway station in Boston, and from there she could make connections to any of her three different offices. So it was silly to move. But Juffie was right about one thing: a change would do her good. And that gave Karen the idea of redecorating her apartment; she'd paint the rooms and buy new furniture.

She had two thousand dollars in her savings account. Probably enough, but she didn't like being without a cushion. She'd get a bank loan and pay it off over a year. It should be easy.

It was. She filled out the forms, saying she wanted to borrow three thousand dollars for twelve months for new furniture, and listed her job titles and the names of her employers and how much she earned: eleven thousand a year when the three salaries were combined. Ten days later the Shawmut Bank of Boston deposited three thousand dollars in her checking account.

Karen left the money there for nearly two weeks before she did anything about it. At the settlement house she was very busy running a project on street gangs, and for no apparent reason she had more than the usual number of patients to test at the hospital. Not until the approach of the long weekend of the Fourth of July did she decide to buy some paint and get started on the decorating. And, so, it was Thursday, the second of July, at four P.M., when she went to the hardware store on Brighton Avenue. It had to be that particular store; it was closest to her apartment and cans of paint were heavy.

She was examining the color charts when Gloria Hanrihan, née Finkelstein, came in. She'd just decided on buttercream walls with colonial crimson trim in the kitchen. She noted the names of the colors and their code numbers on her scratch pad, so she could be efficient about giving her order to the clerk. She was putting her pencil away when she heard the clerk say, "Hi, Mrs. Hanrihan, what can I do for you?"

Bernard had married her barely two months before, but already the storekeepers in the neighborhood knew who Gloria was. And apparently she knew who they were. "Hi, Johnny. I just need three more of those cute little pink juice glasses. You know, the ones I bought the other day."

Karen had been Bernard's mistress for nearly eight years; she did not know that the man in the hardware store was called Johnny . . . nor that Bernard's house was in need of pink juice glasses.

She turned around slowly, wanting to see but not be seen. Gloria was standing by the cash register. Her blond hair was in braids. Braids! Like a ten-year-old's. But there was nothing childish about Gloria's figure. She wore shorts and a halter top. Her breasts were enormous. They all but spilled from the strip of rosebud-printed cotton fabric intended to contain them. She was built like a figure S. Her buttocks formed a voluptuously rounded hillock in the rear, which balanced the thrust in front.

The clerk returned from someplace in the back. "These the ones you mean?"

"Yes, that's right. I think they're cute, don't you? They look real pretty when you serve tomato juice in them. I only bought six before, but Professor Hanrihan has invited seven friends for a barbecue Saturday. And with the two of us that makes nine, so I need three more."

Johnny listened to this spate of information and nodded and waited for Gloria to extract two dollars from her pocket. The shorts were so tight she almost couldn't get her fingers between the two layers of fabric. Eventually she managed, and he took the bills and gave her change, and wrapped the glasses in brown paper and handed them to her. Gloria leaned down to the clutter of shopping bags at her feet. The act of bending over made yet more precarious the containment of her breasts.

"I'll just fit them in here," Gloria said. "I don't need another bag." She stuffed the pink juice glasses between the lacy green top of a head of lettuce and two long loaves of Italian bread. "I hope I haven't forgotten anything for the barbecue. Professor Hanrihan is very fussy about entertaining. Everything has to be done just so."

No, Karen thought. Bernard isn't fussy about it, he doesn't do it. Never. Not once in eight years did they give a party for friends. Bernard would have said that was another silly convention. Besides, they didn't have any friends; given their circumstances, having friends would have been an indiscretion. She watched Gloria leave the store.

The clerk turned in her direction and peered into the shadows of the paint department. "Find the colors you want, miss? Can I get you something?"

Karen stared at him as if he were from another planet. Then she shook her head and walked out.

She had an eleven-inch black-and-white TV in her living room, and when she got home she switched it on and sat down in front of it. She saw nothing, but she sat there until signoff, when some minister said a prayer and they played the national anthem and showed a picture of a waving flag. After which she went into the bathroom and washed her face and brushed her teeth. Then she walked four steps into the bedroom, and removed the spread from her bed and folded it neatly and lay down.

She may have slept sometime during the night, but she was unaware of it. She was aware only of waiting for dawn. When it started to get light she got up and dressed in the red skirt and red and white blouse Juffie had bought for her in New York. She made a cup of instant coffee and drank it, rinsed the dishes she'd used, and put them on the drainboard. Next she got her savings book and her checkbook from her desk and put them in her purse, then she took the trolley to Boston.

Karen went to her branch of the Shawmut Bank on Milk Street and withdrew every penny from both accounts. With the cash jammed into her wallet in hundred-dollar bills, she walked to the Greyhound terminal on Park Street. "I'd like a ticket to Las Vegas please."

"There's nothing direct, lady." The man behind the window studied his routing maps. "You can go to Chicago and change there. Or you can do it via St. Louis."

He discussed with her alternative ways of reaching the city built in the far reaches of the Nevada desert. Karen listened, then said, "Whichever is quicker."

"Can't exactly say. When do you want to go?"

"Now. Right away."

He stared at her, then at his schedules once more. "There's a bus for St. Louis at one. That's two hours."

"Fine. Then I'll go that way."

.   .   .   .

Some things had changed since Karen was there in 1951. The machines themselves were more sophisticated. They had special jackpots, and they flashed pictures of gnomes and "lucky sevens" as well as fruit, and they took quarters, not just nickels and dimes.

Karen played a few machines at the bus terminal when she arrived, a kind of foreplay to the act of love for which she had come. She stopped after fifteen minutes, but that was long enough to realize she was still partial to dimes. They felt right in her fingers as she deposited them in the slot and pulled the lever. But within the boundaries of that choice she had many others. Which casino for a start? Not the Flamingo, where she'd been with Bernard. This time, she decided, she'd play at the Desert Inn.

The casinos themselves were almost identical. You only had to walk a few steps into the lobby to be enveloped in roulette wheels and crap tables and slot machines. The slots were scattered everywhere; so if you were walking through the casino—and you had to do that to get almost anywhere in the hotel—you'd maybe fish out some loose change and try your luck.

It had taken her three days to travel by bus from Boston to Las Vegas, and it was eleven A.M. Monday, the sixth of July, when Karen walked into the casino with a little over five thousand dollars. She didn't register at the hotel and she didn't go into any of its numerous restaurants, though the last thing she'd eaten had been a stale roll and some coffee at four in the morning in someplace called St. George in Arizona.

She examined her surroundings carefully before starting to play. She'd waited so long. Everything had to be as perfect as she could make it. There were three banks of dime machines. Karen chose the ones at the end farthest from the front desk and the entrance. She felt more hidden in this location, more completely anonymous.

The spot Karen chose didn't get quite as much through traffic as the rest of the casino because it was close to the separated area where they played baccarat, a very high-stakes card game where the tables were occasionally all but empty. Behind her were three blackjack tables. Blackjack wasn't a noisy game like shooting craps, and it didn't give rise to the constant stuttering clicks of the roulette wheel. She didn't have to hear anything but the enticing sound of the slot machine.

She found a free stool and sat down, and placed in her lap the plastic bag containing the twenty slender, tightly wrapped rolls of dimes they'd given her in exchange for a hundred-dollar bill. The bag wasn't cloth the way it had been in 1951. Plastic now, like everything else in the world. Karen put her purse on the floor and gripped it between her feet, and cracked the first roll of dimes into the tray at the base of the machine.

At the end of eighteen hours of play she thought of one particular machine as hers. It was the third from the left against the wall, and above the swiftly rotating wheels with their symbols it had a picture of a cowboy with two six-guns in his hands. The guns made shooting noises every time she hit a jackpot.

Her machine was hot. It paid her off with lots of jackpots, and each time the cowboy shot his six-guns, Karen yelped with excitement. She hadn't felt this much enthusiasm, or made such sounds of pleasure since . . . since she was here the last time four years earlier. Certainly nothing she did at work, or anything she and Bernard did together, in bed or elsewhere, ever gave her such a thrill.

When she stopped at five in the morning it was only because she couldn't sit up any longer, she couldn't lift her arm and pull the lever, and she couldn't keep her eyes open. She took her plastic bag of dimes—it was full again because she'd cashed another hundred sometime in the last few minutes, and God only knew how many before that—and her purse, and stumbled toward the reception desk. "I'd like a room, please."

The desk clerk examined her without comment or interest and pushed a registration form across the desk. She hesitated, then, giggling, she wrote her name as Gloria Finkelstein and filled in Bernard's address. She signed it, writing the assumed name with many flourishes, and pushed it back at him. "Any luggage?" he asked.

"No." She giggled again and held up the plastic bag of coins. "Just this."

He looked at her with tired eyes and handed over a key.

·   ·   ·   ·

"That's crazy," Juffie insisted. "There has to be something you can do." She gripped the receiver of the white telephone and paced up and down the white carpet of her bedroom. "She can't have disappeared into thin air. There's something wrong, there has to be."

The police lieutenant on the other end of the line was trying to be patient. "Look, Miss Kane, I understand your concern. I really do. But Dr. Rice is a grown woman, a professional lady. And if she chose to disappear, well, that's her business. There's no reason to think of this as a police matter. The only person with a genuine gripe is her landlord. Her lease has nine months to run. And believe me, he's not likely to demand an all-states search for a broken lease."

"I'm demanding it," Juffie said. "Me, Juffie Kane." She had no compunction whatever about using her celebrity to shake up the Boston police.

The cop was not impressed. "You may be a famous lady, Miss Kane, but you're not an injured party. Now, if you don't mind, I'm very busy. I'll get in touch with you if we hear anything. Anything at all. I promise." He hung up without waiting for Juffie to answer.

The police lieutenant wasn't only stupid and pig-headed, he was wrong. Juffie was injured, terribly wounded, sick in her heart and her soul. Deep inside her was a growing fear that she'd never see Karen again. Failed by Juffie and everybody else who did not recognize the extent of the damage she'd suffered, Karen had gone off and flung herself under a train, or in a river, or from the top of some building. But the police could find no evidence of that, and they'd checked every accident report and every hospital and every morgue.

"Besides," the lieutenant had said to Juffie a few days earlier, "according to her bank, she withdrew all the money from her savings and checking accounts on the third of July. And that's the last anyone's seen her. Why should she take a lot of money out of the bank if she was going to do herself harm?"

Why indeed? Juffie paced some more, then picked up the telephone again. This time she called Karen's mother. "Leah, it's me. I wanted you to know that I've spoken with that lieutenant again. He insists that nothing bad has happened to Karen. He says they'd know if it had."

Leah was crying, Juffie could hear the tears in her voice. "Yeah," she said. "Something bad happened. She met that Irish *momzer* and he twisted up her head, then he broke her heart. I thought I was doing something wonderful, sending her to college. Look what it got her, a goddamn goyisher *momzer* who first made her into an old lady, then dropped her."

"It wasn't your fault, Leah," Juffie said softly. "None of it. You always did the best you knew how for Karen. I knew it and she knew it." She realized she was discussing her friend in the past tense, as if she were dead. "She knows we love her," she added. "Karen will get in touch with us. You wait. I bet we hear something by the end of the week." But the week ended and another began and then another, and there was no word.

In September, when Karen had been missing for nearly two months, Juffie returned to Boston. Leah told her that Karen's landlord was insisting that her things be packed up and moved out of the building. Otherwise he was going to give them all to the Salvation Army. Her rent was overdue and he was reclaiming the apartment.

"I couldn't let Leah do a rotten job like that on her own," Juffie told her father. "So I came up to help."

Myer nodded. "Listen, Juffie. I hate to put it so baldly, but tell me the truth. What do you really think?" He swallowed hard. "Do you think Karen's alive?"

"I don't know," Juffie whispered. "I keep praying she is, and there's that business of the money. Why withdraw every dime if you intend to kill yourself?"

"Yeah." He did not mention that if you were walking around with all that money somebody else might kill you. "Look, I've got an idea. Two ideas really. First, let's pay Karen's rent, what's overdue and then enough to cover another six months. The landlord doesn't care whether she's living there as long as he gets his money. Besides, he doesn't have any legal basis to care. It's her home for the duration of the lease, providing she doesn't default on the rent."

"It never occurred to me," Juffie said. "But it's a great idea, Dad. It's not a lot of money, her rent is ninety-five a month. And if she comes back—when she comes back—it will be good if everything's the way she left it."

"That's what I was thinking. I mean, maybe she's got amnesia and she doesn't remember who she is. But something may lead her back to her own place. So if it's there . . ."

"Great," Juffie agreed. "That's one idea. What's the second?"

"We hire a private detective to look for her. The police are overworked and underpaid. They can't a spend a lot of time if there's not an obvious crime. But a detective is different, he's on his client's payroll and he keeps looking until you tell him to stop."

"God! Why didn't I think of that? You're right; of course you're right. Who do we get?"

"Hold on a minute. Honey, I know you've put every dime of your own into backing your new show. But the fifteen grand I invested in the play isn't going to break me. I'm paying for the detective. I want that understood."

"You pay now, because I'm so cash poor it's a joke," Juffie said. "But Paul will want to help. He'll be in funds again as soon as the D'Oyly Carte tour begins. And I'll be earning a salary when *Morning* goes into rehearsal in November. So we'll straighten out with you in a few months. Agreed?"

Myer nodded.

"Okay, back to my original question. Who do we get? How do you find a private detective?"

"I'll find one," Myer said. "Leave that to me too."

Juffie hesitated and didn't look at him. "Dad, I don't think it ought to be someone . . . someone with a questionable past. I mean—"

"You mean no one connected with the rackets. Don't worry, Juffie. This is one time we're going to be sweet and innocent, like a baby's *tochis*. No Kane-Saliatelli *mishegoss*. We don't need to involve Karen in anything like that." They were in Myer's office and he moved some papers on his desk and paused a moment before he continued. "And since we're on the subject, tell me something, Juffie, is all the financing for this play legitimate?"

She leaned back and stretched her arms over her head. "Yes. Thank God, I can say that and mean it. There were moments when I was tempted. But I never gave in. And we raised the whole thing, five hundred big ones, as Jack says, among ourselves and about a dozen small individual investors. All of whom, I am absolutely convinced, are going to become filthy rich as a result."

Myer smiled. "Good. And forgive me for thinking maybe everything wasn't kosher, but it's been on my mind. Before Pa died he was trying to find out something about Finky Aronson. Something that would give him some leverage. We never talked about it, I don't think he knew I knew he was poking around. But it was for you, wasn't it, Juffie?"

"Yes. Pa had an idea about getting that bastard Aronson off my back. But it's over, Dad. Don't worry about it anymore. I haven't seen Aronson for almost two years. I don't imagine I'll ever see him again. I discharged the debt. Pa told me once that *la cosa nostra* had rules, and even Finky Aronson had to play by them. And according to the rules, he's got no further claim on me."

Myer stood up. "Okay, that's settled. Now let's go see Karen's landlord."

Juffie reached for the telephone on his desk. "As soon as I call Leah and tell her we don't have to pack up Karen's stuff."

· · · ·

The detective Myer hired was a Mr. Schwartz. "A Jewish private eye," he told Juffie when he came to New York to speak with her. "Not like in the books, is it? And I know I don't look the part either."

He didn't. He was short and fat and almost bald, and he wore very thick glasses. "My father tells me you have an excellent reputation for finding missing persons, Mr. Schwartz."

"Yeah, frankly, I do. I get hunches about them. Sometimes I think I'm clairvoyant."

"And do you have any hunches about my friend Karen?"

He shook his head. "So far not a one. But don't be discouraged. We're only starting. And apparently you know Dr. Rice better than anybody, so I figured I'd better talk to you." He took a notebook from his inside pocket and flipped it open. "Maybe you'd like a rundown on what I already got?"

"Yes, please. I would."

"Well, all three places she worked came up with the same story. She was very competent, a first-class psychologist. But she kept pretty much to herself, didn't make close friends with any of the people she worked with. And they all say that last spring, toward the end of May, she changed a lot. She cut her hair and started wearing pretty clothes. They say before that she was fairly dowdy. But nobody can say that she acted any different on the job. They had no warning that she was going to pull a bunk."

"I can explain about the changed image," Juffie said. And she did, ending up, "All we were really doing was restoring her to the way she'd been before she knew Professor Hanrihan. She turned dowdy while she was seeing him. It had something to do with his dead wife. It's pretty complicated and I don't think it will tell us where she is now." She refilled his coffee cup and he added two sugars and stirred it. "Have you spoken with Professor Hanrihan?" Juffie asked.

"Yes. With him and his wife. Separately and together. Which took some finagling on my part. Neither one of them really wanted to talk to me. They both say they haven't seen Dr. Rice since they got married in May, and they haven't any idea where she's gone or why. The hell of it is, I think they're telling the truth."

"What do we do next?" Juffie asked. "Where can you start?"

"A lot of legwork, Miss Kane. A hell of a lot, since the trail is nearly three months old. I'll check the airlines, of course. They make a list of passengers. And I'll have a crack at the train and bus stations, but that's a lot tougher since they don't ask for names. Maybe the best shot will be professional organizations of psychologists in different states. And all the places she could get a job. Five thousand bucks won't last her forever; she'll have to work."

"It sounds overwhelming," Juffie said. "And very depressing."

"No, not really depressing. I've already looked into the hospitals and morgues and accident reports, and so have the police. The one thing that looks likely is that Dr. Rice is alive. It's not certain, mind you. But it looks likely."

Which was all the comfort Juffie was going to get, and the only hope to which she could cling.

"You've got to snap out of your blue funk," Matt told her in the middle of October. "I know how you feel about Karen's disappearance, but you're about to go into rehearsal for what may be the most important show of your career."

It was certainly one which involved her more totally than any other with which she'd been associated. This time, for instance, she had been party to the decision to go way out on a limb with the sets. At Juffie's suggestion, they hired Billy Baldwin to create them. Baldwin did not come cheap, even for Juffie, whom he adored, but his sketches were the most exciting things she'd ever seen. And his models, the miniature three-dimensional sets they were working with at the meeting in Jack Fine's office, were even better.

"This is marvelous, Billy. I love this blue damask drapery; it will fade into the background until it's lit."

"Exactly," he told her. "And when we spin . . . presto! The bed curtains."

When we spin. It had become the byword of the staging. Even freed from Henry Whiteman's original concept of showing the past and the future simultaneously, juggling nine sets in three acts was a prodigious feat. The problem was to be solved by building an electrically operated turntable which would occupy most of the stage. It would be divided into three pie-shaped sections and while one faced the audience, the backstage crew could work on the two others. The blue drapery Juffie had commented on was part of the drawing room of the Boston house in one sector, and the backing of a four-poster in the one adjacent. By such sleight of hand was Baldwin creating a miracle.

"Is damask right?" Henry Whiteman asked anxiously. "Don't forget, it's 1746."

"Dear boy," Baldwin said in his soft voice, "I am in no danger of forgetting. I have two charming ladies with silver hair and encyclopedic brains from the New England Historical Society advising me on every detail. I can't put in a vase or a picture frame without their questioning its colonial authenticity. The fabric and the color are correct. The gentlefolk of Boston imported such stuffs from dear old England. Any other questions?"

Henry shook his head. "No, I guess not. I just want everything right."

These days the boy genius always looked as if any moment he would burst into tears. They were all totally involved and a little worried; it was such an enormous and difficult undertaking, but Henry Whiteman lived in perpetual anxiety. "It's because so many people who can't really afford it have put up money for this show," he'd confided to Juffie. "My parents, your father . . . God! even my mother's optometrist invested five thousand."

So she knew why he was looking at Billy Baldwin with an expression at once hangdog and distrustful. Juffie reached out and covered his hand with hers. "It's okay, Henry. Billy won't make any mistakes. He never does."

"Never ones that show," the decorator said, smiling. "Now, can we go on?"

They went on for four hours. It was after five when the meeting at Jack Fine's office broke up. Matt had been there, too, not just because he'd also managed to scare up some cash to invest in *When Morning Comes,* but because like the others, he felt utterly committed to the project.

He waited for Juffie by the door, holding her coat. "You're back in furs," he said, slipping the silver fox jacket over her shoulders. "Every year that's how I know fall's really come and winter's on its way. It gets a little chilly and one morning I say to myself, summer's over, Juffie will show up in a fur coat any day now. And you do."

"Glad I don't disappoint you," she said. Young Whiteman passed them on his way out and nodded, leaving wordlessly and looking as morose as when he'd come in. "Wonderful how he's enjoying getting his first play on Broadway, isn't it?" Juffie pulled on her gloves. "Let's get out of here."

Fine's office was behind Grand Central, on that atypical street called Vanderbilt Avenue which didn't fit into the strict midtown Manhattan grid. They crossed the road and cut through the station and came out on Lexington Avenue, more intent on their discussion of Baldwin's sets than on where they were going. "We probably shouldn't have come this way," Matt said when he realized where they were. "You could have walked right up Madison to get to Paul's office."

"I'm not meeting Paul; he's out of town until tomorrow. On the West Coast tying up the San Francisco part of the D'Oyly Carte tour."

"Oh."

"That's all?" she asked him. "Just, oh?"

"Is there something else?"

Juffie stopped on the sidewalk and turned and looked at him. "I don't know, is there?" Her heart was pounding and she shoved her hands in the pockets of her navy wool slacks so he wouldn't see them trembling. Usually she could be around Matt and keep perfect control. Only sometimes did the secret rise from its hiding place deep within her. This was one of those times.

Matt hesitated a moment, as tempted as she was. Then smiled at her. "Hello," he said.

The codeword, the exit line he'd devised after their twenty-four-hour affair in London. A reminder of Juffie's own words, a one-act play with a limited engagement and no encores. She tried a grin, failed the first time, and made it on the second attempt. "Hello yourself."

He stepped to the cab rank and opened a door and held it for her. "Give you a ring in a couple of days," he said. "Take care."

"Where to, lady?"

"Wait a minute," Juffie told the cabbie. He shrugged and pushed down his flag. As long as the meter was running he'd sit here for an hour if that's what she wanted.

It didn't take an hour, merely a few seconds while she watched Matt's retreating form. The tall figure, clad in a tightly belted trench coat, and with a rather scruffy dark fedora pushed back on his head, disappeared quickly through the doors of the station. On his way to catch a commuter's train to New Jersey, home to his little house and his wife.

"Okay," she said when she could no longer see him. "Sixty-eighth and Second, East River Tower, the southwest corner." She sat back while the taxi moved uptown through the evening traffic. The driver flicked constant glances at his rearview mirror, trying to decide if it was really Juffie Kane sitting in the back of his cab. Juffie didn't give him an opportunity to ask; she kept her eyes turned to the passing scene, studying the lights of Manhattan winking on seductively in the dusk.

. . . .

In a very short time Karen went through the five-thousand-dollar stake she'd brought to Las Vegas. A vast number of dimes could be spent playing the slots sixteen to eighteen hours out of every twenty-four, and somehow the number of jackpots she hit seldom equaled the amount of money she spent to achieve that pull of the lever which resulted in the cowboy shooting his guns and a shower of dimes falling into the tray.

She'd seen the end of her funds approaching by the beginning of August and she'd moved out of her room at the Desert Inn into a much cheaper place, a cluster of shacks on the edge of town called Belle's Starlight Cabins.

Belle was the name of the woman who was always behind the desk in the two-by-four lobby of the main building. She provided hot and cold running water and clean sheets on Sundays, all for twenty-one dollars a week. The starlight was free; the night sky over the desert was something very special. But Karen seldom returned to her cabin before dawn.

Public transportation in Las Vegas was practically nonexistent. She worried about that. It cost too much to take a taxi back and forth to the Desert Inn twice a day. She decided to hitch. So the second day after moving into her new residence, she staggered out of the casino at a little after·midday and left the hotel on the parking lot side. She stood and looked around, half blinded by the relentless sun, and lifted a tentative thumb.

A car stopped almost immediately. "Hi, you want a ride? I thought you were staying at the hotel."

Karen peered through the window of the flashy late model Chevrolet. The driver was a man she'd spoken to a few times, one of the blackjack dealers. His name was Frank Carlucci. Another time in another life she might have said he was cute, really nice-looking. Now she was aware only of his ownership of an automobile. "I was staying at the hotel. I moved."

"Where to?"

"Belle's Starlight Cabins. Out on Spring Mountain Road."

He leaned over and opened the door on the passenger side. "You're in luck, it's on my way. Hop in, Gloria." That was the name he knew her by. It was the one she'd given him when they met in the hotel coffee shop on one of the rare occasions that she had stopped playing to eat.

His car had red pseudo-leather upholstery and a lot of chrome. It smelled new. They did not talk much. Karen was too exhausted.

Frank said he was tired, too, because he'd just come off the four-to-noon shift. Those were his regular hours, he explained. Because he'd been in Las Vegas only a few months, and what they called the graveyard shift was where they started all the new boys.

"I don't know how you do it," he said as they moved along the deserted road. "You're always there when I come on, and you're usually still there when I leave. I figure you play twelve, maybe fourteen hours a day."

"At least," Karen confirmed. She added no explanation.

"You going to find some slots closer to home now that you've moved?"

Her hair was almost chin-length because it hadn't been cut since May. But it was loose, not pulled back in a bun. When she shook her head the dark blond curls moved around her wan face. "No, I prefer playing at the Desert Inn. I have my own special machine."

"Yeah," Carlucci said. "I've noticed. You always play the one with the cowboy who shoots his pistols when you hit. You figure that's a lucky machine?"

"I don't know. I just like it."

He drove on until they came to the wooden shacks with the peeling paint huddled by the side of the road. He pulled up beneath the neon sign that marked the entrance. "I go back to the Inn around midnight and hang around before my shift. If you want, I'll pick you up."

"No. Thanks, but midnight's too late." She opened the car door.

He put a restraining hand on her arm. "When do you sleep?"

"Now. For a few hours. I don't need a lot of sleep. See you. And thanks for the lift."

"You're welcome. Tell you what, I'll take you home around this same time tomorrow if you're ready to go when I am."

"Around this time," Karen said. "Yes, that's about when I'm usually ready. Thanks again."

It became a pattern. Between eight and nine in the evening she hitched or walked the two miles into town—the Desert Inn was in fact on that part of the Strip near Spring Mountain Road—and Frank Carlucci drove her back the following day sometime after noon. They said little on these journeys, their conversation consisting mostly of Frank asking questions and Karen giving him minimal answers.

In that buried part of her mind which recalled that she was a psychologist, the questions sometimes registered more than average astuteness, as if he were genuinely interested in the obsession that possessed her. But when that happened she turned off both her thoughts and his questions. Down that circuitous path lay memory, and concern for those she'd left so unceremoniously behind, and guilt—all adding up to pain. She gambled in order not to feel the pain, and she would not allow this young man with his wavy black hair and his dark brown eyes to make her remember.

In September she told him she wouldn't be able to ride home with him anymore. "I've got a job from eleven to three."

"Where?"

"In the Angel Grill on Fremont. I'm a waitress."

"Oh, I see. Ever been a waitress before, Gloria?"

"No. But my new boss doesn't know that. And I don't imagine it's too difficult."

"Your money's run out, huh? The stake you brought with you is all gone."

"Something like that," she admitted. "So I won't be riding with you anymore. But thanks for all the times you provided the coach and four."

"Coach and four," he repeated as if testing the words. "Listen, do me a favor. Say 'park your car in Harvard Yard.'"

She actually smiled at him. Something like a grin. Something he would have recognized if he knew the Karen Rice of old; neither the creature who had been Bernard Hanrihan's mistress nor the lady besotted by slot machines named Gloria. "You want to see if you're right and I have a Boston accent, don't you? Pahk your cah in Hahvahd Yahd. See, I do."

"Yes, I thought so. A Boston Brahmin."

"No, that part you've got wrong. A kid from what's known as the West End. Not the best part of town and nothing to do with Beacon Hill or Brahmins."

"Gloria, listen, I know it's none of my business, but what the hell are you doing this for? You're not some chick without a brain in her head, and you're definitely not a waitress. You're an educated woman who refers to things like a 'coach and four.' What is all this in aid of?"

"You're right, it's none of your business. See you around, Frank. Thanks again for all the rides."

Three days later he showed up at the Angel Grill. "Ham and cheese on rye with mustard," he told her as he took his seat at the counter. "How are you?"

"Fine. How are you?"

"Okay. I miss our drives up Spring Mountain Road. I wanted to ask you to have a cup of coffee when I took my break last night, but my boss was hanging around. The management frowns on the dealers getting friendly with the players. Frowns from the management of the Desert Inn are not to be taken lightly."

"No, I don't imagine they are." *Crime and the Immigrant Experience.* No better place to study that than Las Vegas. And a guy named Carlucci dealing blackjack on the Strip must be in the thick of it. "What are you drinking with the sandwich?"

"Coke."

When she left the grill at three-thirty he was waiting for her. "C'mon, I'll drive you home."

"It's your time to sleep. You shouldn't be hanging around here waiting for me."

For answer he simply took her arm and led her to the Chevy. She was staggering with fatigue, far too exhausted to protest. She fell asleep in the car, and when she woke up it was many hours later and she was lying on the narrow, lumpy bed in her cabin.

Karen looked down at herself in the moonlight entering the small, rather dirty window. How did she get here? The last thing she remembered was being in Frank Carlucci's car. Did he . . . ? Did they . . . ? No, she had absolutely no memory of it, and surely she would. Besides, she was fully dressed in the white nylon uniform of a waitress at the Angel Grill. Even her underpants were still on. So, no.

She got up and took a shower and washed her hair and put on her second uniform. She'd wash out the first one when she came home tomorrow. It could dry while she slept. At least getting this job had solved the clothes problem. She didn't have to keep alternating the two pairs of shorts she'd bought since she arrived in Las Vegas, both of which were worn out, and she didn't have to spend money on anything else. She could pull the lever of the slot machine in the same outfit she wore behind the counter of the restaurant.

By the time she came home the following afternoon she was too tired to wash either uniform. She fell into bed and when she woke around nine she was trembling with anxiety because she hadn't played for nearly eleven hours. She was late. Somebody might have grabbed her machine. It didn't matter if it was just a casual player who'd give it up in an hour or less. That had happened before. But what if a regular took it? She could be shut out all night. There wasn't time to worry about how she looked. She pulled on the same uniform she'd worn the day before and ignored the mustard stain on the bodice.

The next day she made a lot of mistakes behind the counter of the Angel Grill. A customer who asked for toast got plain bread and sent his sandwich back. Another told her he didn't want anything on his chicken on whole wheat, but she forgot to say "Hold the butter and the mayo" when she called in his order. He got really mad because he was in a hurry, and he walked out without eating or paying.

"Have to let you go, kid," the owner of the grill said when three-thirty came. "Got no time for losers here." He eyed her soiled uniform with distaste when he paid her the sixteen dollars she had coming.

Karen was crying when she came out on Fremont. "What's the matter?" Frank Carlucci asked, approaching her and taking her arm.

"I got fired. And I made only sixteen dollars, and my rent's due today."

"Well, that's the usual pattern," he said as he got behind the wheel of the car. "Now you'll sneak past the landlady and use the entire sixteen bucks to gamble with tonight. Because, of course, you're going to win big, and all the problems will go away."

"I might," Karen said. "You never know. I do sometimes."

"Yeah. But more often you don't. And sooner or later do you know how it will be, Gloria? You'll be hustling tricks on the Strip to make a few bucks. Just enough to finance another few hours on the slots. Only you won't do very well at that either. For one thing, it's thoroughly organized and you're a babe in the woods. They'll eat you alive. For another, you don't look good enough to peddle your ass. Not at the moment. Though I imagine you were a real cute lady once upon a time."

"Who the hell are you to call me a whore?"

"Nobody. I'm nobody at all. And I didn't call you a whore. I said you were on your way to becoming one. Gloria Finkelstein, big mama. Never mind that she's got bags you could pack under her eyes, and she's shaking most of the time, and she's so skinny you could cut yourself if you put your arms around her."

They were halfway out Spring Mountain Road by now, on a deserted stretch of blacktop road that cut through scrubland. "You've got some kind of nerve. And for your information, my name's not Gloria Finkelstein, goddamn you! It's Karen Rice! *Dr.* Karen Rice, if you want the whole truth."

He slammed on the brakes and the car stopped dead. "Say it again," he said quietly. "Who are you?"

She hated herself for telling him her name, for letting him in. She'd done it only because he made her angry. She did not want to be angry. Or sad. Or happy. She did not want to feel anything. She wanted to pull the lever and watch the fruit spin around. Karen stared straight ahead. The sun beat down, and without the movement of air through the windows the temperature in the automobile began climbing fast.

"Say it," Frank repeated. He turned and grabbed her shoulders. "Tell me who you are!" He was shouting now, shaking her. "Tell me, so you can tell yourself! Who are you?"

"Karen Rice! Karen Rice! Karen Rice!" She screamed the names at him, hurling them in his face as if they were rocks. As if they could hurt him as much as they hurt her. "I'm Karen Rice and I'm a psychologist and I have a bachelor's, and a master's, and a goddamn Ph.D.!"

She collapsed in gulping sobs, sucking in air so fast it made her nauseous and she started to gag and had to fumble open the door of the car and lean over and puke her guts onto the road.

He kept hold of her while she threw up, pressing his hand to her forehead, the way Leah used to do when she was small and was sick to her stomach and vomited over the toilet. Finally she had nothing more to heave out of her belly and she pulled back and lay her head on the red upholstery of the seat.

Sweat poured off her face and Frank wiped it with his handkerchief. "Better?"

"A little. I'm sorry."

"Don't be, I'm not. I think we've made a pretty good start. At least I know your real name. And more to the point, you know it."

He put the Chevy in gear and drove on toward Belle's Starlight Cabins.

. . . .

They began rehearsing *When Morning Comes* on the second of November. The first day all thirty-two members of the cast were assembled they sat around holding pristine scripts, which would soon be much folded and marked, and everybody simply read their lines. Since Marjorie did not come on until halfway through Act One, Juffie had time to look and listen.

She'd been involved in every decision about the hiring of the principals, and she'd come to every casting call, but until now she hadn't seen the entire cast in one place. It was a good mix. Even without costumes and makeup she could see that they'd work well together, physically balance each other on the stage. Initial evidence that Phil Michaelson, the director, knew his job. But she'd already been convinced of that. Michaelson was a man in his forties, a pro from way back with a number of hits to his credit. What remained to be seen was if he'd be inspired . . . if, with this show and this cast in this particular niche of time and space, he could call forth his personal genius.

One very nice thing, she reflected, was that she was working with Harry Harcourt again. He played Jeremiah Slade, the man Marjorie comes to Boston to marry because her father has arranged it. Juffie listened to him trading lines with the fellow who had the part of his lawyer, discussing his forthcoming marriage. They weren't good, not yet, but Michaelson said nothing. This wasn't about direction and interpretation, just about feeling their way in. First readings are always terrible, a truism of the theater.

They were at the bottom of page four. "I do not have to like her, merely to respect and honor her," Harry said. "She's to become my wife, not my friend." There was a great rustling of paper as thirty-two people flipped over the pages of their scripts. Juffie put down the Coke she was sipping. Her entrance was imminent. Three minutes later Harry gave her her cue. "And so, madam, you have arrived."

Juffie read her first words. "Yes, Mr. Slade. I have come a very

far distance and whatever this place may be, I have arrived at it."
She felt a frisson of excitement. Not because she'd delivered the
line well, she had not, but because at last it had begun.

When they broke up, somebody peeked out the door and said
it was snowing. "It can't be snowing," somebody else said. "It's
only the second of November." The first voice insisted it was
snowing.

Juffie came out on Forty-fifth east of Broadway to a white
world. The snow wasn't the heavy wet sort typical of early winter.
It was fine and dry and powdery, and it was sticking. "Get you a
cab, Miss Kane?" someone asked.

"No, thank you. I think I'll walk a bit."

Humming under her breath, hugging close the special joy of
beginning a new show—all the sweeter this time because getting
to the beginning had been so difficult—she walked all the way
home.

Two days later they started blocking; still holding their scripts,
still easing themselves into the act of creation. Now the purpose
was to find their physical way along the streets and alleys and
byways of the world they would make together. Thirty-two people
underlined printed stage directions and wrote in new ones in
colored pencil: enter stage left, cross to center stage, exit right rear,
move to small table center right, take the apples . . .

There were no apples, no props, just as there were no
costumes and no scenery. All was obvious make-believe, in hopes
that eventually it would become believable make-believe.

Before they broke up that afternoon Phil Michaelson posted a
rehearsal schedule on the bulletin board backstage. Like all the
others, Juffie stopped to read it over his shoulder and make notes.
"Okay, Juffie?" Phil asked.

"Fine." She never made a fuss about schedules. She was no
more a prima donna now than she'd been when she played
Hannah Glemp. That fact was well known, but she was still Juffie
Kane, and the director still went through the motions of asking.
"It's fine," she repeated.

She said the same thing to Paul that night when he asked how
it had gone. "It was fine. It's much too early to say anything more.
But for the moment, it's the way it should be."

"Good. I brought you a beginning present." He handed her a
box wrapped in silver embossed paper marked Tiffany.

Juffie opened it to find a fourteen-inch double strand of matched pearls. "Paul, they're lovely. I wasn't expecting anything, it's not my birthday or Christmas or our anniversary."

"It's a starting-a-new-show present, replacement number one of the two I owe you."

She felt tears behind her eyes. "You don't owe me anything, darling."

"Yes, I do. The emerald earrings will appear sooner or later. Juffie, do you remember your promise?"

She leaned forward and kissed his cheek. "I remember."

"We start a baby after you've been a hit for seven or eight months," he said, reiterating the terms.

Juffie pressed her finger over his lips. "Shh . . . You mustn't say that we're going to be a you-know-what. Not now that we're in rehearsals. It's bad luck."

"Bad luck can't touch us," Paul said, hugging her, "We're a charmed couple, *chérie*. We're magic."

Chapter 17

$\mathcal{J}$anuary 6, 1956, was a day a number of people would remember well. It was the day that *When Morning Comes* starring Juffie Kane opened at the Lyceum Theater on Forty-fifth Street.

Despite the fervent advance ballyhoo—the most expensive dramatic production ever staged, the most remarkable sets, the most fabulous costumes, an absolutely brilliant script from the hand of a twenty-four-year-old unknown—there was a lot of skepticism. Because Broadway is naturally skeptical, and because "Juffie Kane may have been great in that television thing, but she didn't make her reputation in drama, and they say this damn play lasts more than three hours . . ."

On any opening day she was a tinderbox waiting for a spark; the morning of the sixth of January she was dynamite with a lit fuse. Juffie knew how many people expected her to bomb, and how much a number of them would enjoy it. "Eat something," Paul urged. "You'll feel better."

"I can't, I just gag."

"Some coffee at least. I'll make a fresh pot."

"No, not coffee. Tea maybe. With lemon and honey."

He made the tea and brought it to her in bed, but she couldn't drink it. Too sweet, he'd put in too much honey. Juffie took one sip and put the cup on the bedside table. The doorbell chimed and Paul went to answer it. He came back holding a big box. "More flowers."

She lifted the lid and discovered white roses and found the card. "You were wonderful, you are wonderful, you will be wonderful," she read aloud. "From Nessa."

"She's right, naturally," Paul said. "Listen, *chérie*, would you rather be alone? I can get out of your way, go down to the office for a few hours. Then—" His words were interrupted once more by the chimes. "I can't leave," he said when he returned. "You need a butler. Here, exactly what you need, more flowers."

These were from her father. Myer was coming to New York to attend the opening. In the meantime he'd sent scarlet camellias and he'd signed the card: "Dad—and Mama and Pop and Pa, in absentia." Juffie started to cry.

"Don't." Paul wiped her eyes with a tissue. "You'll have a hell of a time with your makeup tonight if you keep crying."

"I know." She blew her nose, then tossed back the yellow quilt. "I'm getting up. I can't just lie here and be terrified all day. I'm going for a walk."

"Don't pick up any playwrights," Paul said when she left. At least that made her laugh. For luck she walked up to the Whelan's drugstore on Ninetieth and Lexington. She looked inside, thinking that maybe she'd see Henry sitting at the counter, but he wasn't there. Doubtless his mother was keeping him in bed with a hot water bottle and aspirin every four hours.

When she returned to the penthouse, every flat surface sported an arrangement of flowers. The cleaning woman was muttering something about there not being any more vases. "Leave anything else that comes in the kitchen in a bucket of water," Juffie said. "I'll deal with it later." She walked around checking the cards of the bouquets she hadn't seen before she went out.

Daisies from Matt. They looked wonderfully fresh and innocent among the rarer blooms. The card said: "Don't pull off any petals, I can tell you the answer." For a moment she was startled. What would Paul make of that? Nothing. There was love and there was love, and nobody doubted that Matt loved her and she loved him. The only issue was what kind of love, and Paul didn't seem concerned about it. Since that one time right after she returned from London, he hadn't again referred to Matt as anything other than her friend and agent. She replaced his card and moved on to the others.

"Everybody who's ever met you, I think, has sent flowers," Paul said, coming into the living room. "There are more in the bedroom and in your boudoir. The place is beginning to resemble a funeral home."

"If you don't mind, I can do without that comparison."

He chuckled. "Sorry, I forgot how touchy you are today."

"Not everybody," she told him when she'd completed her tour of the floral offerings. "There's nothing from Karen."

"You didn't really expect it, did you, *chérie*?" he asked gently. "It's been six months."

She'd expected it nonetheless. Just as she'd expected a Christmas card. Karen will get in touch at Christmas, she'd told herself all during December. But she had not done so then, and she wasn't going to do so today.

Mr. Schwartz, the private detective, had given up the search. He refused to keep taking their money when he couldn't turn up any clue, except for a ticket seller at the Greyhound terminal who said that yeah maybe he'd sold a ticket to Las Vegas to a lady who looked like the one in the picture. But he wasn't sure, and Schwartz came up empty in Las Vegas, and Juffie scoffed at the idea. "Karen hates Las Vegas," she insisted. "She told me so years ago." So finally the detective called it quits. Everybody was prepared to call it quits except Leah and Juffie. They went on consoling each other by telephone with empty hopes. Paul was made of different stuff.

"Wherever Karen is," he said, "she probably doesn't know you're opening in a new show tonight. *Chérie*, there are places in the remote wilds of this immense country where maybe they've never even heard of Juffie Kane."

"Karen's heard of me," Juffie said. She glanced at her watch. "It's after three. I'm going to have a long soak in a lot of bubbles."

"Okay, don't drown yourself."

"If it weren't for the fact that I know at least thirty-one people who feel as rotten as I do at this moment, I just might." While she ran the tub she wondered if Karen, wherever she was, was feeling rotten. She hoped so. Oh God, she hoped so. You had to be alive to feel rotten.

· · · ·

In November Karen was fired from the job she'd found sorting dirty clothes in a dry cleaners. "I can't keep people who forget to come to work," the boss said.

She'd played for twenty-three hours straight one day the week before, because she was hot, winning jackpot after jackpot. And by the time she'd given most of it back to the machine, she was so overcome with fatigue she returned to the tourist cabin and slept for nearly two days. Then she played again, with what was left of her earlier winnings. When she finally lost all that, another day and a half had passed, which made five days that she hadn't shown up at the dry cleaners. So she got fired.

"Now what?" Frank asked.

As usual, they were in his car. He never spoke to her while she was playing, though he stood about five yards behind her at his blackjack table. In the Desert Inn Karen concentrated on her game and he concentrated on his. Outside the casino, as he ferried her back and forth between the limited number of places that defined what she called her life, Frank asked the kind of questions she most hated, those which focused her on reality. "Now what are you going to do? Have you got the rent for this week?"

Karen shook her head. "No. But if I can play tonight I'll get it. I'll take the first twenty-one dollars I win and put it aside for Belle and not touch it. I will, really, Frank, I promise. If you'll lend me a stake. Fifteen dollars. That's all I need."

"No dice."

"C'mon. What's fifteen bucks to you? You make a fortune."

"I am not lending you any more money."

She grabbed his arm. "You have to help me, Frank, you're the only one I can count on. Ten dollars. Please, just ten."

At least he didn't push her away. Frank never pushed her away. But he shook his head. "No. I mean it. Unless . . ."

"Unless what? Tell me. Tell me what you want and I'll do it."

"Unless you move in with me."

"What?" She was startled. He'd never touched her, except in the act of moving her from one place to another. It was always she who touched him, grabbing him as she pleaded for one more loan. "Why do you want me to move in with you?" She pushed her hair back from her face. It was a lot longer now, and matted with sweat and tangled curls. She didn't remember the last time she'd washed it.

"Not for the way you look," Frank said. "I didn't say you should share my bed, Karen. Only my house. I have a little bungalow out at the far end of Fremont."

It would take some time, but eventually she would realize that Fremont was the other side of town from Spring Mountain Road.

Every time he drove her to the cabin he was going completely out of his way. She didn't think of that now. "You want somebody to look after it, a live-in maid?"

"Yeah, a live-in maid with a Ph.D. Every boy's childhood dream. I simply want to take care of you. What do you say?"

"Why?"

"Jesus! I'm not going to play Twenty Questions, Karen. Will you do it or won't you?"

She thought for a moment, then shrugged. "I don't have much to lose, do I?"

So in November she moved in with him. At the end of a week they'd established a pattern of existence. She had her room and he had his. His was off limits; she wasn't allowed in. Theoretically they shared the remaining two rooms, but Karen wasn't much good at helping with the upkeep of the living room and the kitchen, and she didn't use either very often.

Her life was little different from what it had been. She slept, ate a tiny bit, and played until she was too exhausted to pull the lever of the machine or her money ran out. Her stake was predetermined; Frank gave her sixty dollars a week to gamble with. It was generous, but not more than he could afford. By his own admission he took down a bundle dealing blackjack six days a week. "I don't expect you to quit," he said. "So I'll stake you. But this much and no more."

He brought her to the casino when he went to work and took her home when he left. If she ran out of money before Sunday, which was the day he gave her the sixty bucks, it was tough shit. He wouldn't give her any more no matter how she begged and pleaded.

A couple of times when she had nothing left and it wasn't Sunday she waited until he went to work, then went out and panhandled on the street. Karen didn't offer anything in return for the money she begged. She did what so many gamblers down on their luck did, stopped strangers and mumbled something about needing a quarter. You had to be very careful, the Las Vegas cops were tough as hell on panhandlers, but Karen got away with it. When she'd begged three or four dollars from the populace who understood so well why she wanted it, she went somewhere and played until she was broke again. Not to the Desert Inn, of course; she didn't want Frank to see her.

If he knew, he never said anything about it. He said other things though. "Take a shower, Karen. House rules. You have to bathe once every twenty-four hours. And wash your hair. At least once a week."

She did exactly as he instructed, like a child. Because she felt no shame at being told she smelled, she was long past feeling shame, and next to playing the slots, the most important thing in the world had become living in the bungalow on Fremont with Frank. She felt safe there, and because she did she realized she had not felt safe for a very long time. Longer than she could remember. Certainly not since before she became Bernard Hanrihan's mistress.

One day Frank went out for a couple of hours and returned with clothes—two skirts, a blue denim wraparound and a pleated green cotton, and four blouses in different colors. "You need something to wear; this way you've got enough so you can wash the stuff between times." Karen dutifully threw away the thread-bare remains of the scant wardrobe she'd had when she moved in, and began wearing the clothes Frank bought her. She also learned how to use his washing machine.

One Saturday night just before Christmas she hit a big jackpot. She won eight hundred dollars and cashed a hundred of it right away. She put the crisp new bill in the sole of her shoe. Before the night ended she'd gambled back almost all the winnings, but she hadn't touched the hundred. "I want to go shopping," she told Frank the next day.

It was four in the afternoon and he was eating breakfast because his shift made such exoticisms necessary. Karen was drinking coffee. She used to take it black, but he'd induced her to add milk and extra sugar. "So you'll get a little nourishment, since it's mostly what you live on."

Now she stirred the coffee and repeated her request. "Can we go shopping?"

"Sure, if you want to." His voice was neutral. If he found her request unusual, or even heartening, he didn't let on.

She wouldn't let him accompany her into the stores; instead, she arranged to meet him on the corner in an hour. "What did you get?" he asked when she returned with three packages.

"Never mind."

She'd bought him gifts for Christmas, slippers and aftershave and a pair of gold cuff links. Well, not real gold, just gold filled. But they were nice, chosen with care from vestigial memories of what was and was not tasteful and elegant. When she gave him the presents on Christmas morning he said he loved them.

"I've got something for you too." It was a cherry-red terry-cloth bathrobe, the classic type that wraps around the body and ties with a sash. She tried it on. "Red suits you," Frank said. He lifted a lock of her hair with the back of his fingers. Clean hair now. "Karen, how did you used to wear it? Before Las Vegas."

"Depends on when you mean." She slicked it all back with her hands. "In a bun like this for a long time. But before and after that, very short. A poodle cut. The way Mary Martin had hers in *South Pacific*."

"I don't think much of the bun, but I'd love to see you with it short."

The following day she had it cut. Frank said she looked terrific. "Do you realize," she asked, "that this month I have spent money on at least two occasions? On something besides playing, I mean."

"Yeah," he said. "I realize."

. . . .

At eight-fourteen P.M., standing in the wings stage left at the Lyceum Theater, listening to Harry Harcourt speak his lines, Juffie Kane was frozen. She was paralyzed, unable to move. She would never walk on that stage, she told herself. This time she couldn't do it. From where she stood she could see the seventh row of the orchestra, where her father was sitting with Matt and Paul and Nessa and Jack Fine. Too bad, Myer was finally well enough to take his first airplane flight and come to New York and attend a performance, and his only daughter was going to embarrass the hell out of him. Not to mention herself.

Phil Michaelson materialized beside her. He touched her arm and smiled. Juffie didn't smile back. The stiff brown brocade gown, plus cape and bonnet and muff, weighed her down. Even if she got up the courage to enter, she'd never be able to move in all these trappings. Fuck that costume designer! Why had she let herself be talked into this outfit?

"She's to become my wife, not my friend," Harry Harcourt was saying center stage. Three minutes now.

She found herself listening for the sound effects. Yes, there it was, that wonderful noise they'd worked out which sounded exactly like the wheels of a carriage on a cobbled street. And then the horse's whinny.

Harry crossed stage left and opened the door in Billy Baldwin's remarkable set. "And so, madam, you have arrived."

And without thinking about it, she was doing it. What she'd been born to do. The only thing she knew. Juffie swept past him, looking first at her surroundings, and only afterward at the man she'd never met who was to be her husband—just the way she and Phil had worked it out. The brown brocade swished elegantly as she turned and faced Harry and loosed with one hand the ties of the bonnet. She removed the hat, waited for the spotlight to pick her up, hung on a second more until the audience could feel the discomfort between man and woman. Finally she spoke. "Yes, Mr. Slade. I have come a very far distance, and whatever this place may be, I have arrived at it."

Walter Kerr, now drama critic at the *Times,* gave her the praise she'd best remember for what remained of her life. Of all the superb reviews she had received, this was the one that made her weep. "Miss Kane is, in a word, perfect. For three hours and twenty minutes Marjorie transports us. She makes us angry and exasperated and frightened, and in the end she makes us proud. She shows us the face of where we have been as a nation, and where we are going as individuals. Juffie Kane, we thank you and we love you."

Every element of the production was reviewed at length. The acclaim was lavish, and not just for the play and the actors; the sets drew raves, as well as the costumes. Readers were told in detail of each moment of opening night—such as that there had been nine curtain calls and a standing ovation for the cast, and that when the traditional cry for the author was sounded and the spotlight picked up young Henry Whiteman, he was sobbing. And that Jack Fine was "a producer of extraordinary astuteness and courage."

"We're a miracle," Jack said when they'd finally read every word at least three times. "A fucking miracle, and you, my darling Juffie, are the biggest miracle of them all."

"Not without you, Jack. None of it would have happened without you."

"That's what I mean. Not that you're a great actress, I already knew that. You're a great person. I'd been such a shit for so long, it took real courage to make me look at this play. And I'll never forget that you did it, and gave me maybe the best night of my life."

That was one of the most precious moments. The other came at about five A.M., when they were all ready to give in to exhaustion and leave Sardi's. Matt carried a bottle of champagne and two glasses to where she was sitting and handed her one and filled them both. "I offer a toast to the first lady of Broadway," he said. Then, very quietly so only she could hear, "My toast is one word, hello."

They looked at each other and they laughed, and were happy because of the wonderfully happy memory. Precisely the way he'd said it would be.

When Juffie and Paul got home she found another silver-wrapped parcel on her pillow. It contained emerald earrings. "Now we're back to where we were," Paul said when she put them on. "Now we can move into the future."

When Morning Comes won the 1956 New York Drama Critics Circle Award for best play of the season. The show also took four Tonys: best play, best dramatic director, best scenic design, and best dramatic actress. Which is how Juffie Kane got her third and final Tony.

She was at the ceremony this time, in the ballroom of the Plaza Hotel, as she'd promised Jack she would be, back when the entire production seemed an impossible dream. The microphones carrying the event to listeners on radio were there too. So were the television cameras. This year for the first time the Tony Awards were being shown on DuMont's Channel 5.

Hundreds of thousands of people saw Juffie dance her way up to the podium. The hot television lights rigged for the occasion followed her and highlighted a green Dior gown and emerald earrings. She said her few well-rehearsed words and accepted graciously another of the standing ovations which had punctuated so many of her soon to be twenty-nine years.

This one was perhaps the sweetest of them all. It was validation that she had come back from the place to which many of the people in this room had tried to banish her. Up yours, she wanted to say. She didn't. She smiled and blew kisses with that inimitable warmth and charm that belonged only to Juffie Kane.

. . . .

"You broke?" Frank asked on a February evening.

"Yes," Karen admitted.

"Okay, you stay home tonight."

By now she knew better than to plead for an additional stake.

He didn't go to work as early on the nights when she wasn't going with him; it was two A.M. before he left for the casino. She lay stiff and wakeful in her bed until she heard the Chevy pull away from the curb, then she got up and dressed in the blue denim skirt and a pink blouse. She added a white cardigan and a navy windbreaker, two items of clothing Frank had recently bought for her, because it would be cold on the street.

She'd decided to go to the bus station; at this hour that was a pretty good place to beg quarters and dimes. The cops would be around, but she could stand in the ladies' room; they wouldn't come in there. And as long as she didn't make a nuisance of herself so somebody got annoyed and reported her, she'd get away with it. She went to the front door. Then she stopped.

Frank would be so angry. If by chance she had a lucky night and made enough money to keep playing, she might get involved and forget to beat him home. That would be terrible. He could even get mad enough to throw her out. No, he wouldn't do it. But he might.

Why was she doing this, putting herself through this mental torture? What the hell did she care? She cared only about playing the slots. She had narrowed her world so that it was contained within borders of spinning cherries and lemons and sevens and gnomes.

Still, she stood with her hand on the doorknob and did not open the door. After many minutes she turned away and went into the living room and sat down in the dark. She was shaking, trembling with her need to play and the conflicting need to please Frank Carlucci. Part of what was happening in her head was an analysis of the struggle, a psychological overview of the motives and the process, but she couldn't get hold of that part. She couldn't keep the facts straight long enough to look at them. Something she'd buried deep was waking from a long sleep, but she could neither grasp nor control it.

Do something, she told herself finally. Don't just sit here, do something. Clean the house. Why? Because it needed it. What did she care? She didn't, but she needed to do something. Jesus, do it! What difference did the why make?

She turned on every light in the bungalow and took off her sweater and her jacket and began. The bathroom first, then the kitchen. Wash the windows and the floor and scrub the sink, and start the refrigerator defrosting. Then find some dustcloths and a can of furniture polish and the vacuum cleaner and go into the living room. When that was done she started on her bedroom. At seven it began to get light and she had finished the three rooms in which she was allowed. She was hot and sweaty, so she took a shower, cleaning the bathroom a second time after she finished.

She came out in the red terry-cloth robe and went into the now-spotless kitchen and made a cup of coffee. Not instant. She'd discovered an old percolator in the back of one of the cupboards and an unopened can of Maxwell House. She started the coffee perking and stood and listened to the sound and inhaled the smell. Food being prepared in a clean kitchen. She thought of Leah. No, she did not want to think about her mother. Close it out. Block out the pain. She was shaking again when she poured the coffee.

After she drank it she washed and dried everything she'd used and put it away. Then she looked at the clock. A little past eight. There was still time. She could scrounge some money on the street and play for an hour or two. The drugstore near the bus station had a couple of machines; everyplace in Las Vegas had a couple of machines. She could be back before Frank was. Maybe.

"Don't do it," she ordered herself, eyes closed tight with tension. She had hung on this long. She could hang on a little longer. Sleep. No, I can't. She'd do something else. What? Clean some more. Everything was clean. Not everything. She hadn't done Frank's room. But he had said . . . The hell with that. He also had said she couldn't have any more money to gamble with. And it had to be one thing or the other.

She found the papers in the bottom drawer of his desk, which she had no excuse for opening other than plain curiosity. While she pulled open the drawer a tiny corner of her mind noted that it was the first time in God knows how long she'd been curious about anything.

The drawer contained a stack of typewritten pages. The top

one said *Just One More Shot: A Study in Compulsive Gambling by Francis T. Carlucci.* Karen lifted them out and turned over the title page and began reading.

She didn't hear his car pull up out front. When he came in she was sitting on the floor of his bedroom, still reading. She didn't look up. Frank lounged against the door frame and watched her a moment. "Hi," he said finally.

She lifted her head and saw him. "What is all this stuff?" she demanded. "Who the hell are you?"

"It's a manuscript. Unfinished, a first draft, I haven't worked on it for months. And I'm Frank Carlucci, just like I said, and it says."

"That's no goddamn answer and you know it."

"No, I suppose it's not." He knelt down beside her and began gathering up the pages she'd discarded, stacking them in a neat pile. "You can read the rest later if you want. Now let's go into the kitchen and get something to eat, I'm starving."

She'd forgotten to turn the refrigerator back on after she defrosted it and things were warm, but Frank said they weren't spoiled yet. "The place looks remarkably clean," he commented.

"Yes, I cleaned it."

"Is that what you were doing in my room, cleaning it?"

"At first."

He fried bacon and eggs and made toast while she sat at the table and watched him. "You want some of this?" he asked when the food was ready. "I made plenty."

"No."

"Have a little, just a few bites." He put an egg and two pieces of bacon on a plate and set it in front of her.

"That's one of the things you say in your book. That compulsive gamblers, like alcoholics and drug addicts, lose any concern for their physical well-being. They require constant urging simply to eat enough to stay alive, the normal hunger/satisfaction response is short-circuited by the compulsion."

"Yeah. But you're the psychologist, do you agree?"

"I'm not sure. I don't know if there's any clinical evidence, and you don't cite any." She heard herself and didn't believe it. Dr. Rice words coming from the mouth of the Karen of Las Vegas.

He sat down and began eating. "There's evidence. You, for instance."

"I eat enough to keep going." As if to prove her point she picked up her fork and took a small bite of egg.

"My mother didn't."

"Your mother?"

"Yeah. She died when I was thirteen. Severe malnutrition, leading to complications resulting in death from lung and kidney failure. She was as hooked on gambling as you are, maybe worse. Her game was roulette."

Karen looked at him as if seeing him for the first time. He was olive-skinned and his nose had an unusually high bridge, and his jaw was slightly squared. The combination looked good on him. She stood up. "I'll make some coffee." She got down the percolator and started it going.

"Where'd you find that?"

"It was in the cupboard. Up on the top shelf. I found it when I was cleaning." Her back was to him. "Frank, where did your mother play? Here in Las Vegas?"

"No. Monte Carlo. I was raised in Monaco, even though I'm an American citizen. My father was a dealer. And his father before him. The Carluccis came from Genoa originally. That's not far from Monaco, and somewhere along the line they became Monegasques. My mother was from California. She met my father in Europe, but after they were married she brought him back here. He went to work for her dad in the newspaper business in Los Angeles. He hated it because, the way I heard it, my grandfather hated him. So after I was born he moved us back to Monaco and returned to his original profession."

The smell of coffee filled the kitchen, and he got up and turned the gas off under the percolator and filled two cups. When he handed her one, Karen asked, "How come you're here now, not in Monaco?"

"When I was twenty my father died and my American grandfather sent for me. I went to California and he put me in UCLA and I got a degree in journalism. I suppose I was meant to take over his business, but somehow that never came off."

"Why?"

He smiled at her. "You're full of questions today. That's not like the Karen I know."

"I'm not sure what Karen I am today. I'll tell you something, though, you wanted me to find the manuscript. It wasn't hidden, the drawer wasn't locked."

"Maybe," he agreed. "But I told you never to go into my room."

"Not enough of a prohibition. That's the kind meant merely to whet the appetite." She ran her fingers through her hair, pushing the short curls off her forehead. "Listen to me. Next thing you know I'll be hanging out a shingle and seeing clients."

"Is that what a psychologist does?"

"Sometimes. I've never been in private practice."

"Tell me what kind of practice you were in."

She shook her head. "No, I can't. I don't want to talk about it. I want to talk about you."

"Okay. Any more questions?"

"Yes, when did your mother start gambling? Why?"

"I don't know exactly when. As long as I can remember she went to the casino every night with my father. He worked and she played the wheel. As to why, you probably know the answer to that better than I do."

Karen hesitated. After a few seconds she said, "To block out the pain."

He gave her a long look. "Maybe," he said finally. "But why do some people choose self-destructive methods to do that? Other people find a way of dealing with pain which doesn't make a shambles of their lives and eventually kill them."

"True," she said softly. "A long time ago I read everything there was on compulsive gambling. It's a limited literature. And nobody has many answers."

"I know, I probably read all the same books. They weren't very satisfactory."

"So you decided to write the definitive text."

"Not exactly. I don't think I'm an expert, but writing is what I do. I'm a freelance journalist. That aborted effort you were reading is my one and only try at a full-length book."

"If you're a journalist, what are you doing dealing blackjack on the Strip?"

"Research. At least that's how it started out. I came to Las Vegas to observe. Then I happened to mention to a guy in a bar that I could deal professionally. I did it before UCLA, for three years in Monte Carlo, when I thought maybe I'd follow the family tradition. Anyway, a few days later I ran into the same guy and he told me they had an opening for a dealer at the Desert Inn. I applied for the hell of it. I don't know why I got the job, usually you need a lot of grease to get in. I walked up to the desk and said I could deal blackjack. Maybe they hired me because my name's Carlucci and they figured I fit with the mob that runs this town, or because being from Monte Carlo sounded classy to them. I don't know."

"Is that why you're still here, research?"

"Sometimes I think so. Sometimes I figure it's the money. You can bank a lot of bread dealing for a few years. If you're careful. But it's boring, for me at least. I don't have the urge, never did. Playing doesn't excite me the way it does you, the way it did my mother. I was getting ready to pack it in when I met you."

"And I became part of the research."

"Not exactly." He leaned over and touched the back of her hand, lightly, with just one finger. "It's not about putting you in my book, Karen. It's about a nice lady who somehow seemed to me to be on the edge, not really over the cliff yet. And I wanted to help."

"You've helped a lot," she said. "Thank you. That's the first time I've said that, isn't it? Thank you."

"I don't know that there's much to thank me for yet. Are you ready to quit? Want to leave Vegas? We could drive out of here this afternoon. You could say good-bye to the slots. Not that you wouldn't find other things to gamble on in other states."

"No," she said. "I wouldn't. I have no interest in other forms of gambling. I never have had. I'm not sure why."

"Okay, how about it? Want to start packing?"

She hesitated, finally she shook her head. "No, I can't do that."

"Right. Well, there's nothing to thank me for, is there?"

"Yes. A whole lot." Then, in a very small voice, she added, "Don't give up on me, Frank. Maybe I'll make it someday."

·   ·   ·   ·

She began to taper off, not so you'd notice at first, it was just that once in a while he didn't have to drag her away from the machine when it was time to leave the casino. Sometimes she'd stop half an hour before his shift ended and walk around and observe the showgirls, and the whores, and the ladies from Kansas City with rinsed blue hair who were on vacation, and the big and little spenders. By May she found that it wasn't so terrible on the nights when her stake was gone and he didn't take her with him to the casino. She could stay home and read a book, and eventually fall asleep. It seemed like years since she'd read a book.

"You have to make up your mind to quit," Frank told her one Sunday afternoon. It was his day off and they'd driven down to Lake Mead and parked the Chevy and they were walking along the lakefront. "It won't automatically happen, you have to decide to do it, then do it."

"I can't. I'm not ready."

"When will you be ready?"

"I don't know."

End of discussion. They drove back to Las Vegas in silence.

On a Thursday toward the end of June she was playing at eleven in the morning, conscious of the fact that Frank's shift would end in an hour and she'd have to stop. She didn't want to stop. Today the buzz from pulling the lever was intense. She wanted to go on and on, and she was winning enough to stay even, so maybe she could.

Above the banks of slot machines was a sign that proclaimed that the Desert Inn paid the biggest jackpots in Las Vegas. Above that sign was another one; it flashed colored lights that spelled "winner" and sounded a siren and hooters when somebody hit what the casino called the premium jackpot.

In nearly a year Karen had heard the siren many times, but it had never been for her. This morning it was. She inserted a dime and pulled the lever and the black letter P with the red circle around it came up in the first and second windows, then the next two, and finally the fifth. The siren blared, the lights flashed, and a torrent of dimes clattered into the metal tray at the base of the machine.

Karen shrieked with delight, and for the first time she turned to look at Frank, standing behind his felt-topped blackjack table in his regulation white shirt and black trousers and green eyeshade. He was looking at her and she gave him a V-for-victory sign. Frank didn't acknowledge it. He went back to dealing.

A floor attendant wearing a change belt and a red three-pocketed money apron approached. "There'll be five hundred in dimes in there, miss," he said, helping her scoop them into a plastic bag. "I'll give you a chit for the rest. You can collect it right over there." He nodded toward the cash desk in the middle of the casino.

"I know," she said. The boy must be new; he didn't recognize Karen as a regular who knew the ropes.

He wrote out a receipt saying that he'd verified her five-bar premium win and gave it to her. "Congratulations. Hope you enjoy it. And come back to the Desert Inn real soon."

She took her heavy bag of dimes and her receipt and walked over to Frank's table. Above his head was a notice saying DEALER STANDS ON EIGHTEEN, and while she watched he folded and paid two of the three players in various colored chips. His movements were deft and tidy when he flicked the money rake, and equally so when he dealt. He didn't have to shuffle, though she knew he could do that phenomenally well, because they had automatic card shufflers and the dealer simply put the deck in, then took it out.

Karen was mesmerized by his movements. She watched him deal another hand, and have to fold again. Two of the players went over twenty-one, but the third had a king showing and turned up an ace in the hole for blackjack. Frank paid him a lot of chips. The player scooped them up, then picked out a red one worth fifty dollars and passed it to Frank, who'd obviously dealt him a lucky streak. "Thank you, sir," Frank murmured. His eyes flicked toward Karen and he made a nodding motion with his head directing her to the cash desk.

She went to it and had to wait while the man who'd been playing blackjack with Frank cashed in his chips. There was only one cashier on duty because it was still morning, and even the casinos slowed down a little at this hour. The blackjack player took a wad of bills and folded them and put them in his pocket and walked away. Karen pushed her winner's receipt over the counter.

"Congratulations," the cashier said when he saw what Karen had presented. He turned and looked at some numbers posted behind him. "The premium is three thousand seven hundred and twenty-six dollars this morning. You've got five hundred in dimes of it right there." He nodded toward the plastic bag she was carrying. "So you're due three thousand two hundred and twenty-six. Hundreds okay?"

Karen nodded to indicate that it was. The amount of the premium changed every few hours; it was figured on a complicated percentage formula that she didn't understand and had never really thought about. The amount was posted all over the casino, but she never paid any attention to it. So until this moment she hadn't realized how much she'd won. When she took the bills her fingers were shaking. Nearly four thousand dollars, almost her entire original stake had been returned to her.

She stood there a moment, still slightly bewildered by it all. Frank came up. "Let's go."

"It's not noon yet," she protested.

"I got somebody to cover for me so I could leave a few minutes early. Let's go."

He led her out of the casino and to the car. "Why did you make me leave before the time was up?" she demanded when they drove out of the parking lot. "I could have played a few minutes more. I'm so damn hot, I might have hit the premium again."

"Yeah, sure." He didn't say anything else until they were in the house. "Let's have something to eat." He started for the kitchen.

"I'm not hungry," Karen said.

"I am. C'mon, you can watch me."

She wouldn't take anything but coffee, and he poured it and made it half milk and put in three sugars. She'd placed her winnings on the counter, the bulging plastic bag of coins and the thick packets of hundreds. Karen kept staring at the money while she sipped the coffee. "Do you know what?" she said finally. "When I came out here last July I had a five-thousand-dollar stake. I won nearly all of it back this morning."

"So you did," he agreed. "You're almost even, if you don't count the money you earned waitressing and working in the cleaners, or the God knows how much you've had from me."

She looked up, startled. "I forgot about that. I'll pay you back. Right now. How much do I owe you?"

"Nothing. It was never a loan. I was just making a point."

"I want to repay you," she said, but there was no enthusiasm in her voice.

"No you don't," Frank said softly. "So think about it, Karen. What do you want to do with nearly four grand? How about buying something? You could get a car. Would you like a car?"

She shook her head. "No, I don't know how to drive."

"Okay, no car. What about a boat? One of those little speedboats we saw on Lake Mead that you thought were so cute. I think three and a half would buy one of those."

"No."

"The lady says no boat. A fur coat then. You can probably have a mink for what's sitting right there. We can go down to one of the fancy shops in the hotels and buy one this afternoon. You'd look good in mink. Isn't that every girl's dream?"

"I'm not a girl, I'm a grown woman, and I don't want a mink."

"Lots of different new clothes maybe? A dozen dresses, a few suits, anything you see that takes your fancy. How does that sound?"

"Awful."

He'd been sitting at the kitchen table; now he stood up and crossed to her. "Awful. Everything I suggest sounds awful. And I bet you think saving the money would be awful too. You do, don't you, Karen? Come on, tell me. Do you want to open a bank account and keep the money safe for an emergency or your old age? Answer me, do you?"

"Stop shouting at me! What are you mad about? I won a lot of money, is that so terrible?"

"No, it's not terrible. Only I want to know what you want to do with the money." He picked up the hundreds and pushed them toward her. "It's just paper, Karen. By itself it's worthless. Its only value is what you buy with it. Things, security, whatever you want." He threw the bills in the air and they fluttered to the floor. She would have dived for them but she couldn't. He'd taken hold of her shoulders and he was shaking her. "Tell me. Come on, tell me. What do you want to do with the money?"

"I want to gamble!" She screamed the words. "I want to use the money to play the slots. So maybe I'll win a lot more. There, is that what you want to hear?"

"No, goddammit! This isn't about what I want to hear. It's about your realizing something, and admitting it to me so you can admit it to yourself. This whole crazy scene, this hole in hell you've made to climb into, is not about money. Do you hear me, Karen? It is not about money! So what is it about? That's what I want to hear. I want you to face what's going on inside yourself and tell me about that."

He kept on shaking her and she started to sob, great wrenching gasps the way she had that day in the car when she'd told him that her name wasn't Gloria. That's what she shouted now. "Gloria! It's about Gloria and Bernard and eight goddamn years when I thought he loved me and turned myself inside out and he didn't love me at all!" She pounded her fists on his chest as if he were the unfaithful lover, as if he were Bernard. "He didn't love me, he didn't love me, he didn't love me. . . ."

And finally she talked. Frank carried her to the living room and put her in a chair and sat across from her. "Tell me," he said, but calmly now, gently. "Tell me what happened. From the beginning."

She did, and what she told him was not simply the facts. She set out to do that, to relate clearly the progression of events that led her to walk out on everything and get on a bus and come to Las Vegas and seek comfort from a slot machine. But Dr. Rice spoke as well as Karen. She had always understood intellectually the true dimensions of all that had happened, but until today she'd shut out the knowledge and an analysis of it.

"That's the thing of it," she said sometime during four hours of a total verbal purge. "That's what I couldn't deal with, and what I turned to gambling to mask. I became involved with Bernard because deep down my own self-image was close to zero. I was so smart-mouthed about getting out of the slums and doing it by becoming a psychologist so I could help the people I'd left behind. But it was all an act. I didn't really believe I could leave the West End. I didn't believe I'd ever be anything but the daughter of a lady who did abortions and a man who cut up fish.

"When Bernard was interested in me, it seemed like a miracle. He was everything I was not, so what if he was thirty-plus years older than I was? He was perfect—father, brother, lover, and teacher, all rolled up into one. Only I wasn't really happy with him. The first time we came out here was a chance thing, because I was fascinated with certain aspects of Las Vegas. I knew almost nothing about gambling as such then. But boy, did I learn fast. From the first dime I pushed into a slot I was hooked. Do you know why? Because I was unhappy when I thought I ought to be ecstatically happy, and the slot machine gave me instant satisfaction when nothing else had." She paused. "My throat's sore. Can I have some water?"

Frank went to the kitchen and got it for her. "Don't stop," he said when he handed her the glass. "Go on, tell me the rest of it.

What happened when you realized you were attracted to gambling? Did you admit to yourself that it was because you were basically unhappy and dissatisfied with your life?"

"No. I looked at the symptom as an isolated fact, which was stupid and contrary to all my training, but it was enough to terrify me. I used aversion therapy to talk myself out of it. Do you know what that is?" He nodded and she went on. "It almost worked. Then my thesis was rejected. My first one. I had to do another to get my Ph.D. I'll tell you the details of that sometime, but not now. Anyway, it was turned down and I was terribly depressed. That's when I found the pictures of Bernard's dead wife."

She told him what Bess had looked like and how she'd made herself into a copy of the dead woman. "But that wasn't what Bernard wanted. Obviously what attracted him was the schoolgirl I'd been. So he got disgusted, and eventually he married an eighteen-year-old mindless blonde with big boobs, somebody who wouldn't even know how to become Bess. And I came out here because I knew all this, and I didn't want to know it. End of story."

"No," Frank said. "It's not the end. It's the beginning."

. . . . .

It was an early September Sunday afternoon in New York, so hot the air-conditioning in the penthouse apartment couldn't keep up. "I'm melting," Juffie said. "Maybe I'll take another shower."

"I've got a great idea." Paul put down the magazine section of the *Times*. "Let's go for a drive." Recently he'd bought a big black Buick sedan and he loved excuses to take it out; there weren't many of those in Manhattan.

"Will it be cooler, do you think?"

"In the car? Sure. Moving makes a breeze. Come on, put something on and we'll go."

Juffie was sitting in nothing but her lacy underpants; now she got up and wandered among her many closets trying to find something to wear that would feel as if she were still naked. She settled for a rust-colored cotton voile sundress and a pair of gold sandals. Paul was waiting in the hall when she came out of the bedroom, twirling the keys of the Buick on his finger.

He kept the car in a brand-new underground parking garage one block east on First Avenue. Juffie waited in the lobby of East

River Tower until he claimed it and drove up to the door, but even walking from the building to the curb was awful. The heat rose off the sidewalk in waves of steam. "New York, New York, it's a wonderful town," she muttered. "Sinatra and Kelly ought to be here today."

"*On the Town* was a great picture, but I think *Anchors Aweigh* was better." Paul slipped into the stream of traffic.

"Me too," Juffie agreed. "It was a lot earlier though, wasn't it? I remember seeing it in Boston at the RKO, we stood in line for hours to get in. That must have been forty-five or forty-six."

"Forty-five, that's when it was released."

She glanced at him. He was looking straight ahead, keeping his eyes on the traffic. God, that profile. Remarkable, truly remarkable. "Where did you see it? I mean, you weren't here. You came in forty-six, didn't you?"

"It was shown at the American bases abroad. I saw it in a big one near Paris, in the officers' club. I was with a colonel. I don't think he enjoyed it much, he was too drunk, but I loved it."

"What were you doing on an American base?"

He shrugged. "By then I had connections. We were allies, there was a lot of mixing."

"Oh," Juffie said. She forgot about the picture and France in 1945. "Where are we going?"

"For a drive. It's not supposed to have a destination. I'm heading downtown, maybe there will be a breeze off Battery Park."

But before they got there they drew level with the Brooklyn Bridge. "Let's go to Brooklyn," Paul said.

"Why?"

"Why not?"

Juffie shrugged. There was a breeze coming through the open windows and it was a little cooler. She lay her head back on the seat and closed her eyes. She must have dozed for a while. When she looked next they were on a broad street of cheap stores with signs printed in Hebrew and English, interspersed with cheaper-looking bars. White men wearing the distinctive garb of the orthodox Hasidic Jew hurried past a few black men slouching on corners. "Where are we?"

"Brownsville, I think. Something called Rockaway Avenue."

"Picturesque, isn't it?" Juffie made a face of distaste. "Let's get out of here. Or are we lost? They say you can be lost for years in Brooklyn. Never heard from again."

"I'm not lost exactly," Paul said. "I'm looking for something."

"In Brownsville? What, for God's sake?"

"A restaurant, a place called Antonelli's. Somebody told me they served the best Italian food in America."

"Paul, I don't want to go to an Italian restaurant dumb enough to open up in Brownsville. Besides, it's too hot. And I'm not dressed for it."

"First, it didn't open up here, not the way you mean. The way I heard it, they've been in the neighborhood for years, since before the Jews and the Negroes moved in. Second, you look beautiful, you always look beautiful, and it's sure to be air-conditioned. Come on, don't be a wet quilt. We may never be here again, and this guy said the food was really wonderful."

"Wet blanket. And I hope we're never here again. I don't even want to be here now."

He ignored her protests. "Look, there it is. Antonelli's. See, there's a sign."

"A neon sign. Pizza. That's what it says, Paul. Pizza. How can a joint in Brownsville with a neon sign advertising pizza have the best Italian food in America?" Paul insisted that it did. He parked the car. Juffie sighed resignedly and got out. "If it's not air-conditioned I refuse to stay."

But it was. A blast of icy air hit them as soon as Paul opened the door. That was a relief, she felt a little better. The front of the place looked exactly as she expected it to look, like every pizza parlor she'd ever seen. "In the back," Paul said. "I was told you have to go in the back." He took Juffie's arm and propelled her past a counter of white tile and booths with worn blue imitation leather seats. Clusters of straw-wrapped Chianti bottles hung from the ceiling, and on the walls were fly-specked posters advertising Firenze and Roma.

The rear, however, was entirely different. Paul pushed open a door and they were in a large room with tables covered in white cloths and a floral-printed carpet on the floor. A man wearing a tuxedo greeted them. "Good evening, Signor, Signora. A table for two?"

Juffie had a momentary sense of déjà vu. She'd been here before, in another life perhaps. No, not here and not in another life. She realized what she was reminded of—Freddie's Restaurant in the North End. A terrible memory because that's where Angel Tomasso took her the night he . . . But a good memory, too, because later Freddie himself had been so kind. She remembered him following her to Dock Square and giving her fifty dollars when that sum of money had meant everything in the world. Which was a funny thing to remember just now. It made her feel very peculiar. Juffie put her hand on her stomach, then dropped it quickly.

The man in the tuxedo was leading them to a table clear across the room. It was beside a door with one of those push-bar handles that had a sign above it saying EMERGENCY EXIT ONLY. The man held a chair for her and Juffie took it. When she was seated he leaned over. "Excuse me," he whispered. "But I have to ask. You are Juffie Kane, aren't you?"

She didn't know why he was whispering, they were practically the only diners in the room. Every other table but one was empty, and the couple at that one were paying their bill and leaving. "Yes," she said. "I am." She didn't feel like it, but she turned on the smile.

"Wait till I tell my wife," he said. "She's a big fan of yours. Used to watch you every week on that quiz show. She didn't care about anything on Sunday nights except to see what Juffie Kane was wearing."

Juffie waited for him to ask for an autograph, but he didn't. Later probably. Now he simply handed them menus. "The lobster fra diavolo is very good tonight, and we have homemade spinach ravioli."

Paul said he'd have both. The ravioli first and the lobster to follow. "You too?" he asked Juffie. She nodded; it sounded far too rich and filling, but she wasn't in the mood to spend a lot of time puzzling over a menu.

"Very good, sir," the headwaiter said. A new group of customers came through the door dividing the restaurant from the pizza parlor, and he left Juffie and Paul and went to greet them. Another waiter approached and brought them water and bread, and lit the candle on their table. In this room the straw-wrapped wine bottles served as candle holders.

Juffie watched while the newcomers were seated at a table on the opposite side of the room. They were an all-male party, six guys in dark suits. She saw the headwaiter speaking to them, then the man with his back to their table turned around and stared at her. She felt a moment's shock. Not because he was so obvious, she was used to that. Because he looked just like Vinnie Faldo. No, he really didn't. It was her imagination, set in train because this place reminded her of Freddie's.

The raviolis were okay, but not great. "Something tells me your informant didn't get it quite right," Juffie said. Paul shrugged.

They'd asked for Valpolicella to be served with the lobster. A complimentary bottle of Asti Spumante was delivered to their table instead. Juffie did not want to drink something fizzy and slightly sweet at a little before seven on a hot Sunday night in September. She wanted to go home. But she had always known how dependent she was on her fans and the whole mystique which was celebrity. She smiled some more and sipped the wine. The air-conditioning in the restaurant was almost too efficient. She felt goose bumps rising on her bare shoulders. "I'm freezing," she said to Paul.

"I've got a sweater in the car," he said. "I'll get it."

"Why did you bring a sweater on a day like this?"

He didn't answer, just got up from the table and headed out the way they'd come in.

Juffie hadn't been alone for more than ten seconds when the man who'd reminded her of Vinnie Faldo got up and started toward her table. Another man rose as well and started to follow him, but the first one waved him off.

"Hey, lady," the strange man said when he was five feet away from her. "You're Juffie Kane, right?" He looked even more like Faldo close up.

Juffie repressed a shudder. She kept smiling and started to acknowledge what he'd meant as a greeting. At that same moment the headwaiter came toward Juffie's table. The two men converged a few inches from her chair. Then only one man was standing, the other one, the Faldo look-alike, was lying on the floor and blood was spurting from a hole which had suddenly appeared in his neck. Her first thought was: so that's what's meant by going for the jugular? A second later she was screaming.

Afterward she would be able to remember the scene only in slow motion. In reality it happened with incredible speed. Two of the men at the table the victim had left jumped up and they had guns in their hands. The headwaiter grabbed Juffie and she thought he was going to use her as a shield, but he pulled her from her chair and out the emergency door in one fluid motion. And most amazing of all, Paul was parked there in the Buick, with the passenger door open and the motor running. She heard gunshots from inside even as the man in the tuxedo hurled her into the car and slammed the door.

Paul didn't ask any questions, not even how she was. He tore away from the restaurant down a series of back alleys and side streets, careening around corners on two wheels and swinging the steering wheel in wide arcs that seemed bound to tip the big car on its side, but did not. Juffie crouched in her seat, hugging herself and trying not to be terrified and to stop shaking. After a few minutes she realized she was going to throw up. "Stop, stop the car. I'm going to be sick." Paul ignored her. "Stop! Please, I can't . . . I have to . . ."

"I can't stop," he muttered through clenched teeth. "I'm sorry, I can't stop."

He was following somebody, that other car in front, the red one. That's how he could find his way through these strange narrow twisting passageways skirting the tenements of Brooklyn. Juffie moaned and in desperation she rolled down the window and vomited into the wind created by the car slicing through the night. Then she wiped her face and crumpled into the corner by the passenger door and huddled there, too frightened even to whimper.

They sped on through the nameless streets and the scene in the restaurant played in her head in a slow motion counterpoint, with all its ramifications gradually revealed. The red car they'd been following peeled off when they got to the Brooklyn Bridge. Paul slowed slightly and crossed it at a more sedate pace. Neither of them had yet spoken. They did not do so until they were going up in the private elevator that served the penthouse.

"You set me up," Juffie said, breaking the silence at last. "You were a party to the whole thing. It's the only explanation."

"*Chérie*, listen—"

"How did you know I'd say I was cold?" she interrupted. "You couldn't have been sure of that."

He was unlocking their door now, and he waited to speak until they were inside and the door was closed behind them. "Sit down. Do you want some cognac? I'll get you some. Please, sit down and I'll explain everything."

Juffie didn't sit and she didn't take the brandy he poured for her. When she refused it Paul gulped it down himself. "It was just lucky," Juffie said. "My complaining that I was cold was nothing more than a stroke of luck. If I hadn't said that, you'd have made some other excuse to leave me alone."

"Yes, but it's not the way you think . . ."

She looked directly at him for the first time in almost an hour. "How is it? I'm waiting to hear. I can't imagine the plot of this script, so you'd better tell me. How does the hero make himself out to be a good guy after all?"

"Not a good guy," Paul said quietly. "Only one who had no choice. They said he was a tremendous fan of yours, the guy who got killed, he kept your pictures everywhere. He was bound to come over as soon as you were alone and he saw his chance."

"They? Who's they? No, don't tell me, that one I can guess. Finky Aronson. Finky Aronson, my other big fan."

"Not just him, a few of his associates. They put me under so much pressure I couldn't refuse. And you were protected every second. They had guys in the kitchen with guns watching every move."

"I was protected? Two gangs of hoods who apparently hate each other get ready for a shootout and I was protected? You—" She started to hurl curses at him. All the words were in her mind, bursting like taste bubbles on her tongue, but she didn't say them. She couldn't. "How much are you into them for?" she asked instead.

"I'm not—exactly. We do business together."

"How much business?"

"I'm not sure. They've invested two, maybe three million in my projects. It's all legitimate, Juffie. Except for tonight. Usually I don't have anything to do with their other . . . activities."

"You fool. You poor misbegotten stupid fool. How long have you been living off their money? Six months? No, longer than that. It would have to be to come to so much. A year? How long?"

"A little over a year. Since I got so short I had to sell your jewelry." He poured himself another drink. "I'm not a fool, Juffie," he said softly. "But I don't know how to get out from under these guys. And I can't face the thought of losing you."

There it was again, the same thing he'd said before in a similar crisis. If he wasn't a success, a big spender, she'd leave him. This time Juffie didn't try to convince him he was wrong. There were too many other things that needed to be said. "Do you realize that a dozen people must have recognized me in that restaurant? The people who were in the pizza parlor when we came in, the couple at the other table who left after we arrived . . . God knows who else. The police will probably be here any second. We've got to figure out what to tell them."

"There won't be any police," Paul said. "It was all taken care of, everybody in the place was a plant. The restaurant belongs to the Taglio mob, it's a regular haunt of theirs. That's the guy Finky and his boys wanted to get, Taglio himself. But they couldn't get near him. You saw, he traveled with five bodyguards. And every Sunday night around seven they always go to Antonelli's. The headwaiter was in Taglio's pocket, too, but he switched sides, sold out to Aronson. So they went in just before we came, and took the place over and set the whole thing up."

"And you set me up so they could be sure. Very neat. Very clever." She sat down now, on the chintz-covered sofa in front of the big window through which you could see the panorama of New York. "Paul, do you remember that night last June when we had our own little celebration? You know, the party for two with the fire in the wastebasket."

They'd gotten a little drunk to celebrate her six-month run in the play; they'd laughed a lot and burnt her diaphragm and all his condoms because Juffie had said she was ready to make good her promise. They could try to start a baby. Paul obviously remembered. He stared at her and wordlessly nodded his head.

"Well, it worked. I was waiting to tell you until I could make a properly dramatic event out of it. But this seems like a good time. The night you set me up and almost got me killed, what better time could I choose? I'm pregnant, Paul. We, you and I, devoted husband and wife, are going to have a baby in March."

Chapter 18

$\mathcal{J}$uffie lay in bed on a wintry January morning in 1957, the beginning of her seventh month of pregnancy. She was drinking a glass of milk because the obstetrician wanted her to cut down on coffee and tea, and she was trying to decide how she'd spend her day.

She could shop for more layette things, but she already had three chests of drawers full of tiny shirts and diapers, and lacy blankets, and hand-embroidered flannelette nighties, and little bonnets and booties. Everything was either yellow or white, no pink and no blue. She wasn't taking any chances, even though Paul was convinced it was a boy. Ah, yes, Paul.

Her husband was ecstatically happy. As far as he was concerned, the night in Brooklyn might never have happened. Paul had put it out of his mind, erased it. She had finally recognized Paul's ability to expunge from the universe whatever he chose not to think about. It explained a lot of things. Not how he could have done it, that she would never understand, just how he managed to live with it afterward. Learning to live with it had been a lot tougher for her.

For two months after Brownsville she scarcely spoke to him. As much as possible she avoided seeing him, though that was difficult since they shared the same apartment. But Juffie never seriously considered throwing him out of it or moving out herself. Not that she hadn't examined the option. Did she want a divorce? Could she get one? What grounds, Mrs. Dumont? a lawyer would ask. *He set me up as an accessory to murder, I was almost killed. Besides, he's tied up with the rackets. . . .* Not an easy story to take to a lawyer, much less a judge. Not when you were Juffie Kane and your name was already associated with the Syndicate.

But that wasn't the real reason she didn't sever her life from Paul's. The real reason was that living with the mob hovering in the background was a fact of existence she'd experienced since she was eleven years old; getting divorced was a concept with which she had no familiarity. Rosie and Myer had shaped her view of marriage, and she was still trying to make her own fit the model of theirs.

Gradually she adjusted to the recognition of Paul's weakness—his ability to forget—his adoration of her, and his delight in her pregnancy, side by side with the risks to which he'd exposed them. It was all simply the way it was, the way he was. And whatever he might be, she was going to have his child, had deliberately set out to conceive his child. It was too late to say she'd made a mistake and wanted out. Slowly they'd resumed the old ways, taken up the familiar patterns of a relationship that had existed for almost six years. And most of the time Juffie, too, managed to forget. Until she left the show, when it became more difficult.

She played Marjorie for the last time on the twenty-seventh of December, 1956. Because of the eighteenth-century costumes her pregnancy didn't show onstage. Eventually it would, however, and in December they found somebody really good to take over the role, and she felt ready to slip into that self-absorbed state that Nessa told her beckoned every pregnant woman. So it had seemed like a good time and she did it. Now she had to adjust to it, and that was proving more difficult.

She loved thinking about the baby and looking at her swelling stomach, but she was accustomed to a life of constant challenge. Lately time often seemed to pass with disconcerting slowness. Like today, for instance. What should she do today? She could buy a new maternity dress. No, she had more of them than she'd ever wear. What then? Call Nessa and see if she wanted to have lunch? Maybe.

Juffie sighed and shifted her position in the bed, patting the bulge beneath the quilt as she did so. Good morning, baby. How are you doing? Are you bored? I'm a little bored. But I'm not supposed to be. I'm supposed to be tranquil and patient and think good thoughts, so you come out perfect. Which I know you will. Talk to you later, baby sweetheart. You just stay happy and keep growing, okay? Right, I knew you'd say that.

She glanced out the window; it looked like snow. She'd listen to the ten o'clock weather forecast on the radio. If they said snow by midday she wouldn't call Nessa, if it was going to hold off she would. That stalling technique satisfied her for the moment and she went back to the copy of the *Times* she'd been reading. These days she read the paper thoroughly, something she'd not often had time for before. She even glanced at the obituaries. She did so now, and the name leapt at her from the printed pages.

"Varley, Patricia, née Thompson, beloved wife of Matthew, at her home after a long illness. Funeral private."

Oh my God! She grabbed the telephone and dialed Matt's office number.

Miss Wilkins answered. "He's not in this morning, Miss Kane. I expect him about two. Shall I have him call you then?"

"No, that's all right. Listen, Miss Wilkins . . ." She spoke slowly, feeling her way because this woman who had been Matt's secretary as long as she could remember was such a cipher, a faceless woman devoid of personality. "Do you know if there's anyplace he can be reached this morning?"

"I'm sorry, I don't. He had some personal business to attend to."

So she wouldn't find out where the funeral was from Miss Wilkins. If she knew, she wasn't saying. "About two, that's when you think he'll be in the office?"

"Yes, that's what he said."

How like Matt. He hadn't called anyone; he hadn't asked for help or comfort. He intended simply to bury his wife and go back to work. As always, he was making a separate compartment for his personal sorrow.

The telephone rang almost as soon as she hung up. She snatched at it, hoping Matt was calling, that he'd changed his mind, that after all he wanted to talk to somebody who cared about him. But it wasn't Matt, it was Nessa. "I don't mean to be morbid, Juffie, but do you happen to read the obits with your breakfast?"

"Yes, I do." Her voice gave her away.

"You know then. I was wondering, should we do anything? Flowers, something like that?"

"No, I don't think he wants flowers, Nessa. She's been ill for a very long time, almost since they got married. I think he wants to close the chapter by himself. What I can't figure out is why he put the notice in the paper if that's true."

"Easy." Nessa was the one with the newspaper background. "He didn't. The undertaker did. They do it as a matter of course, unless you tell them not to. Matt must have forgotten to mention it. He's a funny one, isn't he? Wanting to carry the load all by himself. I wonder if he's as strong as he thinks he is."

Juffie wondered too. And she decided he wasn't. She didn't say anything about lunch to Nessa. She had a cup of soup and some toast at home—the obstetrician insisted she eat regular meals—and got dressed and went to Matt's office. She was there at exactly two.

"He's not here yet, Miss Kane."

"Okay, I'll wait. And, Miss Wilkins, I think maybe it's time you called me Mrs. Dumont. Or just Juffie. I'd prefer that. But Miss Kane doesn't seem entirely appropriate under the circumstances."

Juffie was wearing a royal purple wool smock over a matching skirt. The skirt had a big hole cut out so her burgeoning belly could stick through. The smock belled over it like a battle standard, but it also had an elaborate ruched collar, "to draw attention to the face," as they said in the ads for maternity clothes. But collar or no, even Miss Wilkins could not have failed to notice that she was pregnant.

"Whatever you wish, Mrs. Dumont."

Pie-faced, as always. And doubtless she wouldn't address her as Juffie, because if she did she might have to give her own first name. Even Matt called her Miss Wilkins. "Thank you," Juffie said with corresponding formality. "I'll wait for Mr. Varley, as I said."

She sat down in the blue Queen Anne chair across from the secretary's desk which, like everything else in this office, had been the same since she first saw it in 1949, and picked up the copy of *Variety* lying beside it. When Matt walked in she was halfway through an article about the rising costs of theatrical productions. The author cited *When Morning Comes* as having set a dangerous precedent.

"Hi," he said. "You're a nice surprise. I didn't expect you today. Come on in." His voice was entirely normal and he took a stack of telephone messages from Miss Wilkins and led Juffie into the inner office. The light was better in there, and she could see that he looked unusually tired, but that was all.

He put the message slips by the phone. "More than usual. I must be heading for a surge in business."

"I expect a lot of them are condolence calls, Matt."

He looked at her and didn't answer for a few seconds, then, "How do you know? How does anybody know?"

"It was in the *Times* obit column. I didn't check the other papers, probably they carried the notice too."

"But I didn't put in any notice. I didn't want anybody to find out. I didn't want you to find out. And there aren't half a dozen people who know about Patsy."

"Nessa told me the undertaker does it automatically unless you tell him not to. Apparently you didn't. How did she die, Matt?" It wasn't merely curiosity. He had to talk about it to someone, she was convinced of that. He mustn't bottle it up the way he'd bottled up the whole tragedy of his married life.

"Cerebral hemorrhage, yesterday morning. The doctor tells me it's not uncommon in these cases. He's been expecting it for years. Amazed that it didn't happen sooner. It was quick and painless, thank God."

"Painless for Patsy," Juffie said, coming round to his side of the desk and perching on the corner and putting her hand on his cheek. "How about you?"

He covered her hand with his, pressing it closer. "I don't know yet. It's all too sudden. I haven't had time to feel much of anything. I expect I'll be a little lost for a while. Even the way she was, she was always there, a constant presence in my life. Somebody I always had to think about and provide for."

"Good, I'm glad you recognize that." She leaned over and kissed his forehead. Gently, a friend's kiss, not a lover's. "And there are people always there for you, too, you know. Me, of course, and a lot of others."

"I know." He squeezed her hand, then he patted her belly and said very softly, "Terrible timing for us, isn't it?"

"The baby or Patsy?"

"I meant Patsy. I think any time is good for babies. I didn't mean to imply I wished you weren't pregnant."

I do, Juffie thought. The words came into her head and exploded. They took her breath away and she gasped.

"What is it? Are you okay? It's not labor, is it?"

"Of course not, I have almost three months to go." She managed to smile. "I have to get out of here, I'm late for the hairdresser. But I wanted to see you first."

He took her to the outer door and thanked her again and kissed her cheek before they parted.

She wasn't going to the hairdresser, she'd been two days before. It was an excuse because she couldn't face him. She couldn't face herself. The idea had been so crazy, so awful. No, worse than that. Despicable. I'm sorry, baby. I'm sorry. I didn't mean it. I do want you. Of course I do. I just had this momentary insanity, this sudden realization that if I'd waited a little longer you could have had a different daddy. . . .

And what would Rosie say to that? Juffie didn't want to think about it. She hailed a cab and went home and decided to cook something new and wonderful for dinner. She got down all her cookbooks and began thumbing through the pages.

·   ·   ·   ·

Karen looked at herself in the wavy mirror over the dresser and decided it was time for the third stage. It was May and she'd been in what Frank called the second stage since Christmas. That's when she achieved the miracle of not having pushed a single dime into a single slot machine for four months. That's when he said she was doing great, but she ought to get out of Nevada and away from constant temptation, and begin learning to stand on her own two feet. So he'd moved her to Barstow, California.

Barstow was a town of about ten thousand, in the foothills of the San Bernardino Mountains. It was some hundred and fifty miles southwest of Las Vegas, but the new Interstate 15 ran directly from one city to the other. Frank could get to Barstow in under three hours in the Chevy. He came once a week, on his day off.

Karen always tried to make her days off coincide with his. The people who owned the bakery where she worked were fairly easygoing, so often she could. She'd managed it this week. She wasn't working today and Frank would be there any minute. She peered in the mirror again, fluffed her short curls, and checked her lipstick. Yeah, okay. She had put on another couple of pounds, she looked better than she had in a long time. Frank would be pleased.

He was. "You look terrific. I like that dress."

It was a madras plaid cotton shirtwaist with short sleeves and a full skirt and an elastic cinch belt. She twirled and the skirt flared out around her legs. She still had really good legs, and she'd gone back to wearing high heels. "Glad you approve, sir. How was your week?"

"Okay. Yours?"

"The same. Lots of whole wheat this week though, it definitely outsold the sliced white. I'm thinking of writing a paper on a new national trend."

"Excellent, I'll collaborate. Let's have lunch and discuss it. Where shall we go?"

"In a minute. First I want to ask you something." She sat across from him on the sofa which, with one matching easy chair, a lamp, a dresser, and a table, comprised all the furniture in what was called a furnished studio apartment. "Do you think I'm ready for stage three?"

"What do you think of it as being?" He had on jeans and an open-necked shirt and he leaned back and folded his arms behind his head and crossed one leg over his knee. He was wearing cowboy boots in intricately tooled leather. Karen remembered the day a few weeks before when he'd bought them.

"Are the boots comfortable?"

"Yeah, they're okay. Karen, you're avoiding something, even though you brought it up. What?"

"Leah."

"Your mother?"

"That's the lady. I ought to call her. She loves me, and I just disappeared, and she hasn't heard from me in almost two years. Which is a terrible way to behave."

"Yes, it is," he agreed. "But you've been sick; you're not responsible for how you've behaved. You know that as well as I do. Better. So why the guilt now?"

"Because Leah weighs on me, she always has. She needed me to do what she hadn't done, get out in the big world and make something of myself, and I always secretly resented it. But I do love her, abortions and all. In a crazy way I admire her."

"Then call her." The telephone was next to him on the floor. He'd insisted she get one as soon as she moved in, so she could talk to him if things got tough or if she felt herself slipping. He picked it up and offered it to her. "Call your mother," he said. "You want to do it, so do it."

"Wait a minute. Let me get myself ready. Do you know the

worst part? It isn't really so much that I want to call Leah. It's really because I'm desperate to talk to Juffie, but I know I have to call Leah first or I'll hate myself."

He looked at her a moment. "Juffie who?"

"Juffie Kane, the actress."

"You know her?"

"She's my best friend. Since we were seventeen. At least I was seventeen. Juffie was eighteen, she's a year older."

"Karen," he said evenly, "how come you've never mentioned her before? We've talked about everything, and you never said you knew Juffie Kane."

"I thought you'd think I was lying, or putting on airs. A broken-down gambling addict who says her best friend is a famous actress . . . It sounds like advanced megalomania. Besides, I don't know if Juffie's my friend anymore. She's a lady who's got it all together. I don't know if she can ever forgive what I've done."

He walked to the window and looked at the mountains on the horizon. Even in a cheap place like this furnished hole in the wall you could have a great view in Barstow. If you were lucky and your windows happened to face in the right direction, which Karen's did. "What made you think of all this today?"

Karen opened the drawer in the all-purpose table and extracted a copy of *McCall's* magazine. Juffie's picture was on the cover and the bottom head said, "A new role for fabulous Juffie Kane . . . Exclusive pictures inside." She held it out to him. "I bought this yesterday. Just happened to see it on the newsstand."

Frank took the magazine and looked for a moment at the remarkably beautiful face. "What's the new role mean? Is she in a new play?"

"No. She and Paul have a baby, a boy. Page thirty-two."

"You know her husband too?"

"Of course I do. I told you, we're really close. I was the maid of honor at their wedding. Go ahead, look at the article."

He found page thirty-two and glanced at pictures of the actress and her husband in some fabulous house in New York. In each shot a tiny infant was in the arms of one or the other of them. "Quite a handsome couple, aren't they?" Frank said softly. "The kid's bound to be something special."

"Of course he's special, he's Juffie and Paul's." Karen started to cry. "I feel so rotten. Juffie's had a baby and I wasn't there. I didn't even know about it until I read it in some damned magazine. I'm the closest thing to an aunt that little boy has, and I didn't even know he was born."

Frank closed the magazine and set it aside. "You and she were really close, huh?"

"I told you. She's my best—"

"Yes, I heard what you told me. Wipe your eyes and blow your nose, Karen. And call your mother, so afterwards you can call your famous friend."

Leah didn't explode on the telephone the way Karen expected she would. Karen said, "Mama, it's me." Then there was a long silence.

Until finally, "Karen? Is it really you, *mameleh*?"

"It's me. How are you, Mama?" The only answer was the sound of sobs. "Mama, don't cry. It is me. I'm in Barstow, that's in California. I was sick for a long time, but I'm okay now."

Leah regained enough control to speak, but she still didn't explode, her voice was quiet and gentle. "I never gave up hope, darling. Never. Daddy isn't here now, but when he comes home he won't believe me. He thinks I've been kidding myself all this time. You'll have to call back and talk to him yourself or he won't believe it."

"I will, of course I will. How is he? How's everybody?" She waited for a report on her father, then she asked, "Mama, do you ever talk to Juffie?"

"Of course I talk to her. Once a week at least. She has a little boy, darling. Gorgeous. Juffie's wonderful. And when she hears that you're . . . that everything is okay, she'll be so happy. Juffie and me, Karen. We're the only two that never gave up hoping."

They talked some more, and Karen promised to call again in a couple of hours when her father would be home. And she promised to call Juffie. "Right away, the minute we hang up, darling," Leah insisted. "I'm going to dial her number myself in five minutes and if it's not busy I'll die from disappointment. She'll be so happy," she repeated.

When she hung up Karen kept her hand on the receiver and looked at Frank. "Did you get enough of that to know what's going on?"

He was grinning a happy grin. "Yeah. Your mother's kind of

pleased that you're not six feet under someplace. And everybody still loves you."

"Yes." Karen grinned now too. "Even Juffie. Leah says that Juffie never gave up hope. And I have to call her right away."

She lifted the telephone and dialed. Funny, she remembered the number. A million things that had happened in the past two years were lost in a fog, but not the things that mattered from before. Please God, let Juffie be home, I'll be so miserable if I can't speak to her right away this very minute. Juffie was home. She answered the telephone herself.

"Hi. It's me, Karen."

"Karen? Karen! Oh, my God, Karen!" In a rising crescendo. "Paul, come quick! It's Karen. She's alive!" Then, back into the telephone. "You are, aren't you? This isn't some goddamn seance stuff? It's you, in the flesh?"

"In the flesh. Oh, Juffie. I love you and I'm so happy."

"Where are you? Goddammit, Karen, where the hell are you? Where have you been for nearly two fucking years? Why didn't you let me know?"

Karen told her where she was. "I've been sick," she added. "I couldn't call. I really couldn't. I'll explain when I can, when I see you. Juffie, you're not mad at me, are you?"

"Mad at you? I could kill you. But I'm so happy you're alive that I won't bother. Listen, I have a surprise, a big one. Eleven pounds eight ounces as of this morning, in fact."

"I know. I read it in *McCall's*. Jason Dino Benjamin Dumont."

"Yes. Two months old and he's only the most wonderful, perfect, gorgeous baby ever born. Paul wanted to make him a number two, Paul Dumont II, but I said I couldn't do it. The Jewish half of me couldn't swallow it. So we called him Jason 'cause it's nice, and shoved in Dino and Benny so he'll know where he came from. Dumont is French enough for that part. Karen, when are you coming? You could fly from Los Angeles and maybe be here by tomorrow morning. Is this Barstow place far from L.A.?"

"No, it's not very far. But I can't come yet."

"What do you mean? Why not? Two years is long enough, sweetie. The curtain is overdue on the disappearing act. Get on a plane, goddammit, or if you really can't, I'll come to you. I'll have to bring Jason because I'm nursing, but I can manage all that. Is there someplace we can stay in Barstow?"

"Juffie, no. Not yet. I mean— Hang on a minute." She pressed the telephone to her chest and whispered urgently to Frank. "She wants me to come right away. Tonight. Or she'll come here. I can't, Frank. I'm not ready. I need a little more time before I see her . . ." Her throat was constricting in panic.

"Take it easy," he said gently. "Here, let me talk to her." He pried the receiver from Karen's fingers. "Mrs. Dumont, this is Frank Carlucci speaking. We haven't met, but I'm a friend of Karen's. Look, she told you she's been sick and it's the truth, very sick. She's recovering, doing great in fact, but it's going to take a little more time until she can pick up the threads of her life before the illness."

"Mr. Carlucci, are you a doctor? A psychiatrist perhaps? Are you trying to tell me that Karen has had a nervous breakdown?"

"I'm not a doctor. But yes, something like that."

"You sound a bit guarded," Juffie said. "Am I to assume you can't say more because Karen's listening?"

"That's right."

"Okay. I've got it. But will you please call me back when you can speak more freely? Karen Rice is my oldest and dearest friend and I'm genuinely concerned. Please, Mr. Carlucci. Call collect at any time day or night. My number is in the New York telephone directory. Under the name Paul Dumont. Can you remember that?"

"Yeah," he said. "I will."

. . . .

"What I can't get a handle on," Matt said, "is this guy Carlucci. He told you he's not a doctor. What exactly is his relationship to Karen?"

Juffie adjusted the blanket over Jason's bare foot. She couldn't keep booties on him, somehow they always slipped off, and there was a cool breeze in Central Park on this early June day. The baby slept on, unaware of her ministrations. "I'm not exactly sure. We talked for a long time when he called me back. He described himself as a friend who tried to help when she was at her worst. But he's not a boyfriend exactly, at least I don't think so. When I ask Karen she says the same thing, Frank's her friend."

A vendor with a food cart stood a few yards away. "Do you want another hot dog?" Matt asked. When Juffie shook her head he gathered up the remains of their lunch from the bench and took it to the litter bin. He returned and fussed with his pipe, it was difficult to light in the breeze. After a few seconds he got it going and slouched down, tipping his face to the sun and sprawling his long legs in front of him. "This is nice. You and I and Jason should have lunch more often."

"He only goes to Central Park. Can't stand Sardi's and refuses to set foot in '21'."

"Done. The gentleman can dictate the terms and we'll agree to them. He's a hot property, they always have things their own way." He peered into the imported English carriage. "Not saying much today, is he?"

She glanced at her watch. "Give him about half an hour, then he'll be howling. It's almost feeding time. I wonder if he'll approve of hot-dog-flavored milk; maybe I should have skipped the relish."

Matt smiled a tender smile. "You're like a madonna. You know, I never expected it. I thought you'd hire a baby nurse from day one, or day two maybe. See him for a few minutes of enthusiastic hugging and kissing morning and evening, and leave the slog between to somebody else."

"Truth is, I thought so too. At least before I was actually pregnant, when I tried to imagine what the whole thing would be like. But it consumes you almost from the first minute you know a baby's on the way. Matt, it's the most intense experience in the universe. Having a child colors your view of absolutely everything else. You see the world through a different prism, the angles all changed."

"I believe it if you say so," he said softly.

He turned his face from her and his pain struck Juffie with new force. He must have wanted children, too, years ago when he married his Patsy and expected a normal life. He was thirty-nine, it wasn't too late. Not if he found someone and got married. She felt tears prickle behind her eyelids. When he turned back to her his eyes looked a little moist too.

"So what's the latest with Karen?" he asked. That was a better topic of conversation for them than discussing babies and being a family. "Is she absolutely over the gambling thing?"

"She thinks so. I think so too. It was a response to pain, as she puts it. And she's not in pain anymore. She's figured out the whys and hows of her relationship with Bernard, and it doesn't hurt now. I talked with her yesterday and she didn't say exactly, but I get the feeling she's almost ready to come home."

"That will be nice for you."

"Yes, I've missed her a lot. There are things Karen and I share that no one else in the world knows about or would understand."

"I think women have a greater talent for friendship than men do. And speaking of talent, I'm fielding three and four phone calls a day from producers and directors who want to know if Juffie Kane is interested in looking at a script."

Juffie shook her head. "She isn't, not yet. Not for another six months at least. I don't want to miss this part of Jason's life, Matt. A baby starts growing away from you the instant you get out of the delivery room, but for the moment I'm still the most important being in the world for him. I want to enjoy that while it lasts."

"Okay." He stood up, knocking out the ash of the pipe against the back of the bench. "Now I have to get back to work. I'd offer to put you in a cab, but I don't see how it can be done with that thing." He gestured to the carriage.

"It can't. We'll walk home, it's just six blocks. When I bought the penthouse I never figured it was going to be important that it was an almost straight shot to the Sixty-ninth Street entrance to Central Park."

Jason started crying by the time she crossed Lexington. She managed the last three blocks at a jogging trot, thinking that everyone was looking at her and wondering why that awful woman didn't do something about her howling baby. "Jason darling," she told him when they were going up in the elevator of the penthouse, "the world is not ready for you. It's not ready for babies in general. Most people think you're an intrusion. Which is kind of silly, since babies are a necessary part of the survival of the race."

He wasn't interested in her philosophy, only in the swollen nipple she presented to him when they were finally seated in the rocking chair in the exquisite nursery Billy Baldwin had created from what had been her boudoir. Juffie held him and he suckled, and they both rocked gently in that cocoon of perfection which held them at these moments. Just me and my baby, she thought. Nothing else and no one else matters a damn at this precise instant. Which included her husband, the baby's father. Thinking of that startled her, created a discord in the sweet harmony. As if he felt it too, Jason chose that second to lose his grip on her breast and scream with frustration.

.　.　.　.

Frank was waiting when Karen came out of the bakery on the third Wednesday in June. "Hi," she said, taking both his hands. "What are you doing here? I thought Friday was your day off this week."

"No more days off," he said, leading her to where he'd parked the Chevy. "At least not from the Desert Inn. I've quit. I'm through dealing. It's back to earning my bread with my brains rather than my nimble fingers."

They went to a place called Kay's Kountry Kitchen on the road between Barstow and George Air Force Base, which was a few miles south of the city. Over fried chicken and gravy and mashed potatoes and biscuits he explained his plans.

"I figure I'll spend a couple of months in Los Angeles just getting set up, finding a place to live, and uncrating all my books and files. I put everything in storage when I went to Vegas. Now it all has to be unstored."

The whole thing unsettled her slightly; she was still fragile enough to fear any change in routine. "Will I see you while you're doing all this?"

"Of course, at least once a week, like always. And there's a bus from Barstow to L.A. It only takes a couple of hours, I checked. You can come visit me sometimes, just for a change. You ought to see a little more of California, it's a fairly terrific place."

That made her feel better, especially the fact that he'd checked on the bus schedule. Because, she realized, she still wanted to believe she was the center of his world. And that was not uncommon in a recovering dependency, but not very healthy. But now that she understood she could look at it and see it for what it was. She was integrating her training and what she knew with what she felt—and that was very healthy indeed. She grinned.

"What are you looking so pleased with yourself about?"

She told him. "I'm pleased too," he said. "And I love the way you're tucking into those biscuits. Have another one. Try it with honey, it's delicious."

Karen cocked her head and studied him. "I'm going to turn

the tables on you for a moment, Mr. Carlucci. You have to stop thinking that food is the only bellwether of my state of mental health. Because your mother's pathology led her into a malnutrition-related death, not eating is the thing you fear most in anyone you care about. But it can tip, you can develop a situation where food becomes the pivot of all affection and well-being, then you're headed straight for an eating disorder. So no thanks, I won't have another biscuit. Not because I'm sick. Because I've had three and that's plenty."

He paused a moment in the act of gnawing a chicken leg, then he roared with laughter. "Thank you, Dr. Rice. And of course you're dead right. So what are you having for dessert?"

"Vanilla ice cream and chocolate sauce, naturally. I never said I wanted to be *completely* mentally healthy, that's boring."

Later, over coffee, he said, "Karen, I think you are mentally healthy, I think you're well. What do you think?"

"Pretty close," she said quietly. "Almost there. I can't remember the last time I thought about playing the slots. And I dropped a whole tray of Danish a couple of days ago and my boss screamed at me, and I didn't want to run out and gamble to relieve the tension I felt afterward. I was upset with myself for being clumsy, and annoyed with him for making such a big thing of it, but I didn't feel as if I'd explode if I couldn't play."

She took a sip of coffee and looked at him over the rim of the cup. "Are you going to go on with the book about compulsive gambling? Because if you are, that's an insight I give you free. Tension is part of it. Getting so screamingly tense and uncomfortable and anxious that you know you'll die if you don't let off steam. Of course, it's how you deal with it that separates the compulsive gambler from everybody else."

"Of course. You're right and I'll file it, but I don't think the book's on the cards at the moment. It's too iffy and long-term. I need to reactivate my contacts with editors, find a couple of stories I can do for magazines or newspapers that can be finished and published fairly quickly, so I get back some credibility." He called for the check. "Now I've got to get on the road. And you have to work in the morning."

In the car he picked up on that last statement. "Karen, when are you going to feel well enough to look for some work that is just a little more suitable than what you have? Isn't that a legitimate goal for your recovery?"

"It is. And I'm getting there, Frank. I know I am. The thing is, there's nothing in Barstow, so it means a big change, not a gradual one. Maybe even going back east. Sooner or later I have to do that anyway. I want to see my family, and Juffie and her baby. And there are loose ends flopping all over the place in Boston. I ought to tie them up before I set out to resume my career. It all still overwhelms me, but less than it used to."

"You won't go back to Boston without letting me know, will you?" he asked at her door.

"Of course I won't. What a crazy idea." She reached up and kissed his cheek. "Good luck in L.A."

"I'll call you as soon as I have a telephone. A few days or a week. No more."

Later she thought of his question about Boston. It was an odd remark, as if he were the dependent one. Which he was in a way. His need to purge his guilt about not being able to save his mother when he was thirteen had coincided with her need to be saved. And that's what life was mostly about, she mused. Mutual needs that come together. In the case of her and Frank, it was damned lucky for her. And maybe not so bad for him. Which was very nice.

He called her before the long weekend of the Fourth. "Got me an apartment and a telephone," he said. "And my stuff's been delivered from storage. Life is looking up. What about you?"

"I'm fine."

"Karen, I've been thinking about the fact that it's the Fourth of July. Your anniversary."

"Yes, two years since I blew my mind."

"Is it bothering you?"

"A little, nothing I can't handle."

"Handle it with me," he said. "Get on the bus and come spend a couple of days here. Can you get the time off?"

"I have the time off. The bakery closes two days a year, Christmas and the Fourth of July. And as it happens I have the fifth off as well."

"Great! Will you come?"

She hesitated only a moment. "Yes, sure. I'd love to."

He met her at the bus station a little before midnight on the third. His apartment was three rooms in a new building off Wilshire Boulevard. "Very nice," Karen said. "I'm impressed. Which reminds me that I've never asked what you did about the bungalow."

"It's for sale, a real estate agent's handling it for me. There's no hurry. One thing dealing did for me, I'm not hurting for money." He carried her overnight case through a door that apparently led to a bedroom. "You can sleep in here. I use the third room as an office and there's a couch that opens up, so I'll be okay."

We'll both be okay, Karen thought. And that was another slightly peculiar thing. They were a man and a woman of approximately the same age, neither of them particularly repulsive, at least she wasn't anymore, and he never had been, yet there was nothing sexual about their relationship. No hint of it. She couldn't quite figure out why. Then, while she was drifting off to sleep, she thought of Frank in connection with Las Vegas showgirls. He must have a sexual outlet somewhere, doubtless that was it. Plenty of opportunities for a man in Las Vegas. That thought made her feel a little jealous, but she put it down to her lingering dependency.

They had a great weekend. He drove her around, showing her all the sights, including Hollywood and the movie studios. "Your actress friend's never made a movie, has she?"

"Juffie? No, she says she never will. She needs a live audience."

"Why? I'd think the craft of acting would be the same wherever you did it."

"Not for Juffie. She's not a cerebral-type actress who's studied all the moves. That's not the wellspring of her magic. Juffie needs to feel people loving her and she loves them back. She recognized that when she first started, years ago in college. I remember her talking to me about it. Apparently it's never changed. Juffie's got a lot of love to give, and she needs to give it and get it back."

"What about her husband? Are they in love?"

"Yes, I guess so. I've never had any reason to think otherwise. Frank, what is all this about?"

"Let's go back to my place. I want to show you something."

In the apartment he dragged out half a dozen thick files. "I've been working on this for nearly five years. It's why I was so startled when you mentioned that you knew Juffie Kane."

She looked at him and didn't say anything, only flipped open the first file he handed her. It contained dozens of clippings about Juffie, mostly dealing with her alleged underworld connections. Everything that had been written on the subject, including the savage article from *Confidential* magazine. "I've seen most of this garbage before," Karen said stiffly. "Why do you have it? Why are you showing it to me?"

"Once upon a time I was going to write a story about it, about her. And how the mob takes over everywhere, even in the theater. I've always figured she must be a bitch on wheels. According to you she's not. So does that mean this stuff isn't true?"

Karen shrugged. "It is and it isn't. Her grandfathers were who they say they were, that's true. And Myer Kane is the kind of lawyer they say he is. That's true too. He's also the sweetest, kindest, most concerned man you can imagine. So, as the saying goes, 'What is truth?'"

He looked at her for a long moment. "What indeed? Karen, could you be wrong about her? I mean even Eichmann was supposed to be fond of dogs and children."

"Juffie is a great person and a wonderful friend." She was so angry, the words came out with more force than she intended. They sounded as if she were trying to convince herself, not him. "She is," Karen added more gently. "Really and truly, Frank. Everything you know about her is circumstantial. Wait until you meet her, then you'll see."

He smiled and started putting the papers back in the file. "Yeah, I'd like to meet her someday. Any idea when that might be? When you'll be ready to go back I mean."

"Soon," Karen said. "Not yet, but soon."

·   ·   ·   ·

The Dumonts spent the holiday weekend at a beautiful beach house on Long Island that belonged to someone Paul knew. He'd come home the middle of June and told Juffie that this terrific place in Southampton was going to be unused over the Fourth of July, and it had been offered to them.

"There's a full staff and everything. We only have to drive ourselves out there with the baby and his stuff and our clothes."

"Who owns it?" Juffie asked, not meeting his eyes.

"A man I know, a business associate. Don't get that look on

your face. He's legitimate. He is, Juffie, I swear it. Come on, *chérie*, don't be like this. It will do you good to get out of the city. I was going to suggest a resort somewhere, but a fully staffed private house in Southampton is much better. Easier and more comfortable, for you and for Jason."

She was in the kitchen, preparing cheese for a soufflé. She put down the knife she was holding and gripped the edge of the counter. "Listen to me, Paul. If you do anything, anything, which in any way puts Jason at the most remote risk, I'll kill you. I swear it."

"You think I'd do something like that?"

You already have. She almost said it, but she didn't. It wasn't entirely fair. He hadn't known she was carrying Jason at the time. It was only she he had put at risk. "I hope you wouldn't. I want to believe you wouldn't."

"You can believe it." His voice wasn't angry but pleading. Paul had a disconcerting way of changing an argument into something else. "Who's the one who wanted a child so desperately, Juffie? Who is it who begged you to have one? He's my son, not yours alone. I love him as much as you do."

She'd been stiff with tension; now she sagged. "I know. I'm sorry, it's because . . ."

"I know," he said, "you don't have to explain." He put his hand on her shoulder; one finger stroked the back of her neck. "Relax. You're a bundle of nerves. That's why I want to get you out to the country for a few days. I'll say we'll accept with pleasure, okay?"

"Okay."

"Wonderful. It will be like old times, *chérie*, you'll see."

By which he probably meant that they'd make love. They had not done so for months. There had been a long period right after Brownsville when she wouldn't let him sleep in the same room. Gradually she'd gotten over that, decided to forgive him, but then the obstetrician advised abstinence for the last six weeks of her pregnancy and the first six weeks after the birth. That time was long past. Jason was approaching four months old. And Paul was still sleeping in his study because she didn't want him in the bedroom.

"Like old times," Paul repeated as he went to telephone the man who'd offered them the house.

When they got to Southampton Juffie thought that maybe he'd been right. The place was magnificent, a seaside palace, and the staff was something out of a dream. There were countless numbers of them and they attended to every want before it was voiced. Whoever owned this place had an enormous amount of money. Only fabulous wealth purchased care such as this.

They slept in a huge bedroom with French doors and a balcony looking over the ocean. There was a dressing room en suite and a crib had been set up for Jason there. He was near enough to make Juffie comfortable, and far enough to give them a little privacy.

When they went to bed the first night, Juffie kept to her customary side of the mattress and Paul to his, both stiff and strange as if they were newly met. Then Jason woke them demanding his two A.M. feeding and Juffie nursed him in the bed, with Paul lying beside her and stroking first the baby's tiny hands, then her own. For the first time he was part of the intense experience she shared with her child, and some of Jason's luster rubbed off on Paul. At least that's how she thought of it later.

It had to have been that, because she had not desired him for a long time, longer than she had admitted to herself. Since before Brownsville perhaps, maybe since London and Matt. But that night when he reached for her, after Jason had been returned to his crib and was sleeping soundly, Juffie didn't reject him. She was acquiescent at first, then some of the magic came back and she was enthusiastic.

Paul was as good as ever. He made love to her for three hours. When he buried his head between her legs she had a violent orgasm, and another when he rubbed his rock-hard penis on her buttocks while reaching around and putting his fingers deep inside her. There was a third when he finally entered her. It came in perfect tempo with his, an echo of a rhythm once learned and not forgotten.

They fell asleep when dawn was a pink glow beyond the balcony, and just seconds before she dozed off Juffie thought that she'd only have a very short nap because Jason was bound to demand attention by six-thirty.

That's what woke her, the realization that the baby was overdue for his feeding. She opened her eyes and had to think for a moment to remember where she was. A breeze moved the sheer curtains by the open balcony doors. They hadn't drawn the heavy drapes and she could see the sun sparkling on the water. Yes, of course. Southampton. Beside her Paul was sleeping, his breathing rhythmic and deep. She listened for Jason, but there wasn't a sound. It must be the sea air. Juffie glanced at the bedside clock. Seven forty-five, incredible.

She got up carefully, so as not to wake Paul, and pulled on the robe she'd left folded over the bench at the foot of the bed. Then she padded barefoot into the dressing room. They'd left the door open and she could see the crib before she got there. Jason's little rump was sticking up beneath the yellow and white crocheted blanket she'd spread over him when she put him down during the night.

"Good morning, baby love," she whispered. "I'll have to bring you out to the beach more often. You let Mommy sleep a whole extra hour." She was debating whether to wake him or let him sleep on. What did Dr. Spock say? What did her pediatrician say? She couldn't remember. But she remembered that they both advised her to follow her maternal instincts.

Juffie reached her hand into the crib and touched the back of his head. Jason was cold. But it wasn't cold in the room. Why should he be cold? She put her hand beneath the blanket. His diaper was soaked, but that was cold too. Her fingers found one chubby thigh, also cold. Panic began to rise in her throat. She snatched the baby out of the crib together with his blanket, hugging him to her warmth, willing it to spread to him. His head flopped against her breast and he didn't open his eyes.

"Jason, come on love, it's Mommy." She was still whispering, still acting as if everything were normal and she didn't want to wake Paul. "Time to wake up," she crooned softly to the child. "Time to have breakfast, Jason."

It was another minute before she reacted. For at least sixty seconds Juffie stood there holding her baby and she didn't make a sound, just rocked him back and forth the way she did when he was nursing. Finally a gull soared by the open window. A breeze had drawn the curtain outside the window and the gull actually brushed the curtains with its wings. She was startled then back to reality. That's when she screamed. "Jason! Jason! Jason! He's dead! My baby is dead!" She went on screaming for a very long time.

Chapter 19

*T*hree days later they buried Jason. Rain fell in cold wind-driven sheets that felt more like March than July. The drops spattered Juffie's cheeks, heaven providing for her lack of tears. She couldn't cry, even when the tiny white coffin was lowered into the earth.

Paul had found a young minister. Juffie had no idea which denomination he represented. A kind man no doubt, but he didn't know them, and he'd never seen their child. The clergyman seemed a bit bewildered by these famous people. He kept glancing up from his prayer book and looking at the dozen or so mourners with a perplexed expression, as if their well-known faces were out of place in this setting, as if he thought they were simply pretending to be ordinary mortals.

The Fines lingered a moment at the gravesite when the service ended. Jack leaned down and picked up a handful of dirt and threw it gently into the hole containing the coffin. A moment later Nessa did the same thing.

Juffie watched them and remembered. That's what her father had done the day they buried Rosie, and again at Pa's funeral. An old Jewish custom, he'd told her. An acknowledgment of the biblical words, "Dust thou art, and unto dust shalt thou return." Myer wasn't here today because she'd insisted that he not come, not place such stress on his erratic heart. But she missed him, she missed the sense of continuity, of support come from blood ties. Paul stood beside her, but she did not feel a shared grief with her husband.

The ritual of the funeral, albeit borrowed from some rite alien to them both, provided a structure for the first few hours of that terrible day. Later, at home, there was nothing.

Juffie went to the nursery and opened the door. She didn't go in, she simply stood there and stared. Paul came up behind her and placed a tentative hand on her arm. "Come away, *chérie*, there's no point in torturing yourself."

"Take your hands off me."

"Juffie, please . . ."

"I said take your hands off me. Don't touch me. Don't ever touch me again."

"You're upset, it's natural. So am I. We need each other now, *chérie*."

She turned slowly. It seemed to take a long time before she was actually facing him, studying him, examining his features as if she'd never seen them before. "You don't really feel it. You don't really feel anything." She said the words without emphasis, and yet with absolute conviction.

"Juffie, what are you talking about? How can you say such a thing? Do you think I'm not as sick at heart as you are, as crushed, as overwhelmed? I am. But I know that someday we'll have another child."

"No, Paul. That is one thing we won't have. Another child. You don't understand, do you? Let me put it in words of one syllable. I hate you. I despise you. I have been hiding it for a long time because you were Jason's father. I should have thrown you out of here months ago, but I didn't. That's why you were able to take us to that place and make me forget my son during the few hours when he needed me most, when maybe I might have saved his life. So it's my fault as much as yours. More. But that doesn't make me hate you any less."

He didn't move, didn't flinch or blink. He stood perfectly still and listened. Then, when she'd stopped speaking, "Are you finished? Good, well, let me tell you a few things. There's no way you could 'throw me out of here' as you put it. I know too much, *chérie*, too many skeletons from Juffie Kane's past are in my head. They would make unpleasant reading for your fans, not to mention some other powerful people. As for the rest, I'm prepared to forget what you've said because I know how upset you are today. So go lie down, get some rest. Later, in a few months, we'll talk about another baby."

She shook her head. "I don't believe you. You haven't been

listening to a word I said, have you? No more babies, Paul. Never. I'd die before I'd have another child with you."

He started toward his study, but he turned back to her. "I want a live son, Juffie, not a dead memory. I intend to have what I want."

. . . . .

The death of Jason Dino Benjamin Dumont, whom she'd never seen, was the impetus that sent Karen to New York. "The way I figure it," she told Frank, "most of our lives Juffie's been the giver and I've been the taker. This time she needs exactly what I should be able to give, what all my training supposedly equipped me for. I have to go."

"I agree." He was driving her to the airport. The best way for her to get to New York from Barstow was to take a bus to Los Angeles and fly from there. "It's probably a hell of a time to mention it," Frank said, "but don't forget about my story. I want to meet your famous friend when all this is over."

He paused, and they were both silent for a moment. "Over," Frank repeated finally. "How can it ever be over? How do you get through something like this?"

"That's what I keep asking myself," Karen said softly. "My poor Juffie. I can't bear to think about what she must be feeling. Losing a child to what people call a crib death, it has to be one of the most devastating things a woman can face. She's a tough lady, but tough enough for this? I don't know."

"She'll handle it," Frank said. "You'll help her handle it. And speaking of tough ladies, I know one named Karen Rice who licked a problem other people have let pull them all the way down."

She smiled at him, but they didn't say much after that. Not until they were at the airport gate and she reached up and kissed his cheek. "'Bye. Thank you. It's absolutely inadequate, but there's nothing else I can say."

"Hey," he protested. "Don't make it sound like farewell forever. Have a good flight, call me as soon as you can. You know, to let me know how things are."

It was Paul who met Karen's plane at Idlewild. "Juffie's home in bed," he said. "It's been a week since the funeral, but she hasn't budged out of the bedroom in all that time."

"It's not surprising, Paul." Karen stared at him, trying to figure out what went on in the mind behind the wonderfully handsome face. "What about you, how are you doing?"

"I'm okay, I guess." His jawline was tight and a little blue, as if he hadn't shaved that day. No, he probably had. It was nerves, stretching his skin so taut the veins showed. He swung the big Buick through the traffic with confident, steady hands, but his voice trembled a little. "Losing Jason is bad enough, but what hurts worse is that Juffie doesn't give a damn what I feel."

Karen didn't answer. What he was describing was not uncommon, a textbook case, in fact. But she didn't think this was the moment to try to make him understand Juffie's actions.

The penthouse was as hushed as a hospital—or a morgue. The only sounds were the soft purring noises of the air-conditioners, fighting the July heat wave that had attacked the city. "She's in the bedroom," Paul said. "As I told you, she won't come out, you'll have to go to her."

Karen let herself into the lovely room. Juffie lay on the bed, on yellow and white embroidered Porthault sheets. It was warm despite the air-conditioner, and the quilt was thrown back. She wore a short blue wrap, the kind of thing the Japanese called a happi coat, and she was staring at the ceiling. She didn't move when Karen came in and sat down on the edge of the bed.

"This isn't the way either of us planned it, pet. But I'm back at last." Still no reply, no movement. "Look, I'm more sorry than I can say that I wasn't here to share the happy time with you and Jason. Please let me share at least the sadness."

Juffie turned to her, slowly, as if she were being pulled back from a far place. Karen knew that look, that feeling. Juffie's hair was tangled and matted with sweat, her cheeks were hollow and her eyes, her fabulous gray-violet eyes, were surrounded by ugly black circles. For a moment it was like looking into a mirror a year before. "Hello," Juffie said. "It was nice of you to come."

Nice of her to come. As if she were a casual acquaintance paying a condolence call. "No," Karen said. "It wasn't nice of me, as you put it. I could no more not be here than I could fly. Juffie, like we used to say, this is me, Karen. I know I've abused our friendship pretty badly for two years, but I wasn't in control. I was very sick. And do you know what? When I was sick I looked the way you look now—worse, because I went on a lot longer, but basically the same look. And I felt the way you feel. As if there were nothing in the world that could ever make me happy again. Except maybe playing the slot machines, and that didn't make me happy, it merely covered up the pain. So I know what you're going through, not just professionally, but personally. And I know that the only way it gets better is when you decide to make it get better."

"I'm not about to become a compulsive gambler." Juffie's voice was flat, toneless. There was no hint of the rich vibrancy that had thrilled so many audiences, none of the expansive gestures that were normally so much a part of her personality. "And I'm not going to take to drink. I don't have any compulsions, as a matter of fact. I only want to be left alone."

"I see. Does that include me?"

"Yes, I'm sorry, but today it does. Maybe I'll feel differently tomorrow. Maybe a little better. I don't know. Stay if you can. As long as you like. Paul will make you comfortable. He's got a cook coming in as well as the cleaning lady." She turned her face to the opposite wall.

After a few silent moments Karen left.

Paul was waiting for her in the living room. "Any luck? Did you get through to her?"

"Not yet, no. She's grieving, Paul. It's natural. Her grief is particularly awful because she feels guilty. Every mother who's ever lost a child to crib death thinks that somehow it's her fault. She has to cope with the terrible guilt as well as the pain of loss."

"Juffie doesn't think it's her fault," he said bitterly. "She thinks it's mine."

Karen shook her head. "No, I doubt that. I think you're overreacting, Paul. Why should she blame you?"

He went to the bar and poured himself a drink. "I'll tell you why. Because we were making love. The night Jason died I was making love to my wife, and that's turned into the worst crime of the century. And I'll tell you something else; it was the first time in ages. She'd been shutting me out for a long time. But that night, in that terrific house by the ocean, I managed to turn her on again. And meanwhile my son died."

He gulped the whiskey and slammed the glass on the bar. "And Juffie says that if I hadn't distracted her, she'd have heard something, known somehow that he was in trouble. So it's my fault that Jason is dead."

"Did she actually say that, or do you think she said it?"

"She said it. In a number of ways, all perfectly clear English. Juffie is very good at communicating her feelings, as we all know. But I'll tell you something maybe you don't know. She can be a bitch, Karen. The famous Juffie Kane can be a bitch out of hell."

· · · ·

Not even Matt could reach her. He came every afternoon for the first week of Karen's stay. Each day he went into the bedroom and sat with Juffie, and came out after half an hour and said that nothing had changed. "She won't talk to me. She doesn't say anything. Just lies there."

Karen went through the same explanation with him, the one about how a mother inevitably blamed herself for a crib death. "Women have been programmed to feel that way," she told him. "There are cases on record centuries old. It used to be called 'death from overlying.' In the days when an infant slept in the same bed with the mother, they said she'd turned over in her sleep and smothered the baby. How's that for setting up a giant economy size load of guilt?"

"Awful," Matt agreed. "But that couldn't have happened with Juffie. Jason wasn't in her bed when he died."

"Of course not. And even if he had been, the likelihood of such a thing happening is almost zero. It was nothing but a convenient explanation, it never did have much basis in reality. As medicine goes, it's in a class with leeches and bloodletting." She took a long swallow from a glass of iced tea. "I suppose it's a cut above spells and incantations, but only just."

"Then how did he die?" Matt demanded. "How did Jason die, Karen? He was such a great little kid, and he seemed so healthy."

"I don't have any answers for you. I've been reading everything I can find, but apparently nobody knows what causes crib death. There have been a few studies done lately, in Boston and Chicago. So far all they've managed to prove is that it's nothing to do with smothering. And there's no way the parents could have prevented it. The most terrible thing is that it almost always happens with an apparently perfectly healthy baby." She set down the glass and stared not at Matt but into space. "Think of it, you put a happy, normal child in his crib and go back and find a dead one." She shivered. "Poor Juffie. I can't think of anything worse that could have happened to her."

"There can't be anything worse," Matt said. "It's like a bolt of lightning, like some kind of judgment of the gods. It's devastating, soul-destroying." He got up to go, and she walked with him to the elevator. His last words were an echo of hers. "Poor Juffie."

The following Monday Nessa Fine came. Karen had met her only once, years before when Juffie won the Tony for *Delilah*. "I would have come earlier," she said. "But I hear Juffie doesn't want to see anyone."

"No, she's taking it very badly still."

"God, I'm not surprised. I think I'd kill myself. I probably shouldn't say that, should I?"

"Not to Juffie, please," Karen said quietly.

"I'm not a total idiot. Of course I won't say anything like that to Juffie. I brought her something. I'll put it away."

Karen followed the older woman into the kitchen. She'd brought three jars of homemade English marmalade. "A little crazy, isn't it?" She put them on the kitchen counter. "Why should marmalade make Juffie feel better? But I felt I had to bring something. Flowers seemed too funereal, and I couldn't think of anything else."

"It's very thoughtful, Mrs. Fine. I'm sure Juffie will appreciate the jam when she feels better."

Being in the kitchen had a bad effect on Nessa Fine. "A month or so ago I watched Juffie giving Jason his first solid food. She was sitting in that chair over there. Strained peaches. God, he made a mess." She began to sniffle, and turned brusque to hide it. "By the way, you Americans always think marmalade and jam are the same things. They're not." She found a handkerchief and wiped her eyes. "And call me Nessa, please. Juffie speaks of you so often, I feel as if we're friends." She made a visible effort to compose herself, then went into the bedroom.

An hour later Nessa returned to the living room. Karen was reading a magazine, she looked up hopefully. "Well?"

"I couldn't break through. I kept telling her it couldn't be her fault that Jason smothered to death, but she only lies there staring at the ceiling."

Karen sighed, and wished she'd said more earlier, before Nessa saw Juffie. "Jason didn't smother. It's almost impossible for that to happen. All the latest research proves that in nine hundred and ninety-nine cases out of a thousand, crib death isn't caused by smothering."

"What then?"

A sensible enough question, but there wasn't any answer. Karen shook her head. "I wish to God somebody knew."

"Okay, whatever it was," Nessa said finally. "He's dead, there's nothing going to bring him back. What matters now is Juffie. You're a psychologist, can't you do something? Give her something that will get her over the worst of it?"

"Nessa," Karen said gently. "First of all, as you say, I'm a psychologist. I can't prescribe medicine. But more to the point, there isn't any magic pill we can give Juffie and make everything better. She has to find the will to live with her loss. When she does, she'll need the support of everyone who loves her. And that's why I'm hanging around here waiting, even though I'm not earning my keep at the moment."

In the evening, over dinner, she said much the same thing to Paul. "Look, I know I'm a dead weight right now. Maybe I should go up to Boston. You can call me when Juffie starts to come out of it. And she will," she added.

"Don't go." He refilled her wineglass and took her hand. "You're the only thing that makes me feel it's worth coming home in the evenings. Please stay, Karen."

Karen didn't pull her hand away immediately. She studied Paul for a moment. "Okay," she said finally. "There's nothing much that's waiting for me. I'm happy to stay if it's all right with you?"

"Very all right," he said. "Very."

Tuesday morning she got an idea. She'd told everyone there was nothing to be done, that they had to wait for Juffie to work through her grief. But maybe there was something she could try. She went to the library and found a few articles about crib death in the popular press. Two impressed her particularly, one in *McCall's*, the other in *Today's Health*. Both focused on the fact that the babies had died of some mysterious illness, not smothering, so there was nothing the mother could have done to prevent it.

Karen photocopied the stories and took them home. At two

she went into Juffie's room. Her lunch tray was untouched. Karen didn't comment on that. She picked up the tray and put the articles on the bedside table. "Have a look at these," she said, "I think you'll find them worth reading." There was no reply. "It can't hurt to know what few facts there are, honey," Karen added. "And that other women have been through it, that they felt the way you feel now." Juffie still didn't answer.

When Karen went back in the evening the articles were nowhere in sight. She wondered if Juffie had torn them up and thrown them away. Perhaps she'd read them. She didn't ask because it seemed too much to hope for. Juffie was unchanged, a taut bundle of misery lying unmoving on the bed. When Karen tried to stroke the limp and dirty hair back from her forehead, Juffie pushed her hand away.

On Wednesday morning the reception desk in the lobby phoned through to say that four workmen were on their way up. Karen went to the door because the cleaning woman was somewhere in the back of the apartment. Only one of the four wasn't wearing overalls and a painter's cap.

"I'm Billy Baldwin," the man in the shirt and tie said. "Mrs. Dumont's decorator. This is my crew, we've come to do a tiny bit of work."

Karen noted the pile of boxes and paint cans and bolts of fabric crowding the entry hall, and her heart sank. "I'm sorry, Mr. Baldwin, I know who you are, Juffie's told me, but if she arranged to have something done today, I'm afraid she's forgotten it. She isn't very well at the moment."

Billy Baldwin nodded sympathetically. "I know, and Juffie didn't order this stuff, I did. Now, if you'll let me get on with it, we won't bother anyone. We'll do what we've come to do, then quietly slip away." He didn't wait for an answer, simply slid past her and led his crew and their equipment inside. Karen followed, a protest half formed on her lips. Then she understood what he intended to do—and decided to let him do it.

She didn't see Baldwin again for hours. He closeted himself in the nursery, the high priest performing his secret rituals, but a procession of acolytes and material came and went all day. The smell of paint filled the house. Karen agonized over her instinctive decision to allow him to go ahead. There wasn't any textbook answer to the problem, it was a question that divided the profession. Was it better to let Juffie give up the nursery in her own time, or present her with a fait accompli? Karen wasn't sure.

At six Baldwin emerged and beckoned her. "Come see."

He'd transformed the little room yet again, and he had no training in psychology to muddle his instincts. "Nessa Fine told me Juffie won't get out of bed. But of course she will eventually, and when she does I think it better that she's not confronted with the nursery, don't you? So I've made it a boudoir again. But I thought we needed a few changes. We can't go back in time and pretend dear little Jason was never born, can we? I'm sure what Juffie needs is to go forward."

The room was aquamarine this time, the walls were painted the rich blue-green of the sea and the woodwork bright white. The fabric he'd used was a sheer cotton of the same deep aqua, with an allover print of tiny yellow and white flowers. It was draped lavishly on the window wall and repeated behind a yellow moiré love seat. The rest of the furniture was white wicker with yellow moiré cushions.

"It's lovely," Karen said. "Beautiful. How did you do all this in one day?"

"Organization," he said with a small laugh. "And bribery where necessary. We're still missing two slipper chairs the upholsterer hasn't finished. I'll send them over as soon as they're done."

Karen had long since packed all the baby clothes and taken them to the Foundling Hospital. Now, for better or worse, Billy Baldwin had removed the last traces of Jason Dino Benjamin Dumont's brief life. She started to say something, but was forestalled by a small noise behind her, something between a hiccup and a sob.

Juffie was standing in the doorway, staring at the changes in the room. She still wore the blue happi coat and her legs and her feet were bare, but she'd washed her hair. Very recently. It was hanging soaking wet down her back. Her eyes looked enormous in her thin, drawn face. No tears, however; the noise hadn't been a sob after all.

"It's a good job, Billy," Juffie said quietly. "Good colors, and the fabric's great."

He crossed to her and kissed her cheek. "Thank you, my dear.

I hope you don't think I overstepped myself. But it seemed the right thing to do."

Juffie didn't answer. She walked past him to where Jason's crib had stood, staring at the yellow love seat that filled the space now. Baldwin left the room, murmuring that he'd show himself out. Karen sat down on one of the cushioned wicker stools.

Juffie ran her hands over the back and the arms of the small sofa. "His crib was wonderful. Billy found that too. It was an antique, maple with the most marvelous carving. . . . But you saw it. It was here until this morning. I forgot."

"Yes," Karen agreed. "The crib was beautiful."

"Not as beautiful as Jason," Juffie said. "Jason was the most beautiful baby in the world. I'm so sorry you never met him."

"So am I."

"But I did." Juffie sat down on the sofa, pulling up her feet and hugging her long legs with her arms. "I met him. I had him for four whole months. And nine months before that. Sort of. It was such a short time. Oh, shit, Karen, it was no time at all."

Finally she began to cry. Softly at first, then with great gulping sobs. Karen put her arms around Juffie's shaking shoulders, hugging her hard, longing to take some of her pain. "Fuck everything," Juffie said against Karen's chest, choking out the words between sobs. "Fuck the whole goddamn world. And tell me why this had to happen to me. Why me, Karen? Did I do anything so terrible I deserved this?"

"No. Nobody deserves this. We don't get what we deserve, Juffie. I guess life's not like that."

"No, it isn't." Juffie turned slightly, adjusting her position so she could cling to her friend. "Oh, sweetie, thank God you're here. Hold on to me, Karen, don't let me blow away!"

. . . .

They didn't talk about Paul until early August, after Karen had been to Boston and seen her family, and tied up the loose ends she'd mentioned to Frank so many months before.

"Your father's such a doll," Karen told Juffie. "He's straightened out everything with the contracts I broke, so I won't have bad references. And he's taken care of the bank. I owe the Shawmut three thousand, plus a fortune in interest and penalties, but he got them down to a reasonable figure and told them I'd start repaying as soon as I was working again. And I know what you and he did about my apartment. I'll pay both of you back too."

"Forget that. It didn't amount to much. We kept it up only for the first year. After that it seemed a little silly. The Salvation Army got your stuff, by the way."

They were in the kitchen, drinking glasses of root beer topped with scoops of vanilla ice cream, which Juffie produced because she said it was too beautiful a summer day to worry about calories. Karen scooped up the last bit of half-melted ice cream and ate it. "Not even the Salvation Army deserved my stuff. It was awful. Sensible dark tweeds, like the clothes I wore. Ugh . . ."

"Yes," Juffie agreed. "Ugh and double ugh. Karen, what are you going to do now? Can you find work in New York?"

"Yes, I probably can. Thanks to Matt. He's another very kind man. He talked to some client of his, an opera singer who's on the board of almost every hospital in the city. The singer is checking on openings for me. The only thing that worries me is that rents are so high in New York."

"That's no problem. Stay here, at least until you get on your feet."

"Do you think Paul will object? It's one thing to invade your privacy for a few weeks, something else to do it for months."

"I don't give a damn whether Paul objects. Besides, he won't. He has the hots for you. I've watched him watching you."

"That's ridiculous. And why don't you give a damn? You're not still blaming Paul for what happened, are you, Juffie? It wasn't his fault any more than it was yours."

"No, I know. It's that the whole thing has finally got to me. Paul and his . . . Forget it, it's just too long a story. I haven't the energy to tell it."

"Are you going to leave him?" Karen asked quietly. "Is that what you're trying to say, that you want a divorce?"

"If I could, I would," Juffie said. "I can't."

"What does that mean? If you want to, you can. Oh, not in New York probably, but you could go to Reno, or even Mexico. People in your business do it all the time."

"It's not a legal problem." Juffie took the empty root beer glasses to the sink. "Paul won't let me go. I know the way his mind works. I'm a possession, something nice to look at, something important that he owns. In large measure that's how he felt about Jason—a child completed the image of the successful man. Besides, Paul's thick with the mob. He makes Dino and Benny look like small-time operators. I go up against that and I'm bound to lose. I already have," she added bitterly.

"How?"

"No, I'm not going into all that, not today. Probably not ever. It's too terrible. And basically it's my own fault. I started the whole thing."

"What the hell are you talking about?" Karen demanded.

"Look, let's leave it alone, shall we? I really can't talk about it." Still, it was she who kept the subject alive. "Karen, are you encouraging me to divorce Paul? Don't you like him?"

"No, it isn't that. It's that I don't think you ought to base a decision on anything other than what you really want."

Karen busied herself drying the glasses Juffie had washed and didn't say more. What she felt about Paul Dumont was something she couldn't explain to his wife, because she hadn't yet really explained it to herself. It was something she sensed in him, something hollow at the core. Sometimes she wondered who, if anyone, he really was. But it was too amorphous to discuss. She brought up Frank instead.

"Did I tell you? Frank Carlucci is coming to New York for a few days. I'd like you to meet him. Will you have time?"

"Of course, and if I didn't, I'd make time." Juffie smiled and put her arm around Karen's shoulders. "I've been hoping to have a chance to thank him for bringing back my best friend."

A week later the trio were walking three abreast down Broadway at dusk, Juffie and Karen and Frank Carlucci. Because Frank had never seen the fabled street, and he wanted to watch the lights come on.

Juffie liked him. A lot. She'd decided that about an hour before, over corned beef sandwiches at the Stage Delicatessen. She liked the easy way Frank laughed, and the way he kept smiling at Karen. And that he wanted to do all the tourist things, and had enough self-confidence not to be embarrassed by doing them.

"More movies than theaters," he said now, craning his neck to study the marquees. "I thought it would be the other way around. The Great White Way and all that."

"No," Juffie explained. "Most of the legitimate stages are on the cross streets. Don't tell anybody, but the Broadway houses are really off-Broadway." They were on the corner of Forty-sixth Street and she pointed east to the Lyceum. "Like that."

They paused so Frank could look at the gray limestone facade with its Roman columns, but Juffie didn't offer to take him inside, and she averted her eyes. She knew without looking that the lights over the Lyceum spelled out "Noel Coward in *Nude with a Violin*." A short while ago they'd said "Juffie Kane in *When Morning Comes*." It was less than a year, but in those few months Jason had been born and died . . . changing everything.

Karen picked up Juffie's mood. "Forget the theater, you two. Look at that." She pointed to the marquee of the Embassy Theater. "One broad flashes her bare ass on the screen for ten seconds and the whole world is dying to get in."

The movie was *And God Created Woman*, starring Brigitte Bardot. Everybody knew the film opened with a shot of Bardot's bare bottom in glorious Technicolor and CinemaScope. Which was probably why the crowd waiting for tickets stretched to the end of the block.

"A French movie, with subtitles yet," Juffie said. "A while ago Paul couldn't get an audience of a thousand a week to see a foreign picture, now they're flocking in at a thousand an hour."

"There's no better publicity than a lot of people exclaiming in shocked horror," Frank said with a chuckle. "Best thing that ever happened to this film was being banned in half the cities in America."

"Human nature," Juffie said. "I remember . . ." Whatever she had remembered went unsaid. She'd been scanning the crowd in the ticket line, amazed that it held everything from white-haired grandmother types to kids just out of short pants— even a man with a furled umbrella and a bowler hat who at that moment had turned his face toward hers.

Finky Aronson, the foreign-film fan. They were too far apart to speak, but he smiled at her and doffed his hat in silent greeting.

Juffie had to fight to tear her gaze away. He seemed to exercise a kind of morbid fascination for her, like a snake. But she didn't want him to know that. She flicked her glance to the man beside him, and was startled anew. She recognized the guy with Aronson. She couldn't put a name to the face, but she knew she knew him. He knew it too. He smiled at her. It was not a nice smile. Then he leaned forward and murmured something to Aronson.

"Let's get out of here." Juffie whispered the words fiercely, then started walking. Karen and Frank followed her.

They came to Forty-second Street. "Well, I'll be damned," Frank said gleefully. "There it is." He tipped his head back to get a good look at the huge billboard advertising Camels—the one that blew real smoke rings into the air. It was the symbol of Times Square for most of the world, Americans as well as foreigners. Foreigners. Juffie remembered. "François Fibon," she said.

"What?" Karen wasn't really paying attention, she was fascinated by the smoke rings.

"Nothing," Juffie said. "I was thinking aloud." But it wasn't nothing, it was something eerie, something that sent chills down her spine. Finky Aronson going to the movies with the French-man Paul had met in England. A man he'd denied knowing, but who had definitely unnerved him.

．　．　．　．

"So, Miss Kane, it's been a long time." Aronson was as smooth as ever. "We haven't talked since you did those little errands for me in Mexico."

"Your memory's a bit faulty," Juffie said. "You've forgotten Brownsville."

He didn't flinch. "I haven't forgotten. But we didn't actually meet then. So today is a special pleasure."

"Not for me."

Aronson smiled. He always seemed impervious to her insults, her barely masked hatred. Today he had arranged what he called a brief rendezvous, in a sleazy hamburger joint on Fifty-sixth and Seventh Avenue. He'd telephoned the morning after she'd seen him on Broadway. "I'm sorry about the ambience," he said now. "But it is completely private, isn't it? When you hear what I have to say you'll appreciate that."

"I don't want to hear what you have to say. I don't want to be in any ambience with you. I'm only sorry I ran into you yesterday."

"That was a coincidence," he said. "I might have waited a bit if you hadn't seen me with Monsieur Fibon, but sooner or later we had to have this meeting."

"I don't know who you're talking about," Juffie said. It was one of the few times in her life she'd ever delivered a line badly.

"Not worthy of you, my dear. Both François and I knew instantly that you'd recognized him."

There wasn't any point in denying it again. "I'm not your dear," she said instead.

Finky stirred his weak tea with lemon. Juffie had refused to order anything. "Are you your husband's dear?" he asked softly. "That's much more to the point."

Her head shot up in a startled gesture she couldn't prevent. She'd never doubted Paul would enlist the aid of his mobster friends to keep her in line, but she hadn't thought he'd done so already. She hadn't made a move to rid herself of him, so why was he bringing out the big guns?

"You look puzzled," Aronson said softly. The whole conversation was being conducted in whispers, though there was almost no one else in the place. "Perhaps I should explain that Paul knows nothing of our meeting today."

"Then what are we doing here?" Juffie spat out the words. "What does that Frenchman have to do with anything?"

"Ah, yes," Aronson said with a voluptuous sigh of satisfaction. "Most fortuitous that part. Perhaps I should begin at the beginning. It's rather a long story, Miss Kane. I suggest you make yourself comfortable. A cup of coffee perhaps?"

"I don't want anything," Juffie said dully. But she did, she wanted to get up and walk out. Only she didn't dare. Maybe he was going to produce more pictures. Like that night so long ago, when he'd shown her the one of Myer carrying a banner for the Young Communist League.

"I have some information," Aronson said. "François told me an interesting story."

She clasped her hands on the table and took some small satisfaction in the fact that her fingers weren't trembling. "What story? What does it have to do with me?"

She found herself waiting breathlessly for him to speak, caught up in the process Finky Aronson had set in train. Unable to stop it, though she knew she was sinking deeper into some nameless mire with each passing second.

"I don't suppose you've ever heard of Oberst Klaus Warnheim, a captain in the Gestapo." The unctuous voice lingered lovingly over the word Gestapo.

Juffie felt his eyes studying her from under dropped lids. She was wearing a white linen skirt and a sleeveless blue blouse. A cool outfit for a hot and humid day. But she didn't feel cool. There was no air-conditioning in the restaurant. Her clothes were sticking to her flesh. She could feel perspiration dripping down her back. Which was very odd, since there was a lump of ice in her stomach. "No, I've never heard of him," she said.

"A much-talked-about man, Oberst Warnheim. He disappeared in forty-five, but he's wanted in at least three countries to stand trial for what I believe are called crimes against humanity. Deporting people to the death camps, that sort of thing."

"That can't have anything to do with Paul," she said, feeling a frisson of hope. "He was a member of the Maquis, the French Resistance."

"Indeed," Aronson agreed. "A valuable member of the Maquis, because he'd been conscripted to work for the Nazi high command at Fontainebleau."

"How do you know that?" The details had never been published, he couldn't have read them anywhere. "Fibon . . ." she said tentatively.

"Exactly. Monsieur Fibon was also in the Maquis. But, you see, they sold them out. François and Paul both worked for the Gestapo as well as for the Maquis. You might say the Gestapo was a higher loyalty. Herr Oberst Warnheim paid better. So both young men systematically passed him information about the Resistance."

She knew the nausea she felt must have shown in her face, that he was watching her and saw it. No, enjoyed it. That's why he went on. "Think of it, all those brave young men and women fighting the great Nazi war machine with little more than their wits. And Paul telling the Gestapo who was a member, where they would strike next, which farms and houses they considered safe . . ."

"You haven't any proof," she said. But why this rush to defend him, this wifely concern? Because she wasn't defending Paul, just herself. And even with no time to think it through she knew it was she who was being attacked through her husband.

Aronson shrugged. "I don't think we're talking about legal proof." He pushed away his empty teacup and she noted how carefully manicured his nails were. "Funny how life works out, isn't it?" he said. "Both Paul and François went in the same direction. Unbeknownst to each other, of course. Recently I happened to have some business involving Marseilles. That's where Fibon lives now, as it happens. A respected businessman, and incidentally a member of our organization. I mentioned Paul's name, merely telling one Frenchman about another, casual talk. Then I heard this fascinating story."

"That Paul had been a traitor." She spoke the words tonelessly, but it wasn't really shock that numbed her with horror. The most terrible thing was that she had no difficulty believing the story. The boy collaborator had grown up to be a man who would use his wife as a decoy in a gangland murder. And it was just after they met Fibon in England that Paul rushed back to New York and sold her jewelry to raise money. So Fibon must have been blackmailing him, at least until he found out that they were on the same side yet again. "They got away with it entirely, didn't they?" There seemed no point in a continued pretext to defend him.

"Not exactly." Aronson lit a small cigar before he continued. "Fibon was never suspected, but poor Paul wasn't so lucky. It seems a few people guessed he'd been double-crossing the Resistance. So in forty-four, right after the liberation of Paris, the Dumont vineyards were destroyed, torn up by some men from the village. They even poisoned the ground with salt so it couldn't be replanted."

He looked around for an ashtray, but there was none. Aronson flicked a bit of ash into the saucer of the teacup, too fastidious to drop it on the floor. "Paul's father tried to stop them, so they shot him. His sisters were both stripped and had their heads shaved in the village square, then they were buried in cow dung and left to dig their own way out. Apparently that's a local form of revenge." Like a sociologist commenting on the customs of some obscure tribe. But he was a man who knew all about revenge. *Cosa nostra* were experts at it.

"Afterwards the surviving Dumonts were shunned," he continued. "That's also part of the custom. The village acted as if they didn't exist. I'm told that later the two women moved away, but they don't really concern us, do they?"

"No," Juffie said. "They don't concern us." What was it Paul had told her? "My family were killed by the Nazis. Something happened in the village and they wanted to make an example."

An explanation containing a germ of truth, like everything else he'd said. "And Paul?" she asked. "How did he escape the Maquis's revenge?"

"Ah yes, very enterprising. He simply went to an American base and asked for asylum. He found somebody in intelligence and offered a lot of information in exchange for protection and an eventual ticket to New York. I'm told it was done quite frequently."

"Yes." Juffie murmured. "Very enterprising. He even got to see *Anchors Aweigh*."

Aronson looked puzzled. "The movie?"

Juffie shook her head. "It has nothing to do with anything, it doesn't matter. Okay, you've laid it all out. Now tell me why."

"I'm not quite sure yet," Aronson said. "And if you hadn't happened to see us last night, I probably wouldn't have told you yet. But as it is, well, I thought it best to explain that . . . how shall I put it? The books are open again, my dear. And there's a debit on your side. After all, your public really wouldn't approve of your being married to a Nazi, would they? So my silence is valuable. And I'm a businessman, as you know. I don't give valuable things away for free."

.   .   .   .   .

It took a couple of days for the full horror to build. Then she exploded. In the kitchen, on Sunday afternoon. The air was heavy with the threat of a thunderstorm. She'd been jumpy for the past forty-eight hours, but she felt worse today. This was the kind of weather that always set her teeth on edge. And, because Karen was out somewhere with Frank Carlucci, it was the first time that she and Paul were home alone since her meeting with Aronson.

She was standing at the sink, filling the percolator, when Paul came up behind her. She stiffened as soon as she heard his footsteps, and when he ran his finger along the back of her neck she shivered with revulsion. "Don't touch me."

"*Chérie*, it's been a long time." His tone changed when she didn't respond. "I'm your husband for Christ's sake."

The water kept running into the coffeepot. It overflowed onto her hands and she couldn't make herself move to turn off the faucet. It seemed as if she could see her grandfather's face. Benny Kane was looking at her with such reproach, such disappointment. And Myer. She dropped the pot in the sink and spun around to face him. "Bastard! You lousy Nazi bastard!"

"Juffie, what the hell are you talking about? What's going on?" He reached out and she thought he was going to touch her again and she shrank away, but he was merely turning off the faucet. "I don't know what you're talking about," he said again.

But she could see it in his eyes. All of it. The whole ugly truth. "They were put in concentration camps, gassed to death, burned up in ovens," she shouted. "And you made it happen! You helped them. You're scum, Paul Dumont. You don't deserve to be alive." Her hands were actually fumbling on the counter, looking for a weapon. A knife, a fork, anything . . . He didn't move, didn't say anything. Just stared at her.

She clasped her arms around herself as if she were freezing, made herself stop imagining murder. "Get out, go away so I don't have to look at you." Not screaming now, whispering.

For a long time Paul still didn't move. Then he shrugged. "How do you know?" And when she didn't answer, "Fibon, I suppose. He talked to you."

She shook her head. "No, he told Aronson."

"And Aronson told you. Shit! He's really got us by the balls now."

Astonishment took away every other emotion. "That's all you can say? That's what you're thinking about? That Finky Aronson and *cosa nostra* have us by the balls? Six million people died horrible deaths and you—"

"Shut up," he interrupted. "Spare me the morality lecture. You weren't there. You don't know what it was like."

"I know there were hundreds of people, no, thousands, who didn't sell out. But not Paul Dumont. Not the smart operator who always has his eye on the main chance. You're despicable, you make me sick. Go away," she said again.

He stared at her for a few seconds, then turned and left. Juffie didn't move until she heard the front door open and shut. After that her legs wouldn't hold her any longer. She slid down the wall and crumpled in a sobbing heap on the shiny clean kitchen floor.

Eventually she stumbled into the bedroom and locked the door and made her way into the shower and stood there for what seemed like hours. She felt slimy, contaminated with his filth. But no amount of soap and water could make her clean. Finally she turned off the taps and returned to the bedroom. The storm broke then. It was immediately overhead. Almost no time separated the thunder from the lightning which rent the sky in jagged blue-white flashes.

At ten she heard someone come in and she stiffened and clenched her fists. A moment later she recognized Karen's high-heeled tread, and she relaxed, but didn't go out to meet her. She couldn't face Karen just yet. Not until she decided what, if anything, to tell her. And she couldn't know that until she decided what to do.

She fell into a restless sleep that lasted until sometime in the dead of night when she was wakened by the turning of the bedroom doorknob. Paul. Trying to get in. "Juffie, wake up. Juffie . . ."

He waited a few moments. She imagined she could hear him breathing. Then he moved away. And after the threat was less immediate she began to tremble.

Control. She had to find some control or it would always be like this. She had to find some way to live with what she knew. Because she had no choice. It was precisely as Paul had said. Finky Aronson had her by the balls. He owned her, body and soul. With a few words he could take from her the only thing she had left that mattered, her gift, her talent, and the opportunity to share it. *Cosa nostra* had finally taken ultimate possession, they'd finished the job they started when she was eleven years old—no, before she was born.

At dawn she got up and dressed. A black dress and a black headband holding her hair and black patent pumps. As if she were going to a funeral. Her own.

The door to Karen's room was closed and presumably Paul was sleeping somewhere in the apartment, in his study most likely. She didn't check, just let herself out.

Juffie walked for hours. Hundreds of blocks and God knows how many miles. Around her the city came awake and began its day, but she didn't notice. Shortly after noon she found herself in the Village and faint with hunger. She went into a coffee shop and ordered toast and eggs, but when the food came it made her ill. Still, she managed to eat a few bites. Then she walked some more.

Thinking, thinking. Trying desperately to find something to salvage from the mess that was her life. God, she needed . . .

What? What did she need? She knew. She'd known for a long time. So it wasn't surprising that when she looked around her, clear-eyed for the first time in hours, she realized that she was at Grand Central on Forty-third and Lexington. Instinct had led her here. Back to the only safety and the only joy.

She went into the terminal and found a telephone. "Matt, it's me. Are you very busy?"

"No more than usual. How are you? What's up?"

"I'm okay. At least I think I am, but I need to talk to you. And it won't be a fast conversation."

"Let's see, it's four now, give me half an hour and I'll get clear of business. Do you want to come here?"

"No." She laughed softly. "I'll meet you under the clock at the Biltmore."

·   ·   ·   ·

"We've never been here together," she told him when they were seated in a dark corner of the Biltmore cocktail lounge. "I've been here with Paul, but never with you. Isn't that strange?"

"There are lots of places we've never been together," he said softly. "What's happened, Juffie?"

"Wait. I'll tell you that part later. First I want to ask a question. Will you have an affair with me, Matt darling? That sordid, secretive liaison you told me years ago you'd never settle for, would it be possible now?"

"I told you I'd never let you settle for it. I don't see that anything's any different. I'm a widower, but you're still married."

"But when you first said it you thought I had a reasonably happy marriage. I told you myself that it was working. Now things are different. I hate Paul, and he no longer cares much for me."

He leaned forward and took her hand. "Juffie, listen, sweetheart, this is all just because you've had such a blow. You and Paul have to find your way back from the agony of losing Jason. When you do, it will be like it was before."

"No, that's glib and easy, but it's not true. I've felt the way I do for a long time. I wouldn't face it while I was pregnant with Paul's child, and after Jason was born I couldn't see how I could reject his father. But it's not just because Jason's gone, that's not the only thing that's changed my mind."

"It is. You just think it isn't."

"No." She took a deep breath. "Paul was a Nazi during the war, or near enough so that it makes no difference."

"What? That's crazy. Juffie, that's the craziest thing I ever heard. Paul's a French hero, he—"

"Don't say it," she interrupted. "Don't waste your breath. I know all the lines. But I know something else too. He was a collaborator. He was a member of the Resistance, but he sold them out, gave information to the Gestapo."

"Jesus," he said softly. "Jesus Christ. You're sure it's true?"

"Very sure. He admitted it." She couldn't meet his eyes, afraid he'd see in them the full horror of the scene with Paul, all that hate and despair.

A waitress came by and Matt gestured to his empty glass. Juffie's was still half full. Neither of them spoke until his refill came. Finally Juffie broke the silence. "Well, how about it? Can I have the part of your mistress, Mr. Varley? I had the lead in my high school play."

"No."

"I knew it. That's what I get for lying. I was never in a play in high school. Not until I got to college. Matt, why not, for Christ's sake? I love you and you love me. Why aren't we entitled to a little happiness?"

"That's not happiness, it's a ticket to short-term bliss and long-term misery. I've had that ride before, Juffie. It's not the one I paid for, but it's what I got." He drew rings on the Formica-topped table with the wet bottom of his glass. "I keep waiting for you to mention divorce. How come you're not saying it, Juffie? How come you're not suggesting you'll divorce Paul? Afraid of what it may do to your career?"

She sucked in air, as if he'd hit her. "A little maybe, but there's much more to it."

"What more? You can't expect me to understand unless you tell me."

She gripped her now empty glass with both hands, staring into it as if it contained the answers to all the questions about life and the universe. "Get a room," she said when at last she spoke. "Go over to the desk and register for a room."

"Juffie, what's that going to solve? I want to, of course I do, but . . ."

"Just shut up for once, will you? As you've said, I have to tell you the rest of it. I can't do it here. So please, this time do it my way."

"Mr. and Mrs. Matthew Varley" he wrote on the register. "Any luggage, Mr. Varley?" the desk clerk asked.

"No. My office is across the street. I'm a lawyer. I find I have to spend the night in town unexpectedly. My wife will join me later."

"Of course, sir. Eight forty-six. I'll have the bellman show you up."

"No need," Matt said, taking the key. "I can find my way."

Juffie was watching and she followed him into the elevator. A few people stared at her, obviously recognized her, then looked hastily away. The crib death of the son of Juffie Kane had been in all the newspapers. Most people were unlikely to plead for an autograph at this moment.

"Having an assignation with you is about as secret as taking an ad in the *Times*," he said when they got into the room. He threw the key on the dresser and walked to one of the two windows and turned on the air-conditioner. "Do you want me to call for something to drink?"

"No, I think I'd better do this cold turkey." She sat down on the edge of one of the twin beds. He came to join her, but she stopped him. "No, sit over there, on the other one. I think you'll be happier there after I say what I have to say." She pulled off the black band holding her hair back and shook the long waves free.

Matt took off his jacket and loosened his tie, then he stretched out on the bed across from her. "Okay, we're both stripped for action. I'm ready whenever you are. Only tell me, do I leave the two dollars on the dresser or give you the money now?"

"Don't make jokes, this isn't funny."

"I didn't really think it was," he said softly. "Take your time. I'll shut up and wait."

Juffie took a deep breath. "Paul's in thick with the rackets. A guy named Aronson, a very big wheel in *cosa nostra*. Do you know what that is?"

He shook his head and she translated. "It's Italian, it means 'our thing,' but it's not just Italians. *Cosa nostra* is what people really mean when they talk about the mob or the Syndicate. But if you know them from the inside and you use that phrase, you're saying a lot more. It's a blood brotherhood, and once you're in you don't get out. You can maybe retire with honor, like my grandfather did after he got out of prison. But that's only because he never did anything to make them mad. Usually once you're in, you're in until you die."

"You seem to know a lot about it."

"That's not news. You know I know a lot about it. Anyway, they own Paul body and soul. Aronson for one, and probably a few others whose names I don't know. It all fits with the Nazi thing. Paul's weak, he has to have success, play on what he perceives as the winning side. They offered easy money and he took it. That's one reason I can never divorce Paul. If he doesn't want it, and he doesn't, they won't let me do it. The other one is—"

She stopped speaking and clasped her hands in her lap and stared at them. Matt didn't say a word.

"The other reason is that *cosa nostra* owns me too. In a sense that's how Paul got started. I led him to it. I didn't realize it at the time, but I did."

"Because of your family?" Matt asked quietly. "They own you because of your family? Is that what you mean?"

"No, not just that. For one thing, because they know about Paul and the Gestapo. Finky Aronson told me, in fact. And if he makes that story public, I won't be able to set foot on any stage in the world. On top of everything that's been said about me in the past, well, that would really finish it."

He started to say something but she held up her hand to stop him. "Wait, you haven't heard it all yet. Years ago you asked me if I was working for the mob and I told you I wasn't. That was the truth at the time. But I've done it since." She was crying, tears ran down her cheeks, but she made no tearful sounds, simply went on speaking.

"That's why I was in Mexico. I was a courier for Aronson. That quack doctor was selling him pure heroin, and I brought it back across the border. I did it three times. The time we met was the second. That's what the men in the speedboat were delivering, Matt. Pure heroin for me to bring back to America, so Finky Aronson and his hoods could cut it and sell it and make people—mostly kids—into drug addicts. Isn't that terrific?"

"Why?" His voice was hoarse and harsh. "Why the hell did you do it?"

"Because Paul was in hock up to his eyebrows, he needed half a million to stay alive, and that was the only way he could get it.

But not only that. It was when things were pretty tough for me, too, and he convinced me that if we went bankrupt and were on the street and seen to be losers, it wouldn't help me to make a comeback. I don't know which was the bigger reason, my need or Paul's. But I'd be lying if I didn't say that mine was part of it.

"Oh, and I almost forgot, the night I didn't show up to get my Tony, when I played Vegas, that was for Aronson too. Only that time he had a picture of my father from 1930. He was in a parade with something called the Young Communist League. Aronson threatened to send it to McCarthy or the House Un-American Activities Committee."

"That's different," Matt said instantly. "That I can understand. Why the hell didn't you tell me that when it happened?"

"Because I'd also have to tell you how Aronson got involved with me in the beginning." She explained about the backing for *A Small Miracle* and Vinnie Faldo.

"The guys who scared you to death and cut up your clothes?" Matt asked.

"The very same. But a little later Faldo sold my paper to Aronson. It wasn't real paper, not a signed contract, but with them it comes to the same thing."

"Tell me something, Juffie." His voice had gone hard now. It was brittle and edged with something she'd never heard, not from Matt. "Have you ever told me the straight truth about anything?"

"About most things," she whispered. "All the things that really mattered. Only not about the mob, because I knew you'd look at me the way you're looking now. There's another story, you'd better know about it too." She told him about Brownsville.

"That time Paul set me up. I really did have nothing to do with it. But that doesn't matter, I got spirited away from the scene of the crime, and I didn't report it. Legally I'm an accessory to murder. So it's one more way they sink their claws into me."

"That's all?" he asked finally. "That's absolutely all?"

"Yes. That's everything."

"And your solution to this stinking mess is that you and I become lovers? We have a nice little secret affair, and you go on being Mrs. Paul Dumont in the meantime? That's what you brought me up here to ask?"

She fished in her bag for a tissue, finally acknowledging that she was crying. "It was all I could think of. It seemed like the only

way. At least I'd get a little happiness out of the rest of my life."
She hesitated. "I thought it would make you happy too. A little
happy anyway. But I wouldn't do it without telling you the truth.
Because anything that touches me gets tainted sooner or later. I
wouldn't expose you to that if you didn't know."

It had grown dark while they spoke. Outside on Forty-third
the lights of the city were coming on. Matt got off the bed and
went to the window that wasn't plugged shut by the air-
conditioner and threw it open. He planted his hands on the sill
and gazed down at the street. The sounds of traffic invaded the
room along with the hot humid air. "Come here," he said after a
moment.

Juffie had kicked off her shoes sometime during her long
recital. She padded across the carpet in her stocking feet and stood
next to him. He didn't touch her. "Look down there, Juffie. What
do you see?"

"The same thing you see, Manhattan. All the lights and all the
action. The big time, as they say."

"Yes, that's what they say. And you own it, at least you own a
big piece of it. You're Juffie Kane, top lady on the totem pole in
your particular business, which happens to be one that most of
the world watches avidly and salivates over. And the thing is, like
you told me the day we met, you didn't get there because of your
looks. You are a great and rare talent. So if you want to, if you're
willing to make all the compromises necessary, you will doubtless
stay on top until you have to play little old ladies coming onstage
with a cane. You'll be terrific, no doubt about it. They're going to
love you until you die or quit, Juffie. But what I'm wondering, is
that enough?"

"No," she said quickly. "That's why we're up here, that's why
I've gone through all this. I love you. I want us to be together
however we can. I've done a lot of terrible things, Matt. I just got
through admitting them to the person whose opinion matters
most to me in the world. But I've paid for my sins, at least a little."

She leaned against the windowframe, looking at his profile. It
wasn't perfect, not like Paul's, but it was beloved. "You know
what I think?" she whispered, wrenching the words from someplace deep inside. "I think the reason I lost Jason was a kind of
reparation, a sort of justice. The mothers of children lost to drugs
maybe, paying me back."

"Maybe," he said. He walked back to the bed. She stayed where she was, gazing into the street. "Juffie," he called softly. "Juffie, turn around and face me."

She did. They looked at each other in silence for long seconds. "I love you," he said finally. "I love you more than anything else in the world. And I don't care what mistakes you've made. I'm not in the judgment business. If I can have you, I don't give a damn about anything else."

"Matt, oh, Matt . . ." She started to move toward him.

"Wait a minute," he said, stopping her progress. "I'm not finished. I have one more question. Do you love me that much, Juffie? Enough so it's the most important thing in the world and everything else is secondary?"

"Of course everything else is secondary. How could you think anything else?"

"I can think it because I know you. I mean *everything* else, Juffie. Your career, for a start. Would you give that up? If necessary, would you be willing never to set foot on a stage again, any kind of a stage? Because that's how it may have to be if we're going to be together for the rest of our lives, have something resembling a normal life."

"But why? I don't understand. What does my acting have to do with our being together?"

"This thing you're calling *cosa* whatever, the mob. You've got to get clean of them, you've got to tough it out, sweetheart. I won't settle for part of you, Juffie, I want it all. I won't share you with a bunch of lousy hoods who can make you jump through hoops every time they wag a finger. The only hope for us is for you to tell this Aronson character to go fuck himself. And leave Paul, maybe even blow the whistle on him. Then we get you a bodyguard again. You might have to go into hiding for a while. Maybe even go to the FBI for help and protection. Sooner or later all of that's bound to make the papers. And as you said, you may well wind up a pariah as far as Broadway is concerned."

She didn't answer right away. Matt watched her. After a bit he said, "Tell me now, Juffie. This isn't something you weigh up and think over. This is something you reach into your gut for. Either walk out of here now, or tell me you love me enough to maybe give up what I know has been as necessary to you as air to breathe. And if you do, you'd better mean it. There isn't going to be any turning back."

She stood where she was, a few feet from him, for what seemed a long time. When she moved it wasn't toward Matt. Juffie walked to the bed she'd been sitting on. She picked up her bag and slipped her feet into the black patent leather pumps she'd removed earlier. Then she looked at him wordlessly one more time, and started for the door.

She'd almost reached it, had actually extended her hand to the knob, when she stopped. "I can't," she whispered. "I can't lose you. I don't care what it costs or what I have to do."

She flung the bag to the floor and hurtled herself into the waiting arms that ached for her.

.　.　.　.

It might have worked the way Matt envisioned it—if it were not for Verbier and the avalanche.

Chapter 20

*J*uffie perched on the corner of Matt's desk, one long leg swinging idly, pretending a casualness she didn't feel. Matt didn't feel casual either. The office bristled with the tension between them.

As always, the place was littered with scripts. She picked one up. It was a play by William Gibson, called *Two for the Seesaw*. Gibson's agent had clipped his card to the front and added a brief note: "Perfect for Juffie Kane, we only hope you and she agree."

"When did this come in?" Juffie asked.

"A few days ago."

She flipped it open. A romantic comedy for two characters, the kind of tour de force an actress dreams of. "Good?"

"Excellent." Matt fussed with his pipe and didn't look at her. "Bound to be a huge hit." He paused, then reached out and took the script from her hands, his eyes at last meeting hers. "I've told them you're sorry, but you're still not ready to think about a new production. Juffie," he said softly, "we said no turning back, remember? You can't take a part until you clean up your act. It's just not fair to start a show before you get your life straightened out."

"I know."

"Okay, so when are you going to do it? It's been a month. Have you spoken to Paul?"

"Not yet. I meant to in the last couple of days. I didn't have a chance," she added quickly, seeing his disappointment. "He hasn't come home since last Wednesday. I think he has a bit of something on the side."

"Not surprising. Do you care?"

"Are you crazy? Of course I don't care."

"Okay. Look, you don't owe Dumont any explanations. Move out. I'll get you somewhere to stay. Jersey maybe, someplace in the boondocks where he'll never find you. Then we can set things up with Pinkerton's and you can let the racketeers know you're through, and that they can't use you anymore."

She was listening to him, but not really listening, watching his face. God, she loved him so damned much. And he was so intent on this. So sure his was the right way to do it. He was still talking, pacing the office while he spoke. Juffie put herself in his path, raised her mouth to be kissed. They clung together. Just being in Matt's arms was bliss. What would it be like to live with him, to have breakfast with him every day, to cook his dinners and go to bed each night beside him? Heaven. That's what it would be like.

"It will work." He murmured the words against her cheek. "It will work, sweetheart. As long as you don't get cold feet and chicken out on me."

It wasn't cold feet. Nor even that she might never act again. It was deeper and more complex than that. Matt called doing it his way toughing it out, but it was really giving in to them. Finky Aronson and Paul Dumont were going to drive her into hiding, they were going to take away what had been the center of her existence. They would have won. But not entirely. She would get something in return, something marvelous. Juffie pressed closer to Matt and tightened her grip.

"Okay?" he asked, feeling the tremors she couldn't suppress.

"Yes . . . no, not okay. I feel a great need to lie down, Mr. Varley. Would you care to lie down beside me? On that couch perhaps?"

"Mmm," he said. "Sounds like a terrific idea." Then, before things got really serious, "All these years as an agent and I've finally found out what they mean by a casting couch."

She giggled. Then the laughter turned to wordless joy. For a brief time there was no need to think about the mob or Nazis or bodyguards; nor the fact that Matt really had no idea how tough it was going to be. He didn't, for instance, realize that he, too, would be at risk. Aronson and his people were bound to know about Matt. They knew everything. And he'd be another way to pressure her. . . .

Later, alone in her own bed, that's what Juffie thought about. How dangerous it was to do what Matt suggested. What was it Pa had told her so long ago? "Once you buy from these guys, you're a customer for life." Oh, Matt. You think you're so smart, but in this league you're a kid in short pants.

Four more days went by and she still didn't do anything. "You're vacillating," Matt said accusingly.

"No, I'm not. But I need time to get everything sorted out."

Time. It felt as if each day were something she'd stolen from a pile of forbidden goodies. And there was so much anger inside her. Why did the bad guys have to win? Why had they been able to put her in this position? No, that wasn't accurate. She put herself in the position. They were capitalizing on it. But that still meant they won.

It went on like that until Monday, the twenty-fifth of September, when her telephone rang at four in the afternoon. "Miss Kane, sorry to disturb you, but there's a small favor you could do for me."

Juffie gripped the receiver until her knuckles went white. Finky Aronson was still speaking, not interested in anything she might have to say. "It's a very small favor really. I have some important guests coming from the West Coast. Hollywood people. They'd be delighted to meet you. I'm giving a dinner for them at my home here in Brooklyn. I'd like you to join us, perhaps act as hostess. Saturday night. I'll send a car for you at six. Will that be convenient, my dear?"

"No. It is definitely not convenient. I don't want to come to your party, much less be your hostess."

There was a moment's pause. "I think this conversation is about what I want, not what you want." And when she didn't answer. "Isn't it, Miss Kane?"

Juffie mumbled something and hung up.

She walked slowly into her kitchen and made a cup of tea. She thought for a long time. She had, after all, a great deal to think about. And in the end she reached a decision. Life was about making choices. She had to make one now, and really there was only one possibility. Because she knew things no one else suspected. Not even Matt.

Juffie disappeared on Friday morning. She left behind four letters. The ones for Karen and Paul, like the one she sent to her father, said that she was going to Europe because she needed some time alone to finally come to terms with losing Jason. She'd be in touch and they were not to worry about her. To Matt she wrote, "I'm going away for a time, my darling. Because I have to do this my way. Please trust me, and remember how much I love you."

．　．　．　．

Karen was surprised and a little hurt. It was odd that Juffie would take off like that, not even talk to her about it. But there wasn't time to brood, her own life was very full at the moment.

She'd started work at Lenox Hill Hospital. And she was loving it. And Frank had called to say he was thinking of moving to New York. Which delighted her more than she had imagined it might. So there wasn't a lot of time to worry. Besides, she was convinced that basically Juffie's head was straight. Whatever she was doing now, it didn't seem to Karen to be part of a pathology.

"I'll try to get out of here next week," she told Paul. "I'm looking for an apartment, but it's not easy to find something I can afford."

"What's your hurry?" he asked, dismissing her protests with a gesture. "This place is certainly big enough for two. Stay until you get a little money saved. It will be easier to make the move after you've been working for a while."

At first she tried to stay out of Paul's way. Most of the time he was sullen and morose and not very pleasant company. Moreover, he was involved in some sort of business deal that kept him out of the penthouse from early morning until late at night. That kept them apart until a week after Juffie left. Karen's schedule called for her to be at the hospital only half a day on Fridays. She got back to the penthouse at noon—and found Paul sitting in the living room.

"You're home early," she said. "No meetings today?"

"No more meetings. I had three between seven and ten A.M. I decided that was enough for one day. I wanted to come home, so I did. I've been waiting for you. I thought maybe we'd do something."

"Oh? What?" She sat in one of the chintz-covered chairs, kicking off her shoes and stretching out her legs and wiggling her toes.

"I'm not sure. Something that's fun and different. I think we could both use a break." Paul rose from the couch. His royal blue velour bathrobe was striped in red, it was short and tightly tied around his waist. Karen could see the matted black hair on his chest. "I just had a shower," he said. "I bet you could use one too. But first let me get you a cold drink."

She arched her head back and rubbed her neck. "Sounds nice. A Coke maybe."

"Not a Coke. I made one of my specials. Here, try it."

It was pale pink and full of ice and the glass was frosted. Karen took a sip. "Delicious, what is it?"

"Grenadine and grapefruit juice."

She tasted it again. "And something else. What?"

"Champagne, and a touch of brandy."

He poured some of the cocktail for himself. Refilling a glass, Karen noted, not starting a new one. "You're ahead of me."

"A little. I had to make sure it was good."

"It's good."

She drank almost the whole thing. Paul lifted the pitcher. "Let me top you up."

·　·　·　·

Juffie walked slowly, savoring the unique qualities of this strange time of waiting, of being suspended between two lives and two worlds. There was a special smell to the Swiss forest, something she'd never experienced anywhere else. Not that she'd done much forest walking. There weren't a lot of pine trees on Broadway, or in Newton, for that matter. Not that she was going too rustic.

She laughed at herself when she thought about it, imagine going for a walk in the woods and carrying a shoulder bag with your passport and your Actors Equity card. She had to stop being so paranoid. She kept worrying that she'd turn a corner and Finky Aronson would be facing her and she'd have to run, so she wouldn't move without her papers. Silly. Aronson had no reason to follow her, not yet. Anyway, he wasn't the type to go walking alone in the woods. Ah, but until a few days ago, neither was she.

She stayed on the marked paths, the ones indicated as good for children and old people, where the walking was easy. In that impeccably efficient way the Swiss had, each path was graded for difficulty. They really did make this place a tourist's paradise. She'd decided that as soon as she arrived, so when she heard the noise it seemed an affront.

There was a sudden great howling in the air, a rushing, thundering roar that made her press her hands over her ears. And what she thought was: how strange of these people to allow this, the visitors certainly won't like it.

.   .   .   .

Somehow Paul had maneuvered himself behind Karen. He was rubbing her neck and her shoulders. His fingers were incredibly strong and clever, they found the right muscles, the ones that ached from the tension of the new job, and he manipulated them in wonderful ways. Karen sighed with pleasure. "There's a spot here," he said, putting his thumbs at the juncture of her scalp and her neck, "that makes your whole body tingle if you apply pressure. Have I got it?"

"Yes. Mmm . . . that's heaven." She pulled forward slightly, a little embarrassed by his touch and her response. "Thank you, that makes me feel like a new woman."

"Shh, sit back and enjoy it. Two minutes isn't enough time to relax, a massage isn't really effective until the muscles are conditioned to respond."

.   .   .   .

It took only seconds for Armageddon to happen. The roar preceded all, but almost before Juffie realized that this attack of sound was nothing manmade, rocks and tree limbs started hurtling through the air. Small things first, a shower of debris in advance of the great mass which was careening down the mountain.

She clasped her head with her arms and screamed, terrified, though she did not yet know how justified was terror. There was a great boulder embedded in the earth to her right, a mighty lump of granite as tall as a two-story building, placed by some retreating glacier eons before time. It slanted slightly outward at the top; there was a small declivity at ground level. She pressed herself into that tiny space. In her ignorance she sought shelter beneath the very thing that would batter her to a pulp when it was smashed by the oncoming rush of ice and mud and rocks and trees.

.   .   .   .

Most men, Karen realized later, would have made their move in ten, maybe fifteen minutes. If he'd done that, she'd still have been in sufficient possession of her senses to reject him. Because he was mixed up with the mob, a racketeer, and, she'd been convinced for some time, an all-around bastard—and whatever else, Juffie's husband. But by the time Paul's touch became overtly sexual he'd been massaging her for an hour.

She was jelly, absolutely limp with relaxation. Every muscle in her shoulders and her back and her arms and her legs had been soothed free of every possible kink.

She was lying on the couch on her stomach by then, but she was still fully clothed. When he put his hands on her buttocks she felt his touch through the cotton skirt of her dress and the nylon of her underpants. It heightened the sensation rather than diluting it. Karen didn't object, she was long past objections, long past saying a word. He pressed down, she was intensely aware of her vulva sinking deeper into the yielding fabric of the cushions. Then he slipped one hand beneath her from the side, and it was he she was pressing against, not the sofa.

That was it, he just applied pressure—hard at first, then released, then hard again. She was getting dizzy, there was a ringing in her ears. Paul laughed softly, as if he heard it too. Press, release, press, release. She moaned and strained toward his hand, adding her motions to his. Her torso was pumping up and down on the couch. There was a storm building within her and she wanted desperately for it to break. But it didn't.

Her body was soaked with the perspiration of her effort when he picked her up and carried her to the bedroom. Not the one she was using, his. And Juffie's. The yellow quilt was turned back, the embroidered sheets were cool and crisp and inviting. He lay her on them and began unbuttoning the bodice of her shirtwaist dress.

Karen didn't say a word, she kept staring at him. He looked very serious, very intent.

"You've never had an orgasm, have you?" He whispered the words and somehow they sounded seductive, not clinical. "It's time you did. Relax and let me do everything."

"I shouldn't be—"

"Shh, you should. I'm giving you a gift. You have only to lie here and accept it."

She was naked by now, every nerve alive, every inch of skin tingling. He still wore the robe, and he didn't lie down, he sat beside her. Gently he spread her legs. "Don't move," he whispered. "Stay like that. Open to me." He took her wrists and clasped them with one hand. "See, you can't move, you're my prisoner. So you're not responsible, you don't have to resist because you can't."

His fingers were doing incredible things, unbelievable things. They were rubbing and pulling and pinching—and he'd not yet put them inside her once. It was absolutely concentrated attention directed to one small spot about half an inch in diameter. It made her want to scream; it was so intense it almost hurt. It did hurt. She arched toward him, vaguely wanting to spread the sensations over a wider area of her flesh. But he didn't comply; instead, he increased the tempo of his touch and the pressure behind it. It was harder and faster and deeper. And the dam broke.

She arched higher and shuddered and gasped aloud in a sound that turned into a long moan. "Very good," he said when she was still. His face still wore that grave, absorbed expression. "You were a very good girl. No, don't close your legs. We've only just begun, Karen." He was still holding her wrists and he tightened his grip. "Remember, you're my prisoner. You aren't responsible."

She entered into the game because she wanted to. Later she'd admit that to herself. She could have broken free of him at any moment and he was unlikely to have used physical force to restrain her. That wasn't Paul's style, he was much too subtle. Instead, he found the right button and he pushed it. Let the barriers down, said a voice in her head. Might as well since you have no alternative. There is no guilt because you have no choice.

As an introductory lesson it was quite a revelation, an advanced degree course taken in the space of a few hours. It was shortly before four when Paul stretched himself with satisfaction and lightly smacked her rump. "Okay, you are now a real woman. I lost track of your orgasms after three."

"I don't know what to say," Karen murmured. "I don't know what to say."

"Try thank you. No, don't. I don't require thanks. It was the best time I've had in years. There is absolutely no pleasure to match watching a woman come for the first time. I loved it as much as you did, maybe more. We'll have to do it again soon."

And that's when he got up and went to the kitchen and came

back with the two Baccarat wineglasses and the bottle of chilled vintage Taittinger's. And when he turned on the shortwave radio, because it was time for the news on the BBC.

. . . .

The echo of the words seemed to hang in the air. "There's been an avalanche in the Swiss village of Verbier; among those missing and feared dead is the celebrated American actress, Juffie Kane."

Karen kept watching Paul, even while she tried to sort out her own feelings. His face betrayed a whole range of emotions. Shock first, stunned disbelief, then his eyes went moist and his jaw became slack. Was he crying for Juffie, or was it just self-pity? She wasn't sure and there wasn't time to think about it. She had to take charge or she'd soon have a hysterical man on her hands.

"Go take a shower," she told him. "I'll make a few phone calls. But we have to get up and get dressed. We can't be like this if anybody comes."

It was the sort of appeal he understood, as she suspected he would. A man for whom the image meant more than the reality— just as Juffie said. She waited until she heard the water running in the bathroom, then picked up the telephone and began dialing. She knew Matt's number. He had given it to her right after Juffie left, and he'd made her promise to call him instantly if she heard anything. She wasn't sure why, but she knew that she had to speak to Matt before she could do anything else.

Her hands were shaking so much it took two attempts before she got through and heard his voice. "It's me, Karen. Listen, something came over the shortwave radio a few minutes ago—"

"Karen, you're whispering, I can't hear you very well."

"I have to whisper, Paul's a few feet away." She pulled the long telephone cord a little farther from the bathroom door and spoke a bit louder. "There, is this better?"

"A little. What about the radio?"

"Shortwave, from London. They said there's been an avalanche in someplace called Verbier in Switzerland." She swallowed hard. "They said that Juffie Kane is missing and feared dead."

There was a long silence on the other end of the line. "They could have been mistaken," Matt said finally.

She could hear the sob in his voice and she rushed to reassure him. "Yes, they could be. I'm sure they are. Probably Juffie will call any minute and tell us it was a mistake."

"Yes," he said. "She will. She has to. So we'd better get off the line. Karen, if you hear anything more . . ."

"Of course," she promised.

She hung up at the same moment that the water stopped running in the bathroom. Paul came back, naked and toweling dry his dark curly hair. God, his body was as perfect as his face. What a pair, he and Juffie. She felt a lump rise in her throat. The tears were half grief and worry, half guilt.

"I heard you on the telephone," Paul said. "Who were you talking to?"

"Not the right people." She felt no need to explain to him that initial impulse to call Matt Varley. "I think I'd better try to reach somebody in the State Department in Washington."

She made a number of calls and talked to a number of bureaucrats. She used her title, which earned her instant credibility, and introduced herself as a close friend of the family. She said she was staying in Miss Kane's home, and Miss Kane's husband was naturally distraught, so of course she was making the inquiries.

No official word from the Swiss authorities, that's what they kept saying. "Sorry not to have more information yet, Dr. Rice, but it's still an unconfirmed report. Our people in Switzerland are watching the situation closely. There were a number of Americans in the area. We'll be in touch as soon as there's any definite word."

"If it's definite," Paul asked, "what do we do then?"

The thought made her flesh go cold, but she was still hiding her own reactions, still concerned that Paul not fall apart and complicate things further. "I'm not sure. Somebody will tell us."

Paul disappeared into his study for the next two hours; a few times Karen heard his voice on the telephone. Who was he calling, more officials? No, that was unlikely. His buddies in the rackets probably. Consolidating his position, making sure he'd still be an asset if his famous wife were dead. Oh hell, she didn't know that. She had nothing to gain by getting an active hate on for Paul Dumont. Besides, a few hours ago—Jesus, she felt so guilty. And not only about Juffie, about Frank. Which was insane. Frank was her friend, not her boyfriend. He didn't care whom she slept with. She was under stress, that's all. Control it, make all the right moves. Wait.

The front desk called to say there were reporters and photographers in the lobby. "No statement," Paul said gruffly, and slammed down the phone. As long as they didn't leave the penthouse they were isolated, but they both knew that couldn't go on forever.

It was the cook's day off. Karen made omelettes and they took them into the library and turned on the six o'clock television news. CBS had the story, including a few more details.

"This was what the experts call a glacial avalanche," explained the network's man in Switzerland. "What happens is that at the end of a warm summer, and this one has been very warm, a large chunk of ice may break off one of the eternally frozen alpine peaks. As it tumbles down the mountain it gathers mud and trees and boulders. An enormous mass is formed, so a glacial avalanche can be just as destructive as the more familiar snowslides. Verbier is about twenty-five miles north of the Saint Bernard Pass, and that's not easy country any time of year."

The foreign correspondent ended his report and Walter Cronkite added the fact that fourteen people were known to be dead, three of them Americans. "At least twenty-two more people are missing," he continued. "And on that list is another American, a name many people know well. Broadway's Juffie Kane, whose face was especially familiar to viewers of this station's *What's My Line*, and whose baby son died earlier this year. Miss Kane was recuperating in Verbier from her recent ordeal. She set out for a walk about an hour before the disaster struck, and she's not been seen since."

Cronkite paused for a significant moment, set down the papers he was holding, and looked straight into the living rooms of hundreds of thousands of American homes. "And that's the way it is, Friday, October fifth, 1957."

"Why doesn't somebody call us," Paul said. "What's the matter with those people in Washington?"

"You just heard, the report's still unconfirmed. But I expect somebody will call us."

The telephone rang on cue, Karen picked it up, it was Nessa Fine.

"I just heard the news. I can't believe it."

"Neither can I," Karen said. "I'm not going to believe it. Not unless we have to. She's alive and safe, Nessa. Let's just focus on that. Unless and until we know differently," she had to add.

"Yes, unless we know differently," the other woman said.

As soon as they hung up the telephone rang again, and continued to ring. Everyone called, the concerned and the merely curious. Matt got through a little before ten. "I just spoke with Juffie's father," he said.

Myer! With everything happening she hadn't even thought of him. "How's he taking it?"

"Better than I might have expected. He's a tough old bird."

"Yes," Karen said. "And he's been through a lot. All the same, it's awful to think of him alone in that house. Listen, let me get off the line. I think I can do something about that."

She called her mother. Leah had also heard the news. "I tried to call you, but the line was busy, busy . . ."

"Yes, Ma. I know. Look, Myer Kane's all alone in his house. Do you think you could—"

"I'm hanging up and leaving right now," Leah said, with no need for further explanations. "I'll take a taxi."

At midnight there was still no word from Washington. Karen announced that she was going to bed.

"Sleep in the big bedroom with me," Paul said. "So you'll be there if the State Department calls. I won't know what to say." He didn't seem shocked or pained anymore, not the way he'd been when they first heard the report. Now he was just whining. Karen reminded herself that whatever was between Juffie and her husband, it wasn't love. Hadn't been for a long time.

"I don't know what you should say either," she said shortly. "It depends on what they have to report. You'll manage, Paul. I'm sure you'll manage."

The call came at seven the next morning. Karen wasn't sleeping. She was sitting cross-legged on the bed in the blue and white guest room, staring at the stylized morning glories that twined their way across the wallpaper and the huge panda propped in the corner. Hymie-Lou, a southern relation. The telephone rang and was instantly answered. Then, from across the hall, Paul's voice called to her. "Karen, pick up the extension."

It took a few seconds before she found the courage to lift the receiver. ". . . Very sorry to tell you," the man from Washington was saying. "The Swiss authorities got through to us a little while ago. The body's been found. There doesn't seem any doubt about the identity. A number of people knew what she was wearing, and she had her papers with her. And, of course, Miss Kane was a remarkable-looking lady. They're not likely to mistake her for someone else. So I'm afraid it's definite. Sorry not to have better news."

"I suppose I should go over there," Paul said. "The funeral arrangements—"

"If you'd like, Mr. Dumont," the man from the State Department cut in smoothly. "And we'll help however we can, of course. But frankly, may I say I don't think you will accomplish much. I'm sure you understand the problem. After a disaster like this there's a terrible danger of disease, epidemics. The sanitation facilities are all destroyed, you see. To make it worse, Verbier's sort of at the end of the world, and the hospitals and the police have their hands full. So if you'd let the Swiss bury her quickly, the way they've requested, it would be an enormous help. Later you can have the body exhumed and brought home if you want to."

Karen was dumb. She couldn't open her mouth. All through the long night she'd lived on hope. Now it was gone. They'd found Juffie's body, they were talking about how and where to bury her. She clung to the receiver in silent misery and listened to Paul agree with the diplomat's suggestions.

. . . .

There didn't seem any point in exhuming the body, at least Paul didn't express any interest in doing so. And it was Matt who made arrangements for a memorial service the following week. He decided on St. Clement's Episcopal Church on Forty-sixth west of Broadway because it was known as the theater church, and it was in the heart of Juffie's world, and because despite her background it seemed inappropriate to seek out a Catholic or Jewish ritual. Even Myer approved. He came to New York with Leah and in the back of a cab, on the way to the church, he told Karen and her mother how he felt.

"Juffie always looked for neutral territory, a place where Dino and Benny couldn't fight over her. Like our house in Newton." He took Karen's hand and even managed a small smile. "That's what my father said that first day, when he gave the house to me and

Rosie. 'Dino and me talked it over, we agreed. Not Jewish and not Italian, neutral.' So it's okay for the service to be in a Protestant church. See what I mean?"

The event drew huge crowds and an army of reporters and photographers and television cameras. Harry Harcourt read a poem by Thomas Nashe that was called "Adieu" and he choked when he got to the line, "Brightness falls from the air, our queen has died young and fair . . ." Tim Frank sang Gounod's "Ave Maria," and Jack Fine, wearing a yarmulke and a tallis, read the hundred and forty-third psalm. "Hear, O Lord, my prayer. . . . Turn not away thy face from me. . . . Deliver me from my enemies. . . . Thy good spirit shall lead me into the right land. . . ."

And that was the one time Karen, sitting between her mother and Myer, heard Juffie's father weeping openly.

Matt did not weep. He sat stony-faced throughout, which was why so many people said afterward that he was mourning not Juffie but his ten percent. Karen knew better. She recognized a grief too profound to have a public face.

"A whole world's gone," Myer told her on the steps of the church after the service. "My world. Almost everybody in it has died and left me alone. I think maybe it's time I went too. Wherever they've gone, it has to be better than a place where healthy babies die for no reason, and my daughter is killed at thirty years old in a place I never even heard of."

She didn't know what to say to him. There were no well-learned professional phrases appropriate to assuage his grief. What she wanted most to say was how much she admired his dignity, his raw guts, but somehow she couldn't find the right words for that either.

She wondered if Myer knew how things had been between Juffie and Paul at the end. Paul was obviously avoiding Juffie's father; he didn't even look at him. But Myer went to him and actually took his hand; he was positively gentle with his son-in-law. So he couldn't know that if Paul hadn't had his mobster friends to threaten her with, Juffie would have divorced him, and probably not gone to Switzerland in the first place.

Karen couldn't manage to be so sanguine. Every time she looked at Paul she felt rage, as much at herself as at him. If it hadn't been for that one afternoon in Juffie's bed, she could mourn her friend without all this guilt added to the burden.

"Hang in," Matt said to her in a brief moment's privacy. "Juffie would want us to hang in." Brave words, but he looked terrible.

Finally it was over. The crowd dispersed and the newsmen and the photographers took their equipment and their endless questions to somebody else's misery. They could all decently leave and go home.

Karen didn't exactly have a home to go to. She'd booked herself into the Taft Hotel on Seventh Avenue and Fifty-first, along with her mother and Myer. Paul Dumont could have the penthouse and its ghosts all to himself.

Two days later Frank Carlucci came in from the West Coast. "Sorry I couldn't get back in time for the service," he said. "But I was in the middle of closing up shop in Los Angeles. I've decided to live in New York for a while." He put his hand beneath her chin and tipped her face to the light. "You look exhausted."

"Not physically," she said. "Just emotionally. I'm wrung out. But don't panic. I haven't been tempted to find a slot machine."

"I know. I never thought you would be. Listen, about Juffie. Are they sure she didn't survive? I know that part of the world. It's full of remote little towns and villages cut off from everywhere. She could be—"

"False hope." Karen shook her head. "There's no point in kidding ourselves. They found the body."

.   .   .   .   .

On Tuesday, the sixteenth of October, a small package wrapped in brown paper dropped through the mail slot of the front door of Myer Kane's house on Walnut Street in Newton. He didn't find it because he didn't rush for the mail these days. He didn't rush for anything. He moved slowly through a world and a life that no longer meant much.

Myer did very little legal work now, but he still had a secretary come in three afternoons a week. Miss Gold was many years dead, another familiar face taken from him by time; now the lady who typed his few letters and did his minimal filing was called Mrs. Jablonsky. On Wednesday afternoon she arrived at one and collected the accumulated mail from the basket hanging inside the front door. "Mostly bills, Mr. Kane. But there's this package. It's got a foreign stamp. Do you want me to open it?"

Myer looked at the little parcel. "No, I'll do it." He didn't, however, not until after he'd gone into his office and shut the door. Then he paused and studied the package and finally took a small nail file from the top drawer of his desk and carefully slit the paper so the postmark would not be destroyed.

What the paper surrounded was a cardboard box about four inches square. He opened it. There was crumpled newspaper inside. Myer shook it out as carefully as he'd removed the outer wrapping. Two pieces of jewelry fell to the blotter on his desk. One was a Star of David encrusted with pearls; the other was a gold crucifix adorned with diamond chips.

Myer's hands were shaking as he smoothed out the newspaper. As he'd hoped, there was a fragment with the date intact. If his high school French wasn't failing him, it said October 8, 1957. He reached for the telephone.

"Matt, this is Myer Kane. Look, I hope I'm not disturbing you, but I got something strange in the mail this morning. Or it may have come yesterday, I don't always look every day. Somehow it seemed better to call you than Paul. At the service he seemed very uncomfortable with me. Anyway, what I got was a Jewish star and a cross. Don't think I'm a crazy old man, but Juffie had at least a dozen of each. A whole collection of them. Her grandfathers used to give them to her when she was little. So I was wondering, did you maybe get something similar in the mail?"

"No, nothing. Mr. Kane, I know what you're thinking, it's what I'd like to believe, too, but it doesn't make a lot of sense. Probably the Swiss authorities were sending you something they found on Juffie's person. Or in her room maybe."

"Without a covering letter? And why to me? They'd send anything to her husband, not her father. Maybe you could call him and find out if he got a package. There's something else too. The jewelry was wrapped in torn-up newspaper, Matt. One piece had a date, October eighth. That's three days after the avalanche."

Matt was silent for a moment. "Maybe," he said finally. "I suppose it could be something . . ." Then his tone changed. "Mr. Kane, I think we're kidding ourselves. I think that's only going to make it worse."

"Yeah, probably you're right." Myer sighed. "But it's very funny all the same. Listen, if you get a chance to call Paul, maybe you'll let me know what happens?"

"I will," Matt promised. He put down the receiver and thought for a moment. Then he decided. He'd call Karen. If Juffie were sending messages, she wouldn't send one to Paul. No, the whole idea was crazy. He was tormenting himself.

Still, it could be worth a shot. But Karen wouldn't be in her room at the Taft at this hour, she'd be at the hospital. He didn't want to speak to her there. He'd hang around the office after Miss Wilkins left at five. Karen should be home by six, he'd try then.

It was twenty past five when the telephone rang. "Matt? Thank God you're still there. I took a chance because I don't know your home number. Listen, I just opened a little package from Switzerland. Inside was a—"

"A star and a cross?" he interrupted. His heart started to thud. Easy, he told himself. Easy. Don't go crazy.

"Yes, did you get the same thing?"

"No, Juffie's father did. He called me about it this morning."

"She's alive, Matt! She's alive! What else can it mean?"

"I don't know. But why this? Why such mystery? And why didn't she send me a package?"

"Maybe she did, maybe it hasn't come yet. You know how the mail is. Besides, she had lots of these stars and crosses. She showed them to me years ago. And it's a perfect symbol, Matt. Anybody who knows Juffie really well would know it's a perfect code."

For the next hour and a half he alternated between elation and despair. If Juffie were sending messages, the first one would have gone to him, that's what made it so unlikely that the packages were from her. He repeated that to himself all the way home to the little house in Englewood Cliffs.

After Patsy died he'd thought about moving to Manhattan, but he hadn't found time to look for a bachelor apartment. Then that extraordinary day in the Biltmore happened, and the whole world changed. He began to hope that someday he and Juffie would have a home together. He'd wait until they could find someplace wonderful, where their life could begin. Instead, it had ended in an avalanche. Now it didn't seem to matter much where he lived.

There was a bright green mailbox beside his door. He wasn't expecting anything when he unlocked it, he was simply performing a routine and automatic action. He associated Juffie with his life in New York; she had nothing to do with this New Jersey suburb.

Matt felt the small square box at the bottom of the mailbox before he saw it. He hadn't cried since he was seven years old, not even at Patsy's funeral, or at Juffie's memorial service. But he cried now.

Chapter 21

The postmark said Salvan. Matt went to the Swiss tourist office on Fifth Avenue. Yes, they told him, Salvan was near Verbier. "But fortunately untouched by the recent disaster. On the other side of the mountain." The clerk went on extolling the charms of Salvan. "A lovely village. Few tourists. Superb for skiing. Very remote, you understand, not St. Moritz. Salvan isn't the place for a vacation if you want night life."

It wasn't exactly night life he was after. Rather, a miracle. Was Salvan a place for miracles? It didn't seem like a fair question to ask the Swiss Tourist Bureau.

He convened a meeting, Karen and Myer and himself at Myer's home in Newton. "I don't know what these packages mean, at least I'm not certain. But I know what all three of us are hoping they mean."

Like children who thought that speaking the wish aloud would make it not come true, none of them was able to put it into words, to actually say it. Instead, Myer poured three large shots of Canadian Club whiskey and handed the glasses around. "To Juffie," he said, lifting his drink. "To my daughter and to life, l'chayim."

Matt emptied his glass in one swallow. "There's something I think you two should know. Juffie and I loved each other, we had for years. A couple of months ago we decided to try to make a life together. But there were problems. Some thug named Finky Aronson had a hold over her. And Paul—" He stopped and looked at Karen and Myer. "Paul didn't want to let her go. She was prepared to accept that. Until she found out he'd been a Nazi collaborator during the war."

Karen gasped, Myer hunched forward in his chair, still neither of them spoke. But the silence changed, the palpable difference was stunning. A hope too tenuous to voice had become wordless shock. Finally Myer got up and got the bottle of rye and topped up their glasses. "Who said?" he demanded. "I thought Paul was a hero in the war. Who said he was a Nazi?"

Matt explained. And it was Myer who saw instantly the ramifications. "So after that Aronson had an even tighter hold on her."

"I told her she had to tough it out, tell this guy Aronson she wasn't going to be in his pocket, leave Paul. . . ."

"That was your advice?" Myer asked quietly.

"Yes."

"Matt, excuse me, I know you meant well, but that wasn't advice, it was horseshit. What you wanted Juffie to do was crazy. Certain disaster."

"That's what she said. But she was going to do it."

"No, she wouldn't be that stupid. She knows these people from way back. She knows they have a code of honor."

Matt was incredulous. "Honor?"

"He's right," Karen said. "It's not an uncommon syndrome for a tightly knit minority group. Sorry about the jargon."

"More than honor in the abstract," Myer said. "A set of rules, completely inflexible. What you wanted Juffie to do, betray them, they'd call *infamata*, dishonorable, despicable. Nobody escapes their claim or their vengeance and lives to talk about it. There was no way she would get away with it in the long term."

"So what did she do?" Matt demanded. "How did she do it? What's the meaning of the packages?"

"*What* is easy," Myer said. "If, please God, we're right about the packages, it means she decided to make them believe she was dead. Even *cosa nostra* doesn't go after dead people. As to how?" He shrugged. "I have no idea, but I think maybe you should go to Switzerland, to this Salvan place, and find out. Just you, Matt. Three of us could attract too much attention. And don't underestimate them. Be very careful."

* * * *

Matt flew to Germany. In Frankfurt he hired a car—a Mercedes because it was going to be a long, tough trip—and drove north, across the border at Basel and into German-speaking Switzerland.

At Bern he stopped long enough to buy detailed Michelin maps and spent an evening poring over them. The next morning he set out once more.

He was climbing constantly and the driving was demanding, but at least he was in the French-speaking part of the country. He knew a bit of French.

It was bitter cold; the end of October was winter in the Valais in the high Alps. Once it started to snow and he shook his fist at the heavens, enraged to think he'd have to find somewhere to wait out a storm. Time seemed so precious. And if there was to be a prize at the end of the journey, it was beyond price. God took notice—the snow stopped and the roads stayed open.

According to the maps, the route to Salvan cut off north of a town called Martigny. From there he drove west, then south along a harrowing narrow strip of road. One false move, one thoughtless twist of the wheel, would send the big black car hurtling over a cliff. So there couldn't be any false moves. Concentrate, he kept telling himself. Take it easy. But he was so close. He had to struggle to keep from flooring the accelerator. "You've waited this long," he said aloud. "Don't fuck up now."

All journeys come to an end. This one finished up in a small square in front of a church called Notre Dame de la Victoire. In Salvan. Where three highly unusual packages had been mailed.

Matt parked and looked around. A little picture-postcard village. Chalets with smoke rising from their chimneys, mountainous stacks of firewood alongside every door. Okay, he was here. What did he do now? Find somewhere to wait. If Juffie had sent the packages, she must have a plan. And she'd know that the most logical action he could take would be to come to the place indicated by the postmark.

He studied the faces of the few people on the street. Only local types, no easily identifiable strangers. The only other vehicles in the square were a couple of pickup trucks with enormous tires. He already knew that this was a quiet time between the tourist seasons. It was too late for autumn hikes and too early for first-class skiing.

He got out of the car, conscious that he was being examined, although the sidewise glances weren't obvious. Polite Swiss manners. He'd met nothing else since he entered the country. There was a café across the square. It was the only possible place.

"Bonjour, monsieur." The woman who greeted him was as polite as everyone else. If she found his presence unusual, she didn't let it show. Matt seated himself at a small round table and ordered the local wine.

It came in a carafe, a full-bodied red without distinction but with lots of punch. The waitress asked if he wanted cheese. Matt said he did. Anything to pass the time. Until what? When? That was the problem, he didn't really know what he was doing here. Or what he was supposed to do.

There was a big log fire in the café and he had on tweed slacks and a heavy Irish wool sweater and a ski jacket. Nonetheless, he was freezing. Nerves, of course. And a desperate longing to be right coupled with a conviction deep in his gut that he was wrong. That certitude grew by the moment. Nothing happened. Nothing was going to happen. Juffie was dead. The Swiss authorities had identified her body. Not all the Stars of David or crosses in the world could bring back the dead. But somebody sent them. Who? Why? He had no answer to that. So he was here.

He was the only customer in the café, but the smell of food filled the room. Doubtless the family who owned the place was cooking their midday meal in the back. The minutes passed slowly.

He'd almost finished his wine when the waitress approached. *"Monsieur, nous avons potage à l'oignon si vous voulez. Et le pain frais viendra bientôt."*

He said yes, he'd have the soup, and some bread when it arrived. The woman brought a steaming crockery bowl, and said again that the bread would come soon. She started to say something else, but her French was too rapid and complex for him to follow and he shrugged hopelessly. "I'm sorry, I don't understand."

"You speak English?" she asked. He nodded. *"Bien,* there's a convent near here. The nuns bake the bread and send it over every day. It's late today."

The door opened while she spoke. An old woman came in, not a nun, but a woman dressed all in black. She was bent with age and she wore layers of sweaters above a long black skirt. Her head was wrapped in a black shawl. She carried the crusty, sweet-smelling loaves on a pannier suspended around her neck by a leather thong.

The waitress helped to unload the tray from her curved shoulders. All the while she kept up a rapid stream of French, scolding the old woman for being late when a visitor was waiting for his lunch. The crone didn't reply, a silent response to a long lifetime of harangues. Finally the bread was deposited on a table in the rear. The waitress shoved some coins at the woman and she headed for the door.

Unexpectedly she stopped by the table where Matt sat. *"Bonjour, monsieur."* She held out her hand, as if she were begging. Matt reached into his pocket, looking up at the same time. Her skin was weather-browned and seamed with age, and what he could see of her hair was dark. But she was smiling at him. And her eyes were the most incredible shade of lavender circled with darker rings.

. . . .

Matt gripped the note Juffie passed him before she hobbled out of the café. He watched her go, suppressing the urge to run after her. Anyway, even if he were that stupid, he probably couldn't do it. The exquisite shock of recognition had rooted him to the chair.

When the door closed behind her he hunched forward, cupping the paper in the palm of his hand to read it. She must have prepared it beforehand, probably when she sent the packages and began her vigil. There was a rough map on one side, on the other a note. "Come to the spot marked on the map in thirty minutes. I love you."

He waited a few minutes more, then called for his bill. Outside, the square was deserted, the locals were all having their lunches. The Mercedes started with a quiet purr and he drove out of the village. About half a mile down the road he parked. There were some overhanging trees and they provided cover of a sort. The big black car could still be seen, but there wasn't time for anything else; twenty of his thirty minutes had already passed.

He had to go back a ways. Juffie's map indicated a turning just east of the town. It was a track leading into the woods. The ground was frozen and there were traces of ice and snow. The man who'd been a boy in Hell's Kitchen in Manhattan might normally have found it hard to keep his footing on this forest path slippery with frost and pine needles. But not today.

He broke into a run because today he could do anything. He was reborn. It was a new age in a new world, and nothing in his entire life had ever looked as beautiful as this place at this time. He wanted to shout out his joy. Yodel maybe, if he knew how. But he didn't. So he kept running.

What her map showed was a little house of some kind. She'd indicated a bigger building with a cross and a steeple a bit farther on, the convent the waitress mentioned most likely. But the X on the map was beside the drawing of a small square dwelling with a pitched roof. In minutes he caught a glimpse of that roof, it teased him from behind the pines. Matt quickened his pace.

She was standing outside, still dressed as she'd been in the café, but not hunched over now. Standing and peering in the direction from which he had to come. When she saw him she ran forward and they met halfway across the small clearing. "I knew you'd come! Oh, my darling, I knew you'd understand and come." They stood there holding each other for a long time. "Come inside," she said finally. "It's not much warmer, but it's out of the wind."

It was a cabin, not a house; a solid wood structure with a single room containing nothing but a stove, a cot, and a table. "It's a woodsman's shelter," Juffie explained. "But no one's used it since I've been here. So I took a chance and made it the rendezvous point."

"Don't talk," Matt said. "Not yet. Let me look at you, touch you." He grabbed her, held her close again, kissed her. A dozen kisses, a hundred; water when he was dying of thirst, food when he'd thought he would be hungry for the rest of his life. She tasted of the pines and the cold crisp air and a number of other things he couldn't identify, but mostly of Juffie. His love, his life.

She broke from him finally. "I knew you'd figure it out," she said again.

"Not me, not at first. It was your father who suggested it. He caught on right away."

Juffie heaved a long sigh. "He's all right? My father's okay?"

"Fine. He took it hard, but he was the first to bounce back when you announced your little miracle. Karen and I were a lot slower on the draw."

"I was so scared," she said. "His heart . . . I was afraid the shock might kill him. But I had to do it."

"I know." He was holding her face between his palms, kissing her after each few words. "At least I think I know." Another kiss. "But why like this, Juffie? And how did you manage it? They told us they'd identified your body."

"I'll try to explain everything, but we don't have a lot of time. Sister Mathilde will be expecting me. I don't want any obvious change in routine."

He nodded, caught up in her priorities, however peculiar they seemed. "Got it. Okay, you're producing and directing this show. Tell me whatever I need to know."

Despite the urgency, she leaned back in his arms and frowned at him. "You forgot something. I'm also the star. My name goes on the marquee, bud. Or you'll hear from my agent."

They laughed. Sweet God, he was in some crazy hut in the forest in Switzerland and laughing with Juffie. It was too much to take in, he almost couldn't handle it. But it was real. And deadly serious. Juffie hadn't set up this drama to satisfy her sense of the theatrical. "Tell me," he said again.

"Background first," she said. "I went away intending to stage my own death. I wasn't at all sure how I could do it, just that I had to. There was no other way to be free of them, Matt. What you wanted, the public denouncement, toughing it out—it was suicide. Not only for me, for you and—" She stopped, then went on, "Of course I didn't know in advance about the avalanche. That was just a freak accident. I was hanging around in Verbier because it was so remote. And I took a lot of long walks trying to come up with a plan. Then that . . . that thing happened."

This part came slowly, haltingly, because it was still so terrible to remember. "You can't imagine what it was like. And don't ask me how I survived because I really don't know. I crouched under this huge boulder because it was there, and all my instincts were to find some sort of cover. And somehow when the mountain stopped shaking, that ledge of rock was still standing there, and so was I.

"I had a cut on my leg where something flying through the air had nicked me, but that's all. I waited about ten minutes, then I figured whatever it had been was over and I had to try to get back to the village. It took a long time because the path was completely covered in mud and stones and broken branches. I had to concentrate on staying upright, and I didn't really think about anything else until I found the body."

"The one they identified as yours," Matt guessed.

"Yes. It was a woman and she was lying right across my path. Matt, it was almost as if she'd been put there for me to find. I saw three more bodies afterward, when I got closer to the village, but none of them was perfect the way the first one was. For my purpose, I mean. She was about my height and she had long hair and it wasn't a much different color than mine."

He touched the bit of her hair that showed beneath the shawl. "Not dirty black, like this. What the hell do you have on it?"

"Soot. And I made my skin dark with berry juice and more soot. But that comes later. Let me tell it the way it happened. There was one thing more about the dead woman; it's what convinced me to try. She had no face. She'd been knocked down by a falling tree, not buried under the muck. The tree split her head open. The face wasn't recognizable because there really wasn't any. Just blood and bone and gore." She shuddered, then took a deep breath. "I know how ghoulish it sounds, but I couldn't pass up the opportunity. I took her clothes. God! You can't imagine how hard that was to do. It was cold and the body was starting to get stiff. . . ." She swallowed hard. "Anyway, I did it. I left her in my clothes, and I left my bag beside her."

"What astounds me was your presence of mind, after coming through all that."

"But I told you, it's what I came here to accomplish. I was going to fake some kind of accident, disappear without a trace. So the idea was in my mind. When I saw this poor woman, I figured it was the best shot I was going to get and I'd better take it. Even though there hadn't been a chance to warn you first. I meant to do that if I could. And, at the very least, to warn my father."

"He's fine," Matt assured her again. "And he also said my way would never have worked."

"No, it wouldn't. That's why it had to be something like this."

He took her hand. "Juffie my love, look at me." The violet eyes turned to him. They looked grave and deep and more serious than he ever remembered seeing them. "Sweetheart, you know what this means? You'll never go on a stage again. You have to stay dead, or it will all be for nothing. One thing about doing it my way, at least there was a chance you could make a comeback someday. Juffie, are you sure it's going to be worth it? That I'm going to be worth it?"

They were holding hands and she lifted his palm to her lips. "Oh, yes. I'm sure. But there's something else, something you don't know."

"I'm listening."

"I didn't do it just for you and me. I did it for our baby."

He was speechless for at least ten seconds. Then he said the wrong thing. "We can't be having a baby. We were so damned careful all the time."

Juffie took a deep breath. "I'm going to pretend you didn't say that, Matthew Varley. I'm going to pretend it never crossed your mind that this could be anything other than your child. And I'm going to remind you of that time in the Biltmore in August. We weren't a bit careful then, because neither of us planned to be there."

"Oh God, Juffie, that's not what I meant. But I'm so amazed, so overwhelmed. Hey, a baby! When? How long have you known?"

He was grinning from ear to ear now, and she could forgive him. "I've known since I missed my period and started having morning sickness in September. Don't forget, I've been pregnant before, I know what it feels like. And when is easy. May. Nine months from August. You can use your fingers and count it up."

"A baby in May," he said in tones of awe. They were silent for a few moments, holding each other, sharing this new joy.

"So you see how it was," she said finally. "Maybe you and I could decide to risk everything for ourselves—but we had no right to do that with our child's future. Oh, darling, I grew up in *cosa nostra*'s shadow. My precious Jason was born under it, would have lived under it too. But not this time, not this baby. That's why I even had to take a chance on Dad's heart."

"The new life rather than the old," he said quietly.

Juffie nodded.

"Yes, I understand. Now tell me the rest. After you changed clothes with the dead woman, what did you do next?"

"By then I could see that what had happened was a major disaster and everything was in chaos. Rescue teams were coming out and my biggest worry was trying to avoid them. That meant I couldn't go to the village. I walked for ages, it was the middle of the night when I got to the convent. I didn't so much decide to hide there as face the fact that I couldn't go on. I was at the end of my strength and there was a door and a bell, so I rang it."

They were sitting on the cot now. Matt held her hands. She wore knitted black gloves with the tips of the fingers cut off. A working woman's gloves. Her fingers were cold and he kept rubbing them. "The nuns took you in?"

"Nun. In the singular. Sister Mathilde. She's the extern sister, the one who has contact with the outside world. She told me the others are what's called cloistered, they never see anybody and nobody sees them. They pray and work and do everything behind a high wall. So the only person I deal with is Sister Mathilde, who, thank God, speaks English. That first night she just gave me brandy and soup and put me to bed in a little back room they keep for wayfarers. Hospitality is one of their rules.

"The next day we talked. I think she knows who I am, but she's never said. Neither have I. I told her I needed a place to stay. And that I wasn't running away from the police or anything like that. She didn't agree right away, but when she came back a couple of hours later she brought me these clothes and said that I could stay if I'd deliver the bread to the village once a day. I worked out the makeup and the characterization myself. One of my better roles, isn't it?"

"Fantastic. I predict another Tony. One more question. The stars and the crosses, how did you get hold of them? You said you never went back to the hotel you were staying at in Verbier."

"I didn't. But when I left New York I knew that whatever I didn't take with me I was probably never going to see again, so I picked out some of the stars and the crosses Pop and Pa used to give me." She grinned at him. "The really crazy part is that I put them all on a chain and hung them around my neck. I figured I needed all the luck I could get."

"I've never been religious," he said softly, "but right now it doesn't seem like luck. It's too marvelous for that."

The sun was westering and the cabin grew even colder. He rubbed her hands between his. "Darling, you're freezing, so am I, for that matter. Let's get out of here. I'm parked about a mile away. You can hide in the back until we're clear of the area."

She shook her head. "No."

"What do you mean, no? Juffie, forget what I just said. You haven't got religion, have you? Don't tell me you're going to take the veil."

She giggled. "How many pregnant nuns have you seen lately? Don't be an ass. Though I did cut my hair." She dropped the shawl from her head. Her hair was short, hacked off inexpertly. "It was easier to darken if there was less of it. I had to do it with an old knife. Worse, the nuns don't believe in mirrors. The only way I could see myself full-length was to look in a stream behind the convent. Try doing a characterization like this looking at your reflection in a stream."

Matt reached up and stroked the chopped-off hair. "I still think you're the most beautiful woman in the world. But I don't understand why you won't come with me."

"Look, the thing you've got to get through your head is that they know all about you. Finky Aronson and his friends. Not to mention Paul.

"If you scoot out of New York and take up residence somewhere in Europe a few weeks after I've supposedly died, they're going to smell something. It will all be for nothing. I'm safe here for a while. What I need next is a private clinic where the baby can be born. Very private. I know one in Switzerland. I checked it out when I first came. The Swiss are great at asking very few questions as long as they're well paid for their discretion. I've already left money in various banks under various names. I'm going to make my way to the clinic in three or four weeks. Not directly. A few stops first, a few different disguises."

He saw the wisdom of what she was suggesting. "Okay, but what about me?"

"You go home. You act as if nothing has changed. For a reasonable amount of time, maybe even a year. Then you quietly announce your retirement and sell up and move to Switzerland. By then it won't look suspicious."

In the end he let himself be convinced, at least for the moment, because Juffie said there wasn't much time and she had to get back to the convent. "I don't want to put Sister Mathilde in any kind of awkward position. I don't want her to think there are questions she should ask, and have to decide if she wants to ask them. It's not fair to her, and it will jeopardize my position here. But I can come again tomorrow. I'll meet you here around the same time."

"You come this way every day?"

"Yes. I go out to gather faggots."

"What!"

"Faggots, that's what Sister Mathilde calls them. It's kindling. For the wood stoves. I collect a basketful each afternoon. It's one of my jobs."

"Juffie, this is crazy. For God's sake, let me get you out of here. Somewhere you'll at least be warm and comfortable, and not have to work like an old peasant woman."

"Somewhere as remote as this? A place where they've never heard of Juffie Kane? Like where?"

He was at a loss. And while he was still puzzling about it, she kissed his cheek and murmured, "Tomorrow," and slipped away.

The following afternoon she asked about other people and he told her all about the memorial service. When he got to the part about the readings and Harry Harcourt and the Fines, she started to cry. "I'm sorry, it's silly. I knew it would have to be like this. That I'd never see any of those people again. But I can't help the fact that it hurts." Then, while he brushed away her tears, "What about Karen?"

"She's fine. A new woman since she got your little message. And since Frank Carlucci moved to New York."

Juffie grinned. "Tell her I said Europe is a perfect place for a honeymoon. Switzerland maybe."

After five days of furtive hours in the deserted cabin she knew it was time to send him away. "Matt, you have to go back to New York. We mustn't push our luck. Forgive the corny line, but we've got to stop meeting like this."

He didn't rise to the humor. "Juffie, one more time. Are you absolutely sure you want to do this? Burn all your bridges this way? It's not too late to change your mind. You can still appear and say you lost your memory for a while right after the avalanche."

He was holding her close, his face buried in her funny short dark hair. It wasn't soot anymore, he'd brought her some hair dye from Geneva. "Are you still sure it's worth it?"

"You and me and our baby and a life together, that's worth everything twice over. I'm more sure than I've been of anything."

"Thank God," he whispered. Then he pulled back and looked at her. "Juffie Kane is dead, long live Juffie Kane."

· · · · ·

It was October 1958 when Mr. and Mrs. Frank Carlucci

checked into the Hotel de Paris in Monte Carlo. "Wow," Karen said softly. "Some boyhood home."

Frank took her arm and they followed the bellman. "This wasn't home, it was where I worked."

The lobby was lush and luxe, a spacious place cushioned with thick carpets and glittering with crystal chandeliers. The only noise was the tinkling laughter of beautiful women with deep tans and elegant clothes and sparkling rings on exquisitely manicured fingers. "Where's the casino?" Karen demanded. "I thought this was gamblers' heaven. Where it all began."

"Upstairs, through there." He pointed to a set of huge bronze doors on the mezzanine level and spoke out of the corner of his mouth, like a Hollywood tough guy. "This ain't Vegas, baby. This is what's known as a class act, the big time."

In the afternoon they strolled through the old hilly streets of the town and he showed her the house where he'd grown up. Later they walked to the harbor and admired the yachts. It was while they were standing there, staring at the sleek testaments to incredible wealth and success, that she asked about Paul Dumont. "Do you think it's possible we might run into him in Europe?"

"I doubt it. It's two months since he was deported. He must be hiding out in some remote corner of France, looking over his shoulder, waiting until the Resistance finally gets its revenge."

"Or *cosa nostra*."

"No," Frank said. "Not them. I nosed around a little, a journalist's privilege. It was Finky Aronson who tipped off the State Department. Told them Dumont was an undesirable alien."

She was astounded. "Aronson! But why? An attack of morality?"

"Not on a bet. An attack of pique. With Juffie out of the picture, I guess he figured Paul wasn't useful anymore. This was a nice smooth way to get rid of him."

"Then how come Paul didn't blow the whistle on Aronson and his pals? The FBI might have been interested enough to make a trade."

"A no-win situation for Dumont. He'd wind up having to hide from both *cosa nostra* and the Maquis."

"So he's just slipped quietly into oblivion," Karen said thoughtfully. "I still don't understand why the French didn't prosecute."

Frank shrugged. "If they took every collaborator to court, they'd shut down their country. It was the worst of times, honey. The very worst. Don't be too hasty to judge."

She knew how he felt and didn't press the issue. "These are the best of times," she said instead, taking his arm. "The very best."

When it was time for dinner she admired him in his tuxedo. "You make a gorgeous penguin."

"Not bad, if I say so myself. And you're a terrific swan."

She'd bought the dress in New York a month before, after she told him Juffie was alive and while they were planning this trip. "People still dress for dinner at the Hotel de Paris in Monte Carlo," he said. So she bought a white chiffon dress with a crossed halter neck and a low back, and yards and yards of skirt that swirled around her legs.

They ate in the sumptuous restaurant and had the best table in the room, because the maître d' had known Frank since he was a little kid. The food was wonderful and she was proud of her husband's flawless French, but more proud of his easy camaraderie with the waiters and busboys. This was a snobby place, but there was nothing of the snob about Frank.

"I want to see the casino," she said over coffee and a wonderful aged cognac.

"You sure about that?"

"Of course I'm sure. Frank, nobody can come to Monte Carlo and not see the casino. Come on, let's go."

There was an admission fee designed to keep out the casual and curious. Only bona fide bettors known to the house were admitted free of charge. And Frank Carlucci and his wife, of course. Because the man at the door was Frank's cousin.

The minute she was inside, Karen knew this wasn't the Desert Inn or the Sands or the Flamingo. Even the roulette wheels seemed quieter. And the place reeked of money in a way that no Las Vegas casino did. In Las Vegas the smell was simply of cash, which was entirely different.

They moved slowly up and down the broad aisles between the gaming tables. The crowd thickened as it grew late, and the ice tinkled in the glasses, and the chips changed hands, and the murmured words *banque, rouge,* and *noir* fluttered in the air. Here and there a dealer or a croupier nodded to Frank or smiled at him.

But the intensity of the high-stakes gambling precluded friendly chats.

"Had enough?" he asked after a while.

"Yes."

They left by a different door from the one they'd entered, and suddenly Karen was facing a bank of slot machines, the first she'd seen in Monte Carlo. She stopped and stared at them. Frank looked at her. Finally he took a one-franc coin from his pocket. "Do you want to play?"

She hesitated a moment, then grinned. "Don't be silly, what a boring idea. Besides, we'd better get some sleep if we're leaving for Switzerland in the morning."

· · · ·

Little Rosie was four months old when she met her aunt Karen for the first time. The baby lived up to her name. She was pink and glowing all over. "Perfect," Karen pronounced.

"Naturally," Juffie agreed. "What did you expect? But she's a bit of a tramp. She prefers men to women, her daddy particularly. C'mon, let's leave Matt and Frank to baby-sit and go for a walk."

The farmhouse was near the little village of Aesch, some way from Basel in the Swiss Rhineland. Matt had already explained that the excitement about a Mr. and Mrs. Michael Vernon, the Americans living at the far end of the valley had died fairly quickly. The farmers had their cows and their fruit trees to worry about, the women their children and their busy kitchens. Probably not one of them had ever heard of Juffie Kane, and if they had, they wouldn't associate her with this woman who had short dark hair and didn't go out much and always wore dark glasses.

But to Karen she was still Juffie, though she called herself Jennifer these days, and some things remained to be discussed. "I have to tell you something," Karen said the moment they were alone under the gnarled old apple trees. "I can't talk about anything else until I get this off my chest."

Karen opened her mouth a couple of times, but nothing came out. Juffie waited. "I think I can guess," she said finally. "Shall I?"

Karen nodded, an expression of pure misery on her face.

"You went to bed with Paul."

In a small pained whisper, she asked, "How did you know?"

"Because nothing else would make you look so awful. And

because I know him, and I knew he had the hots for you. You were a challenge. All buttoned-up sexually. Paul could smell that a mile off. Like a hound after a bitch in heat. Sorry, I don't mean to be crude."

"It wasn't crude," Karen said. "A lot of things maybe, but not crude. Juffie, does all this mean you don't care?"

"Of course I care. Not about him, the shit. I care about you. He's fantastic in bed, isn't he? Don't tell me you didn't enjoy it, you must have."

"That's what's so awful. I loved it. Even afterward, when I felt so guilty and so mad at him, I kept thinking about how terrific it had been."

"I'm not surprised. When it comes to sex, Paul has the field all to himself. Even if he is a Nazi and a bastard, in the sack there's nobody like him. Listen, don't let it louse up your life with Frank. There are more important things than being able to hold on to an erection for three hours."

"Yeah?" Karen said. "Name one."

They laughed a lot. Just like old times. Until they heard the baby cry. "Have to get back," Juffie said. "Rosie's hungry."

There was music playing when they approached the house. Matt had brought a collection of records with him when he "retired" to Europe. There were a lot of vintage 78s among them. Like the one he was playing right now. Tommy Dorsey's band, with an unknown vocalist singing the song George M. Cohan made famous in the thirties. "Give my regards to Broadway, remember me to Herald Square. . . ."

TO SET THE RECORD STRAIGHT. . . .

In 1947 *The Voice of the Turtle*, starring Harvey Stephens and Phyllis Ride, was at the Morosco.

Meg Mundy was at the Cort in 1948, in Sartre's *The Respectful Prostitute*.

The National Theater on West Forty-first Street is now the Nederlander. In 1950 the house was first home to Les Ballets de Paris, then to Louis Calhern in *King Lear*.

At the Imperial in 1952 Ethel Merman was starring in Irving Berlin's wonderful *Call Me Madam*—she packed them in for 644 performances.

The musical *Wish You Were Here* followed Merman's star turn at the Imperial, and it was this show which had the first real lake—more of a pool—onstage.

In 1953 Deborah Kerr was at the Barrymore Theater starring in Robert Anderson's *Tea and Sympathy*.

Kitty Carlisle starred in *Anniversary Waltz*, directed by her husband Moss Hart, in 1954–55. It opened at the Broadhurst Theater, then moved to the Booth and ran ten months.

The Happiest Millionaire, starring Walter Pidgeon, was the hit show at the Lyceum in 1956. At the same time *Bells are Ringing*, starring Judy Holliday and Sidney Chaplin, was a smash at the Shubert Theater. Also in 1956, *Li'l Abner* ran for 693 performances at the St. James.

Ingmar Bergman's remarkable film, *The Seventh Seal*, was released in the U.S. in 1956, not 1955. I cheated because it suited my purposes.

In 1949 the Tony for best dramatic actress went to Martita Hunt for *The Madwoman of Chaillot;* that for best musical actress to Rosalind

Russell for *Wonderful Town* in 1953; and Julie Harris's performance in *The Lark* won for best dramatic actress in 1956. That year Francis Goodrich and Albert Hackett's *Diary of Anne Frank* won the Tony as best play of the season and also won the N.Y. Drama Critics' Award. The Tony for best dramatic director was won by Tyrone Guthrie for *The Matchmaker,* that for best scenic design by Peter Larkin for *Inherit the Wind.*

What's My Line appeared on CBS television for seventeen and a half years, and changed hardly at all during the entire time. As many people will remember, the two women regulars for most of the show's run were Arlene Francis and Dorothy Kilgallen.

As near as I've been able to find out, Billy Baldwin never designed the sets for a Broadway show. But no one who knows the work of this remarkable decorator would doubt that he could have done it, so in these pages he did.

Consummate entertainers all. Thus I trust the people listed above—living and dead—to forgive my usurping their achievements and honors and locations for the parallel universe I created for Juffie Kane and company.

And finally, a huge thank you to Louis Botto, senior editor of *Playbill* magazine, for his wonderful book *At This Theater* (Dodd Mead, 1984), which was an enormous help in my research.